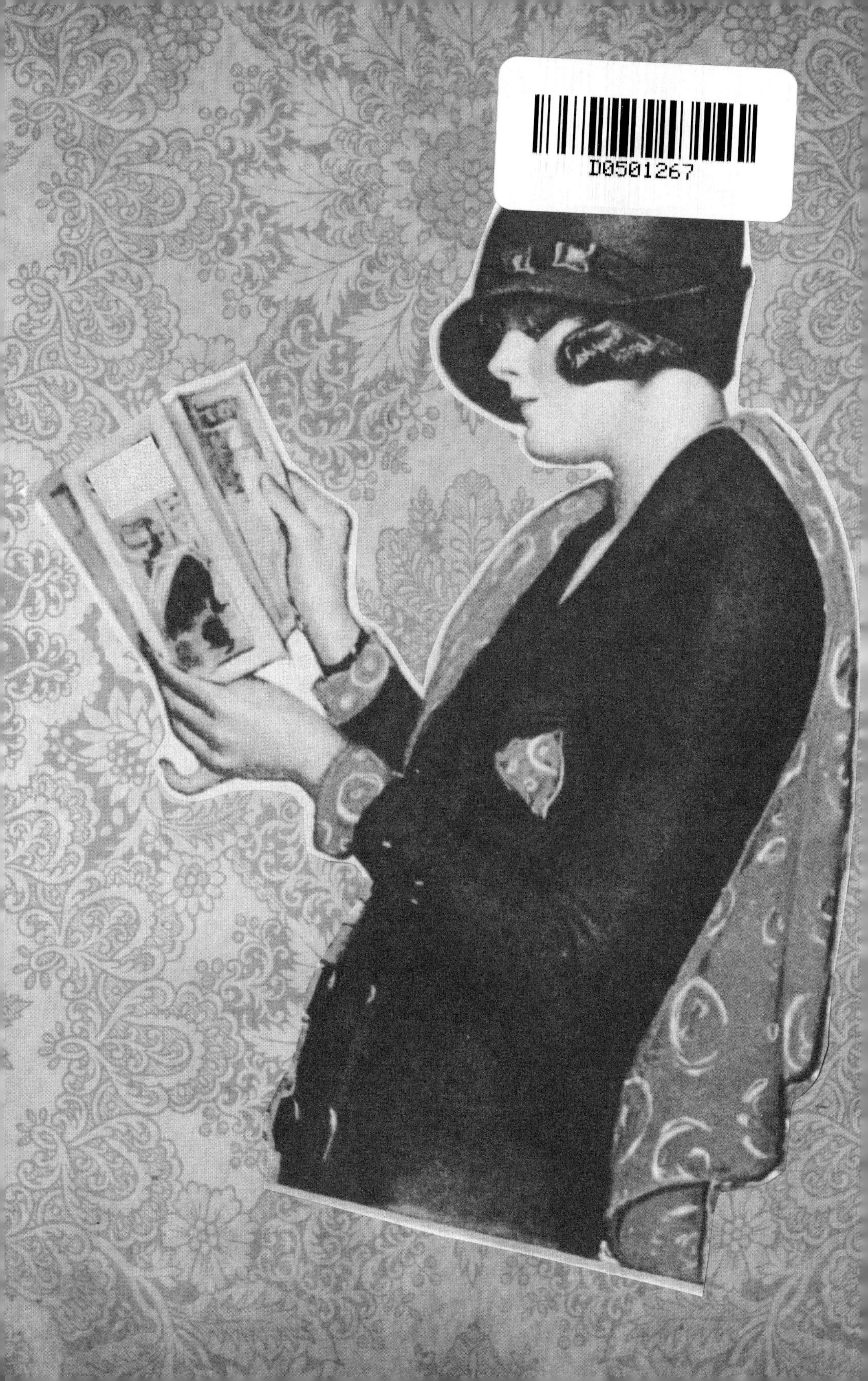

THE SCRAPBOOK

 of

FRANKIE PRATT

a novel in pictures

CAROLINE PRESTON

ecco
ANNIVERSARY
40

An Imprint of HarperCollinsPublishers

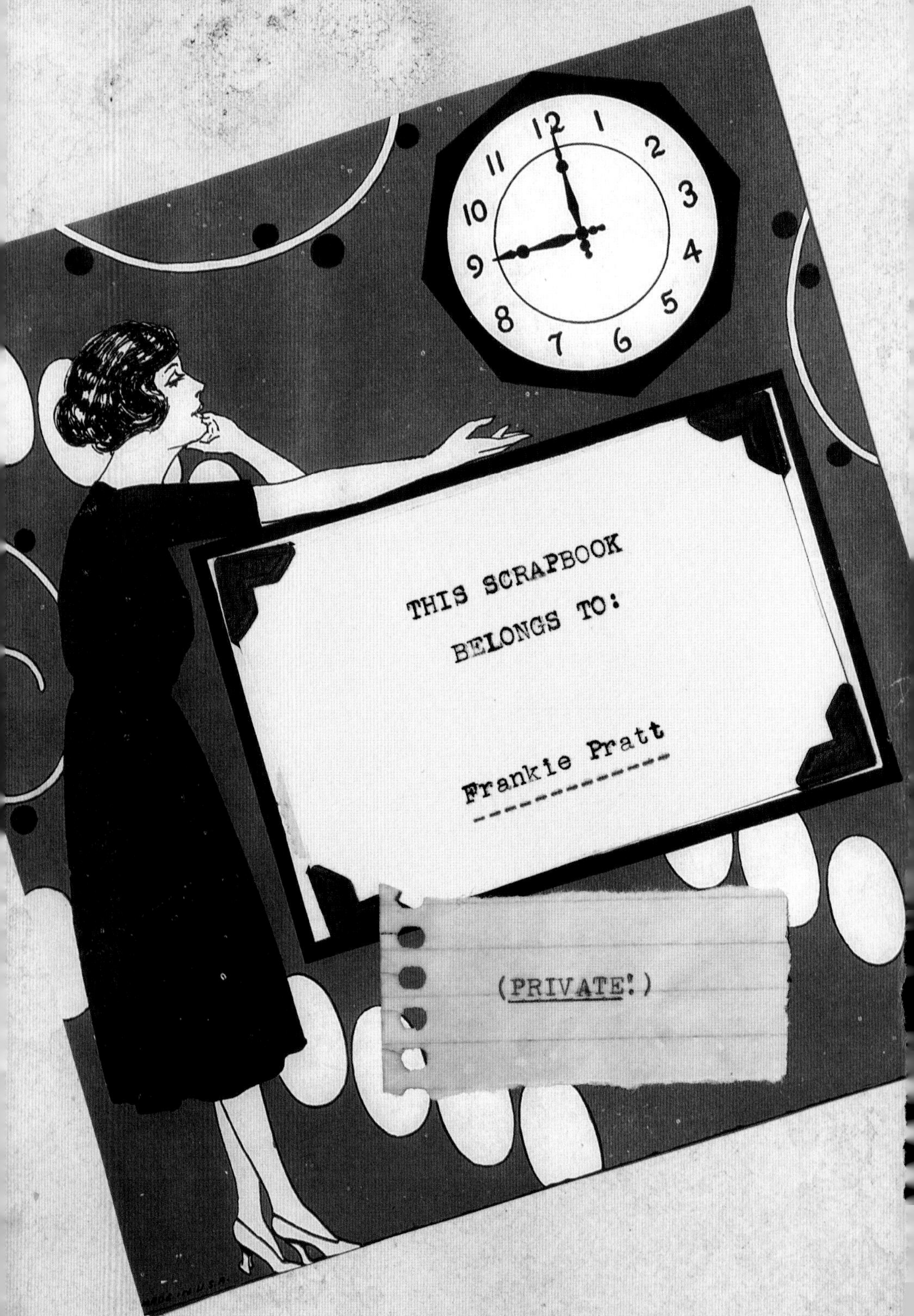
THIS SCRAPBOOK
BELONGS TO:
Frankie Pratt
(PRIVATE!)

The Scrapbook of Frankie Pratt

1920 JUNE 1920

Sun	Mon	Tue	Wed	Thu	Fri	Sat
		1	2	3	4	5
6	7	8	9	10	11	12
13	14	15	16	17	18	19
20	21	22	23	24	25	26
27	28	29	30			

Chapter 1

Cornish,
New Hampshire

1920

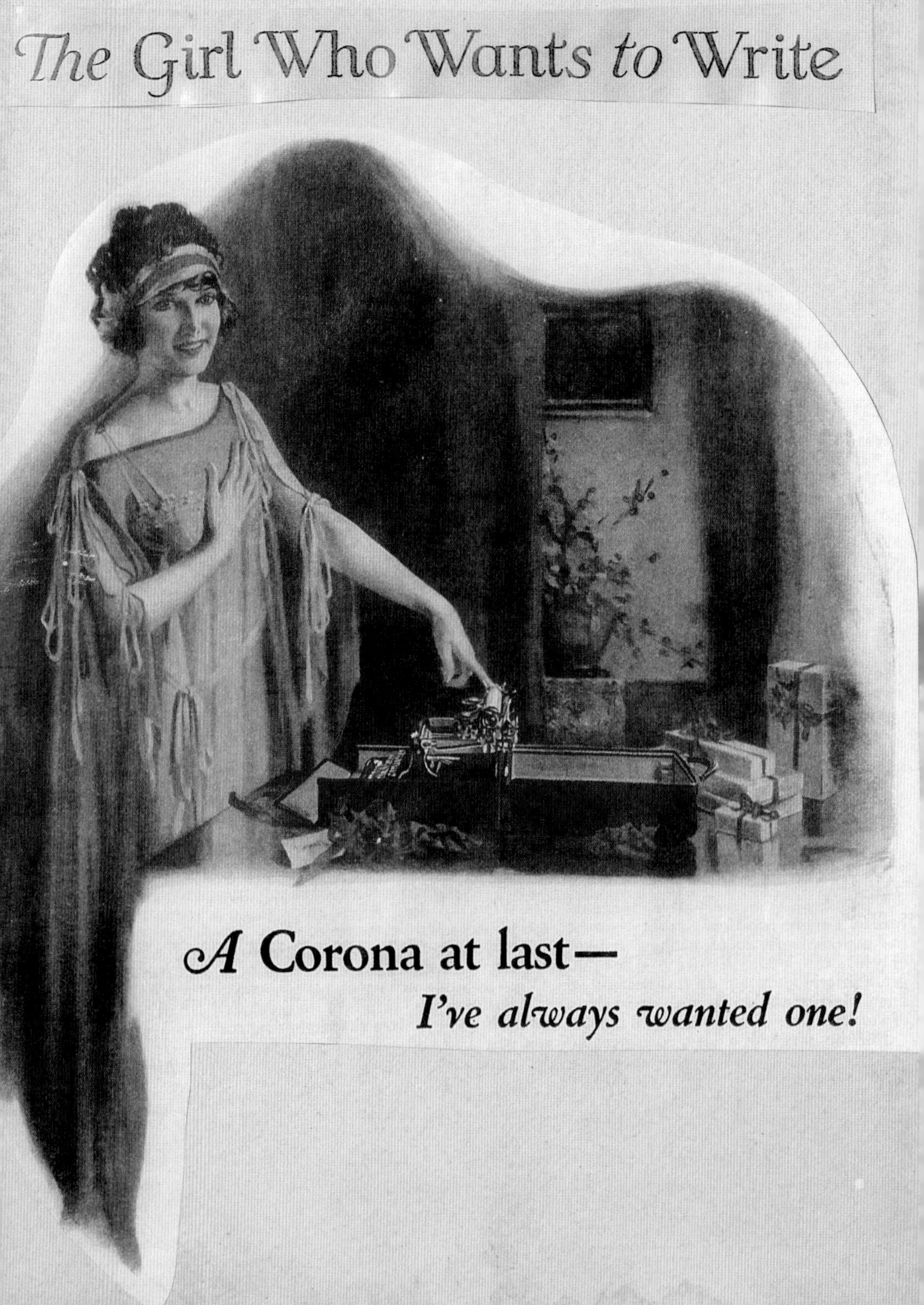
The Girl Who Wants to Write
A Corona at last—
I've always wanted one!

How This Story Begins . . .

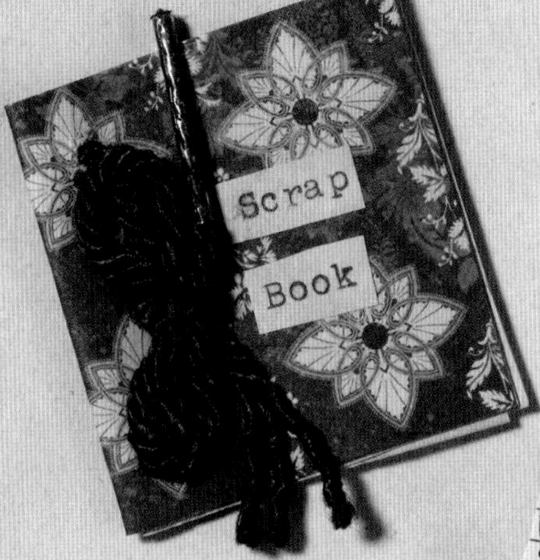
Scrap
Book

Scrapbook was a high school graduation present from mother.

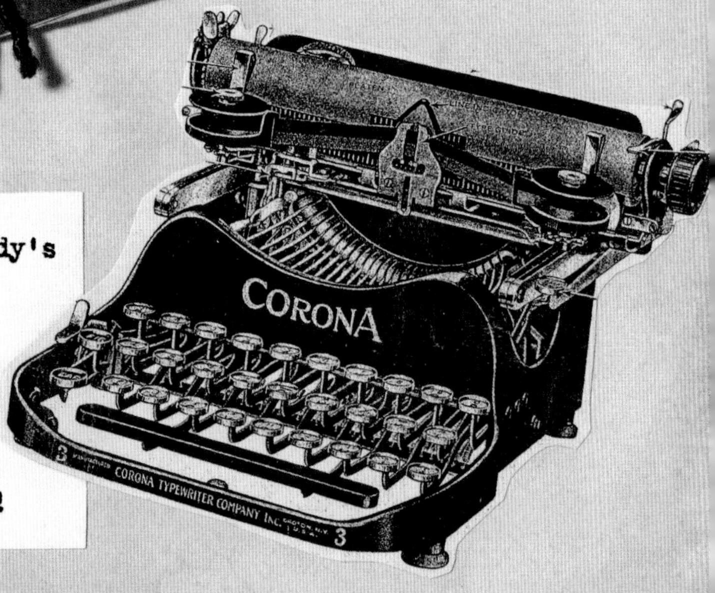
CORONA
CORONA TYPEWRITER COMPANY INC.
3

I found Daddy's old Corona portable in the cellar. Mice had chewed the case but it still works!

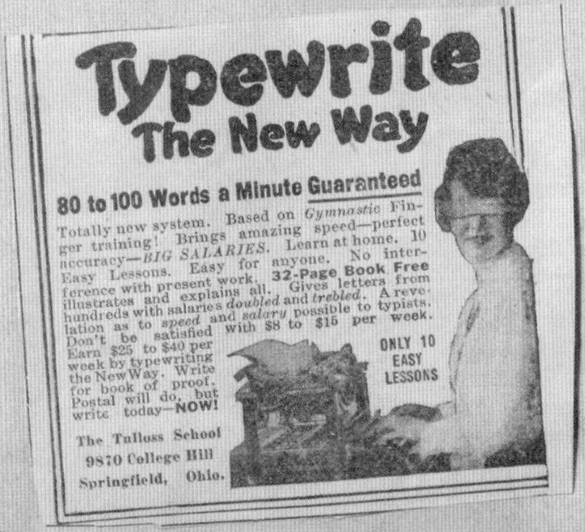
Typewrite
The New Way
80 to 100 Words a Minute Guaranteed
Totally new system. Based on Gymnastic Finger training! Brings amazing speed—perfect accuracy—BIG SALARIES. Learn at home. 10 Easy Lessons. Easy for anyone. No interference with present work. 32-Page Book Free illustrates and explains all. Gives letters from hundreds with salaries doubled and trebled. A revelation as to speed and salary possible to typists. Don't be satisfied with $8 to $15 per week. Earn $25 to $40 per week by typewriting the New Way. Write for book of proof. Postal will do, but write today—NOW!
ONLY 10 EASY LESSONS
The Tulloss School
9870 College Hill
Springfield, Ohio.

I sent away for a free instruction booklet on how to type. I will type one page every day.

Frances Pratt
Personal Information

Nickname: "Frankie" (hate Frances!)

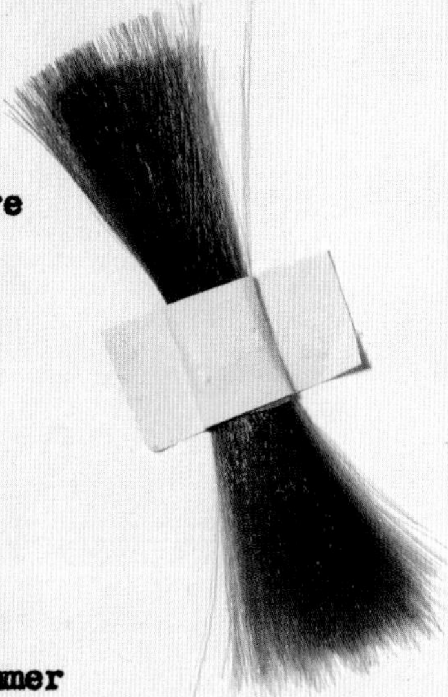

Birthday: Sept 5, 1902

Address: Cornish Flat, New Hampshire

Height: 5 feet 7 3/4 inches
(in stocking feet)

Weight: 116 lbs.
(in stocking feet)

Hair Color: dark strawberry blonde
with honey streaks in summer

Eye Color: blue with hazel green highlights in sunlight

Nose: straight, thin, can look
too pointy from left-hand side

Complexion: too many freckles

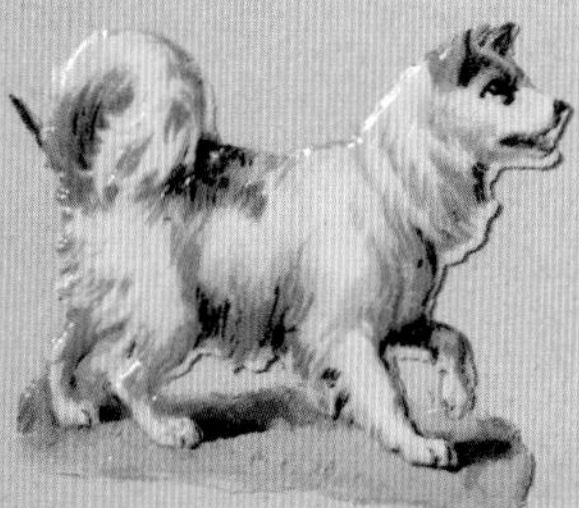

I have a dog
named Fritzy.

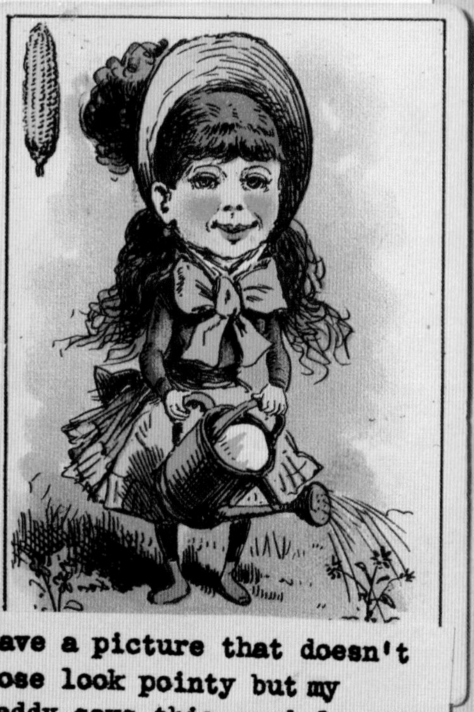

I don't have a picture that doesn't
make my nose look pointy but my
brother Teddy says this card from the
Dr. Busby game looks just like me.

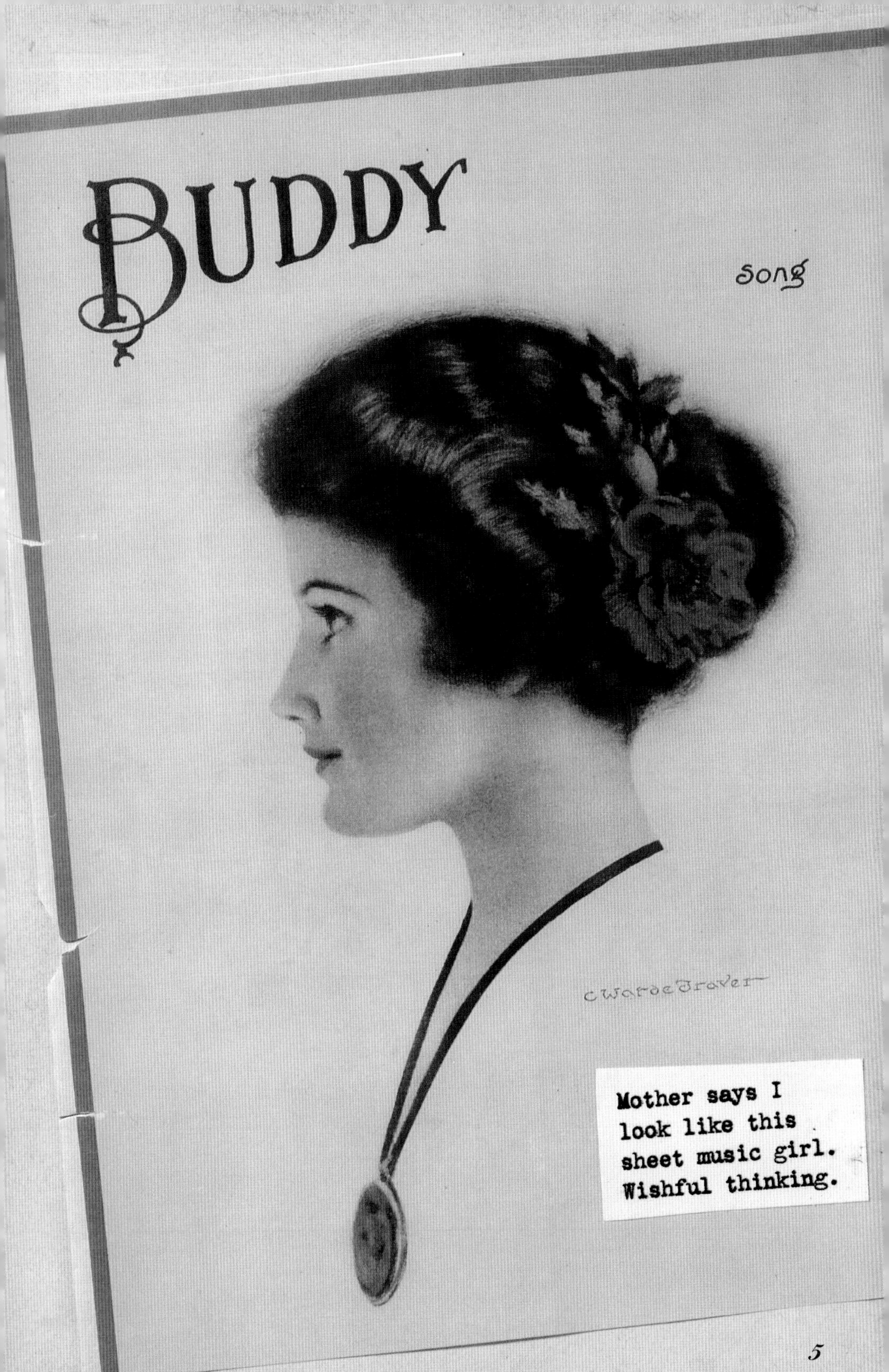
BUDDY
Song
C Warde Traver

Mother says I look like this sheet music girl. Wishful thinking.

My Family

Father

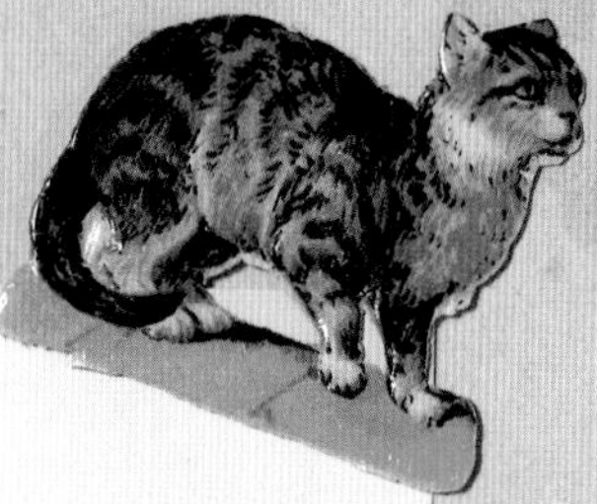

Teddy's cat

Bluebell

Name: George Osborne Pratt

Birthday: October 18, 1872

Education: Windsor High School
Dartmouth College, Class of 1893
Dartmouth Medical School, Class of 1895

Profession: Physician, General Practitioner
Cornish, New Hampshire

Died: January 25, 1915. Dartmouth Hospital

Daddy had a weak heart because he'd had rheumatic fever when he was 5. (Even though his cheeks were always pink and he had arms like a boxer.) Caught influenza which turned to pneumonia. Died 6 days later. They said his heart gave up. I was 12.

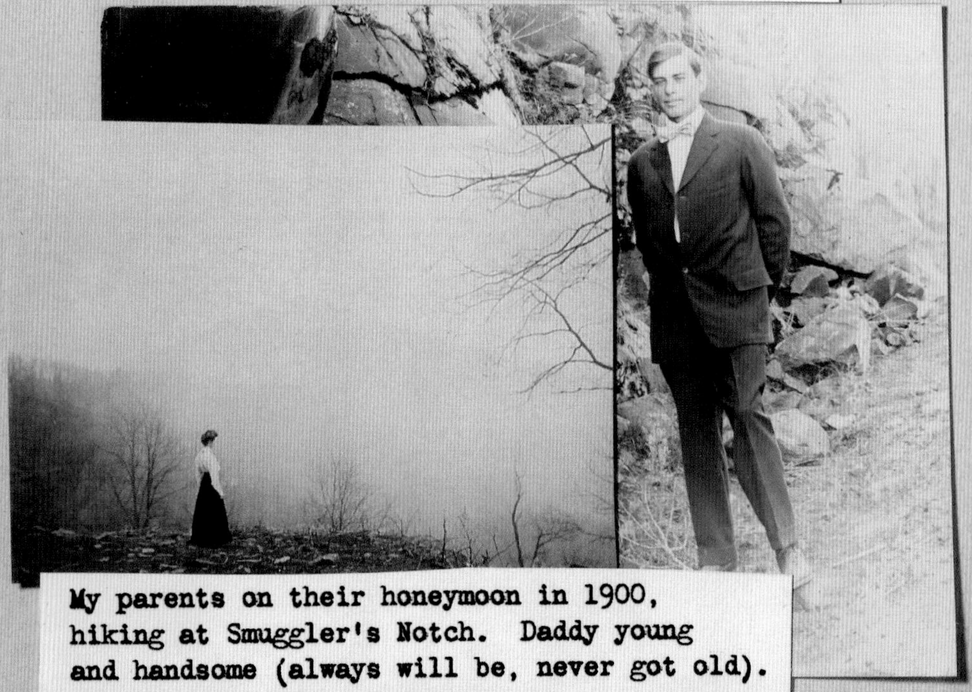

My parents on their honeymoon in 1900, hiking at Smuggler's Notch. Daddy young and handsome (always will be, never got old). Mother still full of dreams . . .

Mother:

Name: Roxanne Bayliss Pratt
Nickname: Roxie

Birthday: April 24, 1878

Education:
Windsor High School
Licensed Practical Nurse Certificate

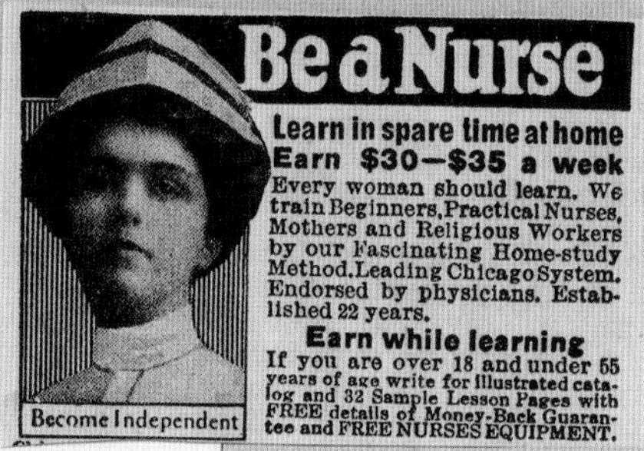
Be a Nurse
Become Independent
Learn in spare time at home
Earn $30—$35 a week
Every woman should learn. We train Beginners, Practical Nurses, Mothers and Religious Workers by our Fascinating Home-study Method. Leading Chicago System. Endorsed by physicians. Established 22 years.
Earn while learning
If you are over 18 and under 55 years of age write for illustrated catalog and 32 Sample Lesson Pages with FREE details of Money-Back Guarantee and FREE NURSES EQUIPMENT.

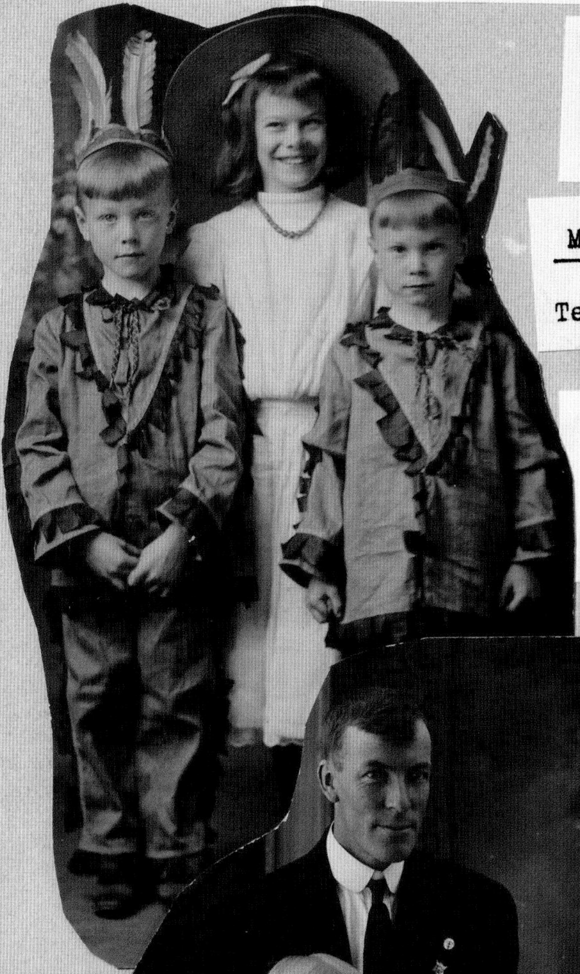

Mother went back to work after Daddy died. Hired as nurse for rich old ladies over on Dingleton Hill.

My Brothers

Teddy & Wally

NO SISTERS

Mother, Daddy, Teddy, Wally, and me. I am five. Mother already getting crease in forehead.

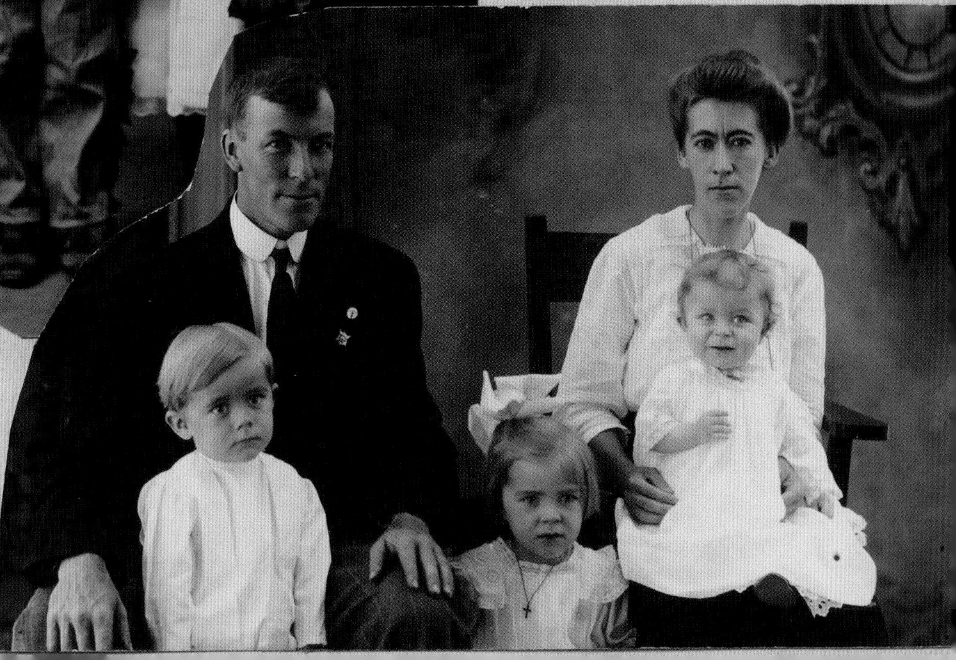

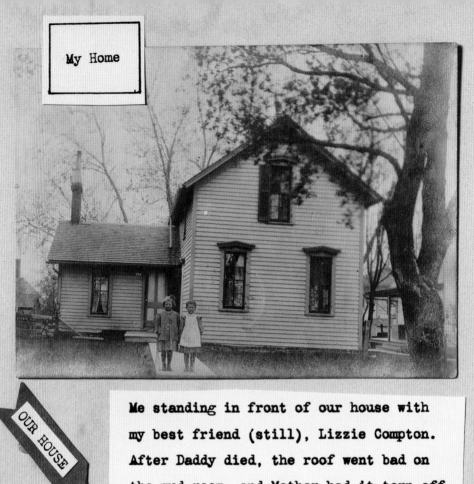

My Home

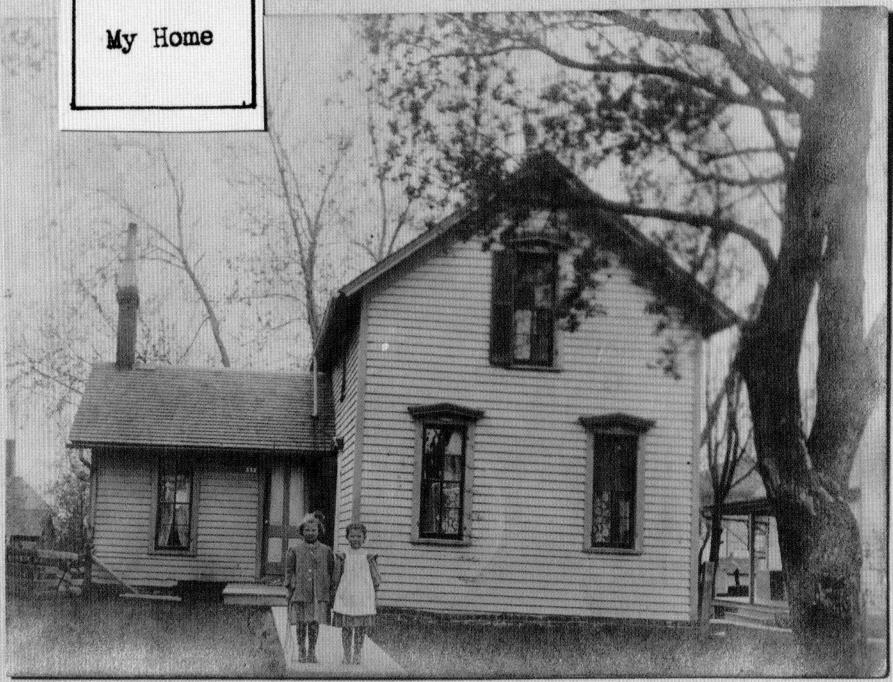

OUR HOUSE

Me standing in front of our house with my best friend (still), Lizzie Compton. After Daddy died, the roof went bad on the mud room, and Mother had it torn off.

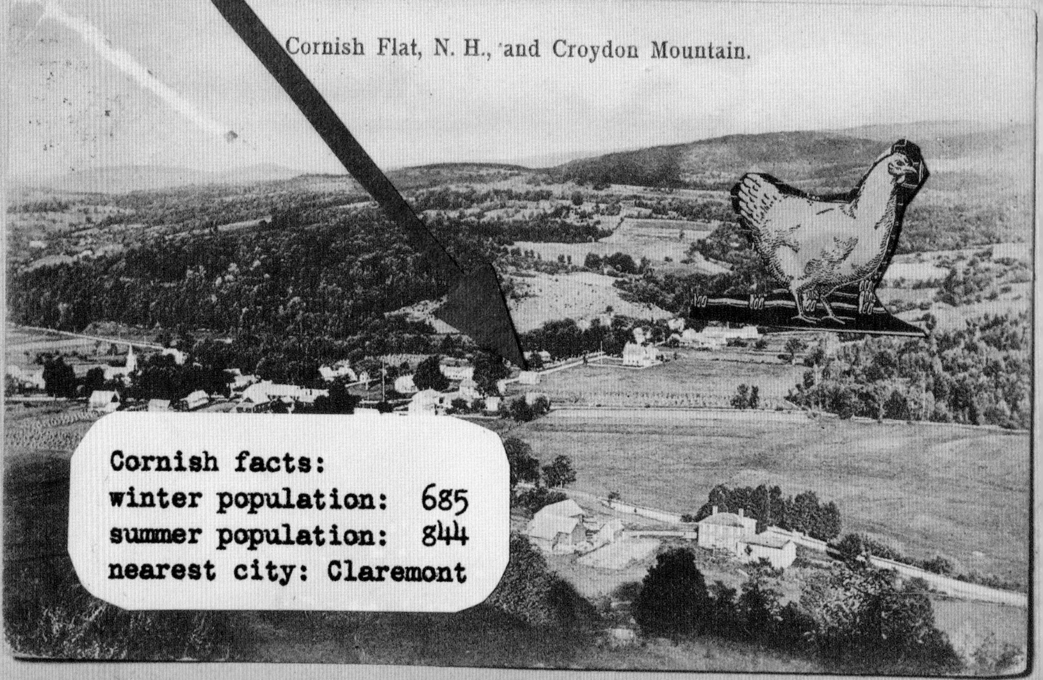
Cornish Flat, N. H., and Croydon Mountain.

Cornish facts:
winter population: 685
summer population: 844
nearest city: Claremont

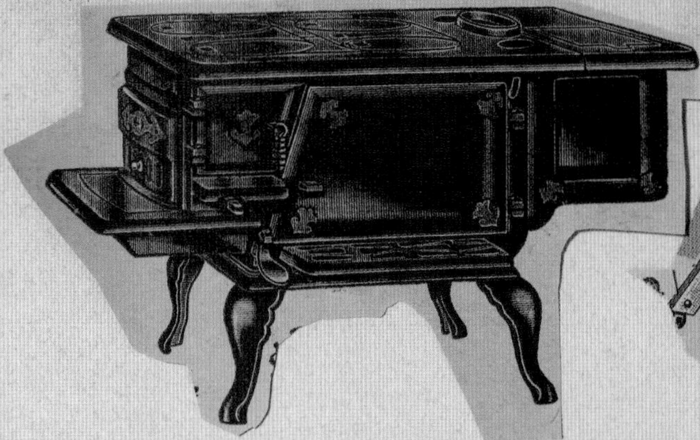

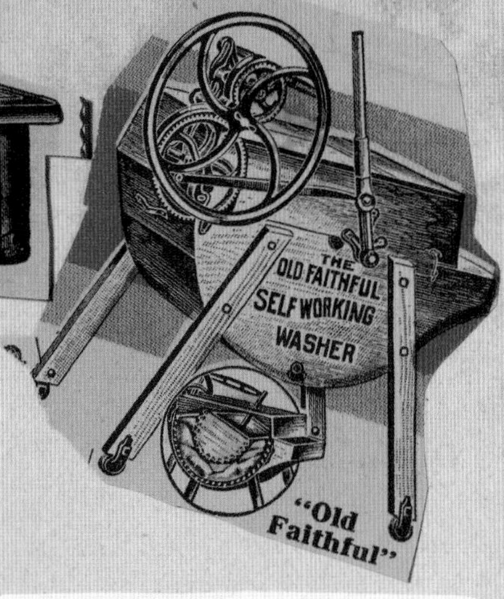
THE
OLD FAITHFUL
SELF WORKING
WASHER
"Old
Faithful"

Our farmhouse still doesn't
have "modern conveniences"
like a gas stove
or a motorized washer

And not likely to get them
any time soon.
*** sigh ***

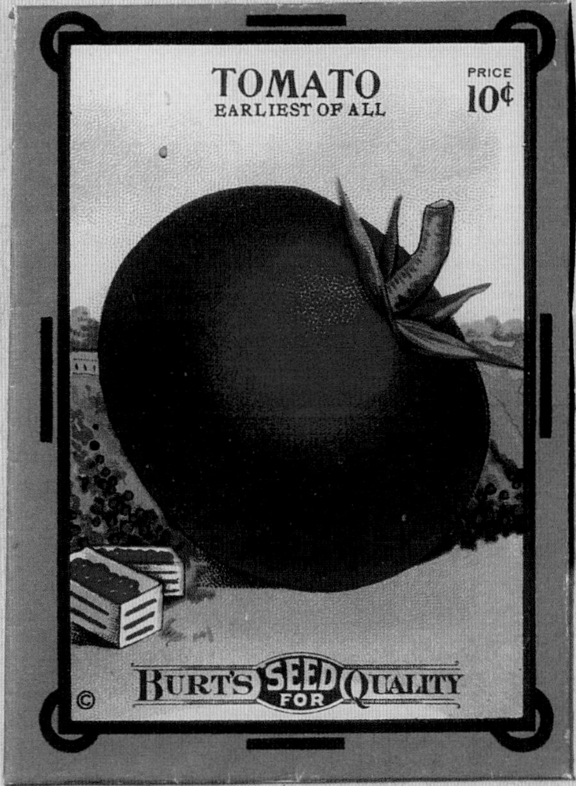
TOMATO
EARLIEST OF ALL
PRICE
10¢
BURT'S SEED FOR QUALITY
©

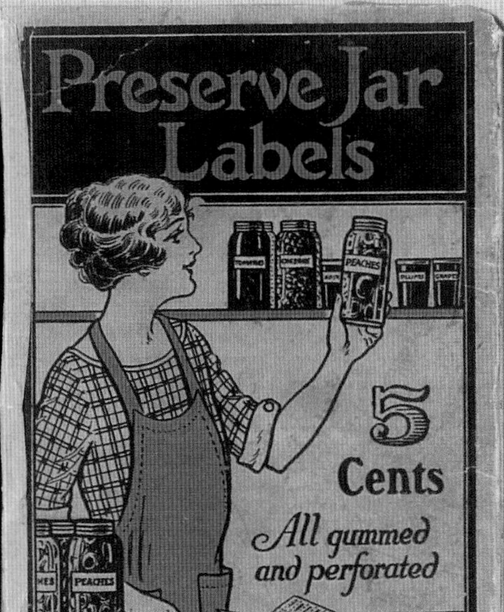
Preserve Jar
Labels
5
Cents
All gummed
and perforated

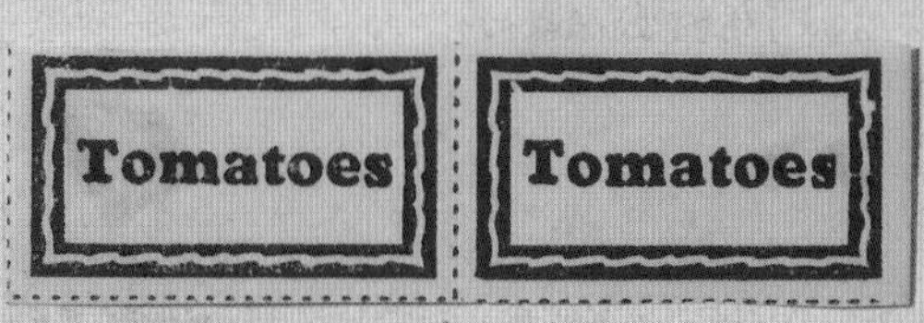
Tomatoes
Tomatoes

Can't afford to buy
food at grocery store
very often either.
Mother keeps a big (weedy)
vegetable garden and a
few scraggly hens.

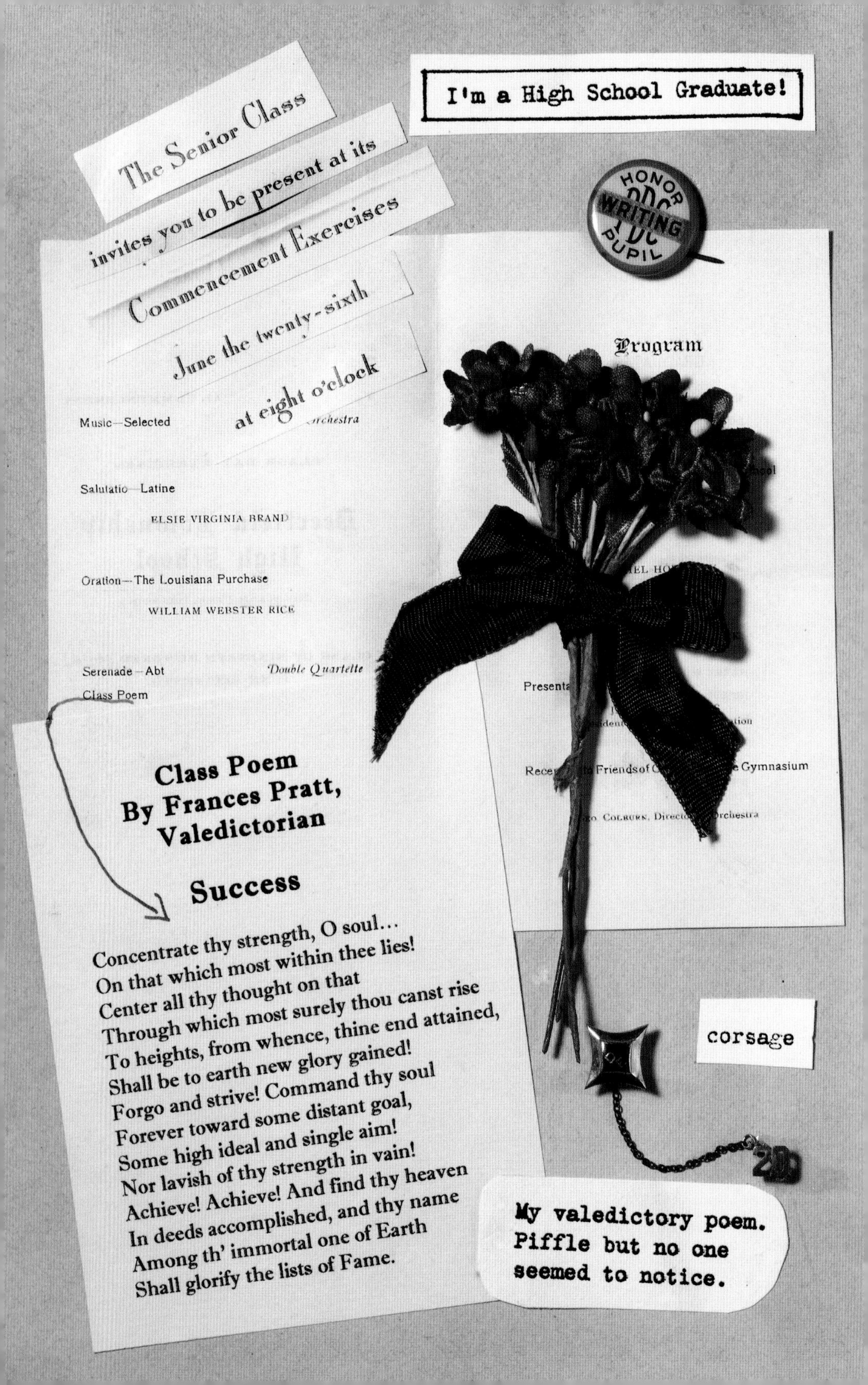

The Senior Class

invites you to be present at its

Commencement Exercises

June the twenty-sixth

at eight o'clock

HONOR
WRITING
PUPIL

Program

Music—Selected   Orchestra

Salutatio—Latine

ELSIE VIRGINIA BRAND

Oration—The Louisiana Purchase

WILLIAM WEBSTER RICE

Serenade—Abt   Double Quartette
Class Poem

Presenta

Recep   o Friends of C   e Gymnasium

o COLBURN, Director   Orchestra

Class Poem
By Frances Pratt,
Valedictorian

Success

Concentrate thy strength, O soul…
On that which most within thee lies!
Center all thy thought on that
Through which most surely thou canst rise
To heights, from whence, thine end attained,
Shall be to earth new glory gained!
Forgo and strive! Command thy soul
Forever toward some distant goal,
Some high ideal and single aim!
Nor lavish of thy strength in vain!
Achieve! Achieve! And find thy heaven
In deeds accomplished, and thy name
Among th' immortal one of Earth
Shall glorify the lists of Fame.

corsage

My valedictory poem.
Piffle but no one
seemed to notice.

My Class

Most Popular Girl: Adelaide Bullard

Most Popular Boy: Tommy Gaines

Prettiest Girl: Adelaide Bullard

Handsomest Boy: Tommy Gaines

Most Sensible Girl: Bessie Fergusen

* Smartest Girl: Frankie Pratt (if I do say so myself)

Smartest Boy: Will Atwater

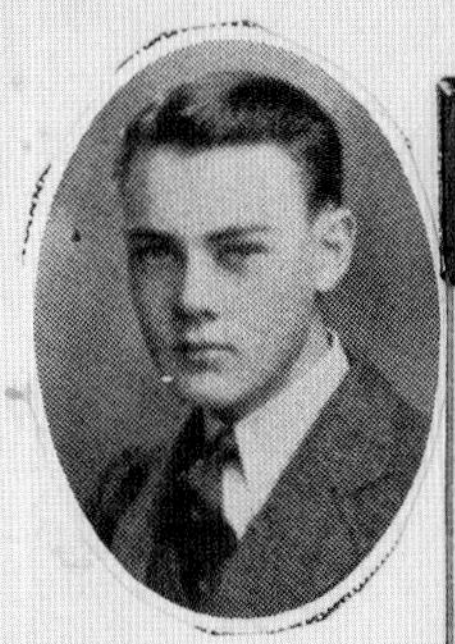

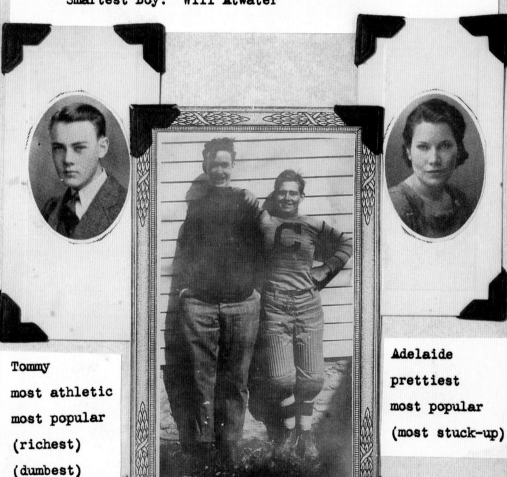

Tommy
most athletic
most popular
(richest)
(dumbest)

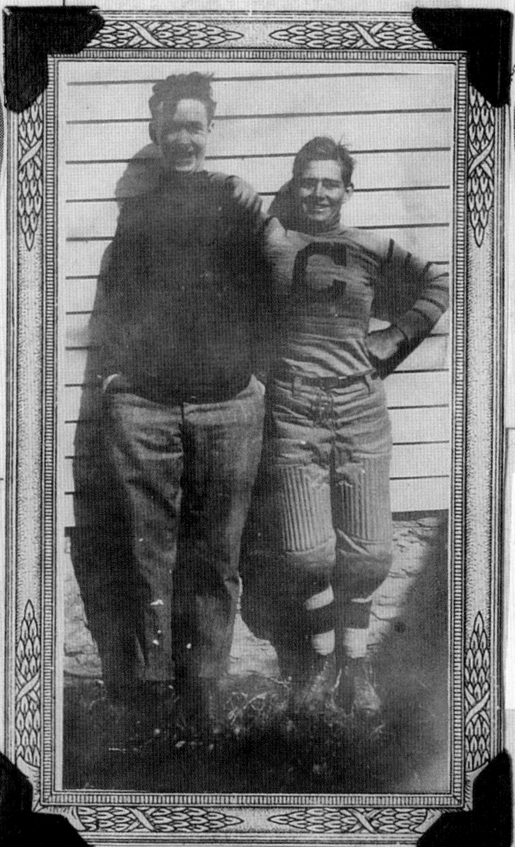

C

Tommy in football uniform
Will (smartest) who didn't
make the team

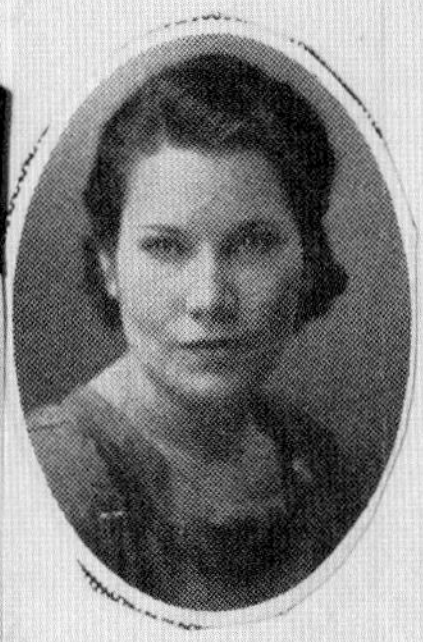

Adelaide
prettiest
most popular
(most stuck-up)

May true friends be around you

MY FRIENDS

Lizzie Compton
My best friend always.
Her father is postmaster.
She's the most cheerful girl
in class and can't understand
why I'm so bookish and serious.
And she CAN'T understand why
either Bessie or I would ever
want to go to college.

Bessie Fergusen
2nd best friend.
Most sensible girl in class.
Is going to go to Plymouth
State to get a degree in
home economics. Can cook
and sew like a demon.

Baking Powder Biscuit

2 cups flour	2 tablespoons lard
4 teaspoons baking powder	¾ to 1 cup milk
	1 teaspoon salt

Bessie is teaching us
how to cook. My biscuits
came out like golf balls.

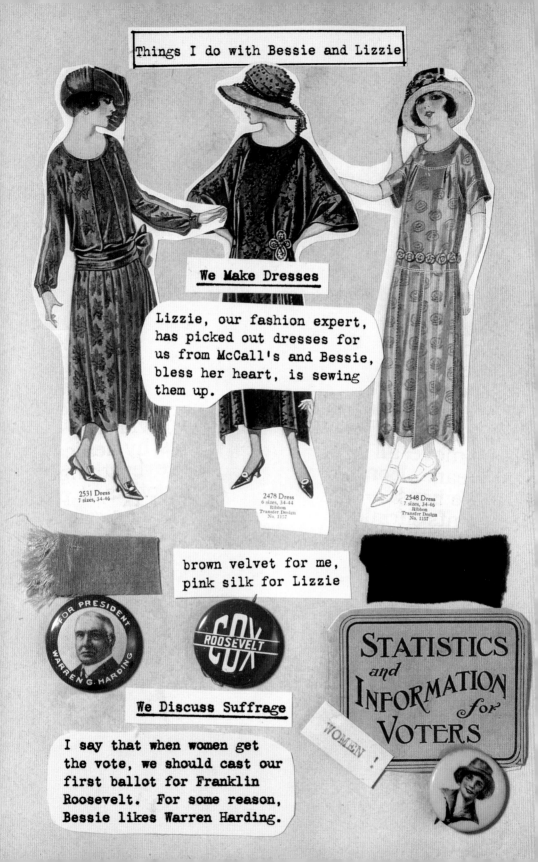

Things I do with Bessie and Lizzie

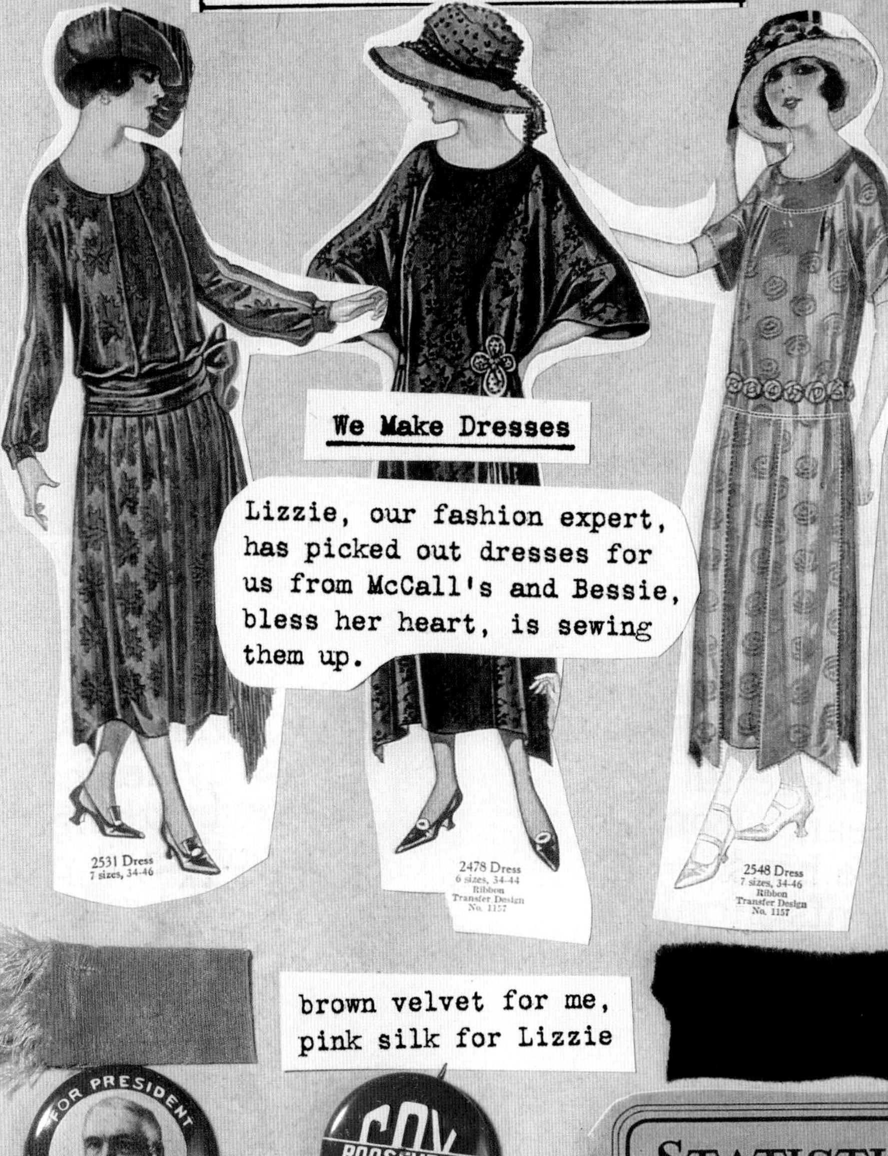
2531 Dress
7 sizes, 34-46
2478 Dress
6 sizes, 34-44
Ribbon
Transfer Design
No. 1157
2548 Dress
7 sizes, 34-46
Ribbon
Transfer Design
No. 1157

We Make Dresses

Lizzie, our fashion expert, has picked out dresses for us from McCall's and Bessie, bless her heart, is sewing them up.

brown velvet for me, pink silk for Lizzie

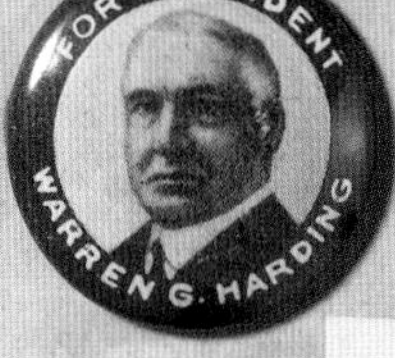
FOR PRESIDENT
WARREN G. HARDING

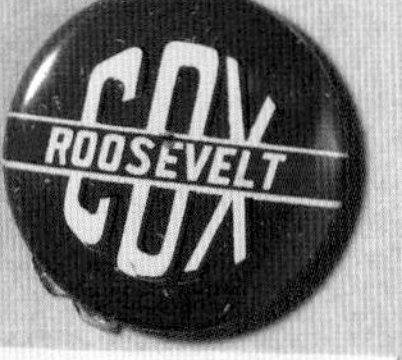
COX
ROOSEVELT
COX

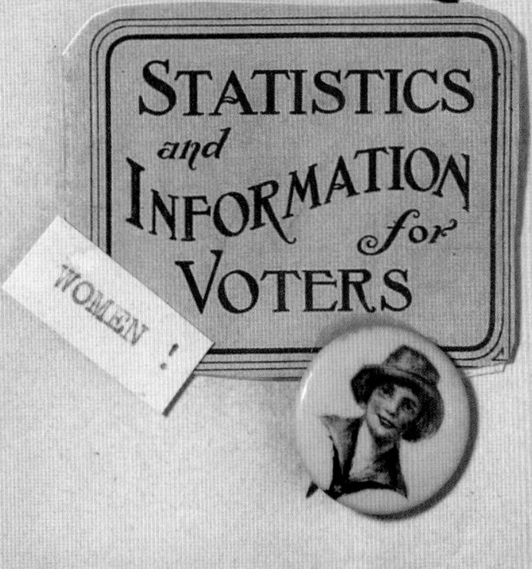
STATISTICS and INFORMATION for VOTERS
WOMEN !

We Discuss Suffrage

I say that when women get the vote, we should cast our first ballot for Franklin Roosevelt. For some reason, Bessie likes Warren Harding.

We Play Cards

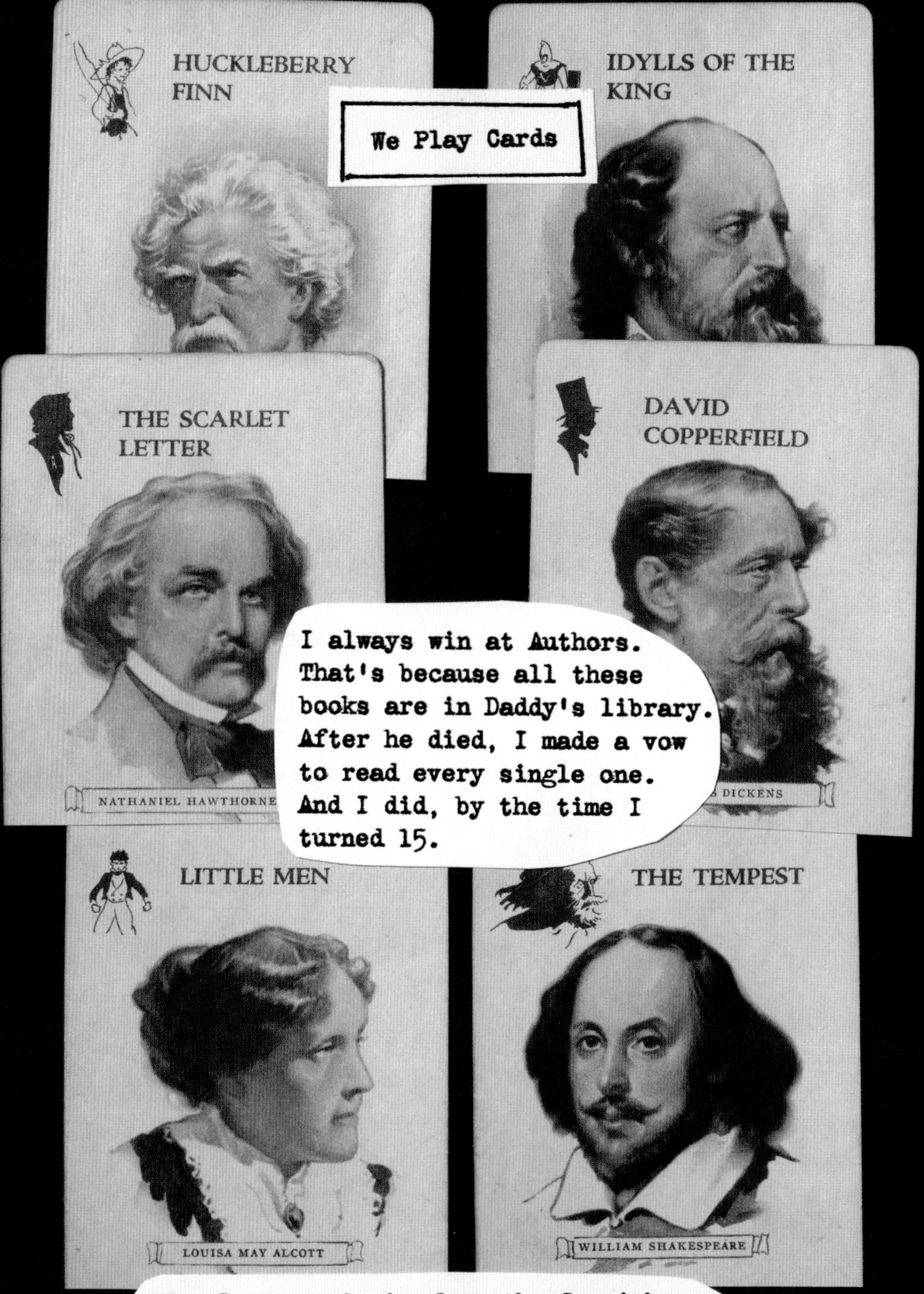
HUCKLEBERRY FINN
IDYLLS OF THE KING
THE SCARLET LETTER
NATHANIEL HAWTHORNE
DAVID COPPERFIELD
DICKENS
LITTLE MEN
LOUISA MAY ALCOTT
THE TEMPEST
WILLIAM SHAKESPEARE

I always win at Authors. That's because all these books are in Daddy's library. After he died, I made a vow to read every single one. And I did, by the time I turned 15.

Now I get my books from the Cornish library. I just finished reading Summer by Mrs. Edith Wharton for the second time. It's about a 16-year-old girl stuck in a New England village. Sounds familiar.

LEARN TO READ THE FUTURE
with
OLD GYPSY FORTUNE CARDS

Shuffle the cards three times and have the ~~~
whose fortu~~~ ~~~ told cut the deck o~~~
each shuffle~~~

Lay the ~~~
rows of ~~~
the cente~~~
in the ~~~
telling ~~~

Wh~~~
repres~~~
and ~~~
inter~~~
he ~~~
No~~~
he~~~

~~~HING CO.

YOUNG WOMAN

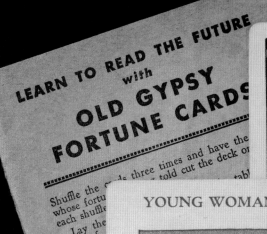

A friend will unknowing~~~
Forgive.

ery careful when you see a certain
blonde.

gift will
Refuse~~~

BEGINNING 1

New admirer in the near future.

Great change for the better.

1

A new undertaking will
be successful.

PROPOSITION

Some event or person will light the way
out of darkness.

A long nourished ambition coming to
realization.

A business offer soon.
Accept.

My fortune.

But what does it mean. . . ?

We Swap Beauty Tips

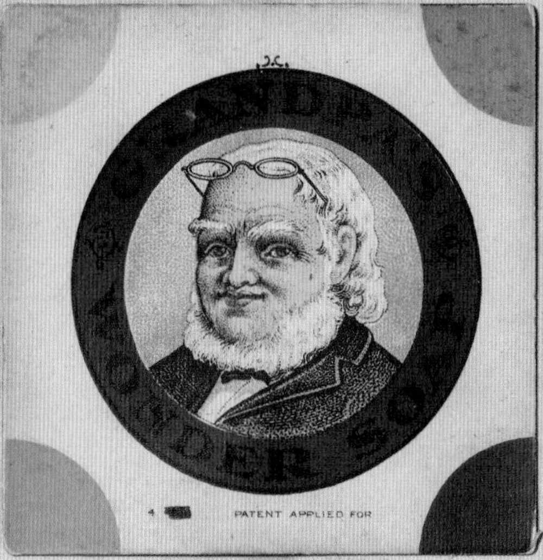
WONDER
PATENT APPLIED FOR

Mother says a bar of yellow soap is all a girl needs, but we use Palmolive to . . .

Keep That Wedding Day Complexion

10c

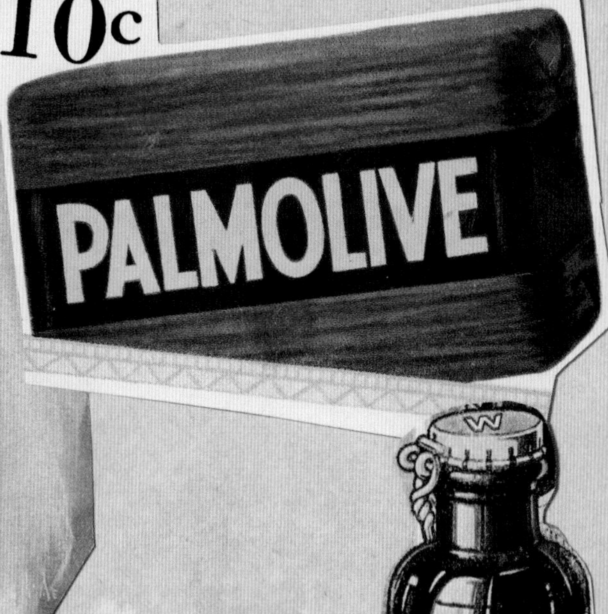
PALMOLIVE

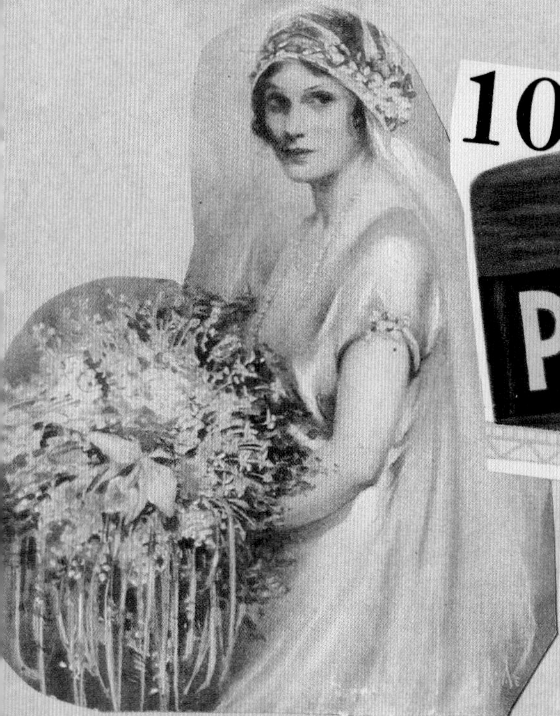

Made our own freckle cream with peroxide, lemon juice, and lard. Got red rash.

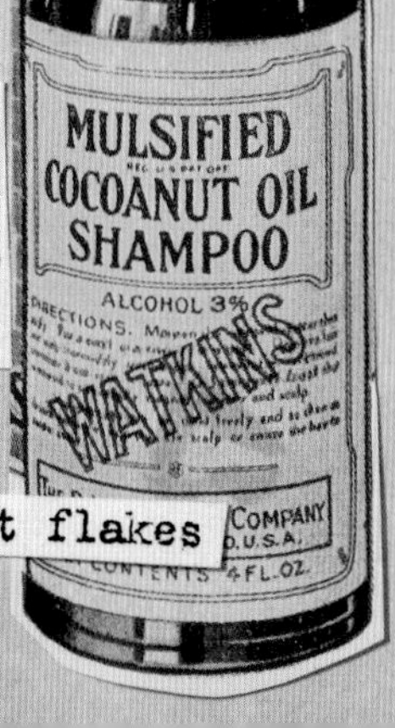
MULSIFIED
COCOANUT OIL
SHAMPOO
ALCOHOL 3%
WATKINS
COMPANY
CONTENTS 4 FL. OZ.

Leaves scalp without flakes

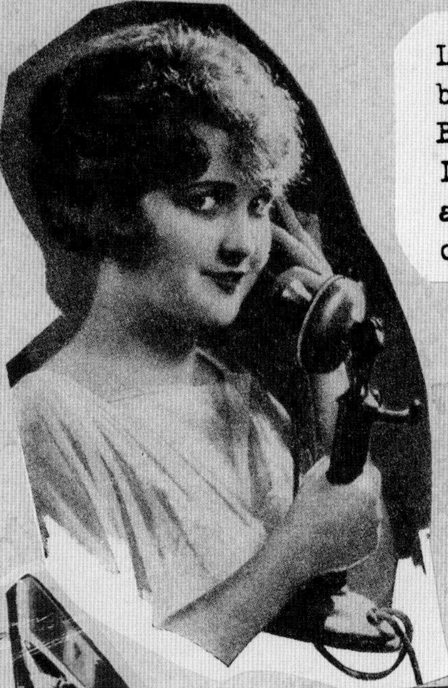

Lizzie got her hair bobbed at Watkins Barbershop in Claremont. I chickened out and just got fringe on the sides.

Lizzie's hair →

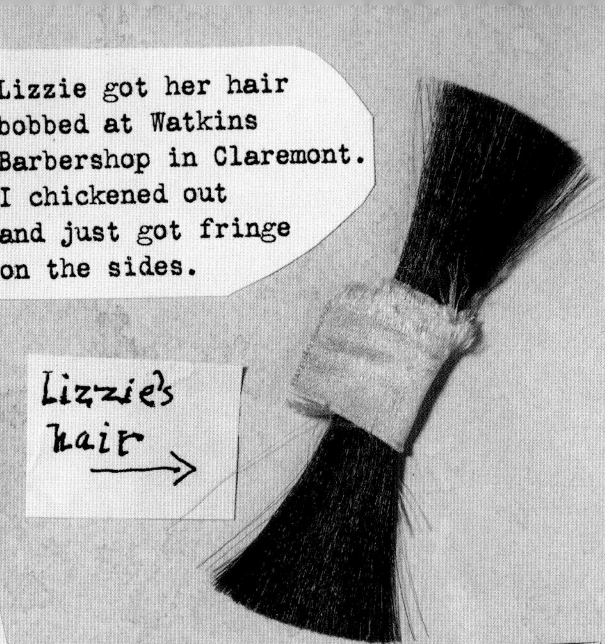

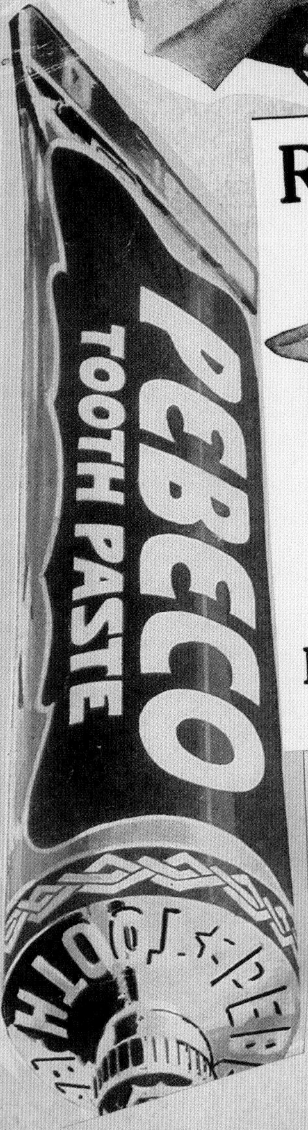
PEBECO
TOOTH PASTE

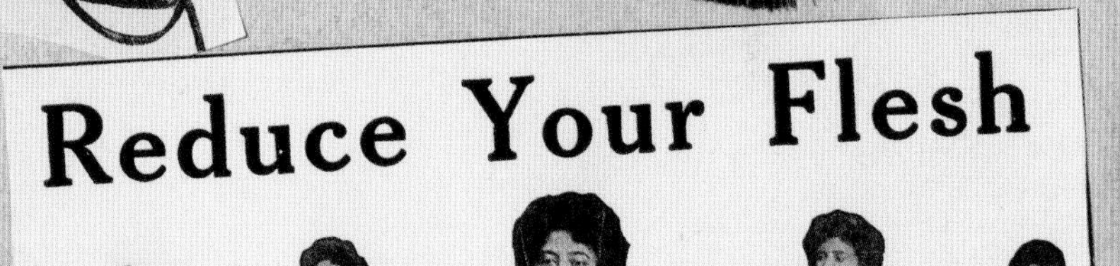
Reduce Your Flesh
You can quickly dissolve superfluous flesh easily and with safety wherever desired by wearing
Dr. Walter's famous medicated reducing Rubber Garments

Bessie ordered one of these for her hips. 3 weeks and hips have not dissolved.

The ads say a girl must be careful she doesn't have halitosis, so we brush with Pebeco.

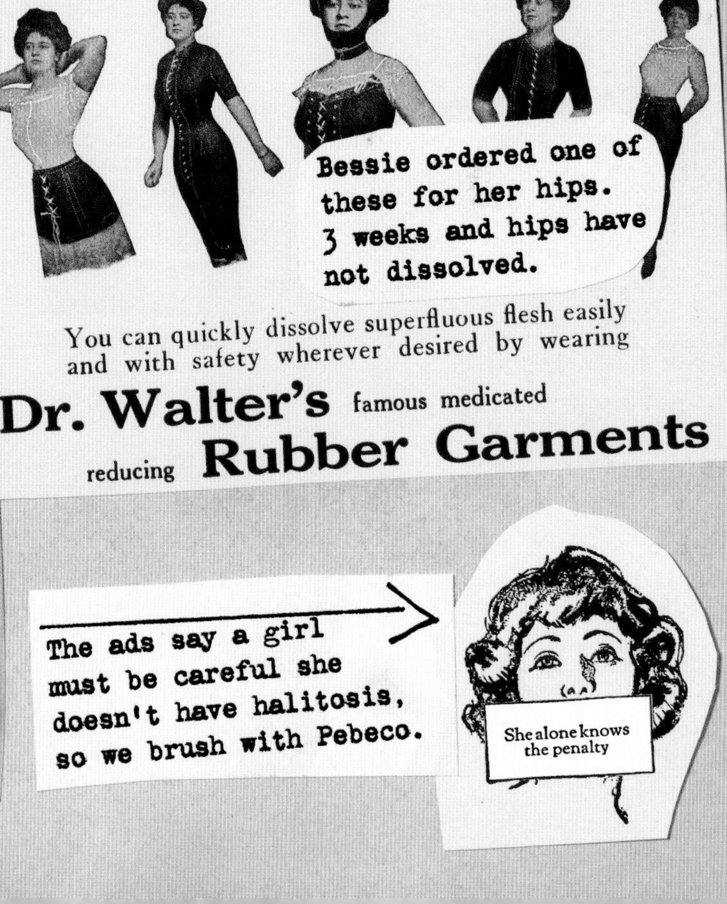
She alone knows the penalty

My First Date

Will Atwater (the smartest boy) asked me (the smartest girl) on an official date.

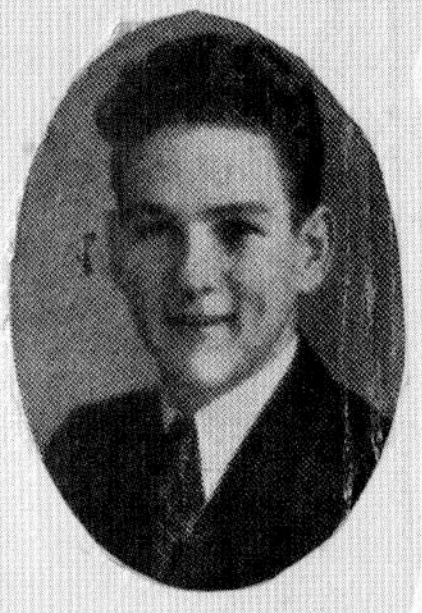

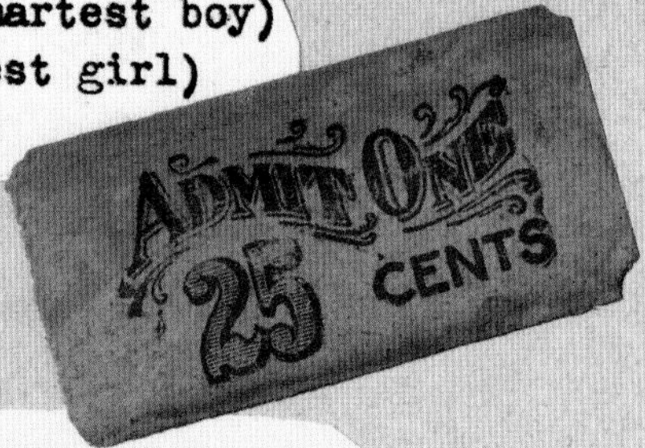
ADMIT ONE
25 CENTS

We drove to White River Junction to see Way Down East in the new picture palace. Movie was actually filmed here on the White River. Fancy that.

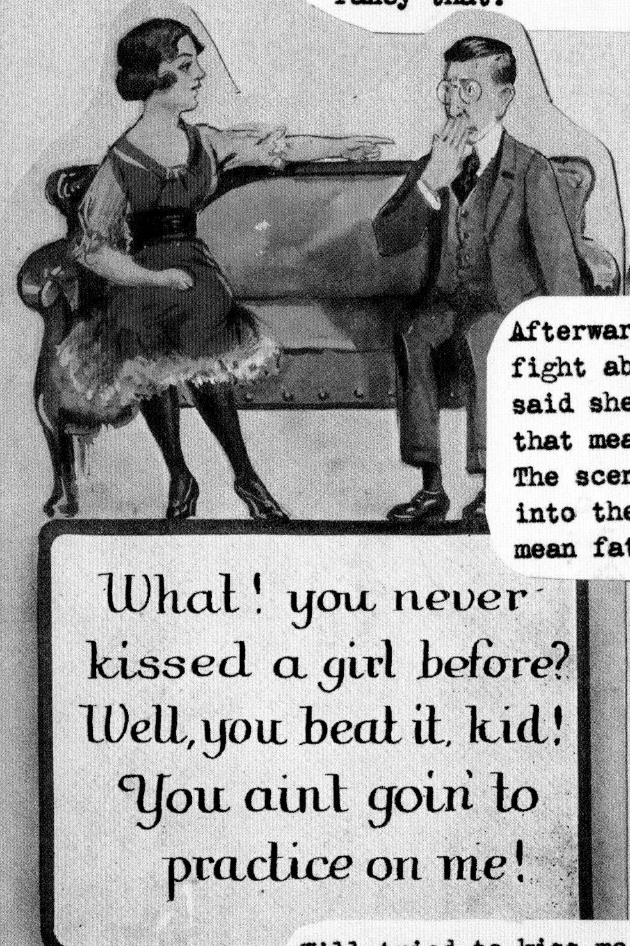
What! you never kissed a girl before? Well, you beat it, kid! You aint goin' to practice on me!

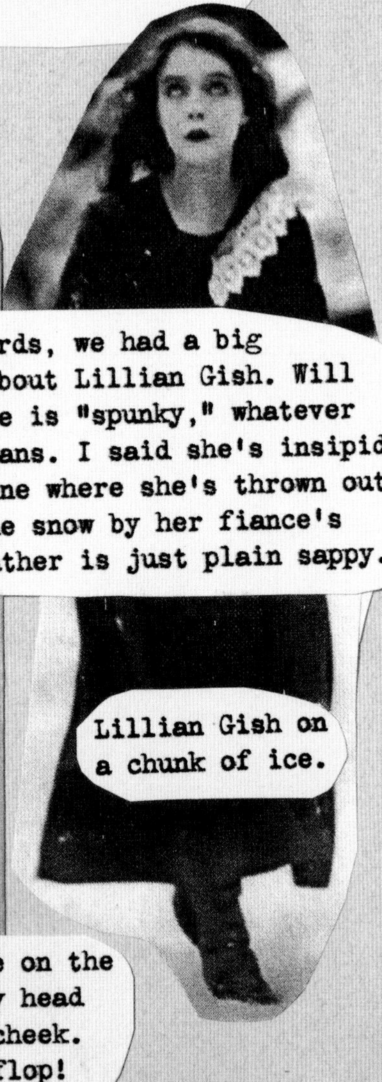

Afterwards, we had a big fight about Lillian Gish. Will said she is "spunky," whatever that means. I said she's insipid. The scene where she's thrown out into the snow by her fiance's mean father is just plain sappy.

Lillian Gish on a chunk of ice.

Will tried to kiss me on the lips, but I turned my head quick, so he got my cheek. Date was a complete flop!

My Idea of the Perfect Male

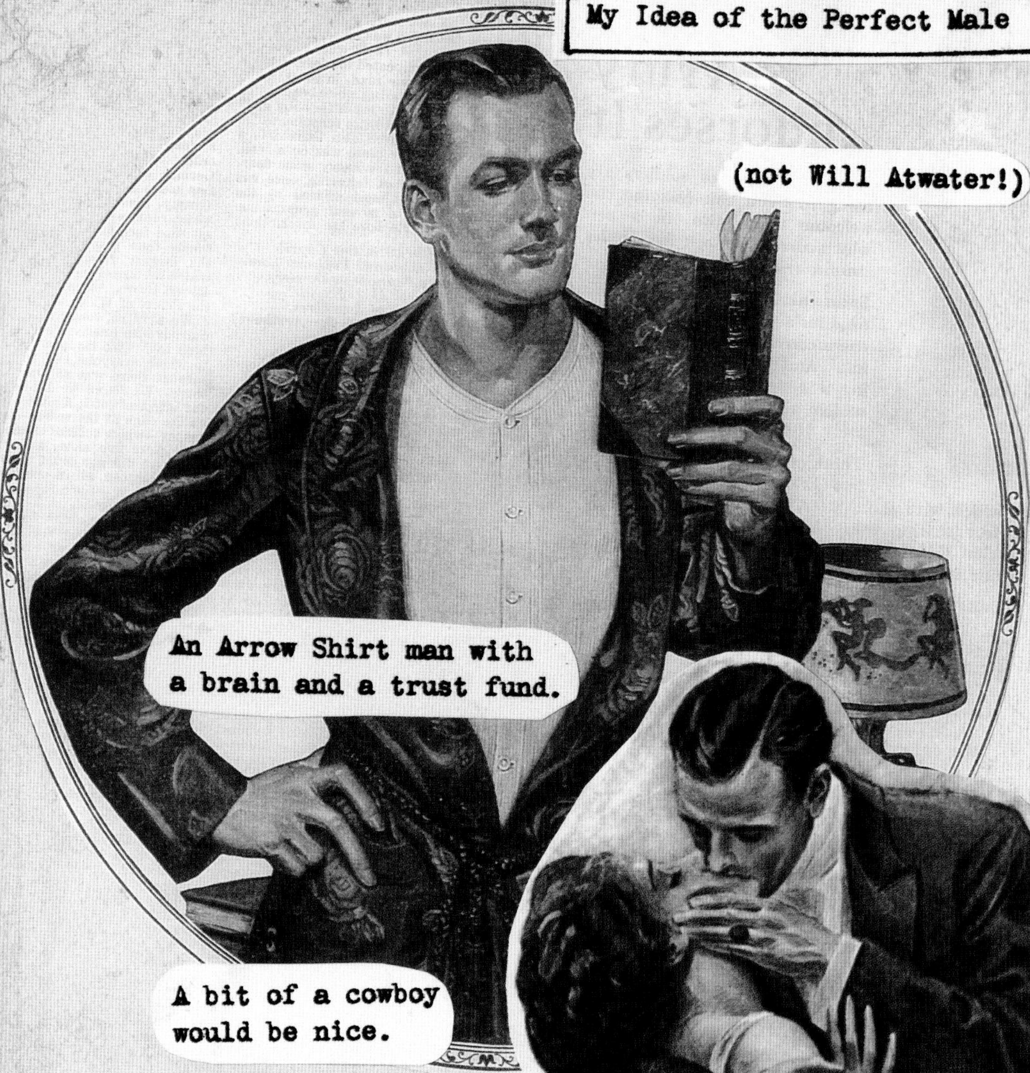

(not Will Atwater!)

An Arrow Shirt man with
a brain and a trust fund.

A bit of a cowboy
would be nice.

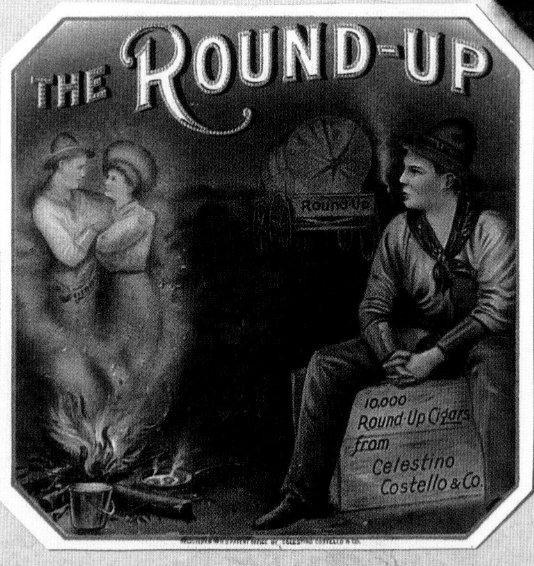
THE ROUND-UP
Round-Up
10,000
Round-Up Cigars
from
Celestino
Costello & Co.

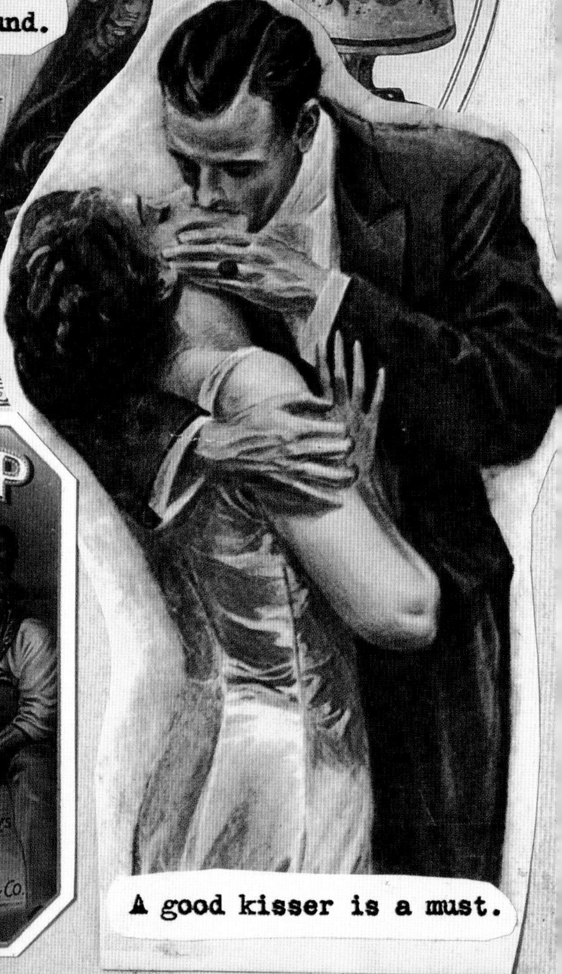

A good kisser is a must.

Daddy always wanted me to go to college.
Miss Vera Jones, the principal,
arranged for me to take the Vassar
entrance exams. She was Class of 1892.
They were d-n hard, and I was sure
I flunked!

Vassar College

Dear Miss Pratt,   wants me . . .

The Vassar College Admission Committee is pleased
to inform you that you have passed the entrance
examinations and offer you a place in the Class
of 1924.

Due to Rev. Phelps's letter concerning your widowed
mother's financial situation, we are prepared to offer
you a half-scholarship. With this stipend, your tuition
for the 1920-21 academic year is reduced to $500. In
order to preserve your scholarship, the Committee
requires that you maintain a B average.

Please accept our congratulation

Sincerely Yours,

C. Mildred Thompson

Secretary, Committee

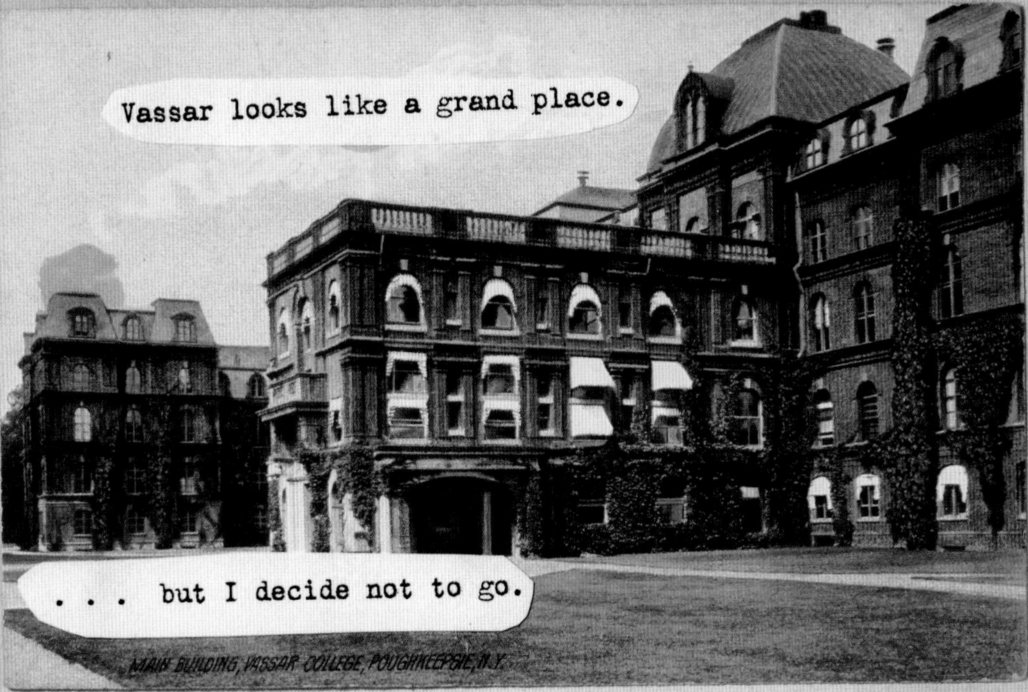
Vassar looks like a grand place.
. . . but I decide not to go.
MAIN BUILDING, VASSAR COLLEGE, POUGHKEEPSIE, N.Y.

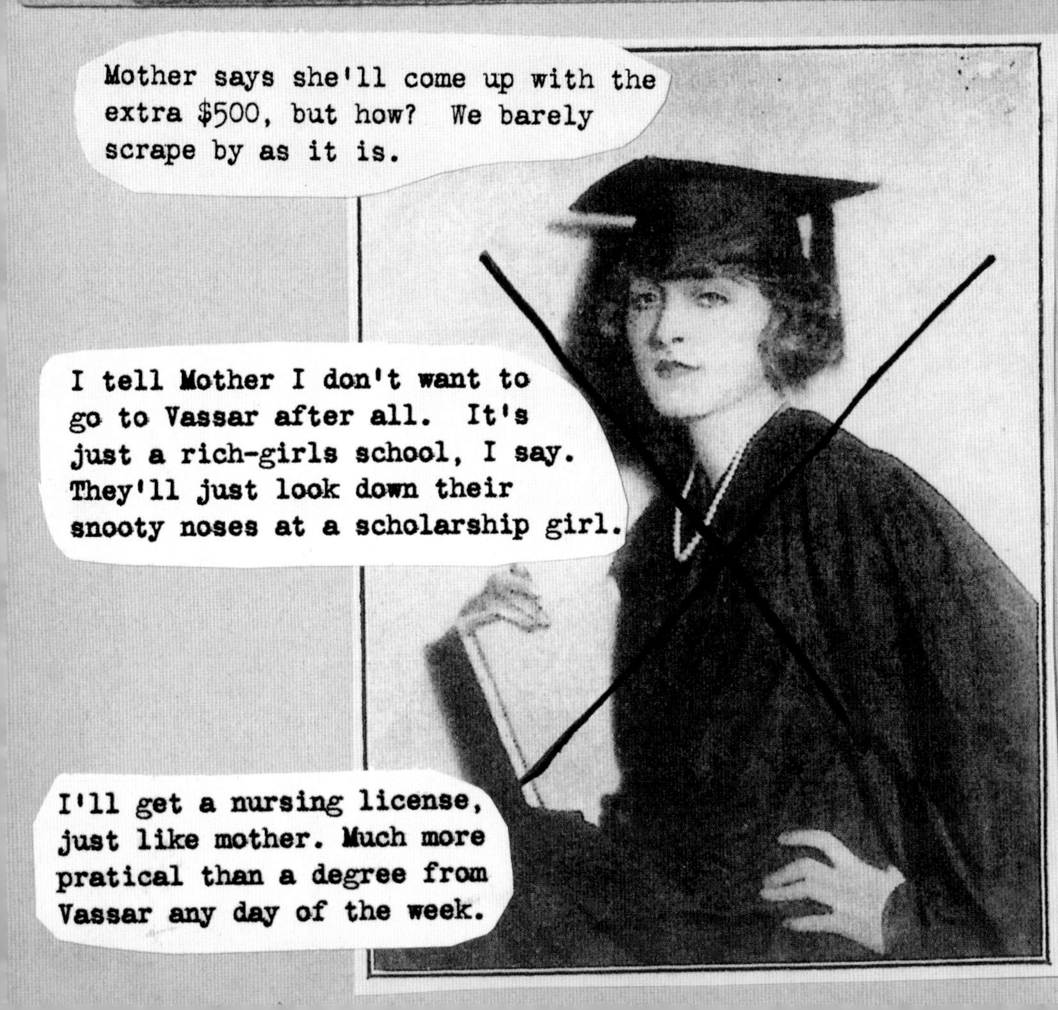
Mother says she'll come up with the extra $500, but how? We barely scrape by as it is.
I tell Mother I don't want to go to Vassar after all. It's just a rich-girls school, I say. They'll just look down their snooty noses at a scholarship girl.
I'll get a nursing license, just like mother. Much more pratical than a degree from Vassar any day of the week.

My First Job

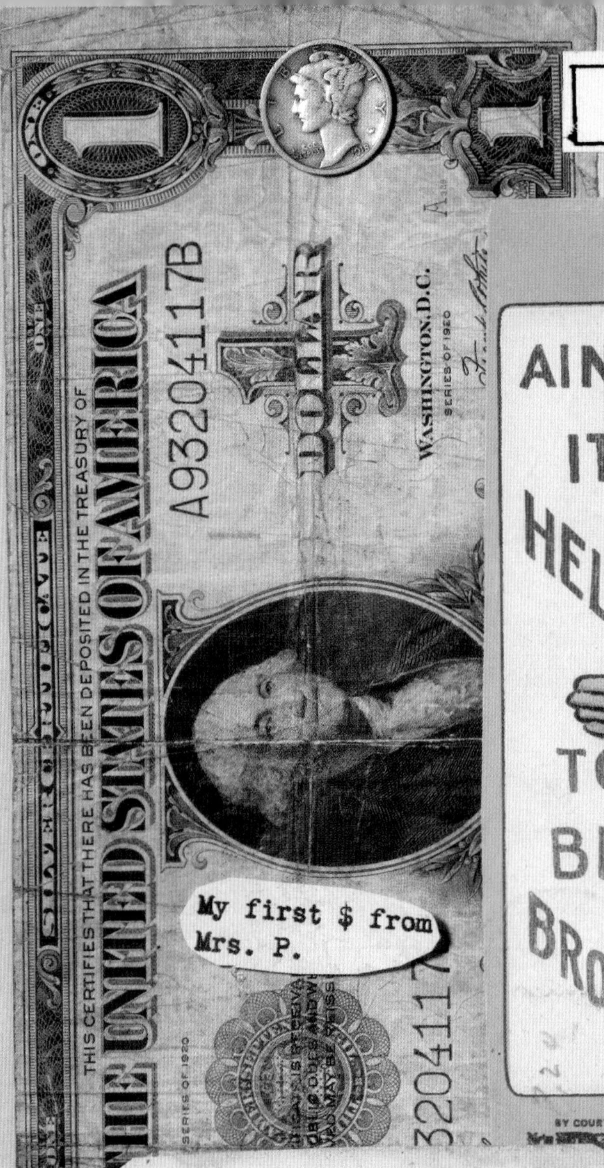
THE UNITED STATES OF AMERICA
THIS CERTIFIES THAT THERE HAS BEEN DEPOSITED IN THE TREASURY OF
ONE DOLLAR
A93204117B
WASHINGTON, D.C.
SERIES OF 1920

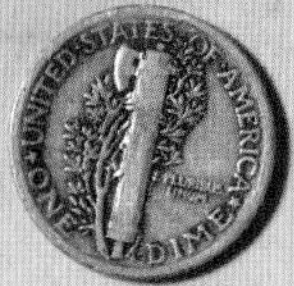

My first $ from Mrs. P.

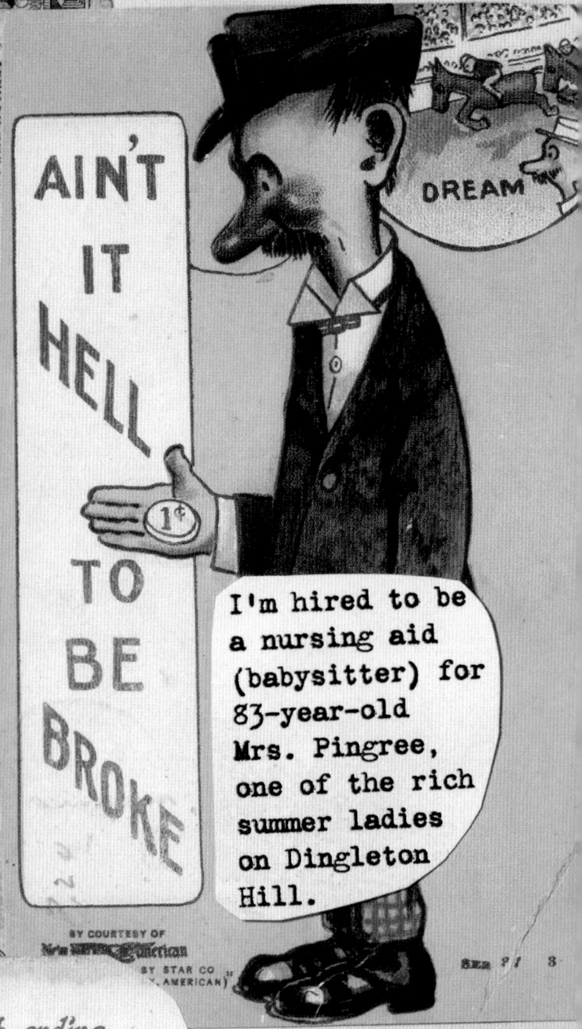
AIN'T IT HELL TO BE BROKE
DREAM
1¢

I'm hired to be a nursing aid (babysitter) for 83-year-old Mrs. Pingree, one of the rich summer ladies on Dingleton Hill.

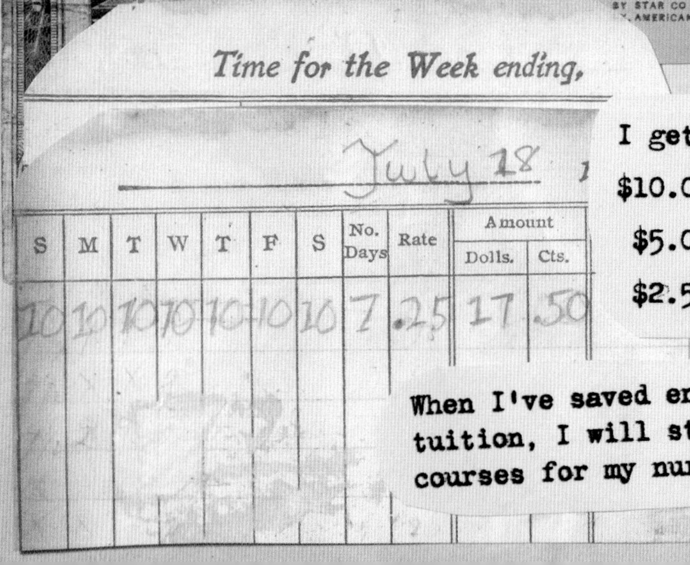

Time for the Week ending,

July 18

S	M	T	W	T	F	S	No. Days	Rate	Amount Dolls.	Amount Cts.
10	10	10	10	10	10	10	7	.25	17	.50

I get paid $17.50 a week.

$10.00 to mother

$5.00 pocket money

$2.50 savings

When I've saved enough for tuition, I will start taking night courses for my nursing license.

A Day with Mrs. Pingree: a Sad Story

By Frances Pratt

POSTUM CEREAL
INSTANT
Reg. U.S. Pat. Off.
HEALTH FIRST
HEALTH FIRST
POSTUM
A BEVERAGE
made of different parts of Wheat and a small portion of Molasses
Postum Cereal Company.
BATTLE CREEK, MICH., U.S.A.
NET WEIGHT EIGHT OUNCES

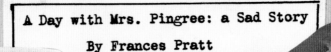

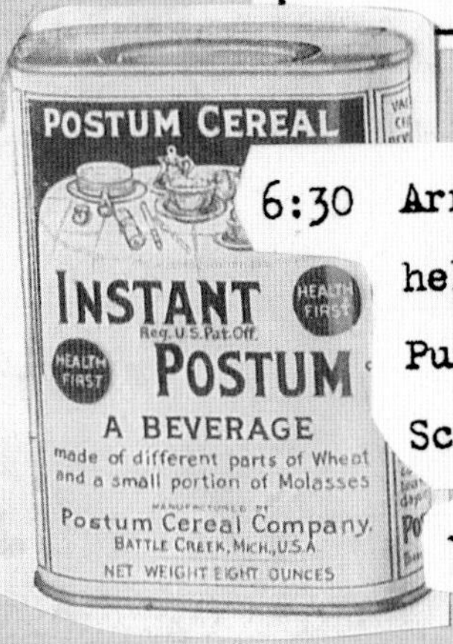

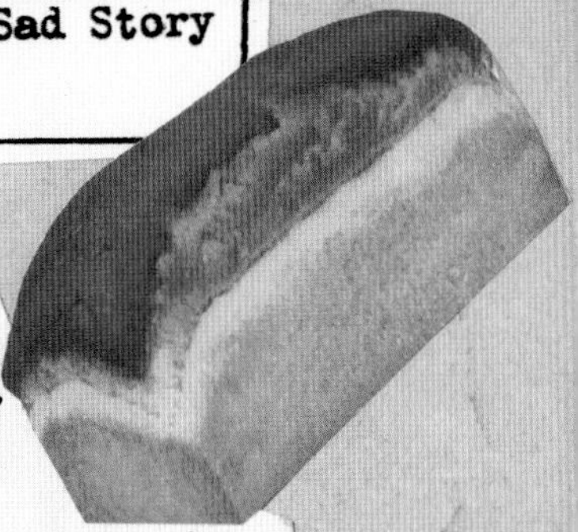

6:30 Arrive, wake Mrs. P up,
help her to the commode.
Put her glasses on.
Scrub her dentures and insert them.

7:00 Bring Mrs. P. breakfast in bed.
1 slice unbuttered toast
cup of Postum

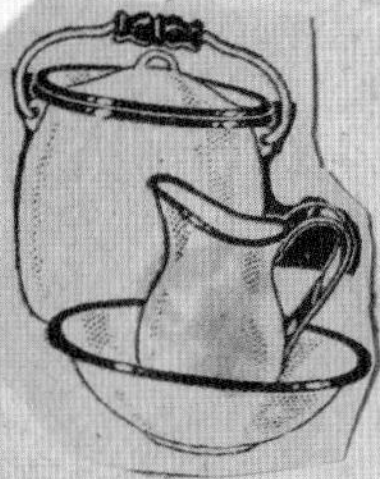

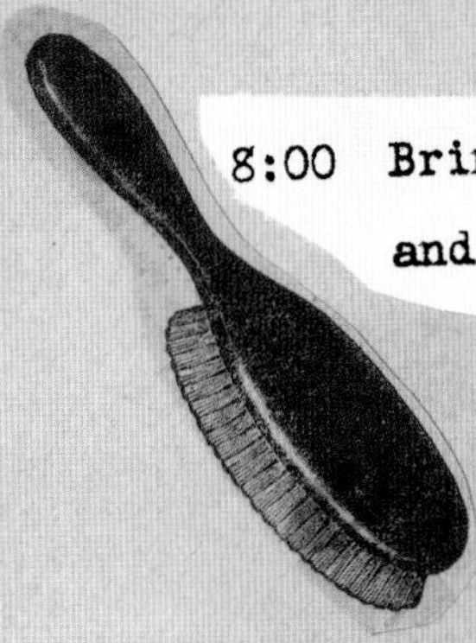

8:00 Bring basin of warm water
and perform her "ablutions."

8:30 Brush out her wisps of white hair.

10:15 dozes off

10:30 Take breakfast tray to kitchen.
Rinse dishes.
Get bored and snoop through stuff in
pigeon-hole in library desk.
Find picture of Mrs. P
as debutante.

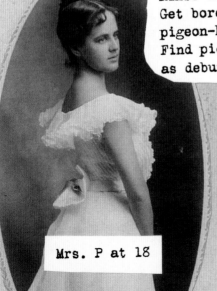

Mrs. P at 18

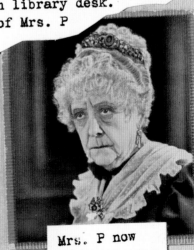

Mrs. P now

Enter Captain Pingree

11:45 Capt. James Pingree wanders down to the kitchen, looking for breakfast. He's been staying with his grandmother since he got out of the army last year. Can't go back to his law firm in New York because lungs are scarred from mustard gas.

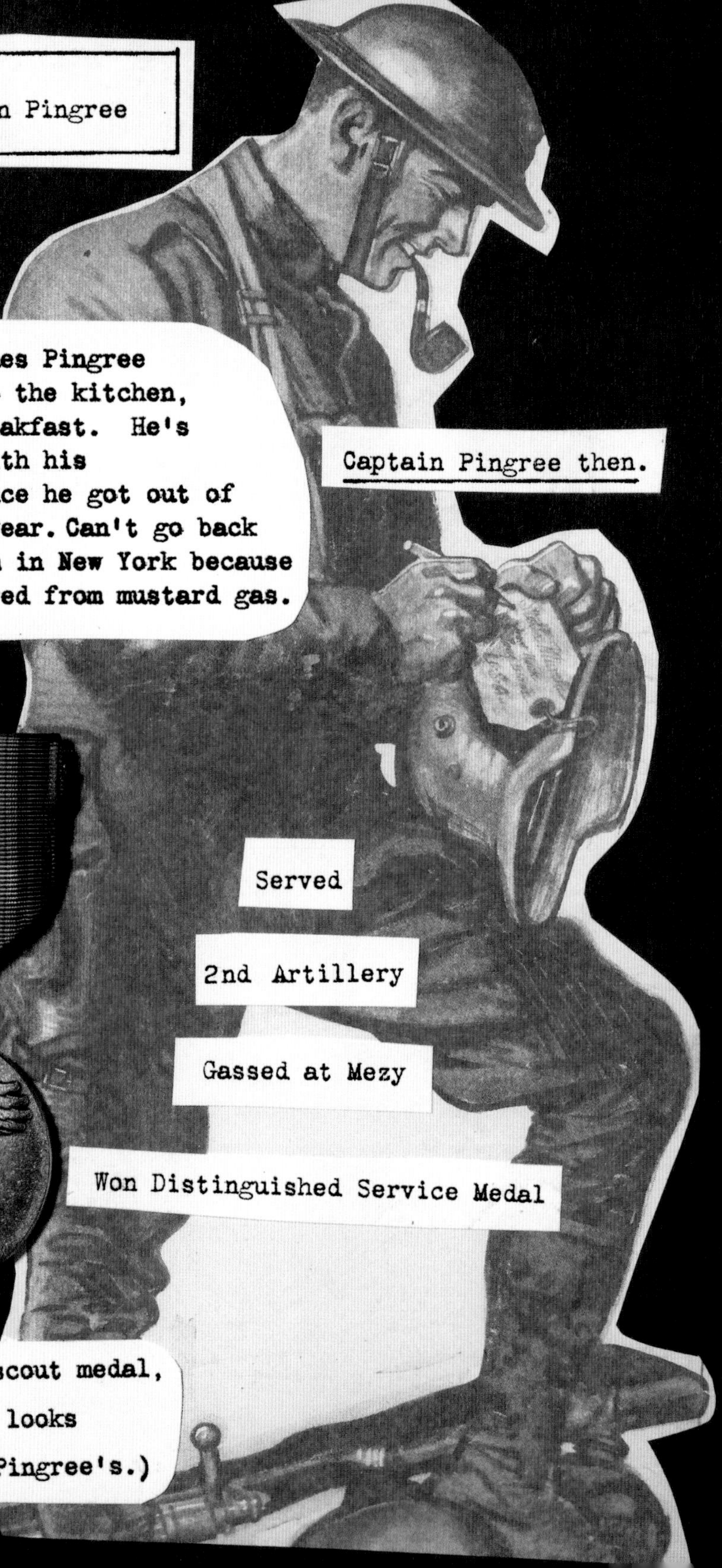

Captain Pingree then.

Served

2nd Artillery

Gassed at Mezy

Won Distinguished Service Medal

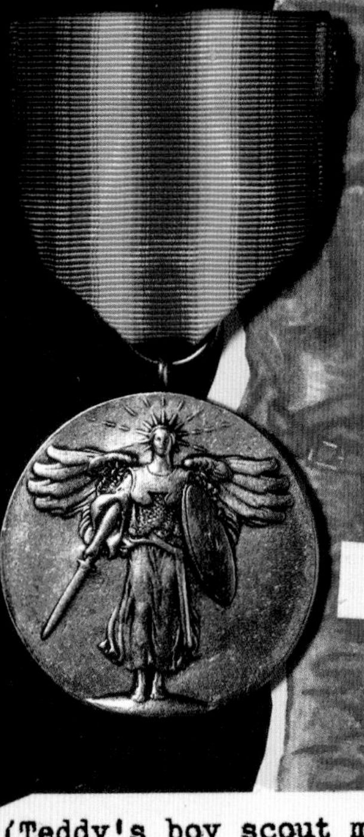

(Teddy's boy scout medal, which sort of looks like Captain Pingree's.)

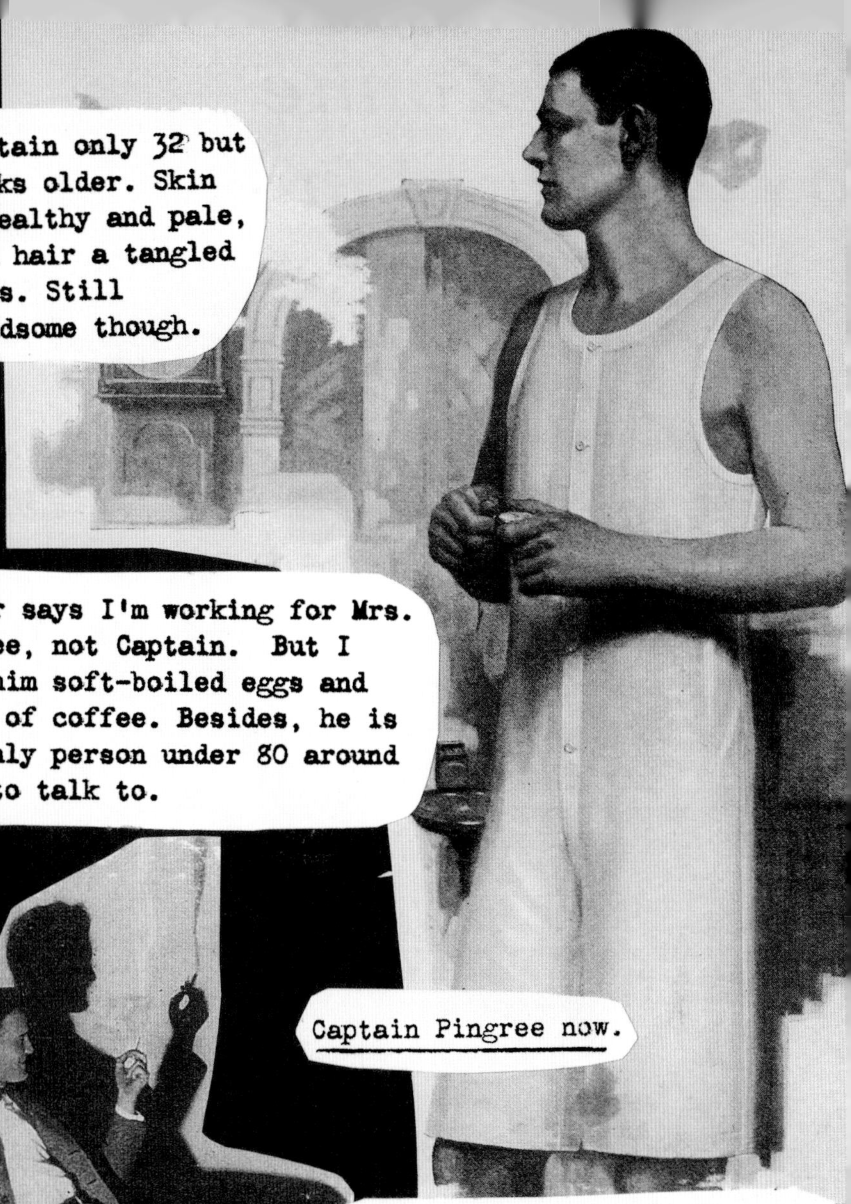

Captain only 32 but looks older. Skin unhealthy and pale, and hair a tangled mess. Still handsome though.

Mother says I'm working for Mrs. Pingree, not Captain. But I make him soft-boiled eggs and a pot of coffee. Besides, he is the only person under 80 around here to talk to.

Captain Pingree now.

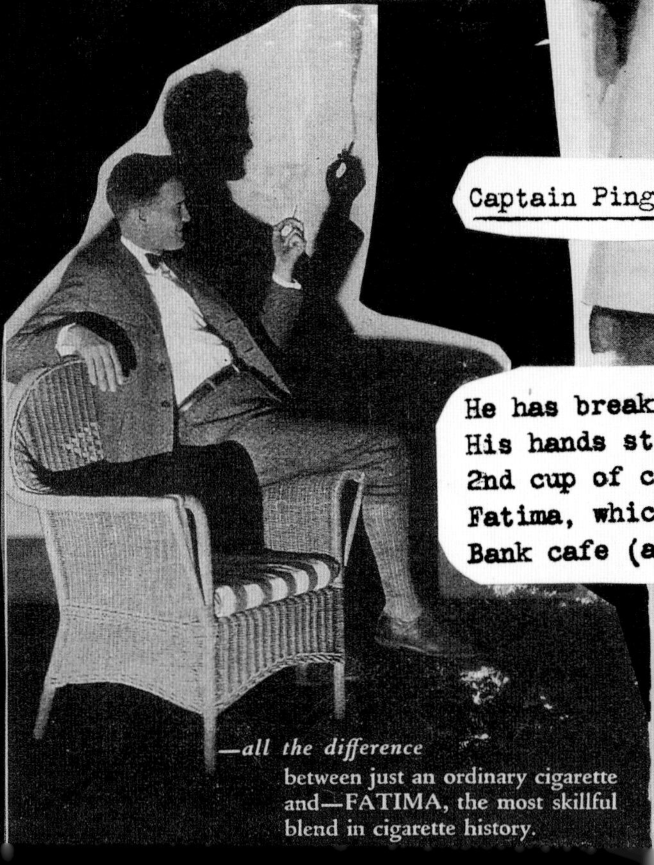
—all the difference
between just an ordinary cigarette and—FATIMA, the most skillful blend in cigarette history.

He has breakfast at kitchen table. His hands stop trembling after 2nd cup of coffee. He lights Fatima, which smells like Left Bank cafe (at least I think so).

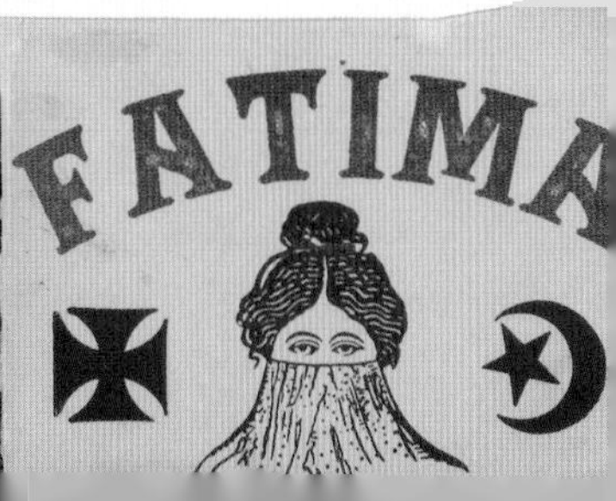
FATIMA

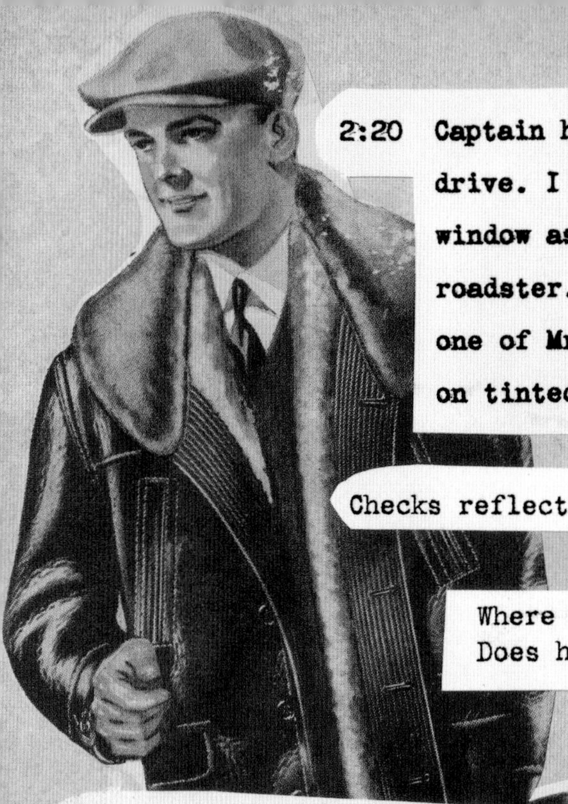

2:20 Captain heads out for his daily drive. I watch from kitchen window as he climbs in Aero roadster. He paid for it with one of Mrs. P.'s checks. He slips on tinted glasses and a tweed cap.

Checks reflection in side mirror. Vain!!

Where does he go every day?
Does he have a girl?

4:30 Heat can of Campbell's soup for Mrs. P's supper.

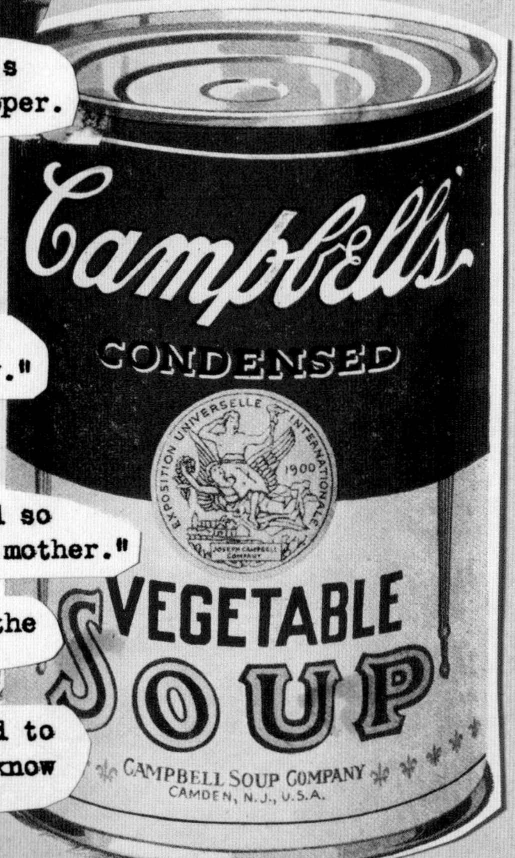
Campbell's
CONDENSED
EXPOSITION UNIVERSELLE INTERNATIONALE 1900
VEGETABLE
SOUP
CAMPBELL SOUP COMPANY
CAMDEN, N.J., U.S.A.

Mrs. P. perks up for the first time all day and wants to talk.

"Your father's my doctor but he hasn't come around lately."
"He's dead."
"Since when?"
"Five years ago."
"Then you should get married so your husband can help your mother."
"I'm only 17."
"Plenty old enough. When's the Captain getting back?"
"I don't know."
"I thought you were supposed to be a smart girl. You don't know much for a smart girl."

Captain Pingree Invites Me on an Adventure !

Frankie—
Come for a drive with
me this afternoon.
I know what you'll say....
You can't leave Gran.
But I've gotten Hobbes'
daughter Tess to come in.
I'll pack a picnic.
Wont take no for an
answer.
Meet you in the driveway
at 1:00....

J.P.

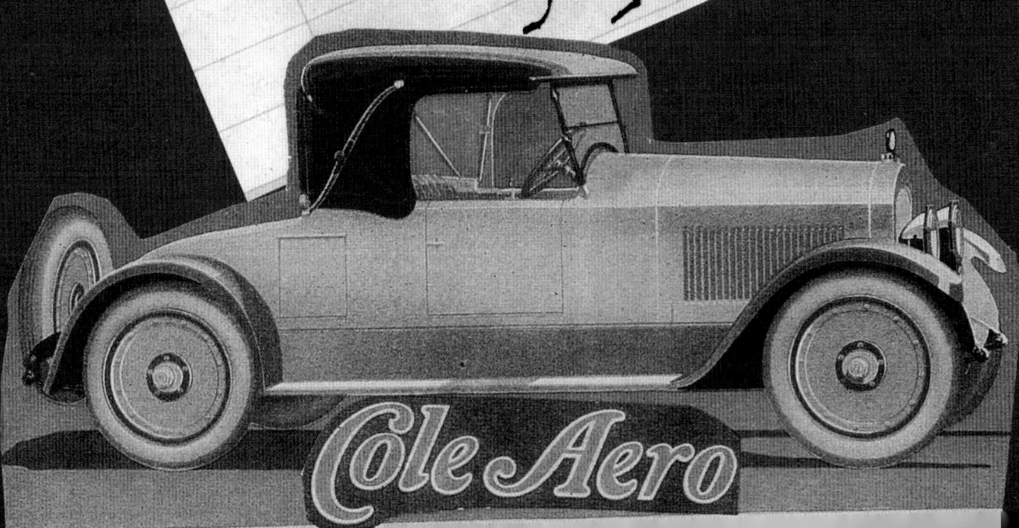
Cole Aero

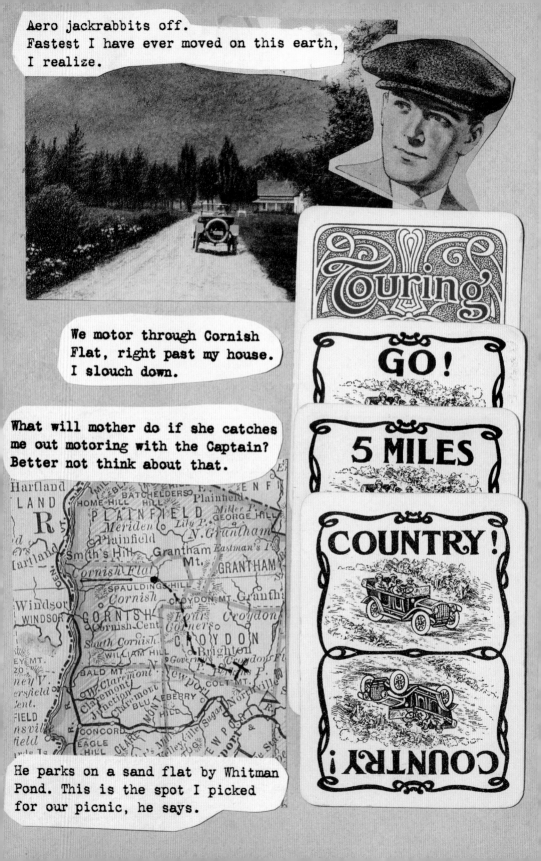

Aero jackrabbits off.
Fastest I have ever moved on this earth,
I realize.

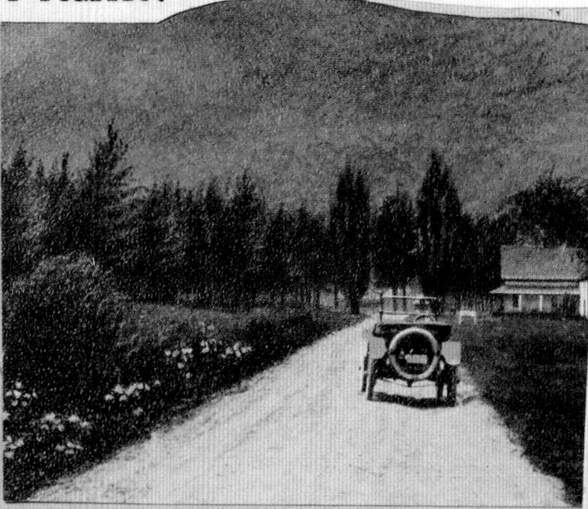

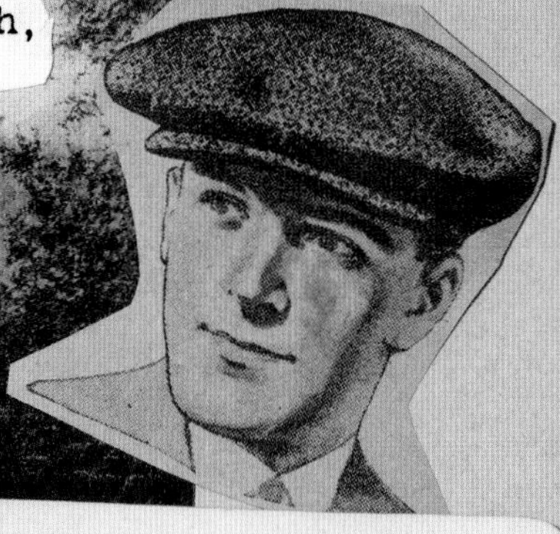

We motor through Cornish
Flat, right past my house.
I slouch down.

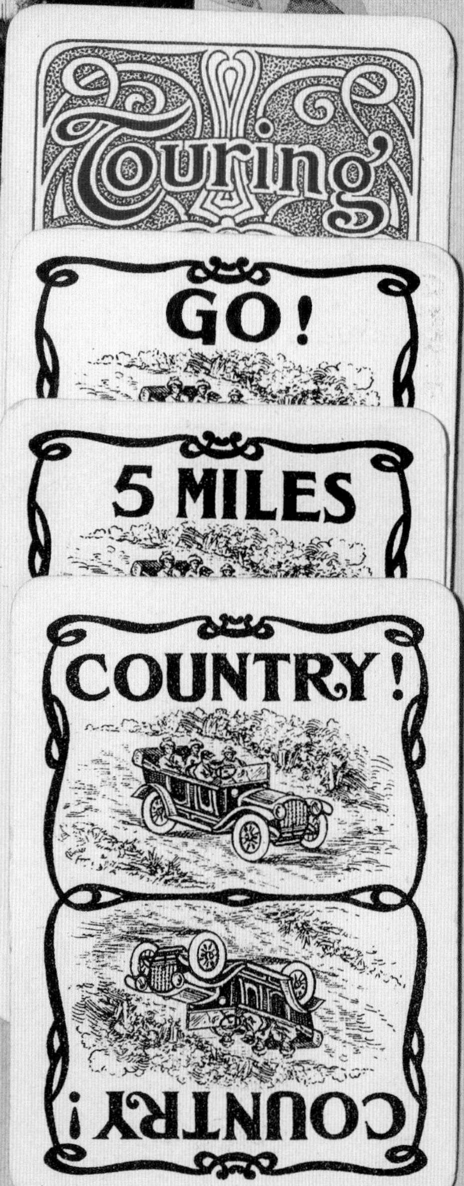
Touring
GO!
5 MILES
COUNTRY!
COUNTRY!

What will mother do if she catches
me out motoring with the Captain?
Better not think about that.

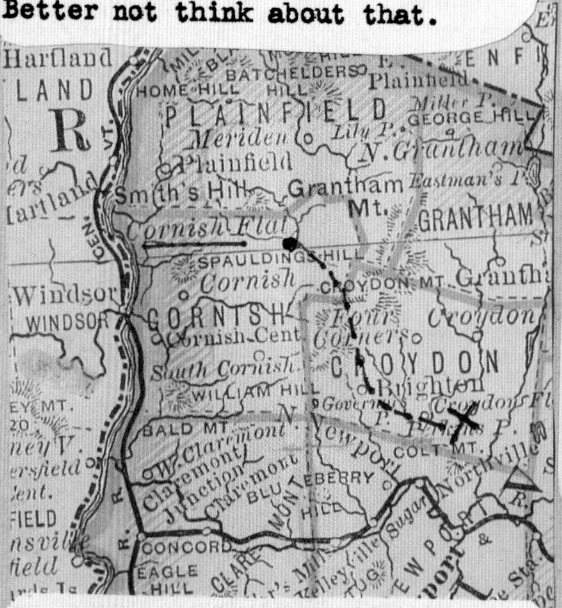
Hartland
BATCHELDERS
Plainfield
HOME HILL
PLAINFIELD
GEORGE HILL
Meriden
N. Grantham
Plainfield
Smith's Hill
Grantham
Mt.
GRANTHAM
Cornish Flat
SPAULDINGS HILL
Cornish
CROYDON MT.
Windsor
WINDSOR
CORNISH
Croydon
Cornish Cent.
CROYDON
South Cornish
Brighton
WILLIAM HILL
BALD MT.
COLT MT.
Claremont
Junction
BLUE
EBERRY
CONCORD
EAGLE
HILL

He parks on a sand flat by Whitman
Pond. This is the spot I picked
for our picnic, he says.

What the Captain Packed in the Picnic Hamper.

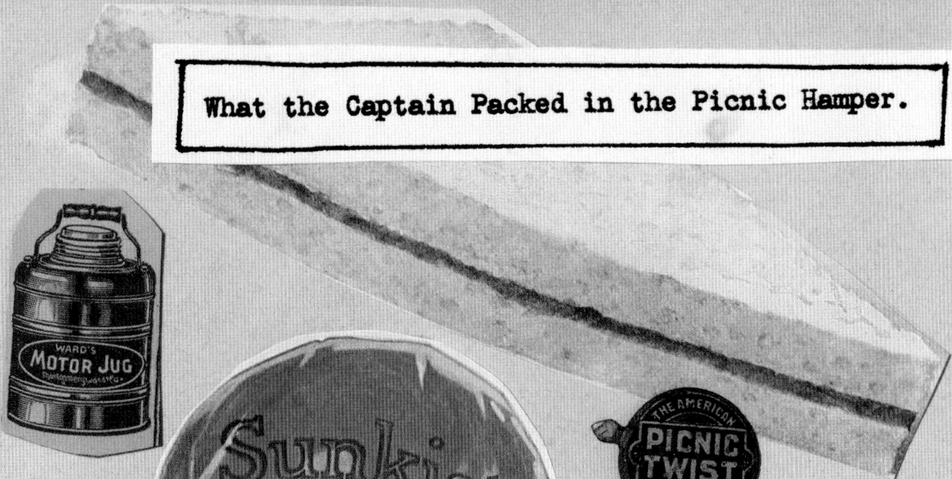
WARD'S
MOTOR JUG
THE AMERICAN
PICNIC TWIST
TOBACCO CO.

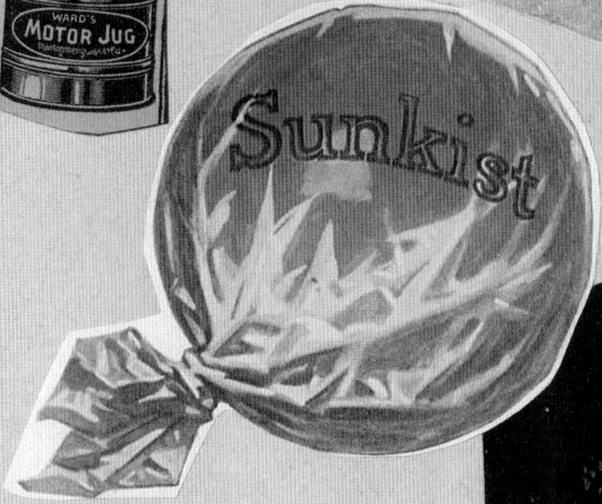
Sunkist

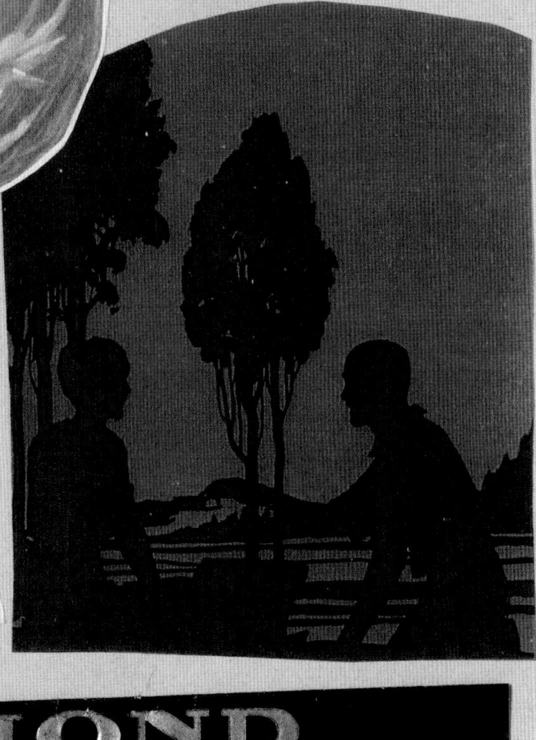

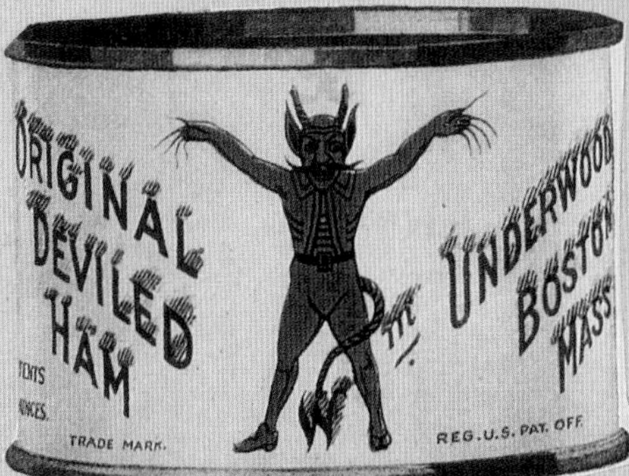
ORIGINAL
DEVILED
HAM
THE UNDERWOOD
BOSTON
MASS.
TRADE MARK.
REG. U.S. PAT. OFF.

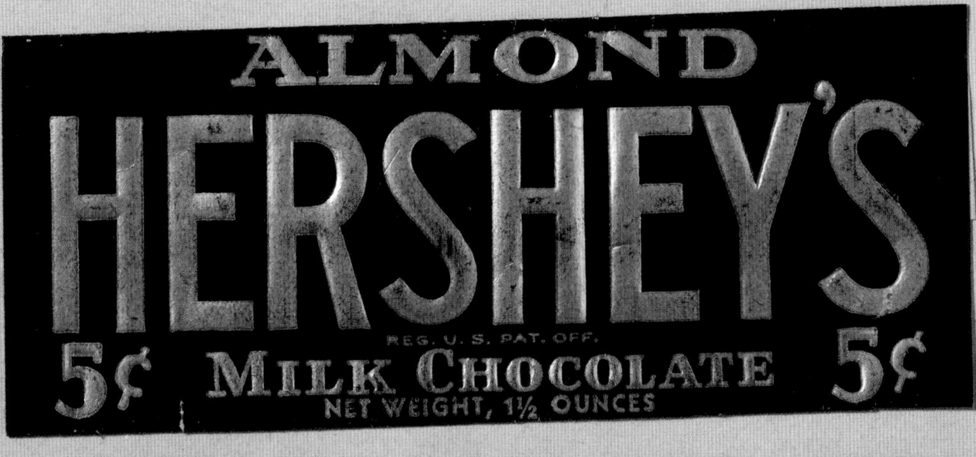
ALMOND
HERSHEY'S
REG. U. S. PAT. OFF.
5¢
MILK CHOCOLATE
5¢
NET WEIGHT, 1½ OUNCES

The Picnic

"Sorry about the mosquitoes."
"They never bother me--I
must not taste very good."
"I find that hard to believe."
"Why is this sandwich pink?"
"Deviled ham. We ate it all
the time in the army."
"Do you think about the war much?"
"I try not to."
"That was a stupid question, I guess."
"I'd rather talk about you. So
you want to be a nurse."
"Not really."

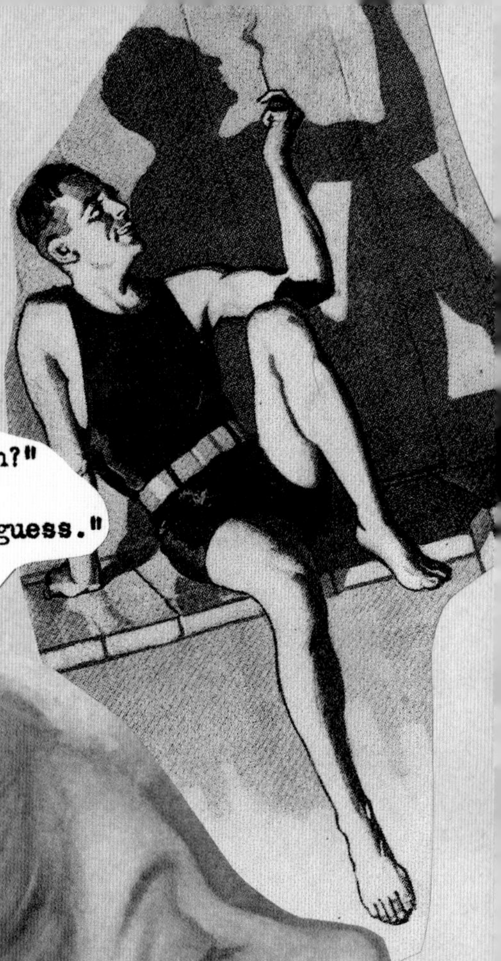

"Well then, what do
you want to be?"
"You'll laugh."
"No I won't."
"I want to be a writer."
"What do you want to write?"
"Novels."
"Like Dickens?"
"More like Mrs. Wharton."
"But her women are
all so sad."
"So you've read
Edith Wharton?"
"Don't sound so
surprised. I wanted
to be a writer once.
A long time ago."
"Why didn't you?"

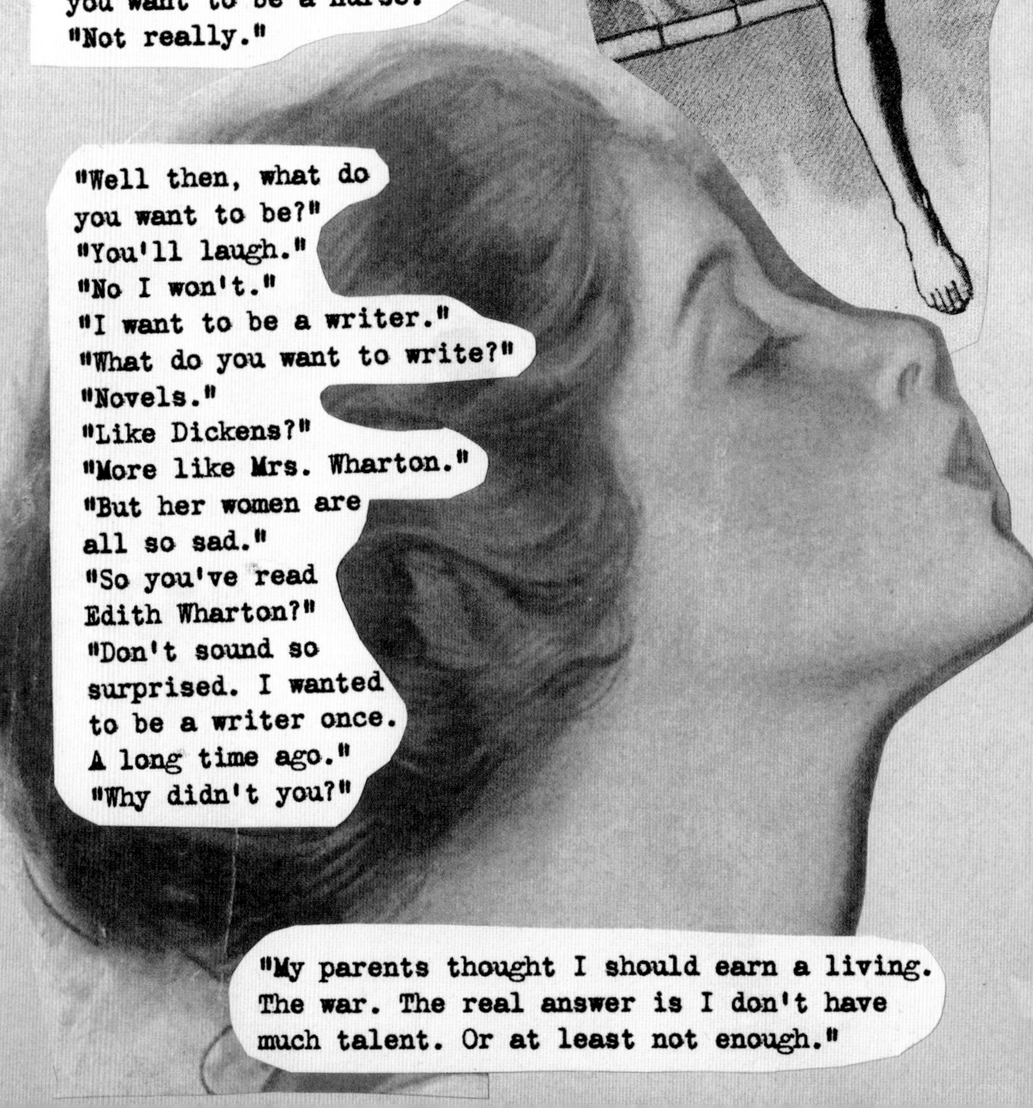

"My parents thought I should earn a living.
The war. The real answer is I don't have
much talent. Or at least not enough."

"It's still not too late. To do what you want."

"Too late for me. But not for you. It's getting hot. Do you want to go swimming?"

"I didn't bring a swim suit."

"Too bad. You could just go in your, you know, slip."

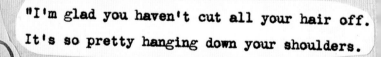

"I'm glad you haven't cut all your hair off. It's so pretty hanging down your shoulders.

Mind if I take a picture? I'm crazy about my Kodak."

"Like this?"   *Snap!*

"Look up. Brush your hair back. Lovely. You're a lovely girl."   *Snap!*

Jamie takes me on a drive almost every afternoon.

Tomorrow at 1:00?

Let ROYSTER'S Start You on the Way to Bigger—Better Crops

ONE

MEMORANDA

SO IT'S 1:00 THEN?

1

AGAIN AT ONE

1

1:00?

By your company you are judged.

43

DRIVING SPECTACLES.

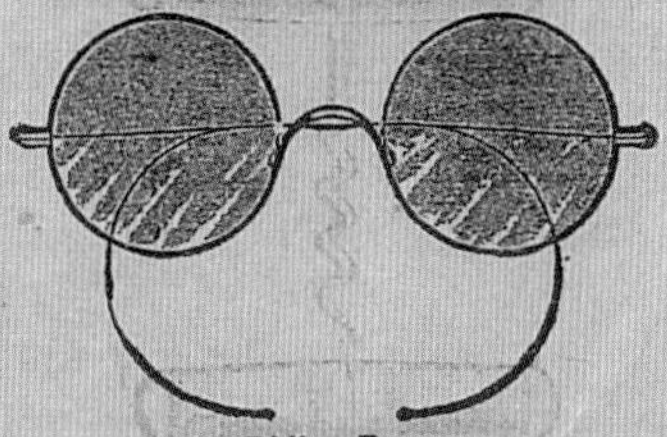

Riding Bow.

He buys me my own pair of driving glasses.

I stop worrying if anyone in Cornish will see us.

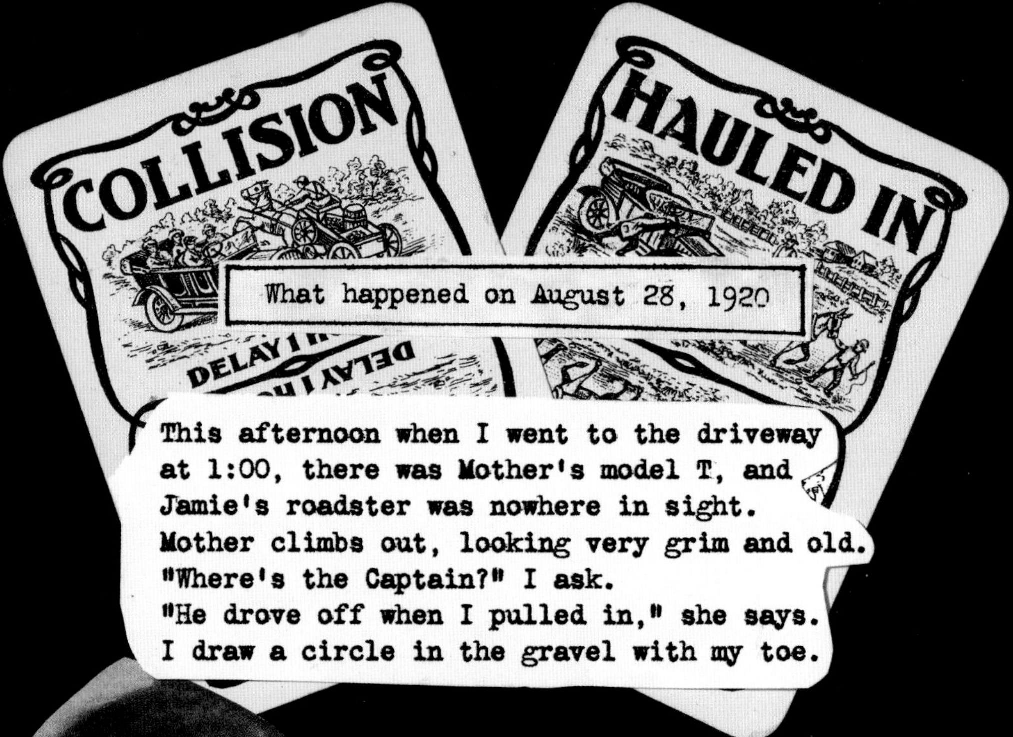
COLLISION
HAULED IN

What happened on August 28, 1920

This afternoon when I went to the driveway at 1:00, there was Mother's model T, and Jamie's roadster was nowhere in sight.
Mother climbs out, looking very grim and old.
"Where's the Captain?" I ask.
"He drove off when I pulled in," she says.
I draw a circle in the gravel with my toe.

"I don't care what you think, Mother. Jamie and I have an understanding."

"Do you?" She sounds so sad. "He's not the man you think he is. I'm going to have a talk with Mrs. Pingree."

She marches in the house and up the stairs.
I chase along behind.

Mother goes into Mrs. Pingree's room without knocking.

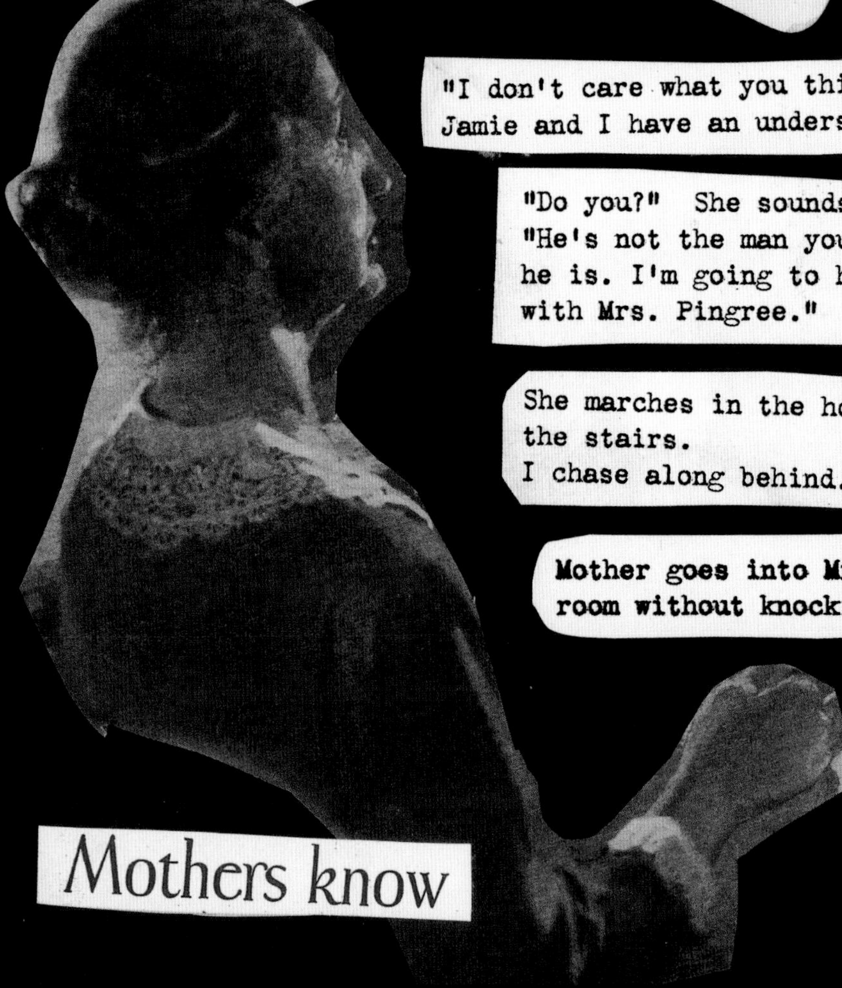

Mothers know

Things I Find in Jamie's Room

I stand in the hallway. Jamie's bedroom door is open. I go inside.

clipping from <u>Town & Country</u> about Jamie's wife (?!)

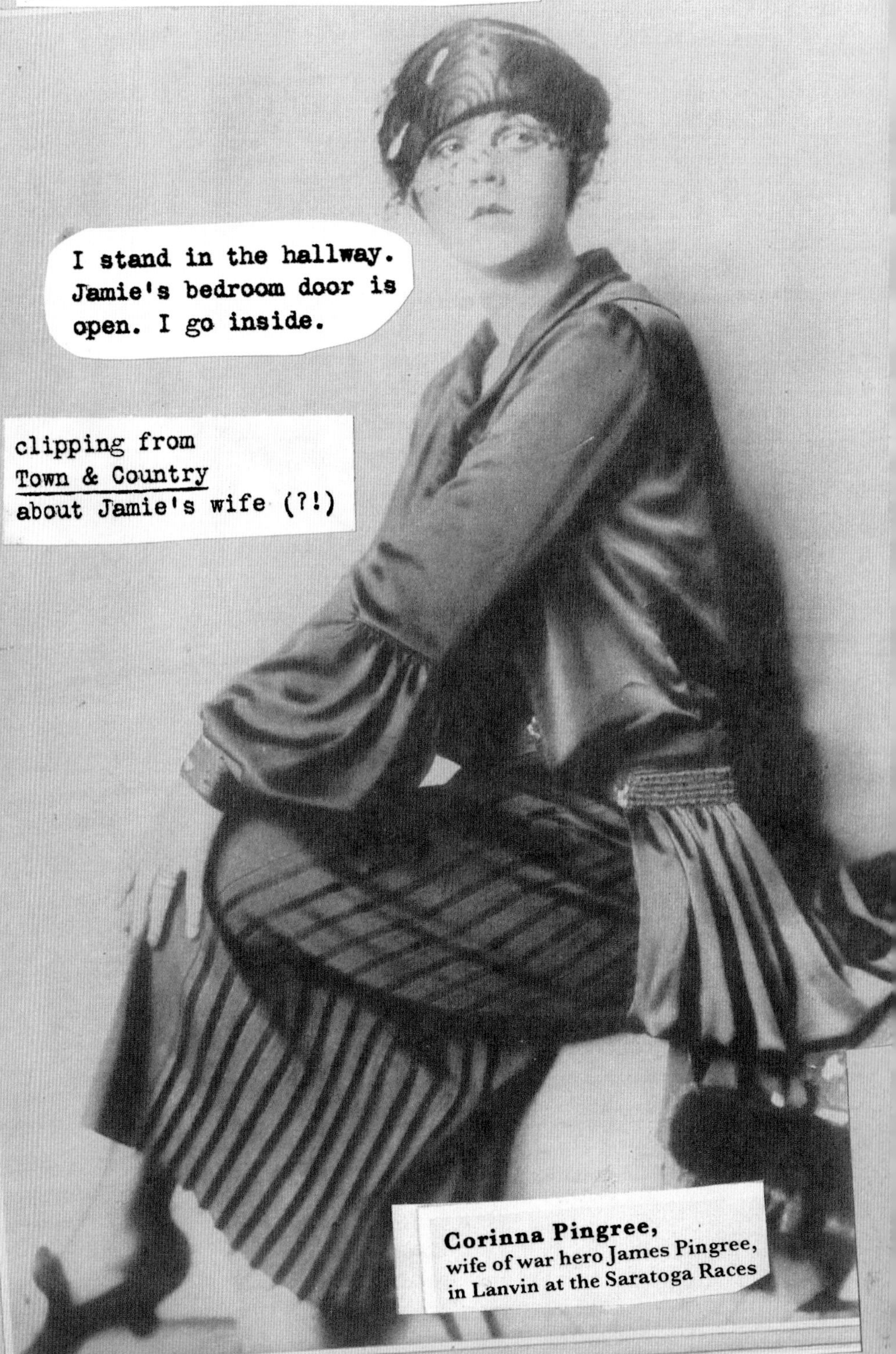

Corinna Pingree,
wife of war hero James Pingree, in Lanvin at the Saratoga Races

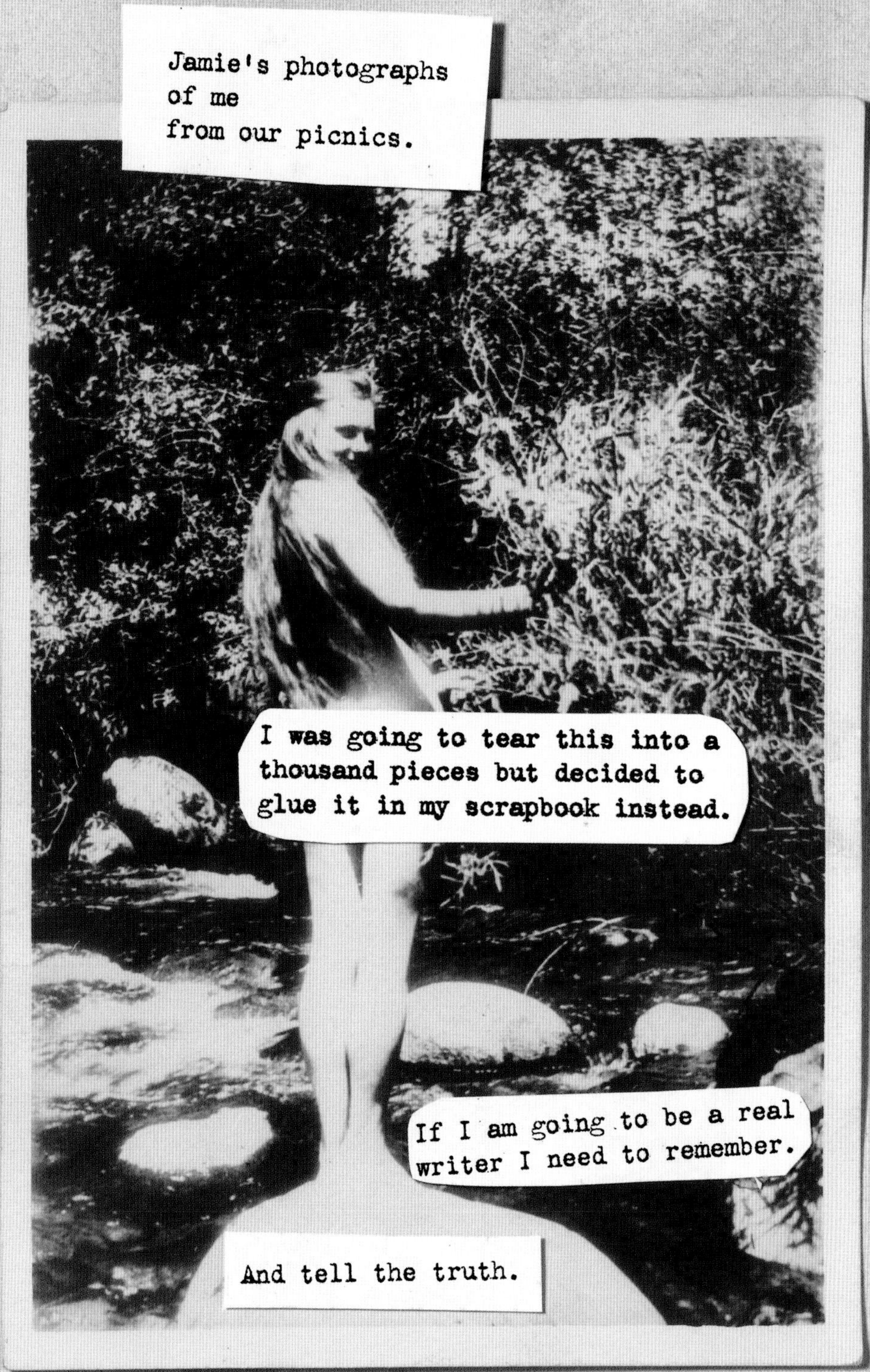
Jamie's photographs
of me
from our picnics.
I was going to tear this into a thousand pieces but decided to glue it in my scrapbook instead.
If I am going to be a real writer I need to remember.
And tell the truth.

What Mrs. Pingree Did

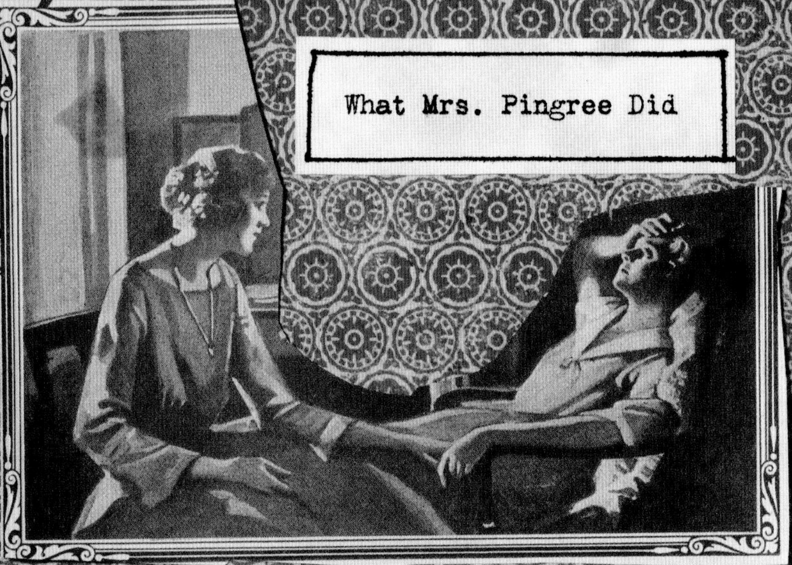

Mother comes out of Mrs. Pingree's bedroom fifteen minutes later and hands me a check.

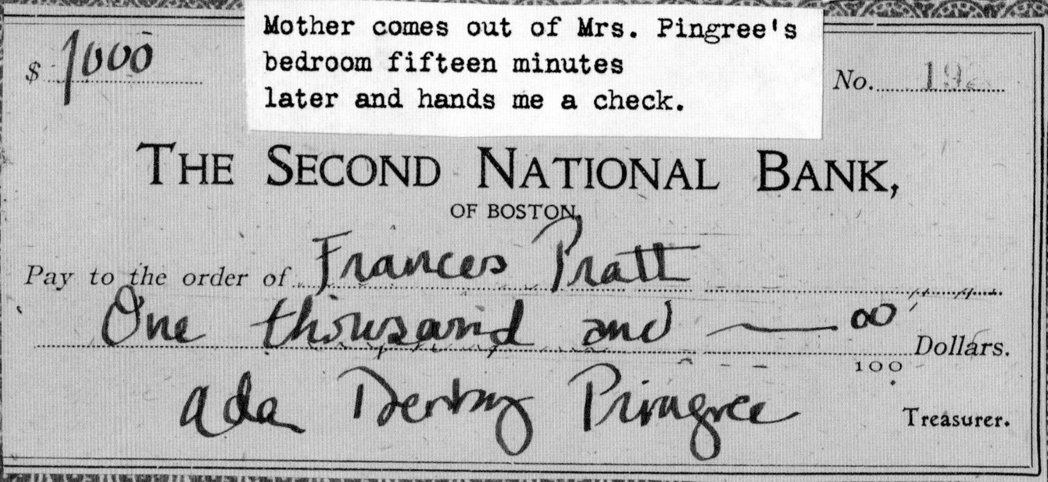

$ 1000

No. 19

THE SECOND NATIONAL BANK,
OF BOSTON

Pay to the order of Frances Pratt

One thousand and 00/100 Dollars.

Ada Derby Pingree

Treasurer.

Dear Miss Thompson,

Is it still possible for my daughter, Frances Pratt, to be admitted into the Vassar class of 1924?

A recent change in our circumstances will allow her to accept Vassar's generous scholarship offer.

Please let me know if arrangements can be made for her to join the freshman class in September.

Sincerely yours,

Roxanne Bayliss Pratt

Vassar is still willing to take me.

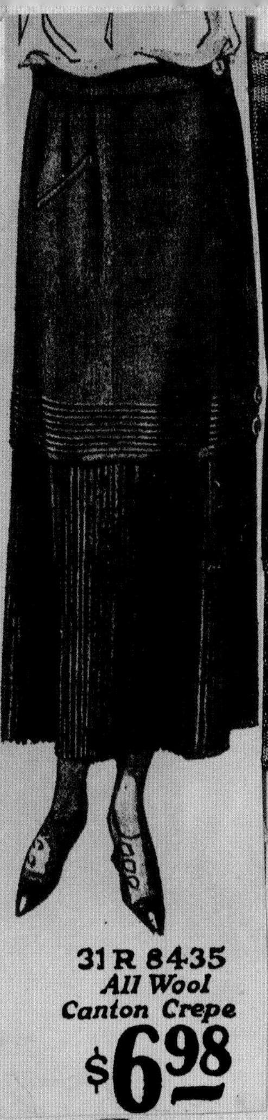
31R 8435
All Wool
Canton Crepe
$6.98

Vassar College
Required Clothing
for Freshman Students
1920

5 white shirtwaists (with collar & modest neckline)
5 skirts (no hemlines above 8 inches from floor)
2 Vassar silk cravats ($2.50 at Campus Store)
1 pair ladies brown oxfords (2 inch heel maximum)
Freshman Beanie & Pin ($1.25; $.75 at Campus Store)
Exercise tunic and bloomers.
Corsets (no "Parisian chemises" or "Teddies")
Stockings (black or white, no "flesh tone")
Garter belts (stockings must be worn with garter belts)

Students are expected to dress modestly in the dormitories.
No men's pajamas or "shortie" nightgowns.

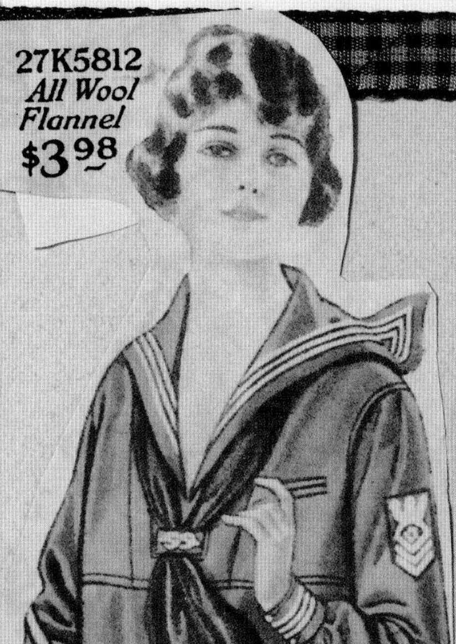
27K5812
All Wool
Flannel
$3.98
I order my Vassar wardrobe from the Sears Catalog.

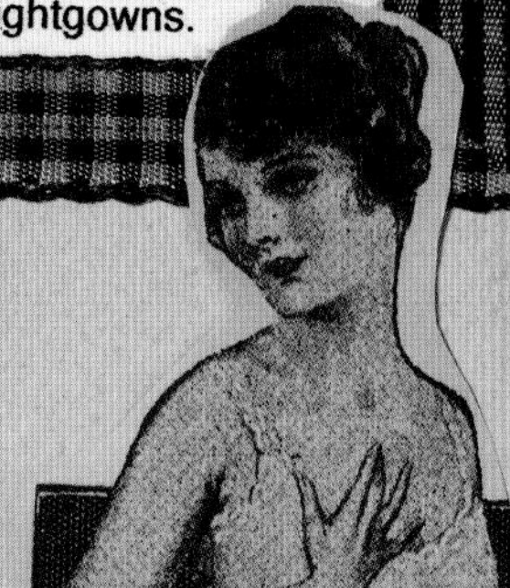
Back Lacing. For Slender and Average Figures.
18T117 $1.79

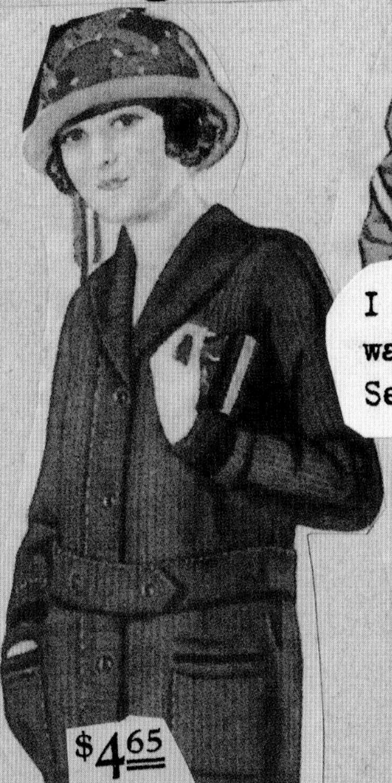
$4.65

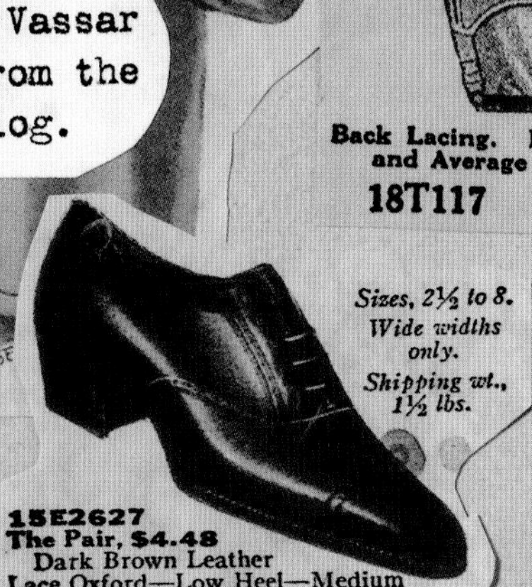
Sizes, 2½ to 8.
Wide widths only.
Shipping wt., 1½ lbs.
15E2627
The Pair, $4.48
Dark Brown Leather
Lace Oxford—Low Heel—Medium
Round Toe—Sewed Sole.

Mother and the boys drive me to the train station in White River Junction before dawn on September 12.

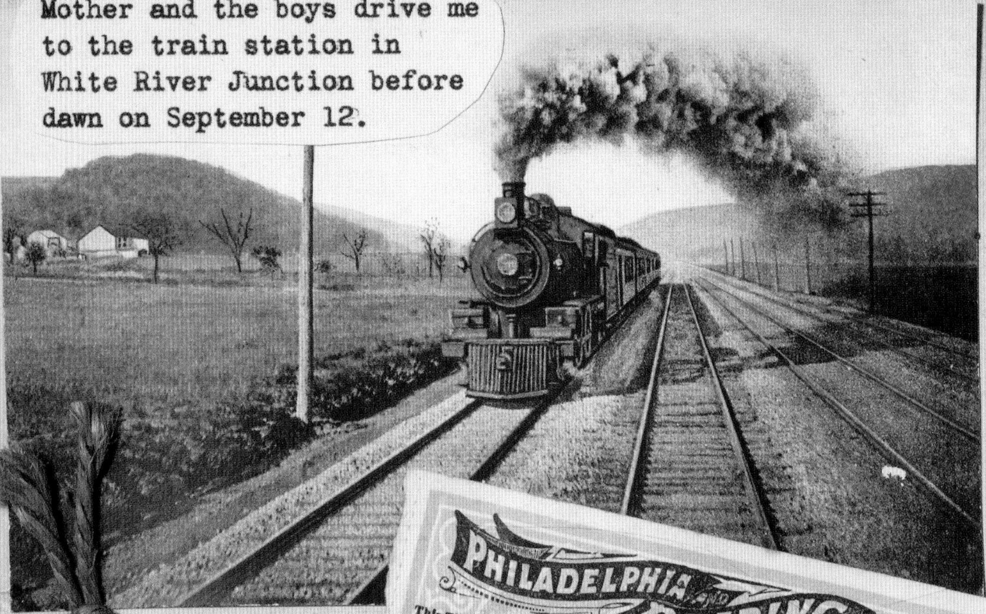

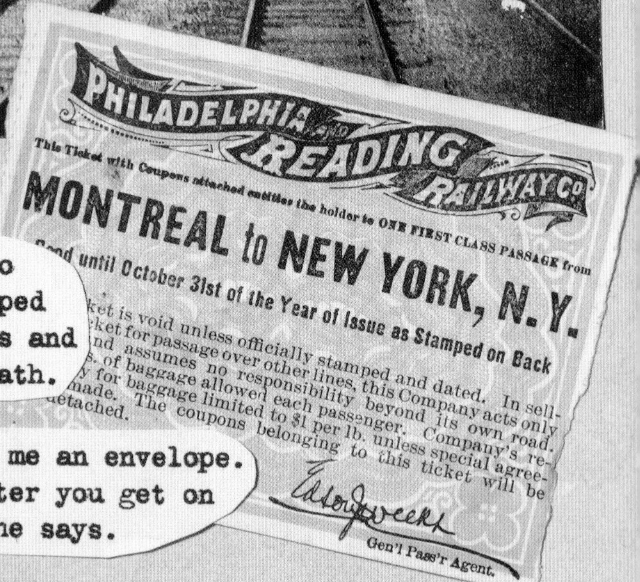
PHILADELPHIA AND READING RAILWAY CO.

This Ticket with Coupons attached entitles the holder to ONE FIRST CLASS PASSAGE from

MONTREAL to NEW YORK, N.Y.

Good until October 31st of the Year of Issue as Stamped on Back

...ket is void unless officially stamped and dated. In sell-
...cket for passage over other lines, this Company acts only
...nd assumes no responsibility beyond its own road.
...s. of baggage allowed each passenger. Company's re-
...y for baggage limited to $1 per lb. unless special agree-
...made. The coupons belonging to this ticket will be
detached.

Gen'l Pass'r Agent.

It is already so cold we're wrapped in wool sweaters and can see our breath.

Mother hands me an envelope. Open this after you get on the train, she says.

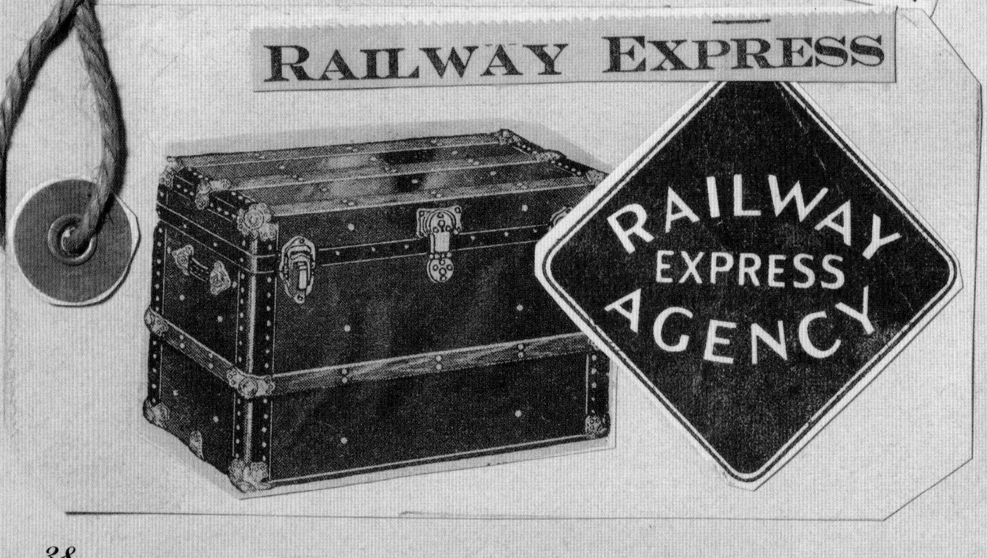
RAILWAY EXPRESS
RAILWAY
EXPRESS
AGENCY

What Was in the Envelope

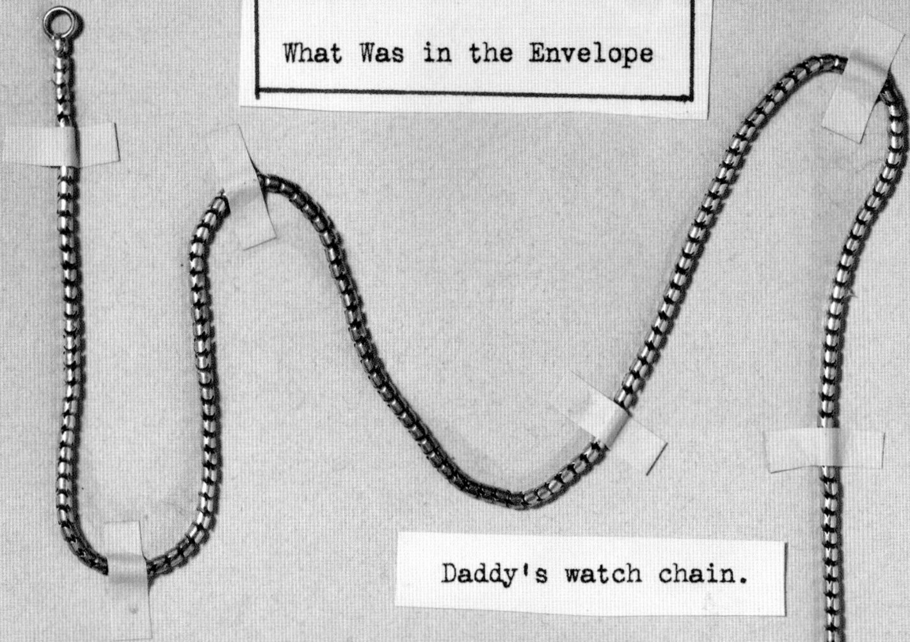

Daddy's watch chain.

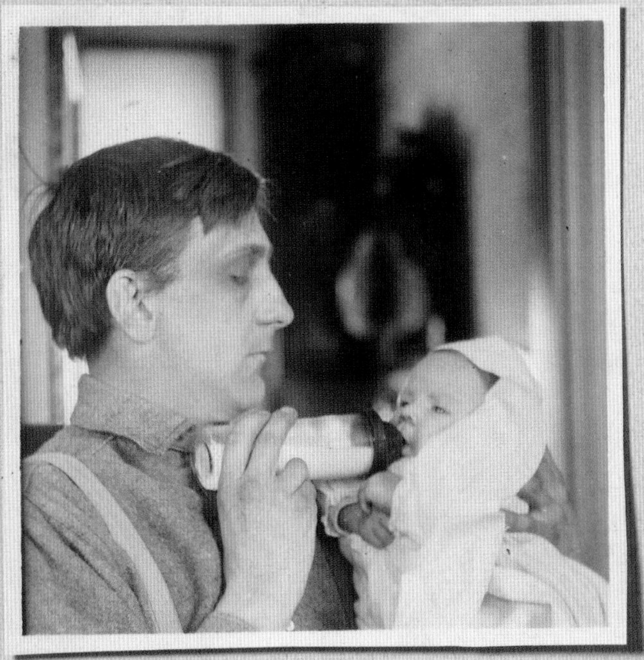

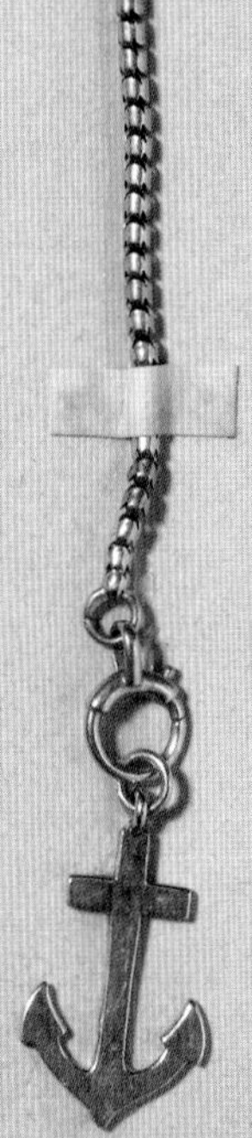

Photograph of
Daddy giving me
a bottle.

The anchor charm Daddy
always wore. He said it
kept him safe.

I stare out the window
and watch the sun rise.
I check the roads at
every crossing.

I can't help it.

I'm looking for an
Aero roadster.

I KNOW WHAT IT MEANS TO BE

LONESOME

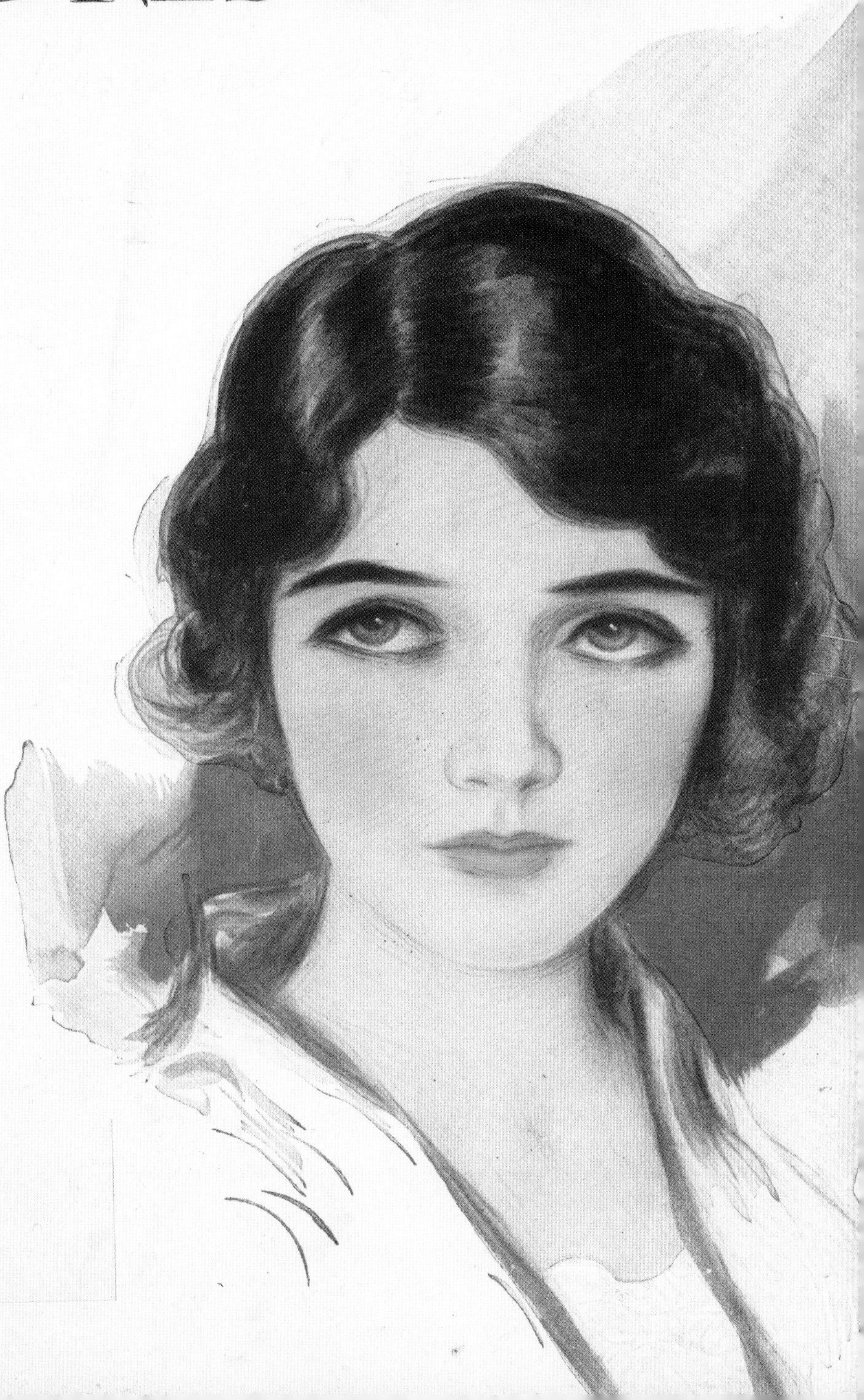

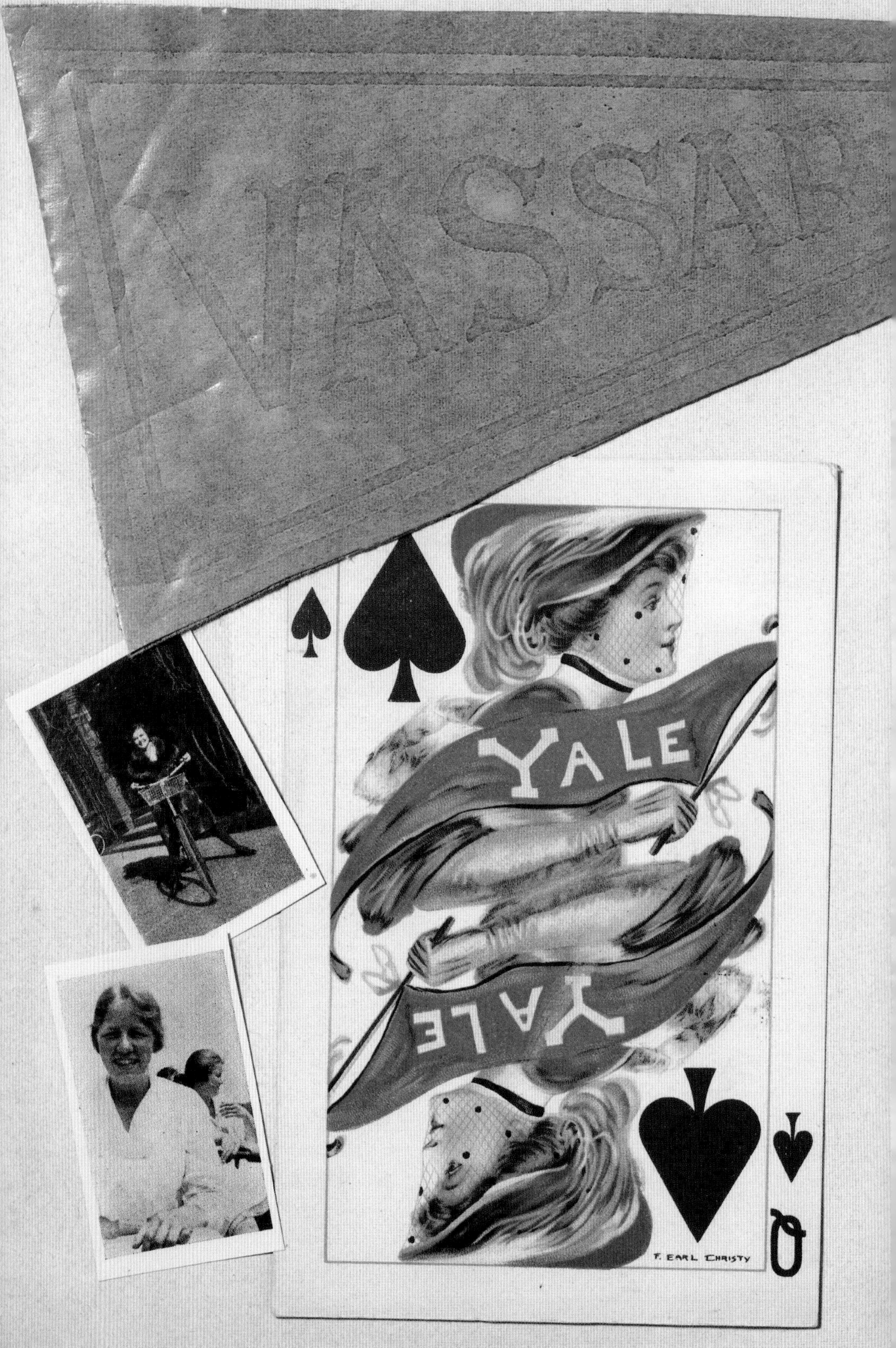
YALE
YALE
F. EARL CHRISTY

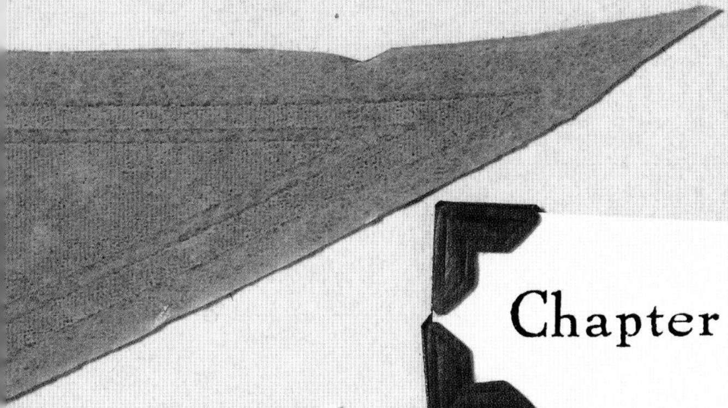

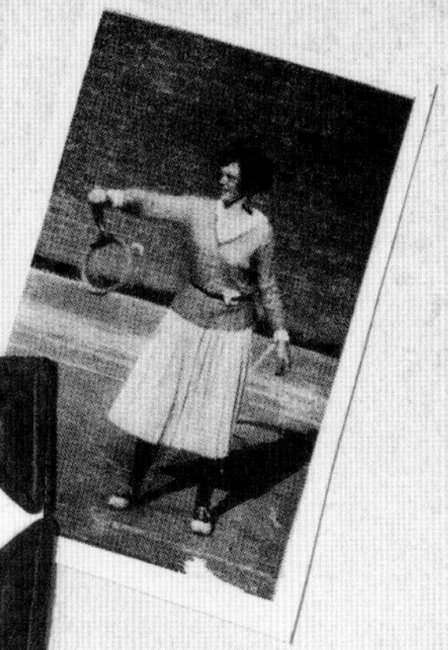

Chapter 2

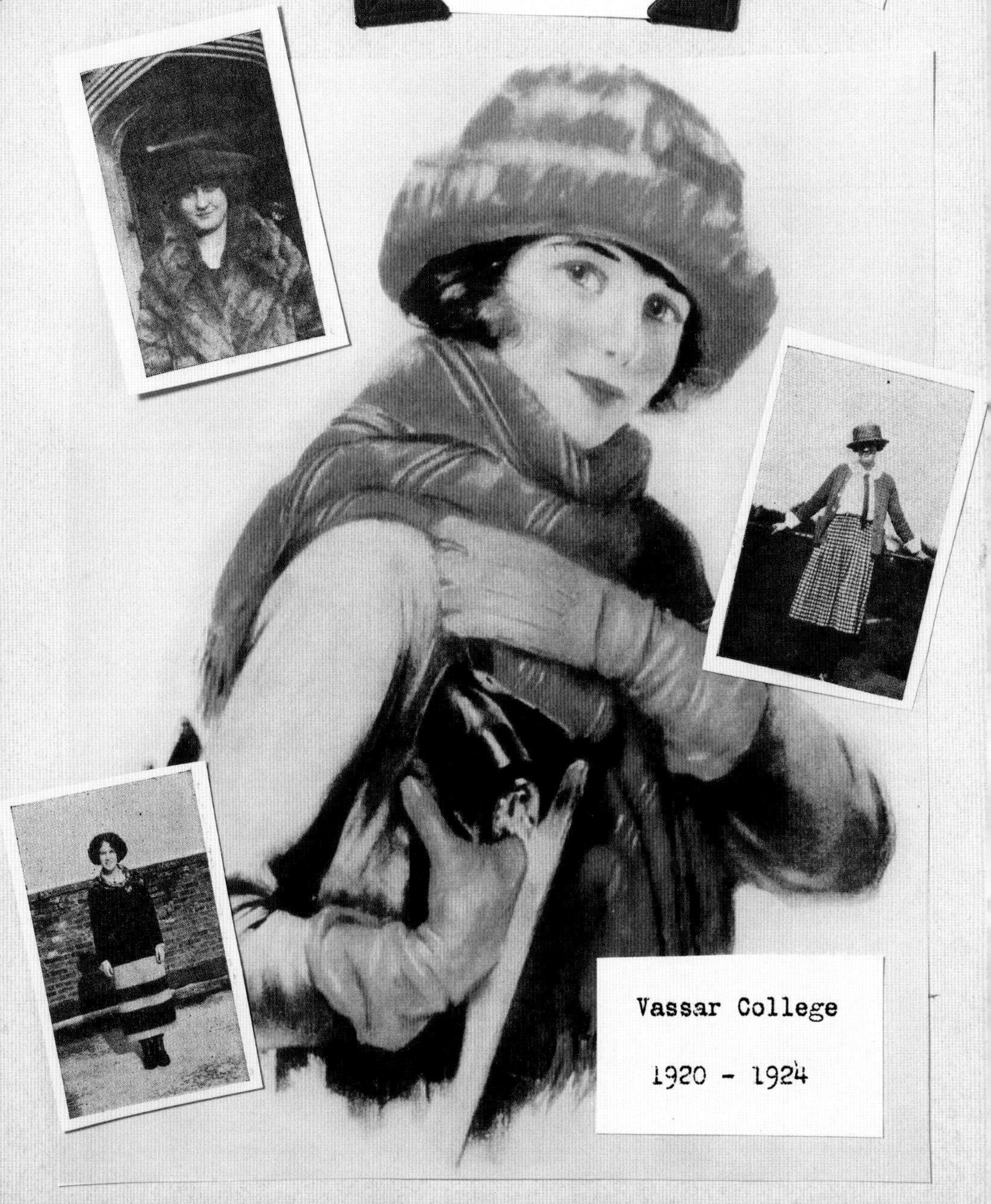

Vassar College

1920 - 1924

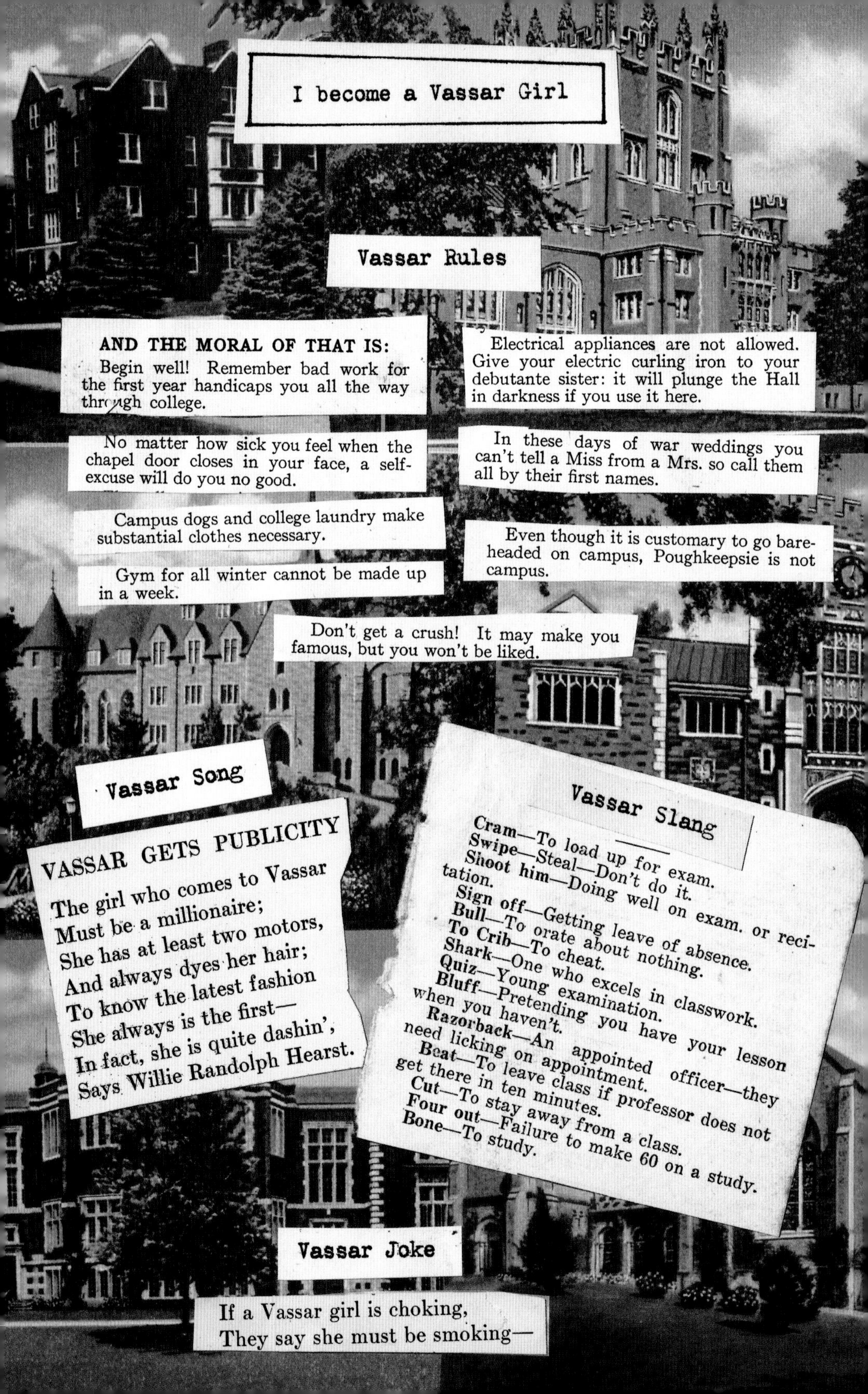

I become a Vassar Girl

Vassar Rules

AND THE MORAL OF THAT IS:
Begin well! Remember bad work for the first year handicaps you all the way through college.

Electrical appliances are not allowed. Give your electric curling iron to your debutante sister: it will plunge the Hall in darkness if you use it here.

No matter how sick you feel when the chapel door closes in your face, a self-excuse will do you no good.

In these days of war weddings you can't tell a Miss from a Mrs. so call them all by their first names.

Campus dogs and college laundry make substantial clothes necessary.

Even though it is customary to go bareheaded on campus, Poughkeepsie is not campus.

Gym for all winter cannot be made up in a week.

Don't get a crush! It may make you famous, but you won't be liked.

Vassar Song

VASSAR GETS PUBLICITY

The girl who comes to Vassar
Must be a millionaire;
She has at least two motors,
And always dyes her hair;
To know the latest fashion
She always is the first—
In fact, she is quite dashin',
Says Willie Randolph Hearst.

Vassar Slang

Cram—To load up for exam.
Swipe—Steal—Don't do it.
Shoot him—Doing well on exam. or recitation.
Sign off—Getting leave of absence.
Bull—To orate about nothing.
To Crib—To cheat.
Shark—One who excels in classwork.
Quiz—Young examination.
Bluff—Pretending you have your lesson when you haven't.
Razorback—An appointed officer—they need licking on appointment.
Beat—To leave class if professor does not get there in ten minutes.
Cut—To stay away from a class.
Four out—Failure to make 60 on a study.
Bone—To study.

Vassar Joke

If a Vassar girl is choking,
They say she must be smoking—

My Classes

CLASS SCHEDULE—First Term.

HOURS	MONDAY	TUESDAY	WEDNESDAY	THURSDAY	FRIDAY
8- 9	FRESHMAN COMPOSITION				
9-10	FRENCH II				
10-11	SOLID GEOMETRY				
11-12	HISTORY of ANCIENT Greece + Rome				
12- 1	L U N C H				
2- 4	ZOOLOGY: MAN + Related mammals				
4- 6	PHYSICAL EDUCATION				HYGIENE

Pecking order of freshman girls:

1. New York City Girls
Went to Miss Chapin's.
Driven to school
by chauffeurs
who hauled in their
many monogrammed trunks.
Fathers are "in
investments."

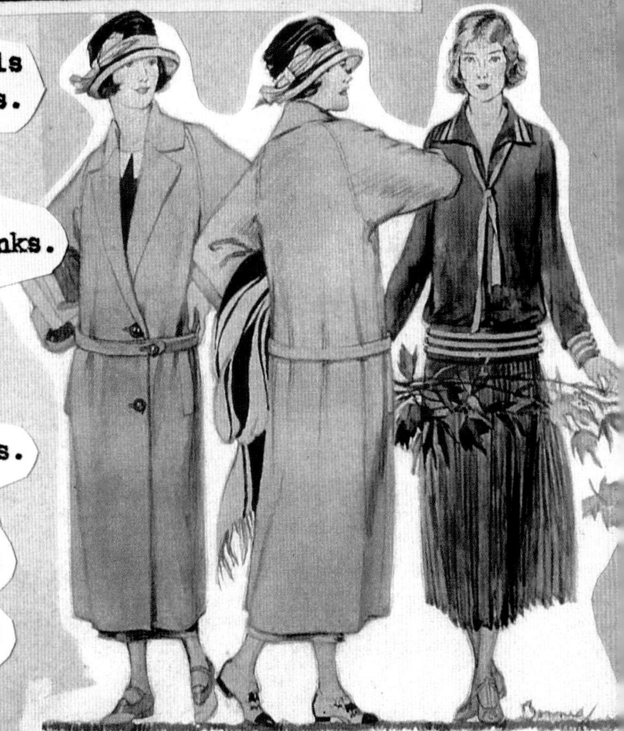

2. Boston Girls
Went to Miss Winsor's.
Have nicknames like
Weezie and Boo.
Sunburned noses from
playing tennis.
Fathers are senators
and ambassadors.

And me, at the bottom of the heap with all
the other poor girls who went to public school.
(Even though none of us would admit being
on scholarship.)

My Roommate

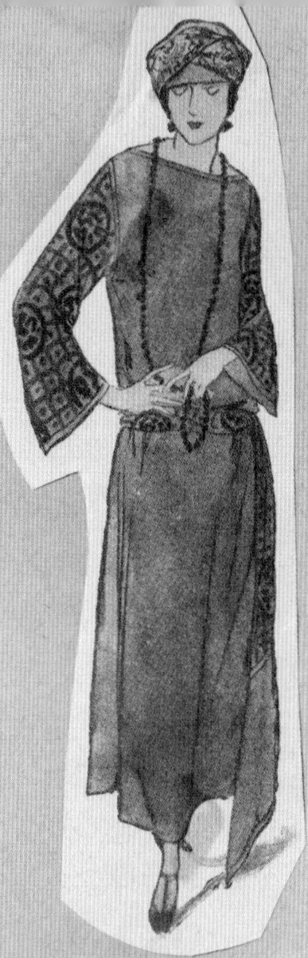

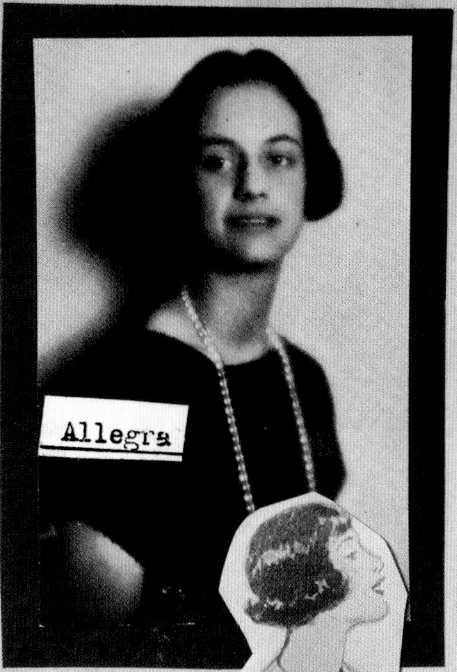
Allegra

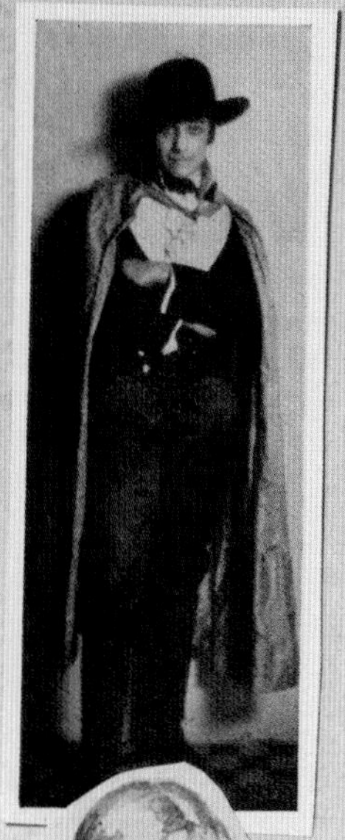

Allegra Wolf
from New York City.
Beautiful, exotic.
Tiny (just 5 feet),
olive skin, onyx eyes,
drastically short
bob. Dresses in
modernist silk swathes.
She's already taken
a shine to me.
"Glad you're not a bore from
5th Avenue," she sniffs.
(Though the Wolfs live on
Central Park West, which
sounds pretty highfalutin.)

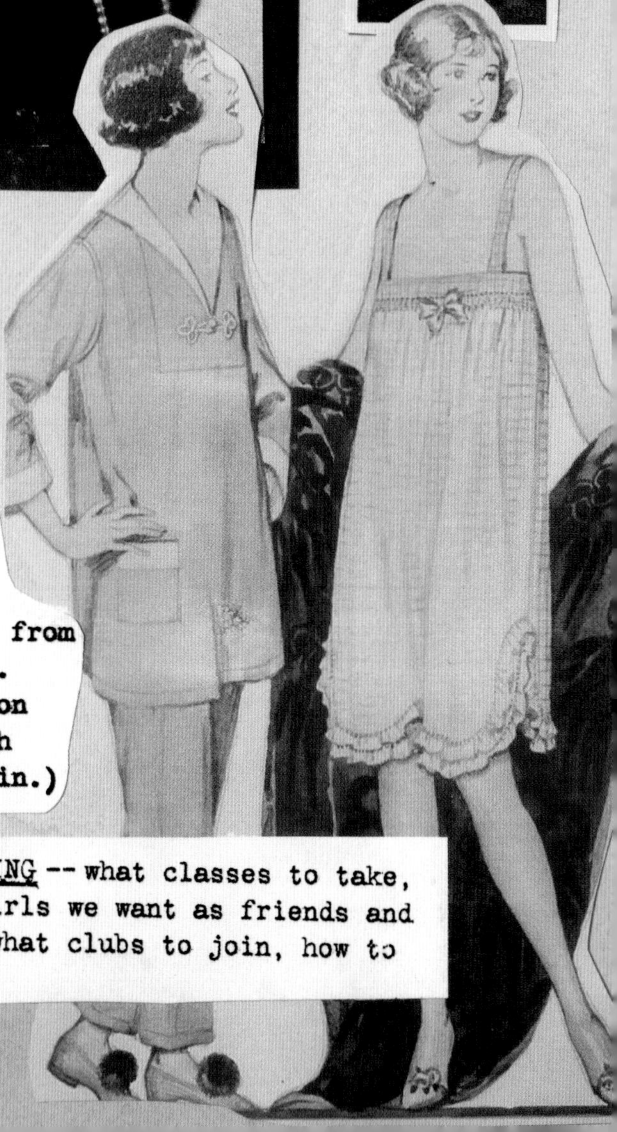

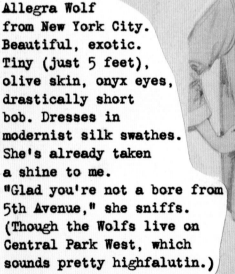

Allegra knows <u>EVERYTHING</u> -- what classes to take, how to dress, which girls we want as friends and which ones to avoid, what clubs to join, how to decorate our room.

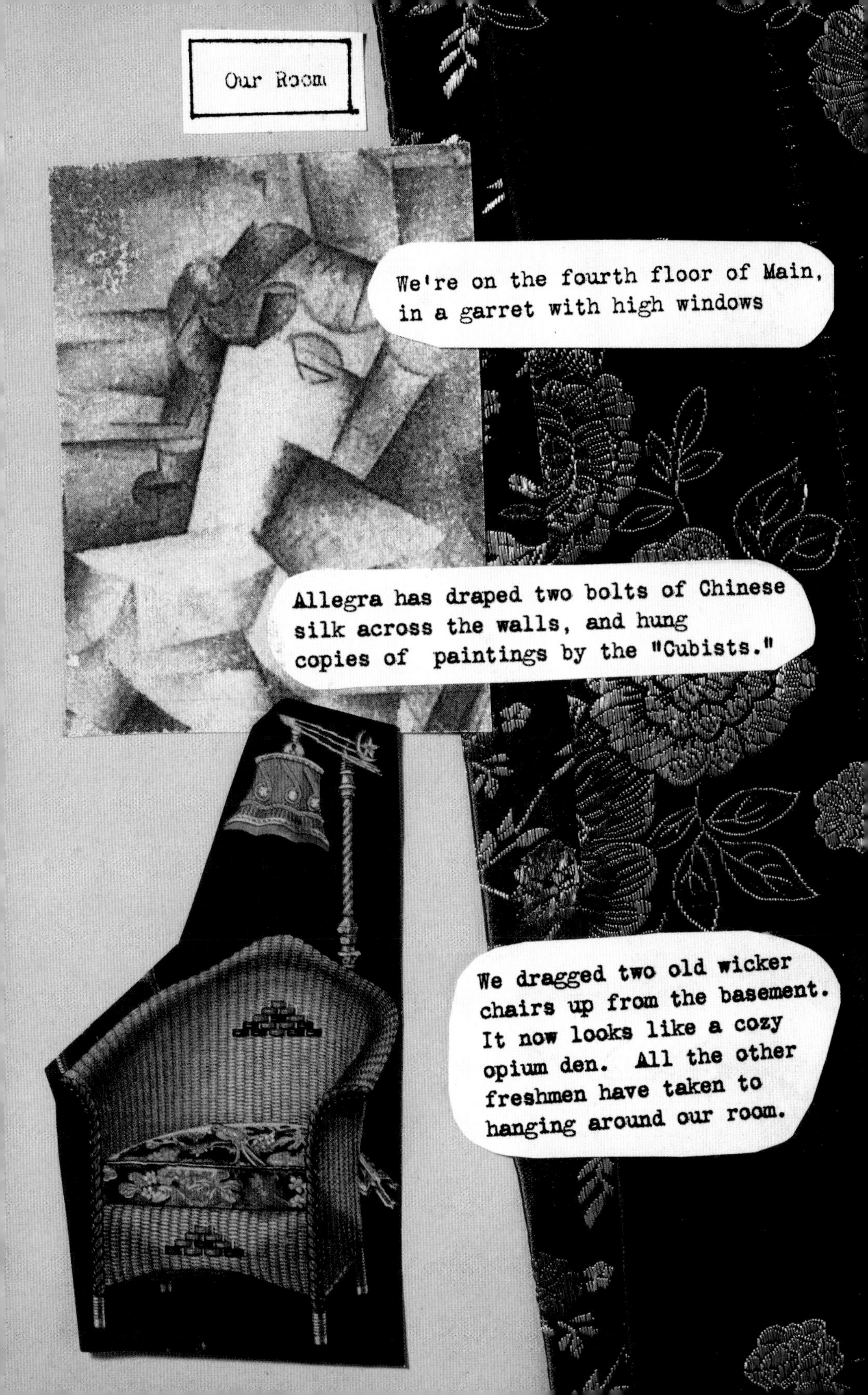
Our Room
We're on the fourth floor of Main, in a garret with high windows
Allegra has draped two bolts of Chinese silk across the walls, and hung copies of paintings by the "Cubists."
We dragged two old wicker chairs up from the basement. It now looks like a cozy opium den. All the other freshmen have taken to hanging around our room.

Allegra Teaches Me Bad Habits

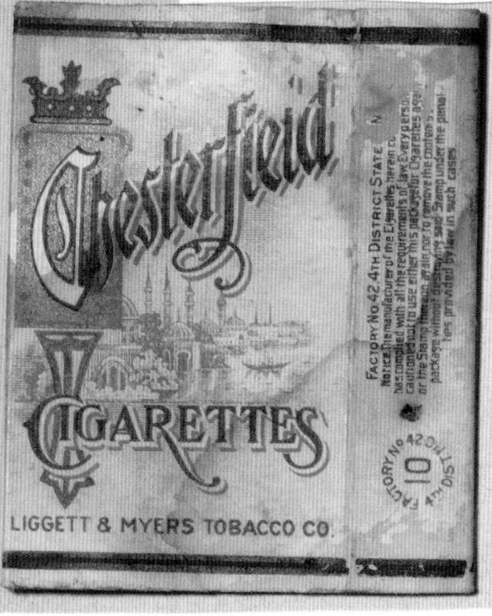
Chesterfield
CIGARETTES
LIGGETT & MYERS TOBACCO CO.

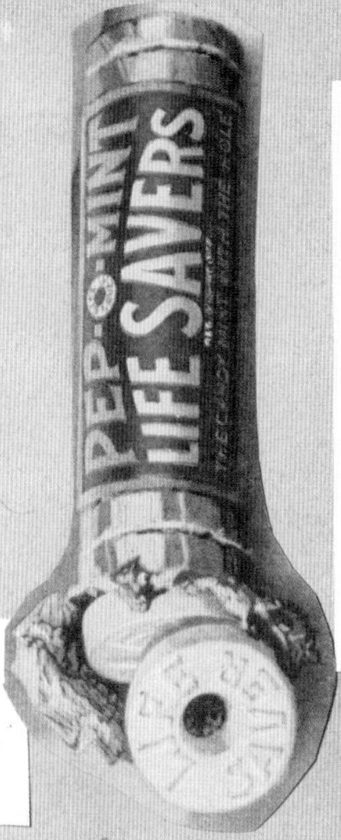
PEP-O-MINT
LIFE SAVERS

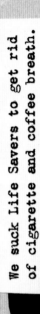

We suck Life Savers to get rid of cigarette and coffee breath.

I am now an official smoker! Smoking is forbidden, so we lean out the window and puff away. I am already up to 5 cigs a day.

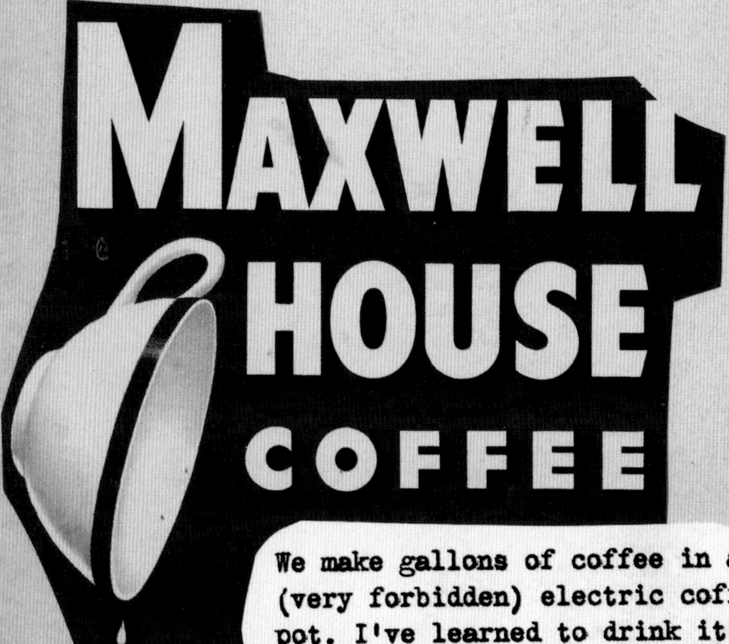
MAXWELL
HOUSE
COFFEE

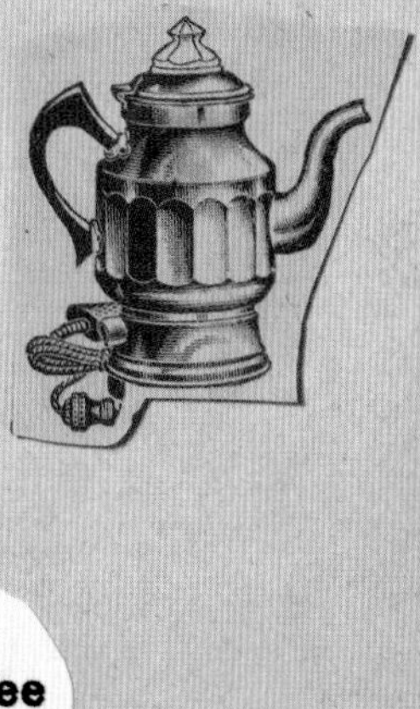

We make gallons of coffee in a (very forbidden) electric coffee pot. I've learned to drink it black, like Allegra.

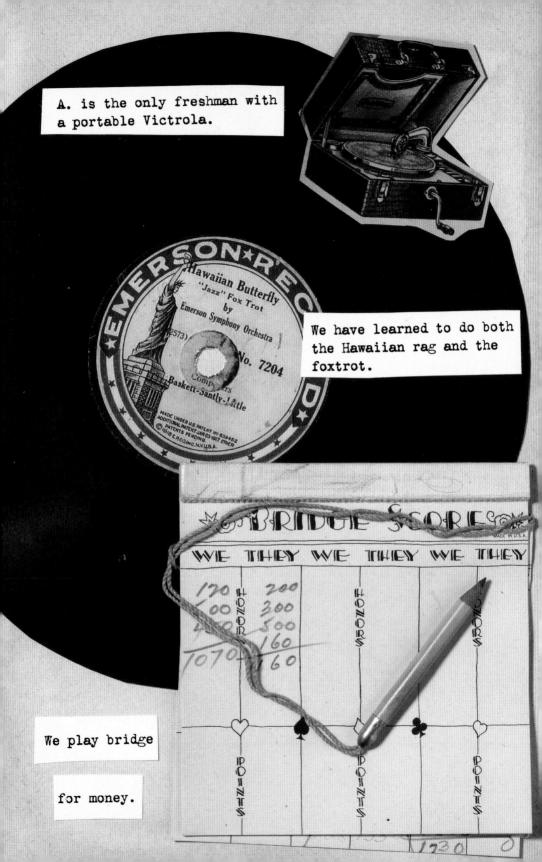

A. is the only freshman with a portable Victrola.

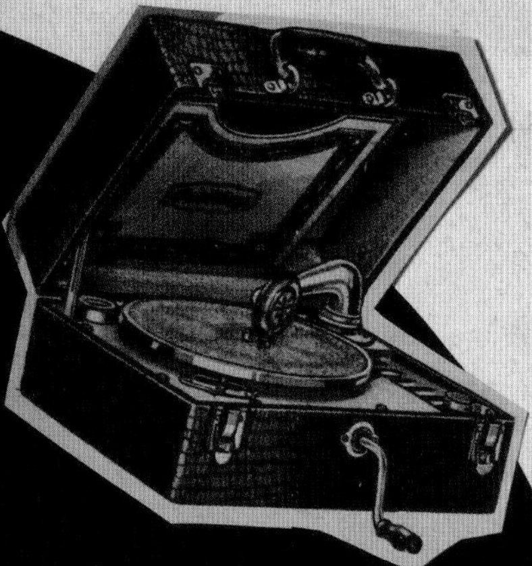

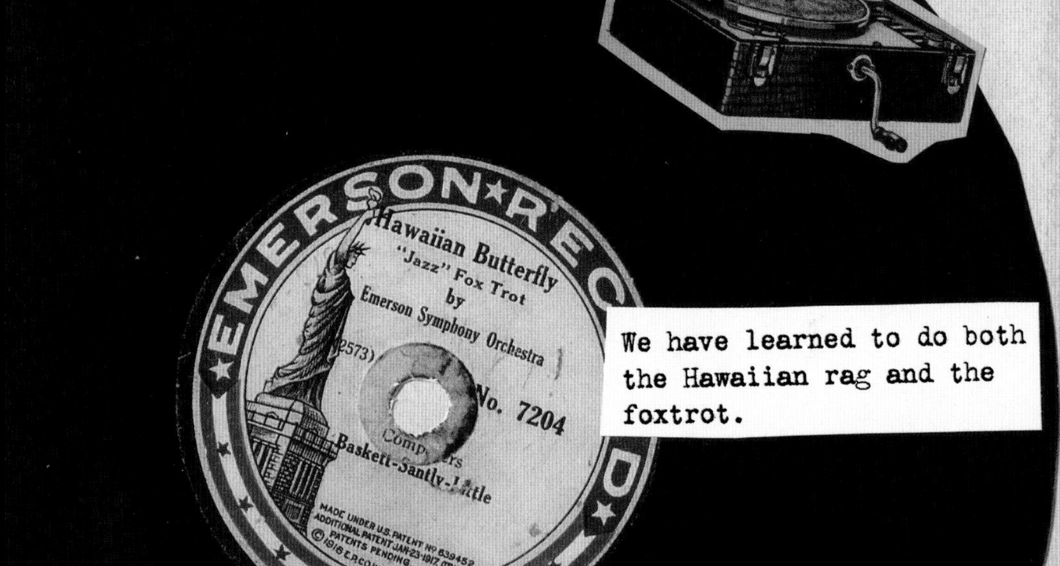
EMERSON ★ RECORD
Hawaiian Butterfly
"Jazz" Fox Trot
by
Emerson Symphony Orchestra
(2573)
No. 7204
Composers
Baskett-Santly-Little

We have learned to do both the Hawaiian rag and the foxtrot.

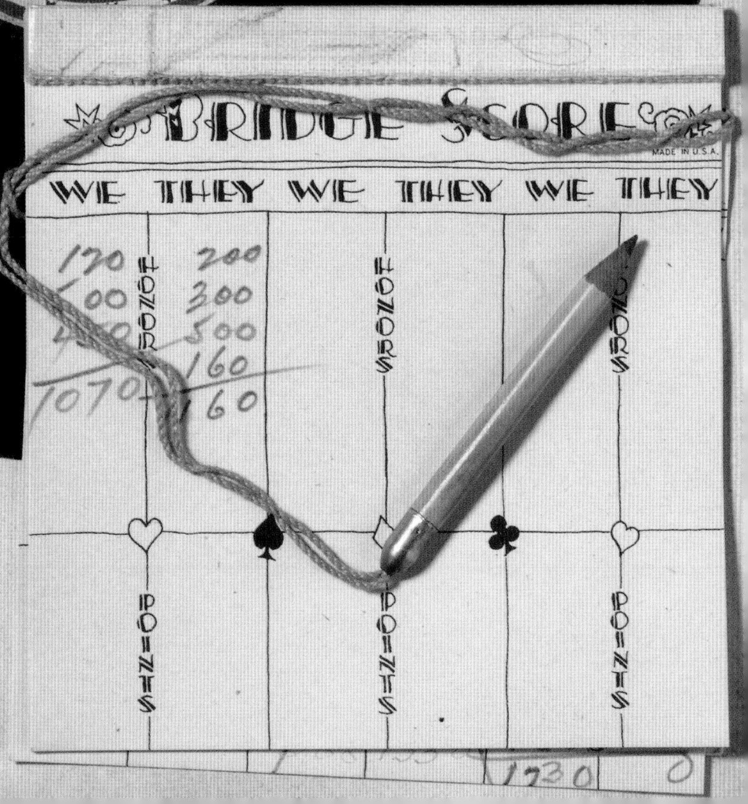
BRIDGE SCORE
MADE IN U.S.A.
WE THEY WE THEY WE THEY
HONORS
POINTS

We play bridge

for money.

I Get My Hair Bobbed

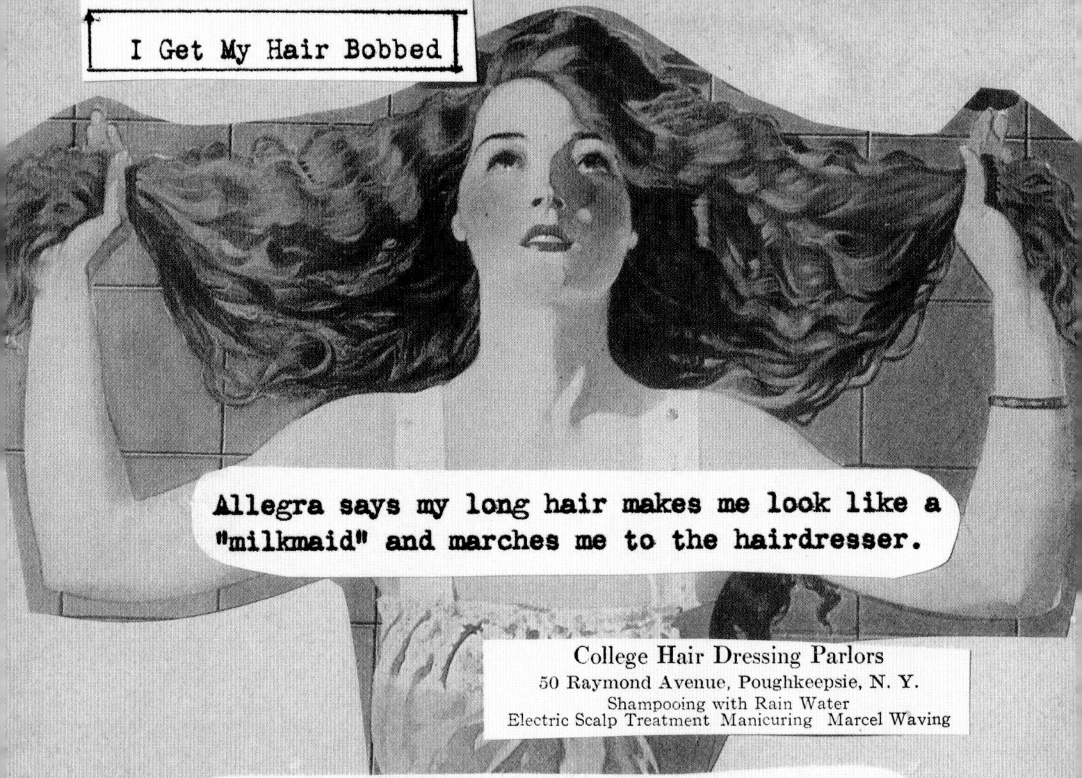

Allegra says my long hair makes me look like a "milkmaid" and marches me to the hairdresser.

College Hair Dressing Parlors
50 Raymond Avenue, Poughkeepsie, N. Y.
Shampooing with Rain Water
Electric Scalp Treatment Manicuring Marcel Waving

(I remember how Jamie was so glad I hadn't cut my hair yet. Relieved to get it whacked off. Haven't told A. about him yet. Know she'd be sympathetic. But I don't want her to think that I'm weak or foolish. Ever.)

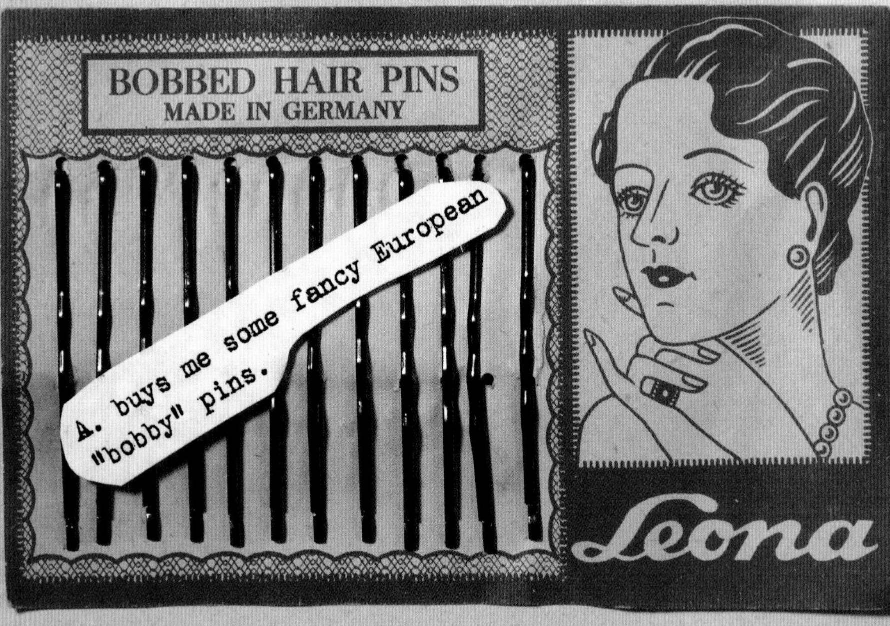
BOBBED HAIR PINS
MADE IN GERMANY
Leona

A. buys me some fancy European "bobby" pins.

Allegra Tries to Make Me Fashionable

A. says gold and platinum are passé. The only jewelry required is a stack of bangles made out of some newfangled stuff called "Bakelite."

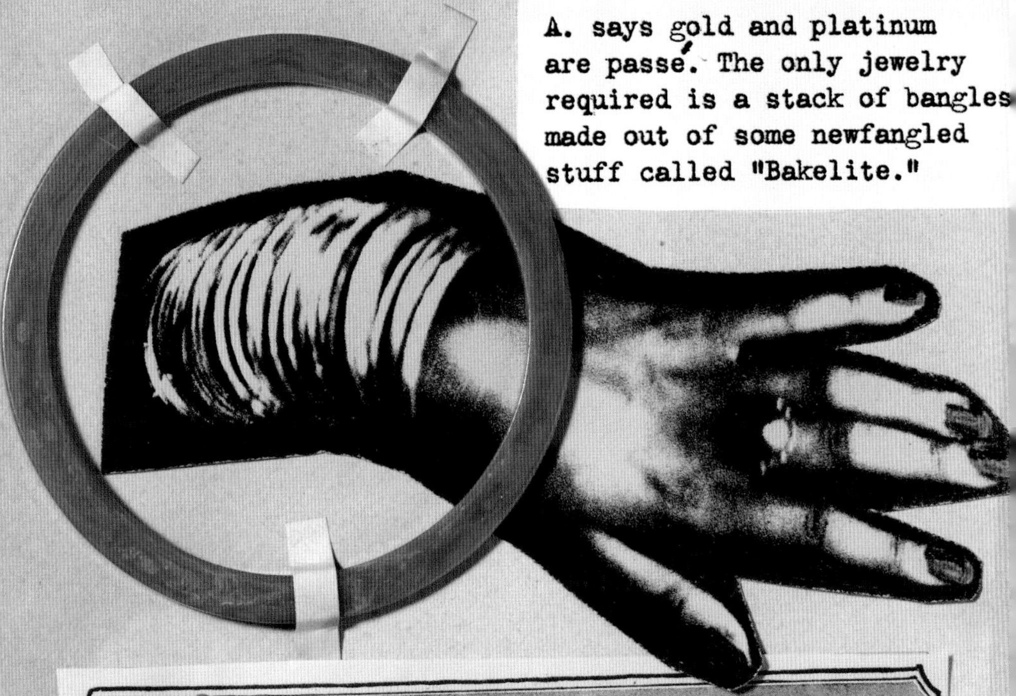

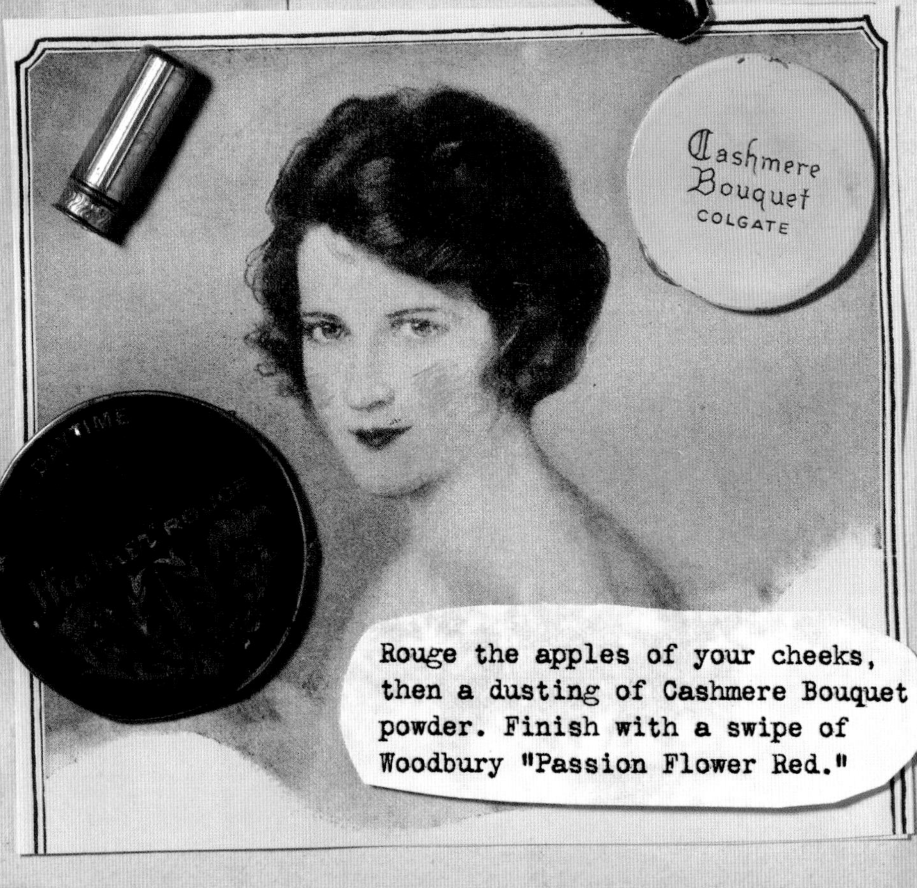
Cashmere
Bouquet
COLGATE

Rouge the apples of your cheeks, then a dusting of Cashmere Bouquet powder. Finish with a swipe of Woodbury "Passion Flower Red."

Allegra and I Disagree About Literature

LITTLE REVIEW

Poetry
A Magazine of Verse

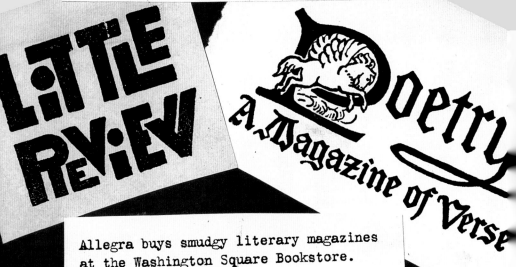

Allegra buys smudgy literary magazines at the Washington Square Bookstore.

She says Stein, Eliot, and Pound are the most important modern poets.

POEMS
BY
EZRA POUND.

L'ART.

Green arsenic smeared on an egg-white cloth,
Crushed strawberries ! Come let us feast our eyes.

GERTRUDE STEIN

In a ribbon.
In a ribbon there is red.
Red white and blue.
Can you know why green is so is so yellow
In a ribbon for a ribbon there is a necklac
Do not say you do like beads.
I likeshells As bells.
Not as door bells.

T. S. ELIOT.

The lamp said,
" Four o'clock,
" Here is the number on the door.
" Memory !
" You have the key,
" The little lamp spreads a ring on the stair,
" Mount.
" The bed is open ; the toothbrush hangs on the wall,
Put your shoes at the door, sleep, prepare for life.
The last twist of the knife.

Amazing, I say. ????????, I think.

I'm crazy about the new novel by
the Princeton boy Scott Fitzgerald.
(A. calls it "Bourgeois")

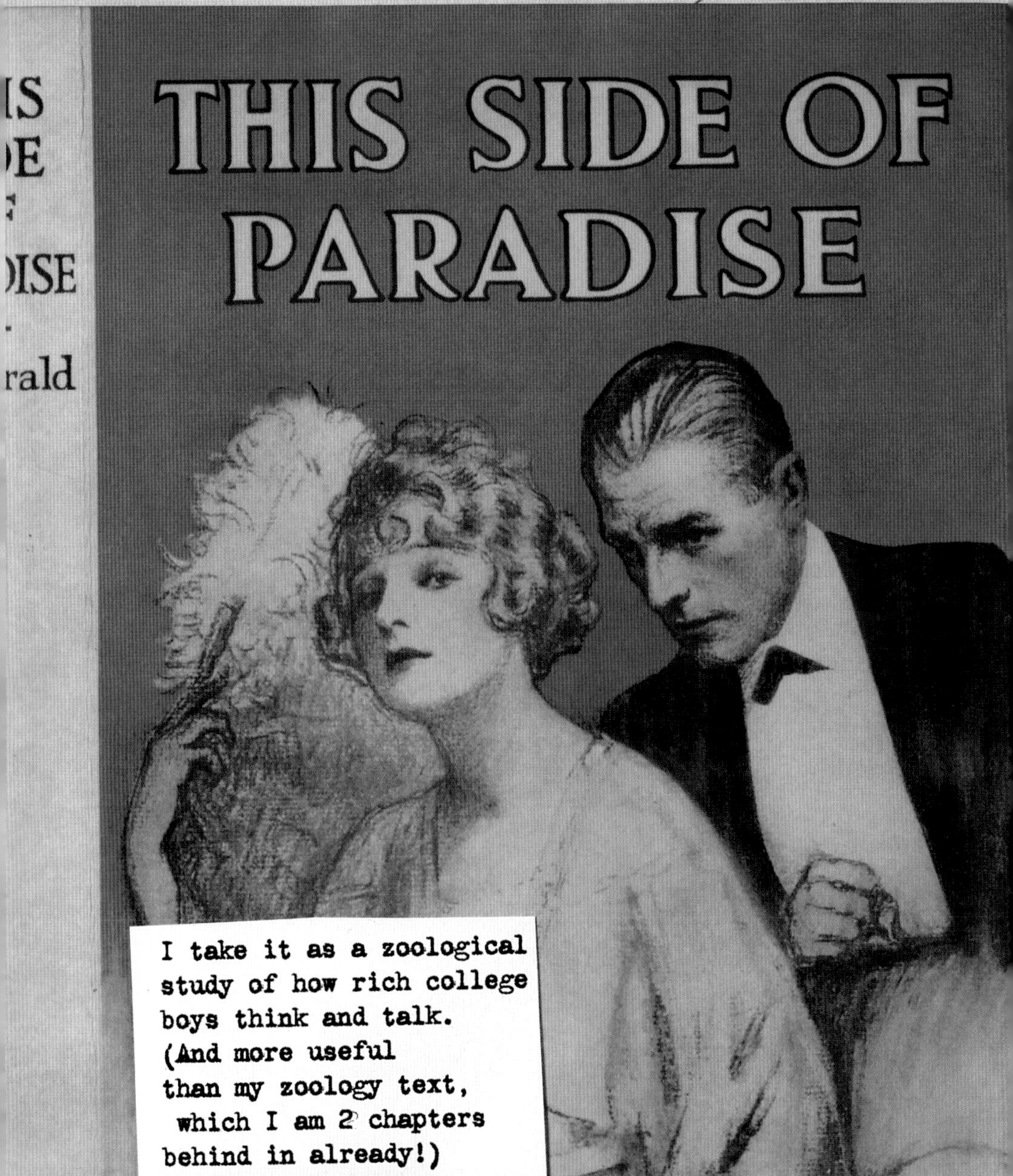
THIS SIDE OF PARADISE
By F. Scott Fitzgerald

I take it as a zoological
study of how rich college
boys think and talk.
(And more useful
than my zoology text,
which I am 2 chapters
behind in already!)

What the Vassar Girl Knows About Men

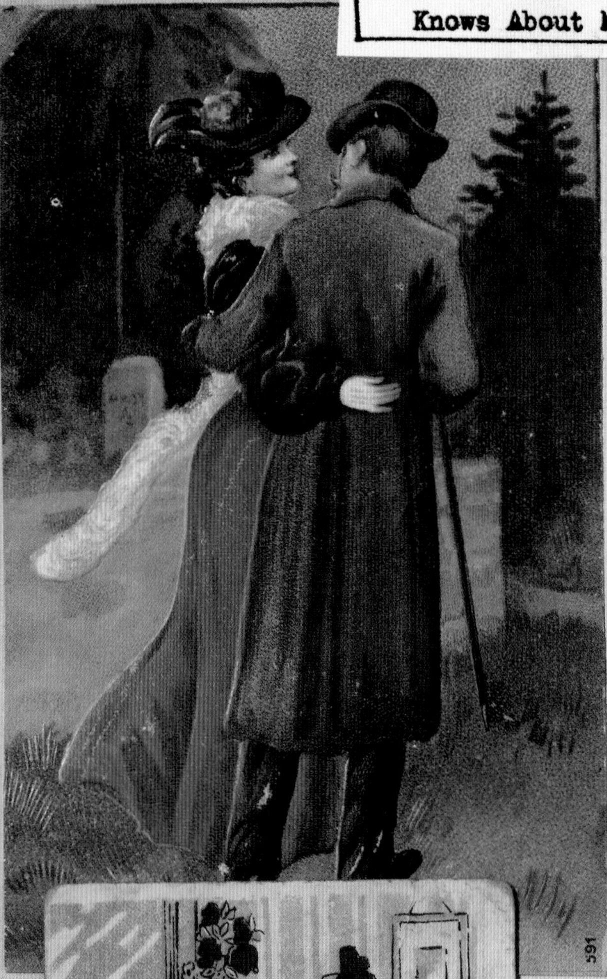
591

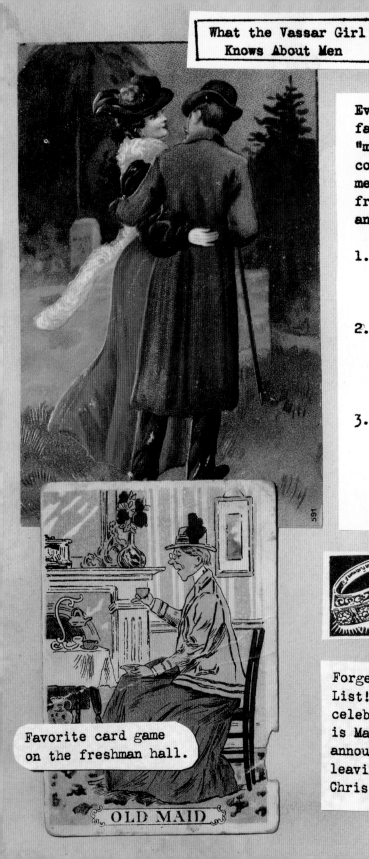

Even though VC girls fancy themselves as "modern," their conversations about men come straight from their mothers and Jane Austen.

1. He has such a nice family.
   (filthy rich)

2. He's awfully keen.
   (going to pop the question)

3. He's not very nice.
   (tries funny stuff with girl, or not rich, or both.)

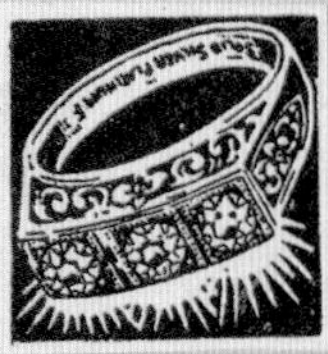

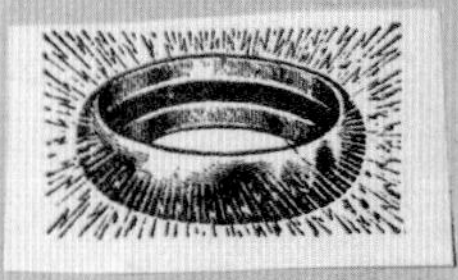

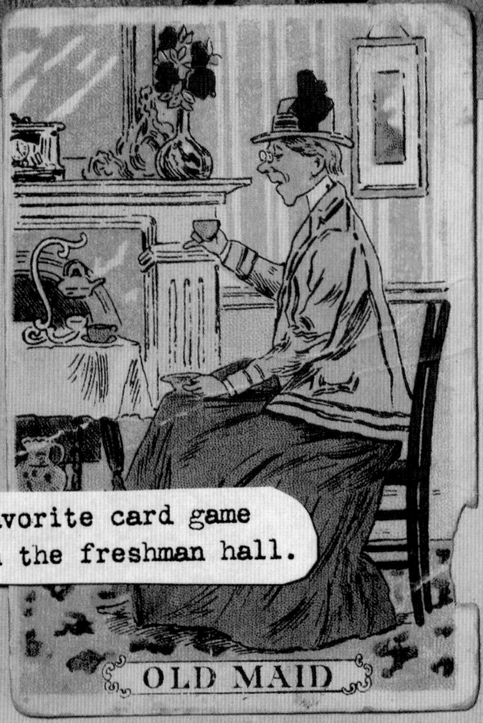
OLD MAID

Favorite card game on the freshman hall.

Forget the Dean's List! The biggest celebrity in our class is May Davenport, who announced that she's leaving VC after Christmas to get married.

What the Vassar Girl Doesn't Know About Men

Women
A
B
C
Men
D

Diagram 1

Seminal Vesicles (cut open)
Bladder nearly empty
Seminal Vesicles (in place)
Prostate and Vas deferens (split open)
Urethra distended
Sperms (enlarged)
head of Epididymis
Spermatic cord
Testicle
Testicle
tail of Epididymis
Scrotum
Meatus

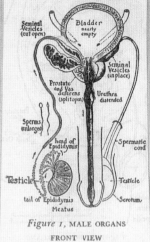

Figure 1, MALE ORGANS FRONT VIEW

In Hygiene Class, Dr. Thelberg shows us vague diagrams and lists.

VENEREAL DISEASE

(*a*) Gonorrhea.

(*b*) Syphilis.

Mutual Adjustment → The Broken Joy

(OR)

→ The Glorious Unfolding

THE SEX TECHNIQUE IN MARRIAGE

"NOTHING ESSENTIAL IS OMITTED OR LEFT IN ANY OBSCURITY."

The marriage manual passed around freshman hall is even more baffling (and alarming).

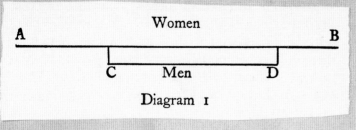

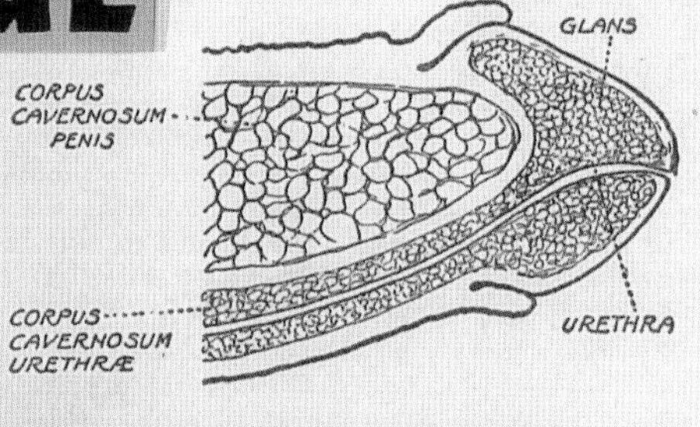

GLANS
CORPUS CAVERNOSUM PENIS
CORPUS CAVERNOSUM URETHRÆ
URETHRA

D. DIAGRAM OF ERECTED ORGAN; SHOWING THE DILATION OF THE BLOOD SPACES.

POSTURES IN INTERCOURSE

1. *The Habitual Posture*

2. *Posterior-lateral Posture*

3. *The Astride Posture*

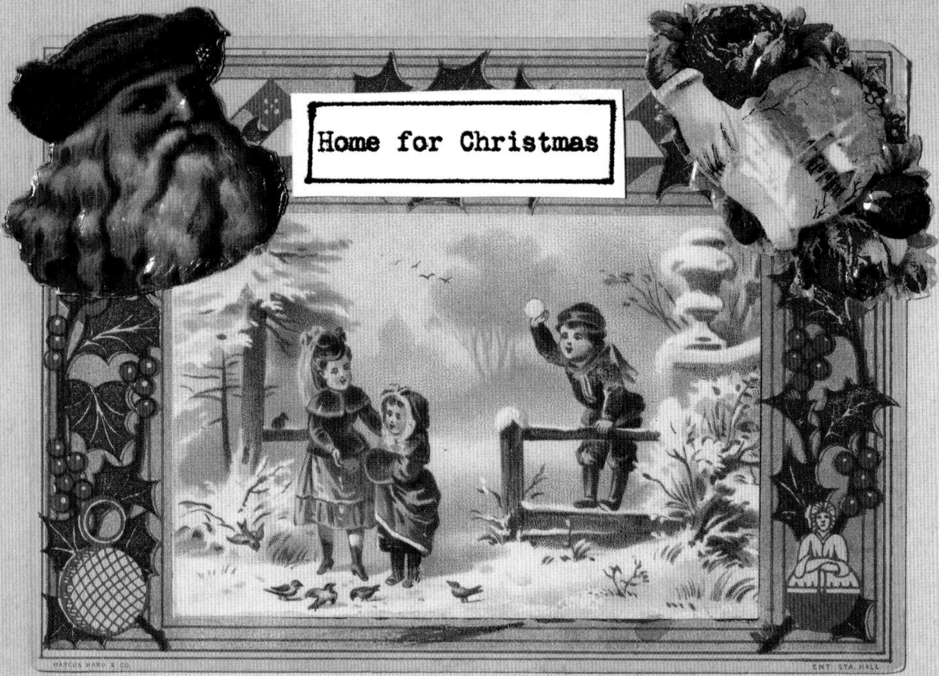
Home for Christmas

The Myth of Winter in New England

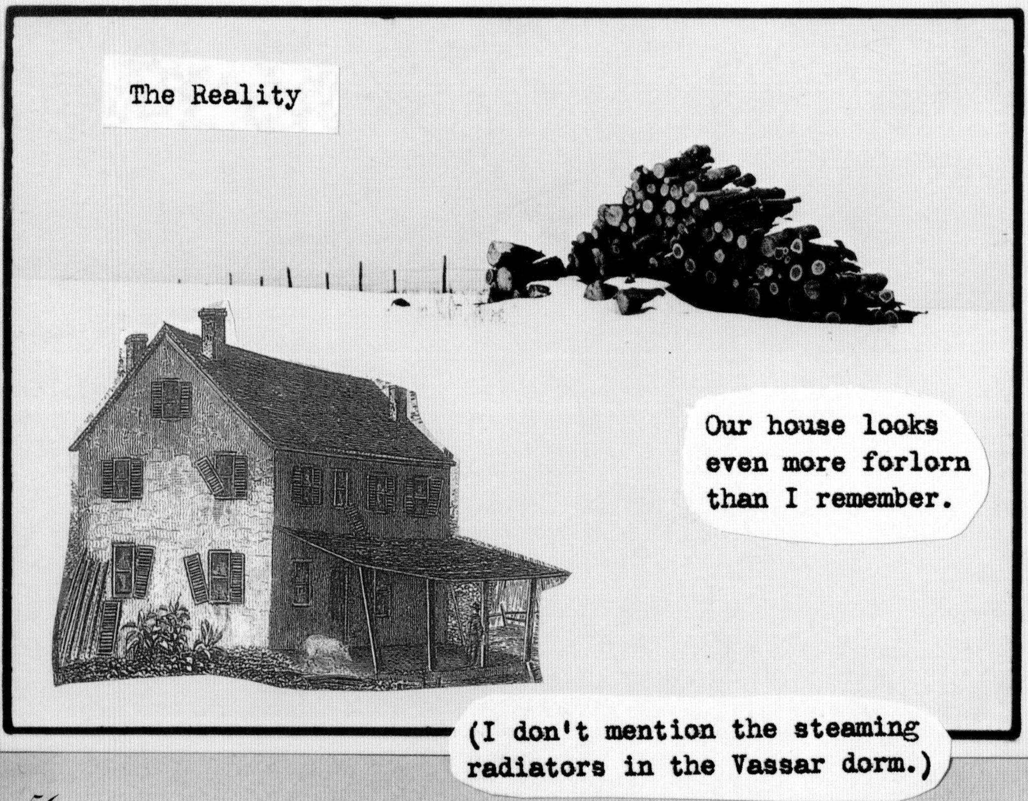
The Reality
Our house looks even more forlorn than I remember.
(I don't mention the steaming radiators in the Vassar dorm.)

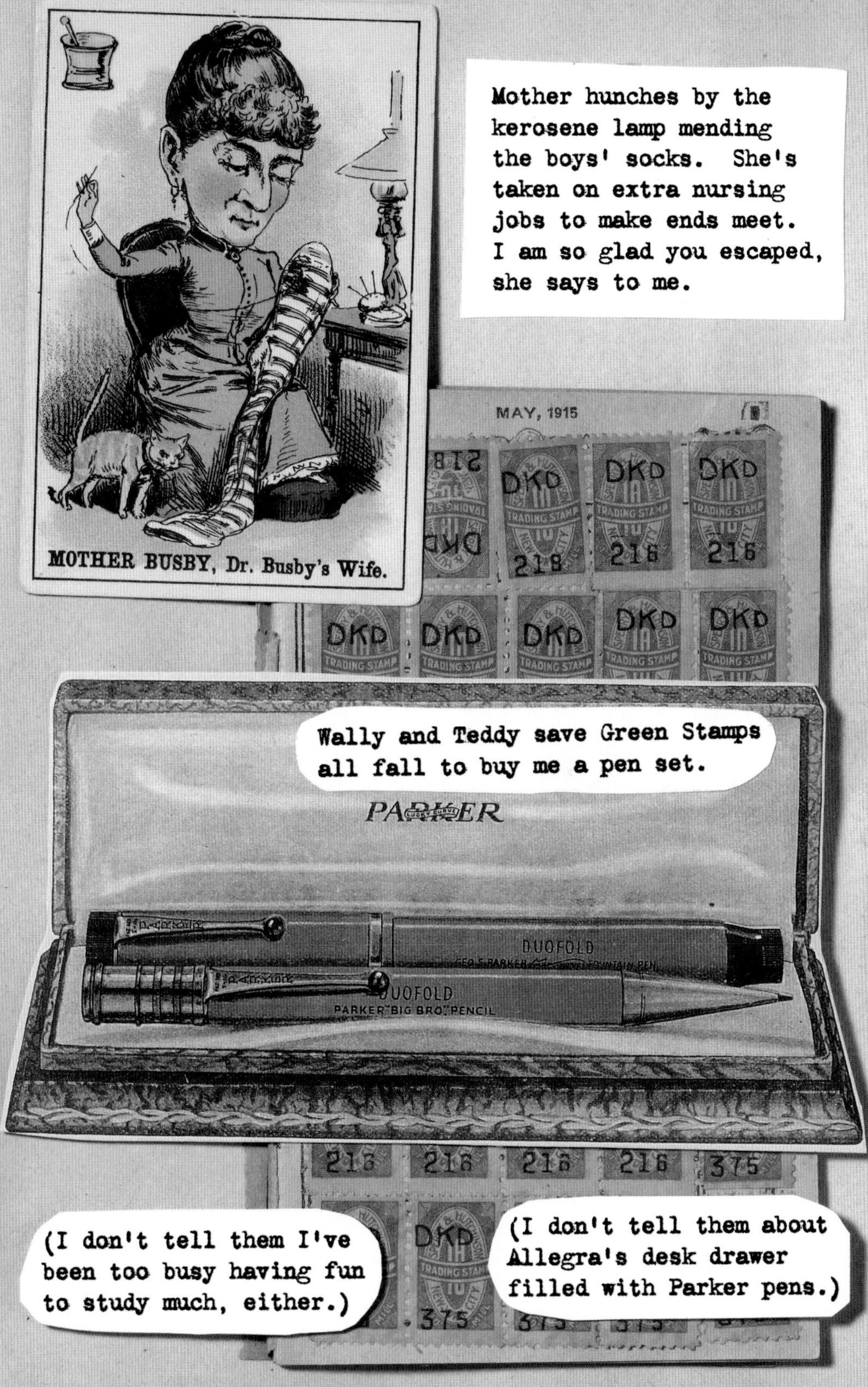
MOTHER BUSBY, Dr. Busby's Wife.
Mother hunches by the kerosene lamp mending the boys' socks. She's taken on extra nursing jobs to make ends meet. I am so glad you escaped, she says to me.
MAY, 1915
DKD
TRADING STAMP
Wally and Teddy save Green Stamps all fall to buy me a pen set.
PARKER
LUCKY CURVE
DUOFOLD
DUOFOLD
PARKER "BIG BRO" PENCIL
(I don't tell them I've been too busy having fun to study much, either.)
(I don't tell them about Allegra's desk drawer filled with Parker pens.)

Exit Captain Pingree

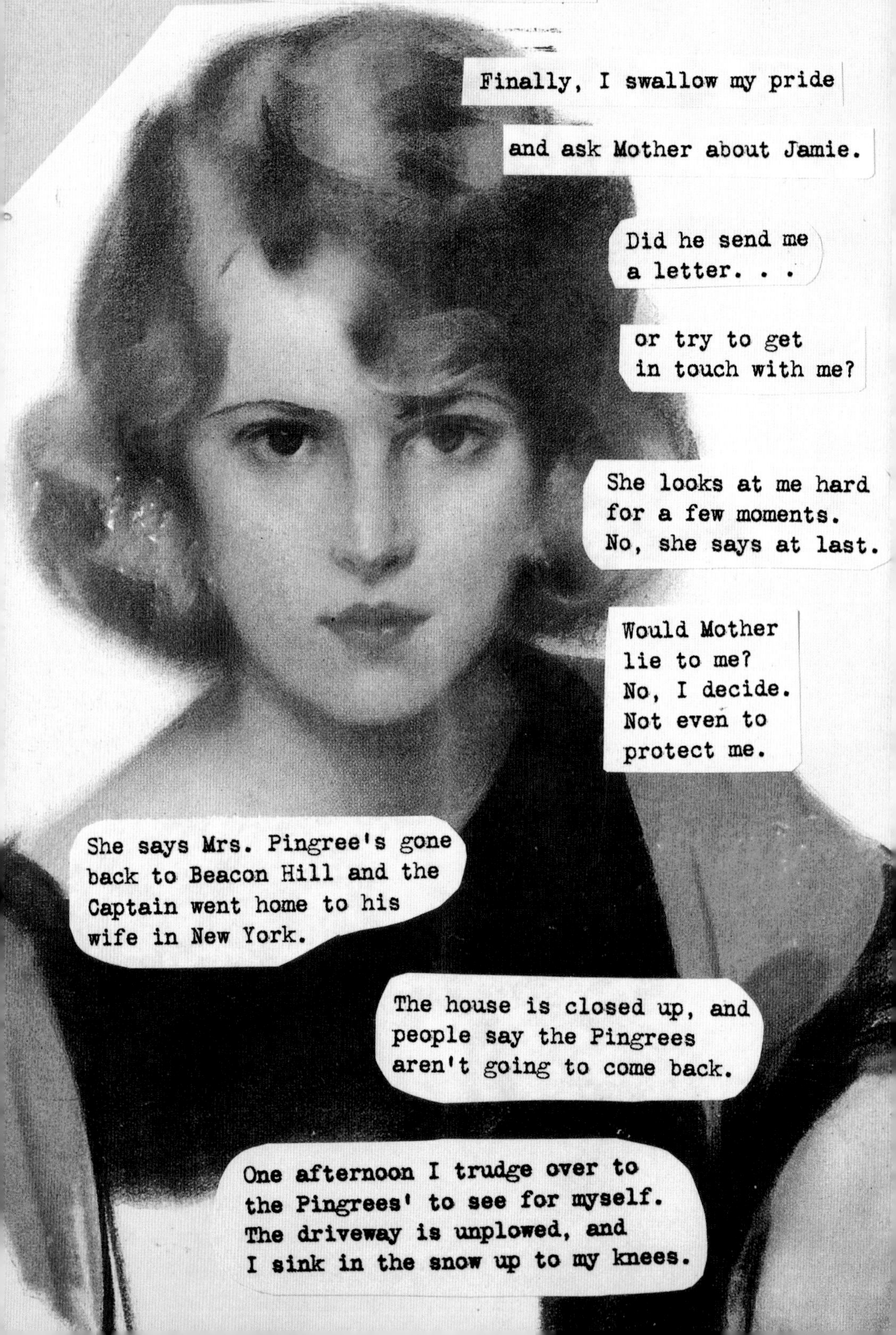

Finally, I swallow my pride

and ask Mother about Jamie.

Did he send me
a letter. . .

or try to get
in touch with me?

She looks at me hard
for a few moments.
No, she says at last.

Would Mother
lie to me?
No, I decide.
Not even to
protect me.

She says Mrs. Pingree's gone
back to Beacon Hill and the
Captain went home to his
wife in New York.

The house is closed up, and
people say the Pingrees
aren't going to come back.

One afternoon I trudge over to
the Pingrees' to see for myself.
The driveway is unplowed, and
I sink in the snow up to my knees.

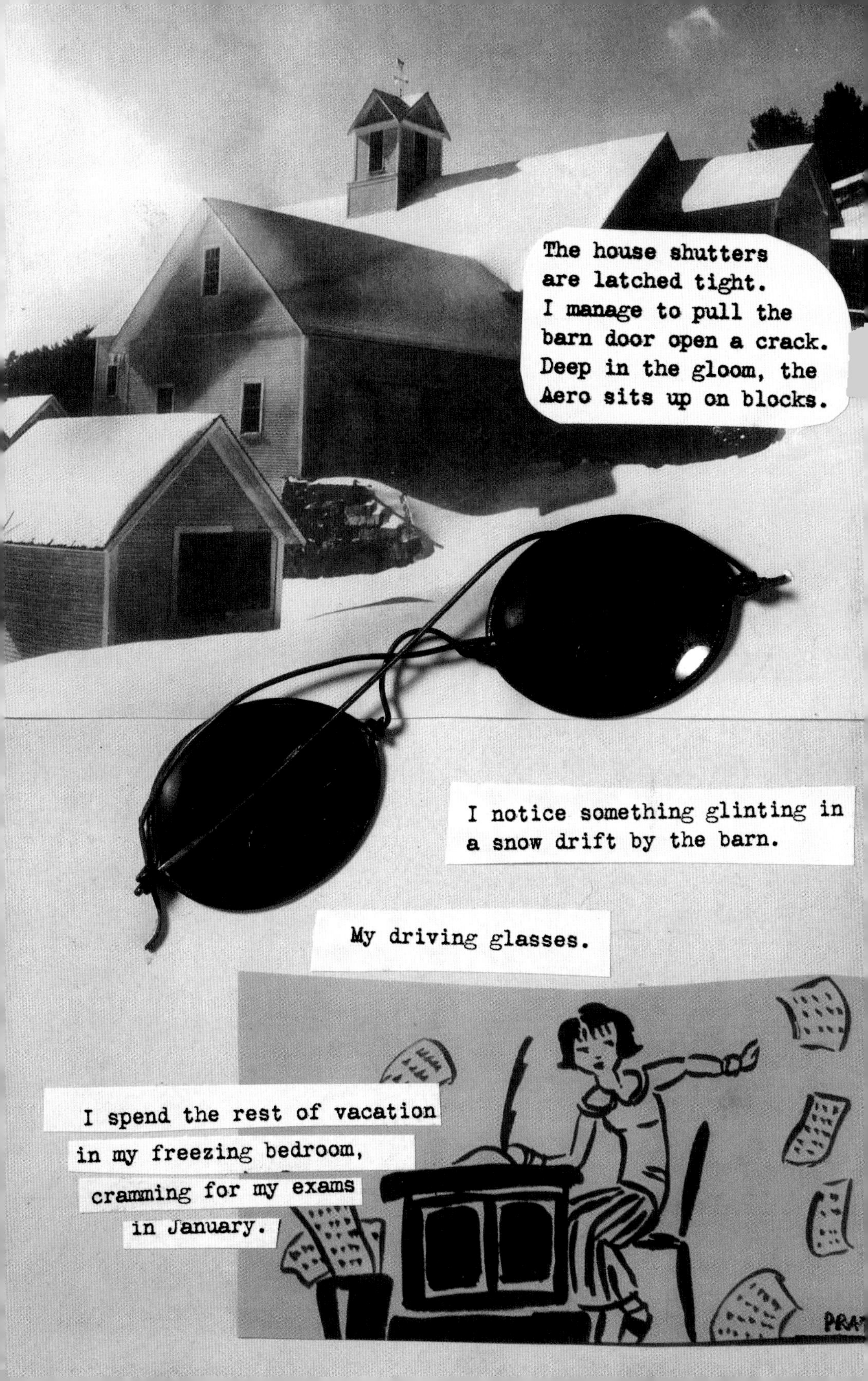
The house shutters are latched tight. I manage to pull the barn door open a crack. Deep in the gloom, the Aero sits up on blocks.
I notice something glinting in a snow drift by the barn.
My driving glasses.
I spend the rest of vacation in my freezing bedroom, cramming for my exams in January.

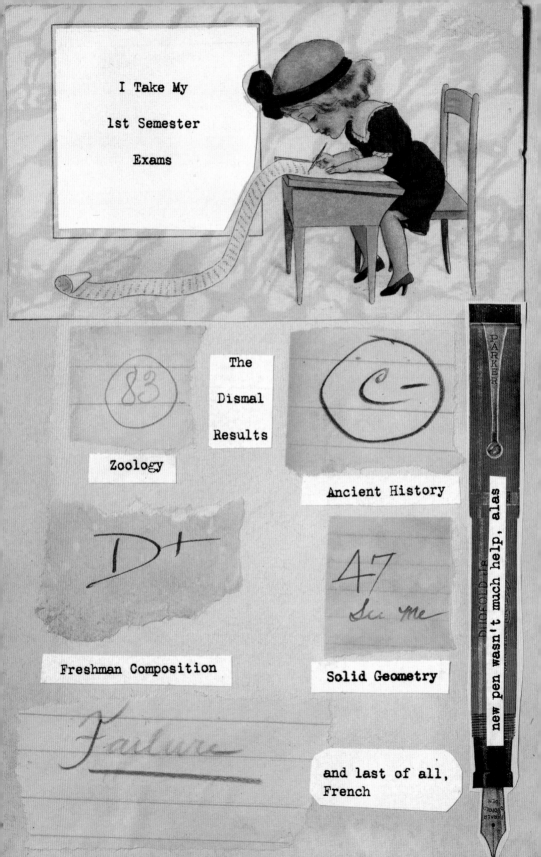

I Take My

1st Semester

Exams

The Dismal Results

83

Zoology

C−

Ancient History

D⁺

Freshman Composition

47
See me

Solid Geometry

Failure

and last of all, French

PARKER

DUOFOLD JR

new pen wasn't much help, alas

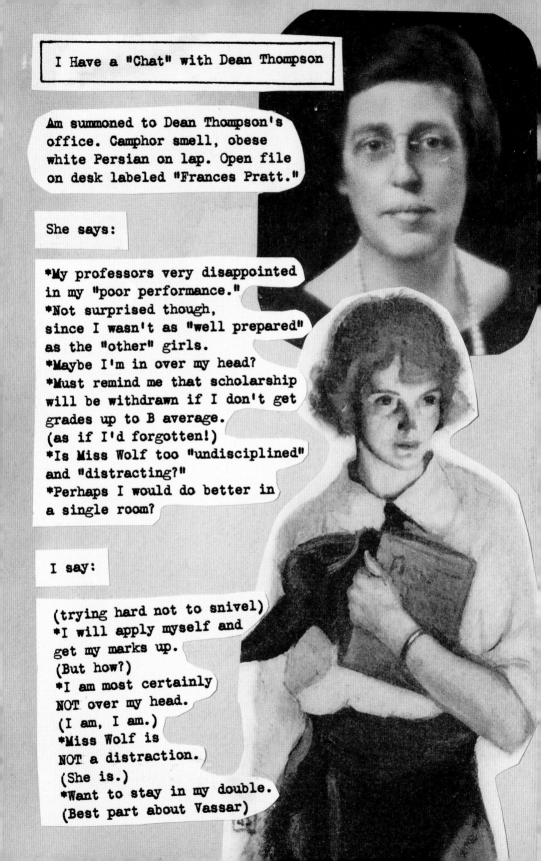

I Have a "Chat" with Dean Thompson

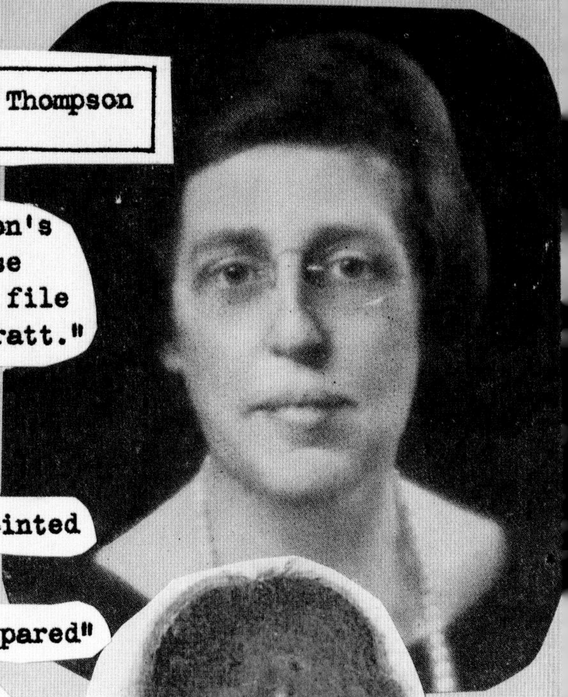

Am summoned to Dean Thompson's
office. Camphor smell, obese
white Persian on lap. Open file
on desk labeled "Frances Pratt."

She says:

*My professors very disappointed
in my "poor performance."
*Not surprised though,
since I wasn't as "well prepared"
as the "other" girls.
*Maybe I'm in over my head?
*Must remind me that scholarship
will be withdrawn if I don't get
grades up to B average.
(as if I'd forgotten!)
*Is Miss Wolf too "undisciplined"
and "distracting?"
*Perhaps I would do better in
a single room?

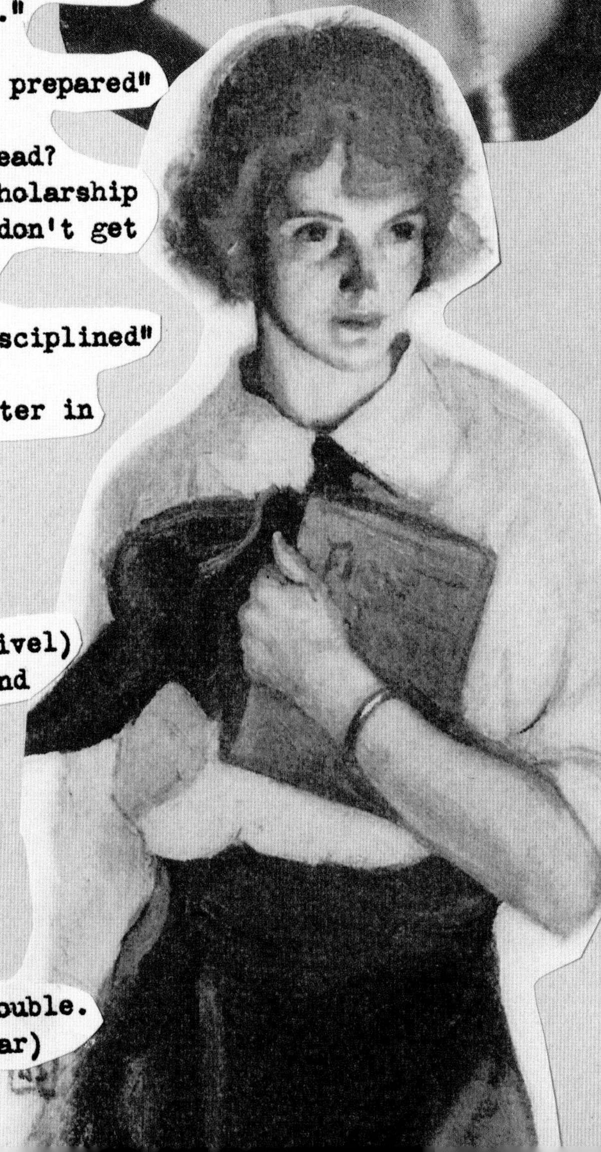

I say:

(trying hard not to snivel)
*I will apply myself and
get my marks up.
(But how?)
*I am most certainly
NOT over my head.
(I am, I am.)
*Miss Wolf is
NOT a distraction.
(She is.)
*Want to stay in my double.
(Best part about Vassar)

I Get a Tutor

Allegra finds me in the wicker chair, weeping.

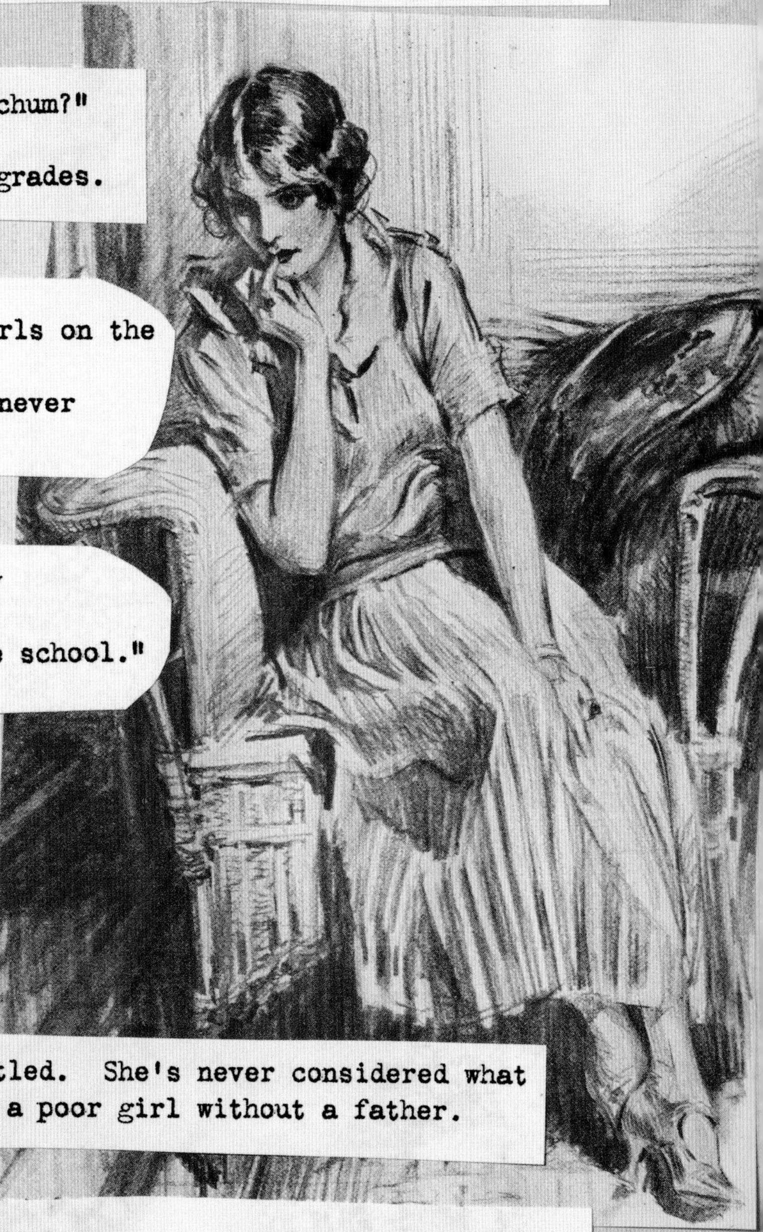

"Why so glum, chum?"

I hand her my grades.

"So? Half the girls on the hall are getting C's and D's, and never crack a book."

"But I'll lose my scholarship, and have to leave school."

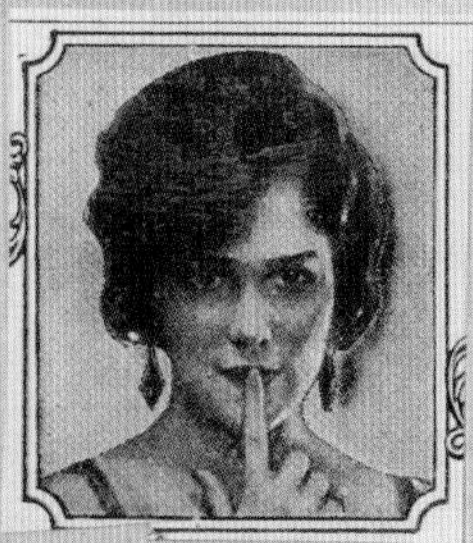

She looks startled. She's never considered what it means to be a poor girl without a father.

"We can't let that happen. I'll tutor you. I'm pretty good in French, and math, and writing too."

Is there anything Allegra isn't good at?

A's Editorial Notes and Crib Cards

opening should be
seduction

repeat word to
show paralellism

insert illustrative
paragraph. should
be no single sub-points

The Theorem of Pythagoras

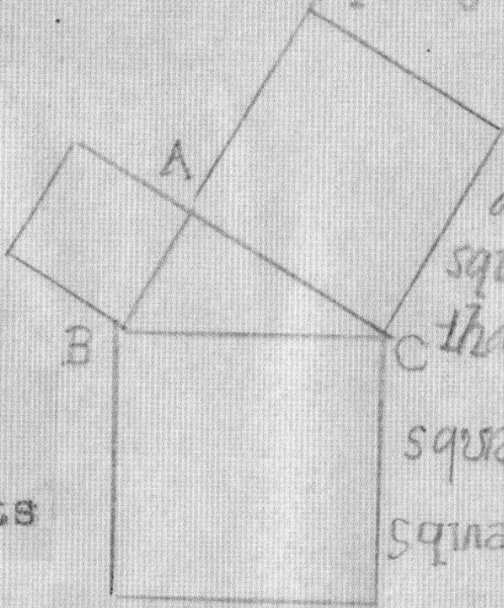

A
B
C

In a right triangle the square drawn on the side opposite the right angle will equal the squares drawn on the sides that make the right angle

square BC =
squares CA + AB

BLOT OUT WORRY

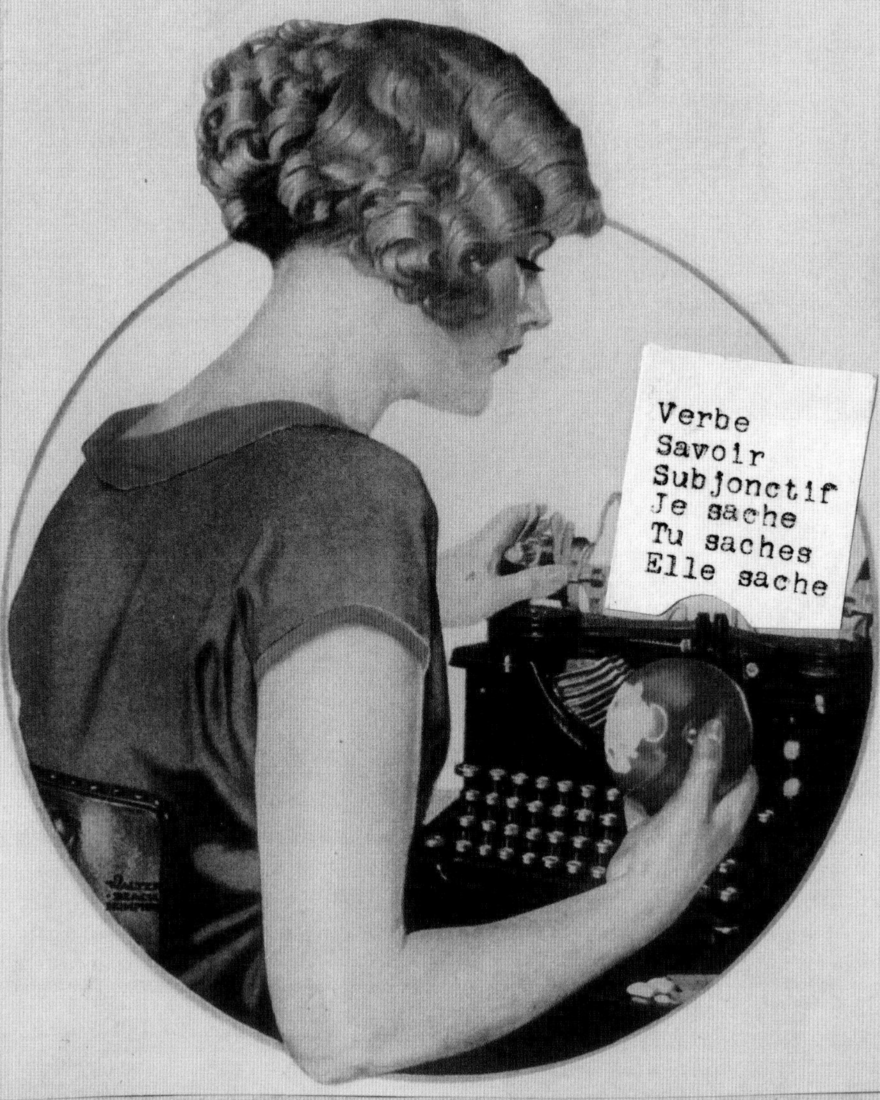

Verbe
Savoir
Subjonctif
Je sache
Tu saches
Elle sache

My First College Boy

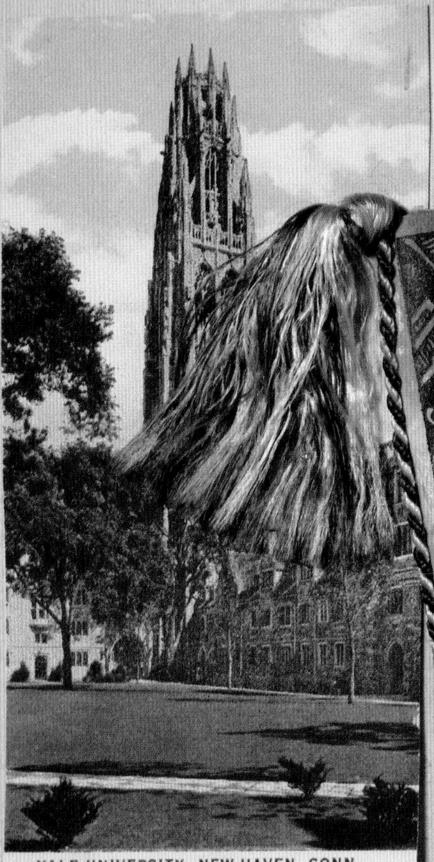

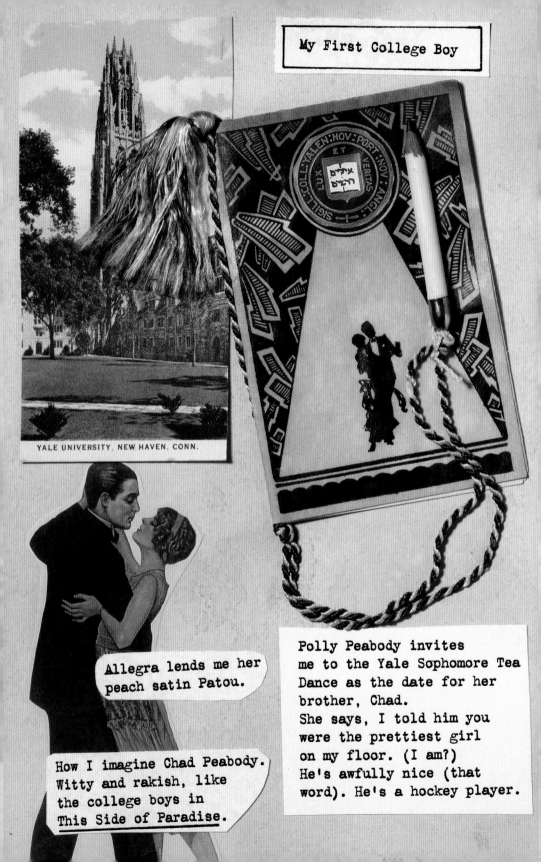

YALE UNIVERSITY, NEW HAVEN, CONN.

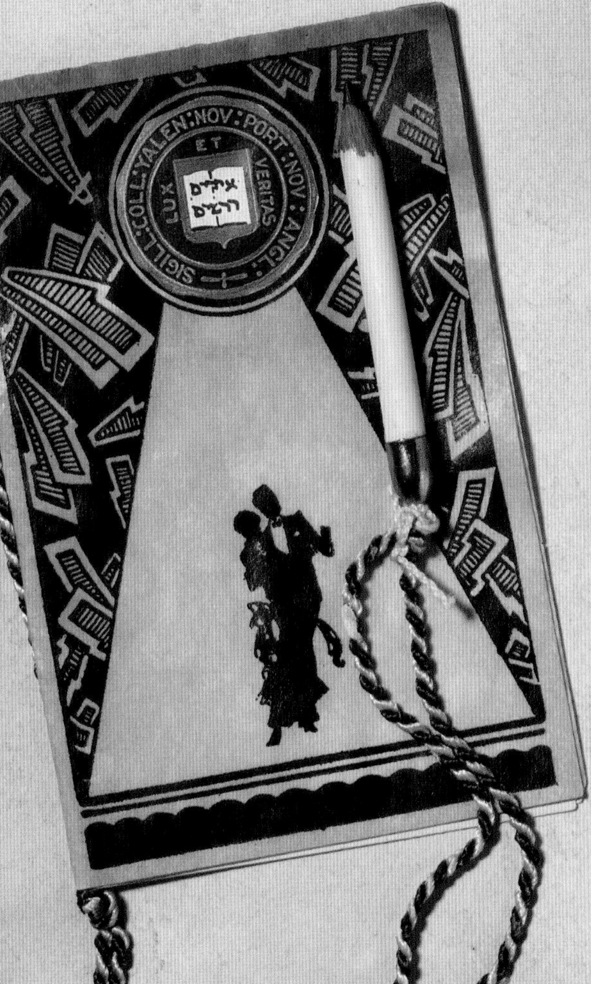
SIGILL·COLL·YALEN·NOV·PORT·NOV·ANGL·
LUX ET VERITAS

Polly Peabody invites me to the Yale Sophomore Tea Dance as the date for her brother, Chad.
She says, I told him you were the prettiest girl on my floor. (I am?)
He's awfully nice (that word). He's a hockey player.

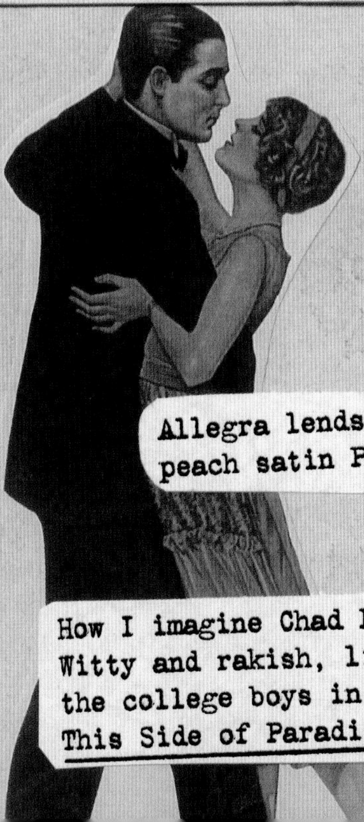

Allegra lends me her peach satin Patou.

How I imagine Chad Peabody. Witty and rakish, like the college boys in <u>This Side of Paradise</u>.

Reality of the College Boy

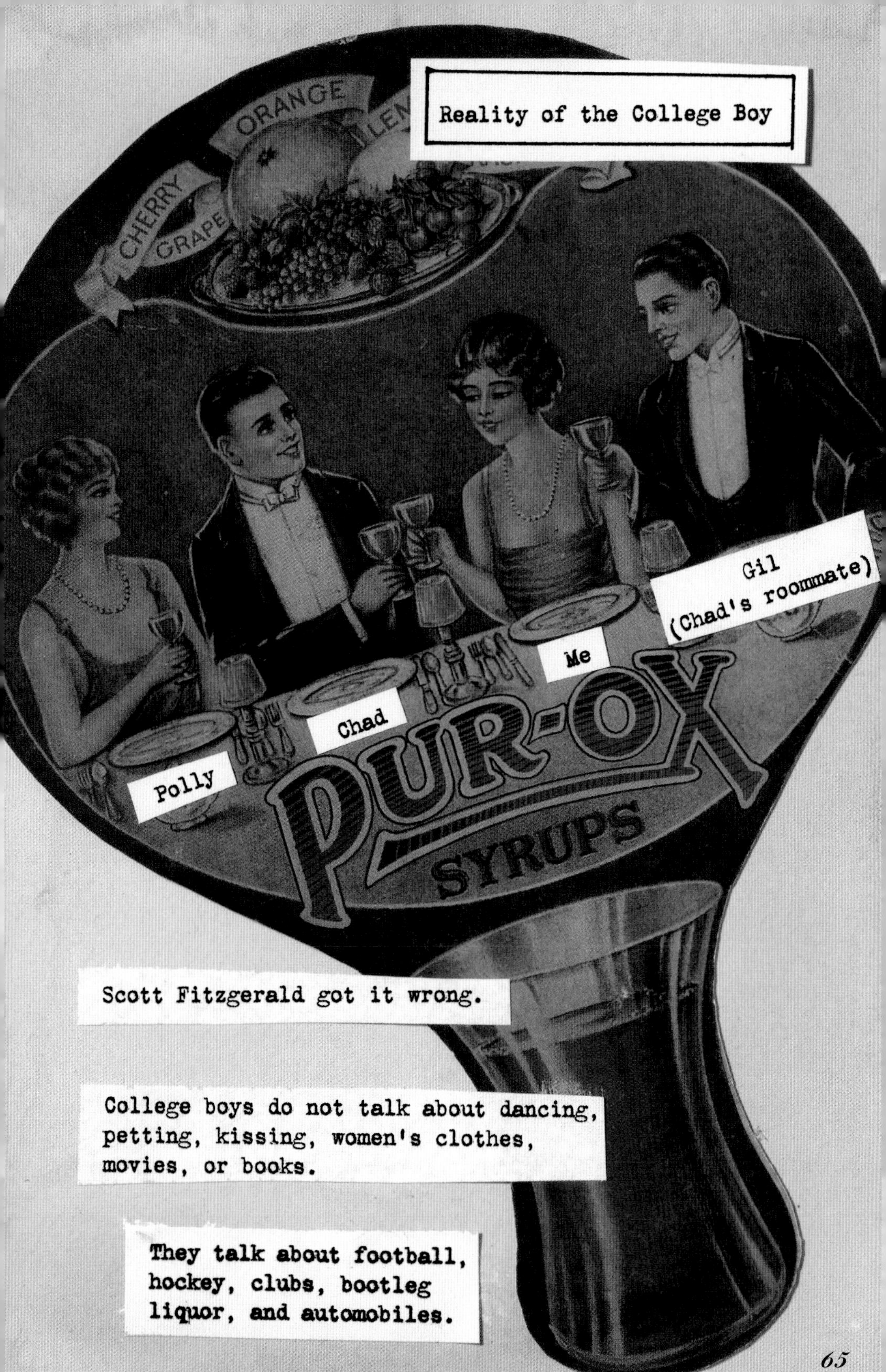
CHERRY
GRAPE
ORANGE
Gil
(Chad's roommate)
Me
Chad
Polly
PUR-OX
SYRUPS

Scott Fitzgerald got it wrong.

College boys do not talk about dancing, petting, kissing, women's clothes, movies, or books.

They talk about football, hockey, clubs, bootleg liquor, and automobiles.

What I Learn from Chad Peabody

C. 'Fraid I'm not much of a dancer.
Especially the colored dances.

F. The what?

C. You know. Rag, shimmy, black bottom.
I can't move like that.

F. So. How are you liking Yale?
(Cringe-- stupid thing to say.)

C. Book stuff is rot, like <u>Theories of the Leisure Class</u>,
which basically makes fun of being wealthy. Getting
3 F's too. Dean says pull them up or I'm out.

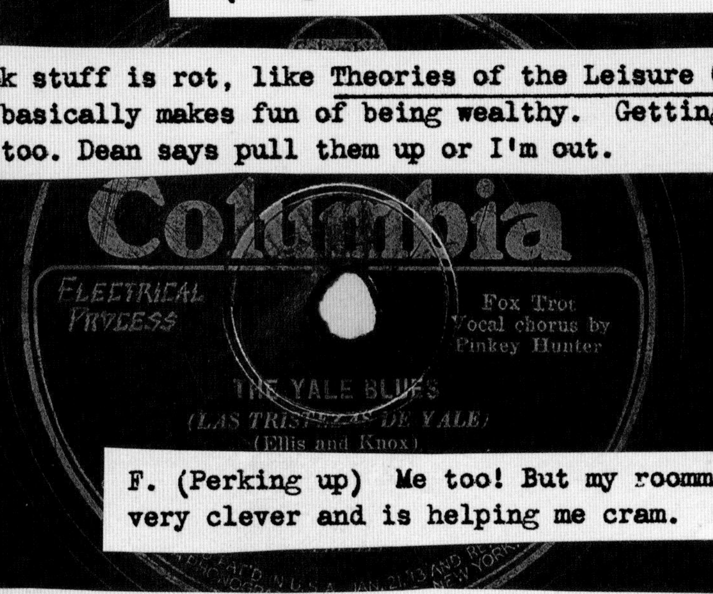
Columbia
ELECTRICAL PROCESS
Fox Trot
Vocal chorus by
Pinkey Hunter
(Ellis and Knox)

F. (Perking up) Me too! But my roommate's
very clever and is helping me cram.

C. Polly told me about your roommate. The Jewish girl.
Her brother's in my class, you know. Oliver Wolf.

F. (A's never mentioned a brother-- why not?
Bet Oliver Wolf knows how to dance and
understands Veblen. I swivel around.)
Is he here?

C. Probably not. They keep to themselves, you know.

F. No, I don't know.

C. Oh, right. Maybe you should switch roommates.

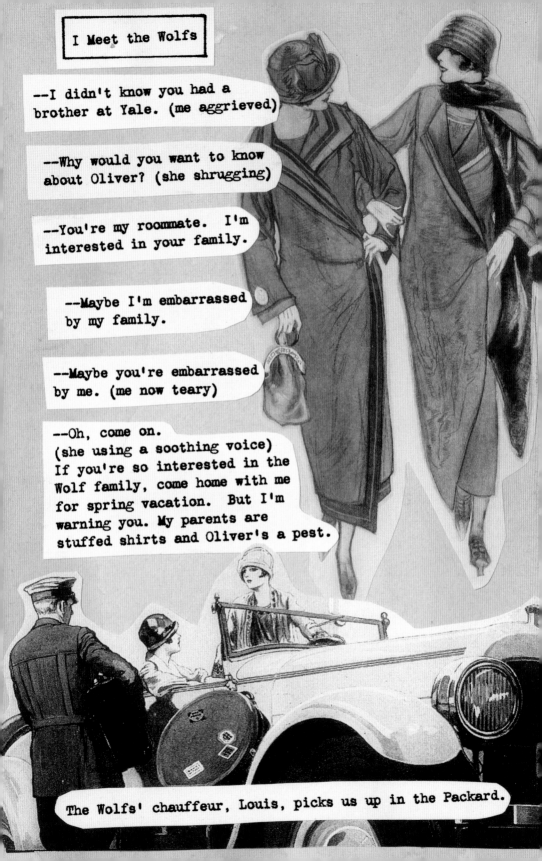

I Meet the Wolfs

--I didn't know you had a brother at Yale. (me aggrieved)

--Why would you want to know about Oliver? (she shrugging)

--You're my roommate. I'm interested in your family.

--Maybe I'm embarrassed by my family.

--Maybe you're embarrassed by me. (me now teary)

--Oh, come on.
(she using a soothing voice)
If you're so interested in the Wolf family, come home with me for spring vacation. But I'm warning you. My parents are stuffed shirts and Oliver's a pest.

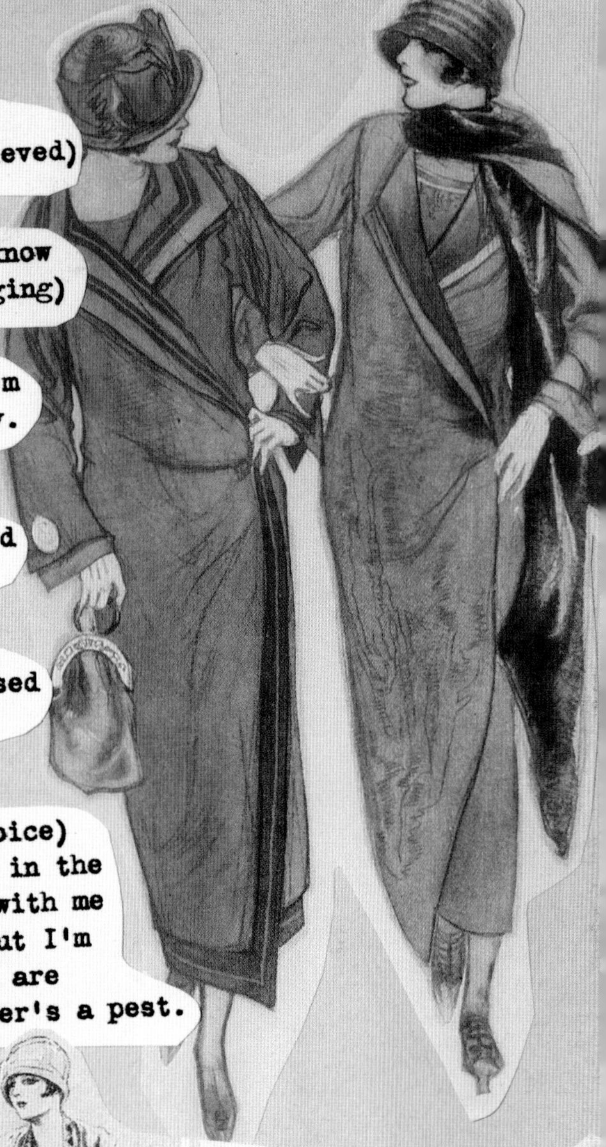

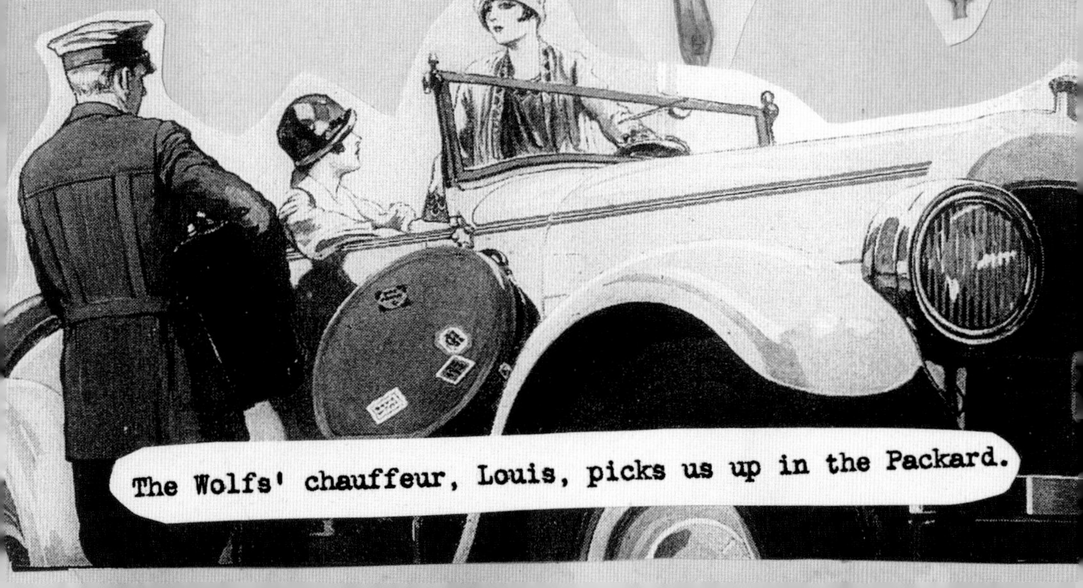

The Wolfs' chauffeur, Louis, picks us up in the Packard.

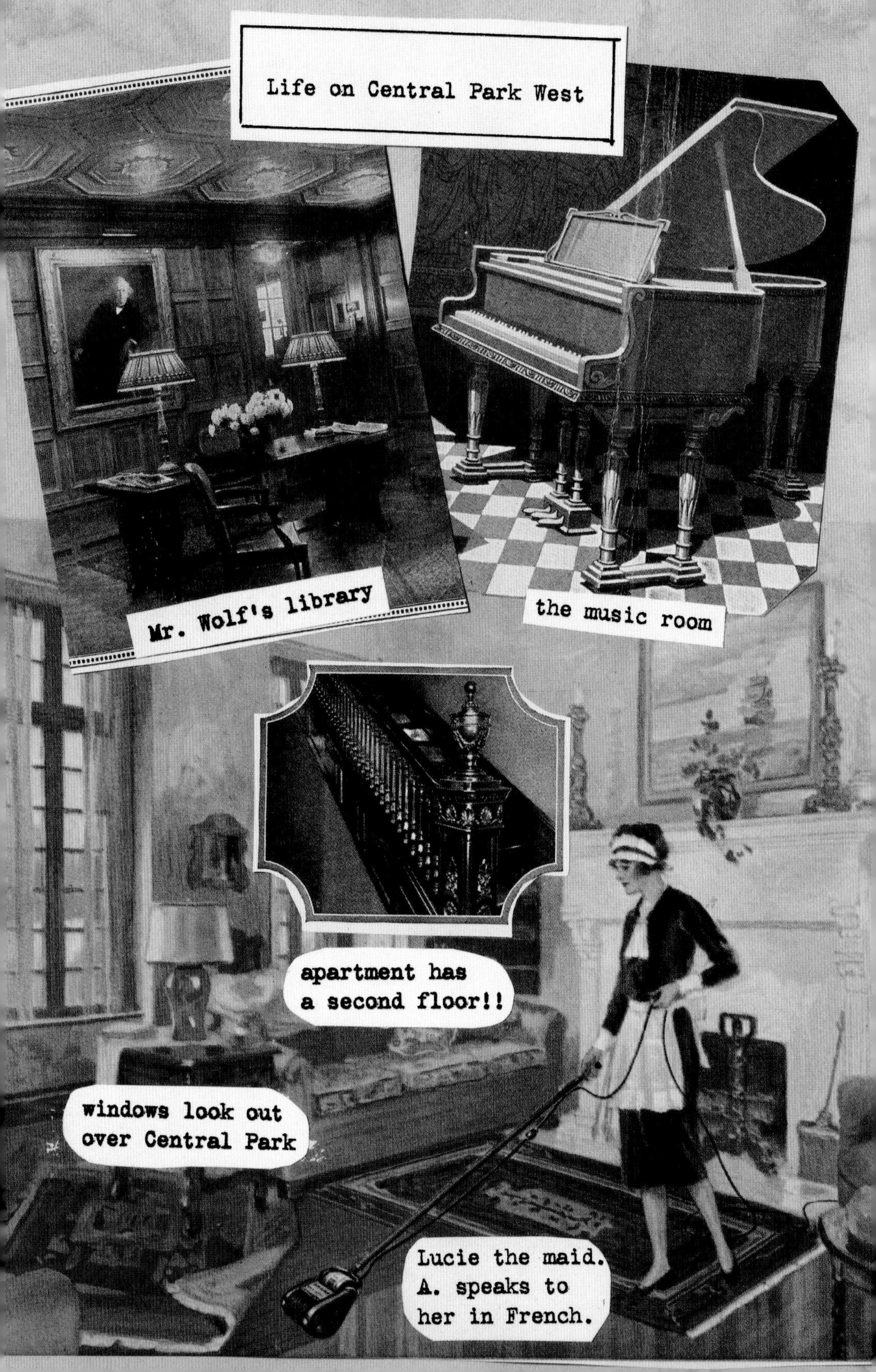
Life on Central Park West
Mr. Wolf's library
the music room
apartment has a second floor!!
windows look out over Central Park
Lucie the maid. A. speaks to her in French.

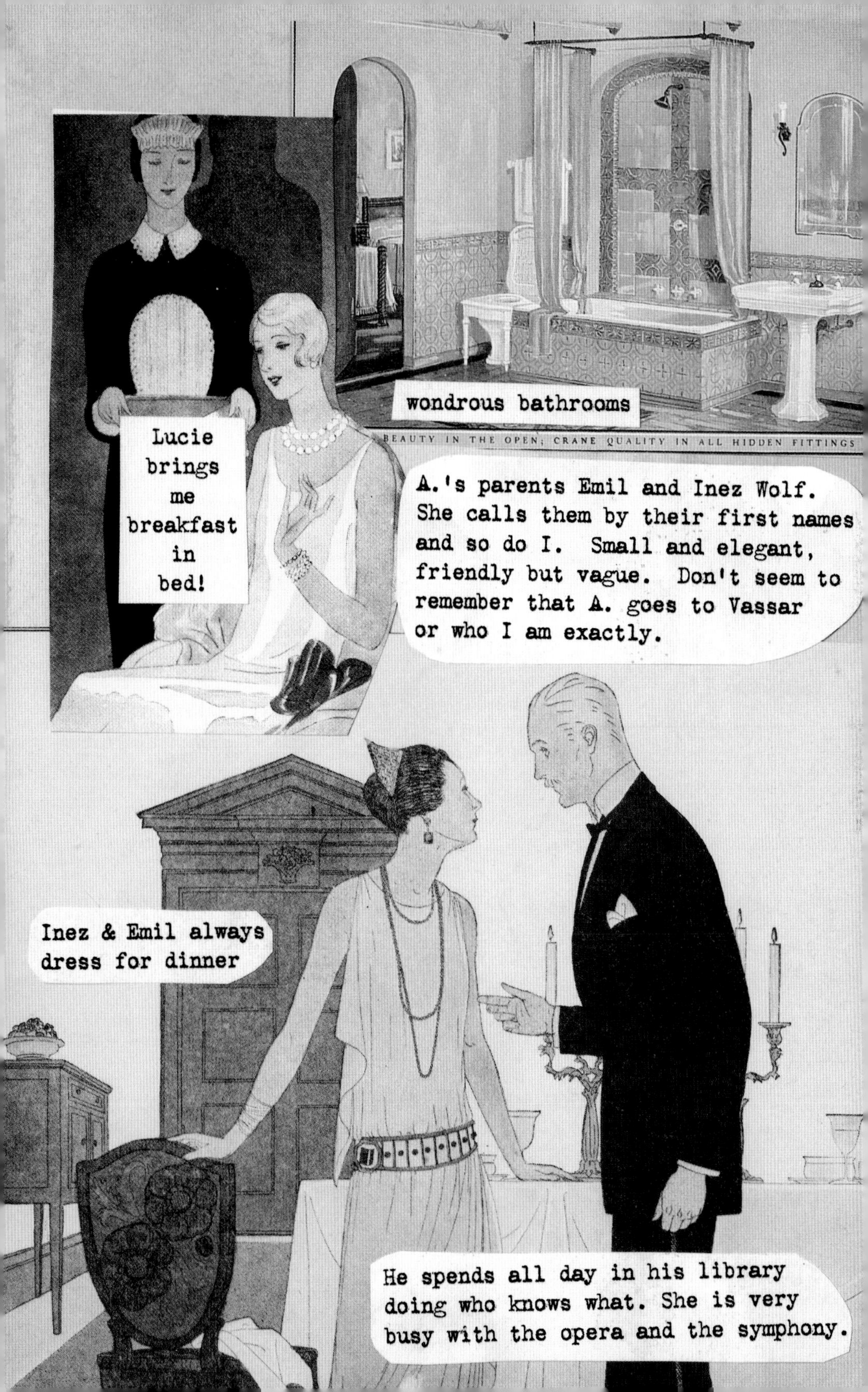
wondrous bathrooms
BEAUTY IN THE OPEN; CRANE QUALITY IN ALL HIDDEN FITTINGS
Lucie brings me breakfast in bed!
A.'s parents Emil and Inez Wolf. She calls them by their first names and so do I. Small and elegant, friendly but vague. Don't seem to remember that A. goes to Vassar or who I am exactly.
Inez & Emil always dress for dinner
He spends all day in his library doing who knows what. She is very busy with the opera and the symphony.

Enter Oliver Wolf

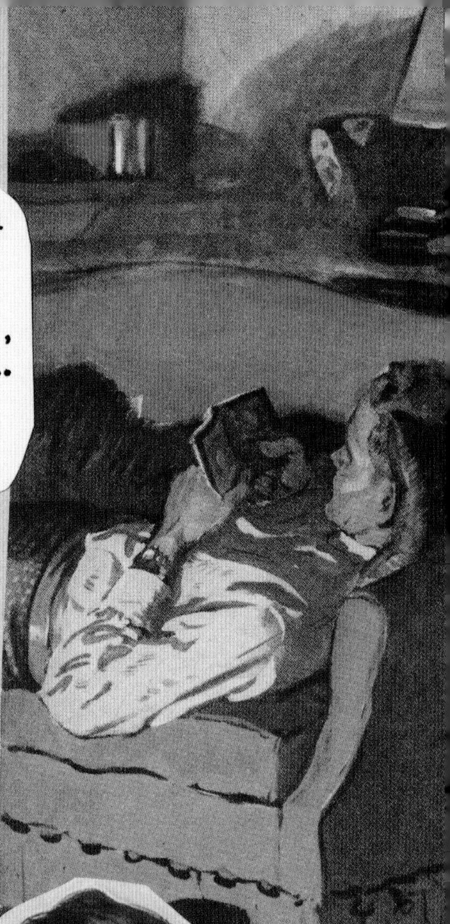

One morning, I find a man stretched across the living room sofa.
Oh, hello, he says, stumbling to his stocking feet (hole in one toe), pushing messy hair off his forehead. "I'm Oliver. I know who you are. The one who gave that dolt Chad Peabody the cold shoulder."

He drinks coffee and peppers me with questions.
Tell me about your parents, your brothers, Cornish.
How do you like Vassar?
How are the other girls?
Who's your favorite writer?
(Fitzgerald, I say, instead of Wharton.)
What do you want to do after graduation? Not get married, I hope.
(Write for a magazine, I say.)
Where do you want to live?
(New York, maybe Paris.
Not Cornish!)
And then he listens closely to my answers, nodding as if they were profound.

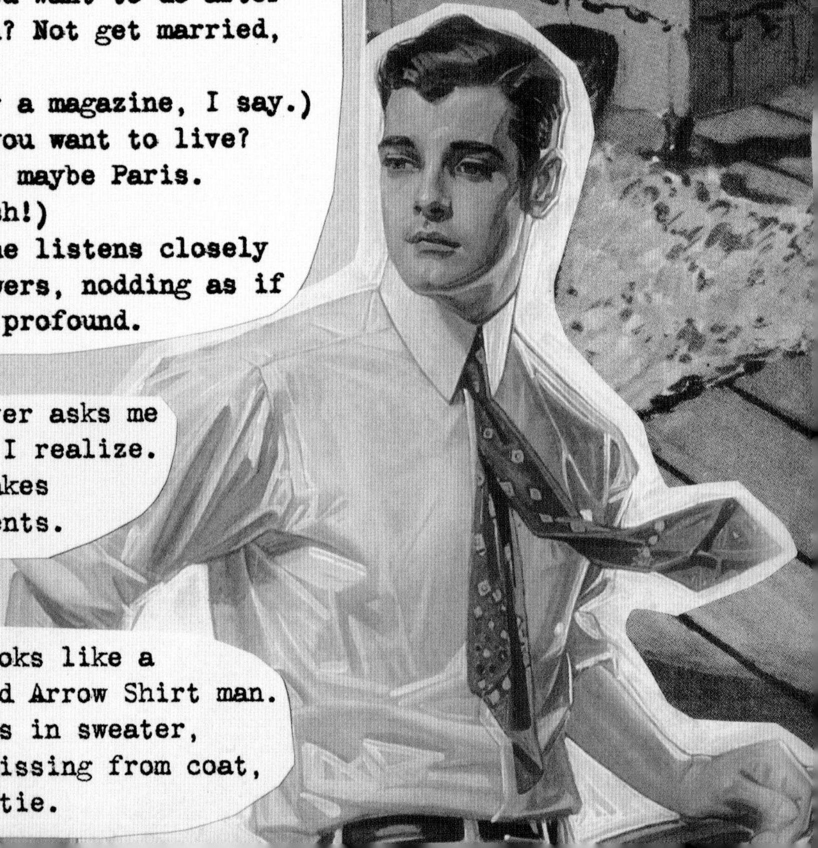

Allegra never asks me questions, I realize. She only makes pronouncements.

Oliver looks like a bedraggled Arrow Shirt man. Moth holes in sweater, buttons missing from coat, spots on tie.

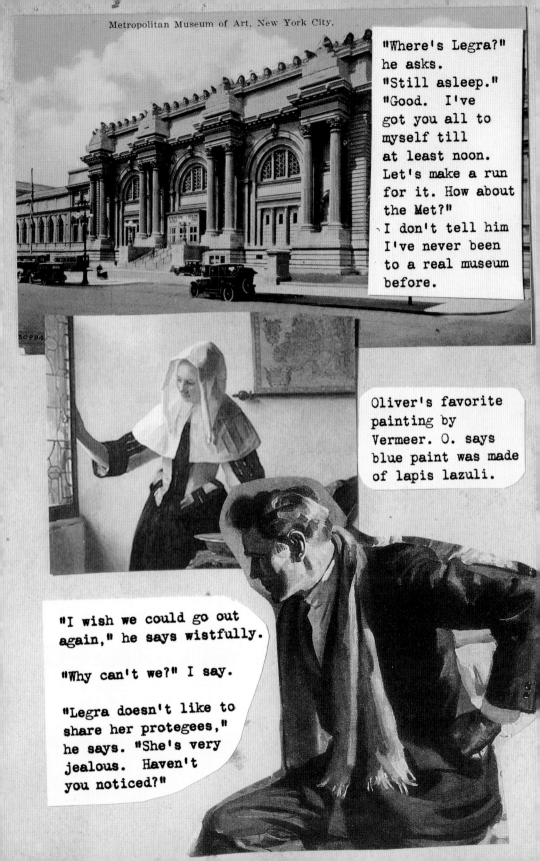

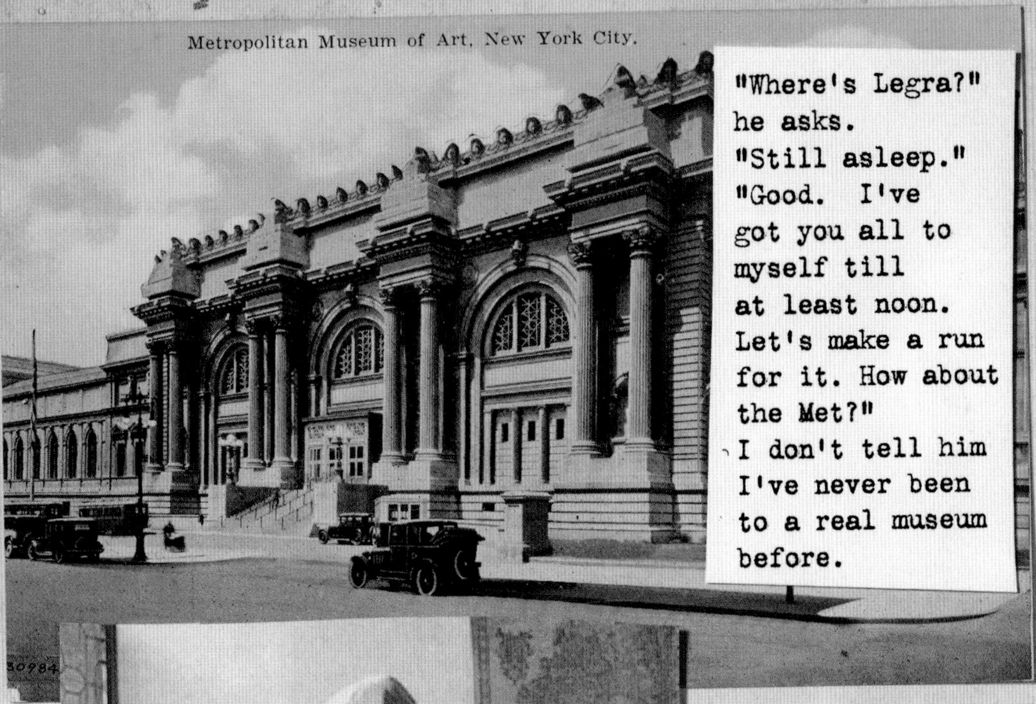
Metropolitan Museum of Art, New York City.
30984

"Where's Legra?"
he asks.
"Still asleep."
"Good. I've
got you all to
myself till
at least noon.
Let's make a run
for it. How about
the Met?"
I don't tell him
I've never been
to a real museum
before.

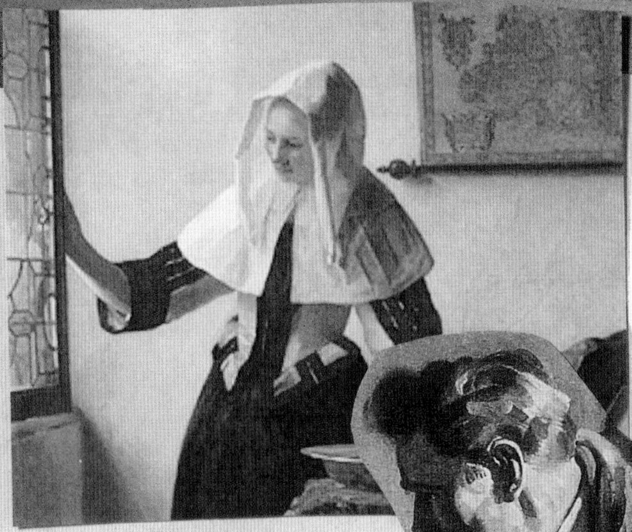

Oliver's favorite
painting by
Vermeer. O. says
blue paint was made
of lapis lazuli.

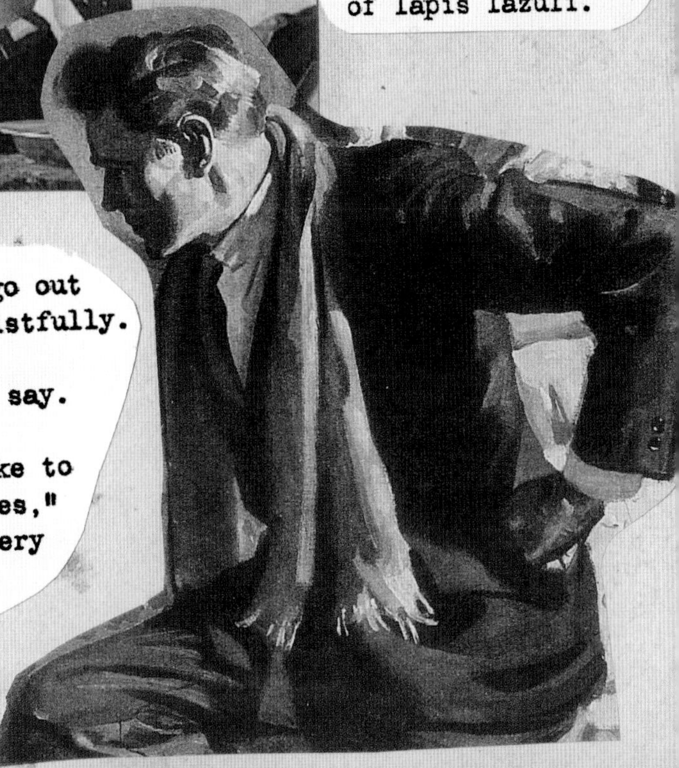

"I wish we could go out
again," he says wistfully.

"Why can't we?" I say.

"Legra doesn't like to
share her protegees,"
he says. "She's very
jealous. Haven't
you noticed?"

Academic Probation!

VASSAR COLLEGE

RECORD FOR 2nd SEMESTER 1920-1921

Frances Pratt

Course	Hours	Grade
English 1		B
History 30		B-
Mathematics 2		B
Zoology 12		B-
French 2		C-
Hygiene		B
Physical Education		B

Total credits received through June, 1921

C. Mildred Thomps

(OVER)

I manage to pull most of my grades up to a low B. Except French, my "bête noire." Dean Thompson puts me on academic probation.

She says I need to spend the summer at Vassar and be tutored in French by Mlle. Monnier. If I pass a make-up exam, I can keep my scholarship.

I can stay in the boarding-house where all the spinster faculty live.

They give me a job in the library typing catalog cards to earn my keep.

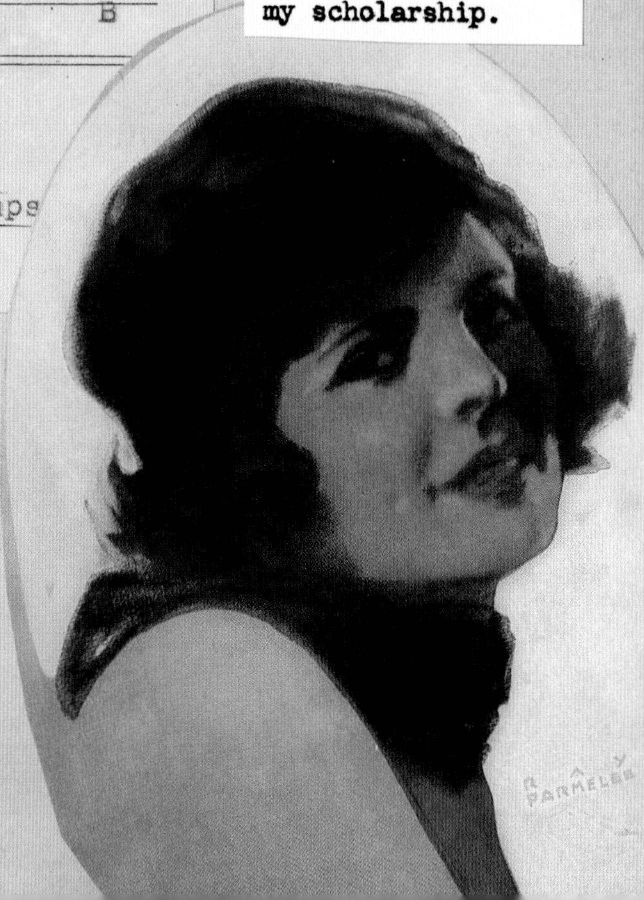
RAY
PARMELEE

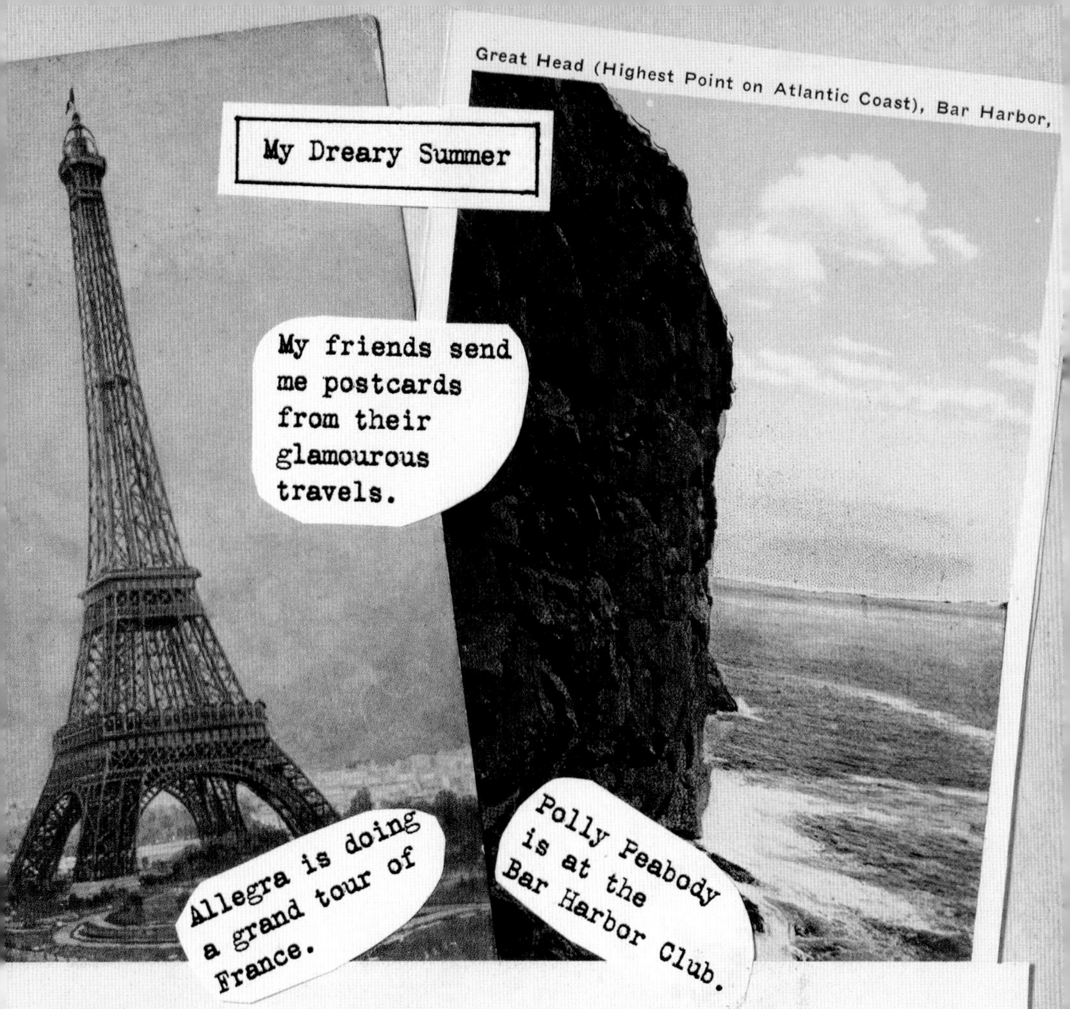

Great Head (Highest Point on Atlantic Coast), Bar Harbor,
My Dreary Summer
My friends send me postcards from their glamourous travels.
Allegra is doing a grand tour of France.
Polly Peabody is at the Bar Harbor Club.

GREETINGS FROM

VASSAR

Dear Allegra,

Thanks for PC's from Chartres, Versailles, Mont-St-Michel, etc. I'm v. jealous.

I'm enduring Mlle. Monnier's endless corrections and learning the Dewey Decimal system. In the evenings, I play cribbage with Dean McCaleb. (some fun!)

I have become great friends with Miss Sandison who says we can both take her advanced fiction writing class next year!! She gave me Women in Love by DH Lawrence, which is banned. Pretty hot stuff! Also short stories by Katherine Mansfield, my new heroine.

Don't run off with a gigolo. . .

F.

My Star Rises

A — much improved

A nice job

Prof. Sandison tells me that my short stories show "promise." First words of praise from a Vassar teacher.

My first A's

I write book reviews for the Vassar Review sophomore year.

I'm the Book Review Editor my junior year.

THE WASTE LAND
T. S. Eliot
Reviewed by Frances Pratt, 1924

The Waste Land is a mosaic made of a thousand patterned bits, some familiar, some old, some new and personal to the their poet, making up a pattern obscure in design and seemingly lacking in unity. One comes away from the first reading confused, amused, and deeply unsettled.

A
clues to th
two book
Bough."

A LOST LADY
Willa Cather
Reviewed by Frances Pratt, 1924

Marian Forrester is the symbolic flower of the Old America West. At first, she appears to draw her strength from that solid foundation, bringing delight and beauty to her elderly husband, to the small town of Sweet Water where they live, to the prairie land itself, and to the young narrator of her story, Neil Herbert. All are bewitched by her brilliance and grace, and all are ultimately betrayed. For Marian longs for "life on any terms," and in fulfilling herself, she loses all she loved and all who loved her.

The VASSAR REVIEW

Senior year, Allegra and I make the masthead.

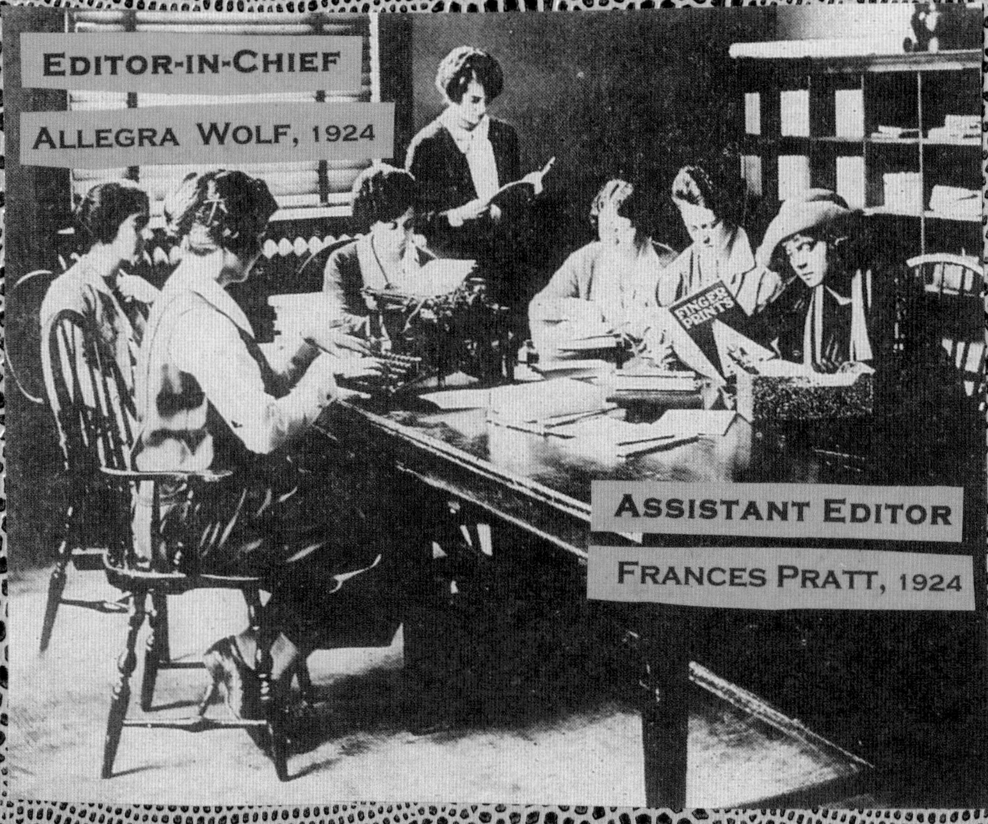
EDITOR-IN-CHIEF
ALLEGRA WOLF, 1924
FINGER PRINTS
ASSISTANT EDITOR
FRANCES PRATT, 1924

Valentines (lack of)

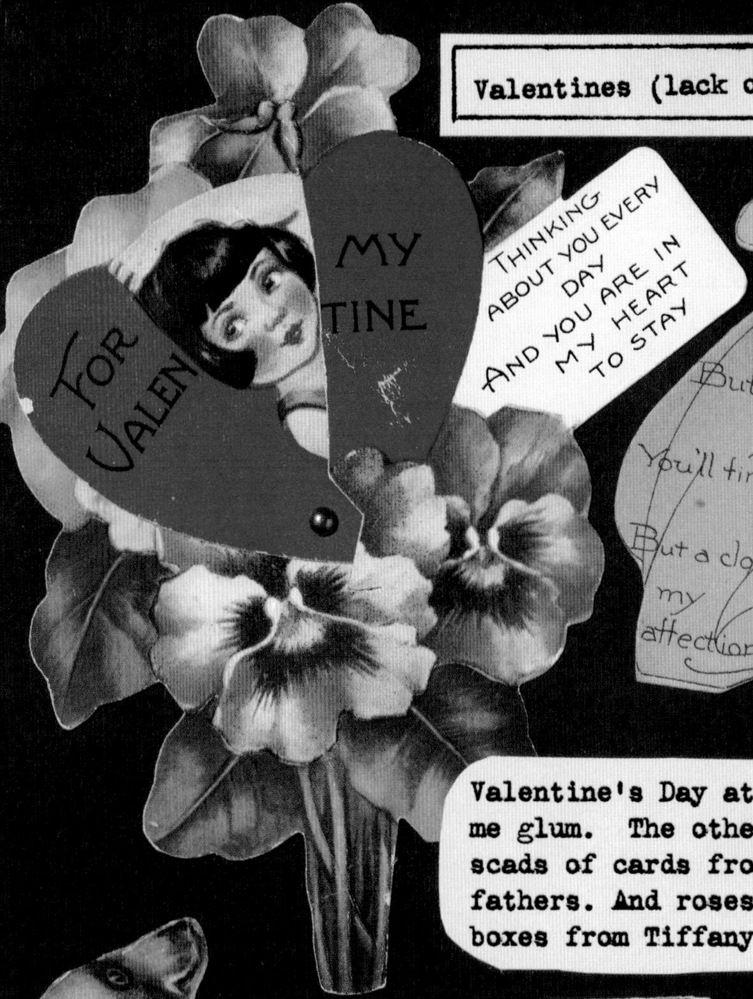
FOR VALEN
MY TINE
THINKING ABOUT YOU EVERY DAY AND YOU ARE IN MY HEART TO STAY

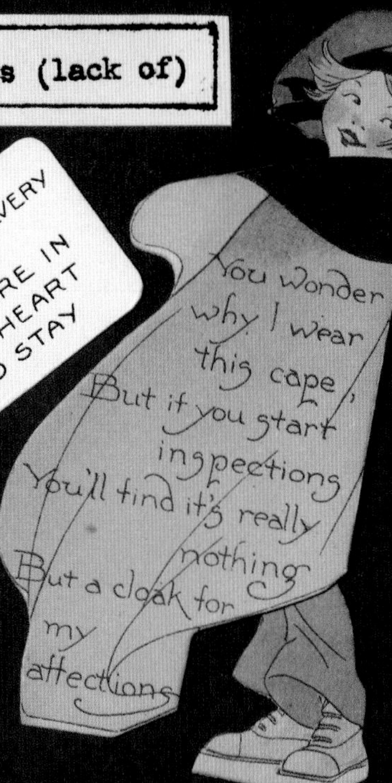
You wonder why I wear this cape,
But if you start inspections
You'll find it's really nothing
But a cloak for my affections

Valentine's Day at Vassar makes me glum. The other girls get scads of cards from beaus and fathers. And roses. And velvet boxes from Tiffany's.

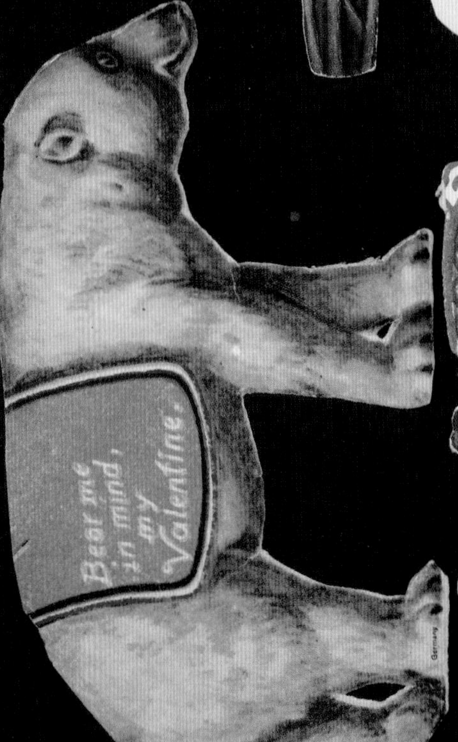
Bear me in mind, my Valentine.

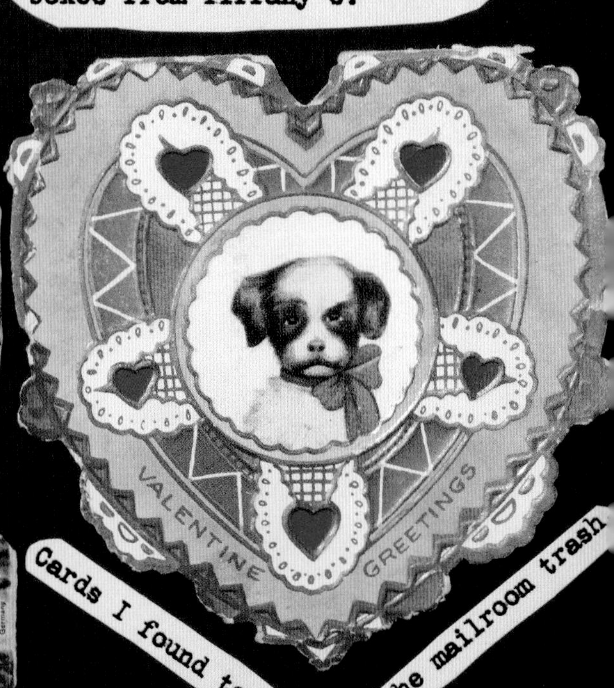
VALENTINE GREETINGS

Cards I found tossed in the mailroom trash

here

is

the

to

My

My senior year,
I get ONE valentine.

A handmade one, like the ones
Lizzie, Bess, and I would
send the boys in our class.

Who is my secret admirer?

I analyze the clues.

* Cornish postmark

* typed address
(because I
would recognize
handwriting?)

Conclusion:

I want to believe
it is from Jamie.

But Lizzie & Bessie
probably sent it as
a gag.

Or my brothers.

There is no great
love on my horizon.

The Falling Out

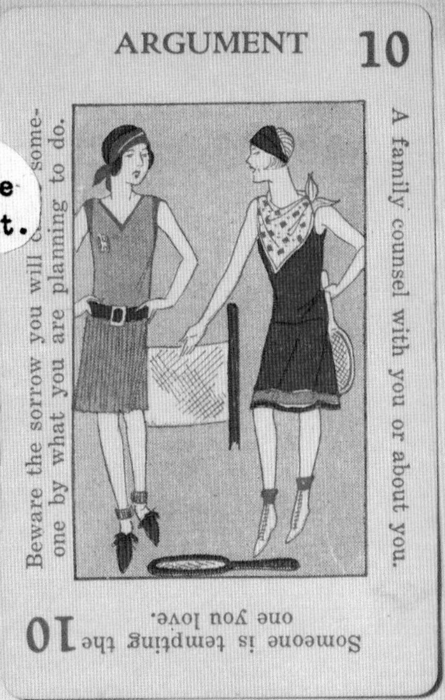
ARGUMENT 10
Beware the sorrow you will
some-
one by what you are planning to do.
A family counsel with you or about you.
Someone is tempting the one you love.
10

Allegra and I both submit stories for the Addison Prize awarded to the best short story by a Vassar student.

The Picnic

short story by Frances Prat

"Sorry about the mosquitoes."

"They never bother me-- I must no

"I find that hard to believe."

"What's the pink stuff in this sandwich?"

"Deviled ham. We ate it

"Do you think about the

"I try not to."

"That's a stupid que

"I'd rather talk abo

"Not really."

"Well, what do you

"You'll laugh."

"No I won't."

Frankie, dear,
Afraid this story comes off as somewhat naive. You imply that the girl feels humiliated and violated by the older man only because he has taken snapshots of her with his Kodak. He certainly would have taken her virginity as well! Remember--write what you know. Nice effort, though. Keep trying.
A.

I make the mistake of showing my submission, "The Picnic," to Allegra for a critique.

March 18, 1924

Dear Miss Pratt,

We are pleased to inform you that your story "The Picnic" has been awarded the 1924 Addison Prize.

Many congratulations.

Allegra's reaction to the news that I've won the Addison Prize.

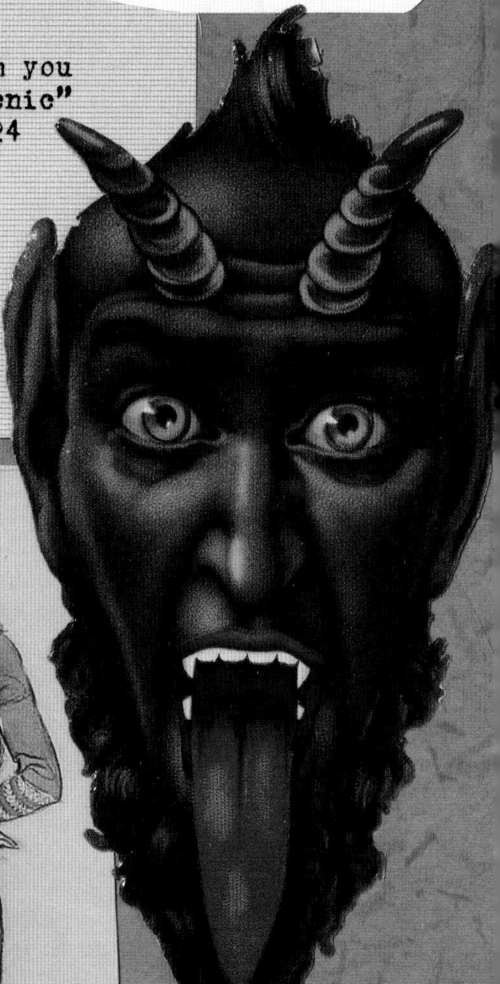

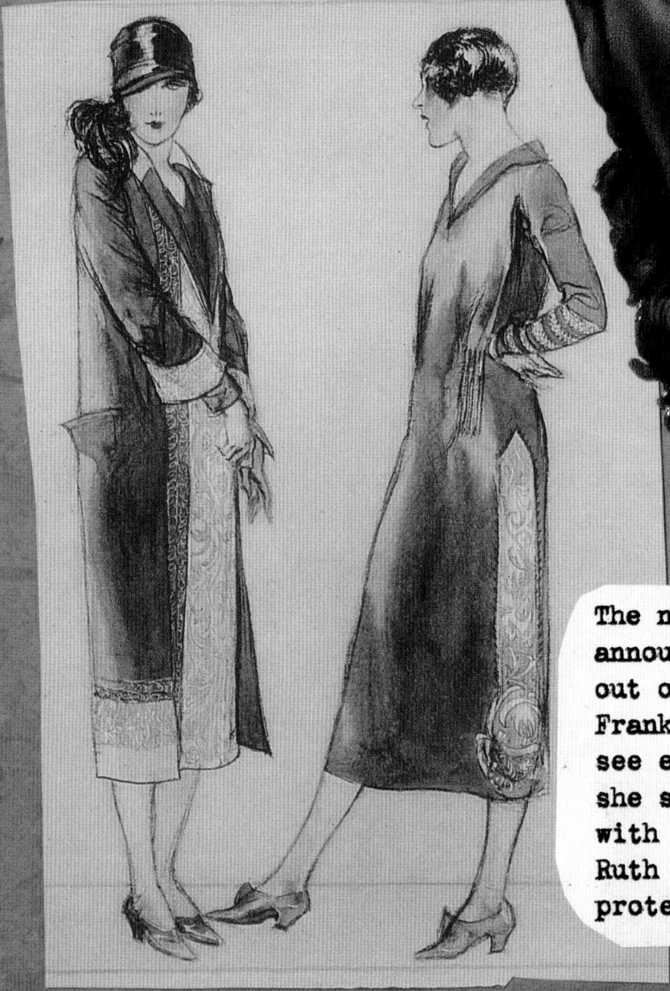

The next week, Allegra announces she is moving out of our room. "Face it, Frankie. We just don't see eye to eye anymore," she says. She moves in with a sophomore named Ruth Wheatley, her newest protegee.

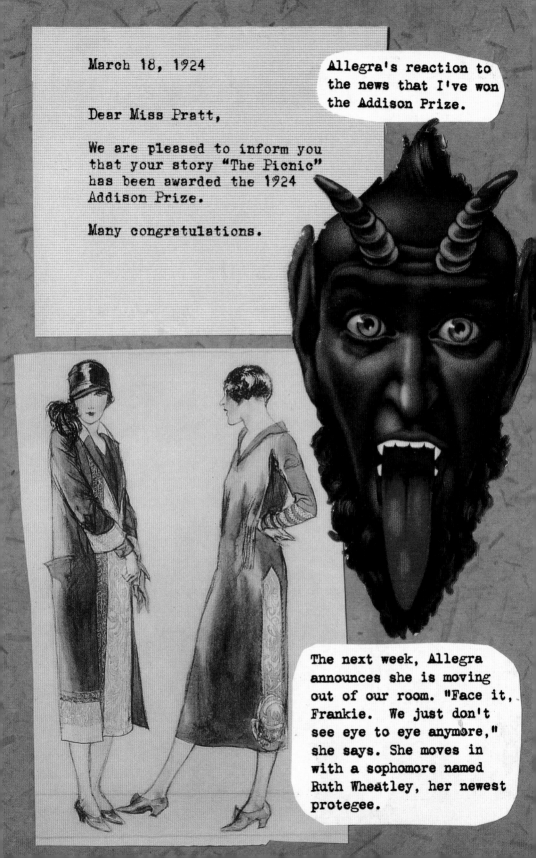

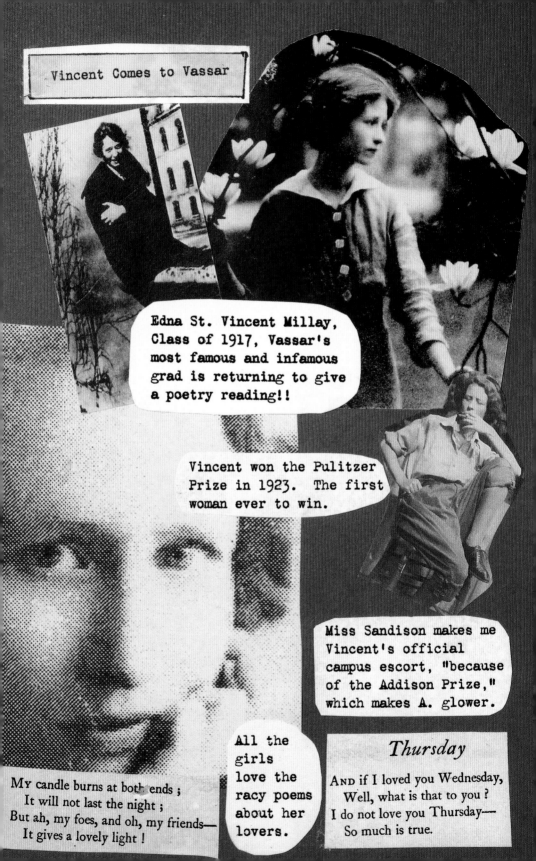

Vincent Comes to Vassar

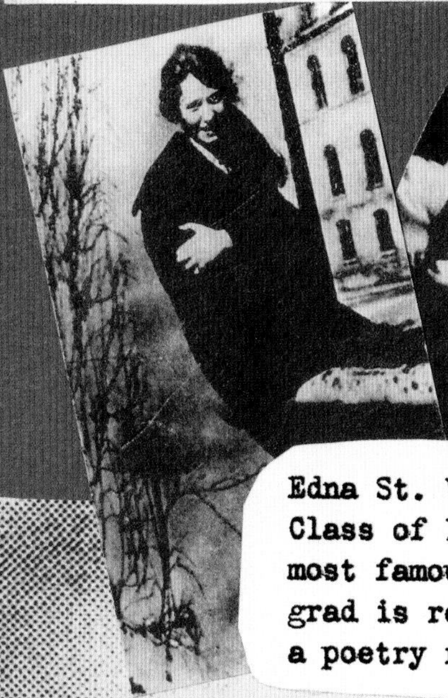

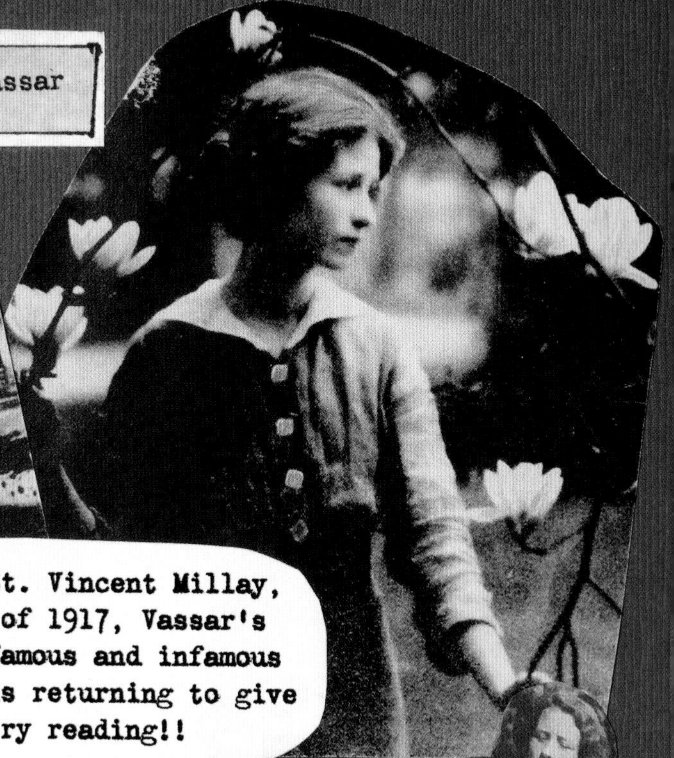

Edna St. Vincent Millay, Class of 1917, Vassar's most famous and infamous grad is returning to give a poetry reading!!

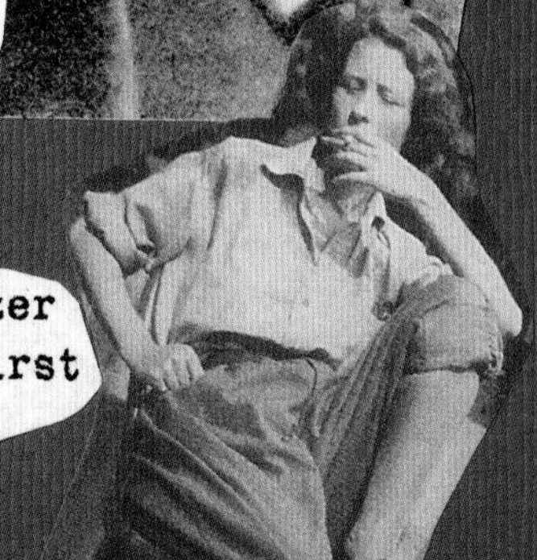

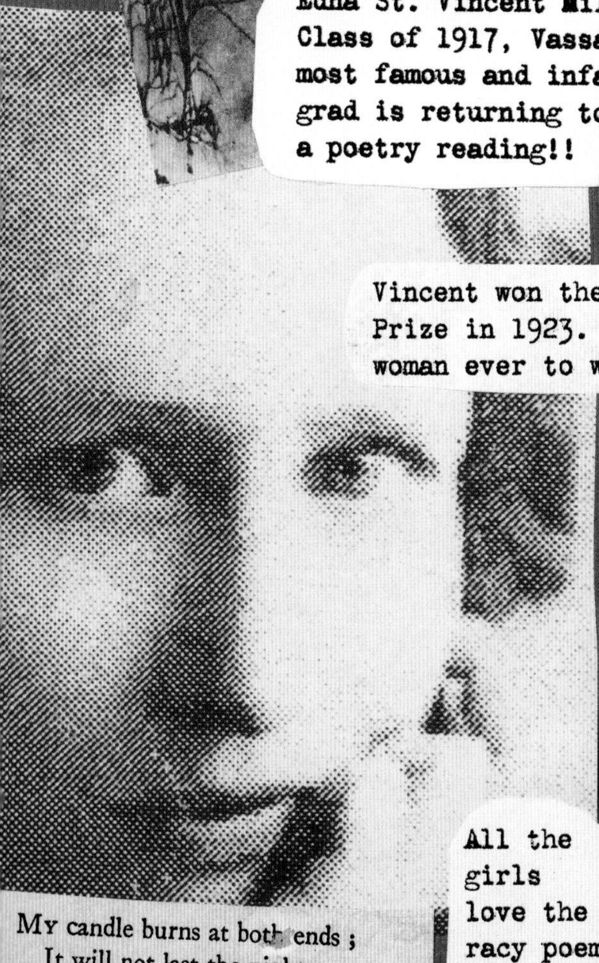

Vincent won the Pulitzer Prize in 1923. The first woman ever to win.

Miss Sandison makes me Vincent's official campus escort, "because of the Addison Prize," which makes A. glower.

My candle burns at both ends ;
It will not last the night ;
But ah, my foes, and oh, my friends—
It gives a lovely light !

All the girls love the racy poems about her lovers.

Thursday

And if I loved you Wednesday,
Well, what is that to you ?
I do not love you Thursday—
So much is true.

Vincent Gives Me Advice

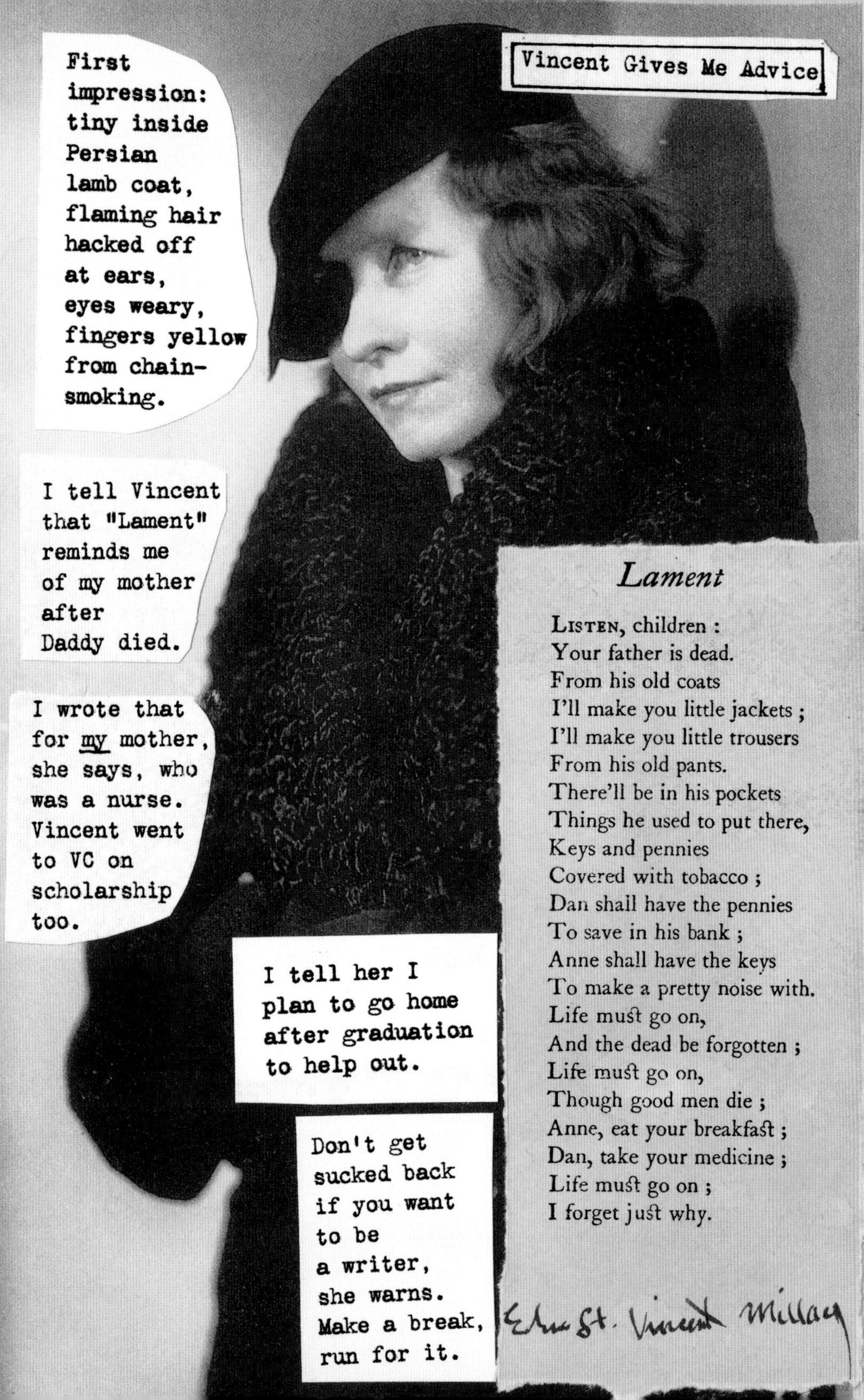

First
impression:
tiny inside
Persian
lamb coat,
flaming hair
hacked off
at ears,
eyes weary,
fingers yellow
from chain-
smoking.

I tell Vincent
that "Lament"
reminds me
of my mother
after
Daddy died.

I wrote that
for <u>my</u> mother,
she says, who
was a nurse.
Vincent went
to VC on
scholarship
too.

I tell her I
plan to go home
after graduation
to help out.

Don't get
sucked back
if you want
to be
a writer,
she warns.
Make a break,
run for it.

Lament

LISTEN, children:
Your father is dead.
From his old coats
I'll make you little jackets;
I'll make you little trousers
From his old pants.
There'll be in his pockets
Things he used to put there,
Keys and pennies
Covered with tobacco;
Dan shall have the pennies
To save in his bank;
Anne shall have the keys
To make a pretty noise with.
Life must go on,
And the dead be forgotten;
Life must go on,
Though good men die;
Anne, eat your breakfast;
Dan, take your medicine;
Life must go on;
I forget just why.

Edna St. Vincent Millay

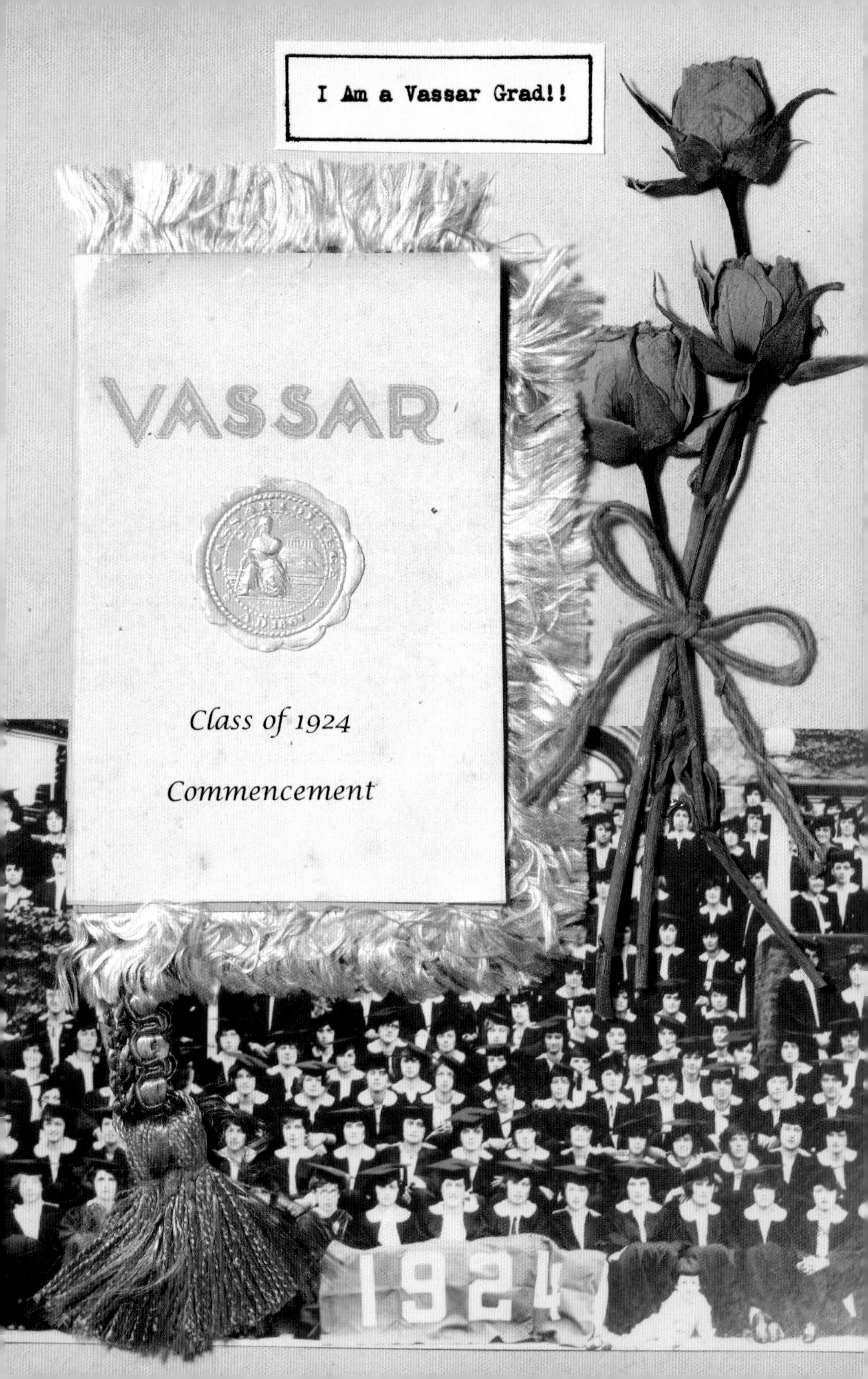
I Am a Vassar Grad!!
VASSAR
Class of 1924
Commencement
1924

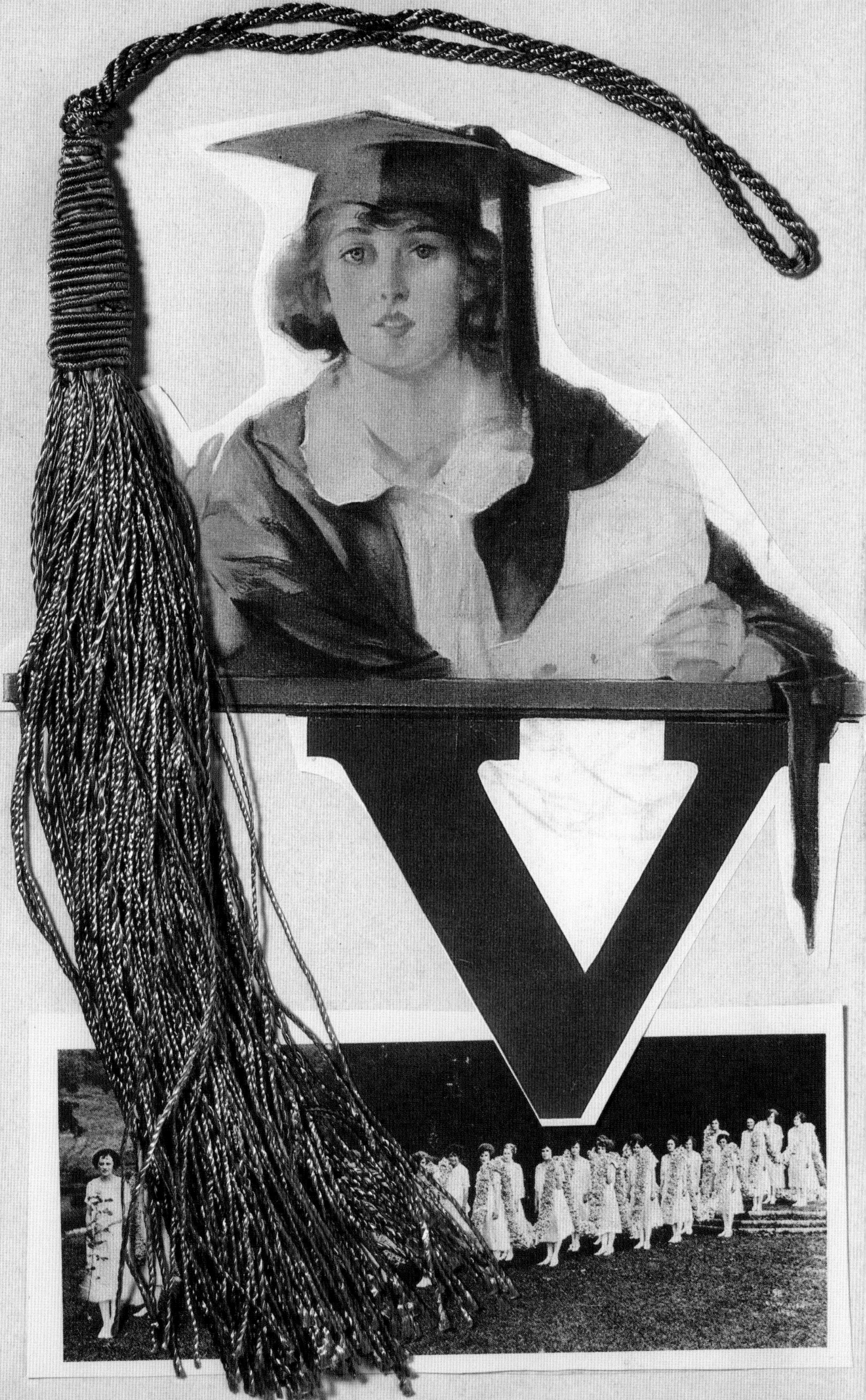

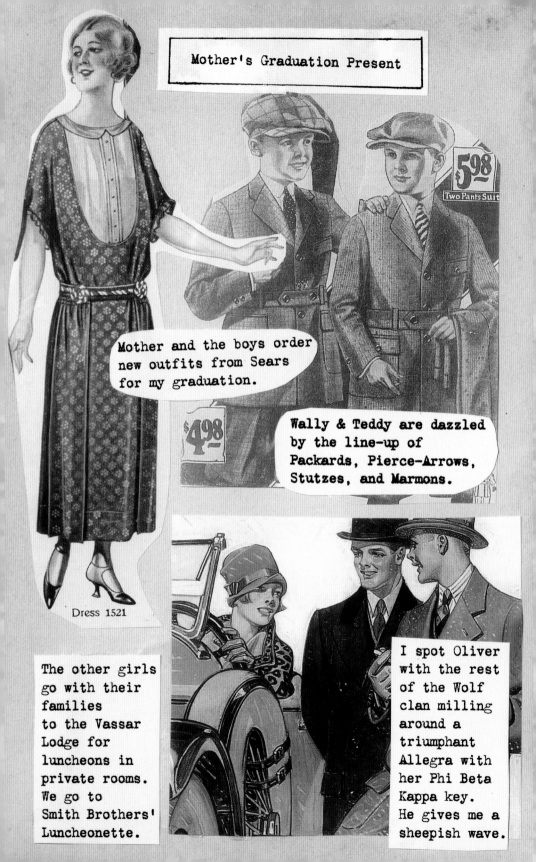

Mother's Graduation Present

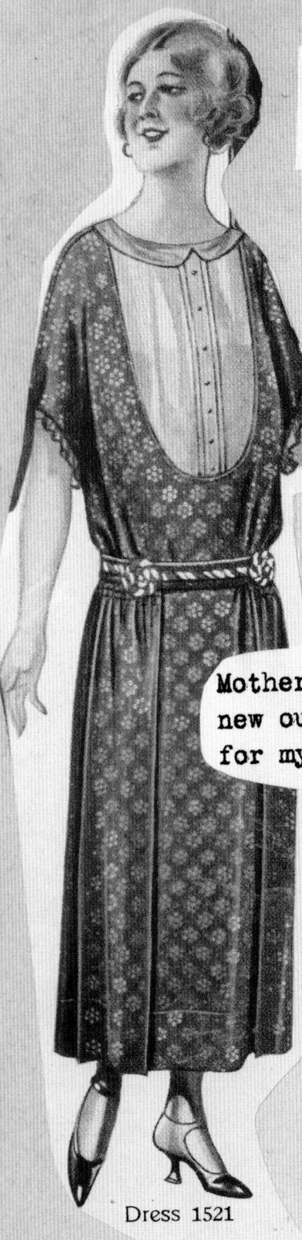

Dress 1521

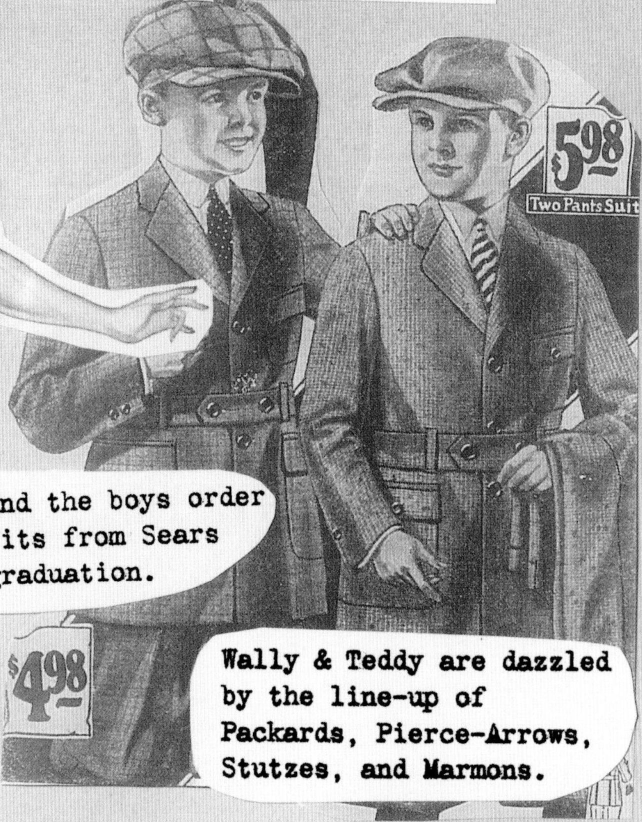
$5.98
Two Pants Suit
$4.98

Mother and the boys order new outfits from Sears for my graduation.

Wally & Teddy are dazzled by the line-up of Packards, Pierce-Arrows, Stutzes, and Marmons.

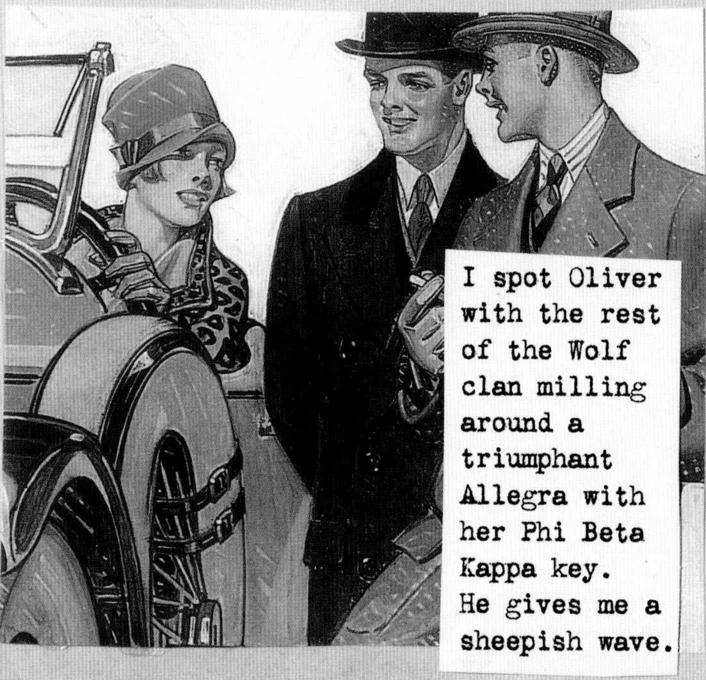

The other girls go with their families to the Vassar Lodge for luncheons in private rooms. We go to Smith Brothers' Luncheonette.

I spot Oliver with the rest of the Wolf clan milling around a triumphant Allegra with her Phi Beta Kappa key. He gives me a sheepish wave.

SMITH BROTHERS
MENTHOL
COUGH
DROPS
SMITH BROTHERS
COUGH DROPS

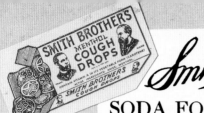

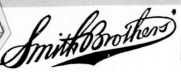

Smith Brothers' RESTAURANT

SODA FOUNTAIN AND LUNCHEONETTE

Operated at the Home and by the Makers of S. B. COUGH DROPS

Breaded Veal Cutlet, Tomato Sauce, Potato			$1.35
Broiled Select Ham Steak, Jelly, French Fried Potatoes			1.35
Chicken a la King on Toast, Whipped Potato			1.35
Griddle Cakes and Syrup	.40	With Bacon	.65
Welsh Rarebit	.75	Golden Buck Rarebit	.90

I have the chicken a la king. Mother has the Welsh rarebit. Wally and Teddy have the griddle cakes with bacon.

PRICE, 10 CENTS

SMITH BROS.
POUGHKEEPSIE, N.Y.
S.B
S.B STAMPED ON EACH DROP
TRADE
MARK
COUGH DROPS

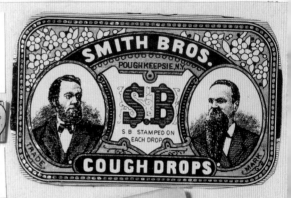

I treat the boys to tins of their famous cough drops.

cat
abc
50
50

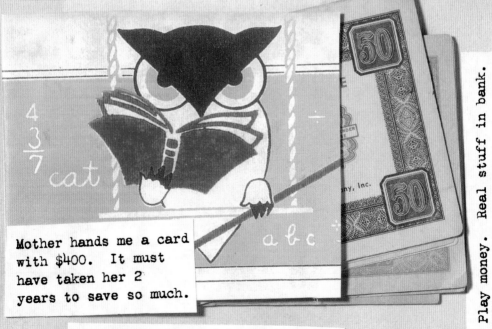

Mother hands me a card with $400. It must have taken her 2 years to save so much.

Something to help you get started in your new life, she says.

Play money. Real stuff in bank.

The Vassar Graduate's Future

85% of the 1924s say their career plans are "wife and mother"

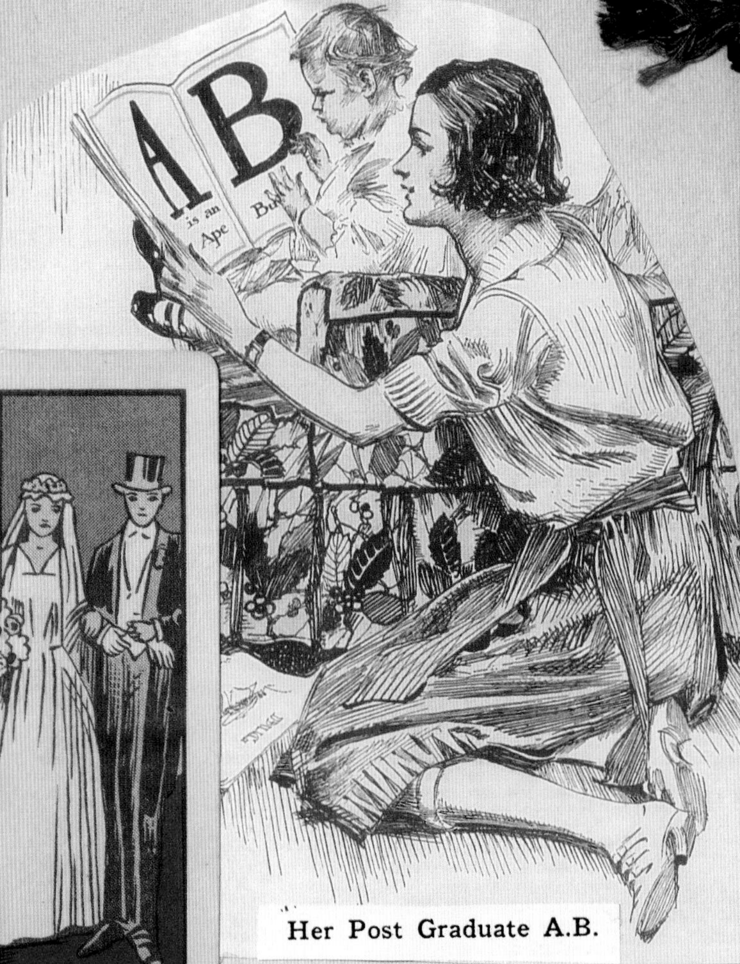
AB
is an
Ape

Her Post Graduate A.B.

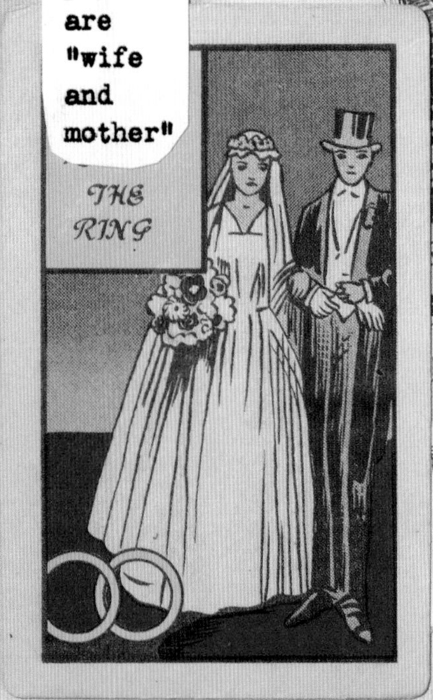
THE RING

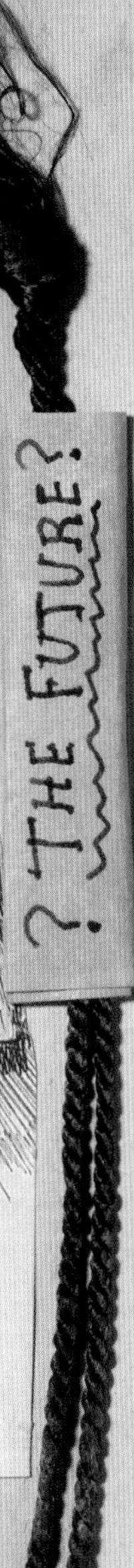
? THE FUTURE?
DIPLOMA

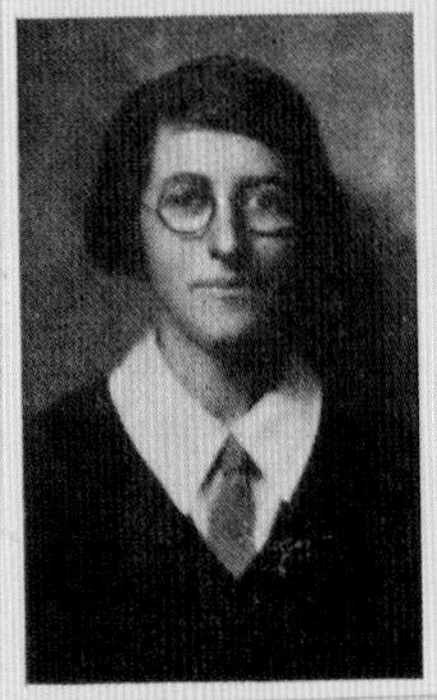

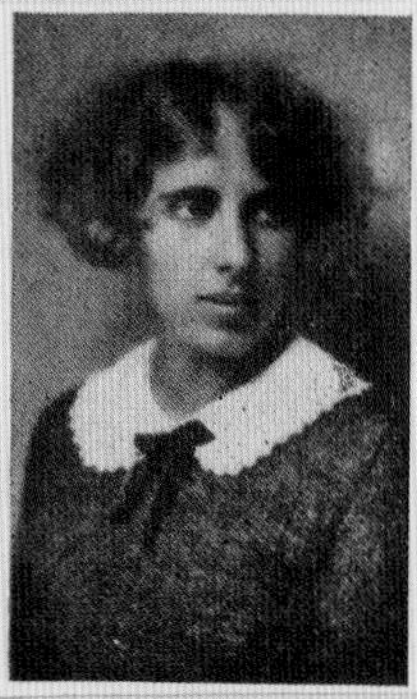

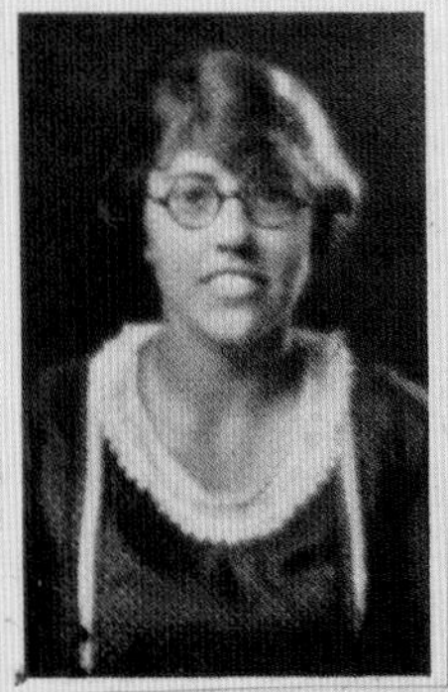

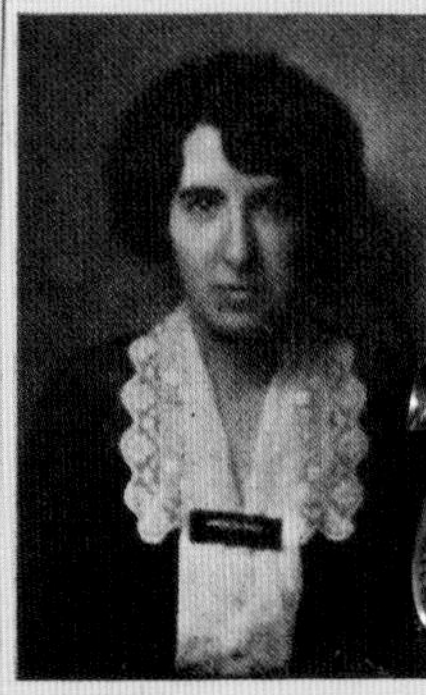

A few serious girls plan to become doctors and social workers. One even wants to be a "union organizer."

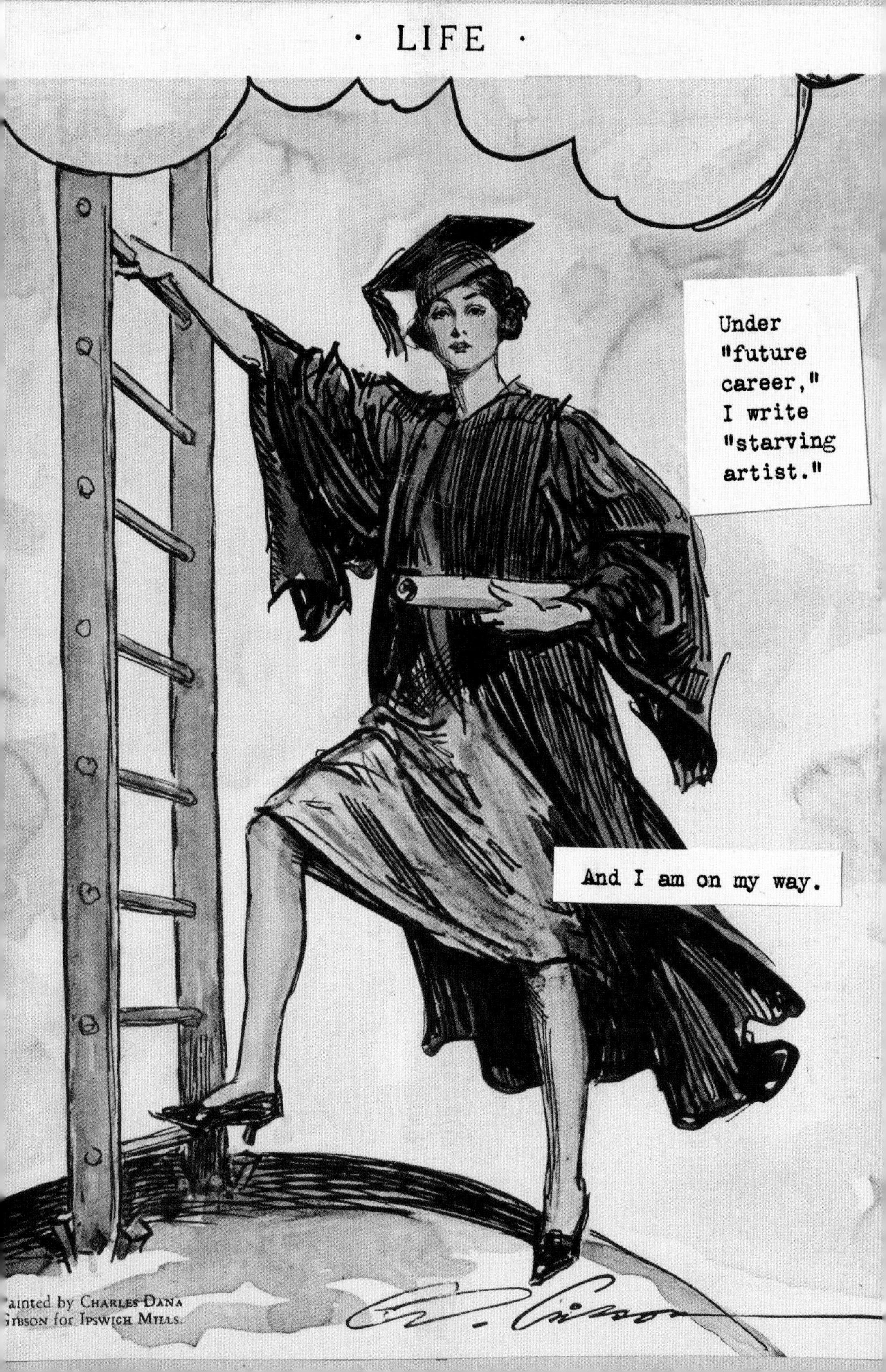

· LIFE ·
Under "future career," I write "starving artist."
And I am on my way.
ainted by Charles Dana Gibson for Ipswich Mills.

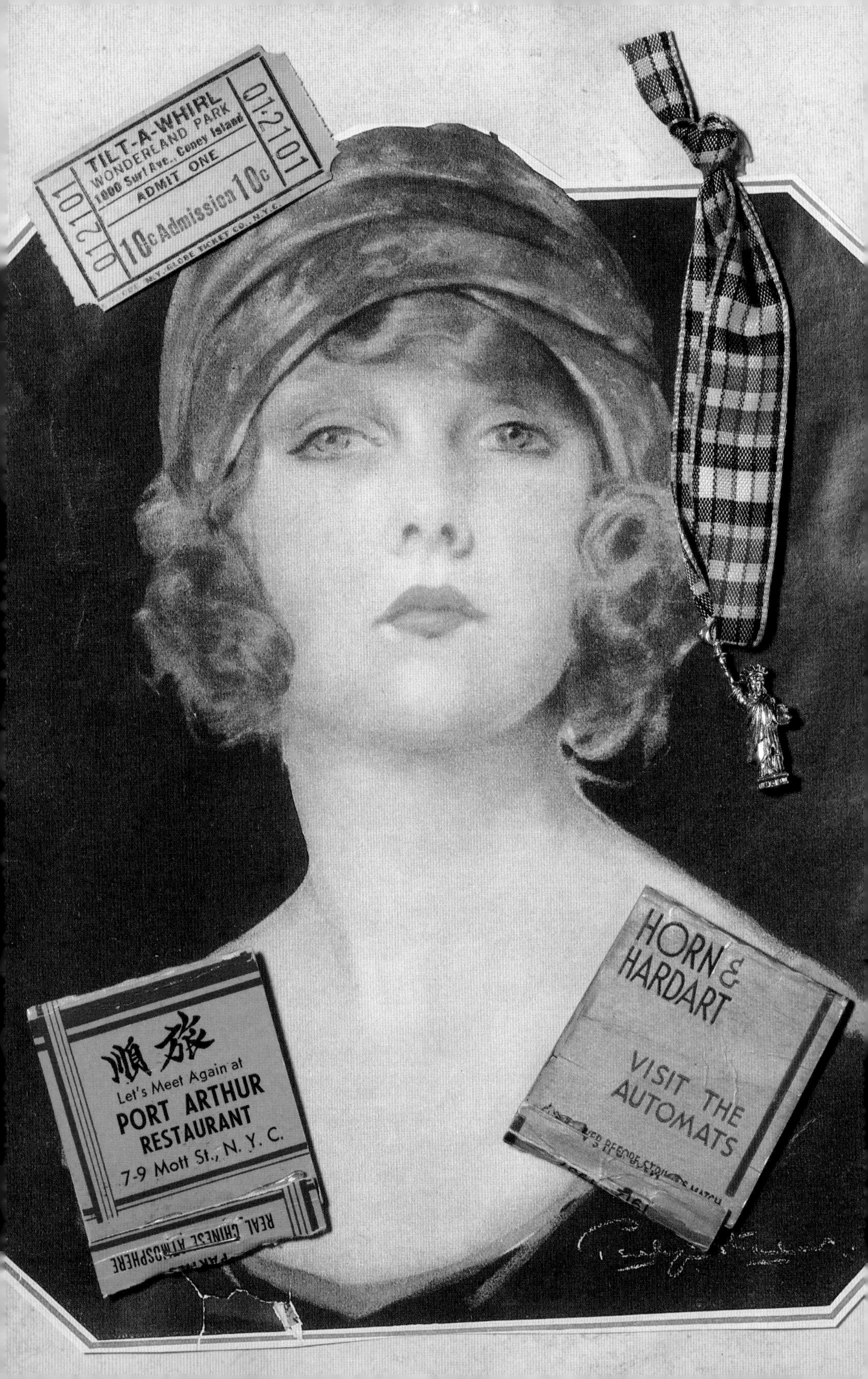
TILT-A-WHIRL
WONDERLAND PARK
1000 Surf Ave., Coney Island
ADMIT ONE
10c Admission 10c
012101
順旅
Let's Meet Again at
PORT ARTHUR
RESTAURANT
7-9 Mott St., N. Y. C.
REAL CHINESE ATMOSPHERE
HORN & HARDART
VISIT THE
AUTOMATS

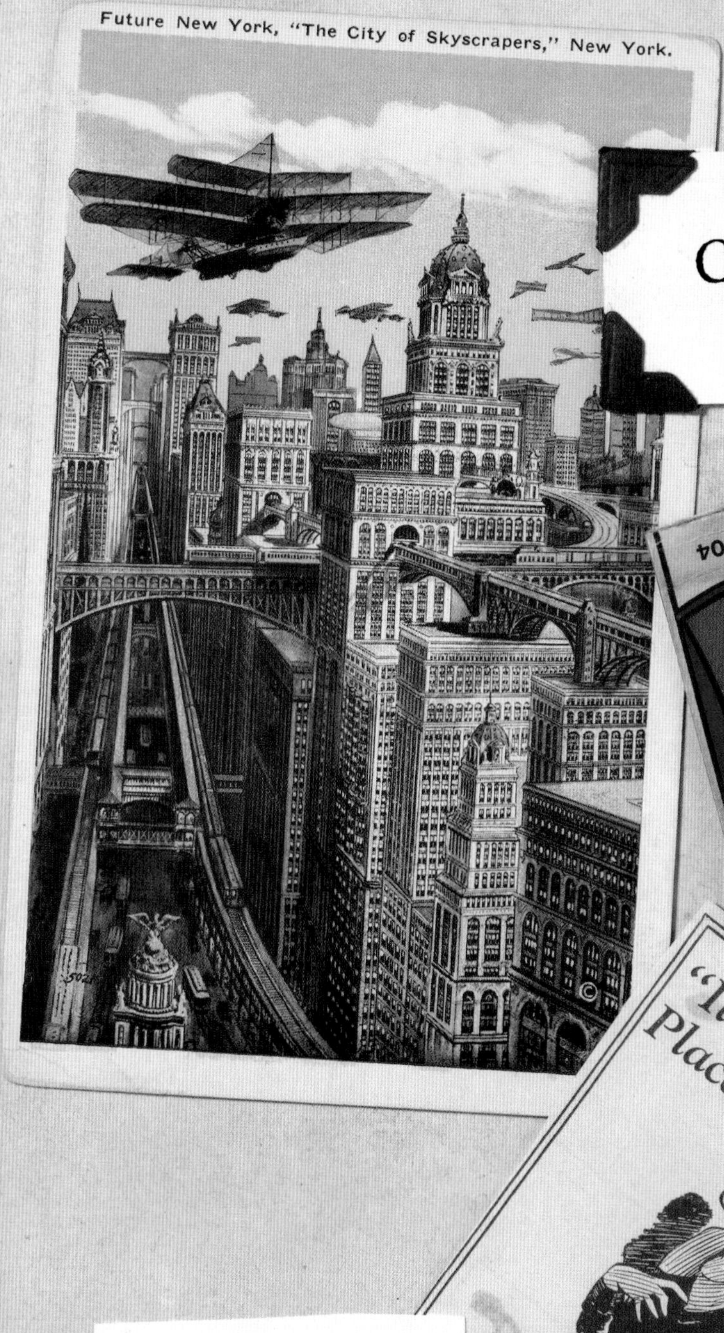
Future New York, "The City of Skyscrapers," New York.

Chapter 3

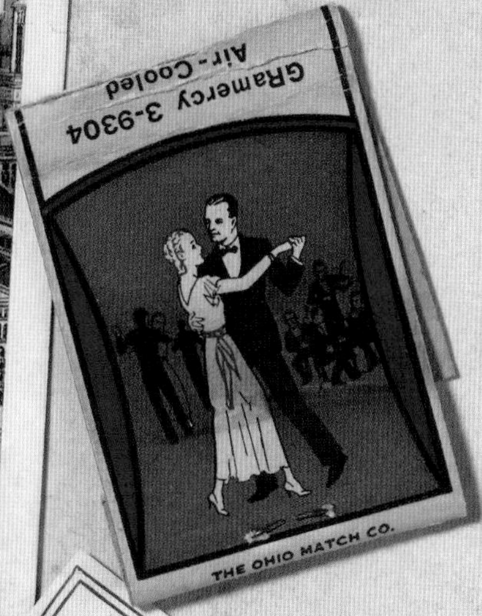
GRamercy 3-9304
Air-Cooled
THE OHIO MATCH CO.

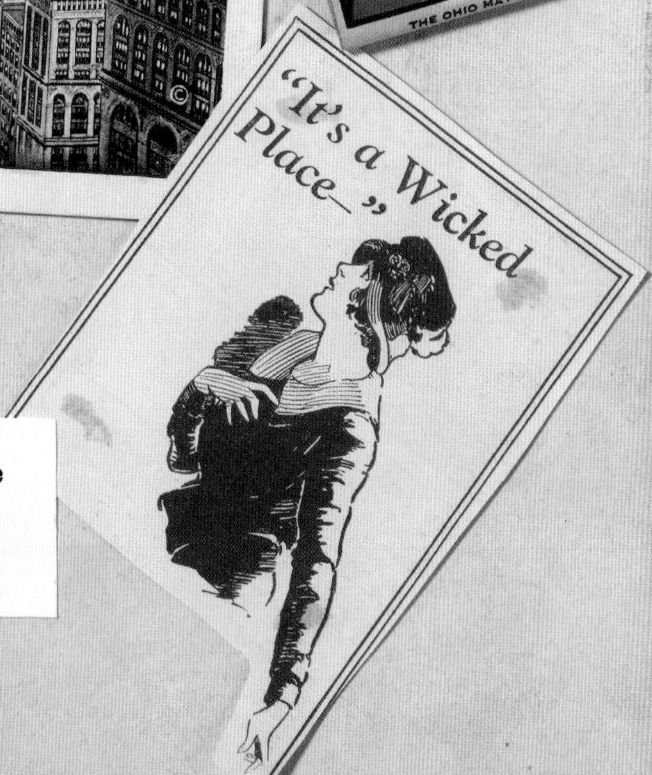
"It's a Wicked Place_"

Greenwich Village

1924 - 1925

I Arrive in New York City

A week after graduation, I roll into Grand Central Station, check my two suitcases and typewriter with a redcap, and buy a guidebook at the newsstand. Vincent told me Greenwich Village was the only place for an artist to live.

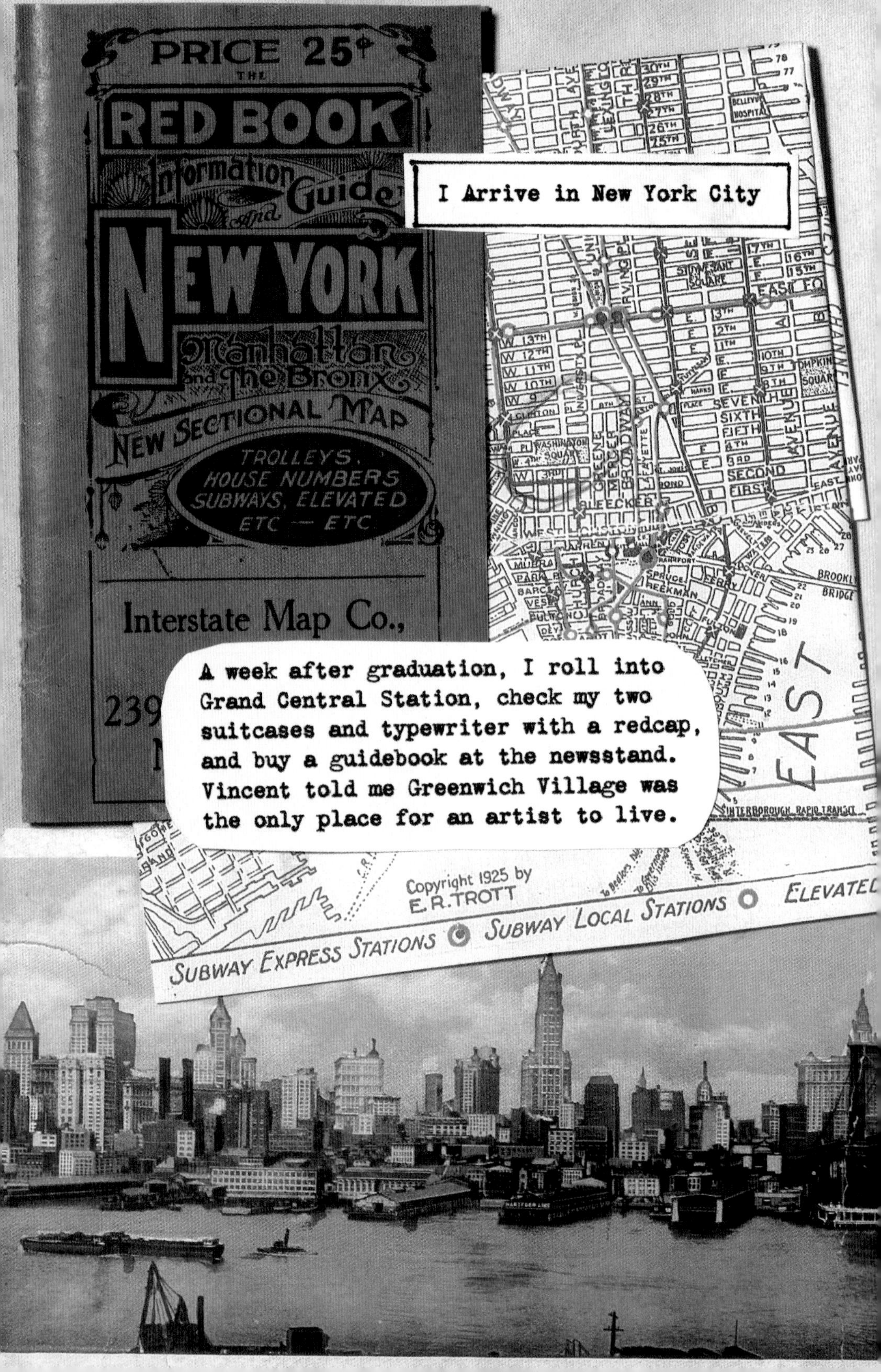
PRICE 25¢
THE
RED BOOK
Information and Guide
NEW YORK
Manhattan and The Bronx
NEW SECTIONAL MAP
TROLLEYS, HOUSE NUMBERS SUBWAYS, ELEVATED ETC — ETC
Interstate Map Co.,
Copyright 1925 by E.R.TROTT
SUBWAY EXPRESS STATIONS
SUBWAY LOCAL STATIONS
ELEVATED
INTERBOROUGH RAPID TRANSIT
EAST
BROOKLYN BRIDGE
WASHINGTON SQUARE
STUYVESANT SQUARE
TOMPKINS SQUARE
BELLEVUE HOSPITAL
BROADWAY
BLEECKER

So how do you start to
seek your fortune?
Here is my to-do list.

1. find way around NYC
   (buy map)
2. figure out subway and buses
   (study map)
3. find place to live
   (check newspaper)
4. open bank account
5. find job
   (check newspaper)
6. write novel
7. get novel published
8. find the love of my life

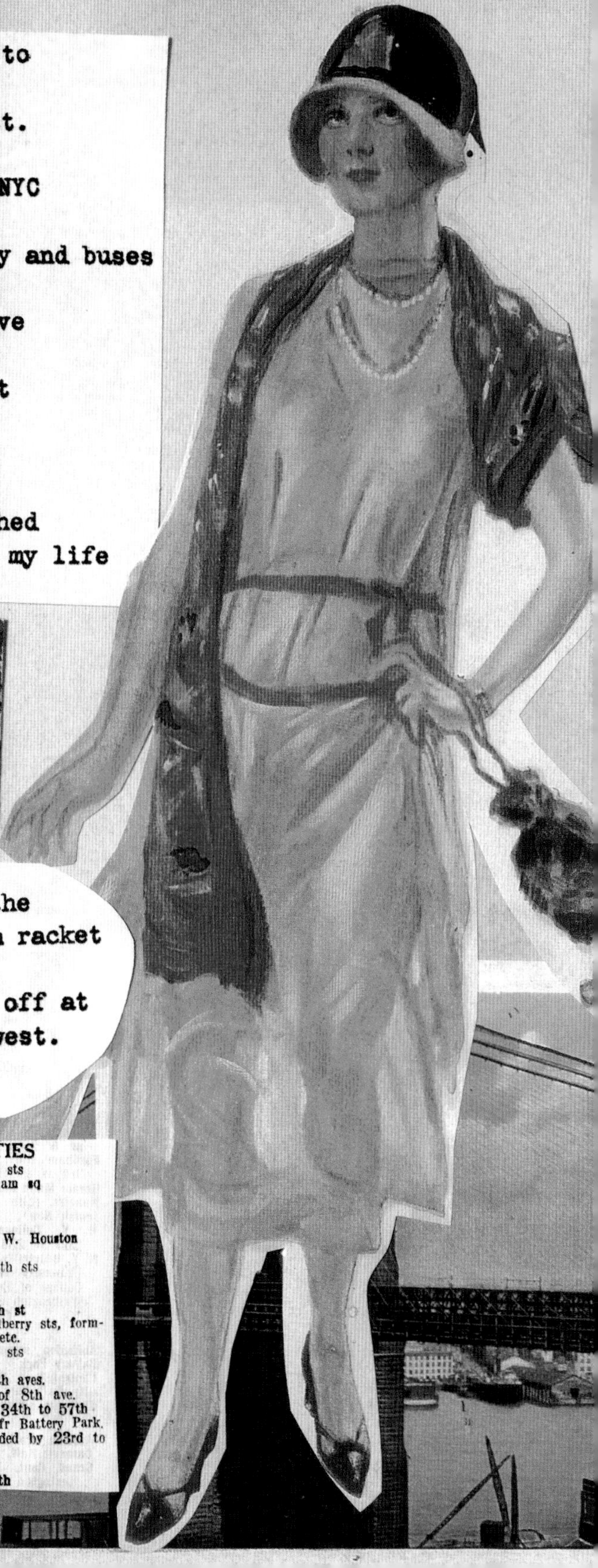

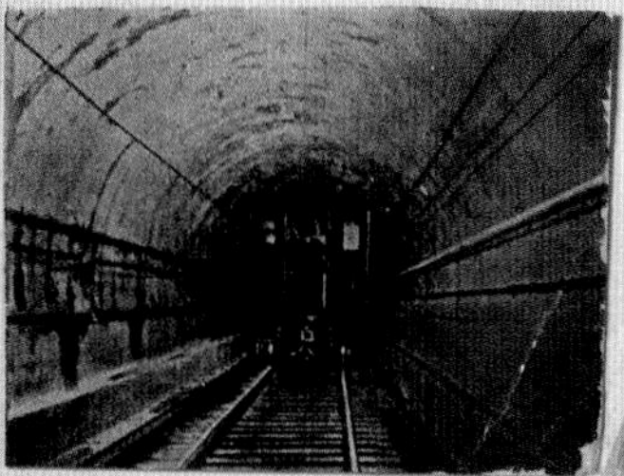

Map in hand, I descend the
iron stairs into the dim racket
of the East Side Subway.
All I need to do is get off at
"Astor Place" and head west.
Sounds easy enough.

DESIGNATED LOCALITIES

Automobile Row, along Bdway 50th to 75th sts
Chinatown, Pell Mott & Doyers st at Chatham sq
Down Town, below Canal st to the Battery
East Side, east of Bowery, below 1st st
Financial, below Wall st to Battery Park
Greenwich Village, West of 6th av, N. of W. Houston
Harlem, 110th to 135th sts, e & w 5th av
Hell's Kitchen, W. of 8th ave, 38th to 59th sts
Italian, S. of Washington Sq.
Latin America, W. 14th st.
Little Church Around the Corner, 5 E. 29th st
Little Italy (Paradise Park) Leonard & Mulberry sts, formerly known as Mulberry Bend, 5 Points, etc.
Millionaires Row, 5th ave, 59th to 110th sts
Newspaper Row, Park Row, opp City Hall
Roaring Forties, 40th to 49th st; 6th to 8th aves.
San Juan Hill Colony, 55th toth st W. of 8th ave.
Shopping Distr., 34th & B'way to 5th & fr 34th to 57th
Syrian Quarter, Greenwich & Wash. sts, N fr Battery Park.
Tenderloin, (Not recognized) formally bounded by 23rd to 50th sts, West of Broadway
Washington Heights, north of 155th st
White Lights Dist., along Bdway 34th to 59th

Greenwich Village

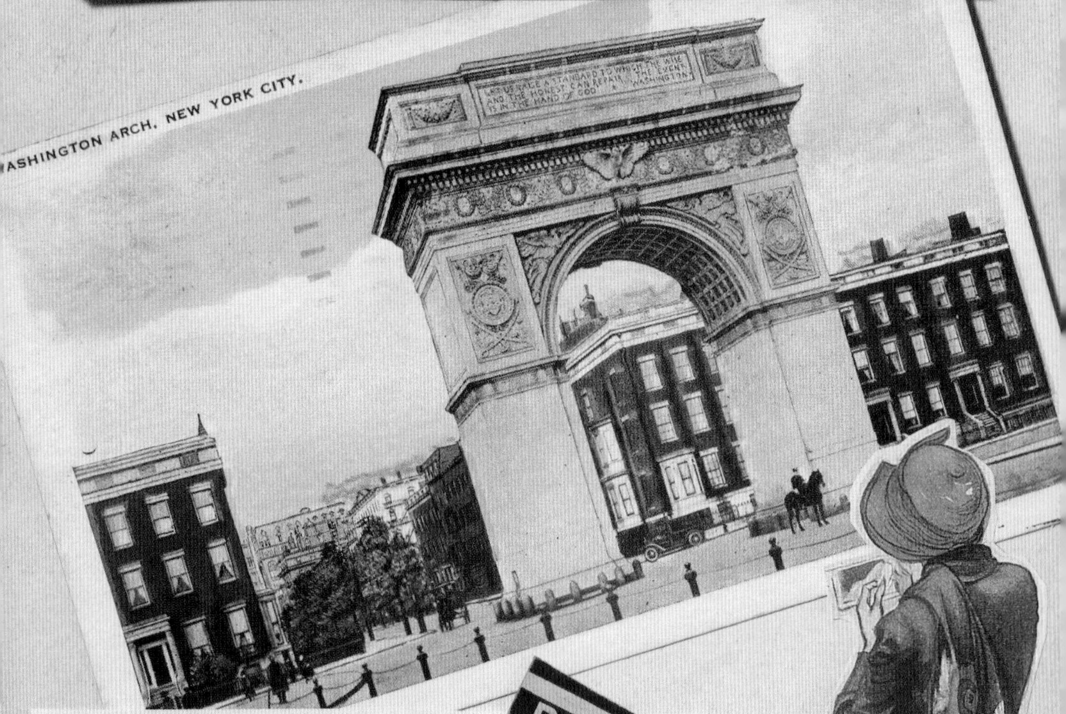
ASHINGTON ARCH, NEW YORK CITY.

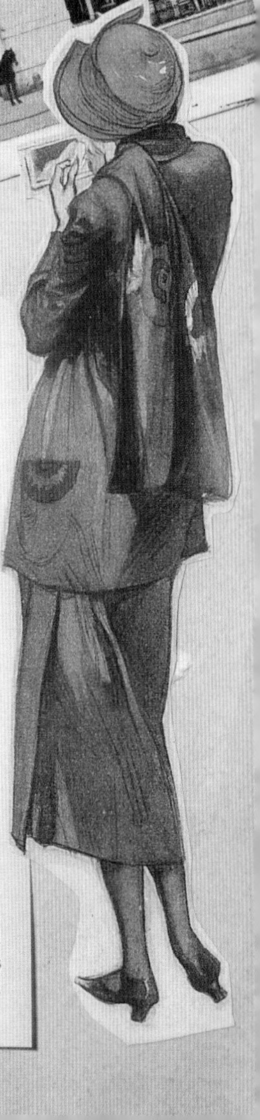

HOTEL BREVOORT

GREENWICH VILLAGE

Just west of Washington Square

The "Latin Quarter" of New York.

Home of artists, sculptors, writers, musicians, etc.

Here is where genius, temperament, smocks and flowing ties predominate—New York's Bohemia! Greenwich Village is famed for its unconventional modes of living and its gay night life.

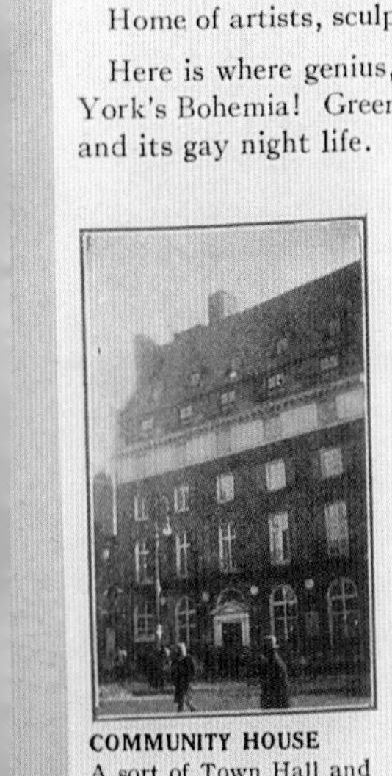

COMMUNITY HOUSE
A sort of Town Hall and general community center.

Cellars, attics and even barns are utilized as studios, cafes, and clubs. A bizarre form of decoration, a unique adaptation of modern embellishment and a disposition to create "atmosphere" all combine in luring tens of thousands to Greenwich Village's "Pepper Pot," "Samovar", "Nut Club," "Pirates Den," and a hundred other popular rendezvous. Here at rough wooden tables with crude chairs fairly good meals are served.

Subdued light of tallow candles socketed in old beer bottles are used to emphasize the "atmospheric" environment and altho tea and "near beer" are supposed to be the popular stimulants which help in making merry at the various dining places of the district, it is whispered that every now and then the Volstead law is violated and that genuine "fire-water" can be located at certain oasis in the desert. Actual speak-easies are so cleverly camouflaged as to fool the cops assigned to the neighborhood—all of which seems to add to the attraction of the community as a whole and augment the crowds of visitors who visit the Village nightly.

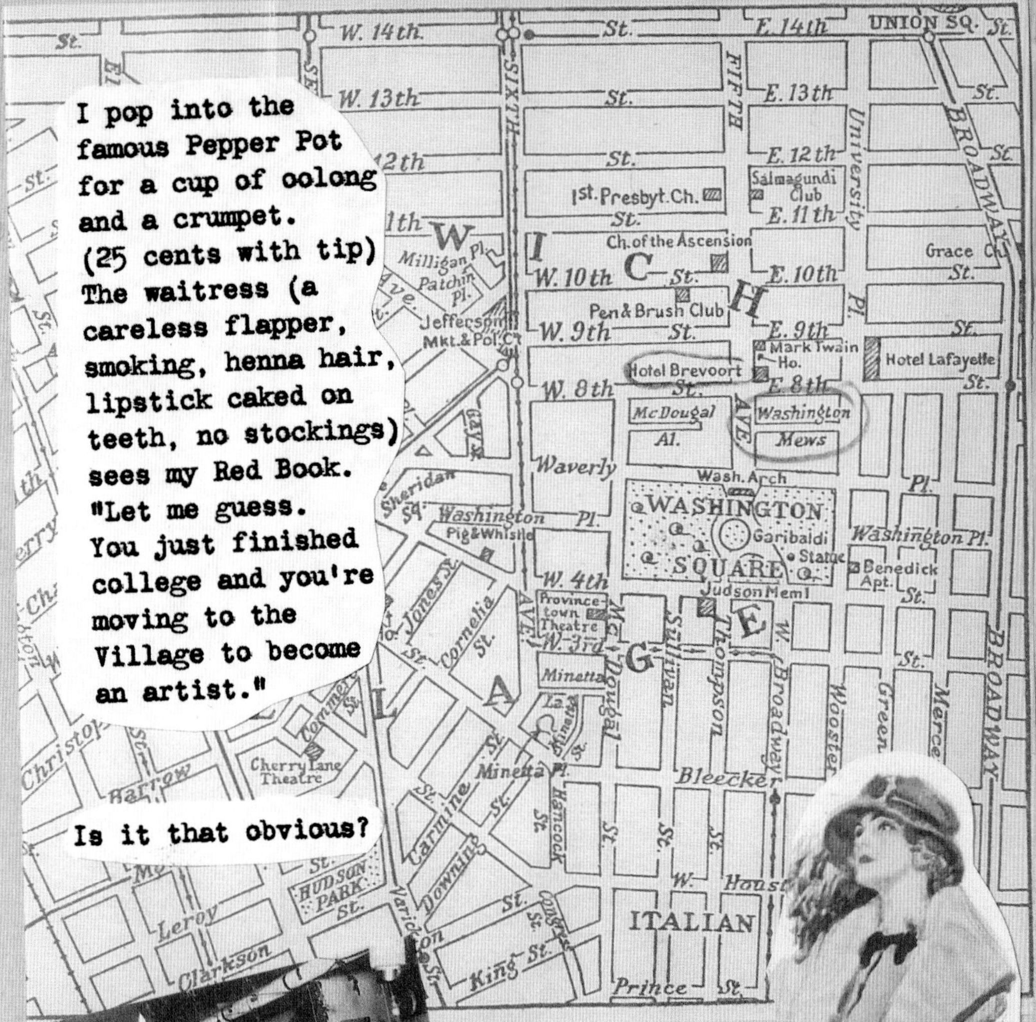
W. 14th St.
E. 14th
UNION SQ.
W. 13th St.
E. 13th
FIFTH AVE
SIXTH AVE
University Pl.
BROADWAY
1st Presbyt. Ch.
Salmagundi Club
E. 11th
Ch. of the Ascension
Grace Ch.
Milligan Pl.
Patchin Pl.
W. 10th St.
E. 10th
Jefferson Mkt. & Pol. Ct.
Pen & Brush Club
W. 9th St.
E. 9th
Mark Twain Ho.
Hotel Lafayette
Hotel Brevoort
W. 8th St.
E. 8th
McDougal Al.
Washington Mews
Waverly Pl.
Sheridan Sq.
Washington Pl.
Pig & Whistle
Wash. Arch
WASHINGTON SQUARE
Garibaldi Statue
Washington Pl.
Benedick Apt.
Judson Meml
W. 4th
Provincetown Theatre
W. 3rd
Minetta
Jones St.
Cornelia St.
Commerce St.
Cherry Lane Theatre
Barrow
Minetta Pl.
Carmine St.
Hancock St.
Sullivan
Thompson
W. Broadway
Wooster
Greene
Bleecker
W. Houston
Leroy
Clarkson
Hudson Park
Downing
Varick St.
King St.
ITALIAN
Prince St.

I pop into the famous Pepper Pot for a cup of oolong and a crumpet. (25 cents with tip) The waitress (a careless flapper, smoking, henna hair, lipstick caked on teeth, no stockings) sees my Red Book. "Let me guess. You just finished college and you're moving to the Village to become an artist."

Is it that obvious?

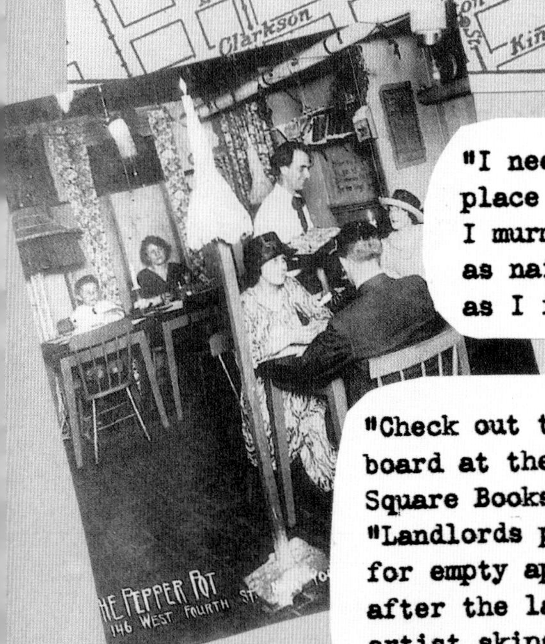
HE PEPPER POT
146 WEST FOURTH ST

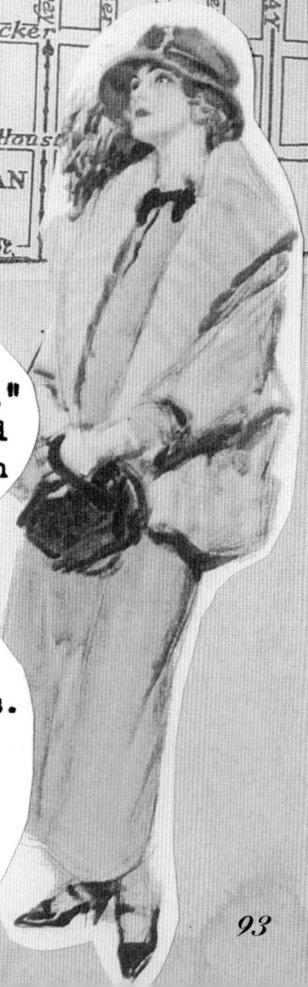

"I need to find a place to stay first," I murmur. Do I sound as naive and foolish as I feel?

"Check out the bulletin board at the Washington Square Bookshop," she says. "Landlords post notices for empty apartments after the latest aspiring artist skips town owing six months rent."

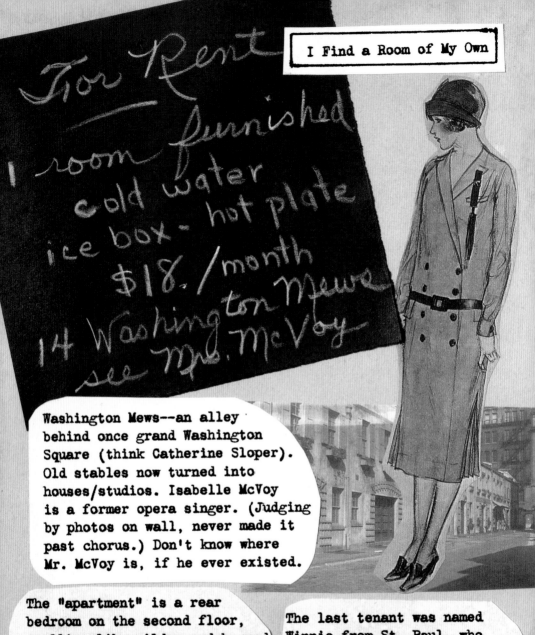

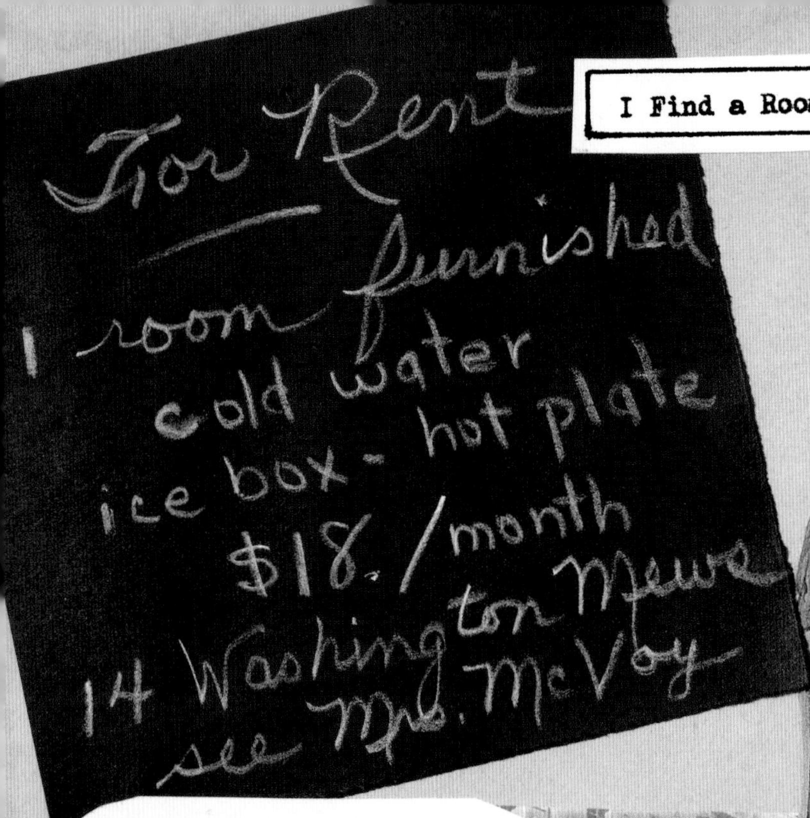
For Rent
1 room furnished
cold water
ice box - hot plate
$18./month
14 Washington Mews
see Mrs. McVoy

I Find a Room of My Own

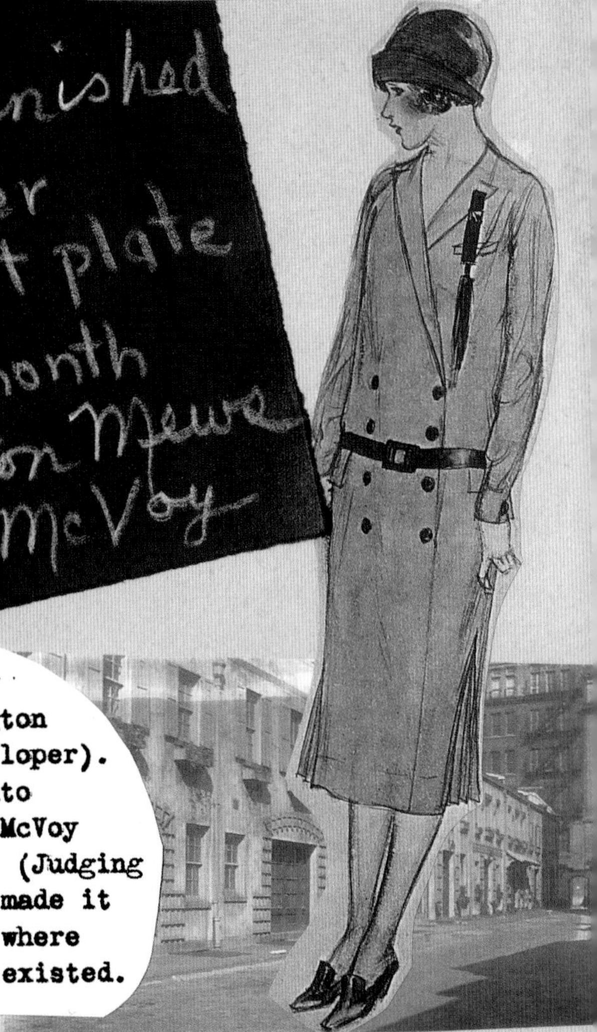

Washington Mews--an alley behind once grand Washington Square (think Catherine Sloper). Old stables now turned into houses/studios. Isabelle McVoy is a former opera singer. (Judging by photos on wall, never made it past chorus.) Don't know where Mr. McVoy is, if he ever existed.

The "apartment" is a rear bedroom on the second floor, smelling like mildew and burned coffee. The bathtub and toilet are on the first floor, shared by 3 other tenants.

The last tenant was named Winnie from St. Paul, who was studying painting at the Art Students League. She left a dragon kimono, a tube of Tangee lipstick, and nude sketches of herself in suggestive poses. "Typical," sniffs Mrs. McVoy.

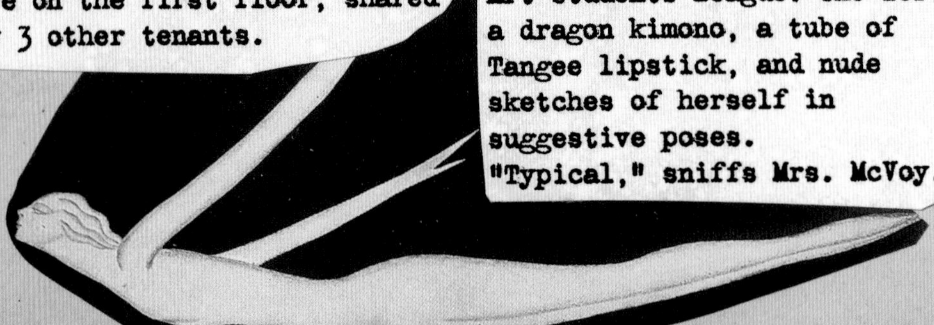

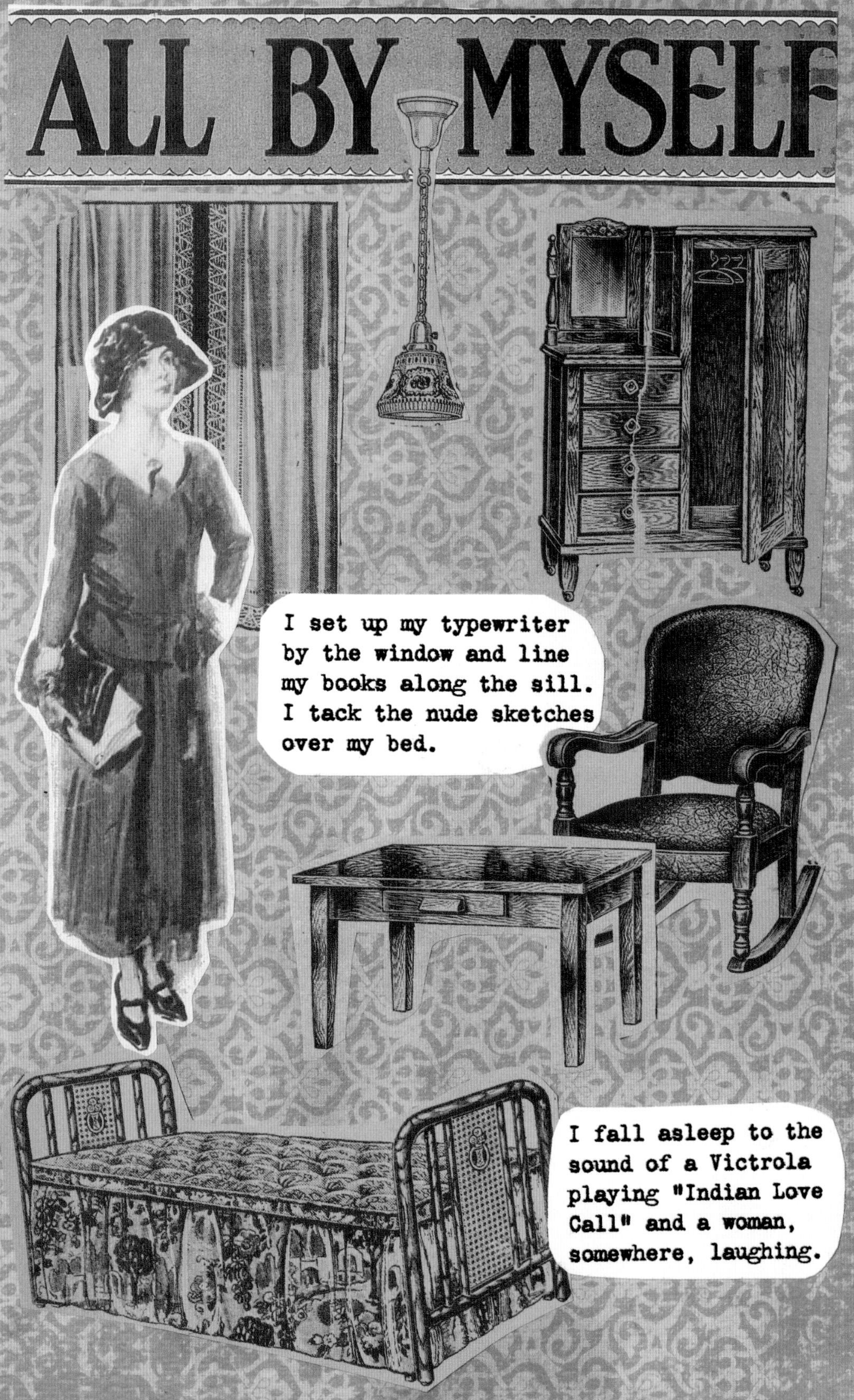
ALL BY MYSELF
I set up my typewriter by the window and line my books along the sill. I tack the nude sketches over my bed.
I fall asleep to the sound of a Victrola playing "Indian Love Call" and a woman, somewhere, laughing.

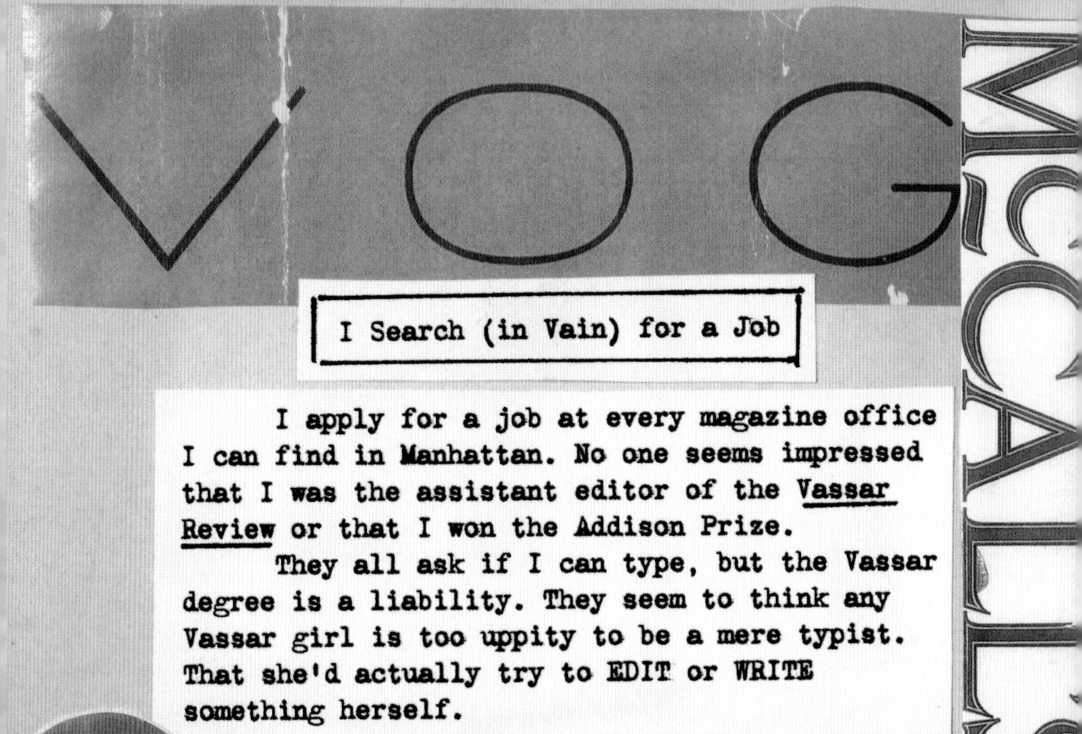
VOG
McCALL'S

I Search (in Vain) for a Job

I apply for a job at every magazine office I can find in Manhattan. No one seems impressed that I was the assistant editor of the Vassar Review or that I won the Addison Prize.

They all ask if I can type, but the Vassar degree is a liability. They seem to think any Vassar girl is too uppity to be a mere typist. That she'd actually try to EDIT or WRITE something herself.

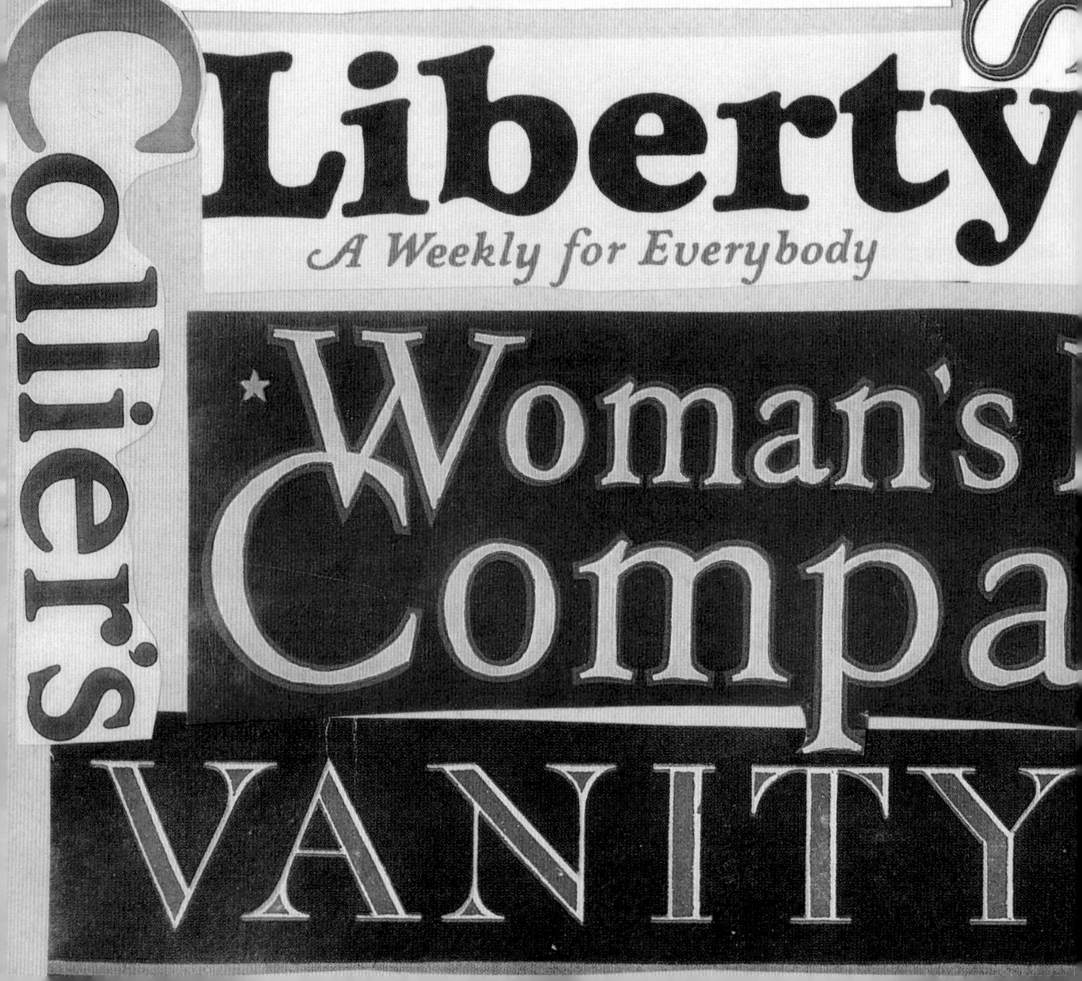
Collier's
Liberty
A Weekly for Everybody
Woman's
Compa
VANITY

The editor at Time says if I'd gone to Yale (meaning if I were a man), he'd give me a try. He means this as a compliment.

Vanity Fair offers me a job as a reporter for their Society page, then withdraws the offer when they learn I expect to be paid. Apparently, a Vassar girl should consider it a privilege to work for free.

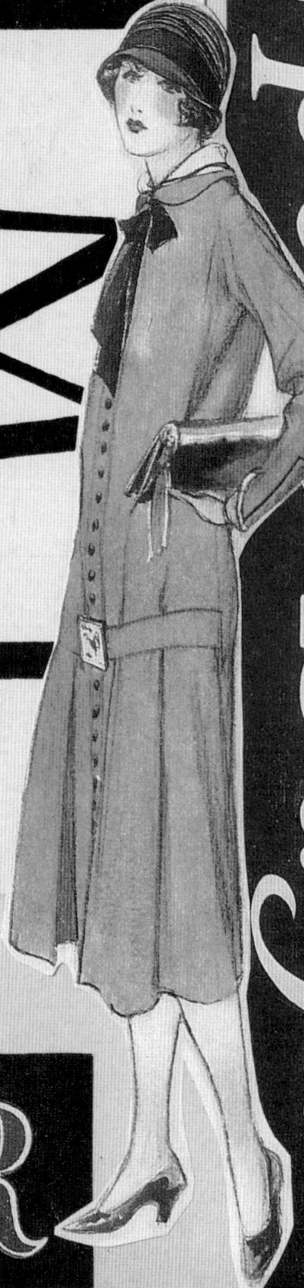
THE SATURDAY EVENING POST
JE
TIME
Harper's Bazaar
lome
nion
FAIR

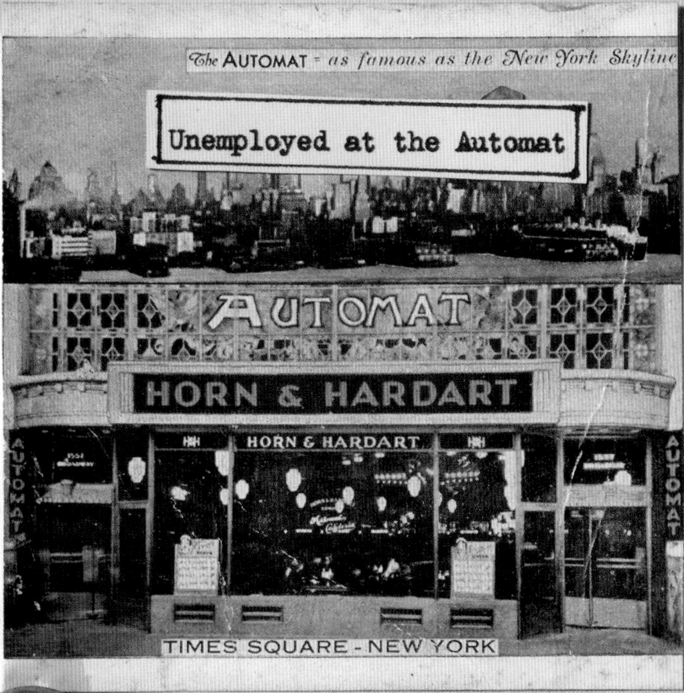
The AUTOMAT = as famous as the New York Skyline
Unemployed at the Automat
AUTOMAT
HORN & HARDART
HORN & HARDART
AUTOMAT
AUTOMAT
TIMES SQUARE - NEW YORK

The most congenial spot for the unemployed is the Automat in Times Square. Search the want ads, read a novel, scribble on a story without any dirty looks from a waitress. Sit undisturbed from 8 until 6-- like going to an office. All that's required is spending a nickel every few hours on a bowl of oatmeal, an egg salad sandwich, a slice of pie (lemon meringue highly recommended), and yet another cup of coffee.

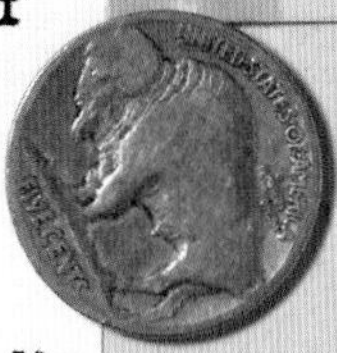

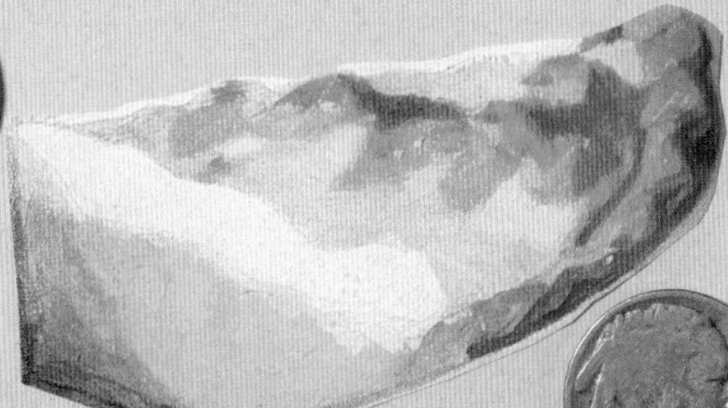

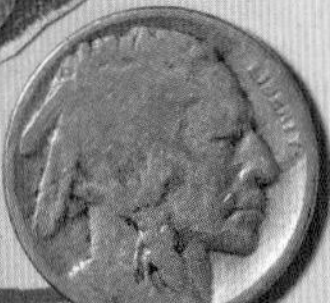

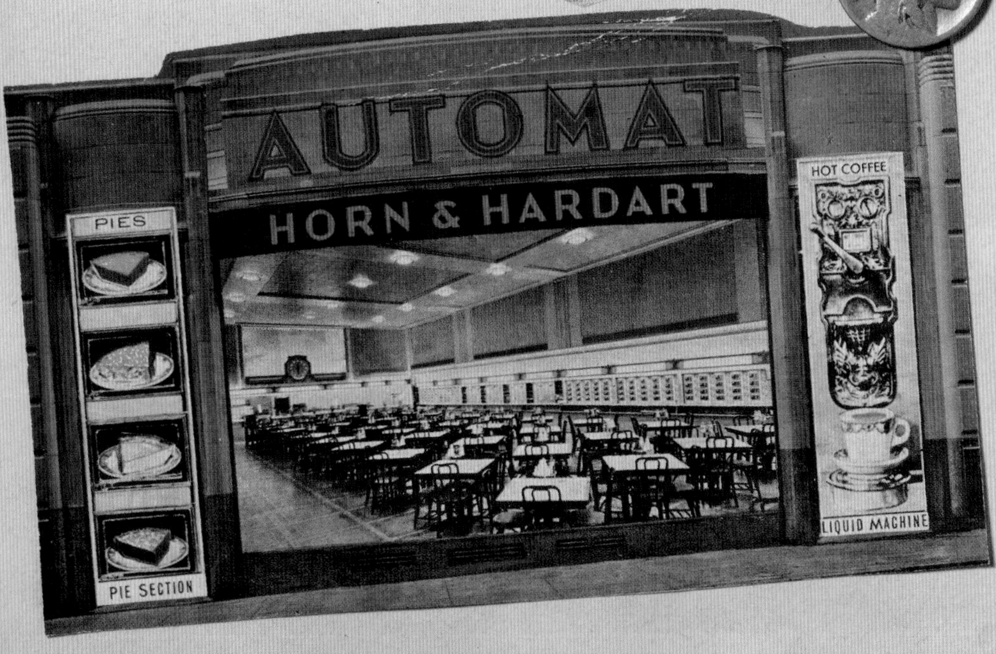
AUTOMAT
HORN & HARDART
PIES
PIE SECTION
HOT COFFEE
LIQUID MACHINE

The Return of Oliver Wolf

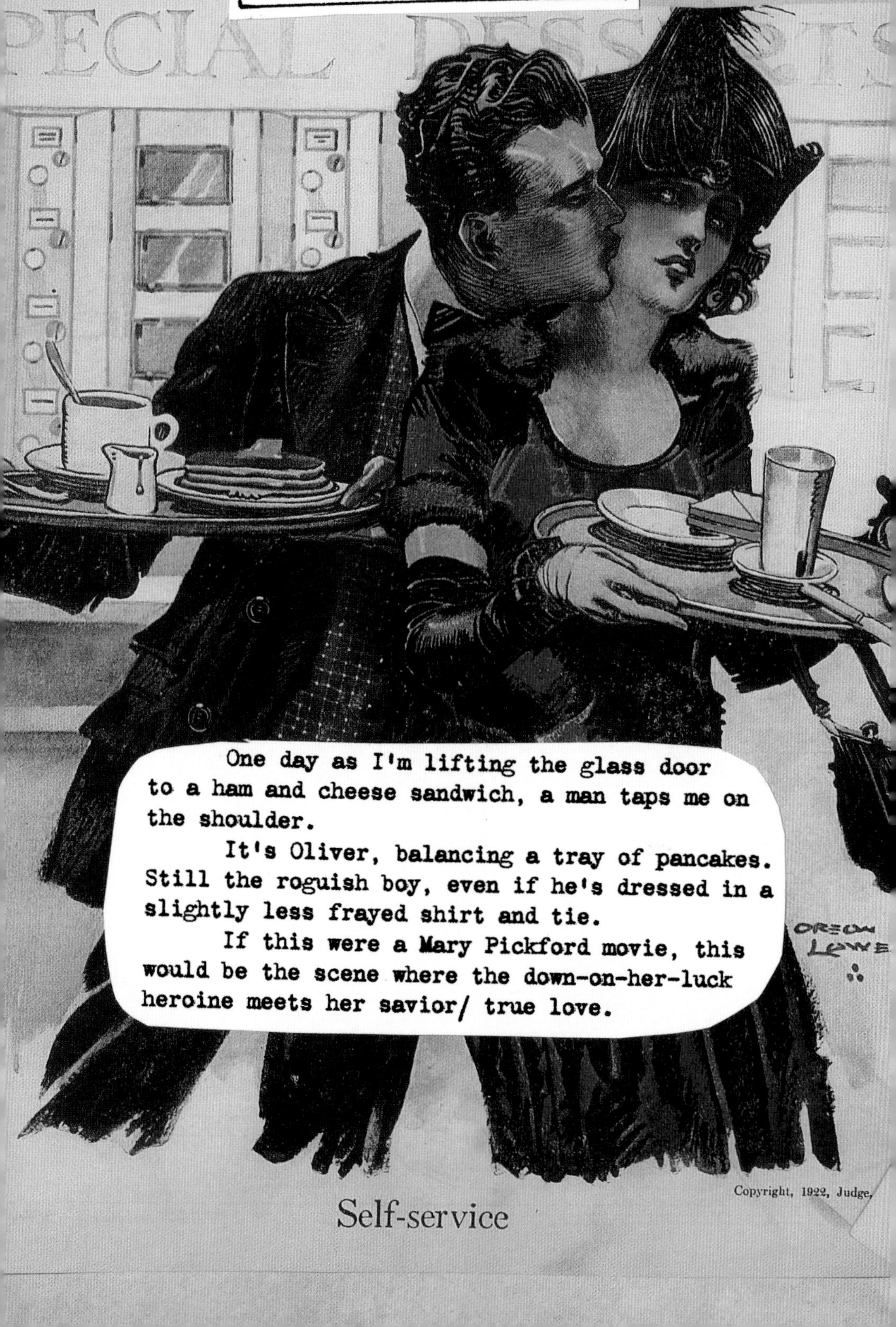
Copyright, 1922, Judge,
Self-service

One day as I'm lifting the glass door to a ham and cheese sandwich, a man taps me on the shoulder.

It's Oliver, balancing a tray of pancakes. Still the roguish boy, even if he's dressed in a slightly less frayed shirt and tie.

If this were a Mary Pickford movie, this would be the scene where the down-on-her-luck heroine meets her savior/ true love.

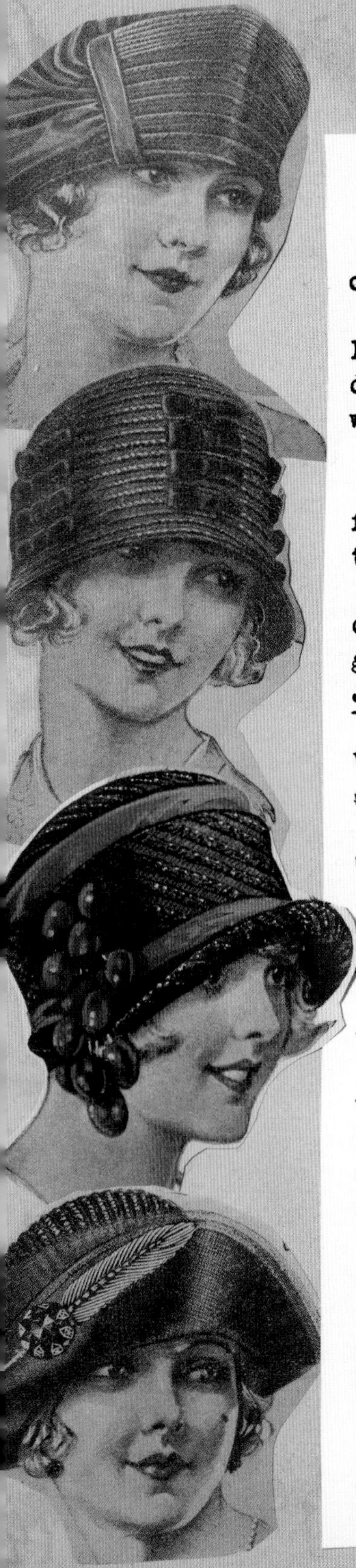

An Afternoon with Oliver

He pulls up a chair at my table.

"Slumming it?" I say.

"Nope. I'm a bona fide member of the proletariat on my lunch break."

"You have a job? Doing what?" It's hard to imagine the rarefied Wolfs doing anything so ordinary as working for a living.

"Staff writer for a magazine."

"Which one?" It figures that feckless Oliver would have an easier time than me.

"It's a new magazine so it doesn't have a name yet. But all the great writers from *Vanity Fair* and *Judge* have come over."

"Could they use a distinguished Vassar grad?" I ask, trying not to sound desperate.

"Sure. . ." he trails off. "Except no one's getting paid yet."

"I'm afraid I need to earn my keep."

"We should go to the movies sometime," he says.

"I thought you weren't allowed to be friends with me."

"Now that you're on the outs with Legra, I'm allowed. Besides, I've moved out so I hardly ever see her. I have a room in a very seedy hotel in Chelsea."

"As I said, slumming it. What's she up to these days?" I dread asking.

"She's going to graduate school at Columbia. She's determined to have Vassar fire that writing teacher and hire her instead."

"You've got to hand it to Allegra. She knows how to carry a grudge."

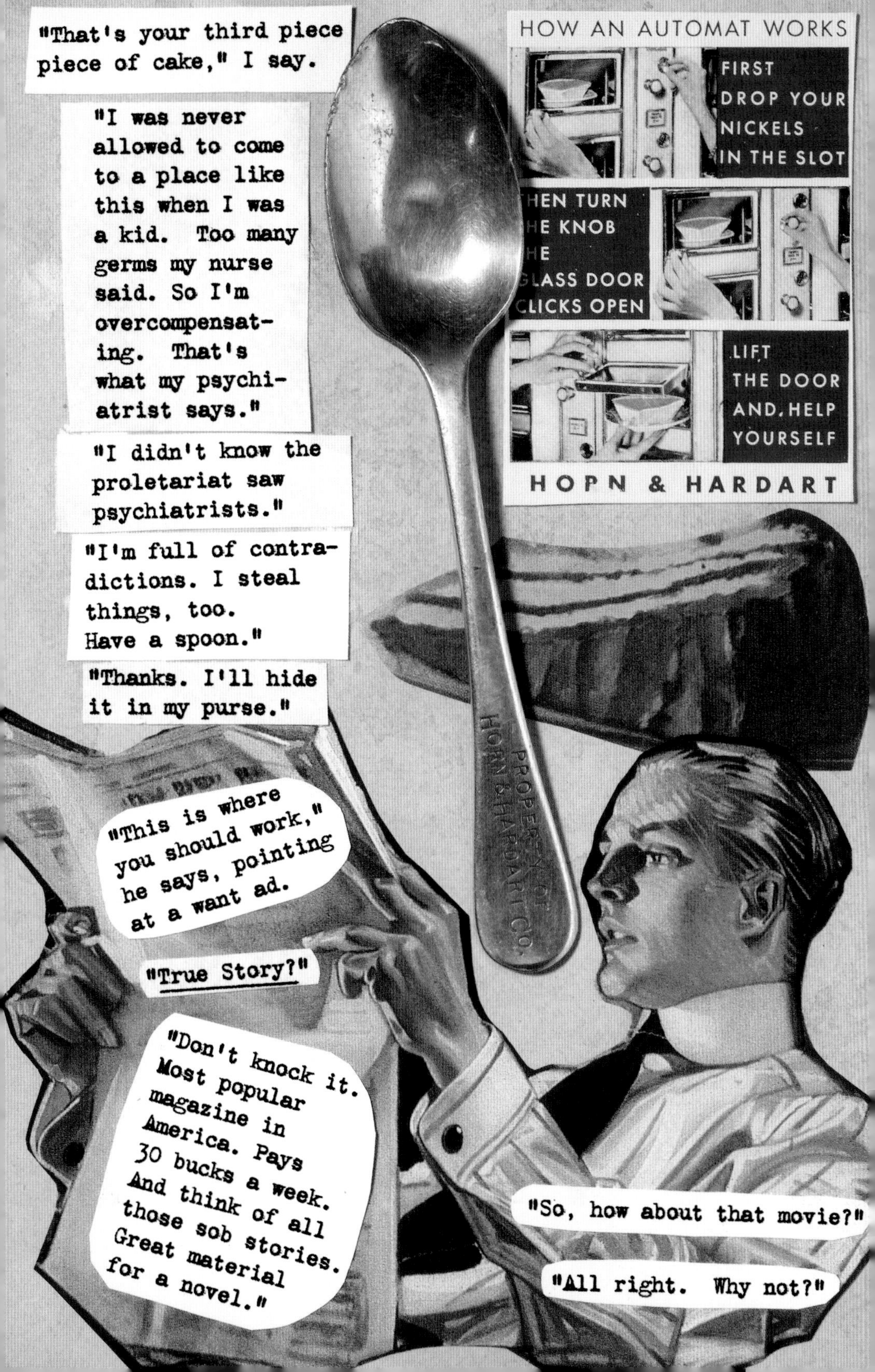

"That's your third piece piece of cake," I say.

"I was never allowed to come to a place like this when I was a kid. Too many germs my nurse said. So I'm overcompensating. That's what my psychiatrist says."

"I didn't know the proletariat saw psychiatrists."

"I'm full of contradictions. I steal things, too. Have a spoon."

"Thanks. I'll hide it in my purse."

HOW AN AUTOMAT WORKS

FIRST DROP YOUR NICKELS IN THE SLOT

THEN TURN THE KNOB THE GLASS DOOR CLICKS OPEN

LIFT THE DOOR AND HELP YOURSELF

HOPN & HARDART

PROPERTY OF HORN & HARDART CO.

"This is where you should work," he says, pointing at a want ad.

"True Story?"

"Don't knock it. Most popular magazine in America. Pays 30 bucks a week. And think of all those sob stories. Great material for a novel."

"So, how about that movie?"

"All right. Why not?"

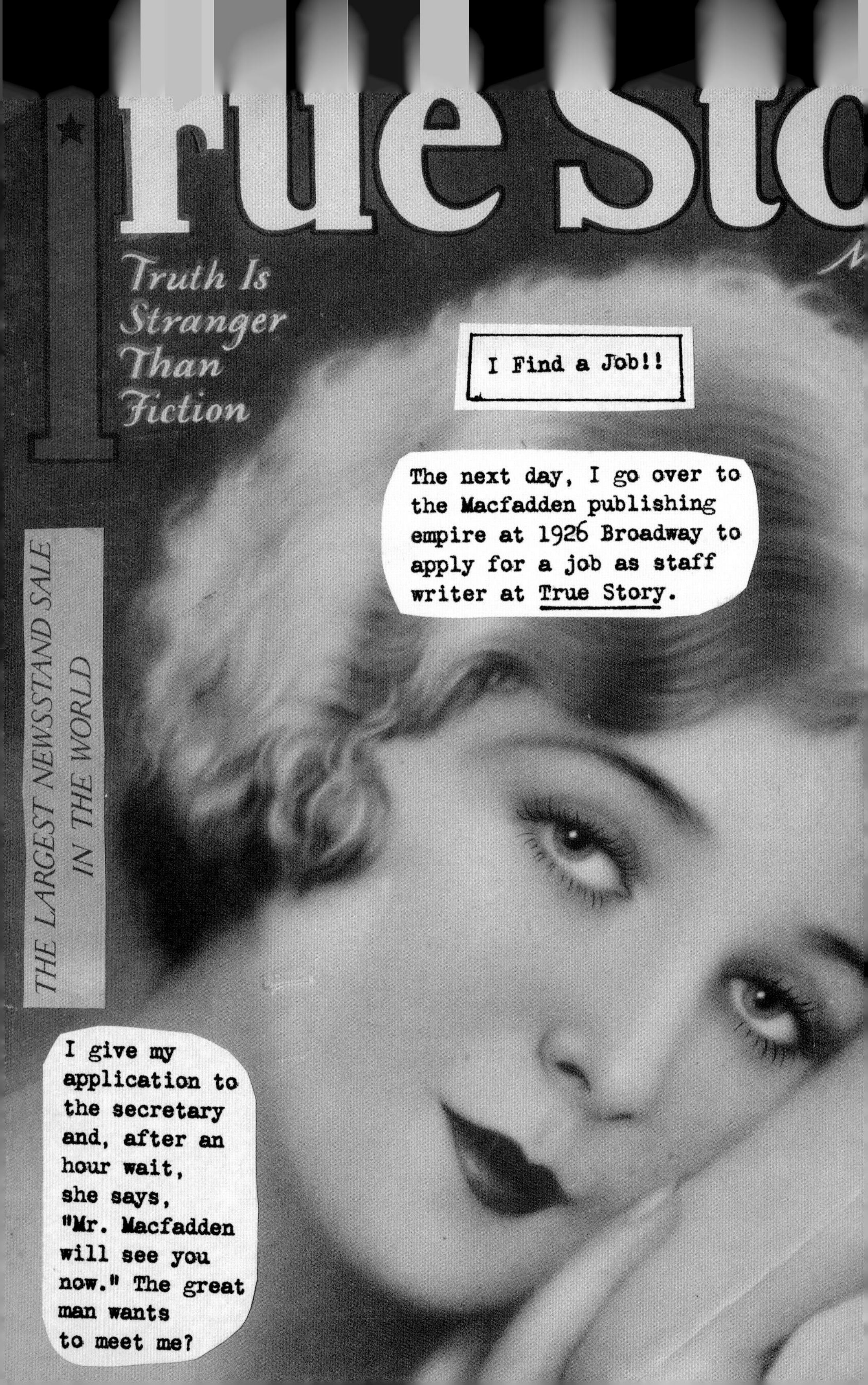
Truth Is Stranger Than Fiction
I Find a Job!!
The next day, I go over to the Macfadden publishing empire at 1926 Broadway to apply for a job as staff writer at True Story.
THE LARGEST NEWSSTAND SALE IN THE WORLD
I give my application to the secretary and, after an hour wait, she says, "Mr. Macfadden will see you now." The great man wants to meet me?

June
ry
azine

A MACFADDEN
25 CENTS
PUBLICATION

Bernarr Macfadden--famous health and physical fitness crackpot and publishing tycoon. Has written dozens of advice books on how to prevent everything from dandruff to sexual frigidity.

An elevator whisks me up to the top-floor office filled with framed covers of True Detective, Physical Culture, True Romance, and Movie Magazine.

Macfadden pops out of a back room like the Wizard of Oz, dressed in a natty windowpane plaid suit. (Thank goodness he's not flexing half-naked like he is in his ads!)

"So, Miss Pratt, what makes a Vassar girl think she's qualified to tell the stories of real people who have actually suffered?

My New Boss, Bernarr Macfadden

"I think I know something about sorrow, Mr. Macfadden. My father died young, leaving my mother to support 3 children."

"Most of our stories are about heartache. What do you know about that?"

I pause-- just say whatever it takes to get the job. "I was involved with a man who turned out to be married." Straight out of True Story!

He looks pleased. "But you lived to regret it?"

"Yes, sir, I did."

"Atta girl. Sin, suffer and repent. That's our motto. You're hired."

He turns to a shelf of Bernarr Macfadden books and pulls out "Womanhood and Marriage." "You may find this useful, Miss Pratt. Let me know if you have any questions."

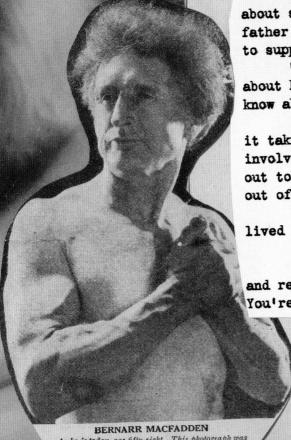

BERNARR MACFADDEN
As he is today, age fifty-eight. This photograph was taken a short time previous to the appearance of this advertisement

50,000.00 in Cash
for TRUE STORIES

Your Own Story May Be Your Fortune!

THE publishers of TRUE STORY Magazine ar
going to pay $50,000 to three hundred an
eleven men and women in amounts rangin
om $5,000 to $100 in exchange for true stories
hy not be among them?

Never was such an offer made
efore. Never before did men
nd women who are not profes-
ional writers have such a glorious
opportunity to turn their life
experiences into handsome sums
of money.

Nearly every man and woman
has lived at least one story which,
because of its unassailable truth,
because it is actually a part of the
life, the sorrows, joys, experiences
of a fellow human being, has more
power for good, more power to
thrill and charm and hold the
reader than any fiction story ever
written.

RULES
TRUE S

All stories m
Typewritte
manuscripts
cepted. Per

Write on
use thin ti
full name
of first p
pages.

Addres
Contest
Unless s
in the c

Encl
envelop

Ever
manus
sible f
to ret

Up
dgm

indefinitely upon the
humanly possible to raise the qual
RY to an even hig
desire and int
d in order to
ignantly in
ghly hel
e do
erience

walk
mainta

TRUE
STORY

The next day, I'm shown to my "office," a pebbled glass cubicle with a metal desk and 3 crates on the floor heaped with letters.

These are the entries for the "True Story" contest. The best sob story wins $5000 and the honor of being published in our magazine.

My job is to plow through, pick out the most "gripping" ones and then "edit" them.

THE LATEST DIRT

their souls for men they loved, an

STORY is

104

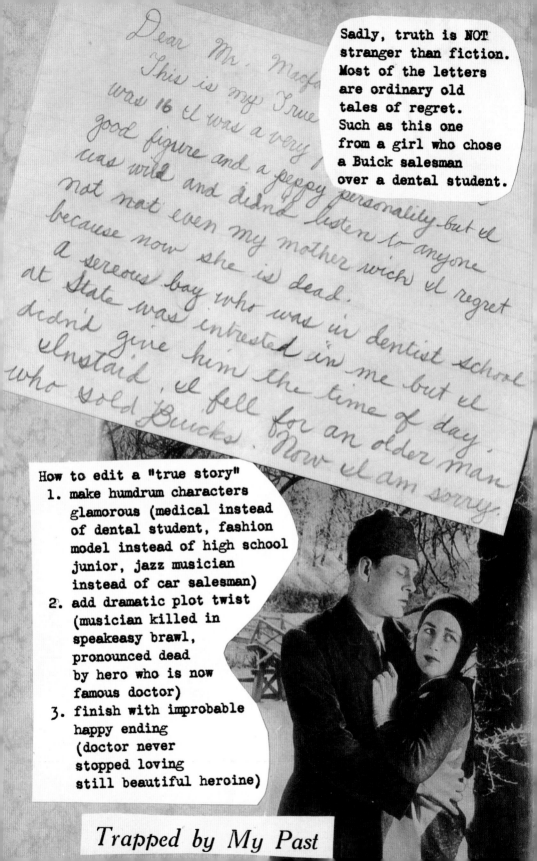

Dear Mr. Macfa...
This is my True...
was 16 it was a very...
good figure and a peppy personality but it
was wild and didn't listen to anyone
not wait even my mother wich it regret
because now she is dead.
a serious boy who was in dentist school
at State was intrested in me but it
didn't give him the time of day.
Instaid, it fell for an older man
who sold Buicks. Now it am sorry.

Sadly, truth is NOT stranger than fiction. Most of the letters are ordinary old tales of regret. Such as this one from a girl who chose a Buick salesman over a dental student.

How to edit a "true story"
1. make humdrum characters glamorous (medical instead of dental student, fashion model instead of high school junior, jazz musician instead of car salesman)
2. add dramatic plot twist (musician killed in speakeasy brawl, pronounced dead by hero who is now famous doctor)
3. finish with improbable happy ending (doctor never stopped loving still beautiful heroine)

Trapped by My Past

Knickerbocker

Entire Week
June 29th

"There's No Place
as Cool as
the Knickerbocker"

We see
I Want My
Man at the
Knickerbocker
with
refrigerated
air.
(Best thing
about movie!)

20¢

GLOBE TICKET COMPANY, PHILA.

"I WANT
MY MAN

a lonesome
sweetheart

LYRIC

LYRIC THEAT

TO-DAY
CHARLIE
Chaplin
OF HIS GREATEST COMEDIES
AND SOUND

I Go
to the
Movies
with
Oliver

Charlie Chaplin
at the Lyric.

D ROW | CENTER 113 | SEAT
BALCONY
LYRIC THEATRE

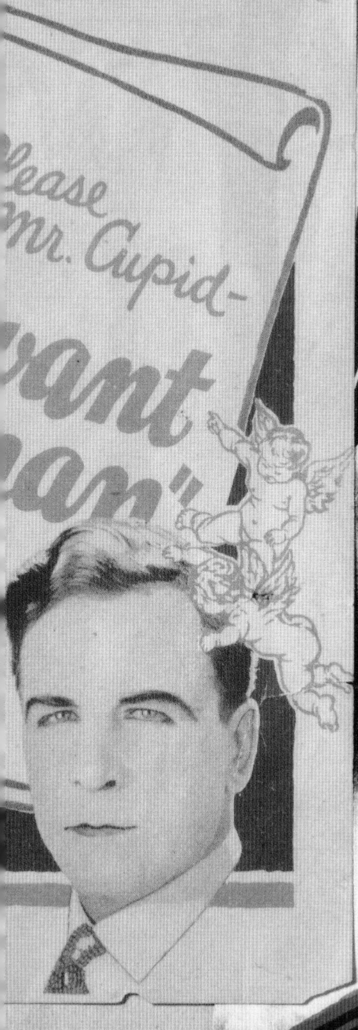

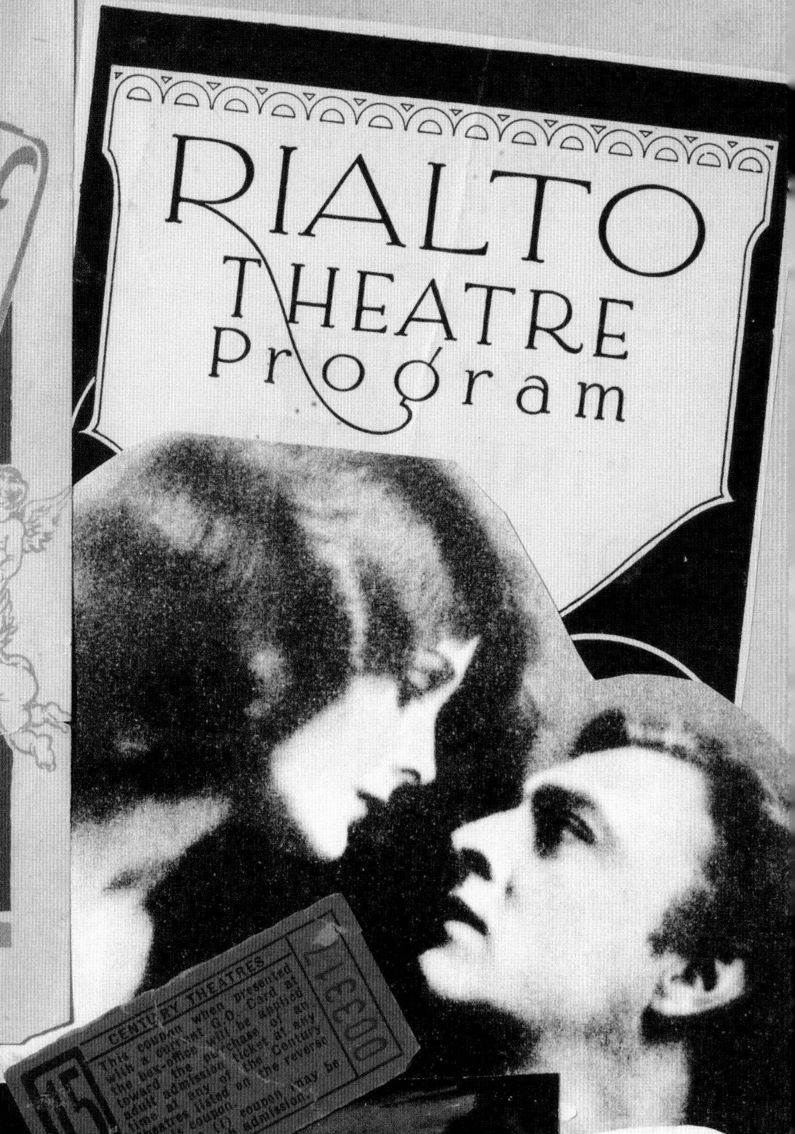
RIALTO
THEATRE
Program
CENTURY THEATRES
This coupon when presented with a current G.O. Card at the box-office will be applied toward the purchase of an adult admission ticket at any time at any of the Century Theatres listed on the reverse of this coupon. Only one (1) coupon may be used for each admission.
15 CENTS
003317

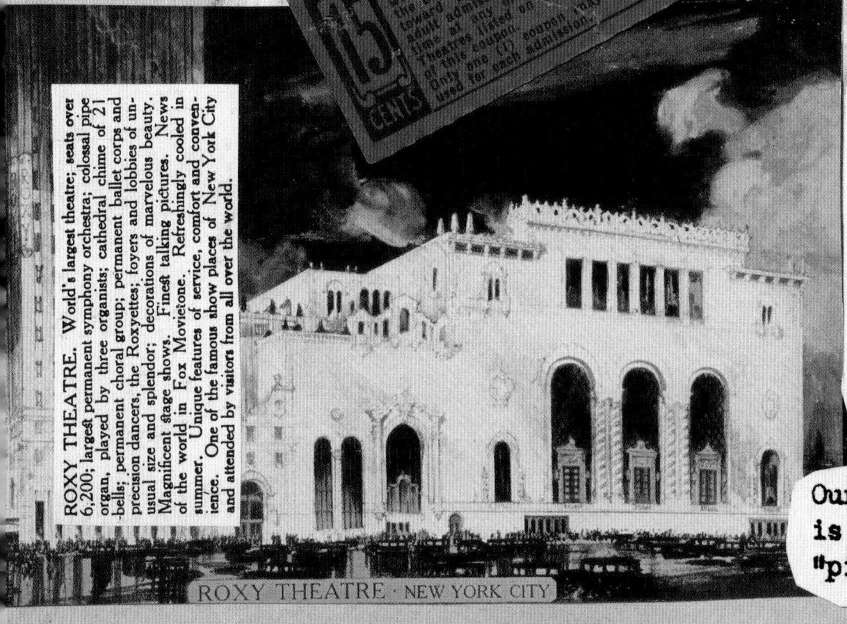
ROXY THEATRE. World's largest theatre; seats over 6,200; largest permanent symphony orchestra; colossal pipe organ, played by three organists; cathedral chime of 21 bells; permanent choral group; permanent ballet corps and precision dancers, the Roxyettes; foyers and lobbies of unusual size and splendor; decorations of marvelous beauty. Magnificent stage shows. Finest talking pictures. News of the world in Fox Movietone. Refreshingly cooled in summer. Unique features of service, comfort and convenience. One of the famous show places of New York City and attended by visitors from all over the world.
ROXY THEATRE · NEW YORK CITY

Mary Astor and John Barrymore in Beau Brummel at the Rialto. The two most famous profiles in the world.

Our favorite is the new Roxy "picture palace."

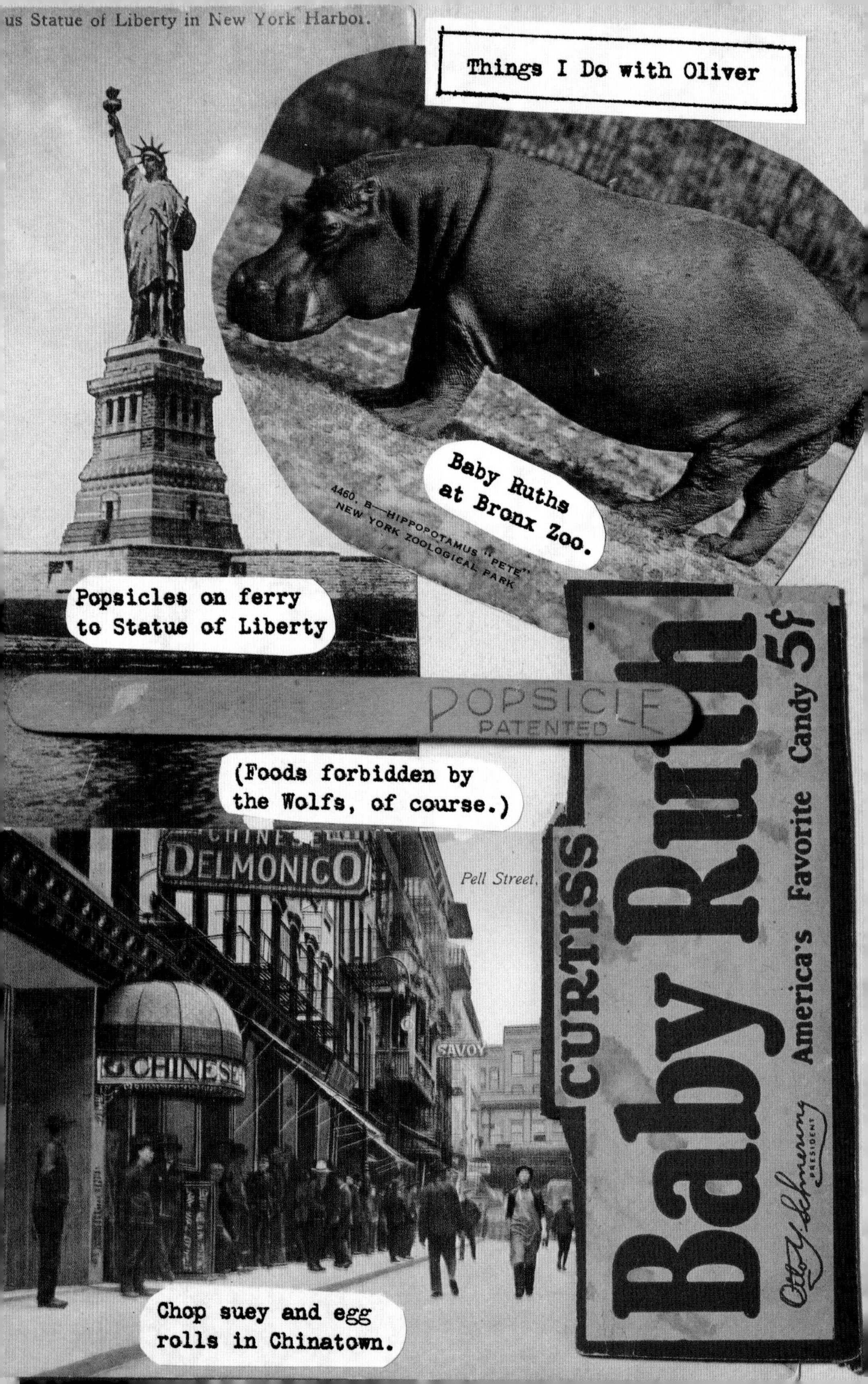
us Statue of Liberty in New York Harbor.
Things I Do with Oliver
Baby Ruths at Bronx Zoo.
4460. B—HIPPOPOTAMUS "PETE"
NEW YORK ZOOLOGICAL PARK
Popsicles on ferry to Statue of Liberty
POPSICLE
PATENTED
(Foods forbidden by the Wolfs, of course.)
DELMONICO
Pell Street.
SAVOY
CURTISS
Baby Ruth
5¢
America's Favorite Candy
PRESIDENT
Chop suey and egg rolls in Chinatown.

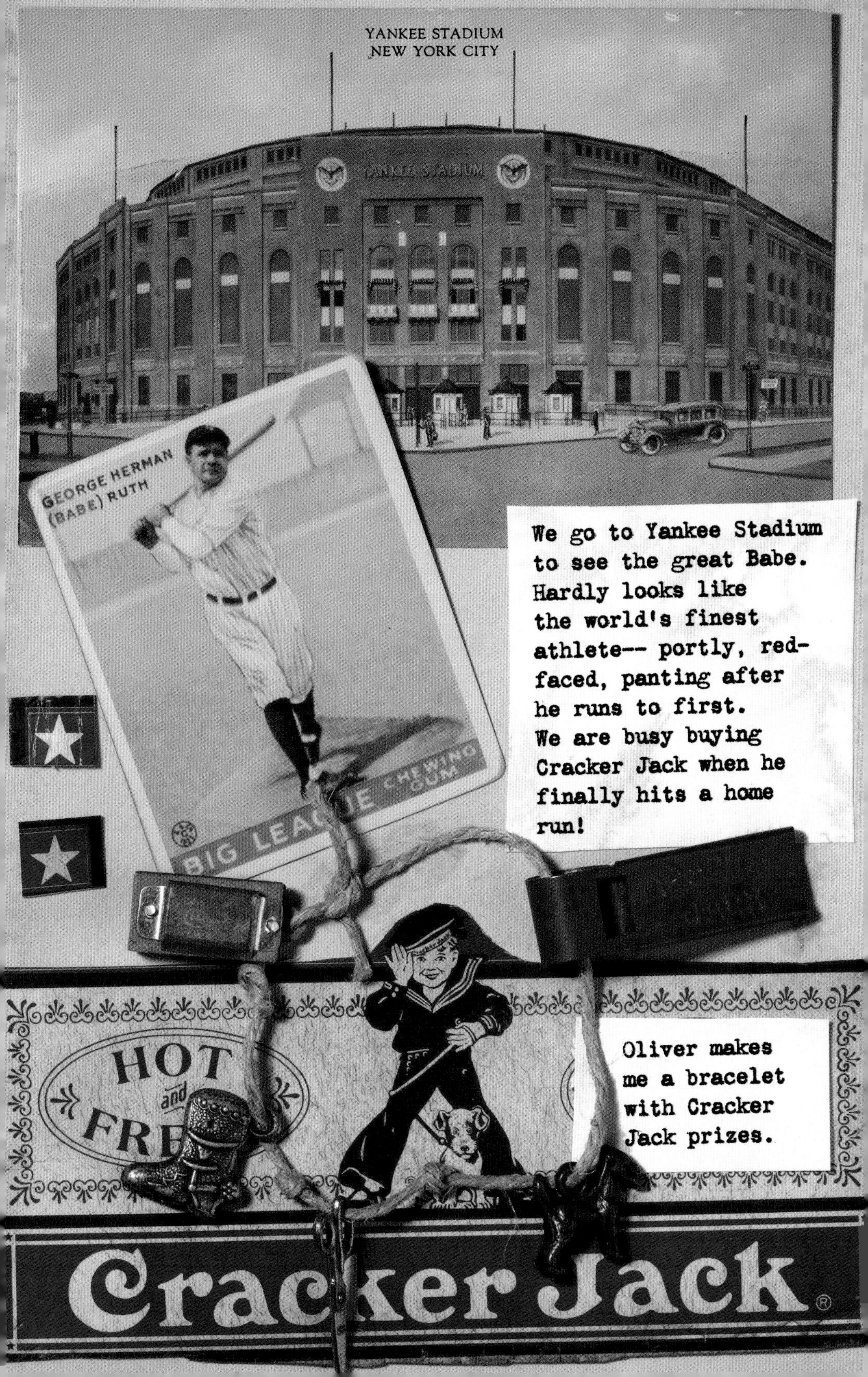
YANKEE STADIUM
NEW YORK CITY
YANKEE STADIUM
GEORGE HERMAN
(BABE) RUTH
BIG LEAGUE CHEWING GUM
HOT and FRE
Cracker Jack®

We go to Yankee Stadium
to see the great Babe.
Hardly looks like
the world's finest
athlete-- portly, red-
faced, panting after
he runs to first.
We are busy buying
Cracker Jack when he
finally hits a home
run!

Oliver makes
me a bracelet
with Cracker
Jack prizes.

We Go to Coney Island

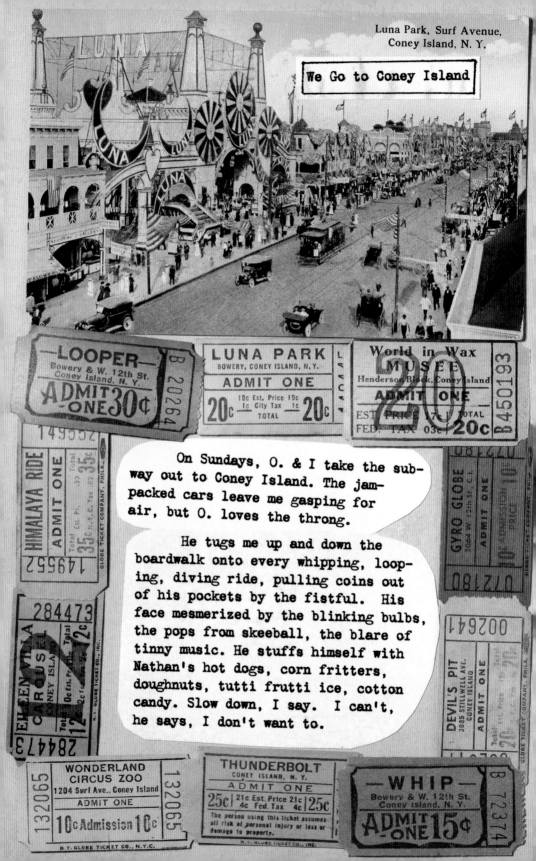

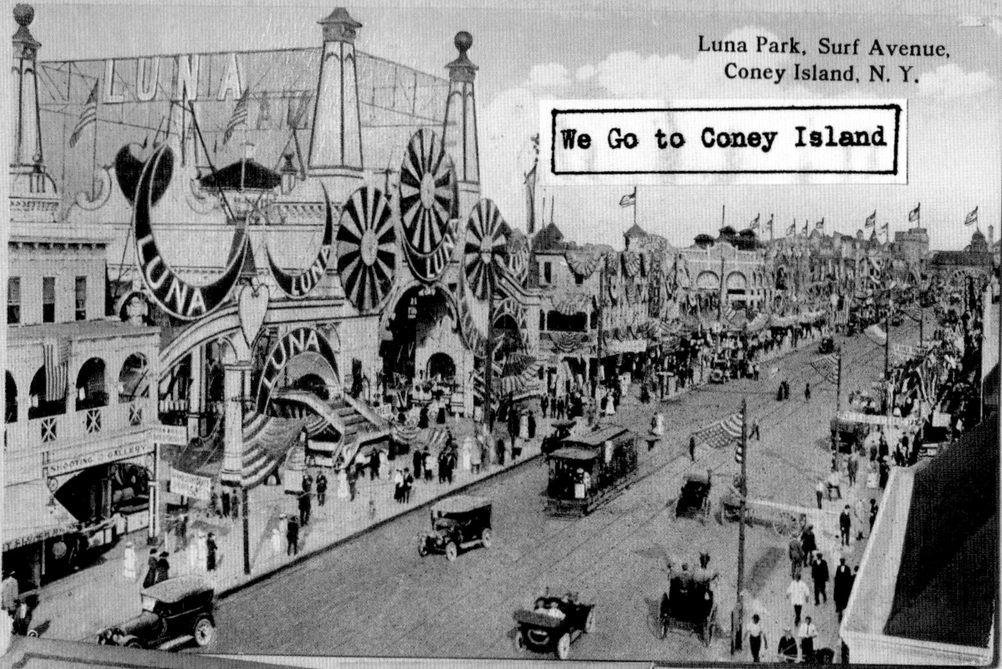
Luna Park, Surf Avenue,
Coney Island, N. Y.

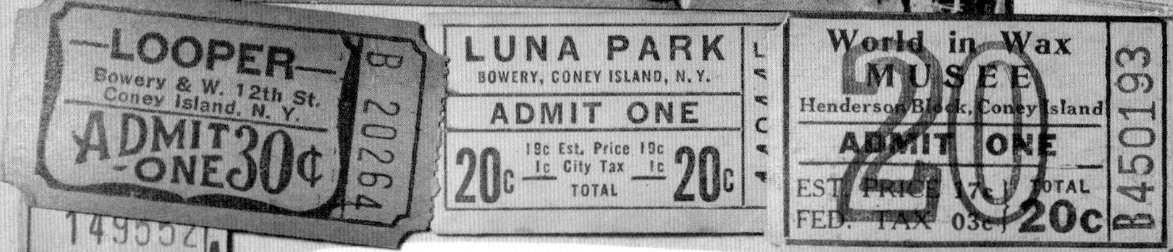
LOOPER
Bowery & W. 12th St.
Coney Island, N. Y.
ADMIT ONE 30¢
B 20264
LUNA PARK
BOWERY, CONEY ISLAND, N. Y.
ADMIT ONE
20c 19c Est. Price 19c 1c City Tax 1c TOTAL 20c
World in Wax
MUSEE
Henderson Block, Coney Island
ADMIT ONE
EST. PRICE 17c
FED. TAX 03c
TOTAL 20c
20
B450193

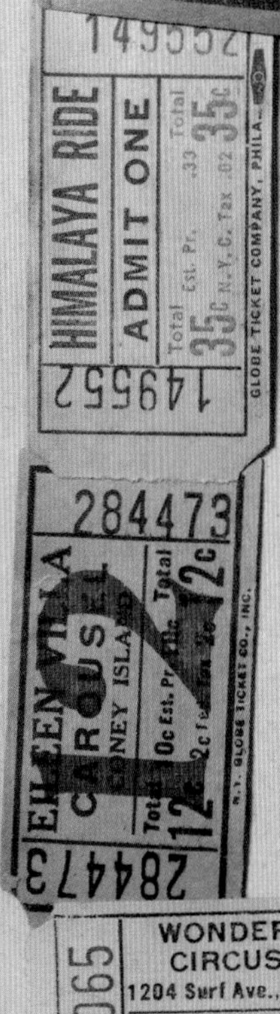
HIMALAYA RIDE
ADMIT ONE
Total 35c
149552
GLOBE TICKET COMPANY, PHILA.
284473
CAROUSEL
CONEY ISLAND
Total 12c
284473
N. Y. GLOBE TICKET CO., INC.

On Sundays, O. & I take the subway out to Coney Island. The jam-packed cars leave me gasping for air, but O. loves the throng.

He tugs me up and down the boardwalk onto every whipping, looping, diving ride, pulling coins out of his pockets by the fistful. His face mesmerized by the blinking bulbs, the pops from skeeball, the blare of tinny music. He stuffs himself with Nathan's hot dogs, corn fritters, doughnuts, tutti frutti ice, cotton candy. Slow down, I say. I can't, he says, I don't want to.

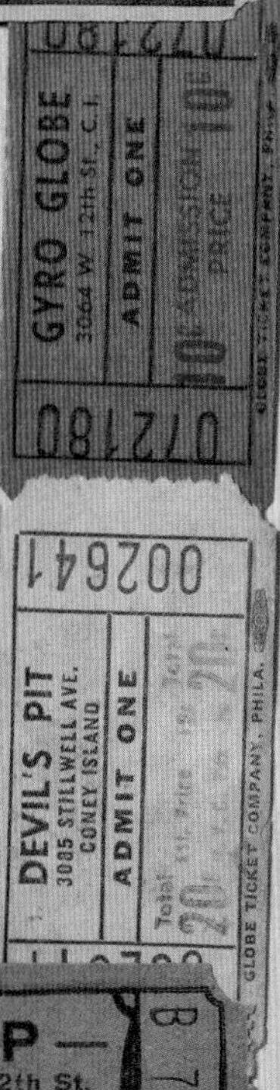
GYRO GLOBE
3064 W. 12th St., C. I.
ADMIT ONE
10c ADMISSION 10c
PRICE
072180
002641
DEVIL'S PIT
3085 STILLWELL AVE.
CONEY ISLAND
ADMIT ONE
GLOBE TICKET COMPANY, PHILA.

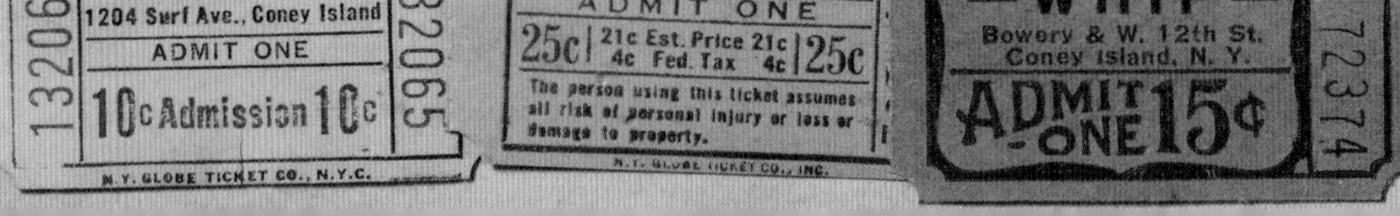
WONDERLAND
CIRCUS ZOO
1204 Surf Ave., Coney Island
ADMIT ONE
10c Admission 10c
132065
132065
N. Y. GLOBE TICKET CO., N.Y.C.
THUNDERBOLT
CONEY ISLAND, N. Y.
ADMIT ONE
25c 21c Est. Price 21c 4c Fed. Tax 4c 25c
The person using this ticket assumes all risk of personal injury or loss or damage to property.
N. Y. GLOBE TICKET CO., INC.
WHIP
Bowery & W. 12th St.
Coney Island, N. Y.
ADMIT ONE 15¢
B 72374

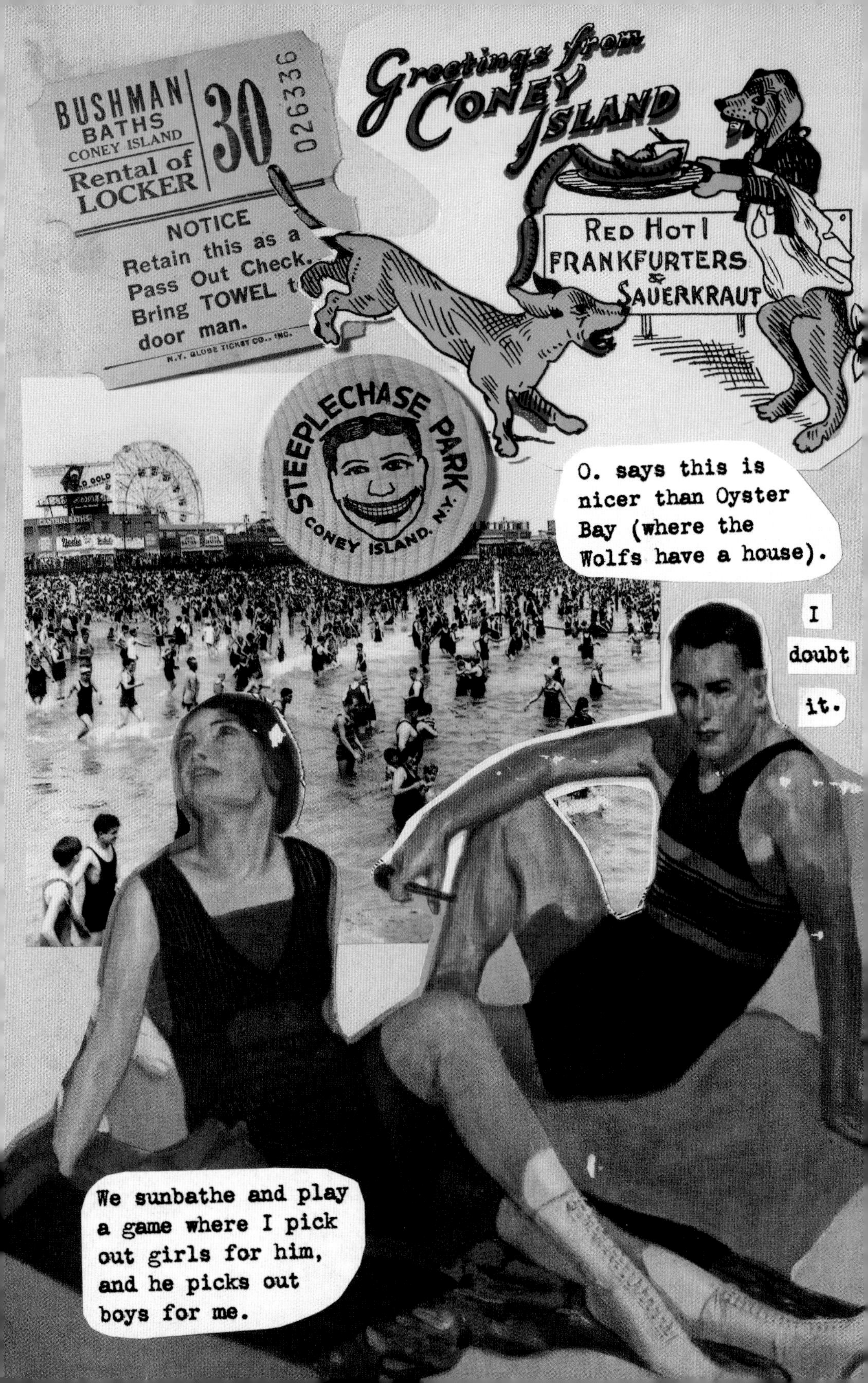
BUSHMAN
BATHS
CONEY ISLAND
Rental of
LOCKER
30
026336
NOTICE
Retain this as a
Pass Out Check.
Bring TOWEL t
door man.
N.Y. GLOBE TICKET CO., INC.
Greetings from
CONEY ISLAND
RED HOT!
FRANKFURTERS
&
SAUERKRAUT
STEEPLECHASE PARK
CONEY ISLAND, N.Y.
O. says this is nicer than Oyster Bay (where the Wolfs have a house).
I doubt it.
We sunbathe and play a game where I pick out girls for him, and he picks out boys for me.

DANCE

Dancing with Oliver

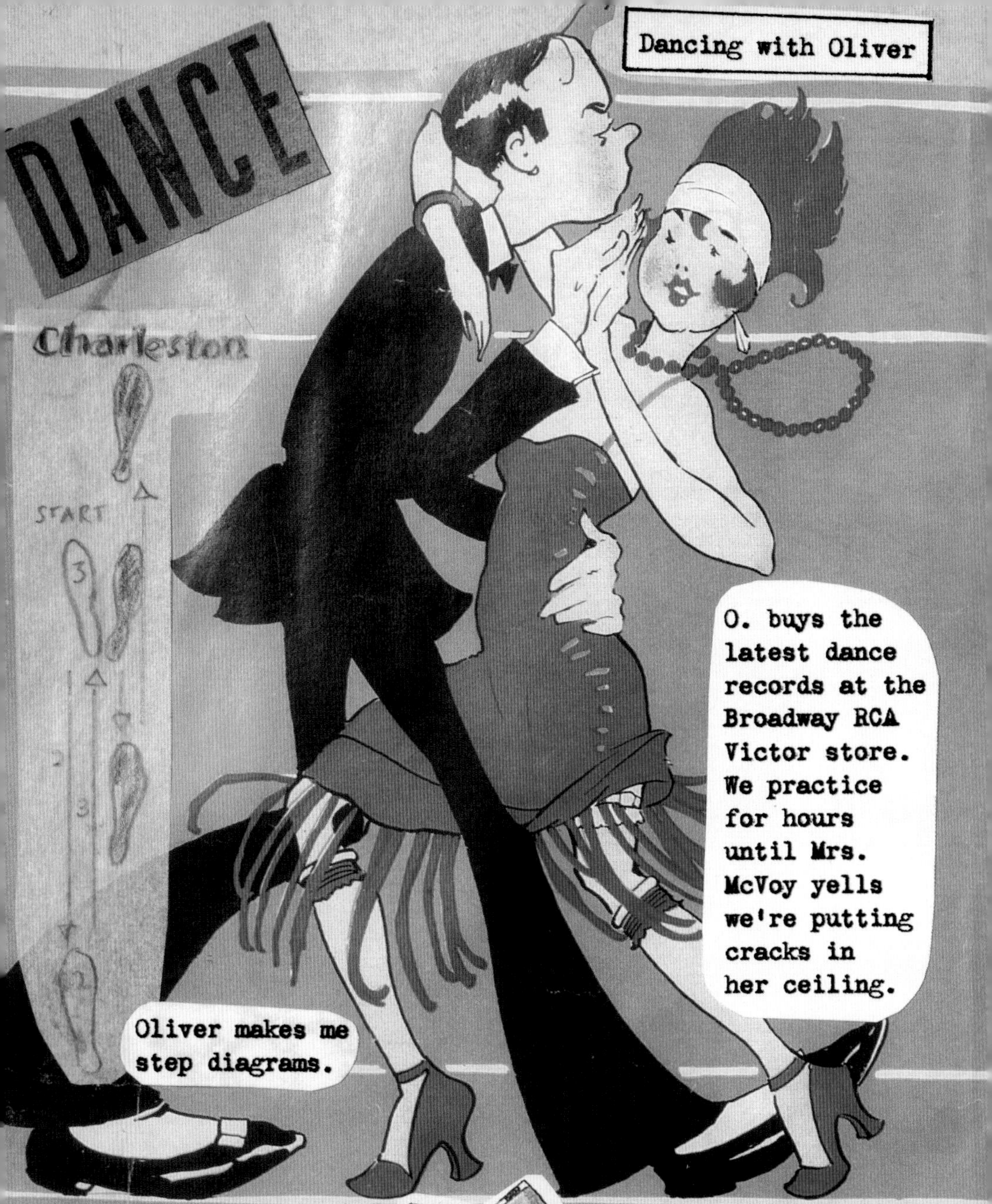
Charleston
START

Oliver makes me step diagrams.

O. buys the latest dance records at the Broadway RCA Victor store. We practice for hours until Mrs. McVoy yells we're putting cracks in her ceiling.

I splurge half a week's salary on blue & silver dancing slippers from Saks!

PRESSÉ

A formal slipper of mauve, flesh, purple, tango, peacock blue, green or black satin. Vamps, hand-embroidered in France with pastel ribbons. Silver or gold kid heels and straps. 18.50.

O. skips me across the floor in perfect time, whirls me round on the tips of my toes like a tin top. I press my face into his neck, which always smells like sandalwood soap.

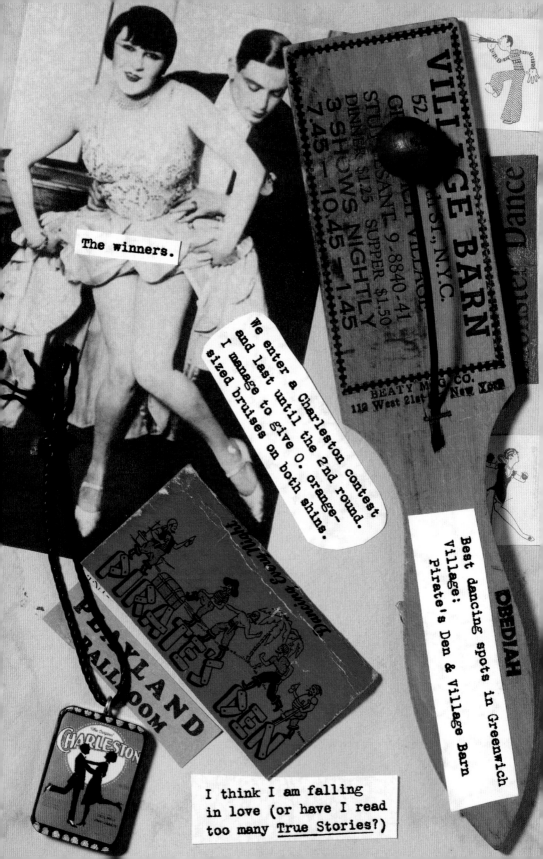

The winners.

VILLAGE BARN
52 ... GREENWICH VILLAGE
...AL ST., N.Y.C.
STUY...SANT 9-8840-41
DINNER $1.25   SUPPER $1.50
3 SHOWS NIGHTLY
7.45 — 10.45 — 1.45

BEATY MFG. CO. New York
112 West 21st ...

We enter a Charleston contest
and last until the 2nd round.
I manage to give O. orange-
sized bruises on both shins.

PIRATE'S DEN

PINKLAND BALLROOM

CHARLESTON

OBEDIAH

Best dancing spots in Greenwich
Village:
Pirate's Den & Village Barn

I think I am falling
in love (or have I read
too many True Stories?)

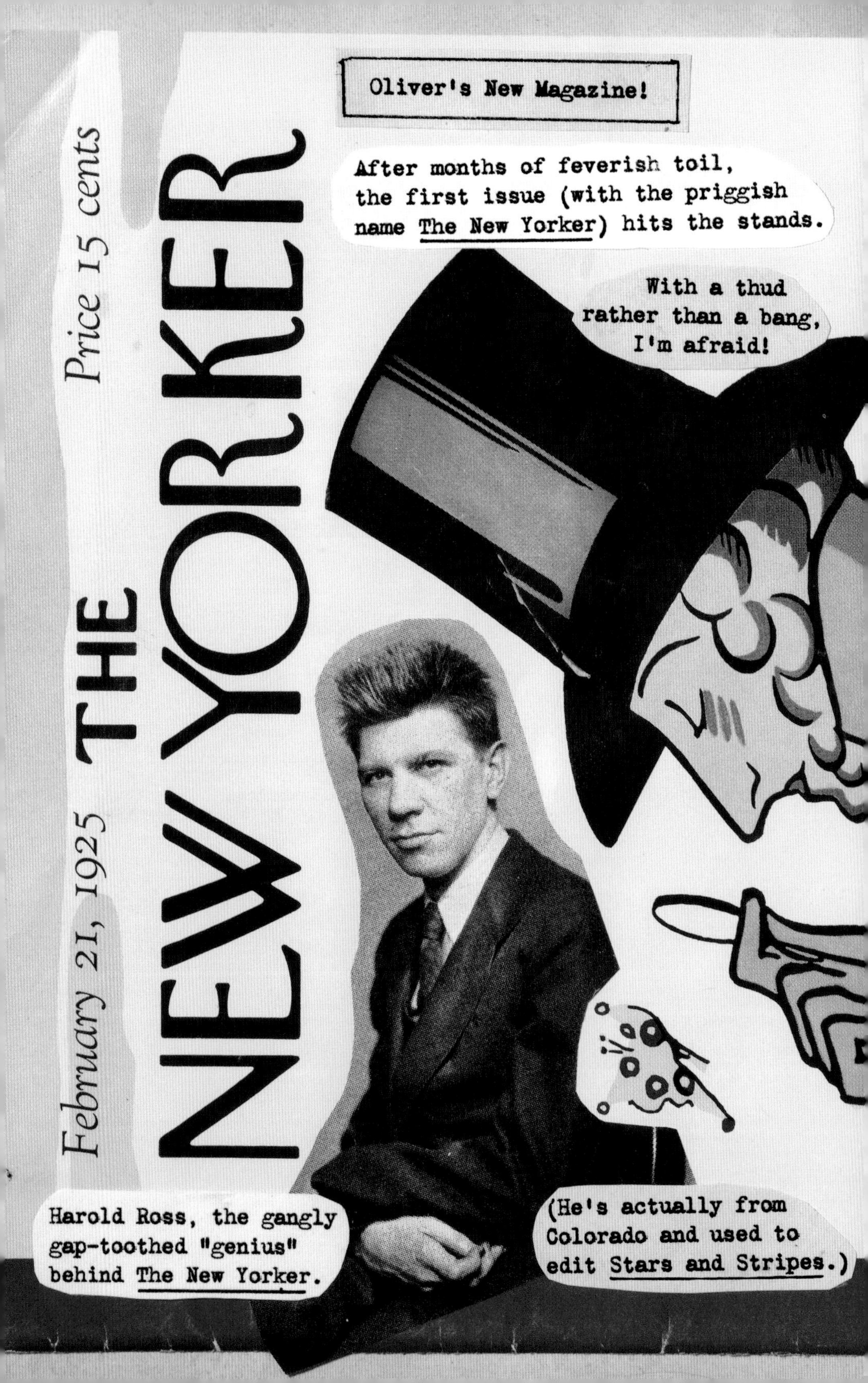
Oliver's New Magazine!
After months of feverish toil, the first issue (with the priggish name The New Yorker) hits the stands.
With a thud rather than a bang, I'm afraid!
THE NEW YORKER
Price 15 cents
February 21, 1925
Harold Ross, the gangly gap-toothed "genius" behind The New Yorker.
(He's actually from Colorado and used to edit Stars and Stripes.)

The New Yorker boasts that it will have a brand new style of cartoons. But what could be more ho-hum than a flapper cartoon?

Ethel Plummer

UNCLE: *Poor girls, so few get their wages!*
FLAPPER: *So few get their sin, darn it!*

THE NEW YORKER asks consideration for its first number. It recognizes certain shortcomings and realizes that it is impossible for a magazine fully to establish its character in one number. At the same time it feels a great deal of pride in many of its features and heart-felt gratitude for the support it already has received.

THE NEW YORKER starts with a declaration of serious purpose but with a concomitant declaration that it will not be too serious in executing it. It hopes to reflect metropolitan life, to keep up with events and affairs of the day, to be gay, humorous, satirical but to be more than a jester.

It will publish facts that it will have to go behind the scenes to get, but it will not deal in scandal for the sake of scandal nor sensation for the sake of sensation. It will try conscientiously to keep its readers informed of what is going on in the fields in which they are most interested. It has announced that it is not edited for the old lady in Dubuque. By this it means that it is not of that group of publications engaged in tapping the Great Buying Power of the North American steppe region by trading mirrors and colored beads in the form of our best brands of hokum.

The New Yorker

Why the first issue is (in my humble opinion) a bore:
1. British fop on cover
2. self-important editorial
3. no color pictures
4. no table of contents
5. no author bylines

GOINGS ON

Mr. Ross calls O. "Wolf" and only lets him write the theatre and art listings in the "Goings On" section. Mostly he sends him on errands to fetch cigarettes and hooch from the bootlegger.

I don't tell O. that I think The New Yorker will fold in a month. Poor Wolf -- he had such high hopes!

Polly Peabody Sends Me a Letter from Paris

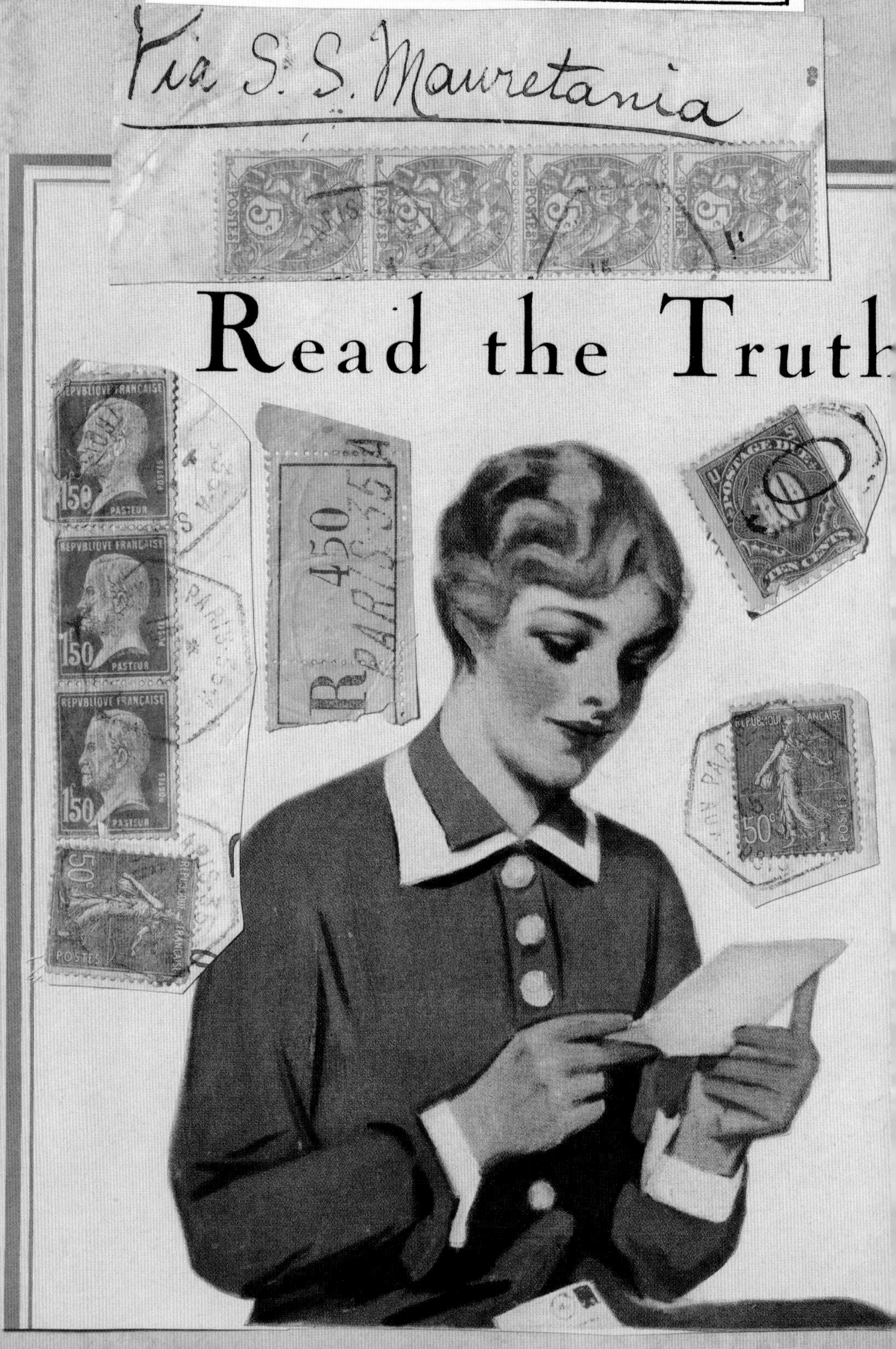
Via S. S. Mauretania
Read the Truth
450
PASTEUR
POSTES
50c

Dear Frankie,

I was at the Café Select yesterday (a
favorite hang out for American expats) drinking
a café au lait and struggling miserably through
Pere Goriot (for my $%&* French literature
class at the Sorbonne).
A man settled into the table next to mine
and ordered a brandy (even though it was only
11 in the morning). Mid 30s I'd guess, dark and
very handsome in a going-to-seed kind of way.
"American?" he asked. (How does
everyone always know?)
We struck up a desultory conversation and
he seemed completely bored until I said I'd just
graduated from Vassar.
"You didn't by any chance know a girl named
Frankie Pratt?" He kept his eyes on the pavement,
very nonchalant, but I could tell it was an act.
"Frankie! She's one of my best friends." I
told him you'd been the star of my class and won
the writing prize. (No surprise there, the
mystery man said.) That you were living in
Greenwich Village and writing for a magazine.
I asked him if he wanted your address.
"No. I promised I wouldn't contact her."
(What the h-e-l-l does that mean??) "But
next time you write her, please tell her that
James Pingree sends his regards."
So there you are. Message delivered.
Sometime you'll have to tell me the whole
story!
Chad's in New York too. I told him to
ask you out for dinner some time. . .

Love,
Polly

Jamie hasn't forgotten me after all.

But have I forgotten him?

117

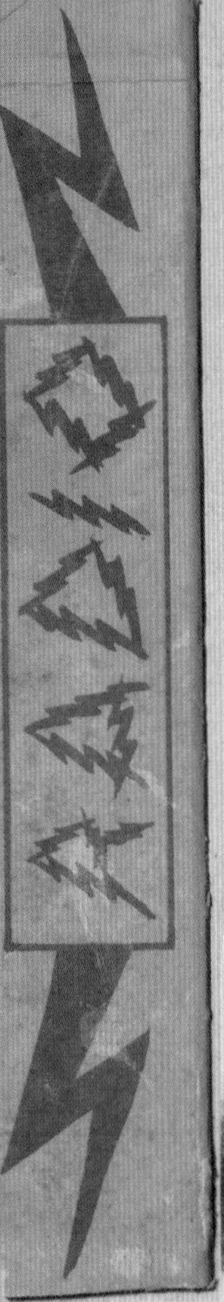

My First Radio

Radiola Super-Heterodyne

—gets distance with no antenna —noground wires —noconnections. Once mark the stations on the dials, and you can turn to the marked spots and tune in—clear—true—real!

Operates entirely on dry batteries.

With 6 Radiotrons UV-199 and Radiola Loudspeaker. With compartments to hold the batteries. Entirely complete except batteries . . $269

RCA Radiola AN RCA PRODUCT

On my birthday, O. comes staggering up to my room with a huge crate.

I pry open the top and blow away the excelsior.

It's a Radiola!

It runs on batteries & is totally portable.

It only weighs 39 pounds.

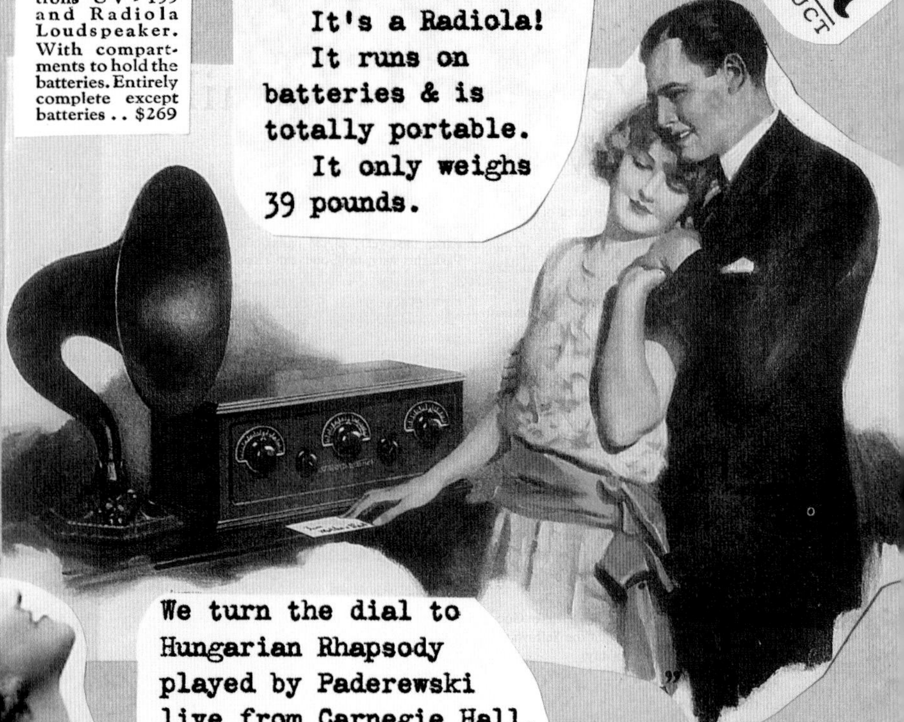

We turn the dial to Hungarian Rhapsody played by Paderewski live from Carnegie Hall. So scratchy and distant, it sounds like it's broadcast from the moon.

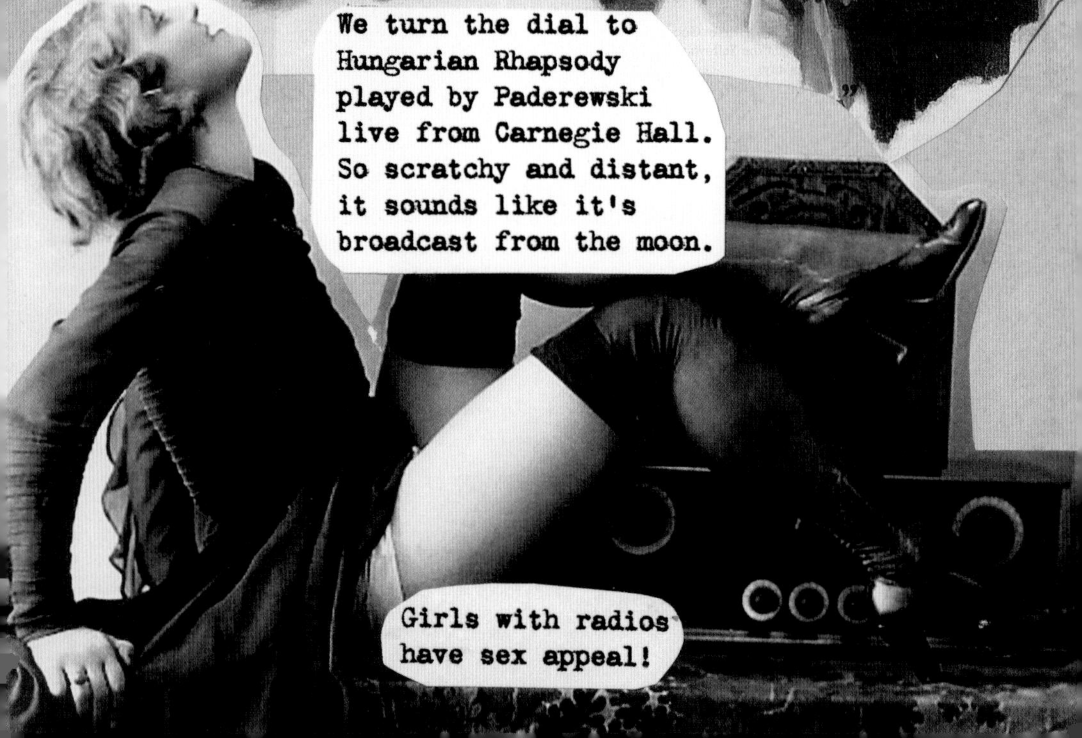

Girls with radios have sex appeal!

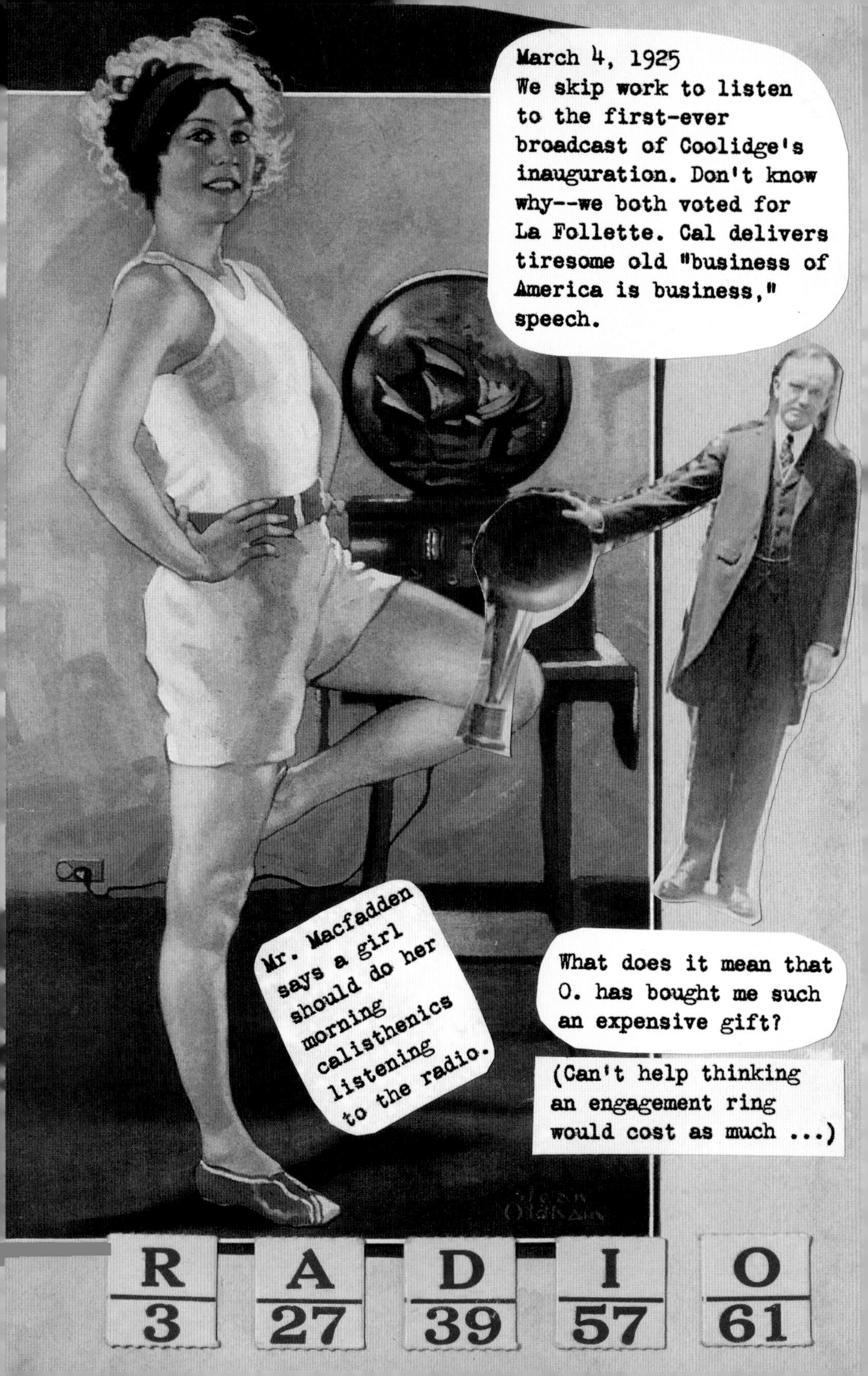
March 4, 1925
We skip work to listen to the first-ever broadcast of Coolidge's inauguration. Don't know why--we both voted for La Follette. Cal delivers tiresome old "business of America is business," speech.
Mr. Macfadden says a girl should do her morning calisthenics listening to the radio.
What does it mean that O. has bought me such an expensive gift?
(Can't help thinking an engagement ring would cost as much ...)
R A D I O
3 27 39 57 61

DUPLICATE

PRESCRIPTION FORM FOR MEDICINAL LIQUOR

F98524

Rx

Oliver Teaches Me How to Drink

KIND OF LIQUOR   QUANTITY   DIRECTIONS

DATE PRESCRIBED

STREET   CITY   STATE

PRESCRIBERS PERMIT NUMBER

CITY   STATE

PERMIT   PERMIT NUM

AND CANCELED   STRIP STAMP NUMBE

CITY   STATE

UNDER   47

Oliver's psychiatrist prescribes gin for his "nerves."

THE NEW YORKER

THE LIQUOR MARKET: Sharp rise in genuine whiskies and wines due to tightening along Canadian border. Scotches: Grand Old Parr, $100@ $105; King George the 4th Top Notch Scotch, $105@$110. Champagnes: Mumms Cordon Rouge, 1911, $140@$150; Pol Roget, 1919, $140 @$150. Bacardi Rum, brandies and Sloe gins available at $125. Canadian Liquor Commission alcohol, per gallon, $30, supply short; Montreal flooded with low-grade alcohol imported from New York for illegal manufacture.—THE NEW YORKERS

O. is writing the "Liquor Market" column in the "Talk of the Town" —which he considers a great honor. Every week, he runs around town and interviews a dozen bootleggers. They give him free samples, and he has set up a fully stocked bar in my bottom bureau drawer.

CHAMPAGNE BRUT

← OLIVER   ME →

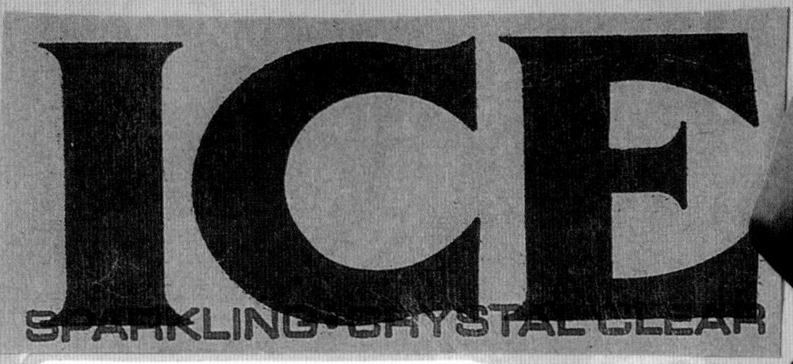
ICE
SPARKLING • CRYSTAL CLEAR

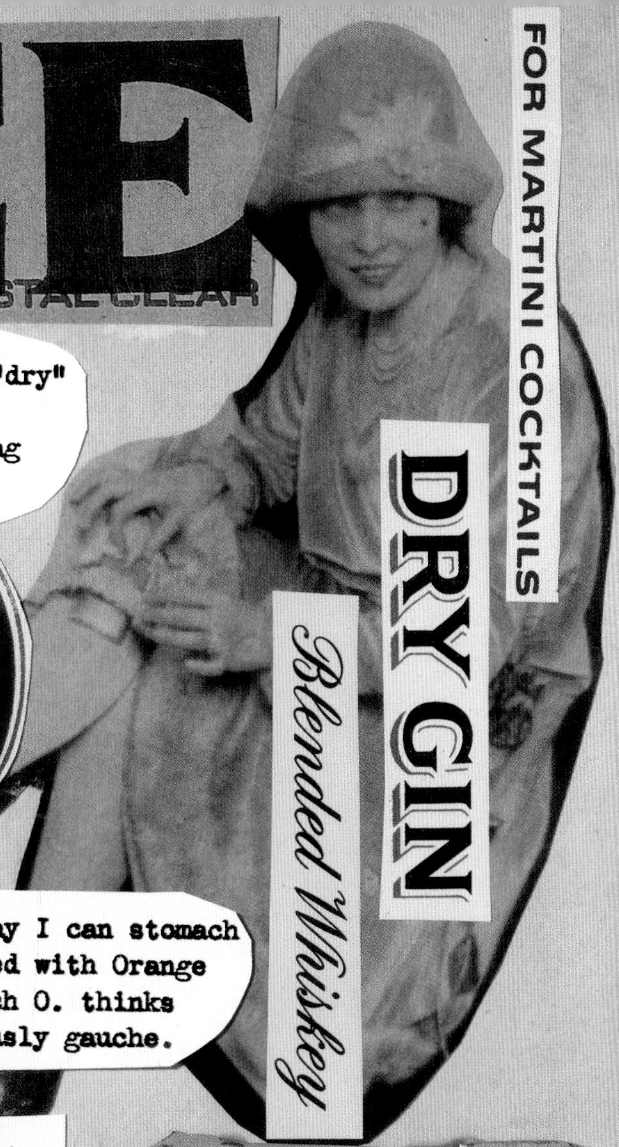
FOR MARTINI COCKTAILS
DRY GIN
Blended Whiskey

O.'s favorite drink is a "dry" martini or bourbon on the "rocks." (He smashes a bag of ice on the fire escape with a hammer.)

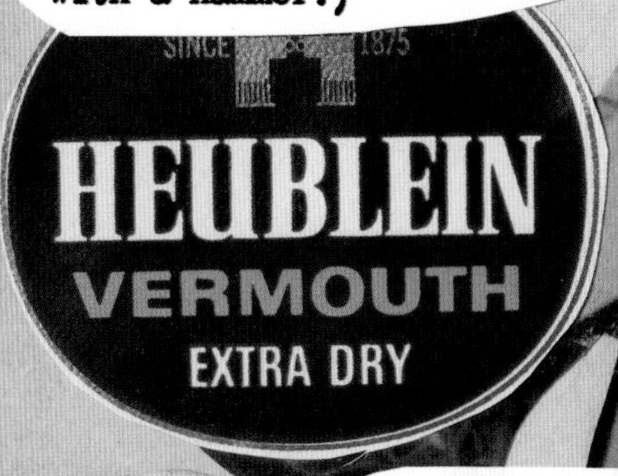
SINCE 1875
HEUBLEIN
VERMOUTH
EXTRA DRY

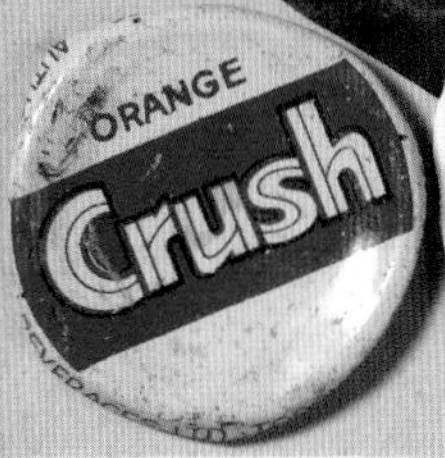
ORANGE
Crush

The only way I can stomach gin is mixed with Orange Crush, which O. thinks is hilariously gauche.

After a couple of martinis, O. gets very romantic. He puts on "Rhapsody in Blue" and pulls me onto his lap. He runs a finger down my cheek and gives me long, deep kisses that make me giddy. "I love you," he says, "more than anyone in the world."

"Thank you," I say stupidly, wondering what he really means.

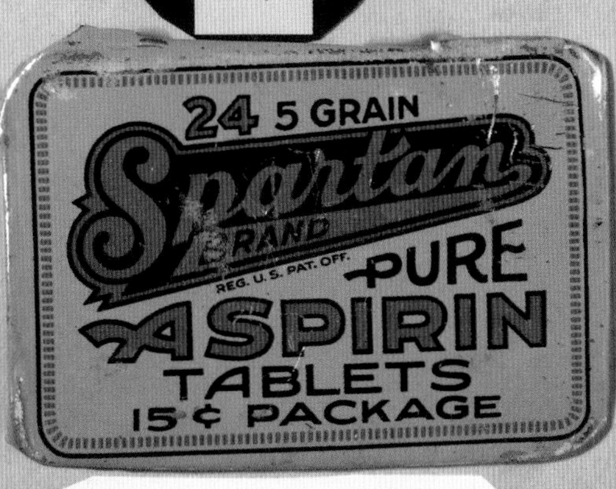
24 5 GRAIN
Spartan
BRAND
REG. U.S. PAT. OFF.
PURE
ASPIRIN
TABLETS
15¢ PACKAGE

For hangover: Take 2 Spartans with quinine water at bedtime, and 2 with Listerine before breakfast.

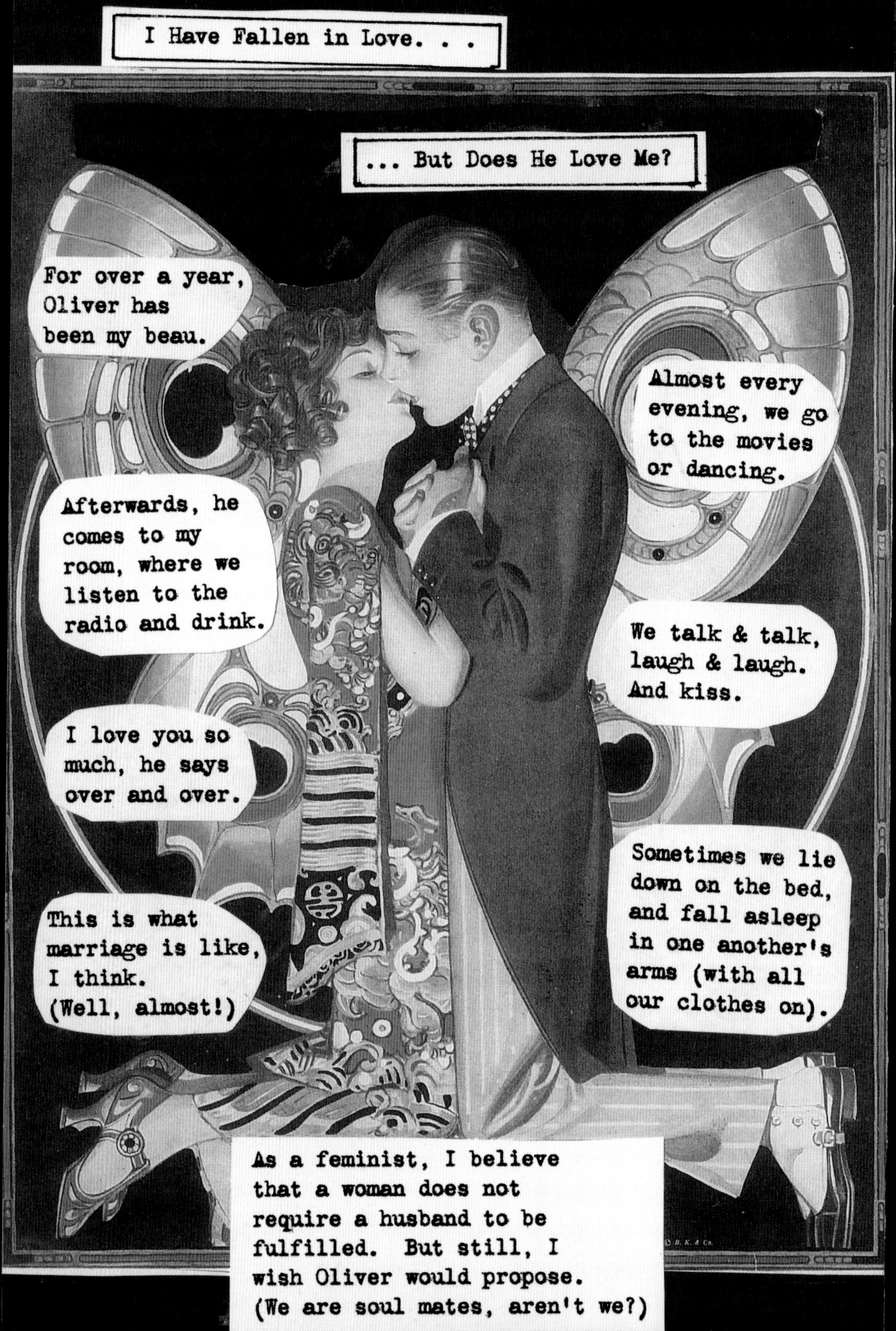
I Have Fallen in Love. . .
... But Does He Love Me?
For over a year, Oliver has been my beau.
Almost every evening, we go to the movies or dancing.
Afterwards, he comes to my room, where we listen to the radio and drink.
We talk & talk, laugh & laugh. And kiss.
I love you so much, he says over and over.
Sometimes we lie down on the bed, and fall asleep in one another's arms (with all our clothes on).
This is what marriage is like, I think. (Well, almost!)
As a feminist, I believe that a woman does not require a husband to be fulfilled. But still, I wish Oliver would propose. (We are soul mates, aren't we?)

‘Womanhood and Marriage”

By Bernarr Macfadden

Don’t Make the Mistake of Choosing the Wrong Life Partner!

By Bernarr Macfadden

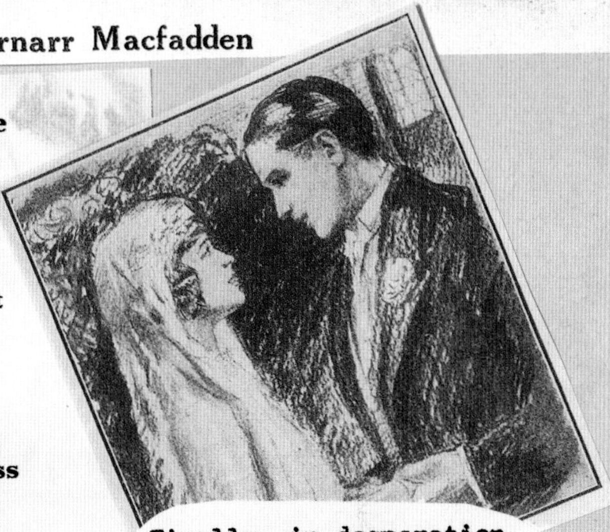

Fill out this easy checklist to ascertain whether your suitor is a compatible match.

Finally, in desperation, I turn to Mr. Macfadden's book for romantic advice, and fill out this checklist.

I. Judging A Man’s Fitness

Y Is he of equal intelligence?
Y Is he physically attractive?
N Does he have robust physical fitness?
N Does he have sound mental fitness?
N Is he ambitious?
N Is he a good provider?
N Is he responsible about money?
N Does not drink alcohol to excess?

II. Are You Compatible?

Y Do you have common interests?
Y Do you enjoy his company?
Y Are you physically attracted to him?
Y Is he usually agreeable?
N Do you have the same friends?

III. Do You Have Shared Values?

N Do you get along with his family?
N Are you the same religion?
? Does he believe in matrimony?
? Does he want children?
? Would he be a good father?

6 # Yes

12 + He is a fine match!
8 + He is a fair match.
7 - He is completely unsuitable! !

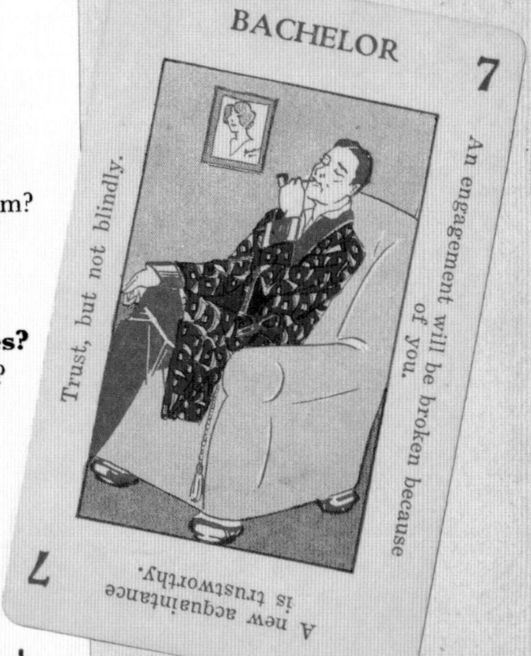
BACHELOR
7
Trust, but not blindly.
An engagement will be broken because of you.
A new acquaintance is trustworthy.
7

Maybe Oliver is just a confirmed bachelor.

Oh, dear . . .

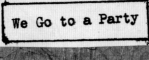

We Go to a Party

BERGDORF GOODMAN
616 FIFTH AVENUE
NEW YORK

Alden Fisher, O.'s roommate at Yale, invites us to a black tie house warming for his penthouse in a brand new building on Sutton Place.

Can't go, I sigh. Nothing to wear.

Next day, Oliver presents me with a dress box from Bergdorf's. Nestled in lavender tissue, a Premet gown in the latest color, "Acid."

We look like the haughty couple from the Arrow Shirt ad.

I use Neet to make myself downy smooth!

Neet
A fragrant antiseptic cream that removes hair
MADE IN THE U.S.A.

HIS QUICK EYE SAW THE SOFT WHITE
BEAUTY OF HER UNDERARM

According to Oliver, Alden's job is sinking his family's money into "little plays no one understands."

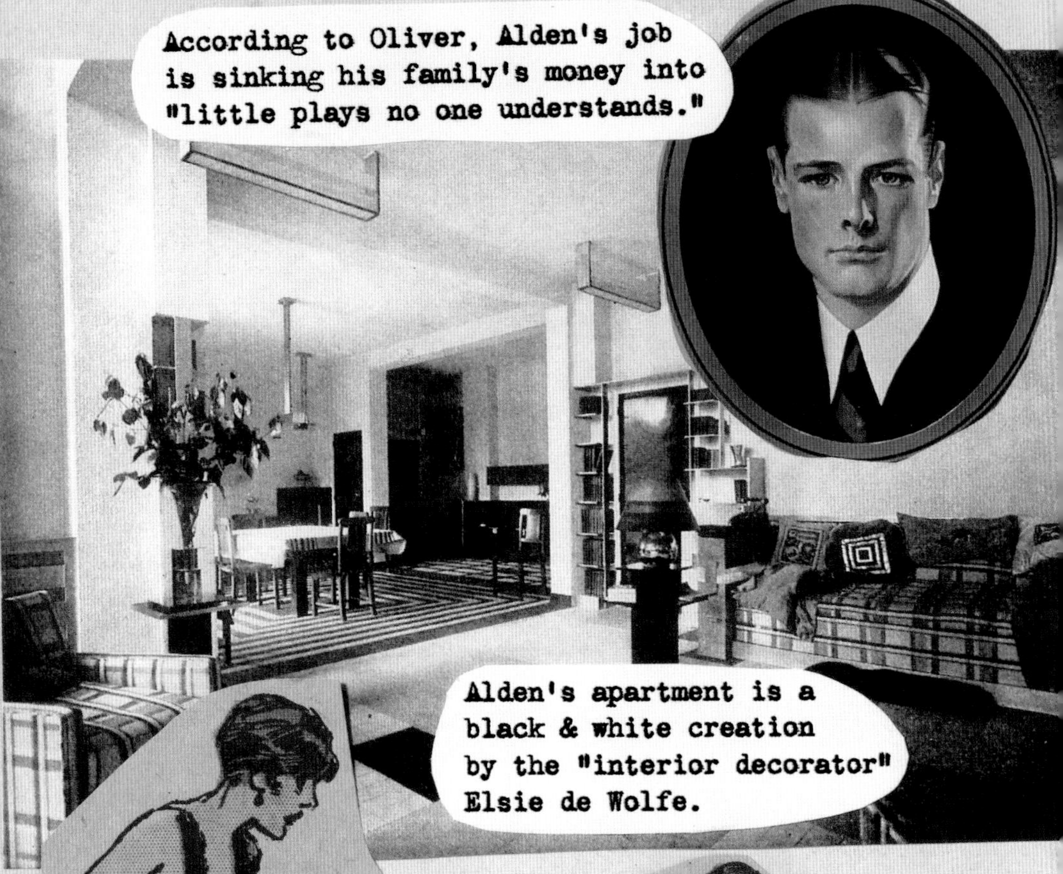

Alden's apartment is a black & white creation by the "interior decorator" Elsie de Wolfe.

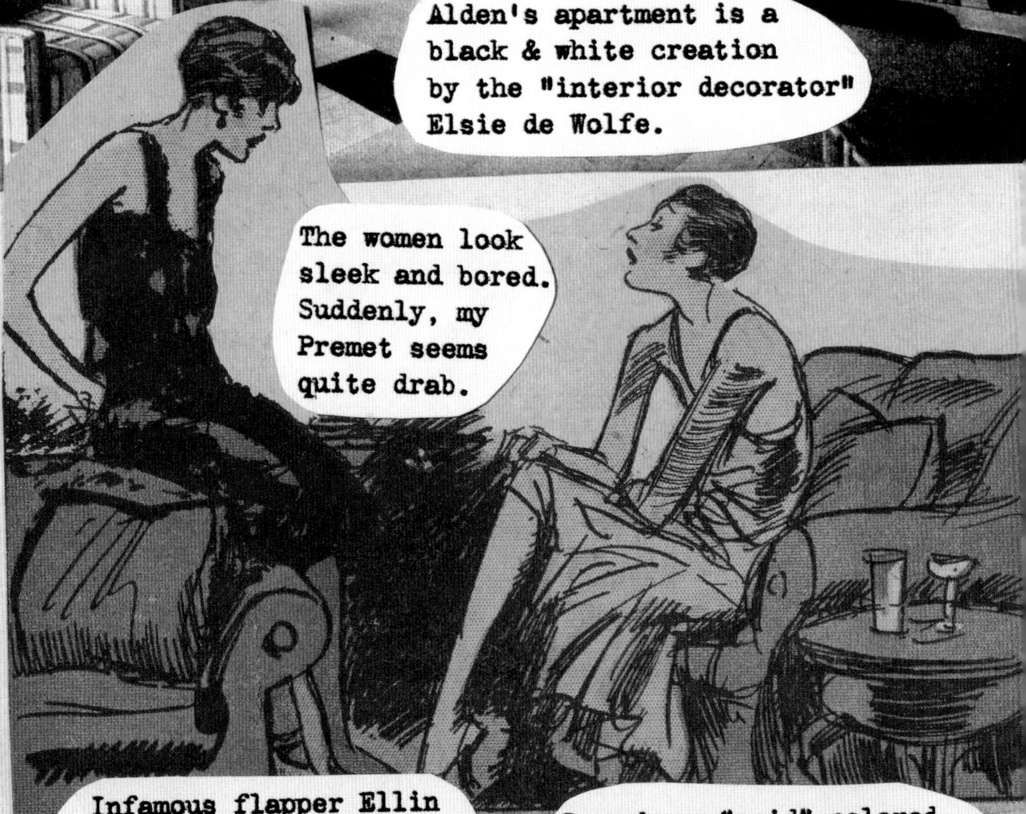

The women look sleek and bored. Suddenly, my Premet seems quite drab.

Infamous flapper Ellin Mackay, who shocked high society by running off with (older, divorced, Jewish) Irving Berlin.

I grab an "acid"-colored cocktail from a chrome tray. (No Orange Crush here.)

A Spin Around the Dance Floor

A hand grasps my upper arm and
steers me towards the rubber
dance floor (rolled over the
parquet to prevent scuff mark
. . . It's Chad Peabody.

"Well, now. You've spruced up
not a dowdy Vassar girl anymor

"I guess that's a complime
What are you doing these
You look prosperous." (Co
word for getting stout.)

"Selling stocks. Making a b
of course, like everyone els
Just bought my own penthouse
Madison. Bigger than this o

"Sounds impressive. Congratulat:

"Thanks." (Sarcasm flying ove:
thick head.) "Let me take you
to dinner sometime."

"I'm not really very availab

"Oh, right. You engage

"Almost."

"Anyone I know?"

"Yes, actually. Oliver Wol

(A perplexed pause.) "I'm surprised. He doesn't seem like your type."

"Oh, really? What is my type?"

(A shrug.) "I dunno. Probably said enough. I need another cocktail."

Where's Oliver? I think. He shouldn't abandon me to the likes of Chad Peabody.

I wander down a long hallway, open doors, peek inside. I find him in the butler's pantry.

Kissing

Alden Fisher

on the lips.

A two to one favorite

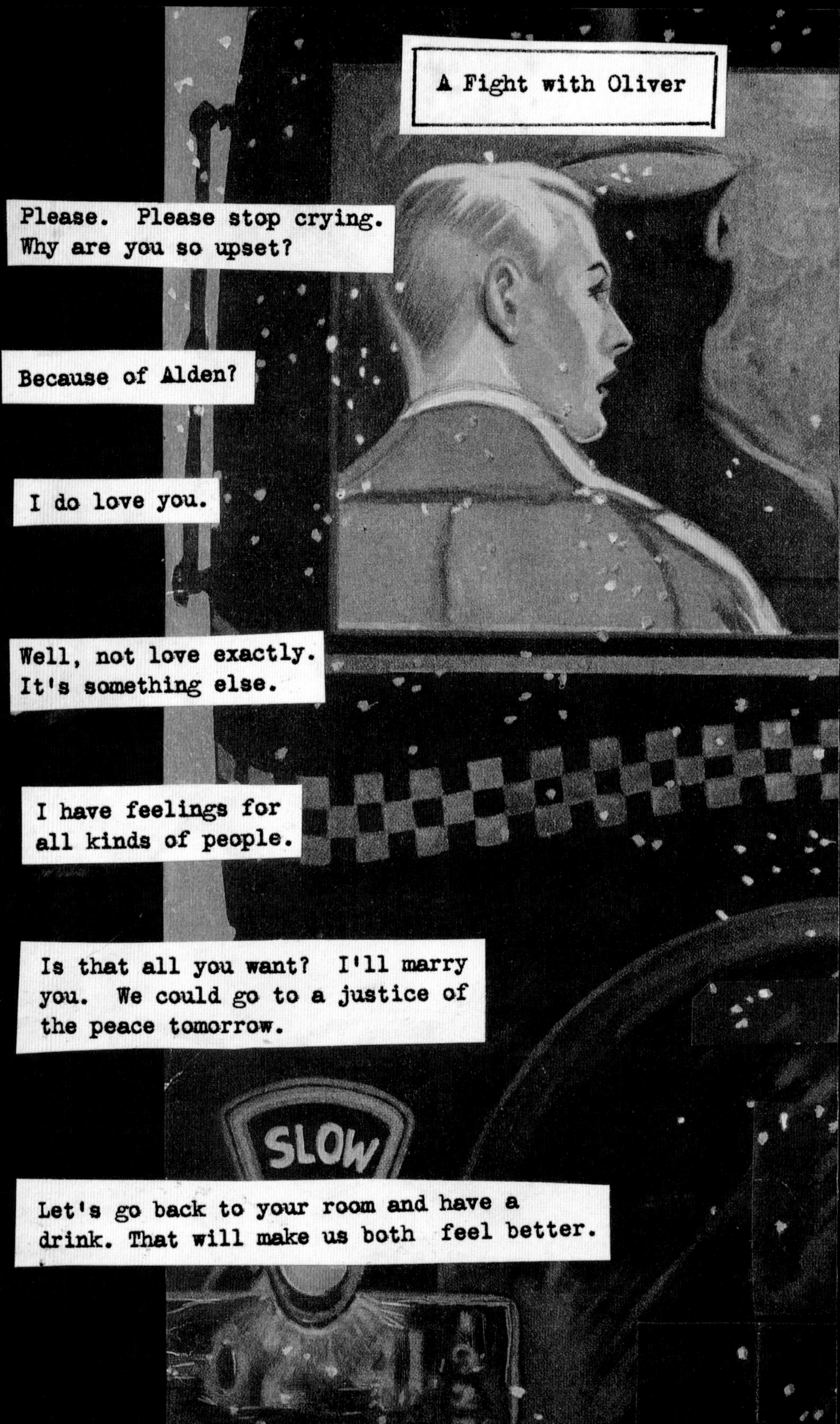
A Fight with Oliver
Please. Please stop crying. Why are you so upset?
Because of Alden?
I do love you.
Well, not love exactly. It's something else.
I have feelings for all kinds of people.
Is that all you want? I'll marry you. We could go to a justice of the peace tomorrow.
SLOW
Let's go back to your room and have a drink. That will make us both feel better.

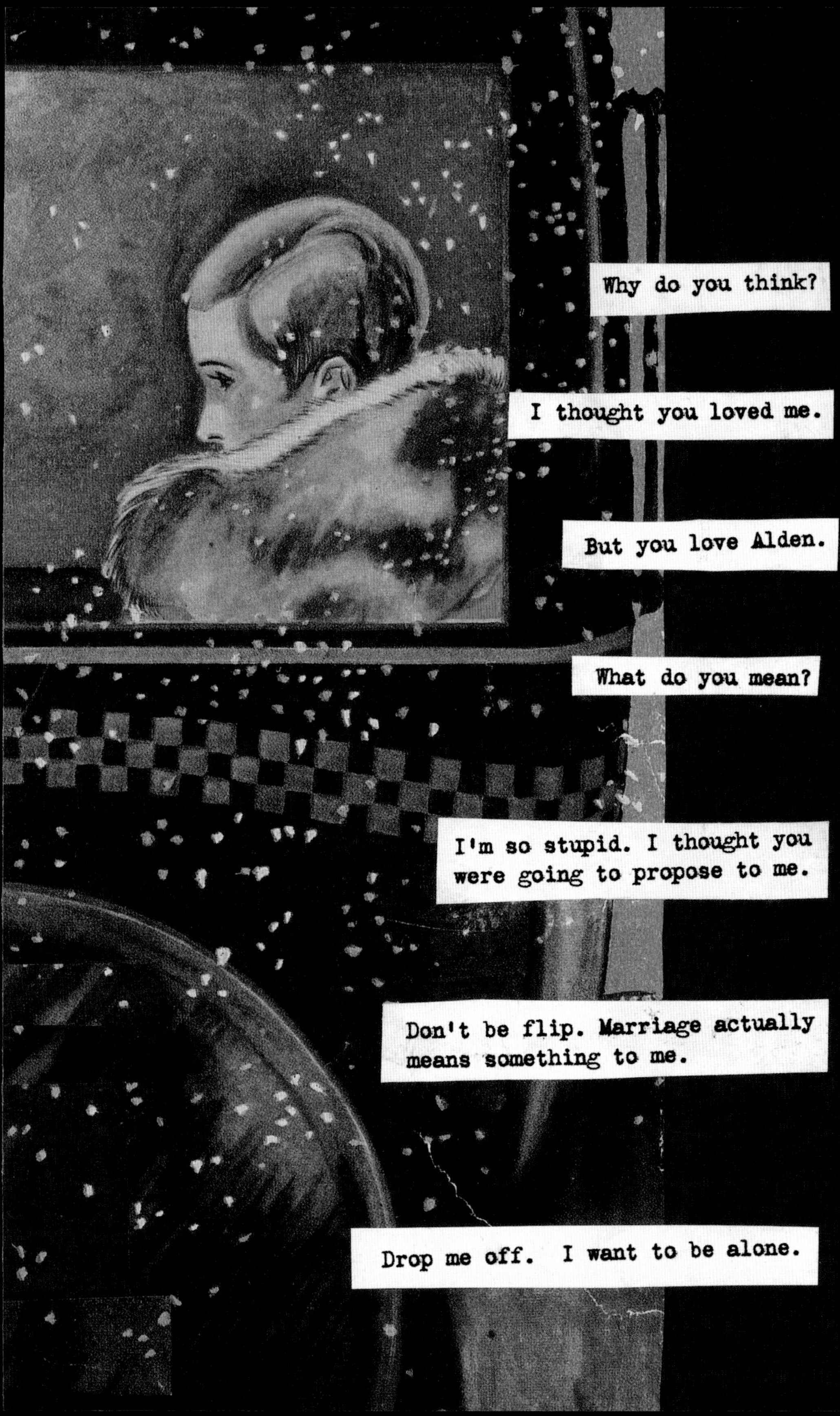
Why do you think?
I thought you loved me.
But you love Alden.
What do you mean?
I'm so stupid. I thought you were going to propose to me.
Don't be flip. Marriage actually means something to me.
Drop me off. I want to be alone.

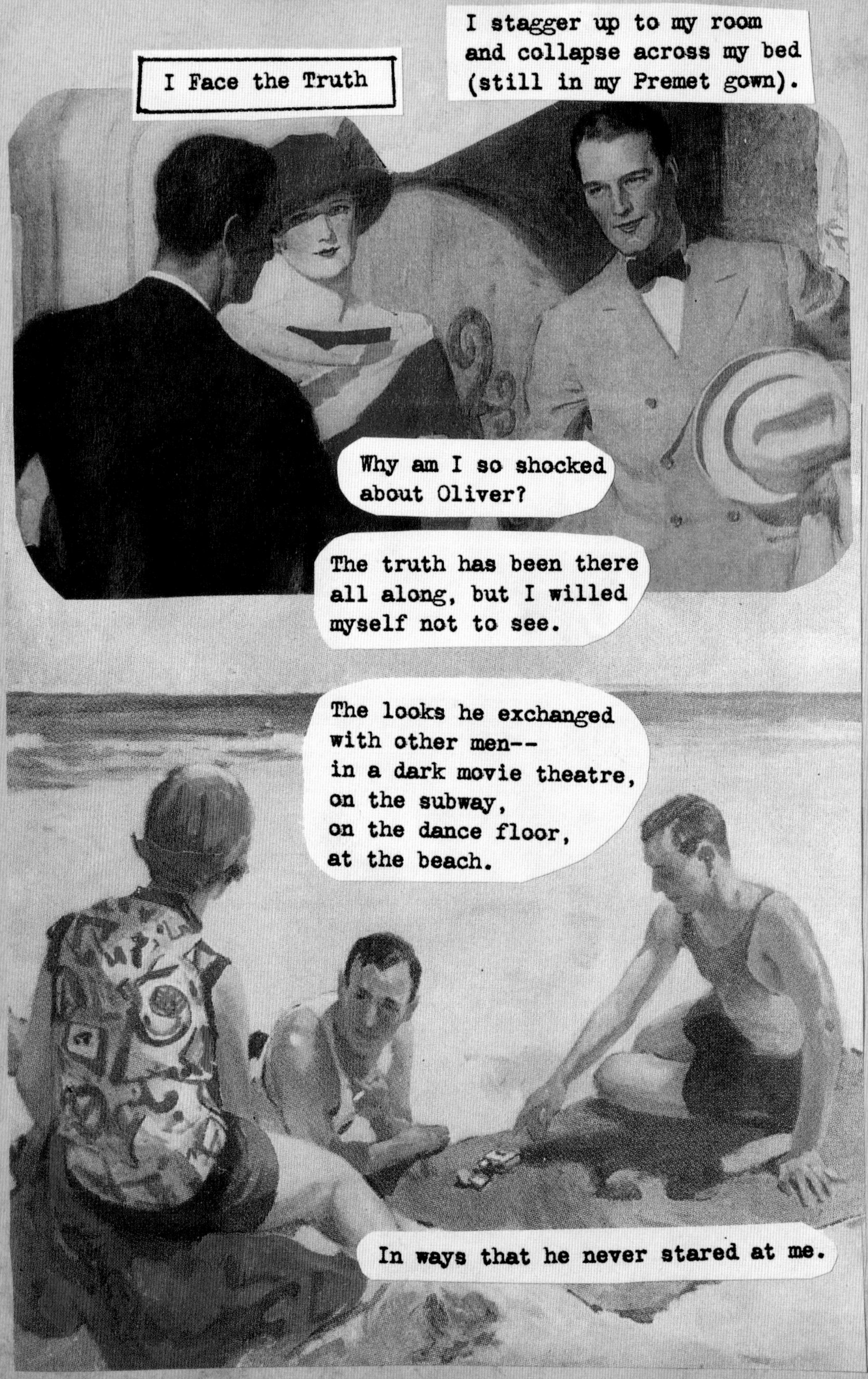
I Face the Truth
I stagger up to my room and collapse across my bed (still in my Premet gown).
Why am I so shocked about Oliver?
The truth has been there all along, but I willed myself not to see.
The looks he exchanged with other men-- in a dark movie theatre, on the subway, on the dance floor, at the beach.
In ways that he never stared at me.

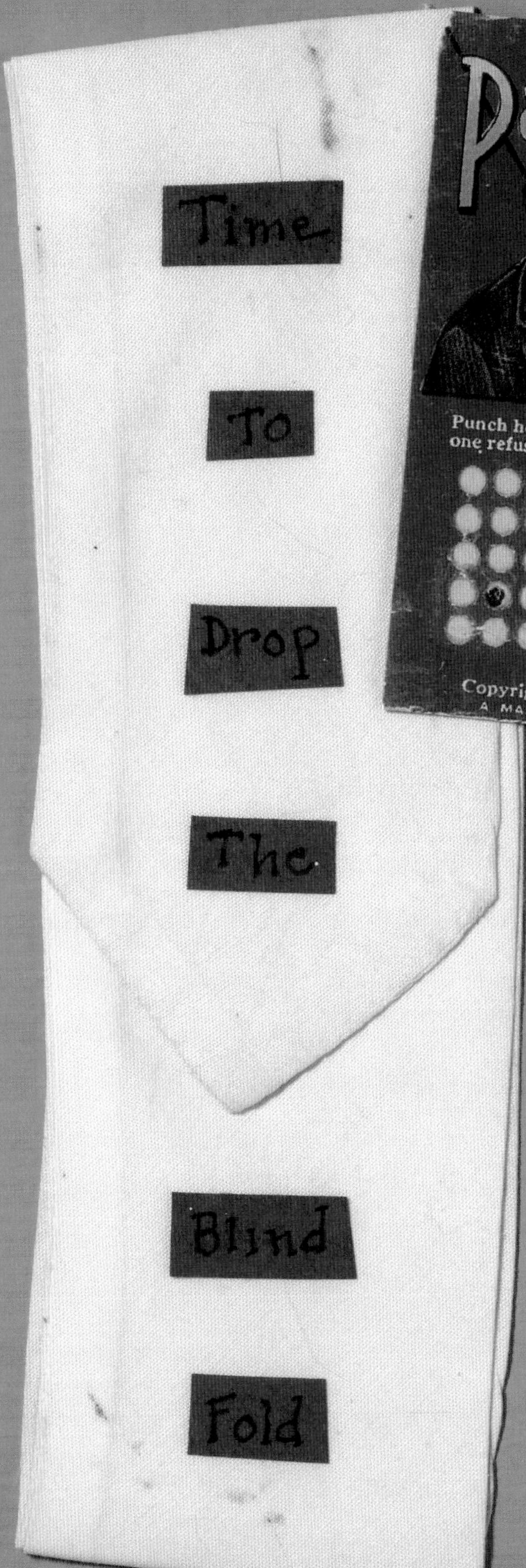
Time
To
Drop
The
Blind
Fold

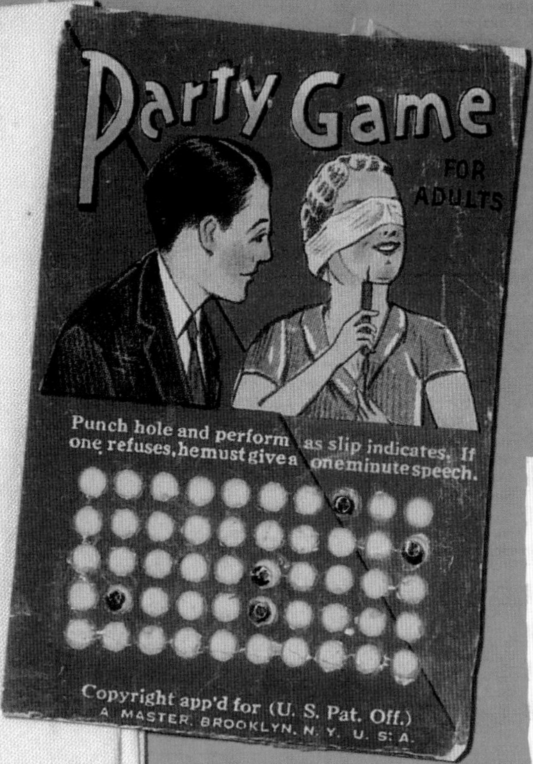
Party Game
FOR ADULTS
Punch hole and perform as slip indicates. If one refuses, he must give a one minute speech.
Copyright app'd for (U. S. Pat. Off.)
A MASTER, BROOKLYN, N. Y. U. S. A.

Answer any question given you.

The Facts

1. Oliver does love me, but it's love without passion. (Could only kiss me when he was drunk!)

2. At heart, I'm just like all those Vassar girls who only want rings on their fingers.

3. I say I want to be a writer, but all I've done so far is write True Stories.

4. It's time for a drastic change!

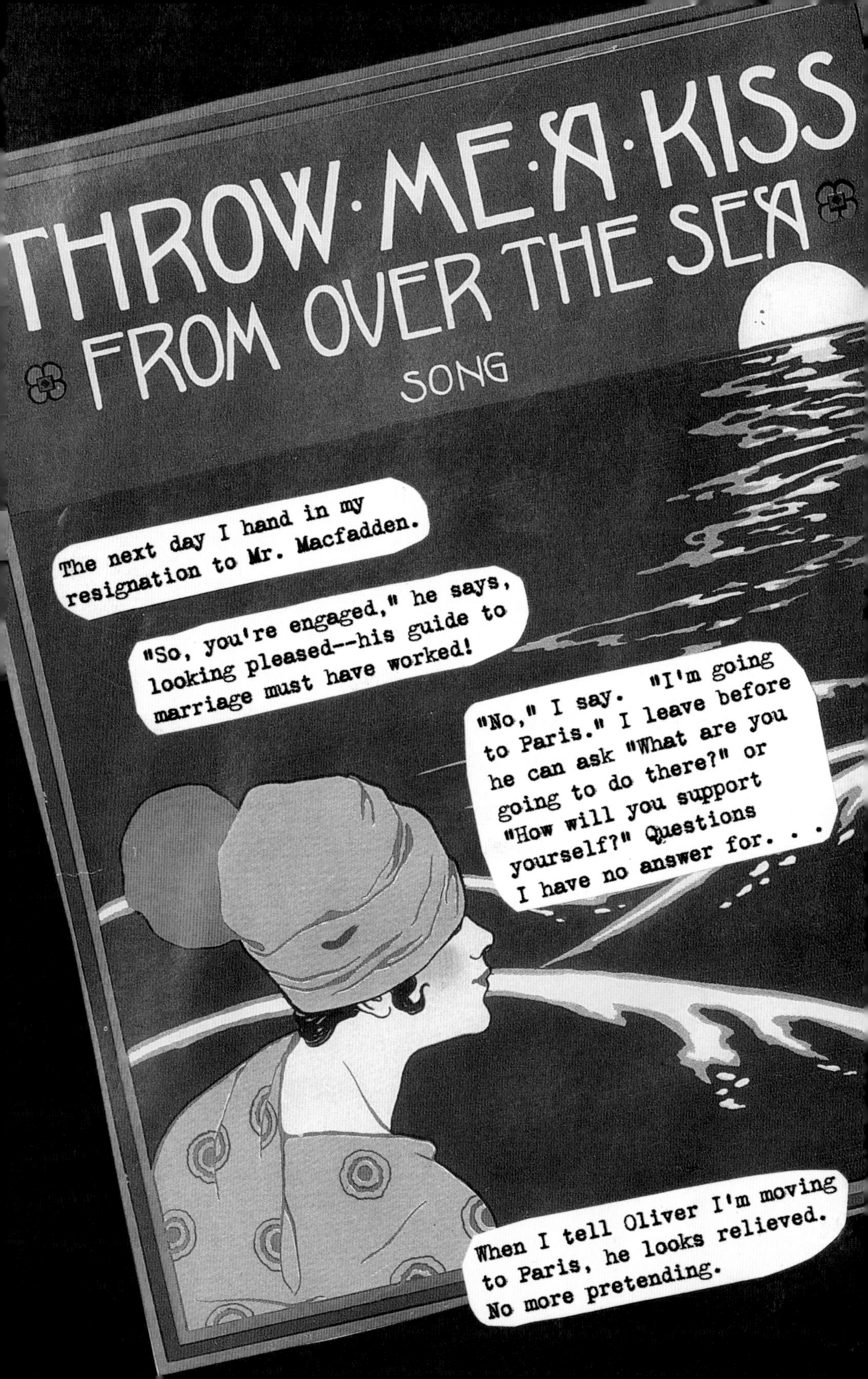
THROW·ME·A·KISS
FROM OVER THE SEA
SONG
The next day I hand in my resignation to Mr. Macfadden.
"So, you're engaged," he says, looking pleased--his guide to marriage must have worked!
"No," I say. "I'm going to Paris." I leave before he can ask "What are you going to do there?" or "How will you support yourself?" Questions I have no answer for. . .
When I tell Oliver I'm moving to Paris, he looks relieved. No more pretending.

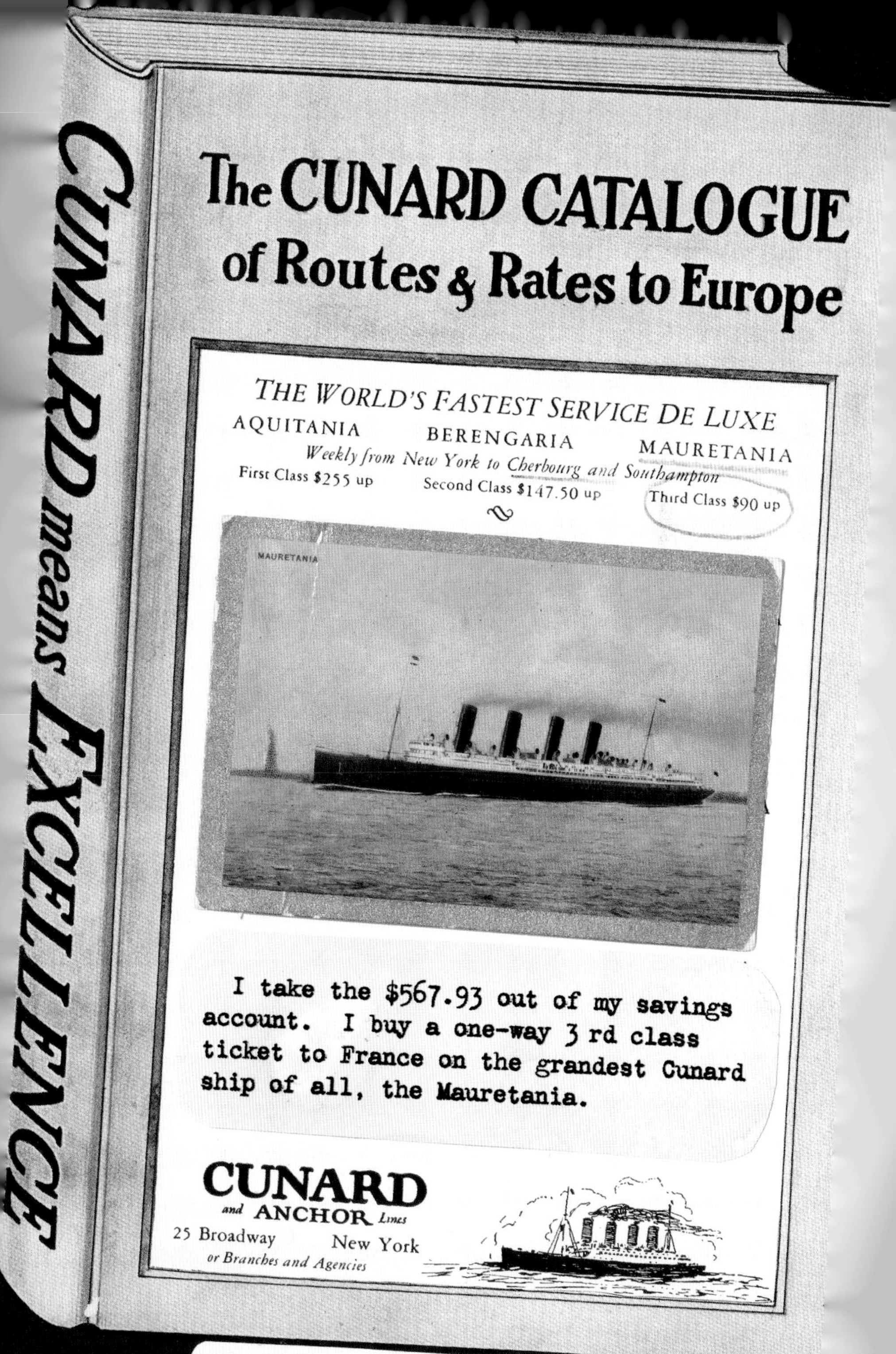
CUNARD means EXCELLENCE
The CUNARD CATALOGUE
of Routes & Rates to Europe
THE WORLD'S FASTEST SERVICE DE LUXE
AQUITANIA BERENGARIA MAURETANIA
Weekly from New York to Cherbourg and Southampton
First Class $255 up
Second Class $147.50 up
Third Class $90 up
MAURETANIA
CUNARD
and ANCHOR Lines
25 Broadway New York
or Branches and Agencies

I take the $567.93 out of my savings account. I buy a one-way 3 rd class ticket to France on the grandest Cunard ship of all, the Mauretania.

And I bid NYC & Oliver au revoir.

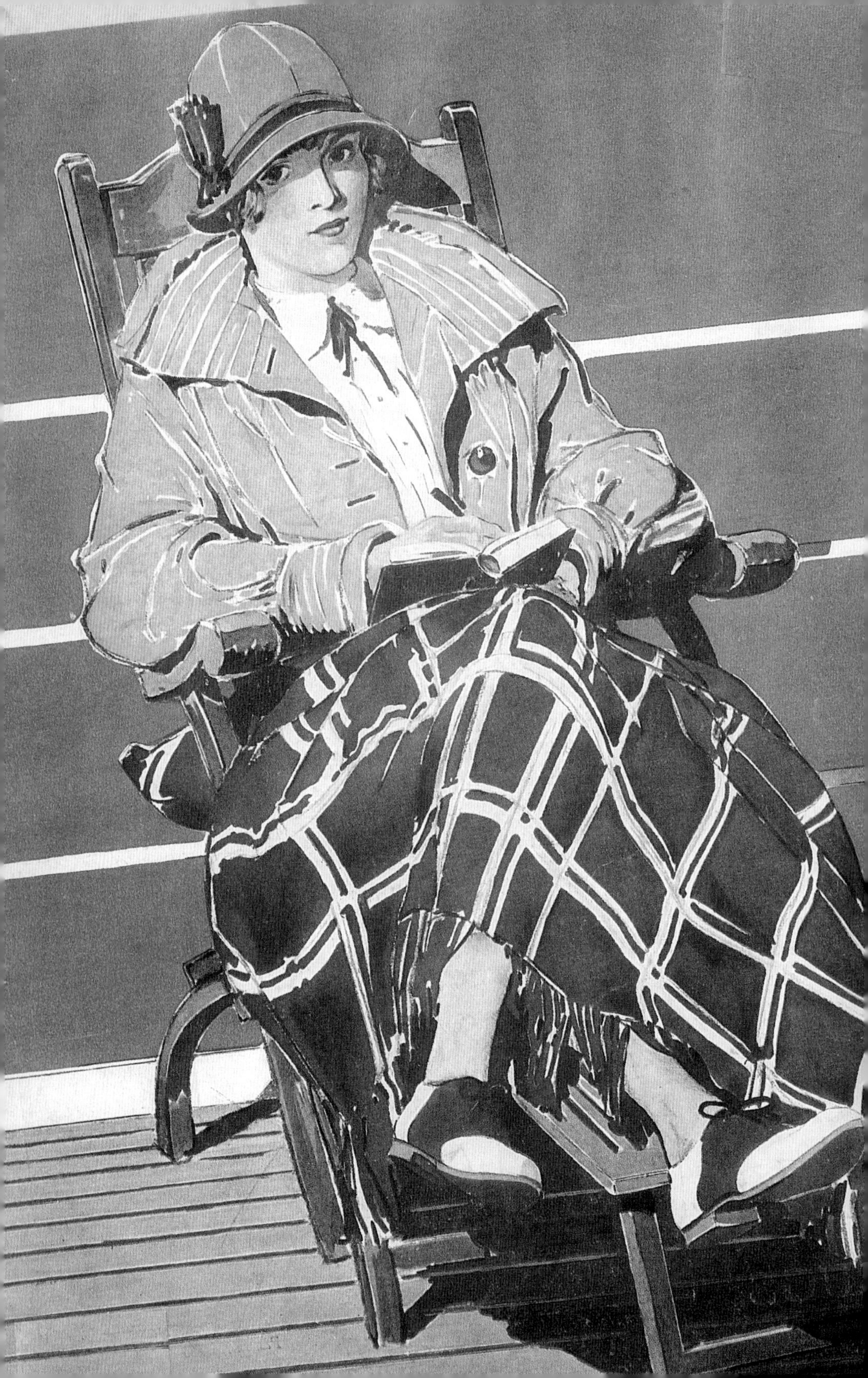

Chapter 4

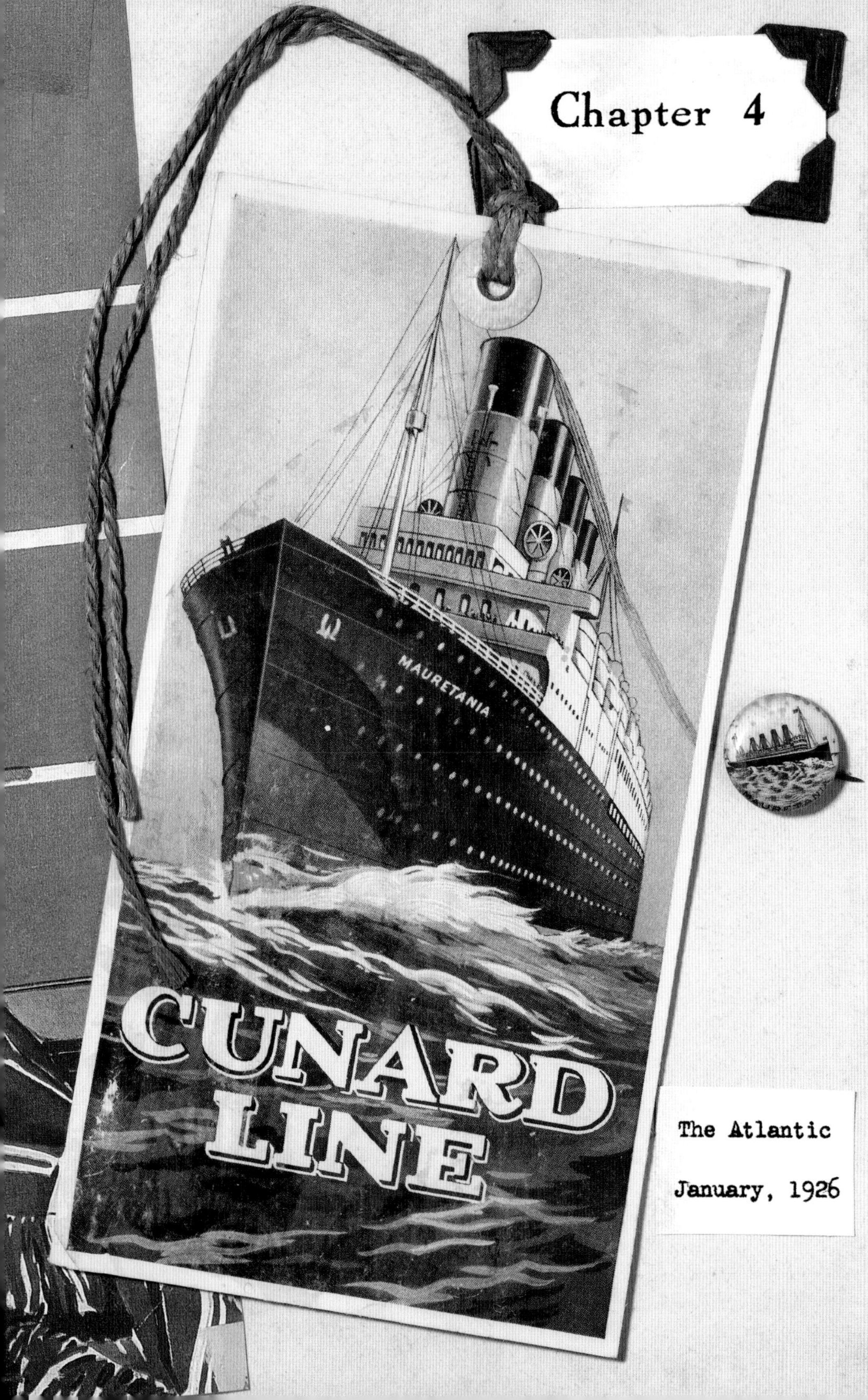
MAURETANIA
CUNARD LINE

The Atlantic

January, 1926

My Cabin

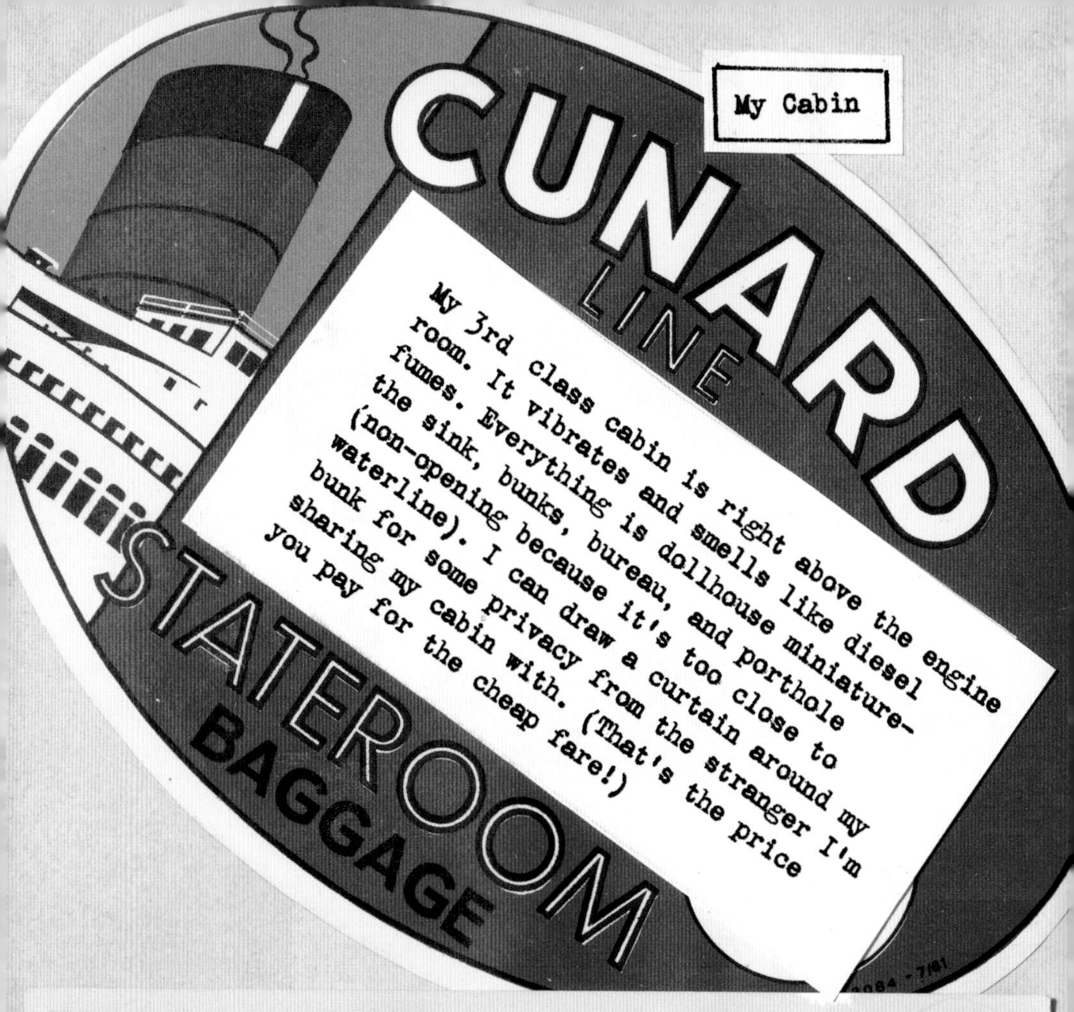
CUNARD
LINE
STATEROOM
BAGGAGE

My 3rd class cabin is right above the engine room. It vibrates and smells like diesel fumes. Everything is dollhouse miniature—the sink, bunks, bureau, and porthole (non-opening because it's too close to waterline). I can draw a curtain around my bunk for some privacy from the stranger I'm sharing my cabin with. (That's the price you pay for the cheap fare!)

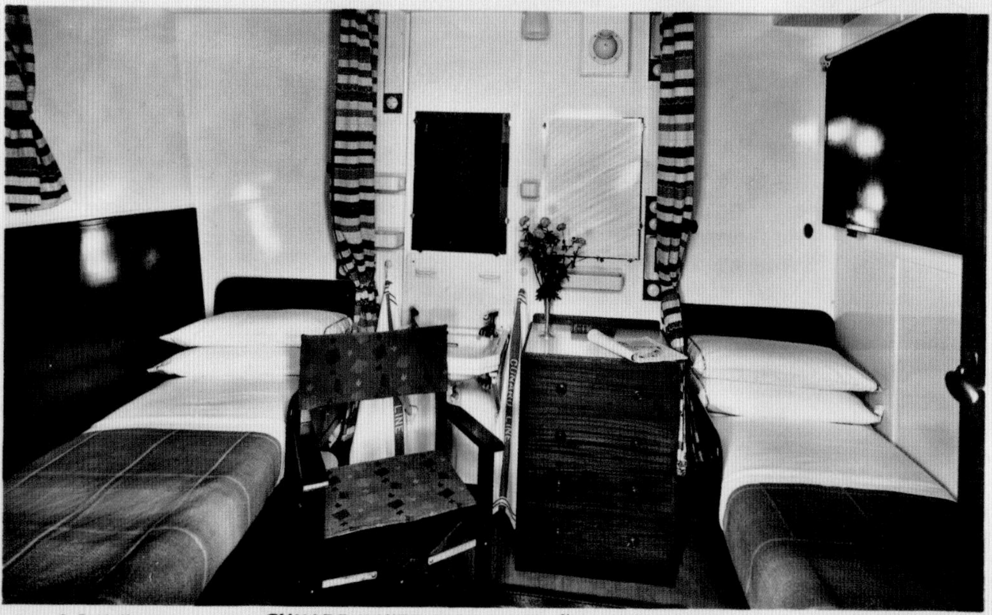

1288 C. R. Hoffmann, Southampton. CUNARD WHITE STAR LINER "MAURETANIA." 34.000 TONS

THIRD CLASS CABIN.

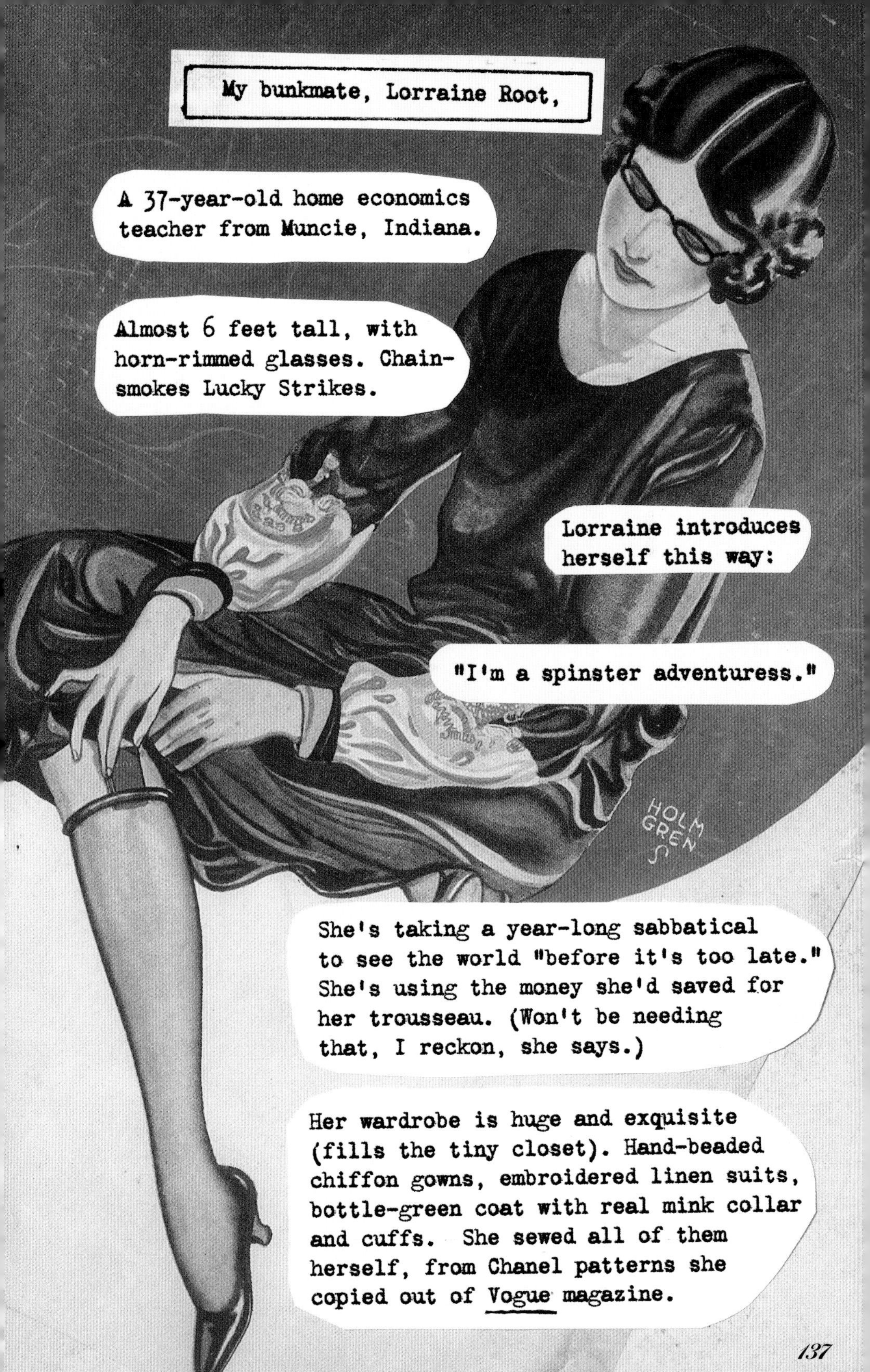
My bunkmate, Lorraine Root,
A 37-year-old home economics teacher from Muncie, Indiana.
Almost 6 feet tall, with horn-rimmed glasses. Chain-smokes Lucky Strikes.
Lorraine introduces herself this way:
"I'm a spinster adventuress."
HOLMGREN
She's taking a year-long sabbatical to see the world "before it's too late." She's using the money she'd saved for her trousseau. (Won't be needing that, I reckon, she says.)
Her wardrobe is huge and exquisite (fills the tiny closet). Hand-beaded chiffon gowns, embroidered linen suits, bottle-green coat with real mink collar and cuffs. She sewed all of them herself, from Chanel patterns she copied out of Vogue magazine.

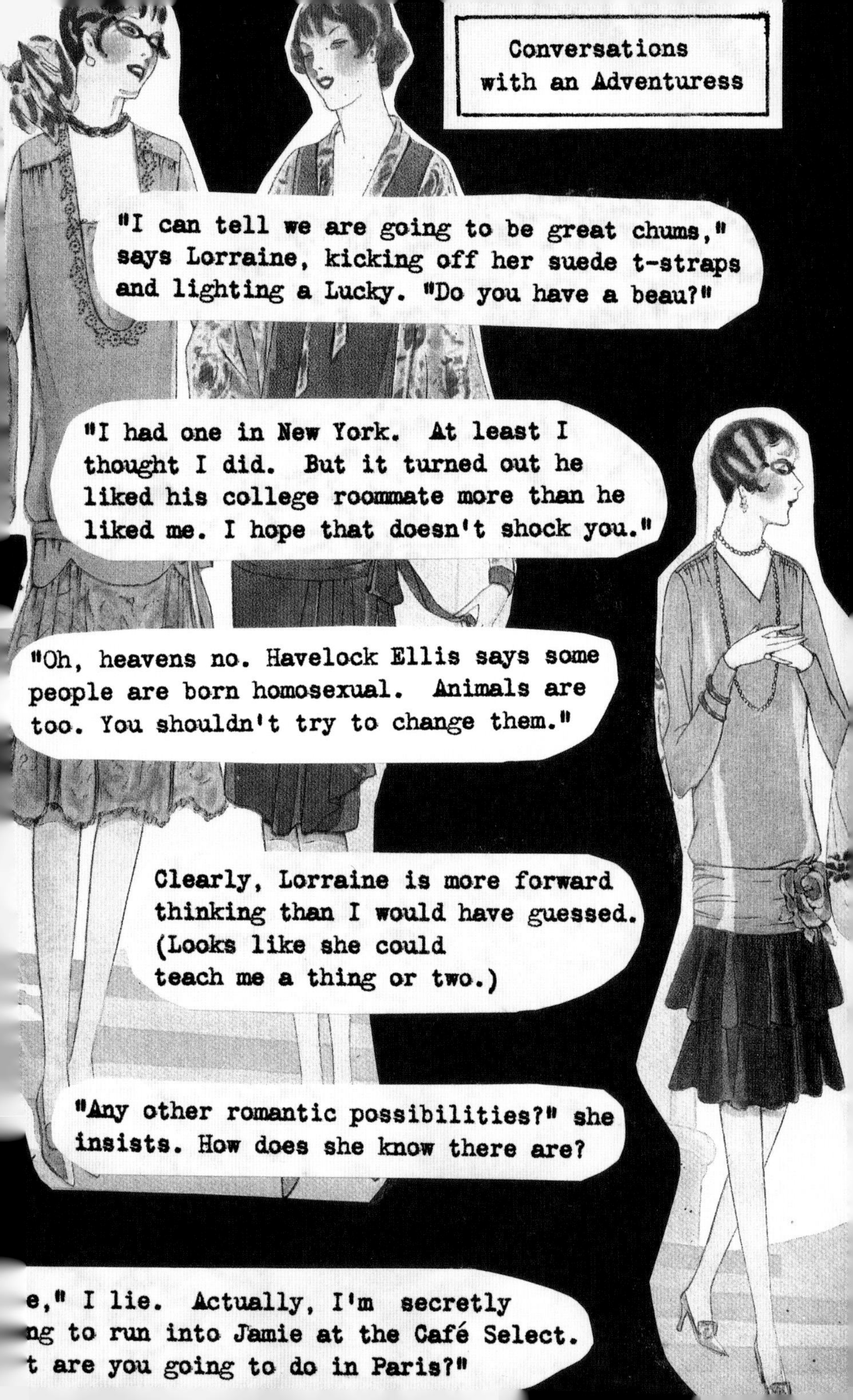
Conversations with an Adventuress
"I can tell we are going to be great chums," says Lorraine, kicking off her suede t-straps and lighting a Lucky. "Do you have a beau?"
"I had one in New York. At least I thought I did. But it turned out he liked his college roommate more than he liked me. I hope that doesn't shock you."
"Oh, heavens no. Havelock Ellis says some people are born homosexual. Animals are too. You shouldn't try to change them."
Clearly, Lorraine is more forward thinking than I would have guessed. (Looks like she could teach me a thing or two.)
"Any other romantic possibilities?" she insists. How does she know there are?
e," I lie. Actually, I'm secretly
ng to run into Jamie at the Café Select.
t are you going to do in Paris?"

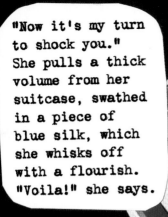

"Now it's my turn to shock you." She pulls a thick volume from her suitcase, swathed in a piece of blue silk, which she whisks off with a flourish. "Voila!" she says.

It's Ulysses by James Joyce, the <u>notorious</u> banned novel! Everyone in New York talked about it, but I've never seen a real-life copy.

"Mr. Joyce lives in Paris. I've written and he's agreed to autograph my book. Have you read it?" she says.

"Not yet," I admit. Even Oliver said it was too hard to understand.

"You must." She presses <u>Ulysses</u> into my hands. "Pure genius!"

ULYSSES

CUNARD LINE

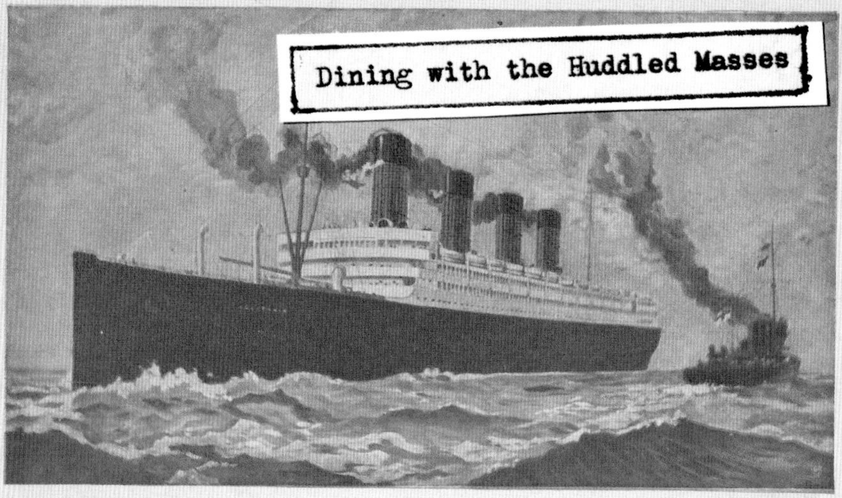

Dining with the Huddled Masses

TOURISTS' THIRD CABIN

- - LUNCHEON - -

Consomme Pauvre Homme   Barley Broth

Fried Plaice

Ox-Tail—Jardiniere

Puree of Turnips   Mashed Potatoes

COLD

Bologna Sausage

A sample of the swill they serve the lowly third class. We hear rumors of the feasts up in first-- oysters, beef Wellington, and flaming baked Alaska.

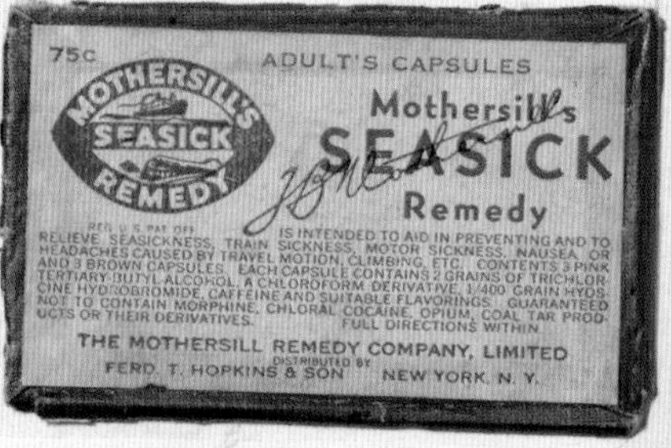
75c
ADULT'S CAPSULES
MOTHERSILL'S SEASICK REMEDY
Mothersill's
SEASICK
Remedy
REG. U.S. PAT. OFF.
IS INTENDED TO AID IN PREVENTING AND TO RELIEVE SEASICKNESS, TRAIN SICKNESS, MOTOR SICKNESS, NAUSEA, OR HEADACHES CAUSED BY TRAVEL MOTION, CLIMBING, ETC. CONTENTS 3 PINK AND 3 BROWN CAPSULES. EACH CAPSULE CONTAINS 2 GRAINS OF TRICHLOR TERTIARY BUTYL ALCOHOL, A CHLOROFORM DERIVATIVE, 1/400 GRAIN HYOSCINE HYDROBROMIDE, CAFFEINE AND SUITABLE FLAVORINGS. GUARANTEED NOT TO CONTAIN MORPHINE, CHLORAL, COCAINE, OPIUM, COAL TAR PRODUCTS OR THEIR DERIVATIVES.
FULL DIRECTIONS WITHIN
THE MOTHERSILL REMEDY COMPANY, LIMITED
DISTRIBUTED BY
FERD. T. HOPKINS & SON NEW YORK, N. Y.

Coffee   Cheese

Most everyone in third is seasick. (Except Lorraine and me-- we are of hearty pioneer stock.) Is it the food or the fumes?

..., NEW YORK

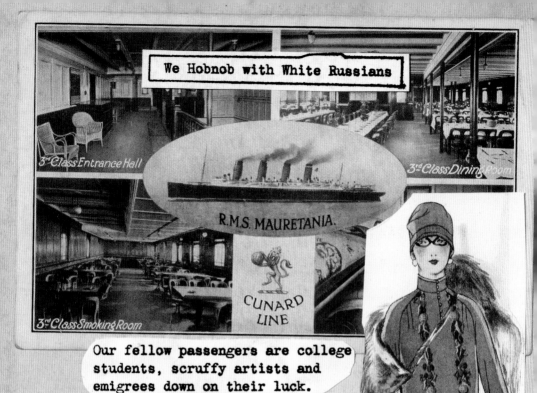

We Hobnob with White Russians

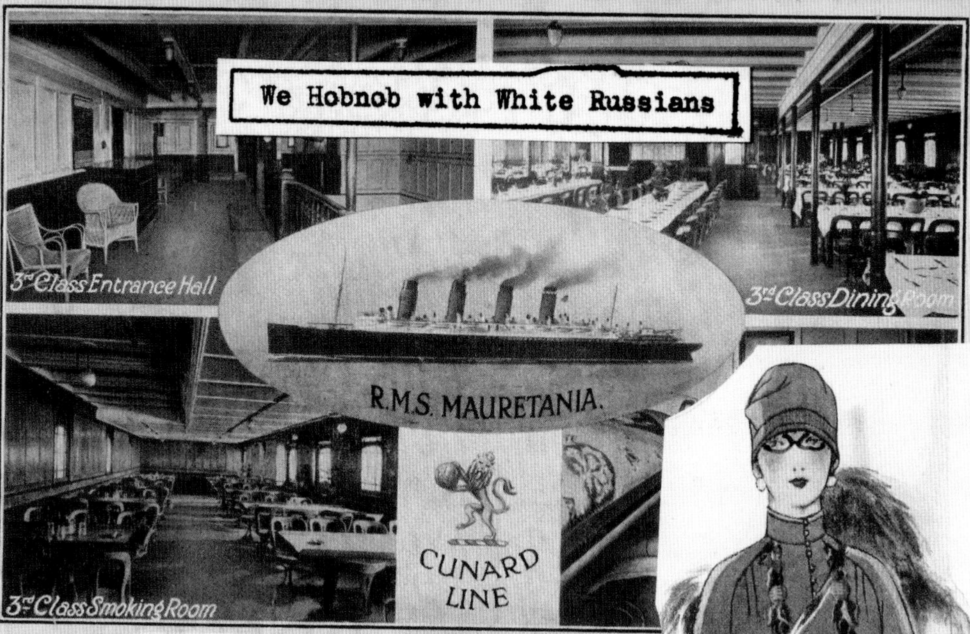
3rd Class Entrance Hall
3rd Class Dining Room
R.M.S. MAURETANIA.
CUNARD LINE
3rd Class Smoking Room

Our fellow passengers are college students, scruffy artists and emigrees down on their luck.

We sit next to Russian royalty! Princes Gregor and Alexei Volkonsky, who fled the Bolsheviks in 1919. Only 32 and 29, but seem prematurely aged. Their dinner jackets have moth holes, and they slip the Parker House rolls into their pockets.

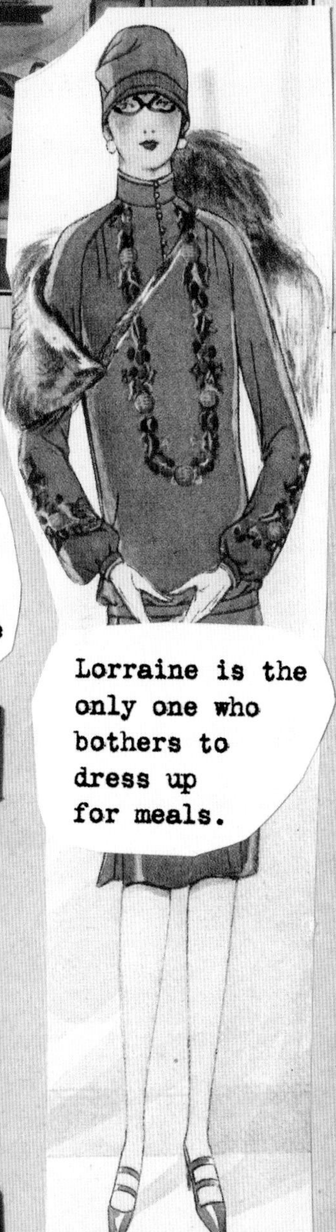

Lorraine is the only one who bothers to dress up for meals.

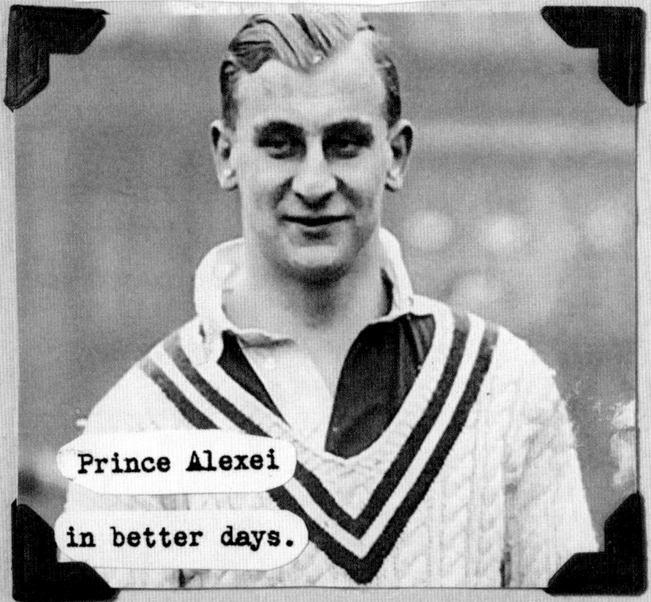

Prince Alexei in better days.

Shipboard Amusements

After dinner, Lorraine steers us to the saloon for "the games." The princes, who seem to have taken a shine to us, tag along.

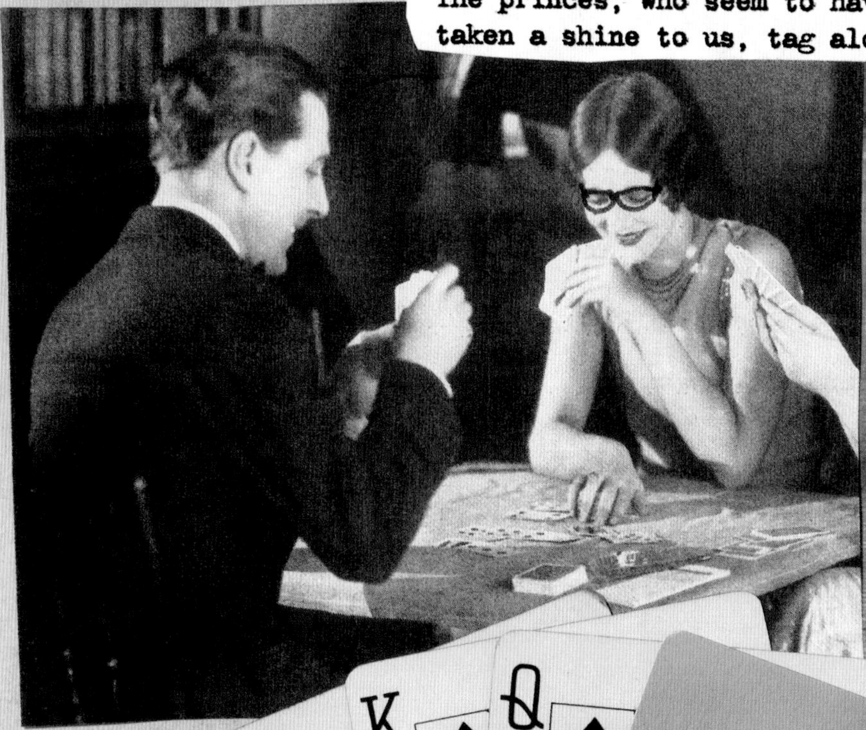

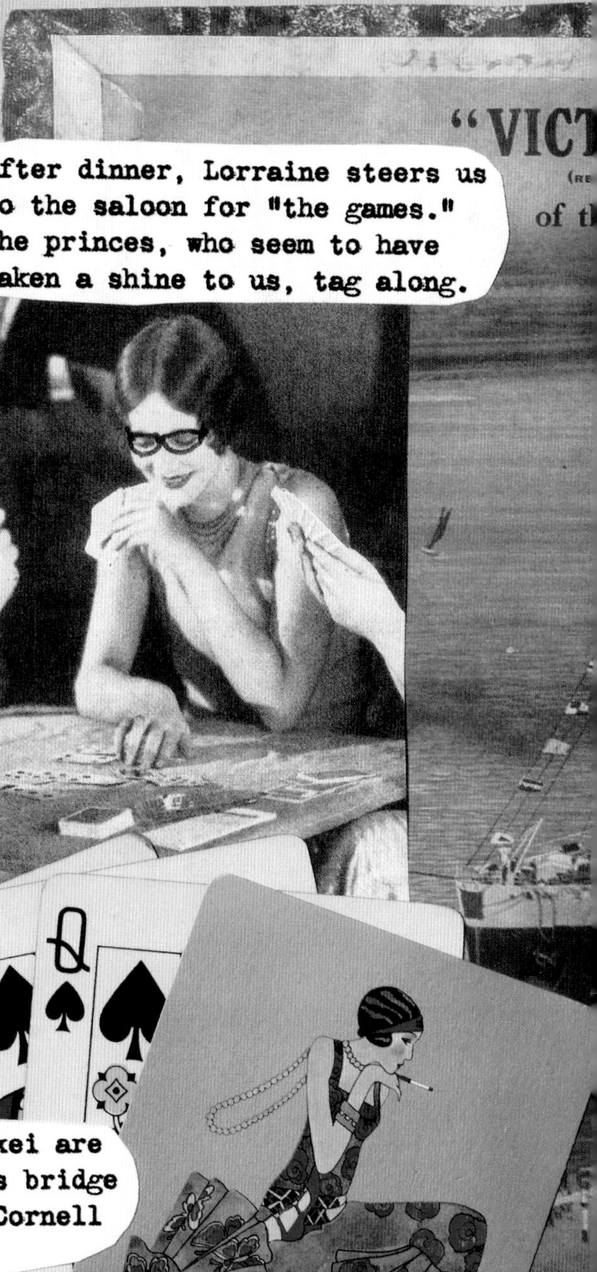

Lorraine and Prince Alexei are swept into a high-stakes bridge game against a pair of Cornell students.

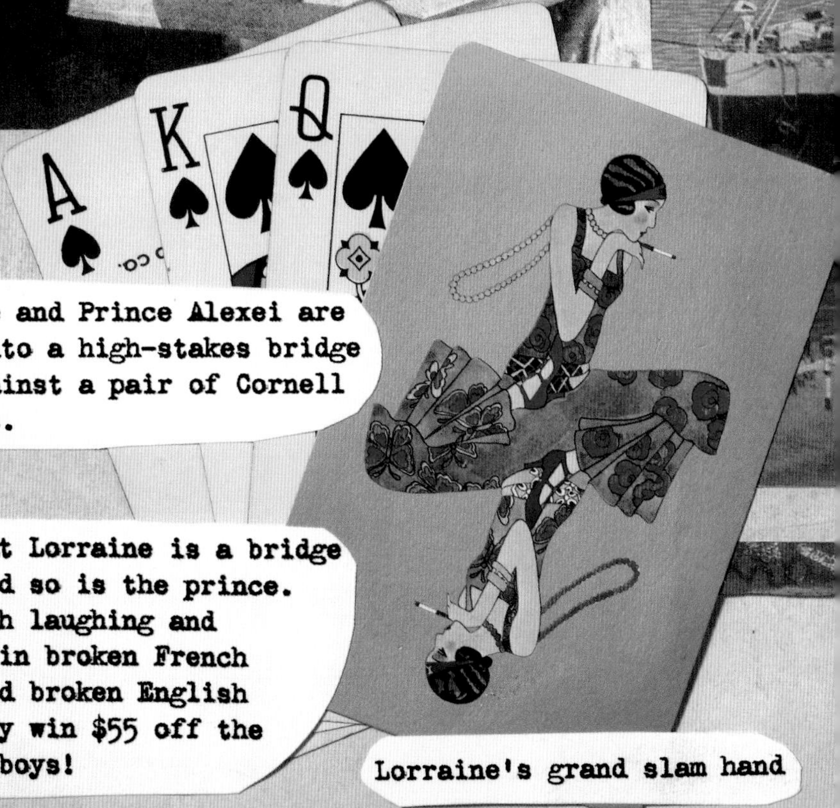
A
K
Q

Turns out Lorraine is a bridge whiz, and so is the prince. With much laughing and bidding in broken French (she) and broken English (he),they win $55 off the college boys!

Lorraine's grand slam hand

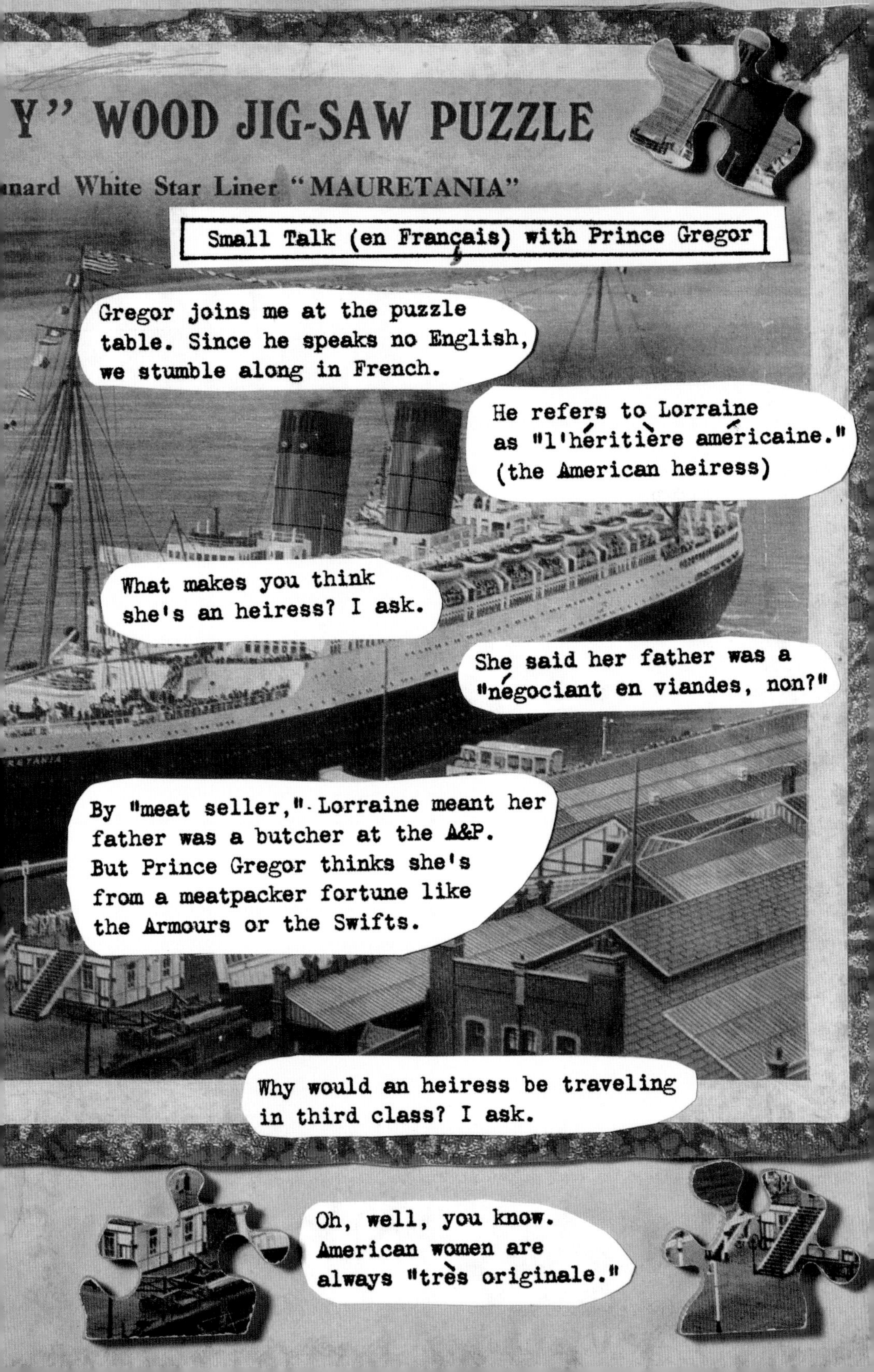
Y" WOOD JIG-SAW PUZZLE
nard White Star Liner "MAURETANIA"

Small Talk (en Français) with Prince Gregor

Gregor joins me at the puzzle table. Since he speaks no English, we stumble along in French.

He refers to Lorraine as "l'héritière américaine." (the American heiress)

What makes you think she's an heiress? I ask.

She said her father was a "négociant en viandes, non?"

By "meat seller," Lorraine meant her father was a butcher at the A&P. But Prince Gregor thinks she's from a meatpacker fortune like the Armours or the Swifts.

Why would an heiress be traveling in third class? I ask.

Oh, well, you know. American women are always "très originale."

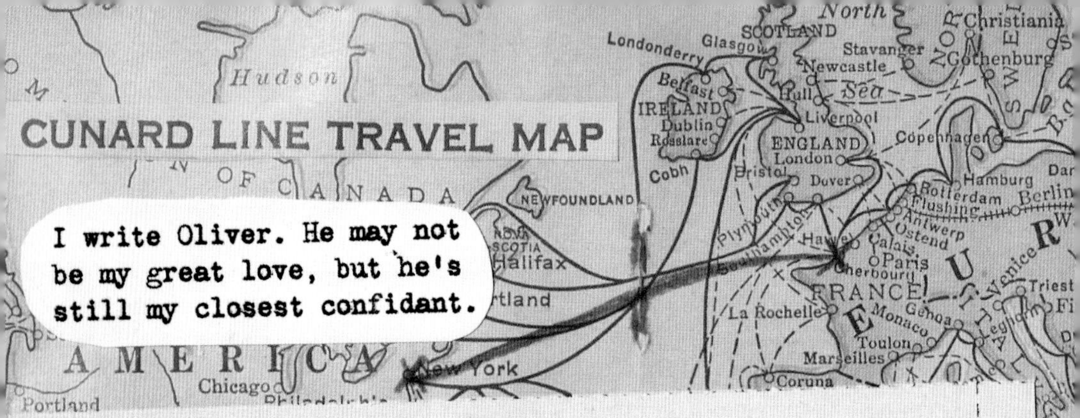
CUNARD LINE TRAVEL MAP
Hudson
OF CANADA
AMERICA
NEWFOUNDLAND
NOVA SCOTIA
Halifax
New York
Chicago
Portland
North
SCOTLAND
Londonderry
Glasgow
Stavanger
Christiania
Gothenburg
Newcastle
Belfast
Hull
Sea
IRELAND
Dublin
Rosslare
Liverpool
ENGLAND
London
Copenhagen
Cobh
Bristol
Dover
Hamburg
Rotterdam
Berlin
Flushing
Antwerp
Ostend
Plymouth
Southampton
Havre
Calais
Paris
Cherbourg
FRANCE
Venice
Triest
La Rochelle
Monaco
Genoa
Leghorn
Toulon
Marseilles
Coruna

I write Oliver. He may not be my great love, but he's still my closest confidant.

Cunard White Star

R·M·S "Mauretania"

Dear Oliver,

I am holed up in my stuffy cabin typing letters. Don't dare venture into the lounge because I am being madly pursued by a threadbare Russian prince who is missing a few teeth and appears by his thumping limp to have a wooden leg. His younger (and far more presentable) brother is wooing my jolly cabin mate Lorraine (who he mistakenly thinks is filthy rich).

Guess what-- I've already found a place to live in Paris! James Joyce's publisher (who also runs an English bookstore called Shakespeare & Company) has offered Lorraine a room to rent above the shop, and I can stay there too. So I will be in the beating heart of the expat Left Bank. Stay tuned.

Speaking of James Joyce, I have spent most of the voyage on a deck chair wrapped in a steamer rug, trying to read Ulysses. (The prince has weak lungs and has to avoid Atlantic winds.) Mostly I skip around to the shocking parts. Leopold Bloom in the outhouse, in the brothel, leering at a girl's knickers on the beach. Not sure I appreciate such Highfalutin lit-ar-a-tour, but at least now I can claim that I have (mostly) read Ulysses.

I miss you lots! Hugs,

F.

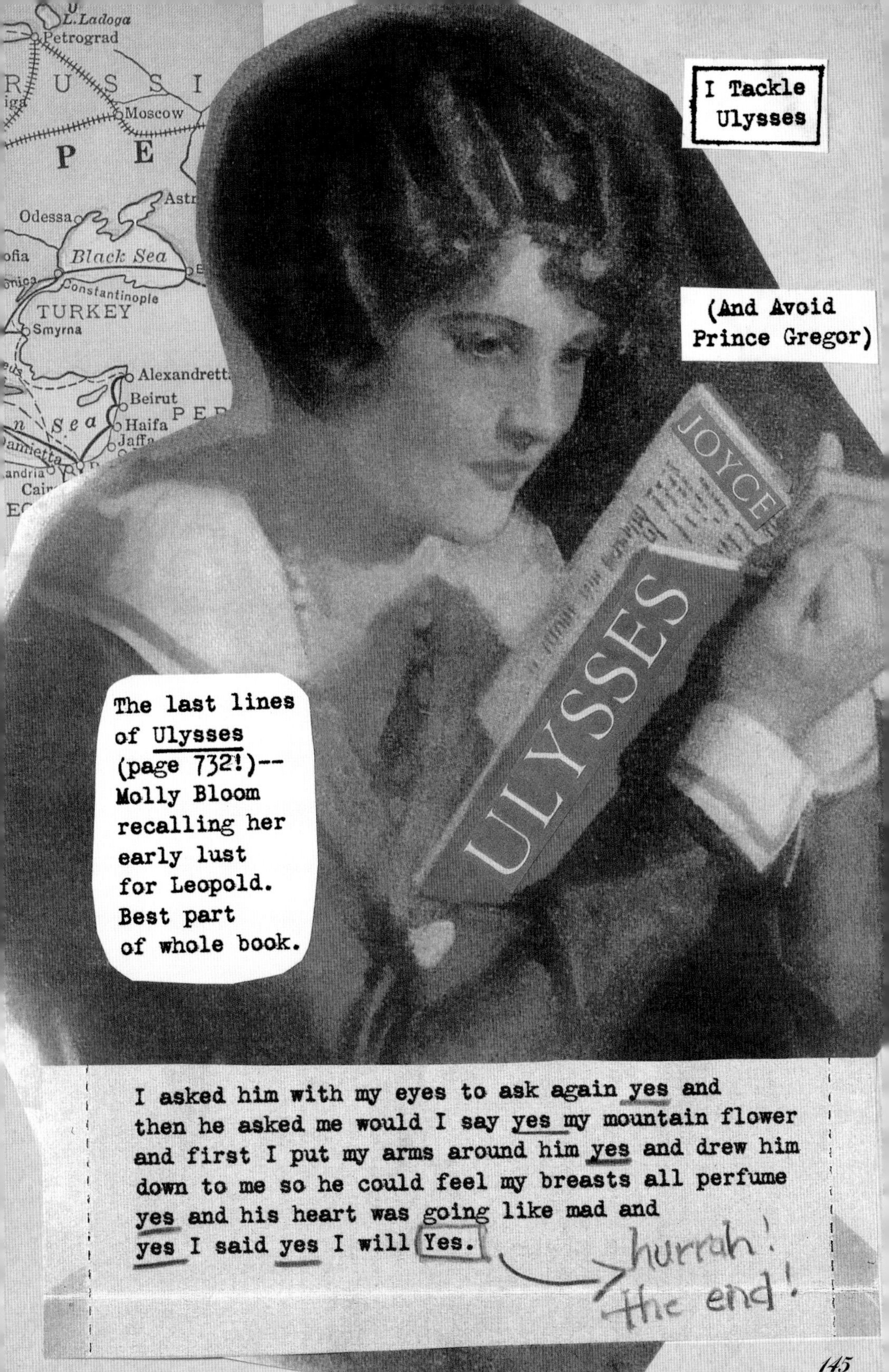

I Tackle Ulysses
(And Avoid Prince Gregor)
L. Ladoga
Petrograd
RUSSI
Moscow
PE
Odessa
Black Sea
Constantinople
TURKEY
Smyrna
Alexandrett
Beirut
Haifa
Jaffa
JOYCE
ULYSSES
The last lines of Ulysses (page 732!)-- Molly Bloom recalling her early lust for Leopold. Best part of whole book.
I asked him with my eyes to ask again yes and then he asked me would I say yes my mountain flower and first I put my arms around him yes and drew him down to me so he could feel my breasts all perfume yes and his heart was going like mad and yes I said yes I will Yes.
hurrah! the end!

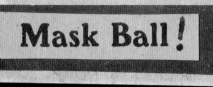

Mask Ball!

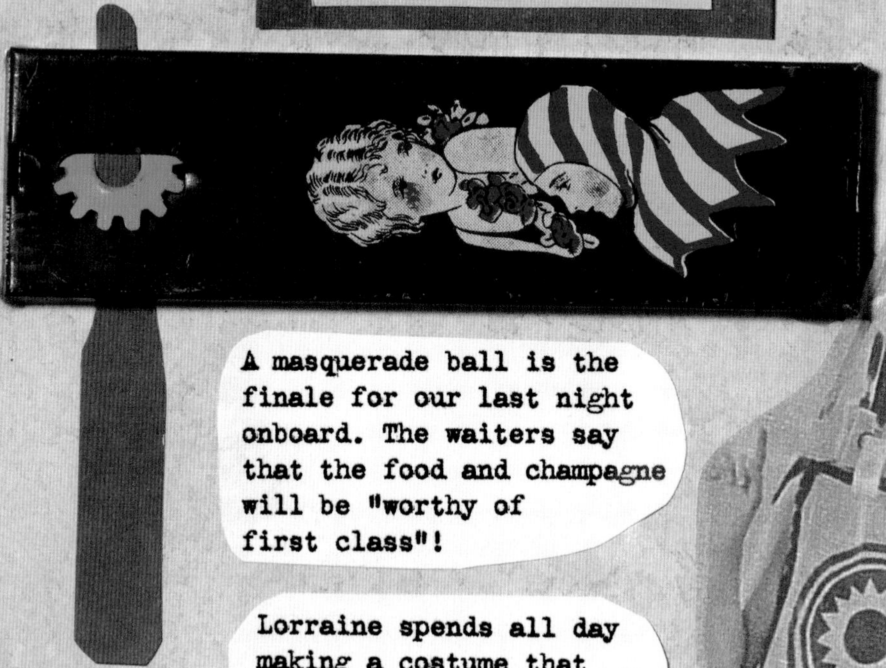

A masquerade ball is the finale for our last night onboard. The waiters say that the food and champagne will be "worthy of first class"!

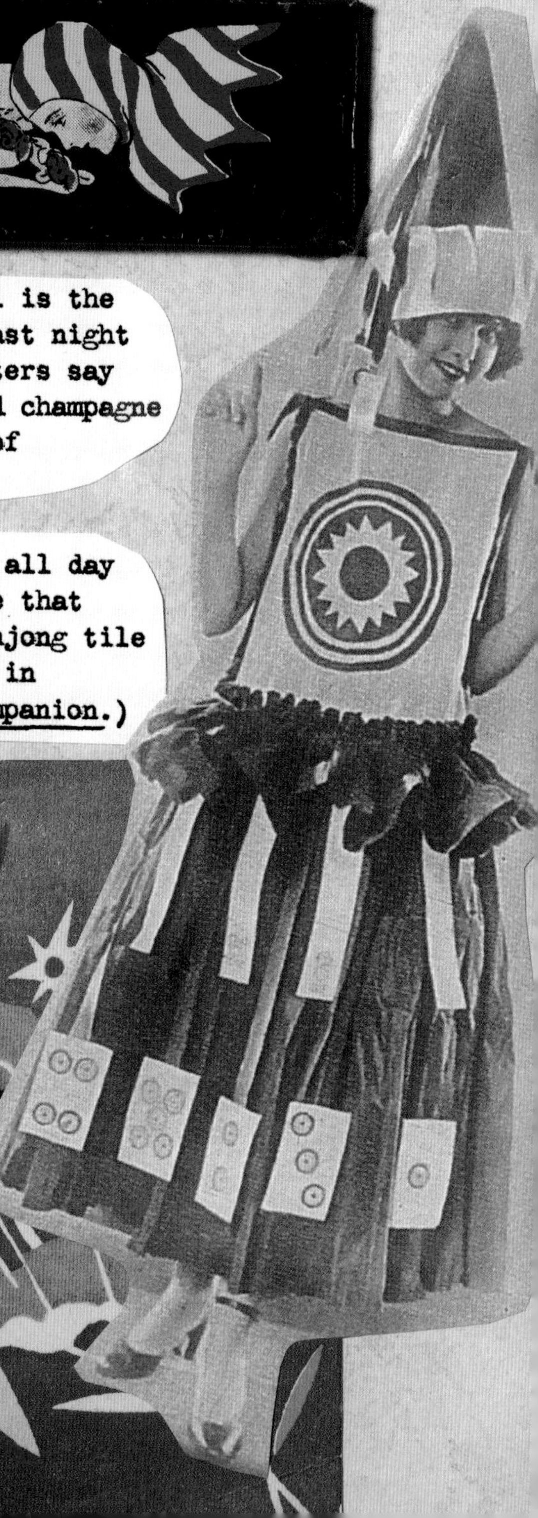

Lorraine spends all day making a costume that looks like a Mahjong tile (from a pattern in Woman's Home Companion.)

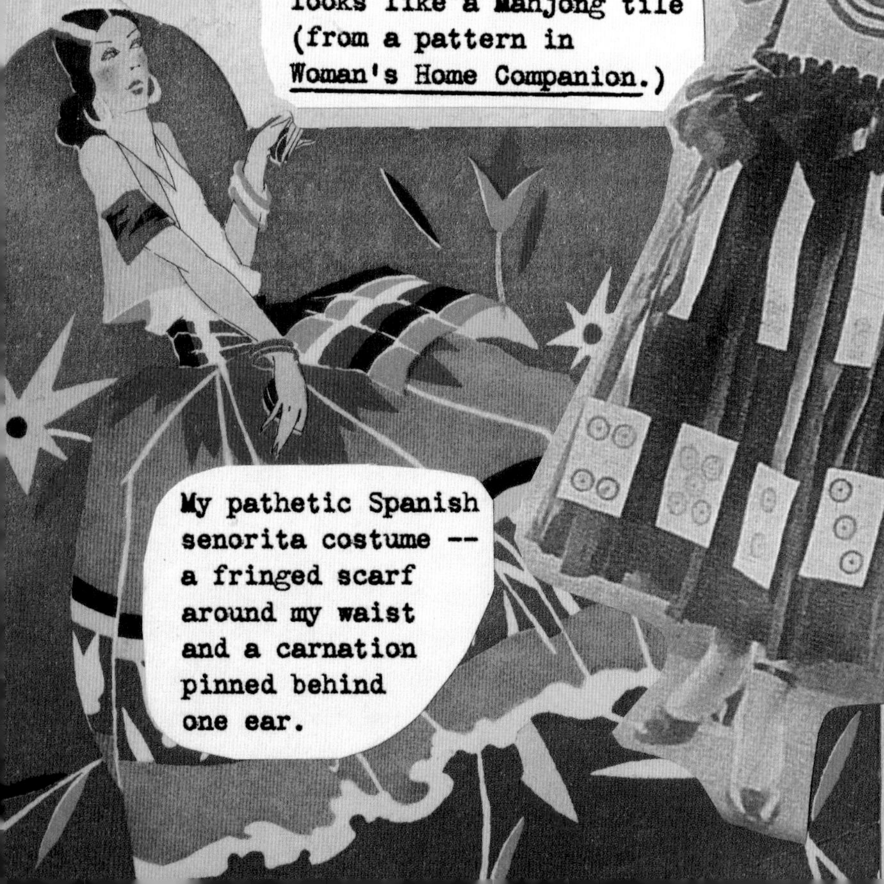

My pathetic Spanish senorita costume -- a fringed scarf around my waist and a carnation pinned behind one ear.

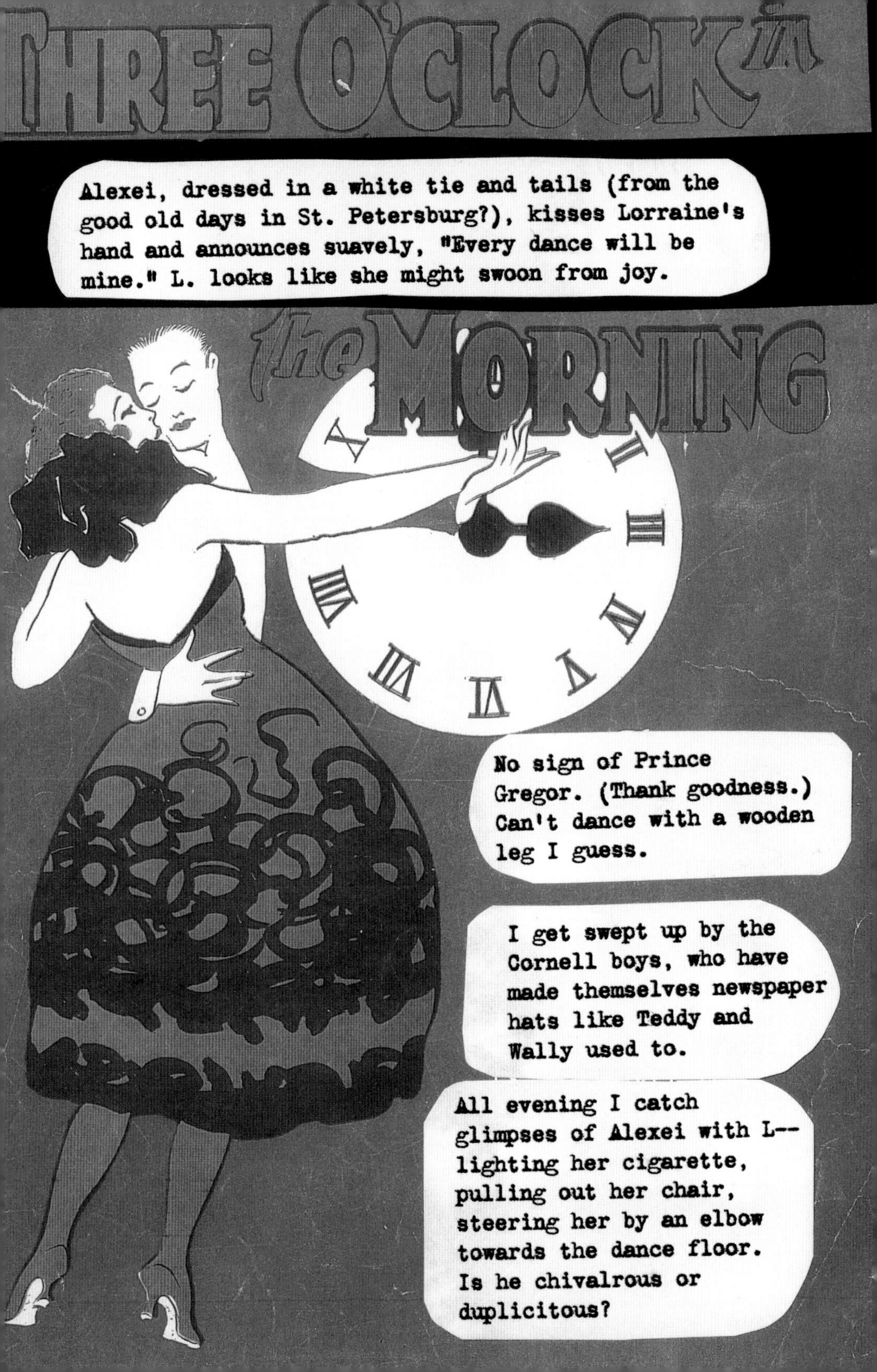
THREE O'CLOCK in the MORNING

Alexei, dressed in a white tie and tails (from the good old days in St. Petersburg?), kisses Lorraine's hand and announces suavely, "Every dance will be mine." L. looks like she might swoon from joy.

No sign of Prince Gregor. (Thank goodness.) Can't dance with a wooden leg I guess.

I get swept up by the Cornell boys, who have made themselves newspaper hats like Teddy and Wally used to.

All evening I catch glimpses of Alexei with L-- lighting her cigarette, pulling out her chair, steering her by an elbow towards the dance floor. Is he chivalrous or duplicitous?

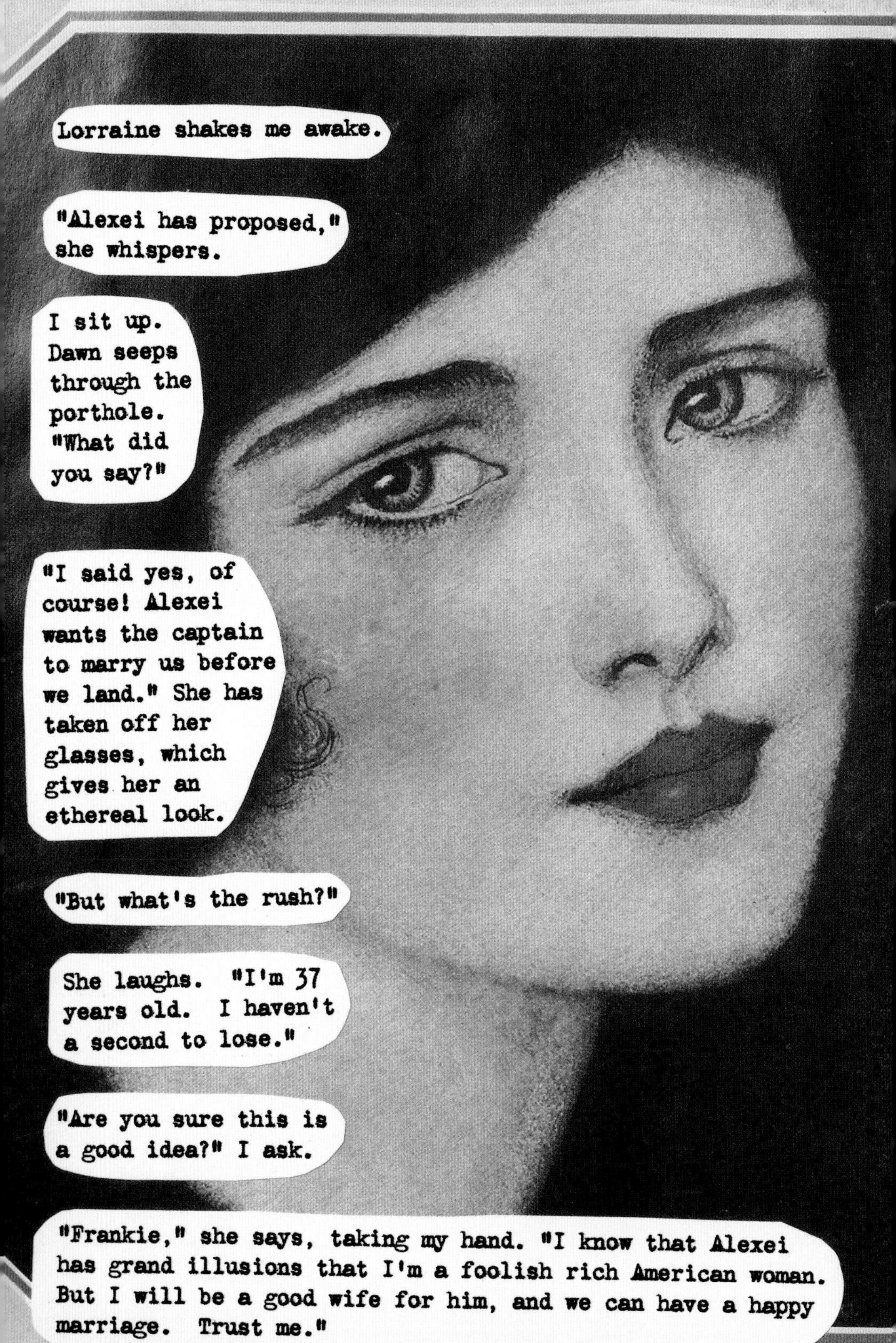
Lorraine shakes me awake.
"Alexei has proposed," she whispers.
I sit up. Dawn seeps through the porthole. "What did you say?"
"I said yes, of course! Alexei wants the captain to marry us before we land." She has taken off her glasses, which gives her an ethereal look.
"But what's the rush?"
She laughs. "I'm 37 years old. I haven't a second to lose."
"Are you sure this is a good idea?" I ask.
"Frankie," she says, taking my hand. "I know that Alexei has grand illusions that I'm a foolish rich American woman. But I will be a good wife for him, and we can have a happy marriage. Trust me."

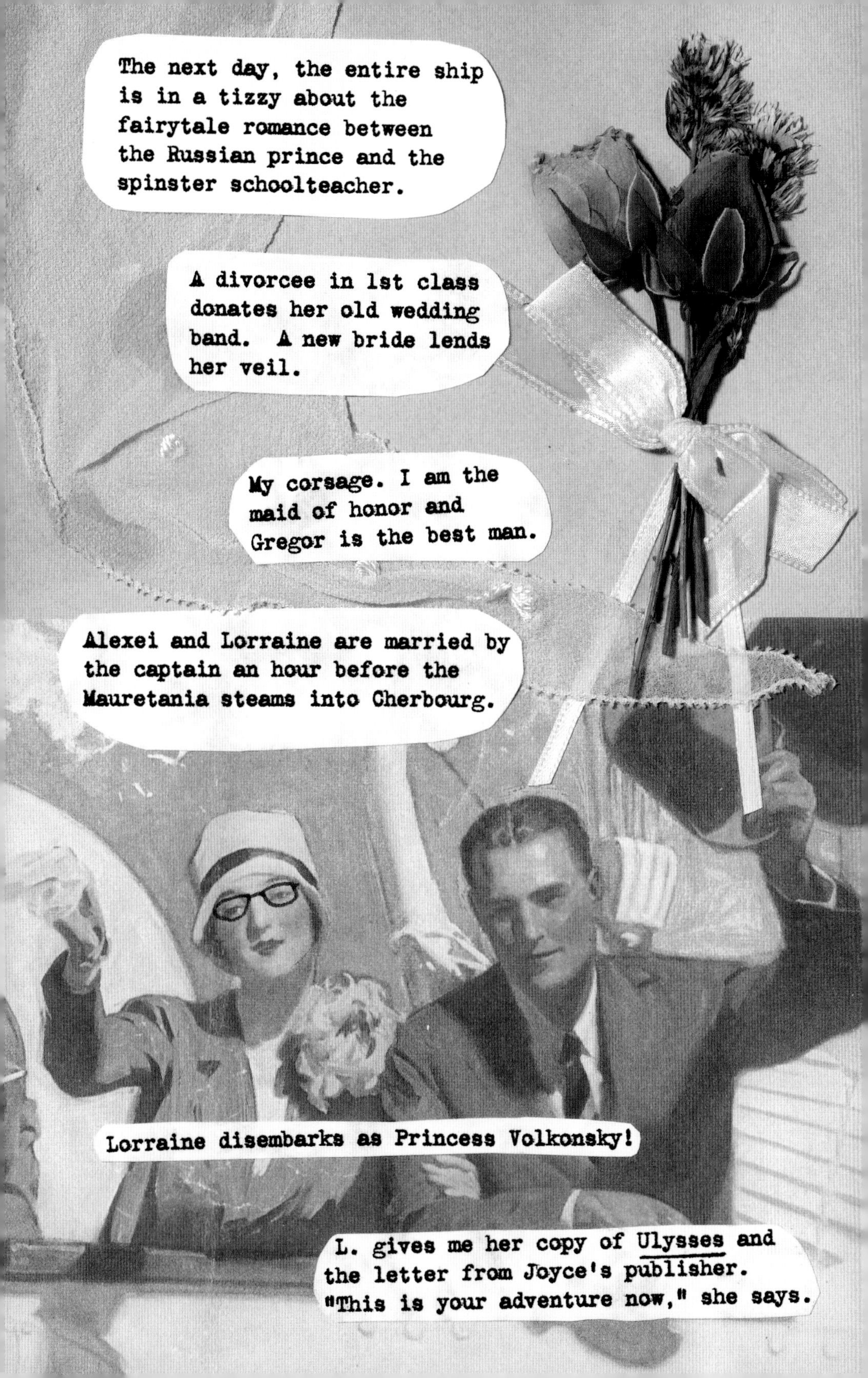
The next day, the entire ship is in a tizzy about the fairytale romance between the Russian prince and the spinster schoolteacher.
A divorcee in 1st class donates her old wedding band. A new bride lends her veil.
My corsage. I am the maid of honor and Gregor is the best man.
Alexei and Lorraine are married by the captain an hour before the Mauretania steams into Cherbourg.
Lorraine disembarks as Princess Volkonsky!
L. gives me her copy of Ulysses and the letter from Joyce's publisher. "This is your adventure now," she says.

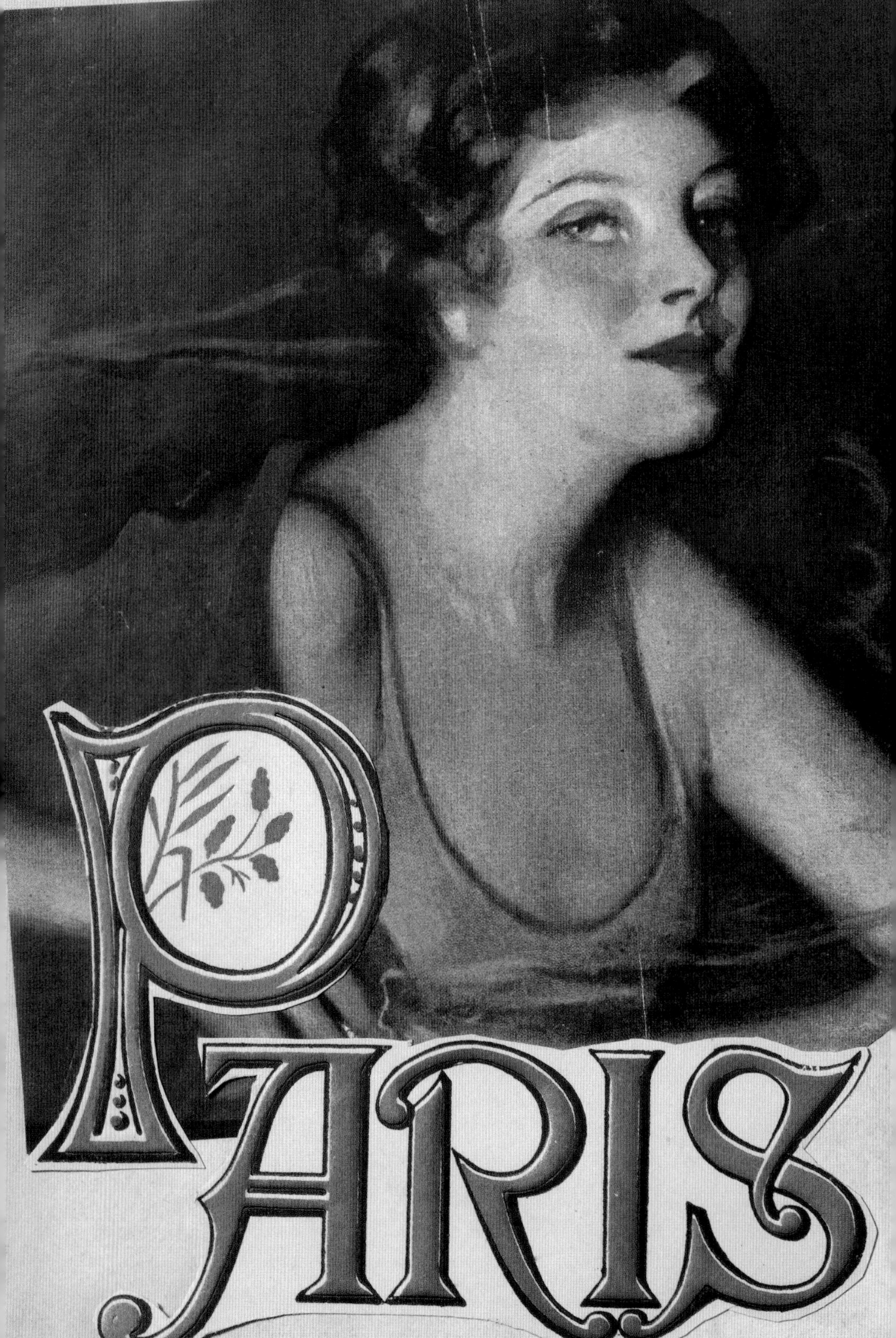
PARIS

Chapter 5

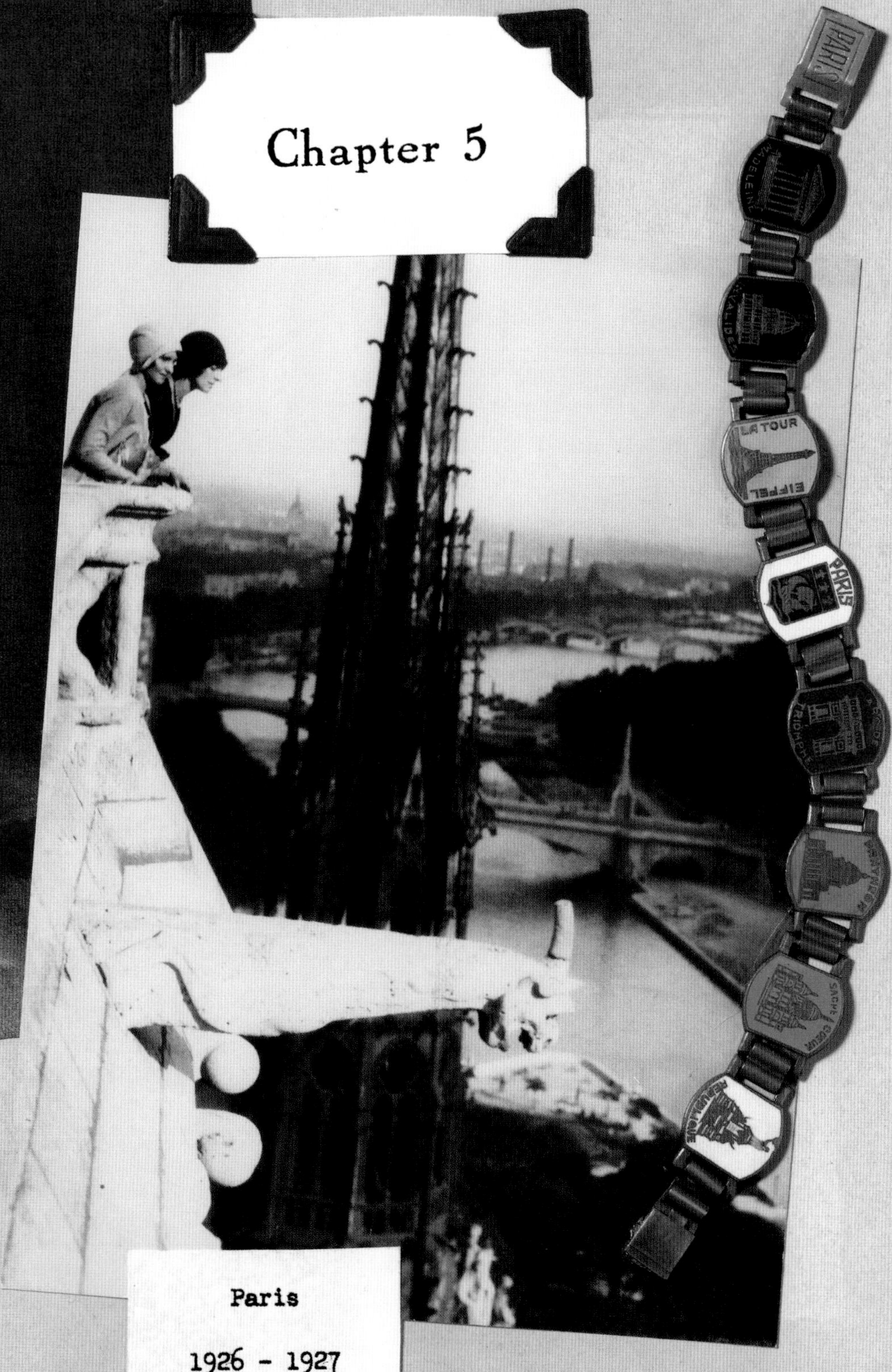
PARIS
LA TOUR
EIFFEL
PARIS

Paris

1926 - 1927

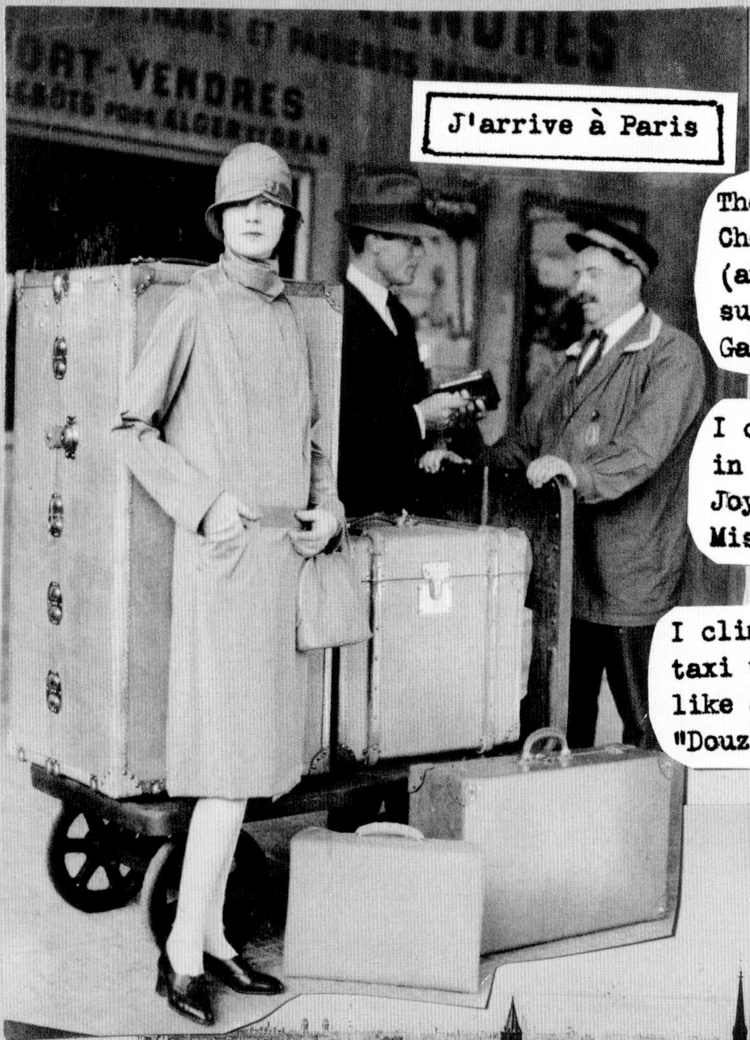

J'arrive à Paris

The train from Cherbourg dumps me (and my 2 measley suitcases) at Gare St. Lazare.

I check the address in the letter from Joyce's publisher, Miss Sylvia Beach.

I climb in a toy-sized taxi with a canvas seat like a beach chair. "Douze Rue de l'Odeon."

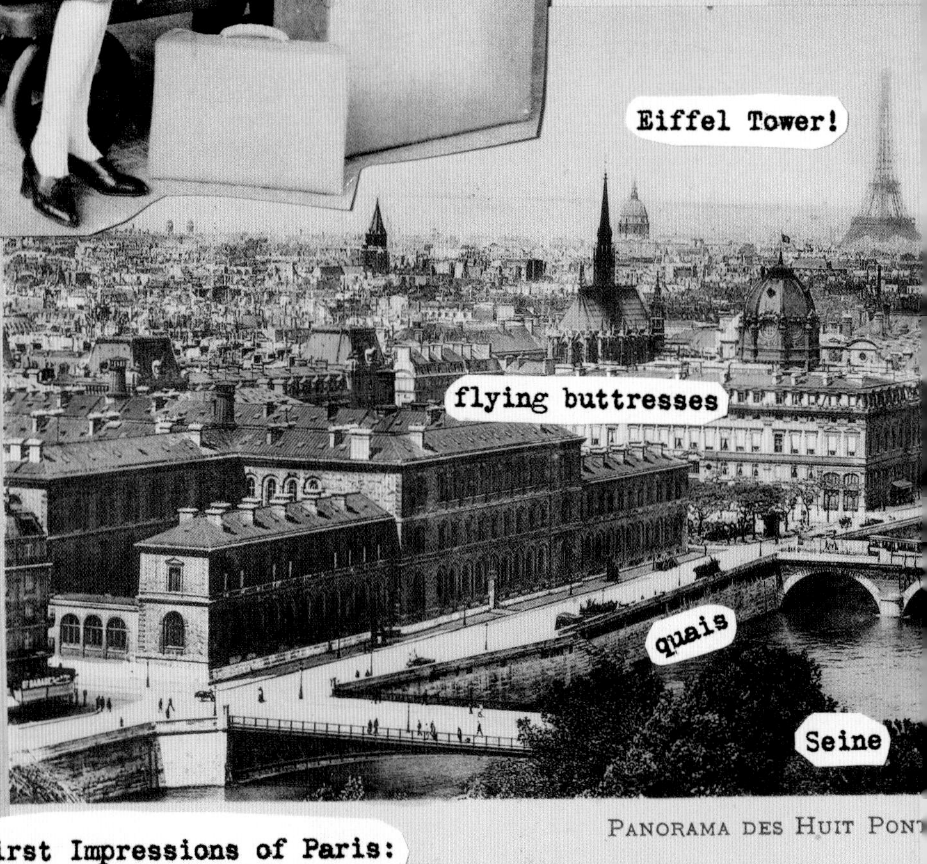
Eiffel Tower!
flying buttresses
quais
Seine
PANORAMA DES HUIT PONT

First Impressions of Paris:

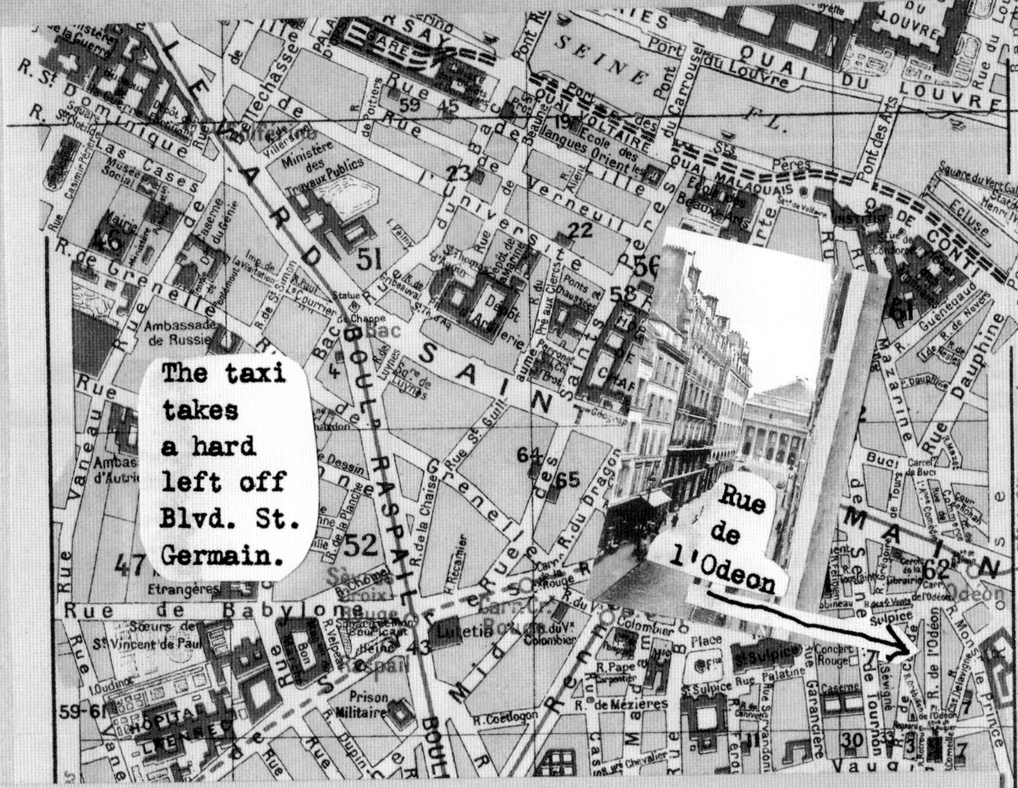
The taxi takes a hard left off Blvd. St. Germain.
Rue de l'Odeon

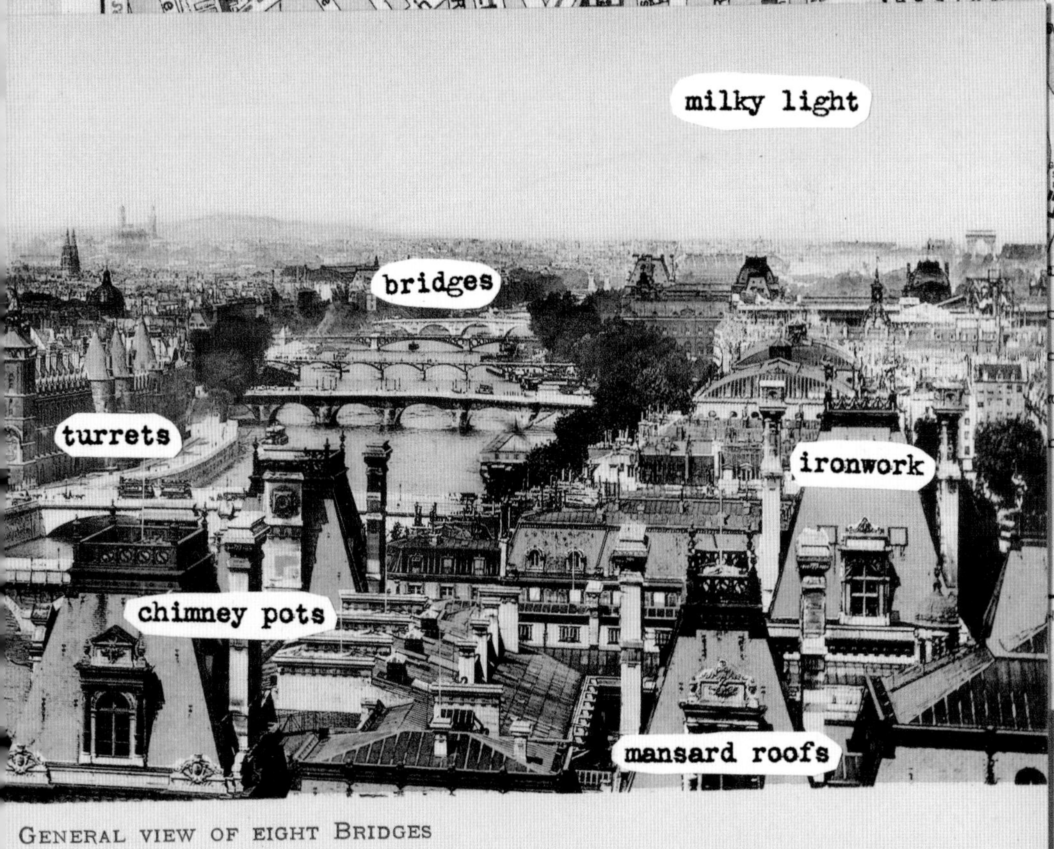
milky light
bridges
turrets
ironwork
chimney pots
mansard roofs

GENERAL VIEW OF EIGHT BRIDGES

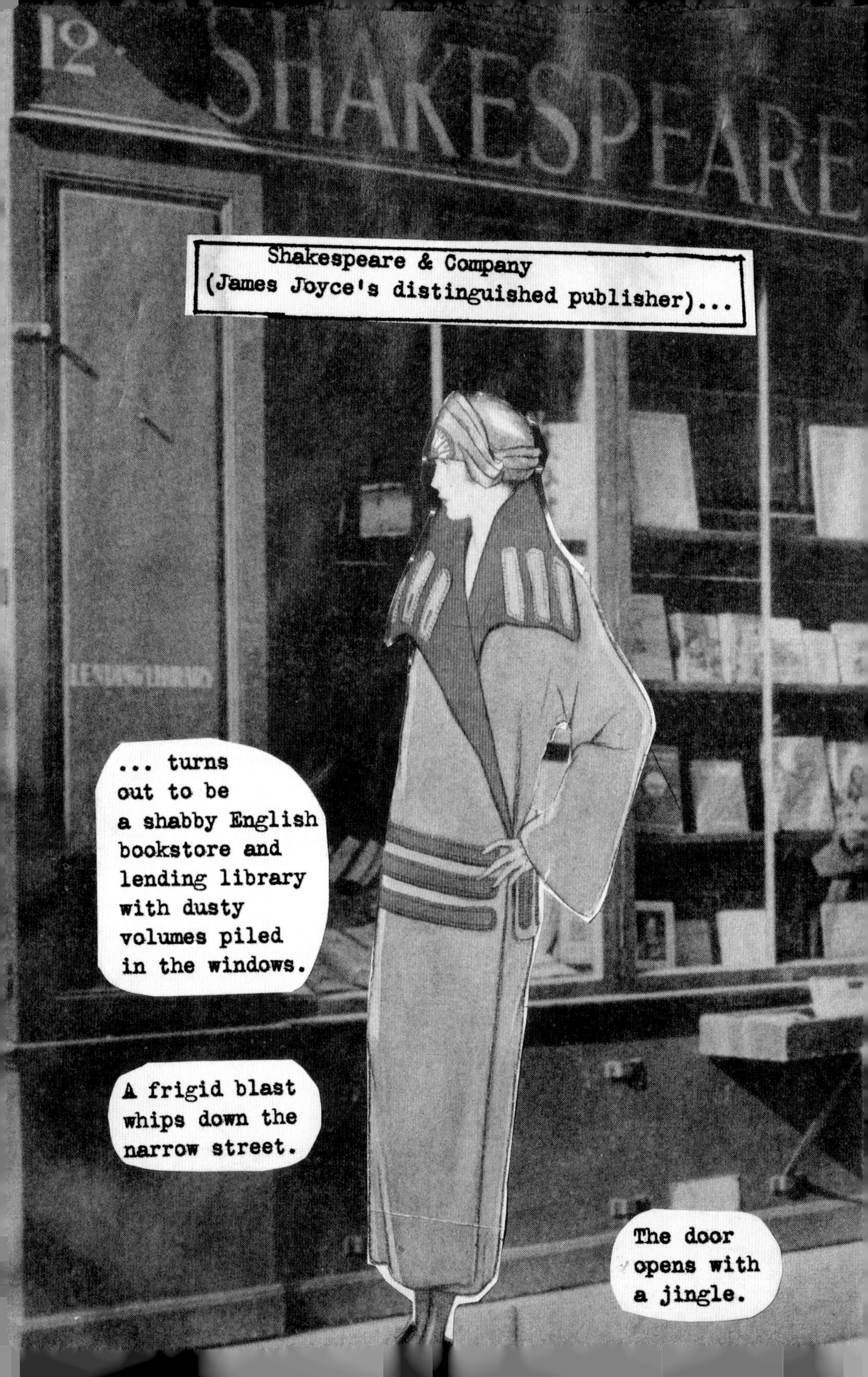
12
SHAKESPEARE
Shakespeare & Company
(James Joyce's distinguished publisher)...
... turns out to be a shabby English bookstore and lending library with dusty volumes piled in the windows.
A frigid blast whips down the narrow street.
The door opens with a jingle.

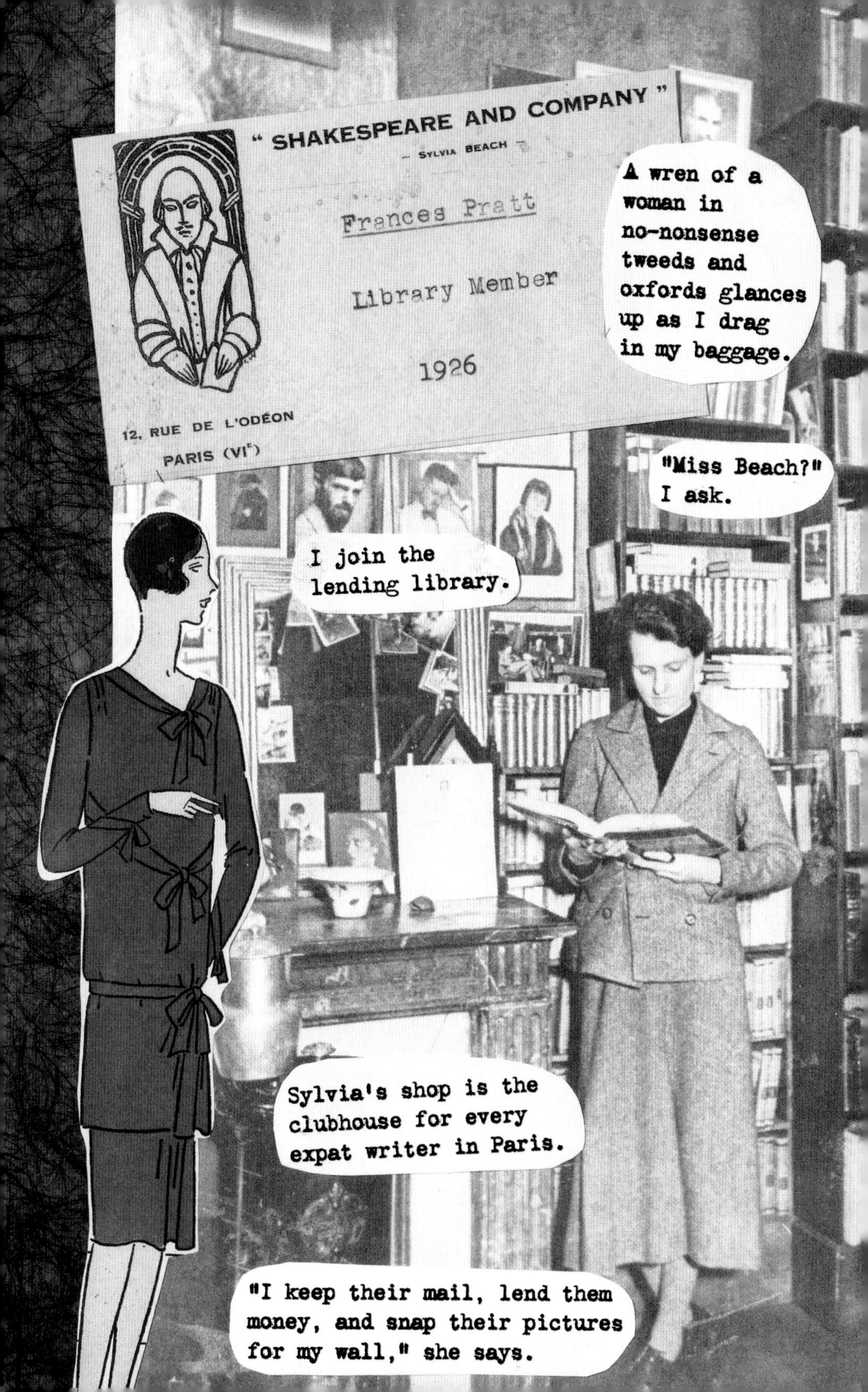

" SHAKESPEARE AND COMPANY "
— SYLVIA BEACH —
Frances Pratt
Library Member
1926
12, RUE DE L'ODÉON
PARIS (VI^{E})
A wren of a woman in no-nonsense tweeds and oxfords glances up as I drag in my baggage.
"Miss Beach?" I ask.
I join the lending library.
Sylvia's shop is the clubhouse for every expat writer in Paris.
"I keep their mail, lend them money, and snap their pictures for my wall," she says.

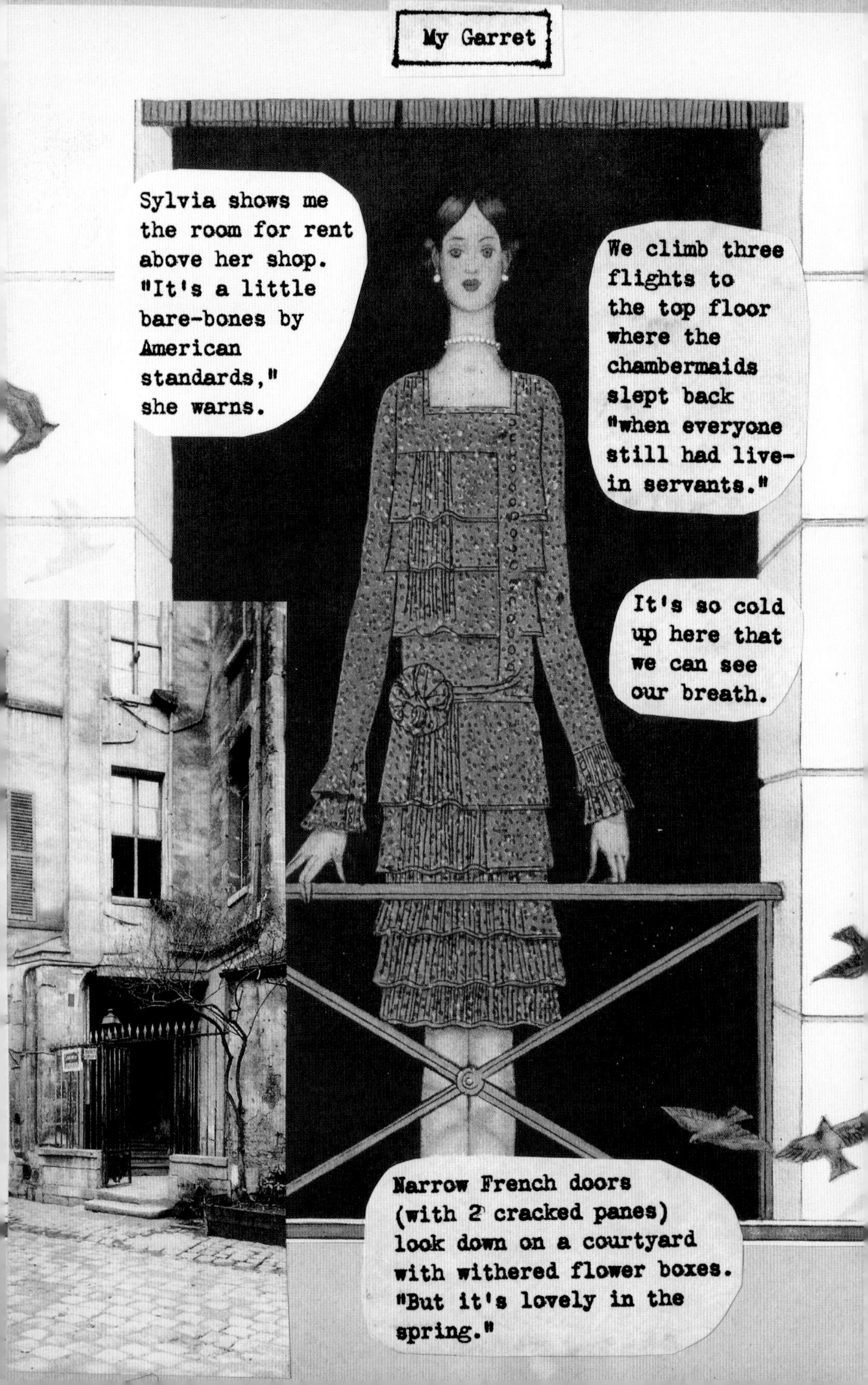
My Garret
Sylvia shows me the room for rent above her shop. "It's a little bare-bones by American standards," she warns.
We climb three flights to the top floor where the chambermaids slept back "when everyone still had live-in servants."
It's so cold up here that we can see our breath.
Narrow French doors (with 2 cracked panes) look down on a courtyard with withered flower boxes. "But it's lovely in the spring."

The minute coal stove can heat a teakettle "and not much else."

The furniture looks like castoffs from a petit bourgeois in a Balzac novel.

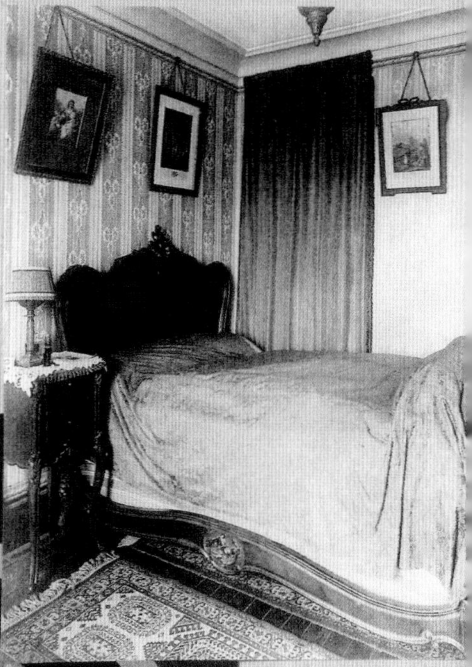

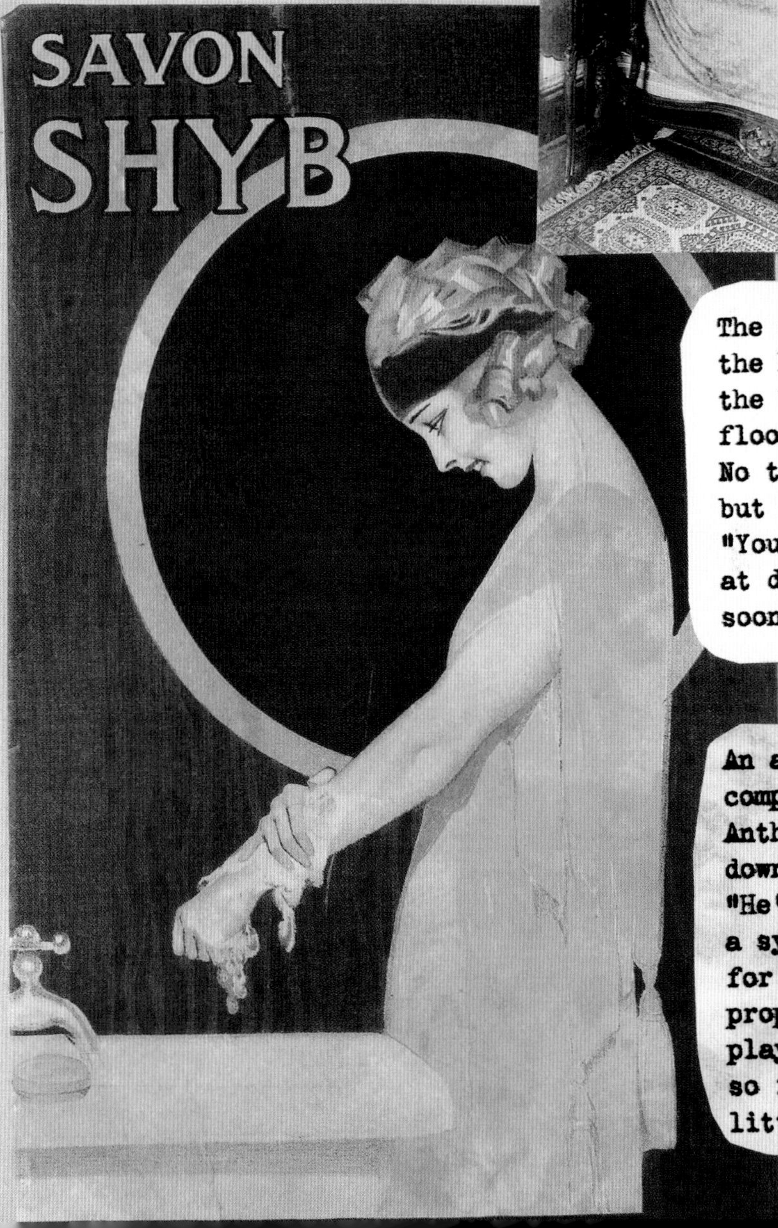
SAVON
SHYB

The sink is in the hall, and the WC on the floor below. No tub anywhere, but Sylvia says, "You get expert at doing without soon enough."

An avant-garde composer named Anthiel lives down below. "He's writing a symphony for airplane propellers and player pianos, so it can get a little noisy."

A Tourist in Paris

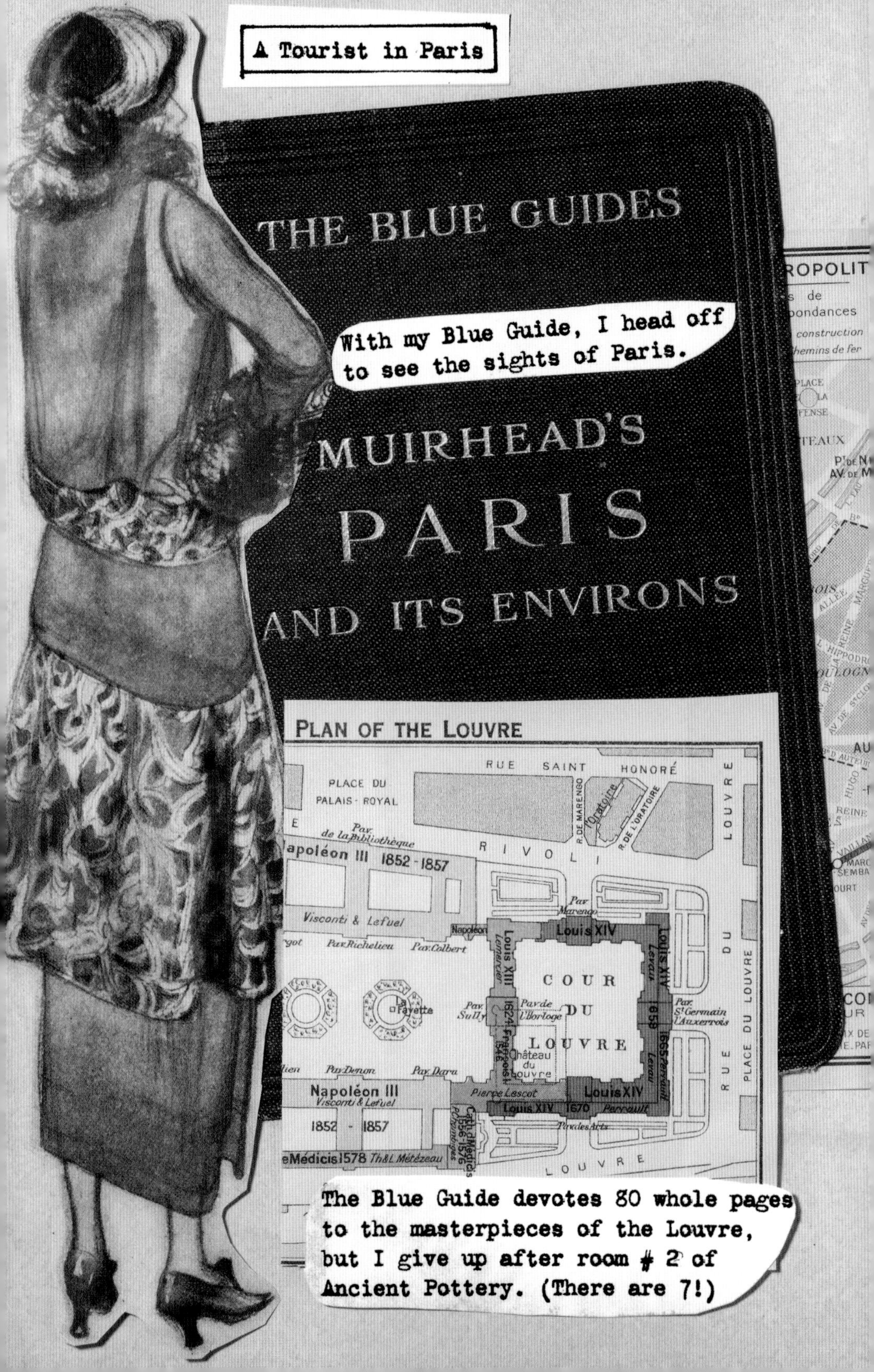
THE BLUE GUIDES
MUIRHEAD'S
PARIS
AND ITS ENVIRONS
PLAN OF THE LOUVRE
RUE SAINT HONORÉ
PLACE DU PALAIS-ROYAL
RIVOLI
RUE DU LOUVRE
PLACE DU LOUVRE
COUR DU LOUVRE
Napoléon III 1852-1857
Visconti & Lefuel
Pav. Richelieu
Pav. Colbert
Pav. Sully
Pav. de l'Horloge
Pav. Denon
Pav. Daru
Pav. Marengo
Louis XIV
Louis XIII
Pierre Lescot
Château du Louvre
Pav. des Arts
Perrault
La Fayette

With my Blue Guide, I head off to see the sights of Paris.

The Blue Guide devotes 80 whole pages to the masterpieces of the Louvre, but I give up after room # 2 of Ancient Pottery. (There are 7!)

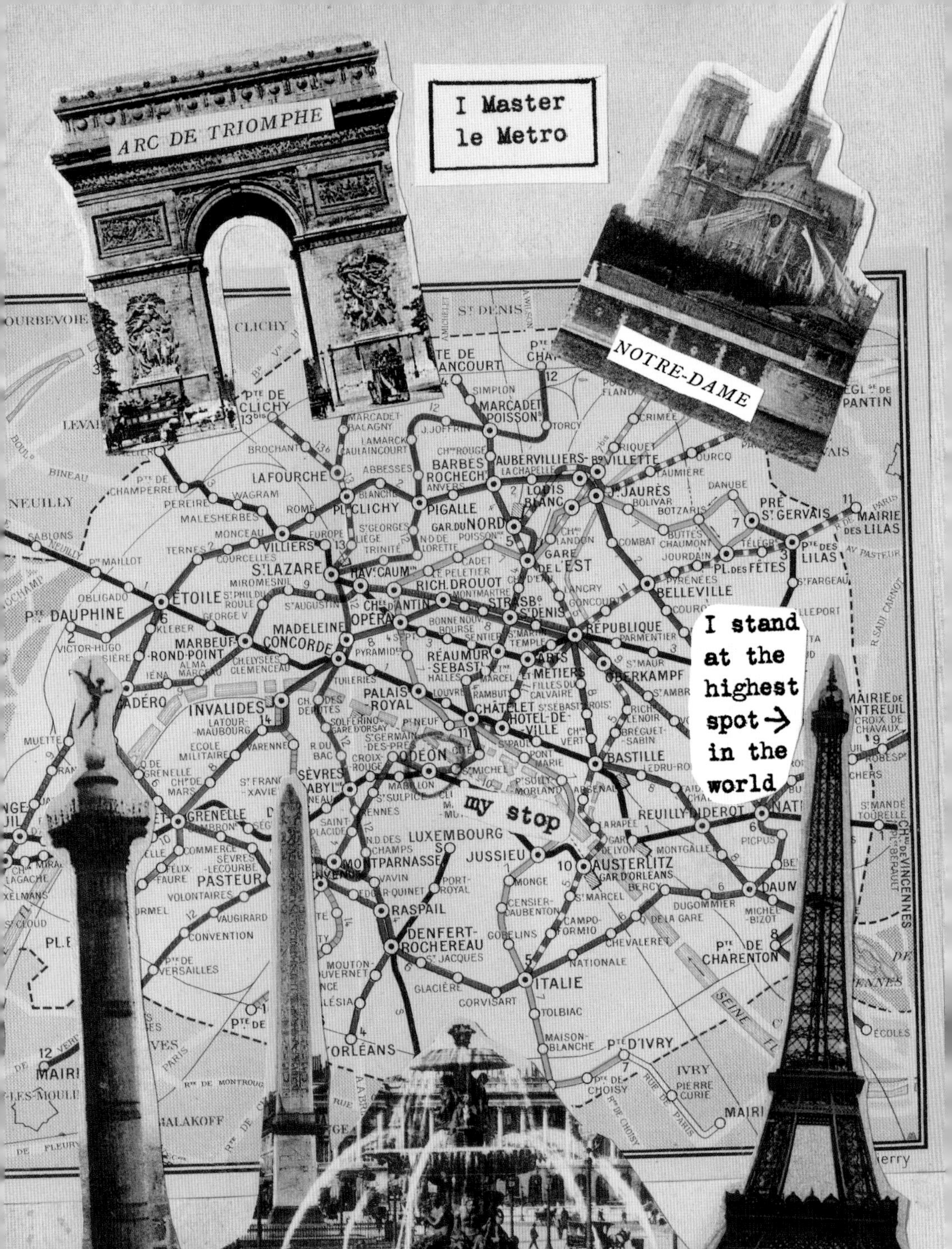
ARC DE TRIOMPHE
I Master le Metro
NOTRE-DAME
I stand at the highest spot → in the world
my stop
PLACE DE LA CONCORDE

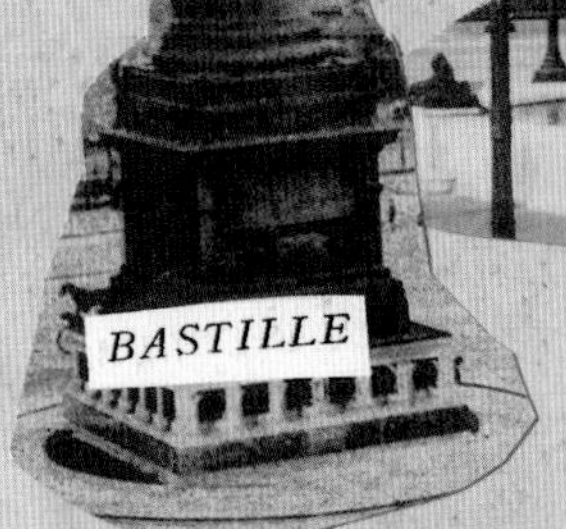
BASTILLE

At the river end of the Champ-de-Mars, facing the Trocadéro, rises the ***Eiffel Tower** or *Tour Eiffel* (Pl. R 26, *B*), 984 ft. high, the tallest structure in the world (Woolworth Building at New York 750 ft.; Washington Obelisk 555 ft.; Great Pyramid 450 ft.), dominating the W. end of Paris.

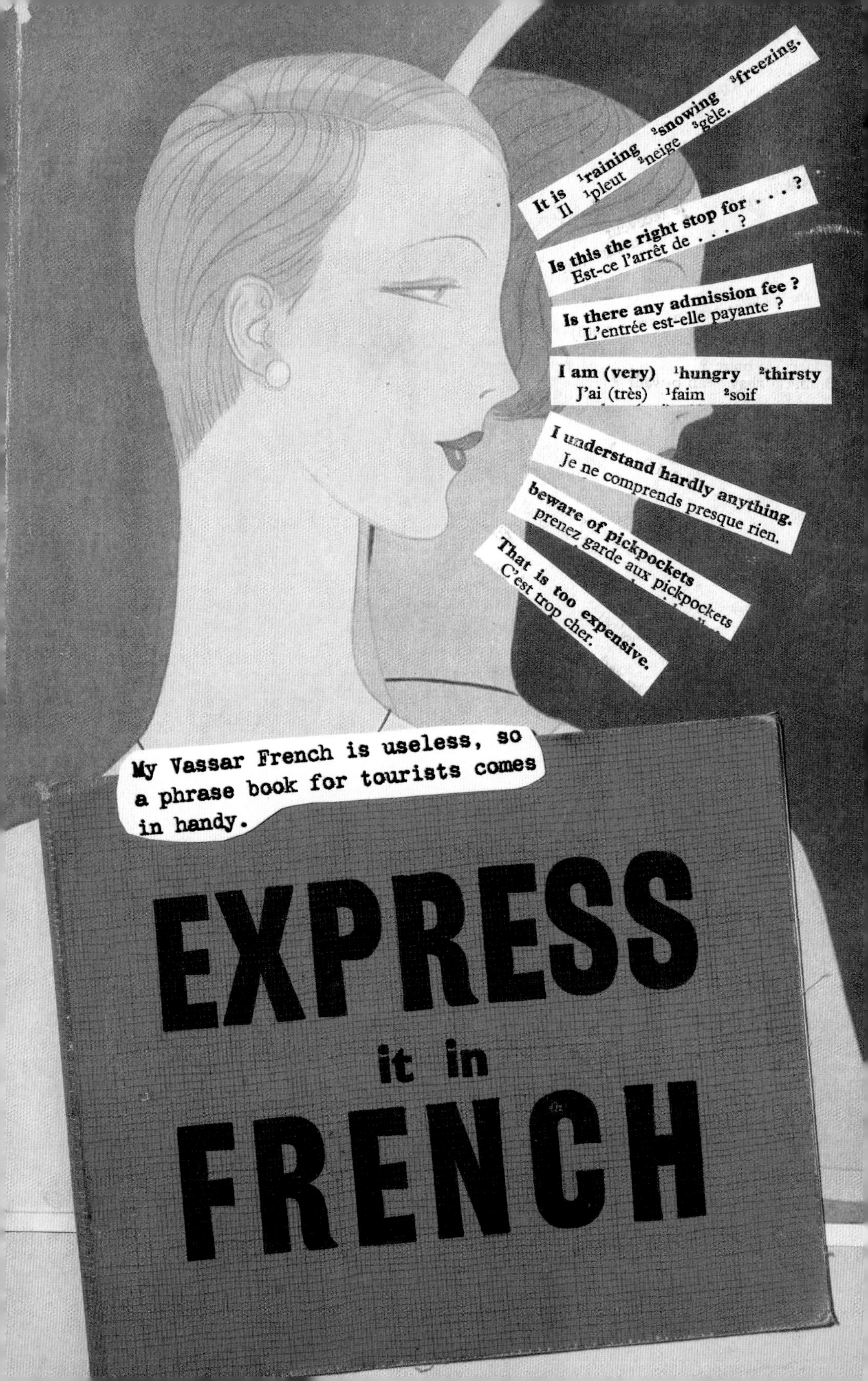
It is ¹raining ²snowing ³freezing.
Il ¹pleut ²neige ³gèle.
Is this the right stop for . . . ?
Est-ce l'arrêt de . . . ?
Is there any admission fee ?
L'entrée est-elle payante ?
I am (very) ¹hungry ²thirsty
J'ai (très) ¹faim ²soif
I understand hardly anything.
Je ne comprends presque rien.
beware of pickpockets
prenez garde aux pickpockets
That is too expensive.
C'est trop cher.
My Vassar French is useless, so a phrase book for tourists comes in handy.
EXPRESS
it in
FRENCH

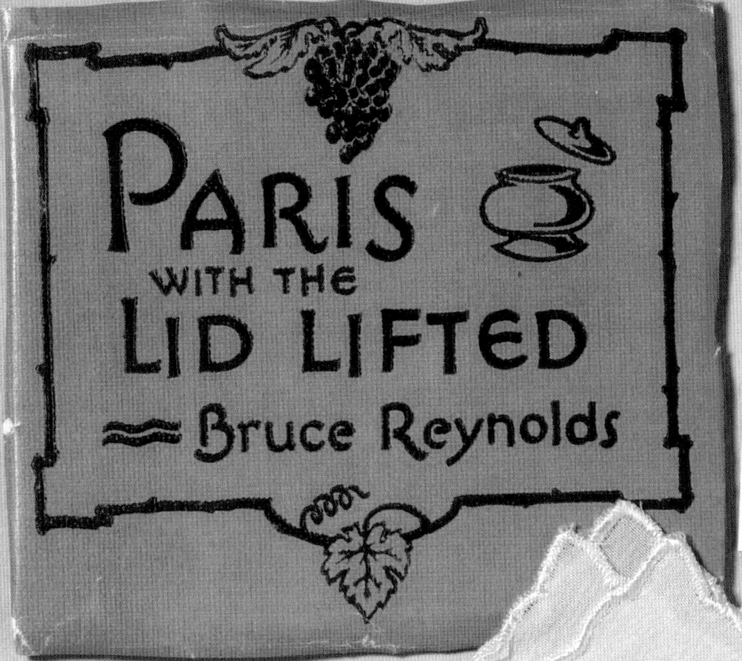
PARIS
WITH THE
LID LIFTED
Bruce Reynolds

I find a naughty guide to the "real" Paris. (Brothels, bars, dance halls, nude folies...) Much more fun than the Blue Guide.

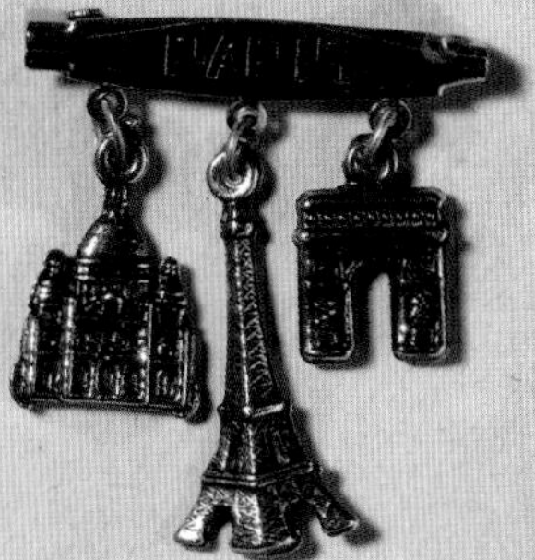

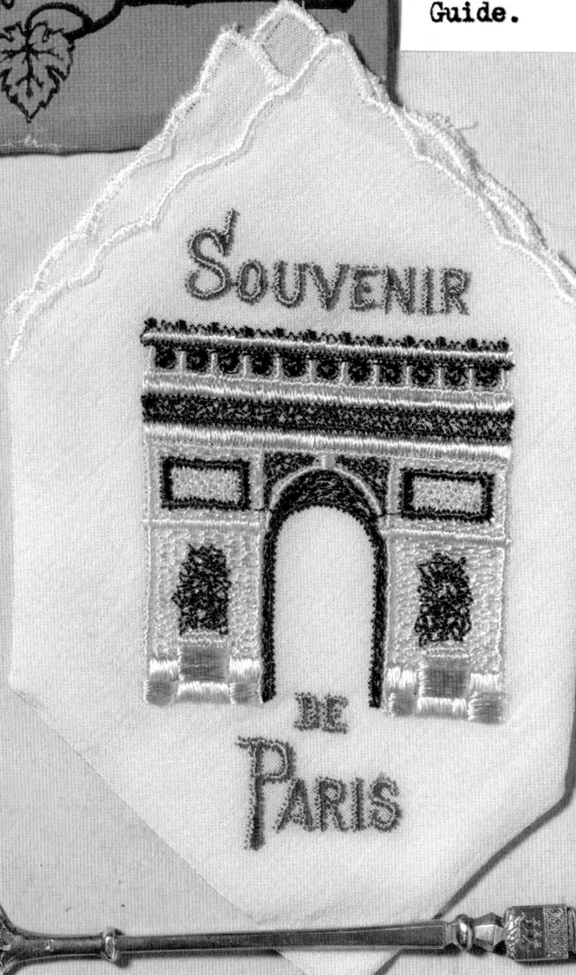
SOUVENIR
DE
PARIS

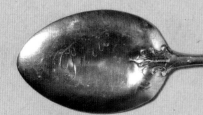

Souvenirs from a shop in the Eiffel Tower.

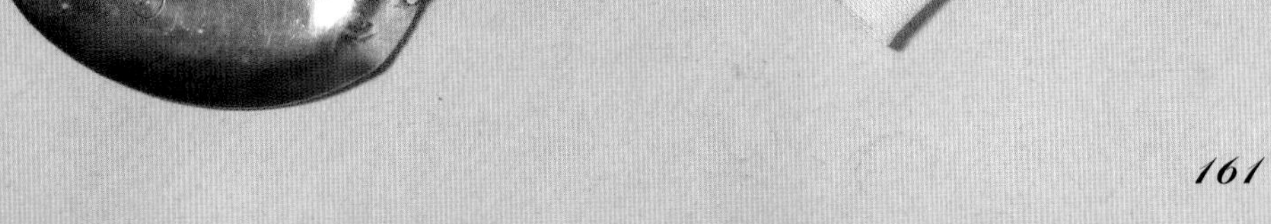

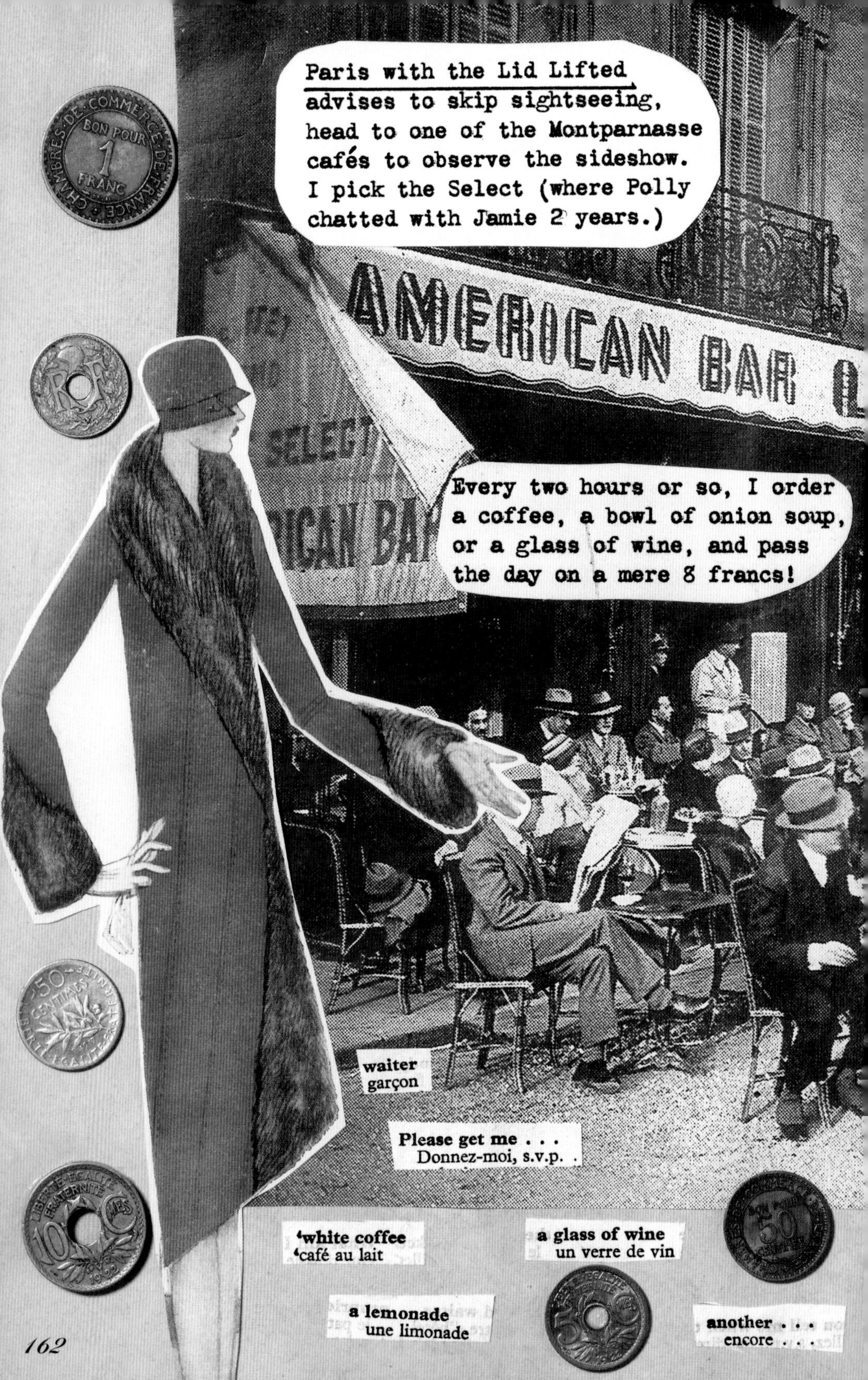
Paris with the Lid Lifted advises to skip sightseeing, head to one of the Montparnasse cafés to observe the sideshow. I pick the Select (where Polly chatted with Jamie 2 years.)
AMERICAN BAR
SELECT
Every two hours or so, I order a coffee, a bowl of onion soup, or a glass of wine, and pass the day on a mere 8 francs!
waiter
garçon
Please get me . . .
Donnez-moi, s.v.p. .
'white coffee
'café au lait
a glass of wine
un verre de vin
a lemonade
une limonade
another . . .
encore . . .
BON POUR 1 FRANC
50 CENTIMES

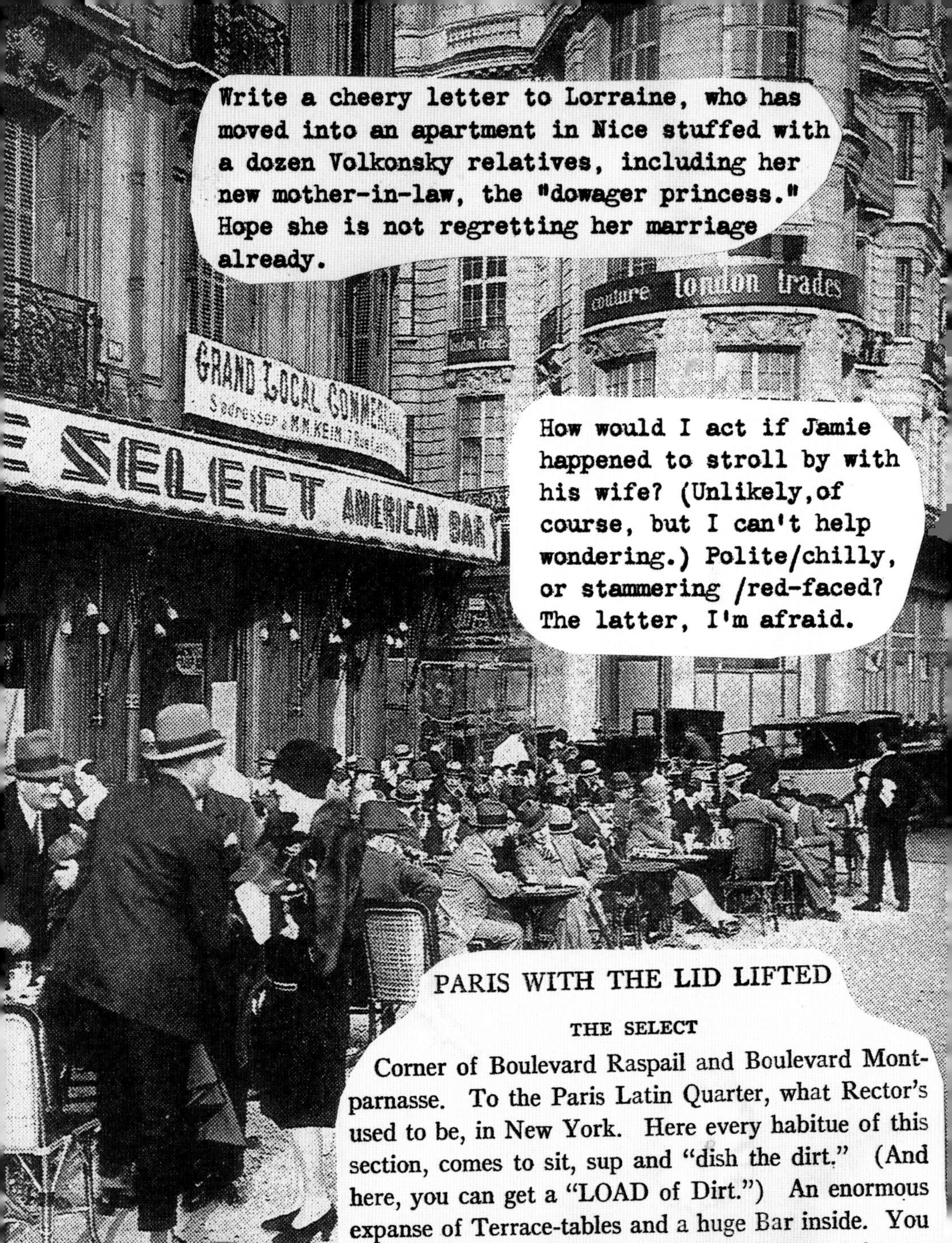
SELECT
AMERICAN BAR
couture london trades

Write a cheery letter to Lorraine, who has moved into an apartment in Nice stuffed with a dozen Volkonsky relatives, including her new mother-in-law, the "dowager princess." Hope she is not regretting her marriage already.

How would I act if Jamie happened to stroll by with his wife? (Unlikely,of course, but I can't help wondering.) Polite/chilly, or stammering /red-faced? The latter, I'm afraid.

PARIS WITH THE LID LIFTED

THE SELECT

Corner of Boulevard Raspail and Boulevard Montparnasse. To the Paris Latin Quarter, what Rector's used to be, in New York. Here every habitue of this section, comes to sit, sup and "dish the dirt." (And here, you can get a "LOAD of Dirt.") An enormous expanse of Terrace-tables and a huge Bar inside. You see all the Nuts and all the Freaks, plain and fancy; broke and affluent; mangy and modish, glassy-eyed and goo-goo eyed; long haired and bald-domed; Van Dyke bearded and pasty-faced; decorous and degenerate; pious and perverted; mademoiselle-ish young men and young-men-ish mademoiselles. Every sort, type, and figured male and female you ever beheld, inside or outside a side-show.

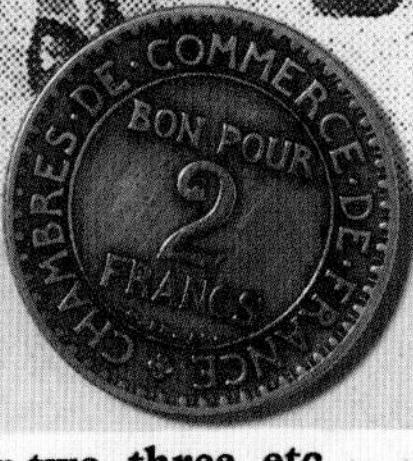
CHAMBRES DE COMMERCE DE FRANCE
BON POUR
2
FRANCS

another two, three, etc. . . .
encore deux, trois, etc. . . .

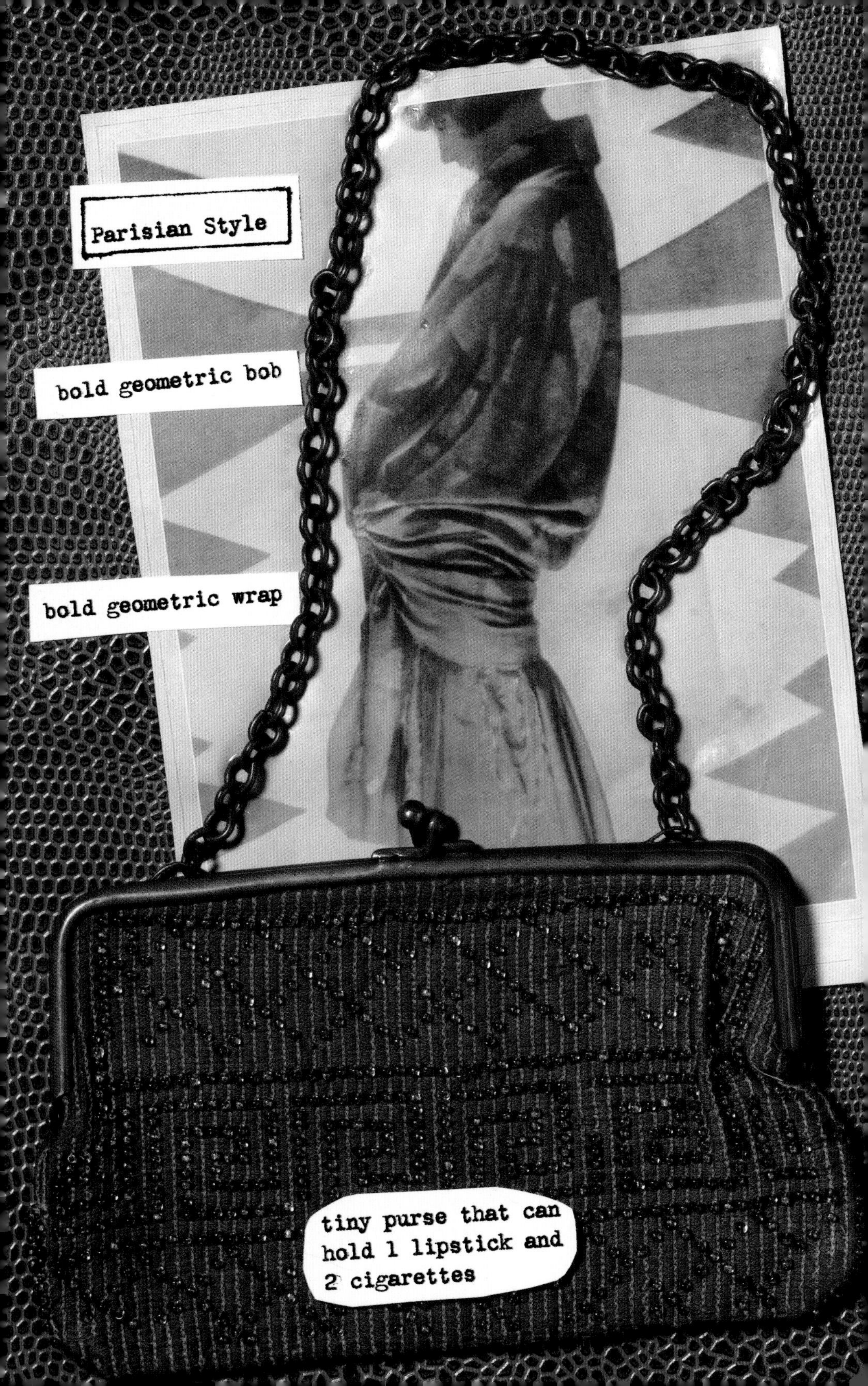
Parisian Style
bold geometric bob
bold geometric wrap
tiny purse that can
hold 1 lipstick and
2 cigarettes

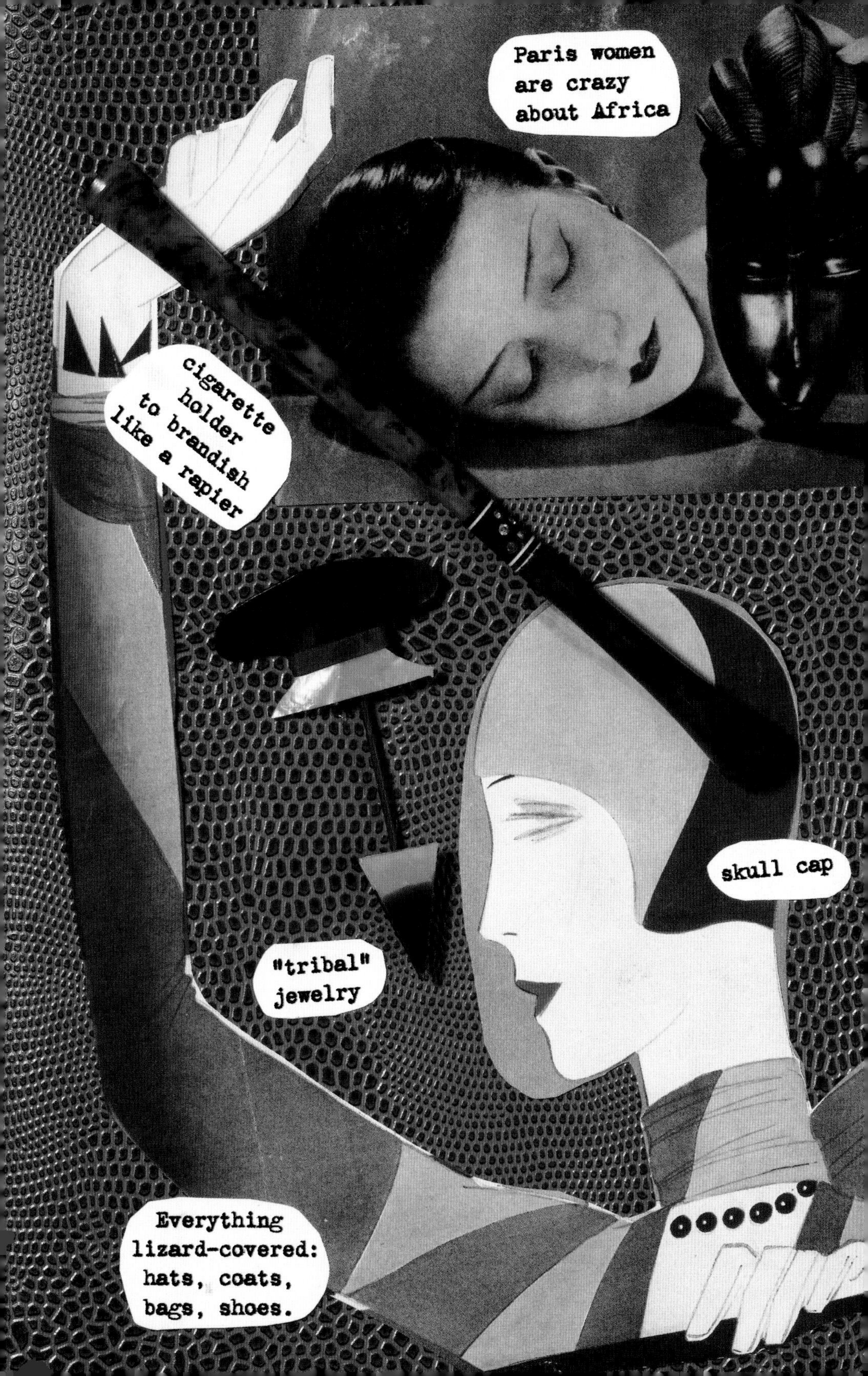

Paris women are crazy about Africa
cigarette holder to brandish like a rapier
skull cap
"tribal" jewelry
Everything lizard-covered: hats, coats, bags, shoes.

Finding a Job: Paris Edition

The Chicago Tribune AND THE DAILY NEWS NEW YORK

EUROPE'S AMERICAN NEWSPAPER

LA SEMAINE A PARIS

Features of the week in Paris

Sylvia says the best way to find an editing job is to advertise in all the English language newspapers.

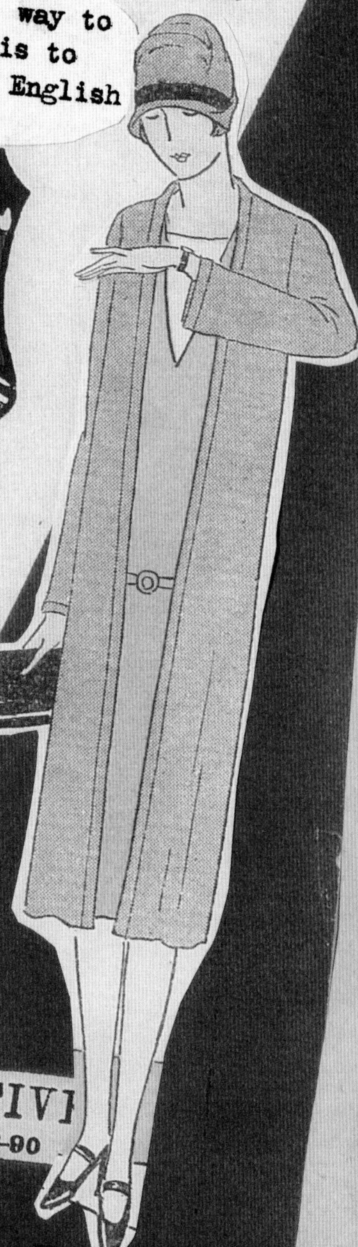

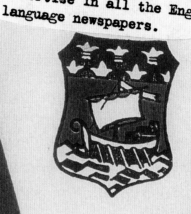

ENGLISH EDIT

my ad

Copy Editing & Proof Reading Services: Vassar grad., experience with major NY mag. Contact: Frances Pratt, c/o Shakespeare & Co., 12 rue de l Odeon, Paris VI

YNDICAT d'INITIATIVI

4, rue Volney (2e) — Louvre 08-90

Friday

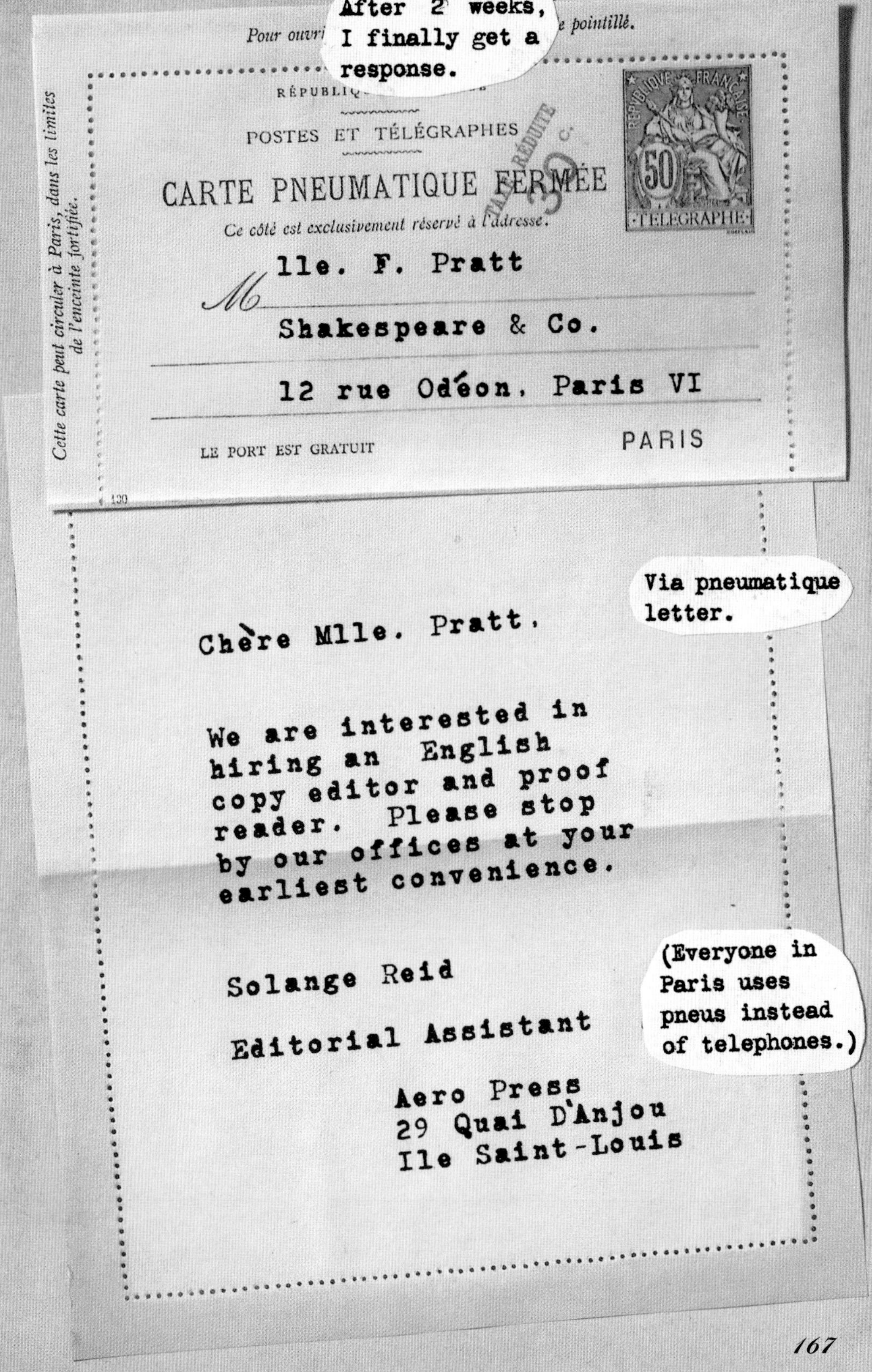
After 2 weeks, I finally get a response.

Pour ouvri … e pointillé.

RÉPUBLIQ…

POSTES ET TÉLÉGRAPHES

CARTE PNEUMATIQUE FERMÉE

Ce côté est exclusivement réservé à l'adresse.

TAXE RÉDUITE 30 c

RÉPUBLIQUE FRANÇAISE 50 TÉLÉGRAPHE

Mlle. F. Pratt

Shakespeare & Co.

12 rue Odéon, Paris VI

LE PORT EST GRATUIT PARIS

Cette carte peut circuler à Paris, dans les limites de l'enceinte fortifiée.

130

Via pneumatique letter.

Chère Mlle. Pratt,

We are interested in hiring an English copy editor and proof reader. Please stop by our offices at your earliest convenience.

Solange Reid

Editorial Assistant

Aero Press
29 Quai D'Anjou
Ile Saint-Louis

(Everyone in Paris uses pneus instead of telephones.)

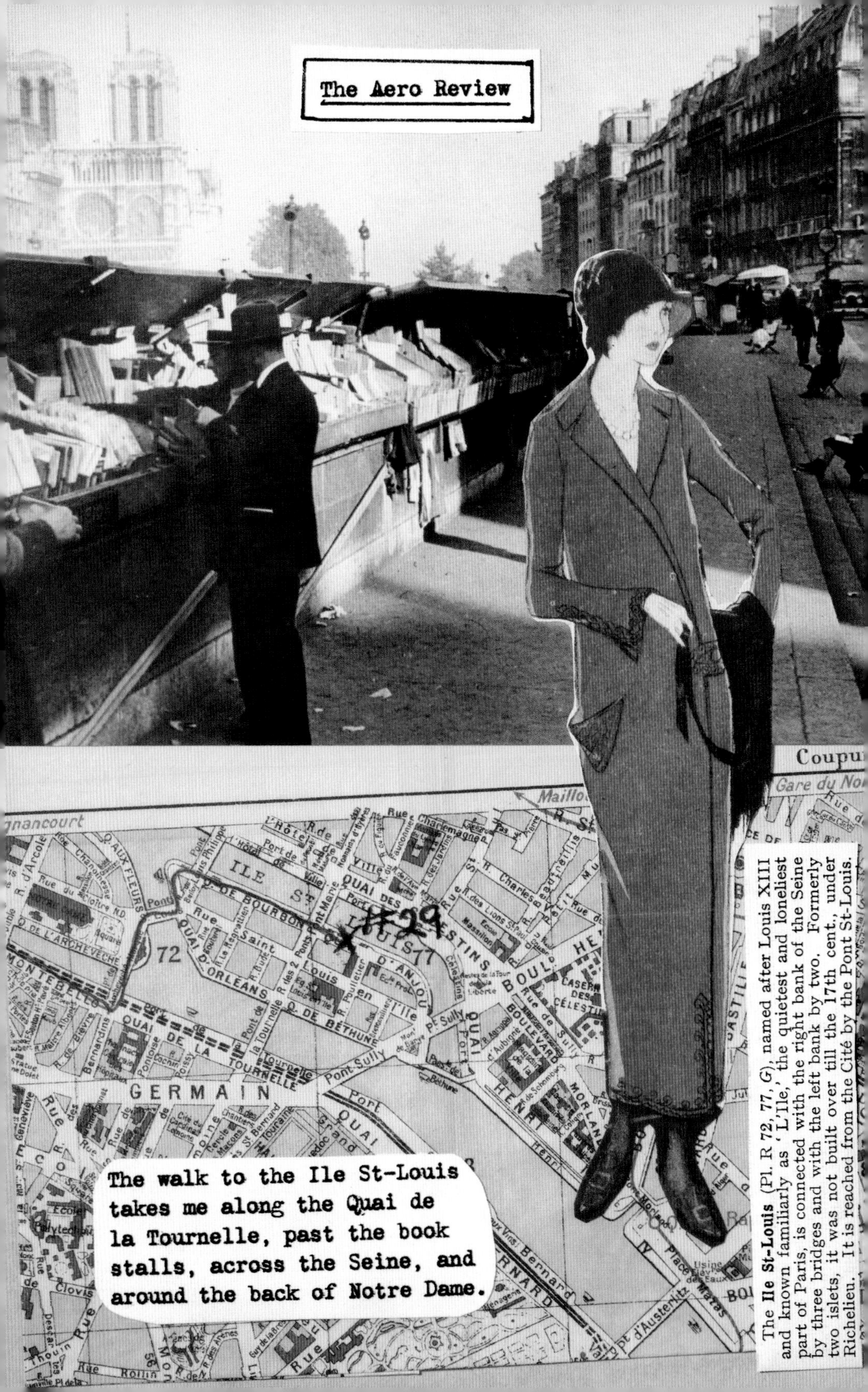
The Aero Review
The walk to the Ile St-Louis takes me along the Quai de la Tournelle, past the book stalls, across the Seine, and around the back of Notre Dame.
The **Ile St-Louis** (Pl. R 72, 77, *G*), named after Louis XIII and known familiarly as 'L'Ile,' the quietest and loneliest part of Paris, is connected with the right bank of the Seine by three bridges and with the left bank by two. Formerly two islets, it was not built over till the 17th cent., under Richelieu. It is reached from the Cité by the Pont St-Louis.

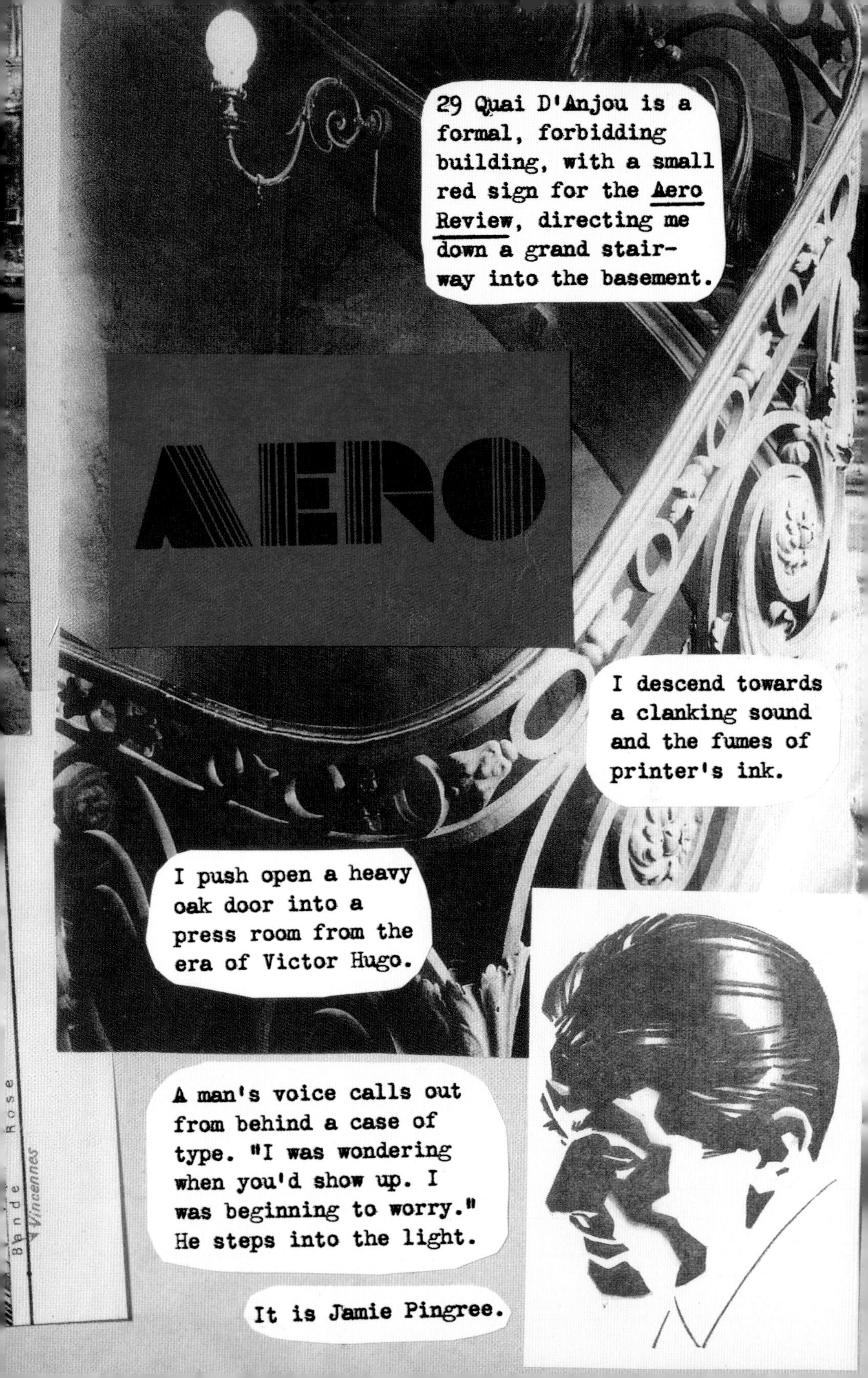
29 Quai D'Anjou is a formal, forbidding building, with a small red sign for the Aero Review, directing me down a grand stairway into the basement.
AERO
I descend towards a clanking sound and the fumes of printer's ink.
I push open a heavy oak door into a press room from the era of Victor Hugo.
A man's voice calls out from behind a case of type. "I was wondering when you'd show up. I was beginning to worry." He steps into the light.
It is Jamie Pingree.

The Return of Jamie

I stare dumbly for a few seconds, trying to take him in. Dressed like a Breton peasant, in a linen shirt with ink-stained sleeves. Older, of course, with wide streaks of gray at the temples. Healthier than in 1920, with the softness of middle age. But still darkly handsome (alas). Finally, I find my voice, which I manage to keep cool, indignant.

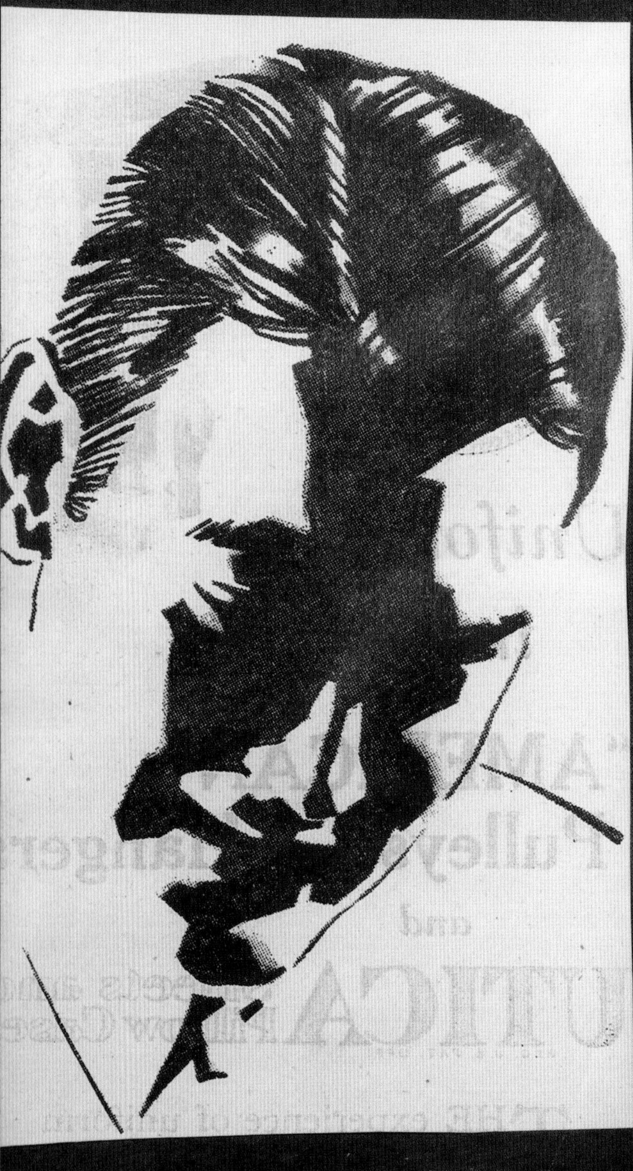
and
UTICA

* What are you doing here?
* I own the <u>Aero Review</u>.
* Since when? I thought you'd gone back to your law practice in New York.
* I did, for about a year. Then I remembered a girl saying it's still not to late to do what you want. So I chucked it all and came to Paris.
* What did your wife think about moving to Paris?
* She didn't care much. She'd already divorced me by then.
*Is that supposed to make me feel better about the way you've tricked me?
* Frankie, no. I've felt nothing but guilt. . . and shame.
* So why didn't you write me?
* I promised I wouldn't.
* Promised who?

* Your mother. She came to see me after you'd left for Vassar. Told me I'd done you enough harm and I should leave you alone. Said you could do a lot better than a wastrel like me.
* (I smile. My dear old mother!) So why write me now?
* Because you're old enough and wise enough not to be damaged by me. And because I wanted to see you again. And because I really do need a copy editor.

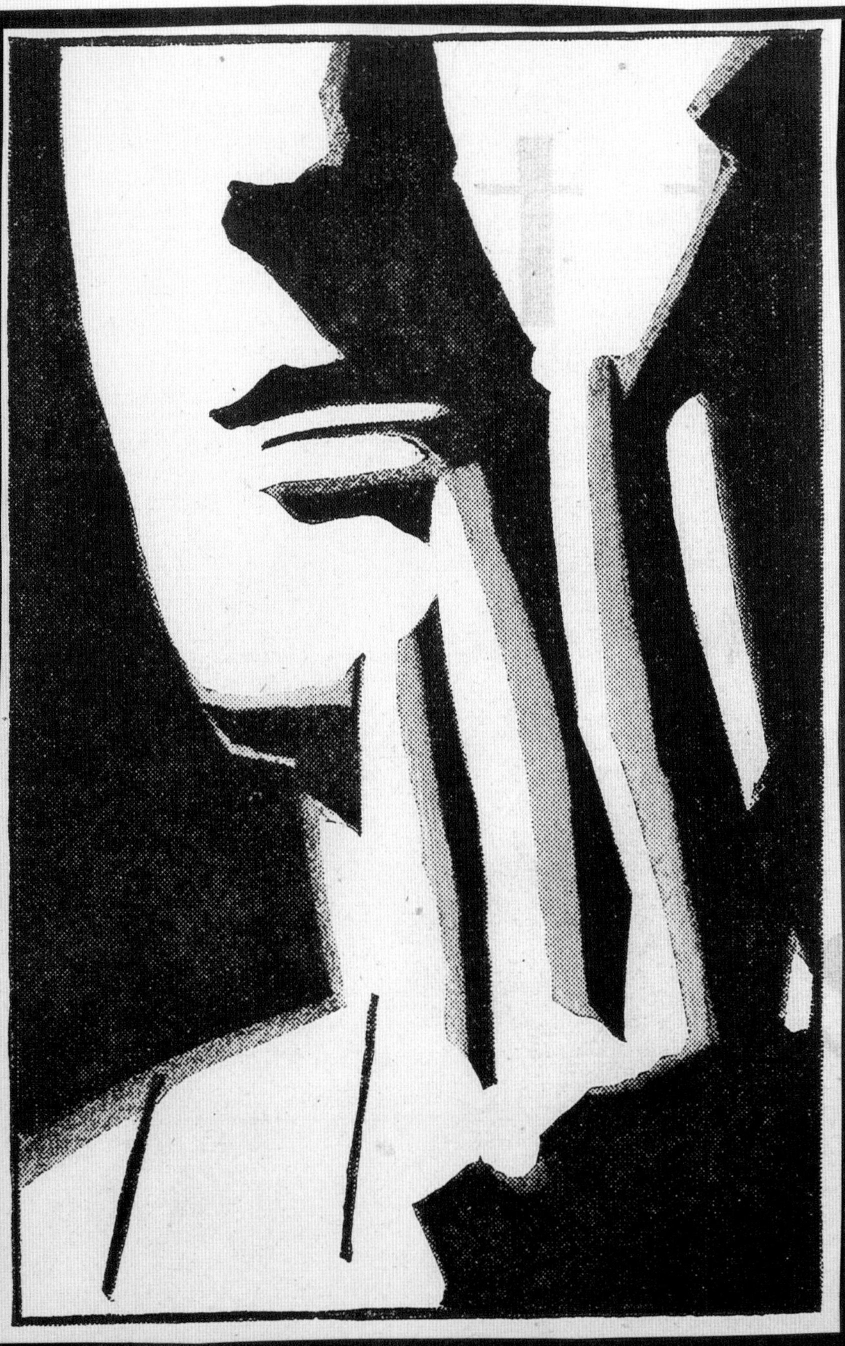

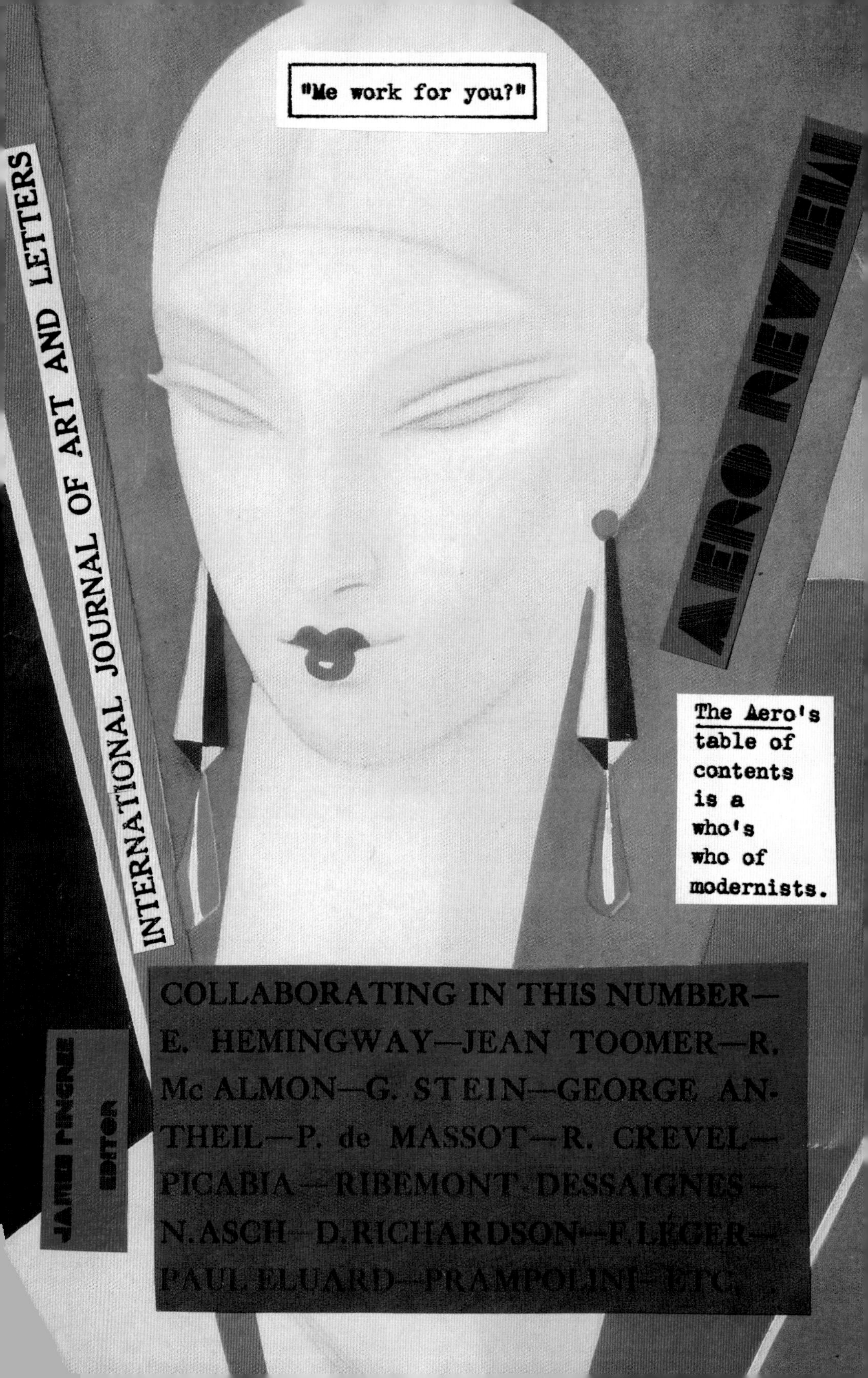
"Me work for you?"
INTERNATIONAL JOURNAL OF ART AND LETTERS
AERO REVIEW
The Aero's table of contents is a who's who of modernists.
JAMES
EDITOR
COLLABORATING IN THIS NUMBER—E. HEMINGWAY—JEAN TOOMER—R. Mc ALMON—G. STEIN—GEORGE ANTHEIL—P. de MASSOT—R. CREVEL—PICABIA—RIBEMONT DESSAIGNES—N. ASCH—D. RICHARDSON—F. LEGER—PAUL ELUARD—PRAMPOLINI—ETC.

He holds up a hand.

THE ELECTRIC CHAIR

JOHN D. ROCKFELLER JR.

HOOVER

GARY

GOMPERS

DUPONT FAMILY

BILLY SUNDAY

SUNDAY OBSERVANCE

Y. M. C. A.

THE MAN WHO INVENTED THE ELECTRIC CHAIR

DR. FRANK CRANE

COFFEE HOUSE (ENTIRE)

BISHOP MANNING

PAUL ROSENFELD

THE BARRYMORES

DARIUS MILHAUD

100 PER CENT OF THE ACTORS

98 PER CENT OF THE PAINTERS

98 PERCENT OF THE POETS

99½ PERCENT OF THE MUSICIANS

YOU'RE NEXT (STIEGLITZ FOR MSS)

The Aero publishes radical manifestos (like this one about who deserves to get the electric chair).

"Before you say no, hear me out. I'll pay you 100 francs a week.

And my behavior will be 100% professional. No funny business, I promise. Give it a thought."

My Thoughts:

* Pay is twice what any other English paper offers.

* I'll work with every big shot writer in Paris.

* Jamie & I have unfinished business.

So I say yes, I will. Yes.

do be devils to flirt. I could sit on one side till the bark of the day laughing lazy at the sheep's lightning, till I'd followed through my upfielded naphewscope the rugaby moon cumu- rously godrolling himself westasleep amuckst the cloudscrums for to watch how carefully my nocturnal goosemother would lay her new golden sheegg for me down under in the shy orient. What wouldn't I give — my socks, my shoes, my shirt, honest! — for a feast of grannom with the finny ones, flashing down the swansway, leaps ahead of the swift 'macEels and the purse- winded carpers, rearin aut___g perches astern of me, or, when I'd like own company be___ help of a norange and bear, to be reclined by the las____ ther, with the jealosomines wilting away to their hear___ and the king of saptimber getting down his special odou____ onsternation, burning water in the spearlight or, catching____ king's royal college of sturgeone b___le armful f____ while. O twined' __ abower in ___ ___entyforu Dorian blackbirds o___ ___cal airs, I give, a king, to me, ___uble give. And what sensitive c___ ___k it sumtotal in subdominal po___ ___whole ounce you half on your back ___ ___at'd make pay like cash registers ___ ___ophole on the mart as a factor. And ___ ___wouldn't hold me. Nothing would stop me. ___ __ knew where you weren't I stake my 'ignit___ ___ggering humanity and loyally roliing you ove___ __ tons of red clo- ___ __d spoil ver al-

The Aero is publishing a section of James Joyce's new novel called (for the time being) "Work in Progress."

Jamie can't make heads or tails of Joyce's scribbled page proofs.

"You're just going to have to sit down with Joyce and have him spell it all out. Literally," Jamie tells me.

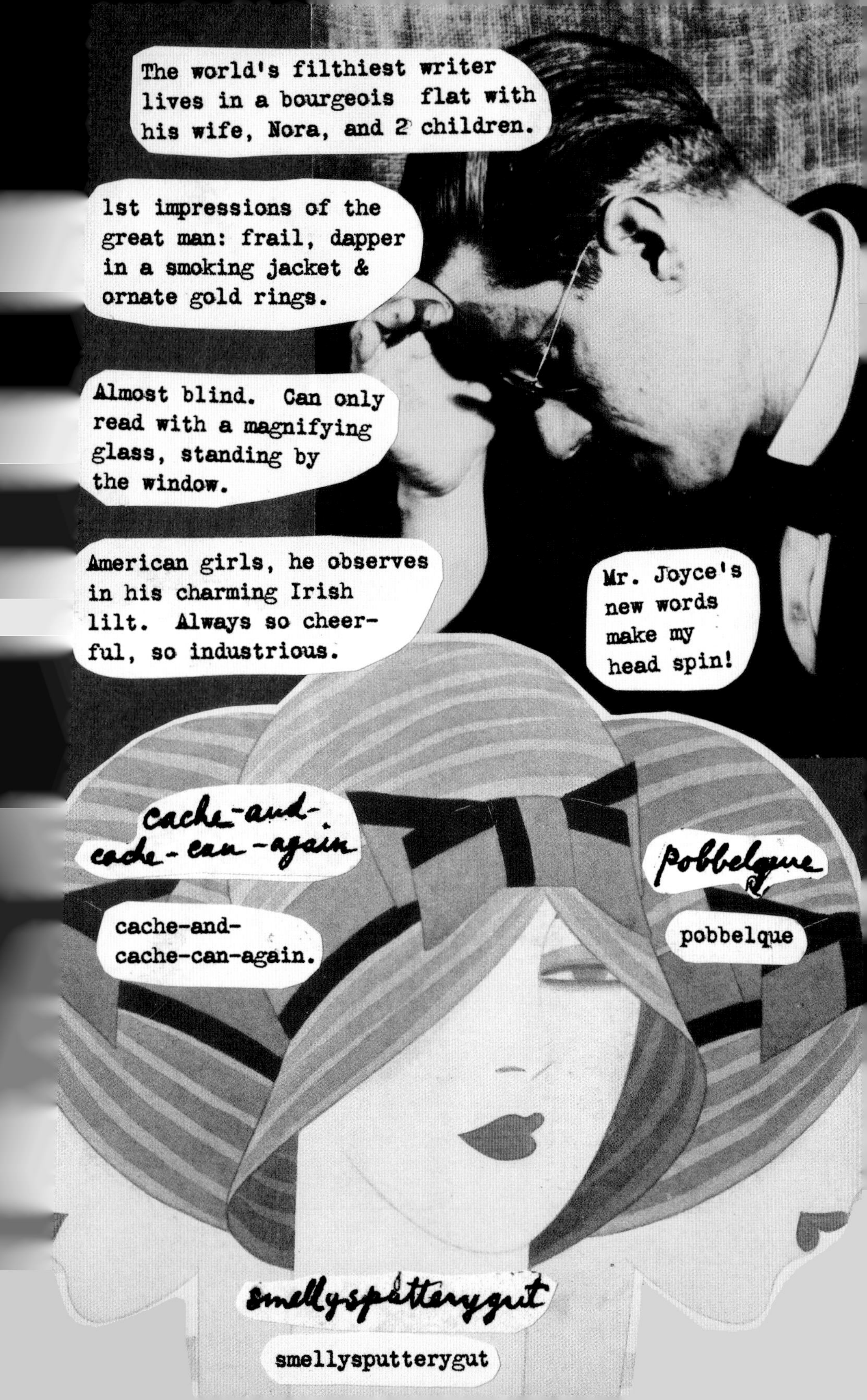
The world's filthiest writer lives in a bourgeois flat with his wife, Nora, and 2 children.
1st impressions of the great man: frail, dapper in a smoking jacket & ornate gold rings.
Almost blind. Can only read with a magnifying glass, standing by the window.
American girls, he observes in his charming Irish lilt. Always so cheerful, so industrious.
Mr. Joyce's new words make my head spin!
cache-and-cache-can-again
cache-and-cache-can-again.
pobbelque
pobbelque
smellyspatterygut
smellysputterygut

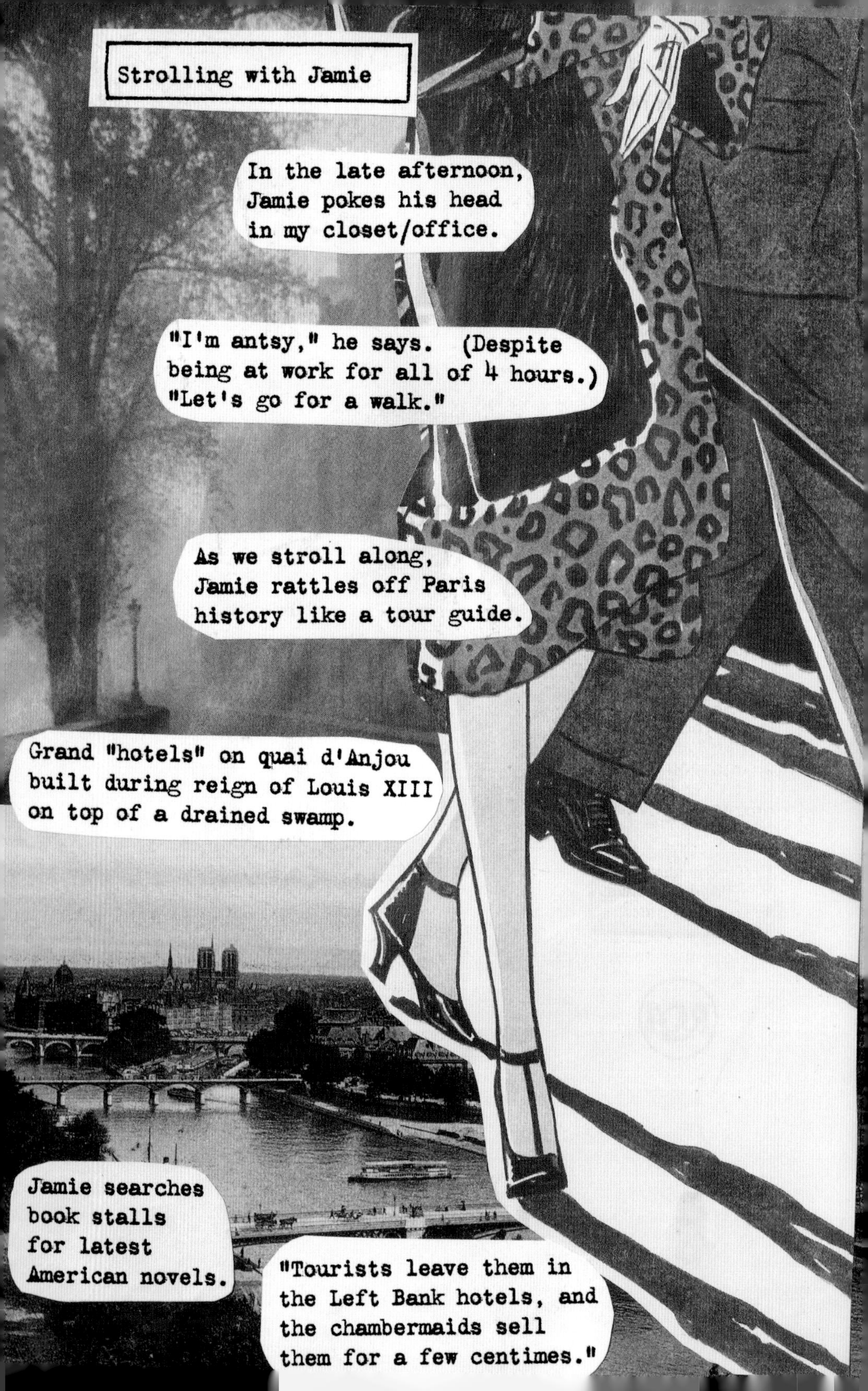
Strolling with Jamie
In the late afternoon, Jamie pokes his head in my closet/office.
"I'm antsy," he says. (Despite being at work for all of 4 hours.) "Let's go for a walk."
As we stroll along, Jamie rattles off Paris history like a tour guide.
Grand "hotels" on quai d'Anjou built during reign of Louis XIII on top of a drained swamp.
Jamie searches book stalls for latest American novels.
"Tourists leave them in the Left Bank hotels, and the chambermaids sell them for a few centimes."

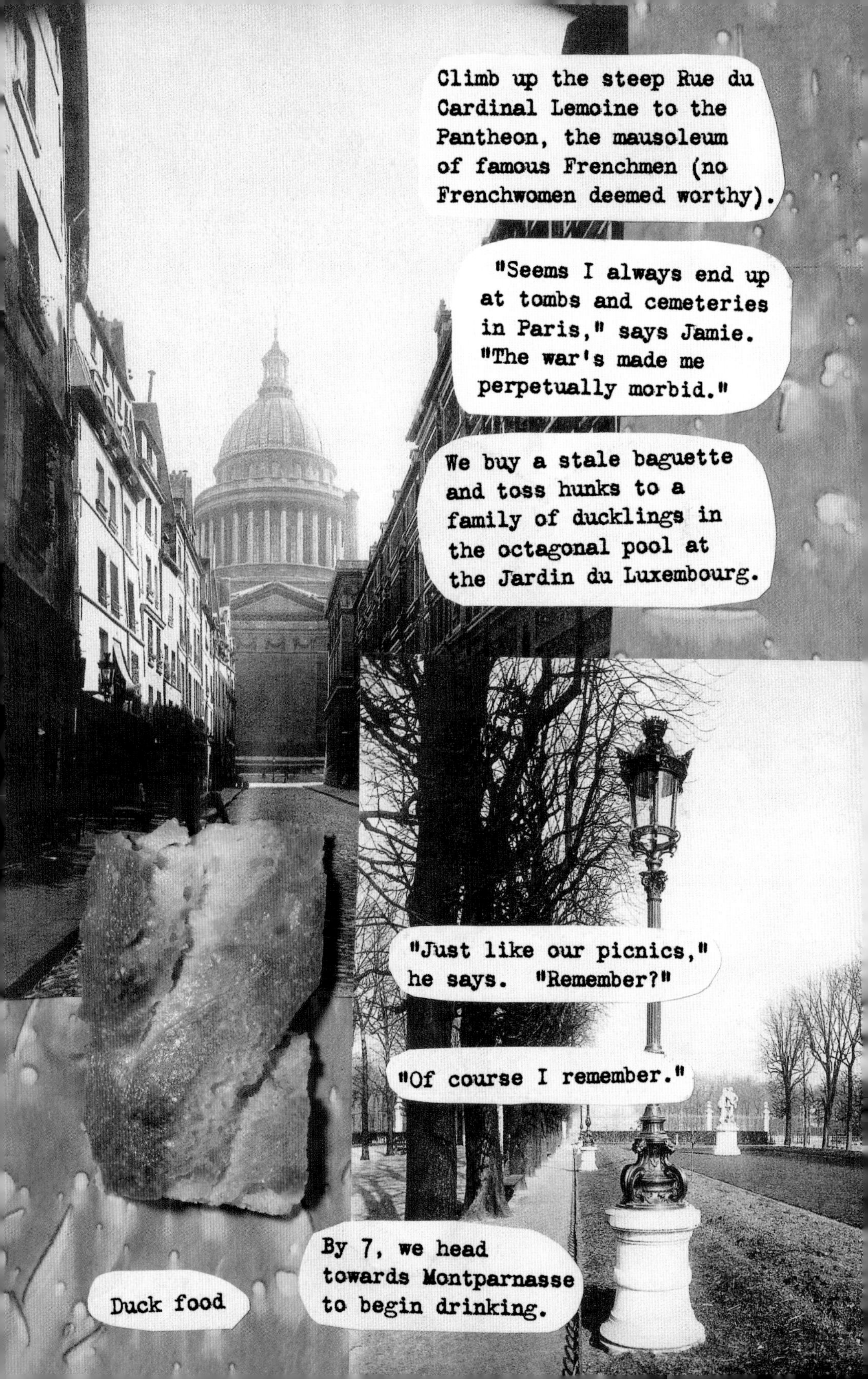
Climb up the steep Rue du Cardinal Lemoine to the Pantheon, the mausoleum of famous Frenchmen (no Frenchwomen deemed worthy).
"Seems I always end up at tombs and cemeteries in Paris," says Jamie. "The war's made me perpetually morbid."
We buy a stale baguette and toss hunks to a family of ducklings in the octagonal pool at the Jardin du Luxembourg.
"Just like our picnics," he says. "Remember?"
"Of course I remember."
Duck food
By 7, we head towards Montparnasse to begin drinking.

The Expats of Montparnasse

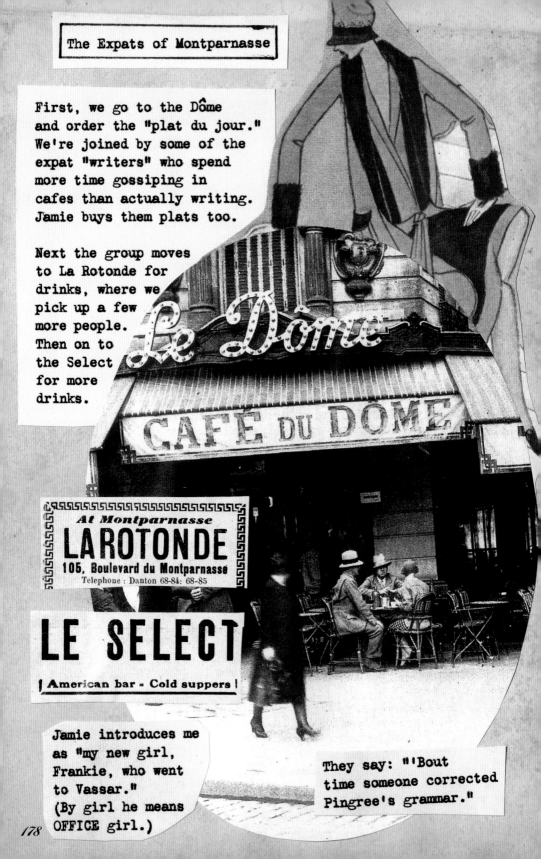

First, we go to the Dôme and order the "plat du jour." We're joined by some of the expat "writers" who spend more time gossiping in cafes than actually writing. Jamie buys them plats too.

Next the group moves to La Rotonde for drinks, where we pick up a few more people. Then on to the Select for more drinks.

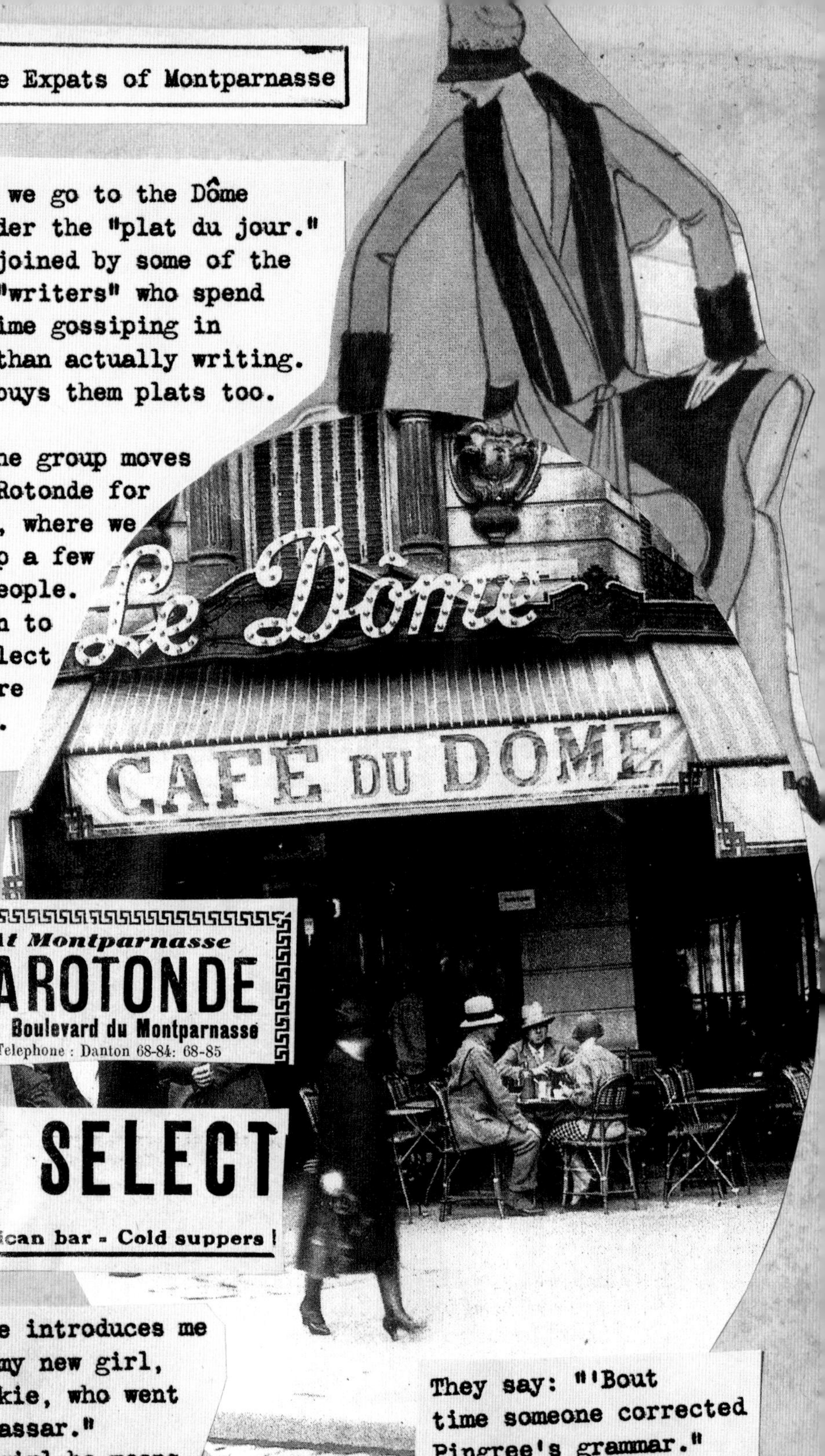
Le Dôme
CAFÉ DU DÔME

At Montparnasse
LAROTONDE
105, Boulevard du Montparnasse
Telephone : Danton 68-84: 68-85

LE SELECT
American bar - Cold suppers

Jamie introduces me as "my new girl, Frankie, who went to Vassar." (By girl he means OFFICE girl.)

They say: "'Bout time someone corrected Pingree's grammar."

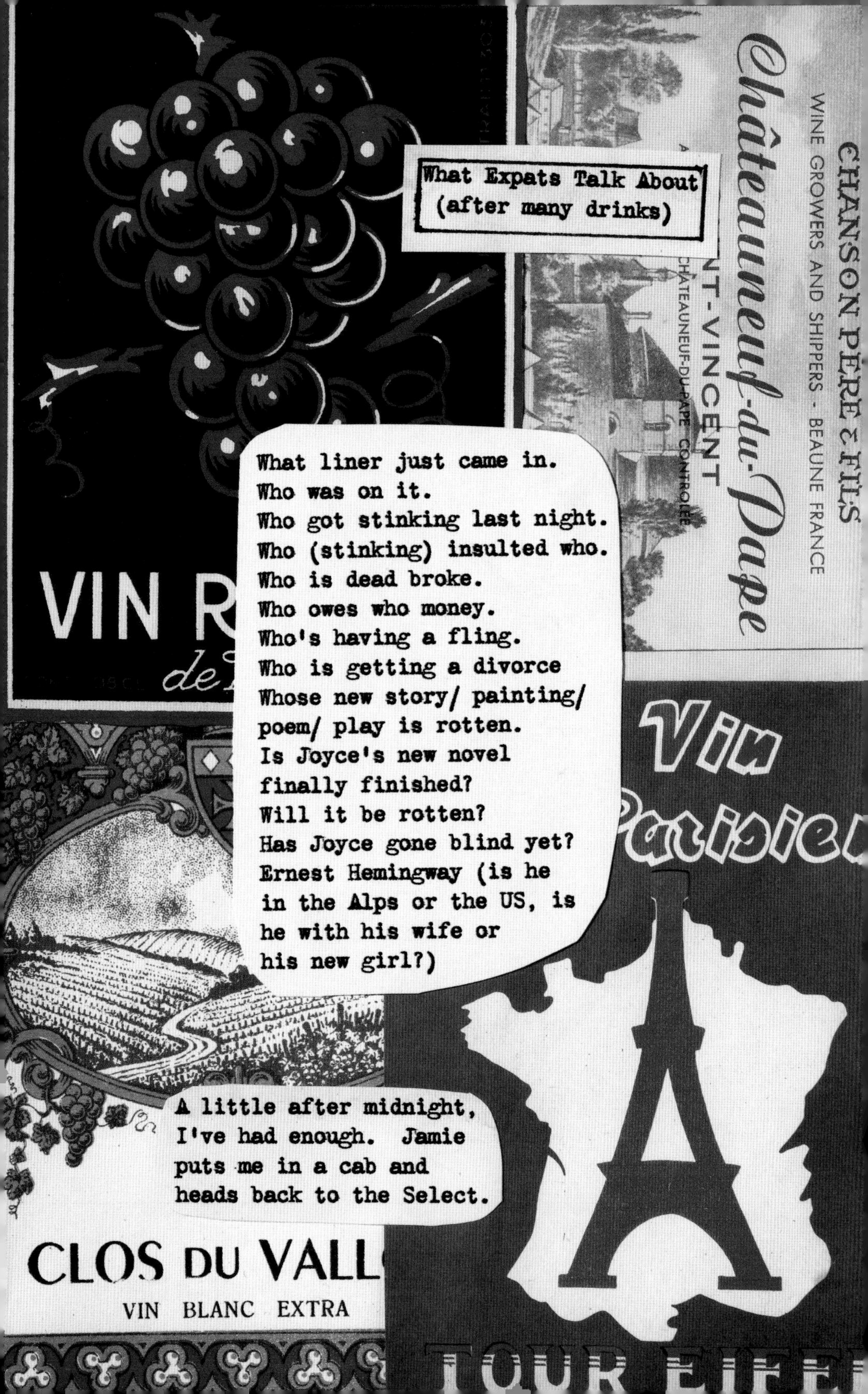
CHANSON PERE & FILS
WINE GROWERS AND SHIPPERS - BEAUNE FRANCE
Châteauneuf-du-Pape
CHÂTEAUNEUF-DU-PAPE CONTRÔLÉE
Vin
VIN BLANC EXTRA

What Expats Talk About
(after many drinks)

What liner just came in.
Who was on it.
Who got stinking last night.
Who (stinking) insulted who.
Who is dead broke.
Who owes who money.
Who's having a fling.
Who is getting a divorce
Whose new story/ painting/
poem/ play is rotten.
Is Joyce's new novel
finally finished?
Will it be rotten?
Has Joyce gone blind yet?
Ernest Hemingway (is he
in the Alps or the US, is
he with his wife or
his new girl?)

A little after midnight, I've had enough. Jamie puts me in a cab and heads back to the Select.

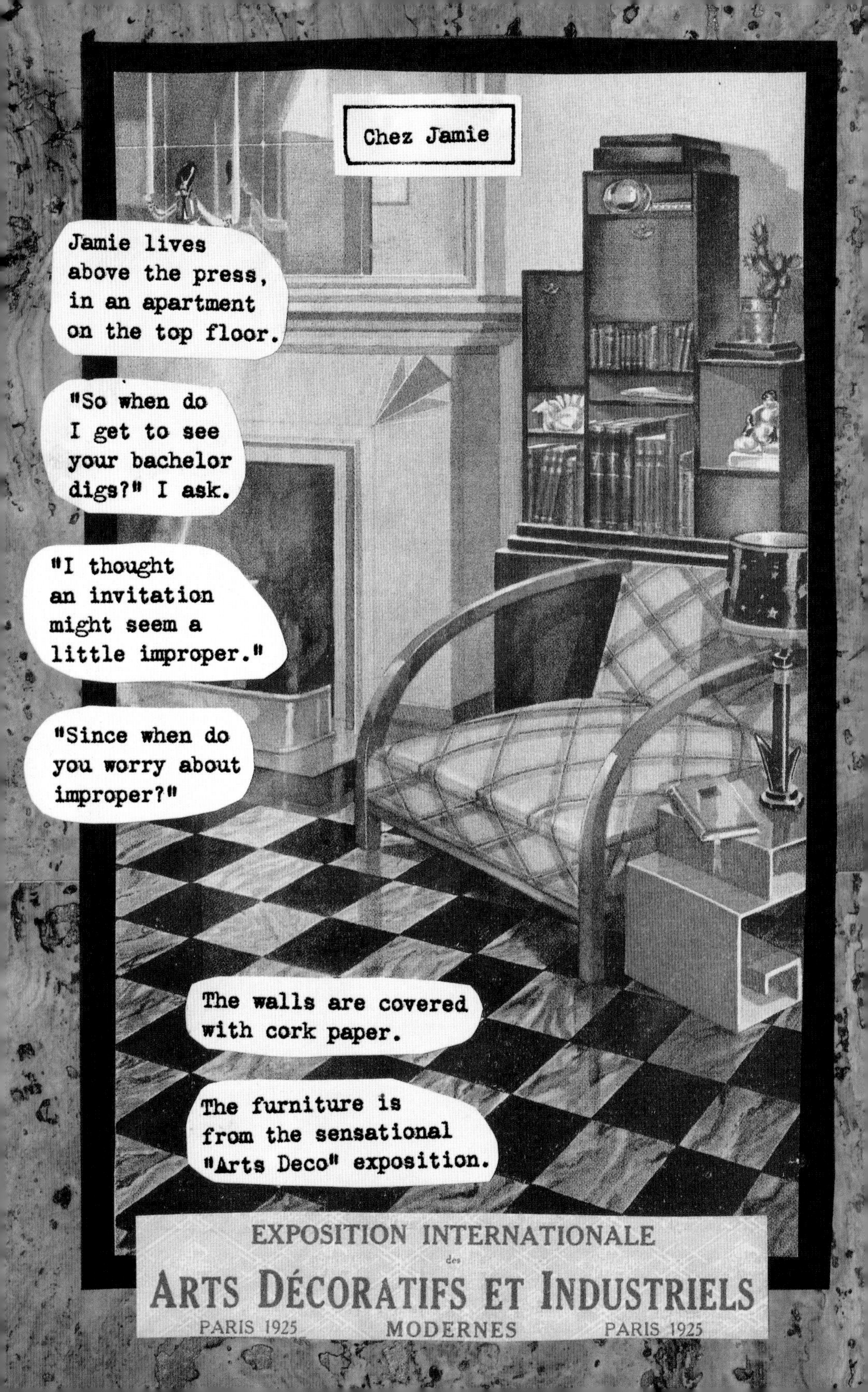
Chez Jamie
Jamie lives above the press, in an apartment on the top floor.
"So when do I get to see your bachelor digs?" I ask.
"I thought an invitation might seem a little improper."
"Since when do you worry about improper?"
The walls are covered with cork paper.
The furniture is from the sensational "Arts Deco" exposition.
EXPOSITION INTERNATIONALE
des
ARTS DÉCORATIFS ET INDUSTRIELS
PARIS 1925 MODERNES PARIS 1925

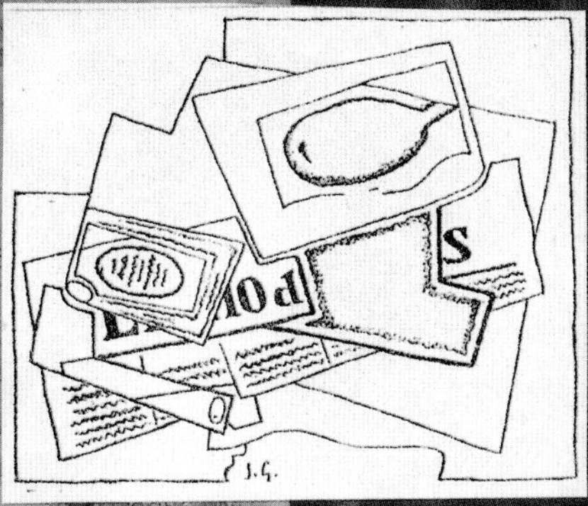

Drawings by Jamie's pal, Juan Gris.

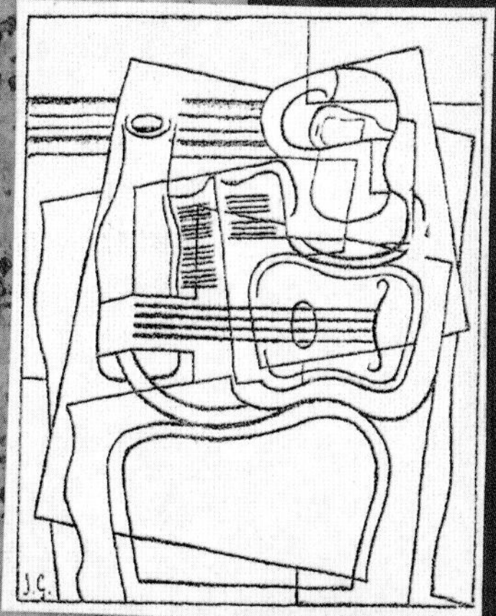

GRANDE FINE CHAMPAGNE

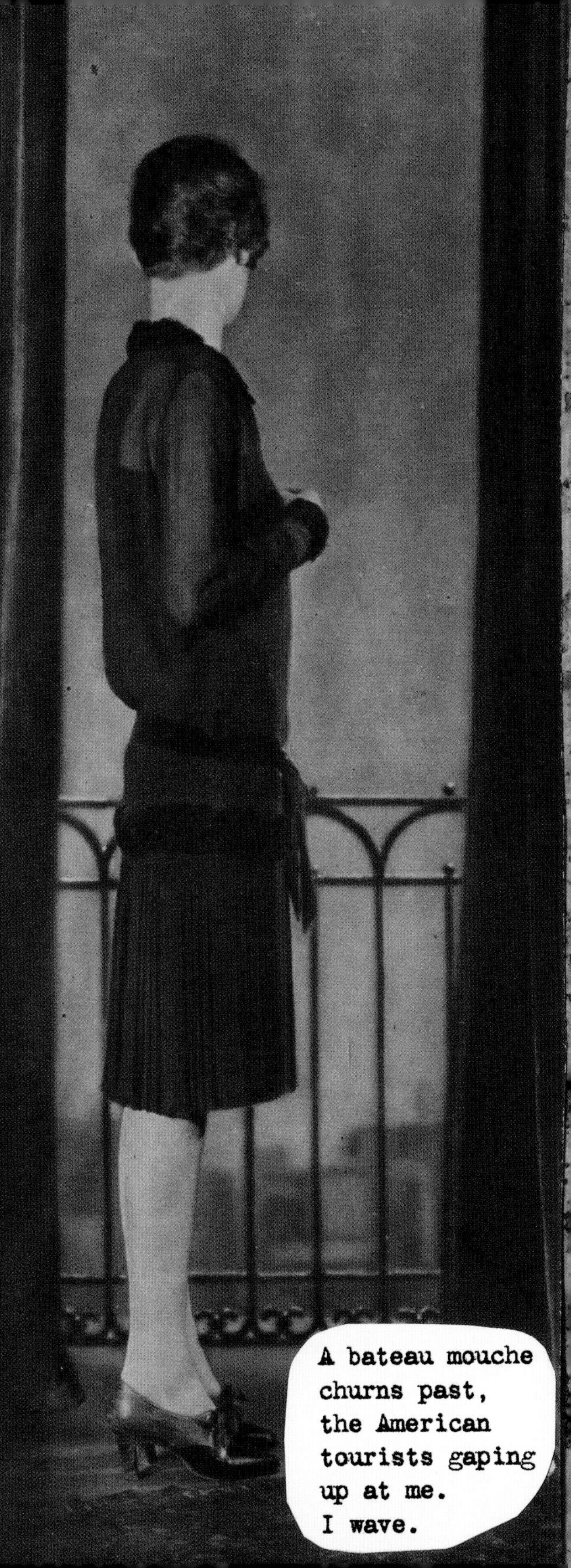

He pulls a bottle of champagne from a lead ice chest while I take in the view down the Seine to the gargoyles of Notre Dame.

A bateau mouche churns past, the American tourists gaping up at me. I wave.

The Seduction

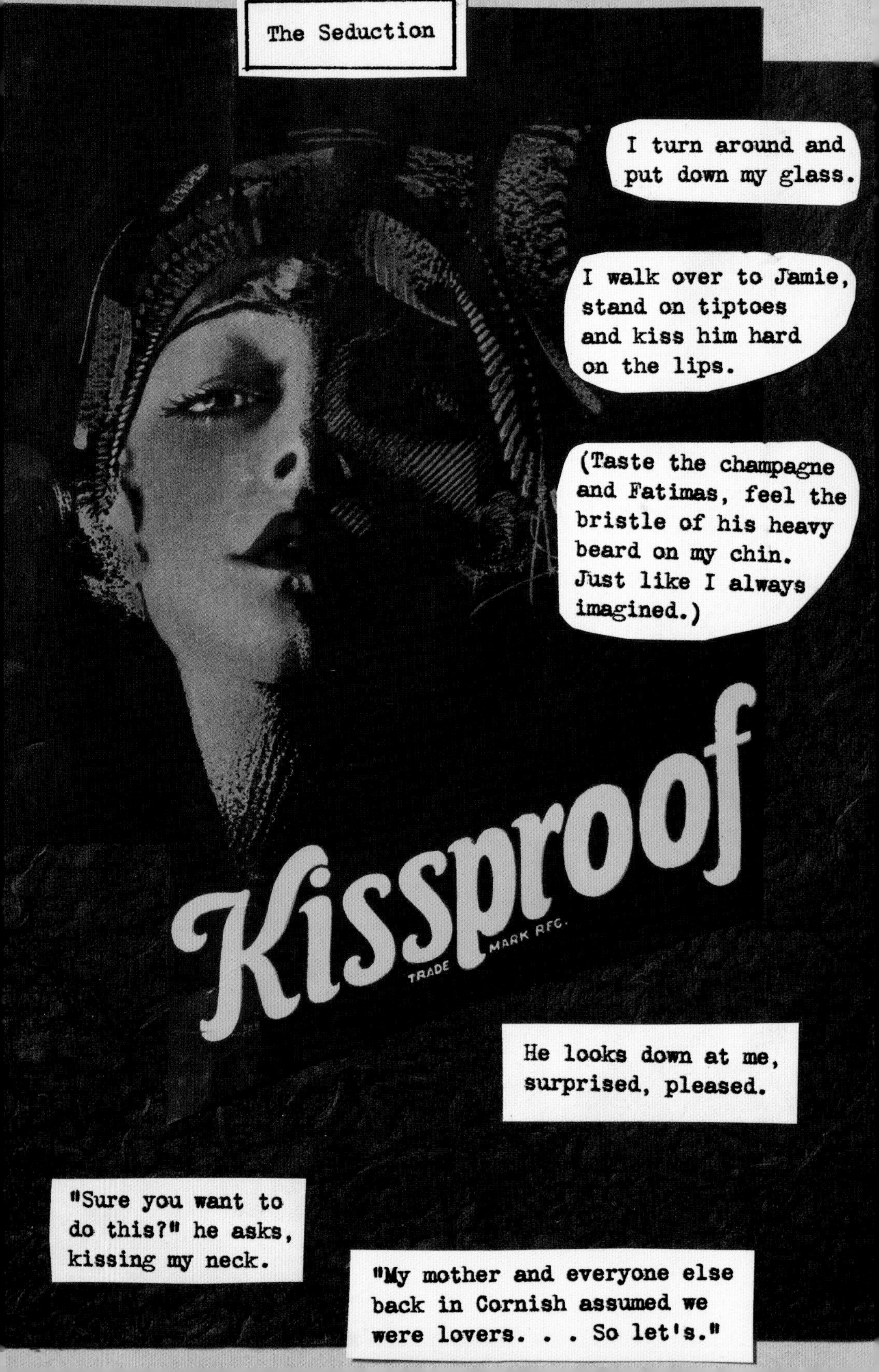

I turn around and put down my glass.

I walk over to Jamie, stand on tiptoes and kiss him hard on the lips.

(Taste the champagne and Fatimas, feel the bristle of his heavy beard on my chin. Just like I always imagined.)

He looks down at me, surprised, pleased.

"Sure you want to do this?" he asks, kissing my neck.

"My mother and everyone else back in Cornish assumed we were lovers. . . So let's."

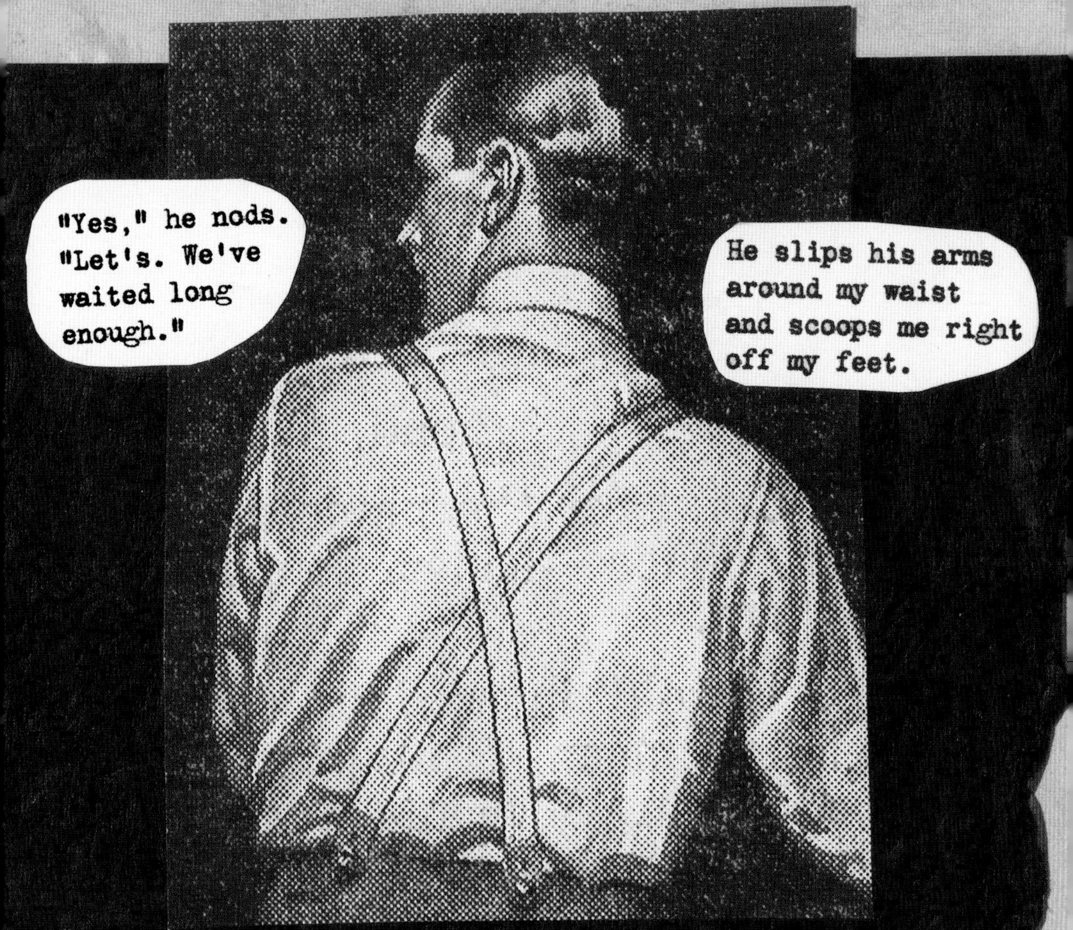
"Yes," he nods. "Let's. We've waited long enough."
He slips his arms around my waist and scoops me right off my feet.

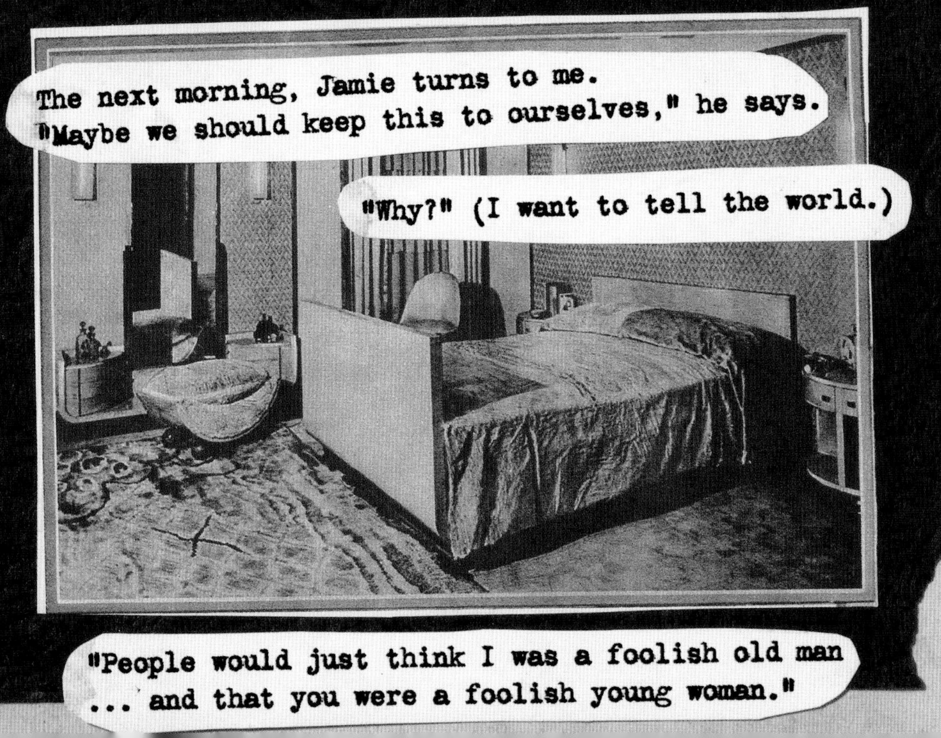
The next morning, Jamie turns to me. "Maybe we should keep this to ourselves," he says.
"Why?" (I want to tell the world.)
"People would just think I was a foolish old man ... and that you were a foolish young woman."

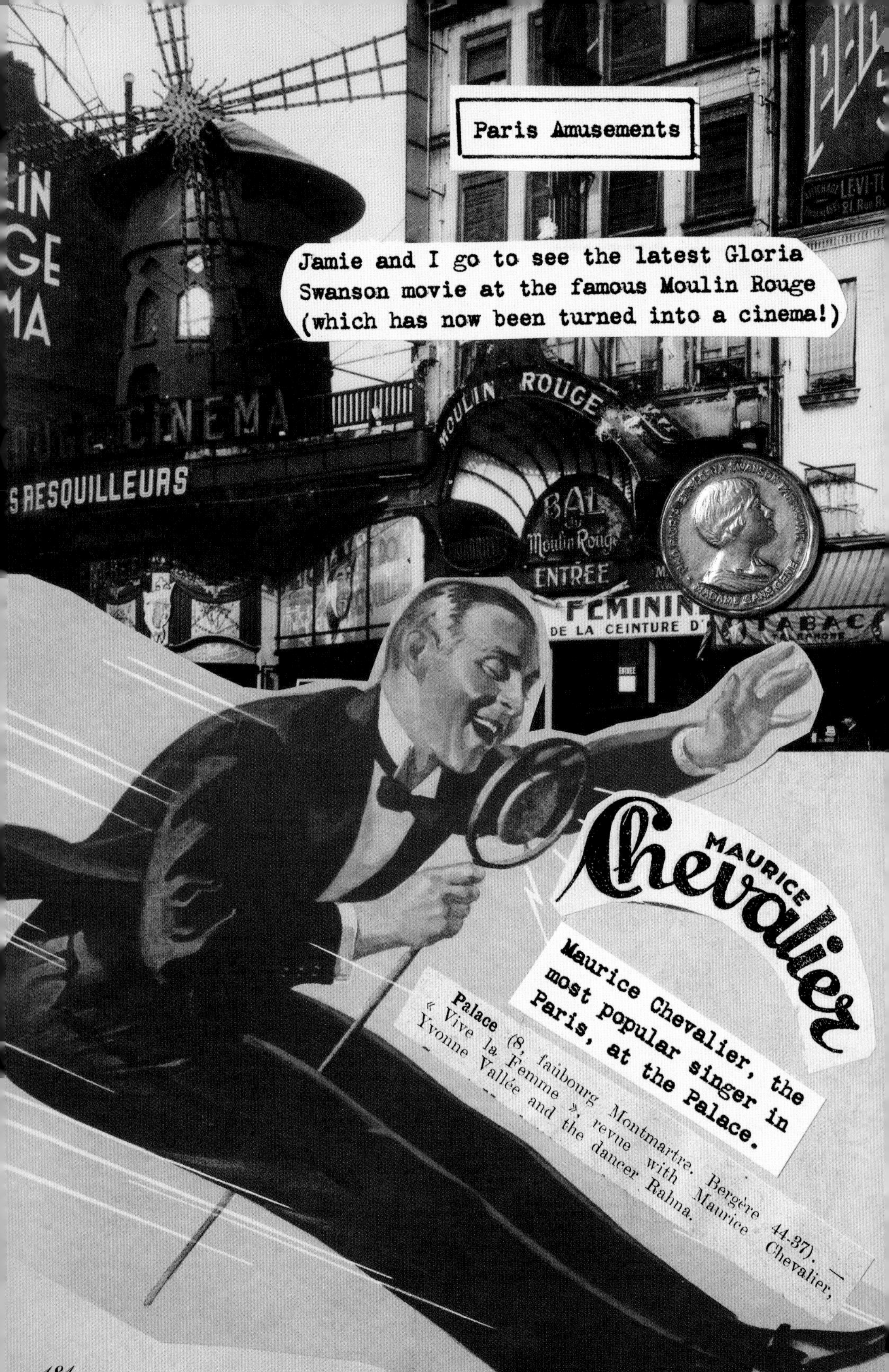
MOULIN ROUGE
CINEMA
LES RESQUILLEURS
BAL du Moulin Rouge
ENTRÉE
FEMININ
DE LA CEINTURE D'
TABAC
MADAME SANS-GÊNE
MAURICE Chevalier

Paris Amusements

Jamie and I go to see the latest Gloria Swanson movie at the famous Moulin Rouge (which has now been turned into a cinema!)

Maurice Chevalier, the most popular singer in Paris, at the Palace.

Palace (8, faubourg Montmartre. Bergère 44.37). — « Vive la Femme », revue with Maurice Chevalier, Yvonne Vallée and the dancer Rahna.

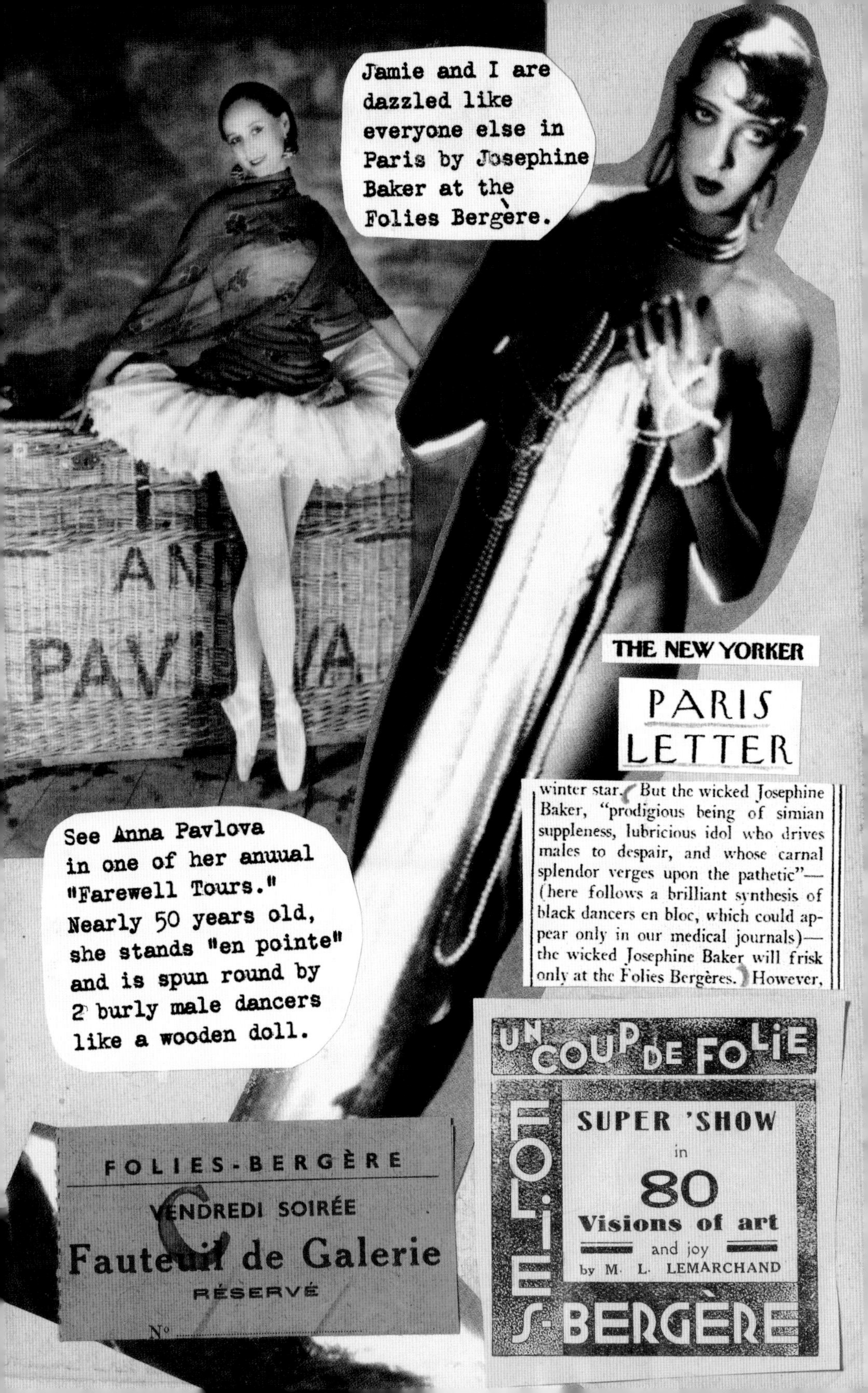
Jamie and I are dazzled like everyone else in Paris by Josephine Baker at the Folies Bergère.
ANNA PAVLOVA
See Anna Pavlova in one of her anuual "Farewell Tours." Nearly 50 years old, she stands "en pointe" and is spun round by 2 burly male dancers like a wooden doll.
THE NEW YORKER
PARIS LETTER
FOLIES-BERGÈRE
VENDREDI SOIRÉE
Fauteuil de Galerie
RÉSERVÉ
N°
UN COUP DE FOLIE
FOLIES-BERGÈRE
SUPER 'SHOW
in
80
Visions of art
and joy
by M. L. LEMARCHAND

winter star. But the wicked Josephine Baker, "prodigious being of simian suppleness, lubricious idol who drives males to despair, and whose carnal splendor verges upon the pathetic"—(here follows a brilliant synthesis of black dancers en bloc, which could appear only in our medical journals)—the wicked Josephine Baker will frisk only at the Folies Bergères. However,

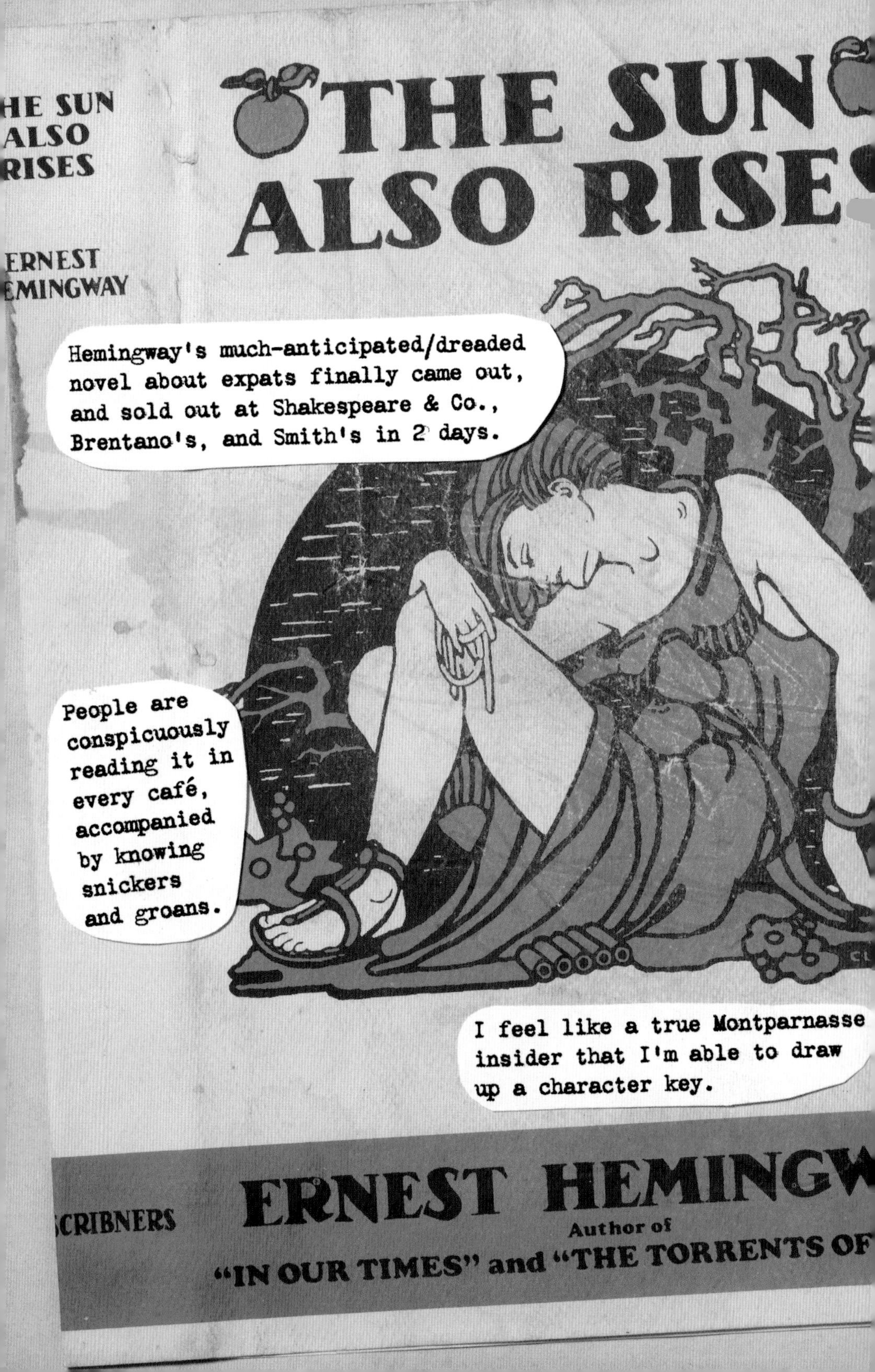
THE SUN ALSO RISES
ERNEST HEMINGWAY
THE SUN ALSO RISES
Hemingway's much-anticipated/dreaded novel about expats finally came out, and sold out at Shakespeare & Co., Brentano's, and Smith's in 2 days.
People are conspicuously reading it in every café, accompanied by knowing snickers and groans.
I feel like a true Montparnasse insider that I'm able to draw up a character key.
SCRIBNERS
ERNEST HEMINGW
Author of
"IN OUR TIMES" and "THE TORRENTS OF

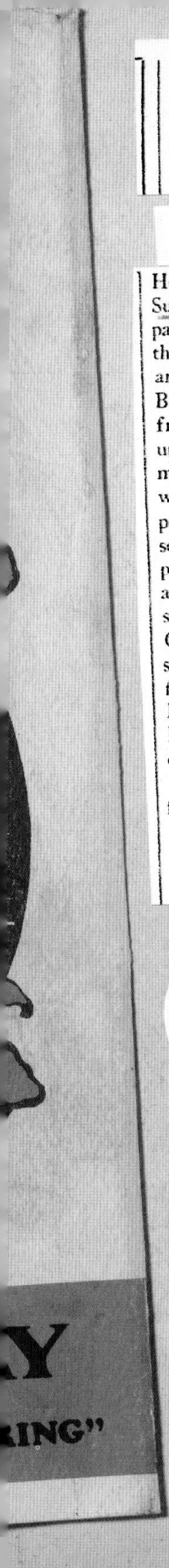

PARIS LETTER

PARIS, Dec. 4, 1926

The appearance here of Ernest Hemingway's *roman à clef*, "The Sun Also Rises," has stirred Montparnasse, where, it is asserted, all of the four leading characters are local and easily identifiable. The titled British declassée and her Scottish friend, the American *Frances* and her unlucky *Robert Cohn* with his art magazine which, like a new broom, was to sweep esthetics clean—all these personages are, it is maintained, to be seen just where Hemingway so often placed them at the Select. Not being amorously identified with the tale, it should be safe to say that Donald Ogden Stewart is taken to be the stuffed-bird-loving *Bill*. Under the flimsy disguise of *Braddocks*, certainly Ford Madox Ford is visible as the Briton who gives, as Mr. Ford does, dancing parties in the *bal musette* behind the Panthéon. Because it is also from the life, René Crevel's "La Mort Difficile" has been criticized. It is another Montparnasse episode of American love and French despair.

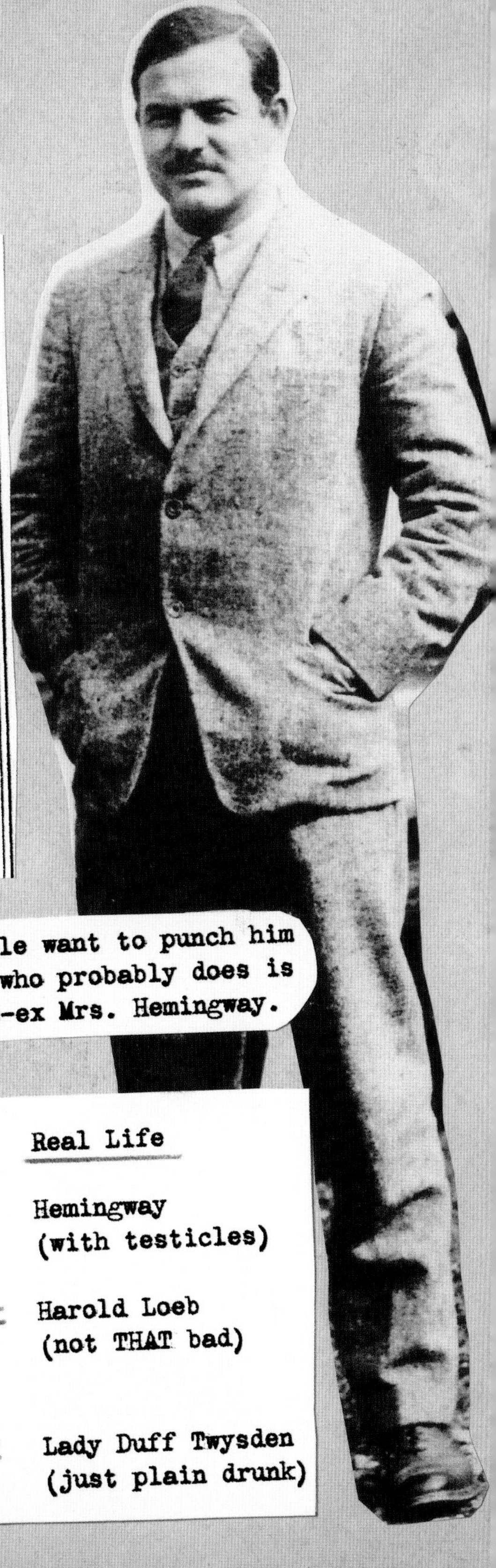

Ernest brags that people want to punch him out, but the only one who probably does is Hadley, the soon-to-be-ex Mrs. Hemingway.

Character		Real Life
Jake Barnes (with no testicles)	=	Hemingway (with testicles)
Robert Cohn (writes bad novel, whines, cries about girl)	=	Harold Loeb (not THAT bad)
Lady Brett Ashley (charming drunk)	=	Lady Duff Twysden (just plain drunk)

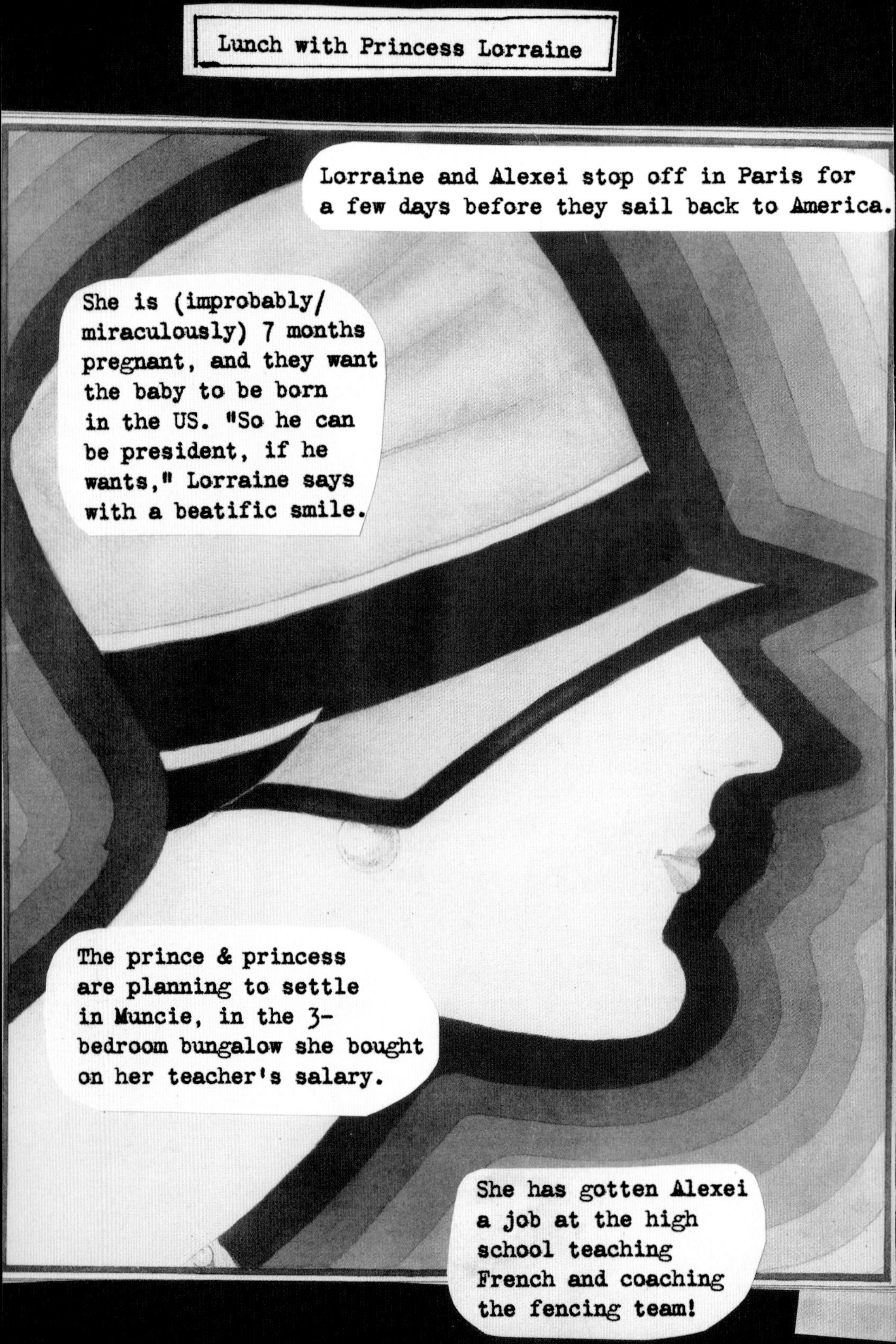
Lunch with Princess Lorraine
Lorraine and Alexei stop off in Paris for a few days before they sail back to America.
She is (improbably/ miraculously) 7 months pregnant, and they want the baby to be born in the US. "So he can be president, if he wants," Lorraine says with a beatific smile.
The prince & princess are planning to settle in Muncie, in the 3-bedroom bungalow she bought on her teacher's salary.
She has gotten Alexei a job at the high school teaching French and coaching the fencing team!

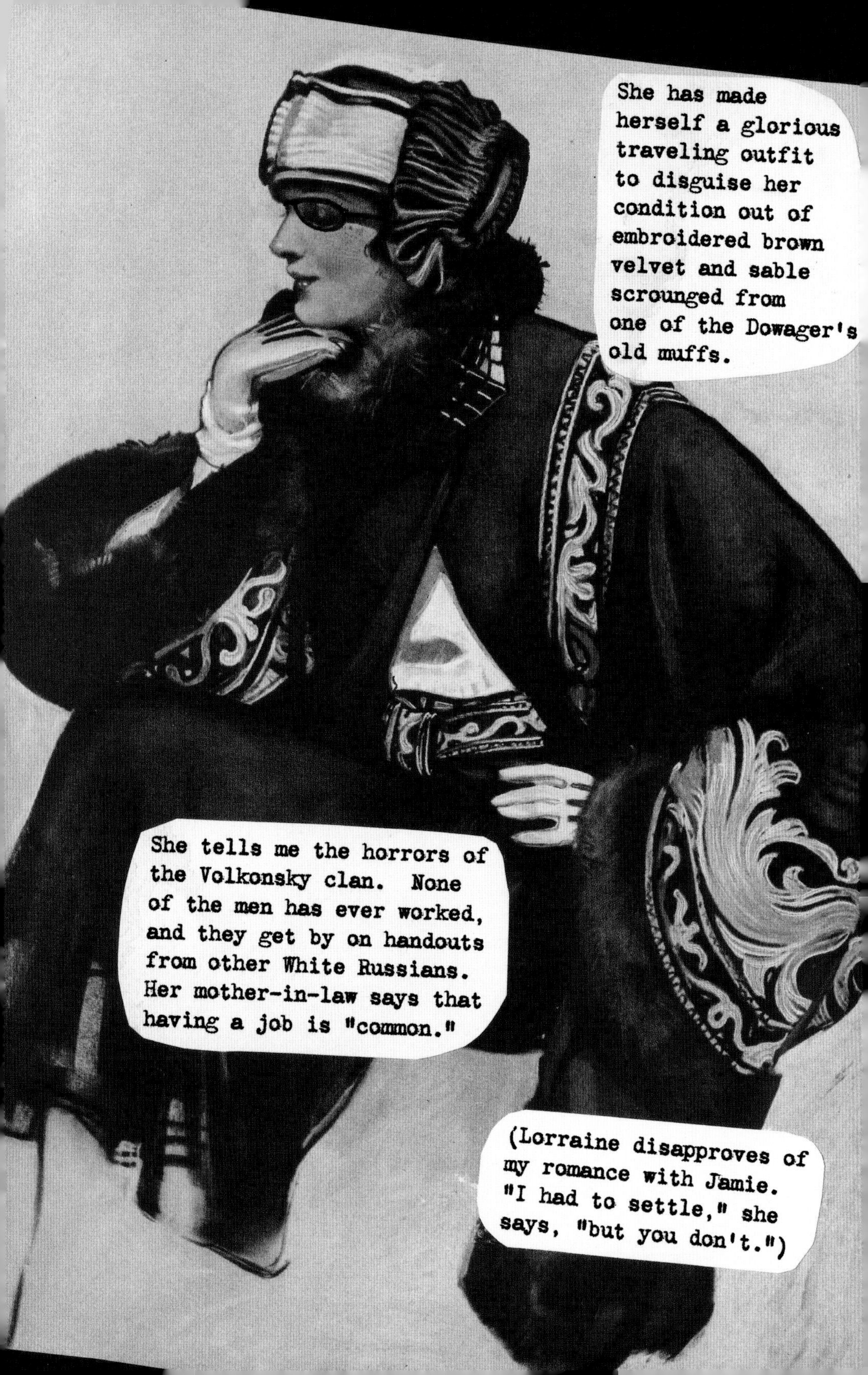
She has made herself a glorious traveling outfit to disguise her condition out of embroidered brown velvet and sable scrounged from one of the Dowager's old muffs.
She tells me the horrors of the Volkonsky clan. None of the men has ever worked, and they get by on handouts from other White Russians. Her mother-in-law says that having a job is "common."
(Lorraine disapproves of my romance with Jamie. "I had to settle," she says, "but you don't.")

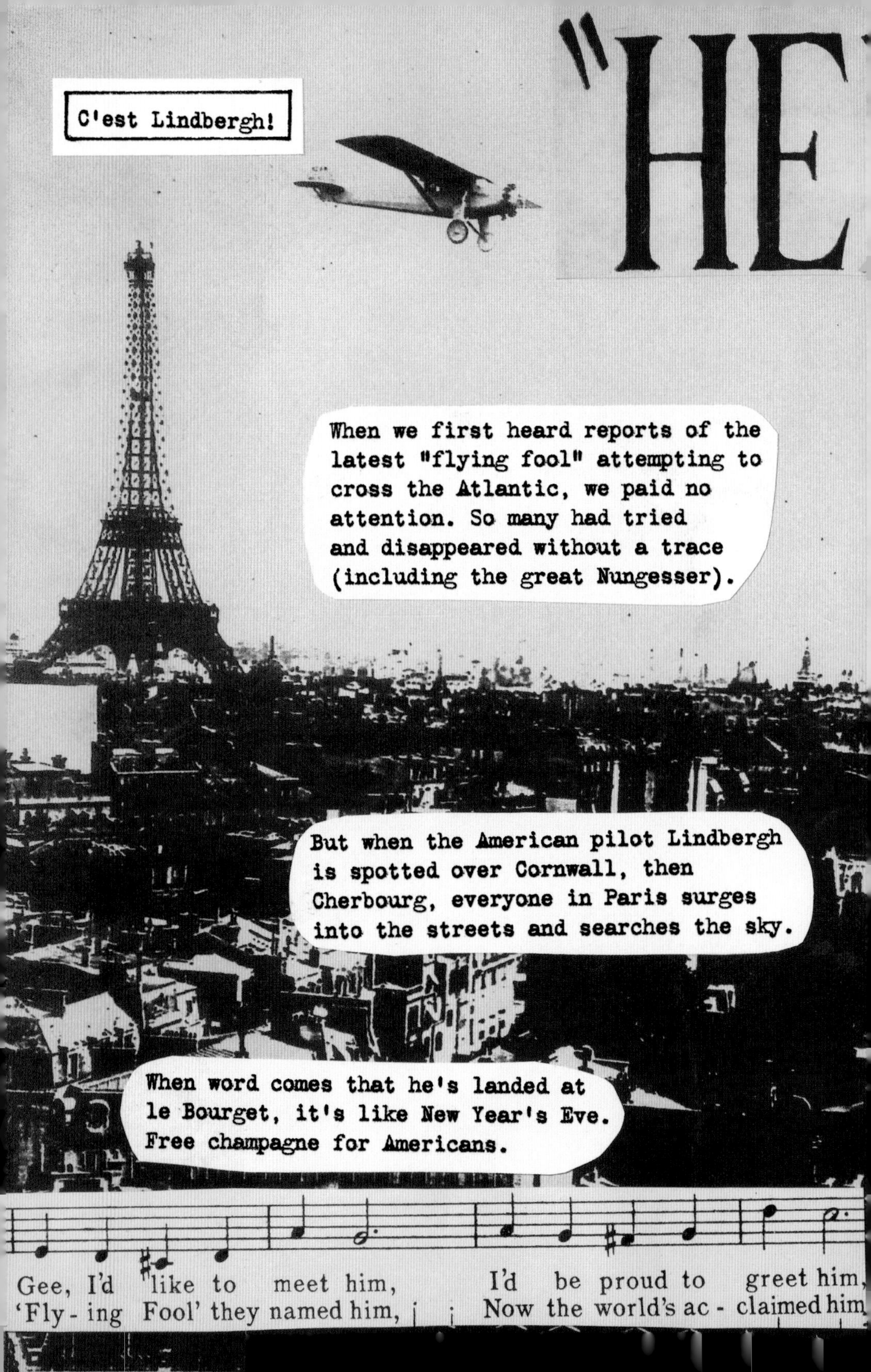
C'est Lindbergh!
"HE
When we first heard reports of the latest "flying fool" attempting to cross the Atlantic, we paid no attention. So many had tried and disappeared without a trace (including the great Nungesser).
But when the American pilot Lindbergh is spotted over Cornwall, then Cherbourg, everyone in Paris surges into the streets and searches the sky.
When word comes that he's landed at le Bourget, it's like New Year's Eve. Free champagne for Americans.
Gee, I'd like to meet him, I'd be proud to greet him,
'Fly - ing Fool' they named him, Now the world's ac - claimed him

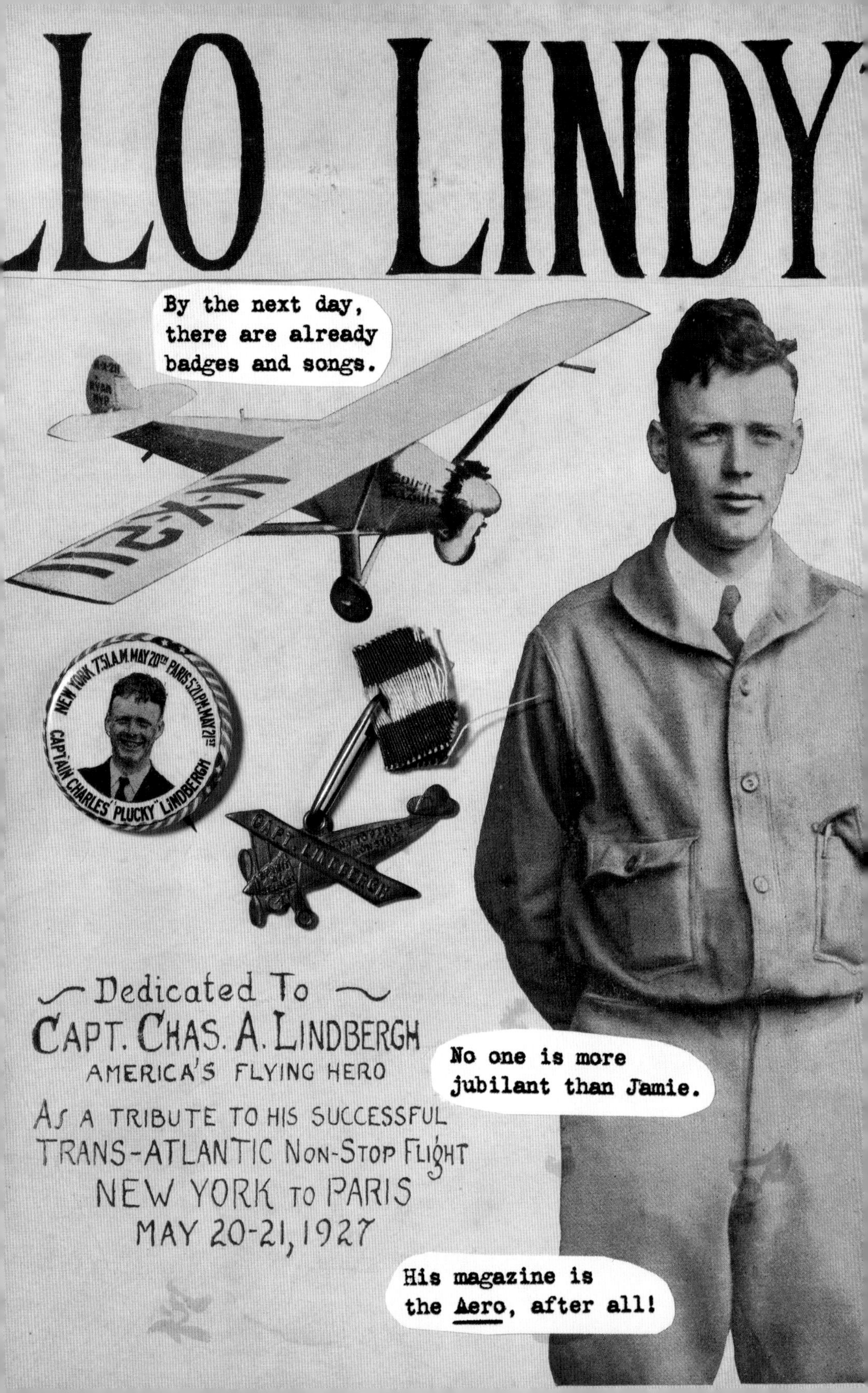
LO LINDY
By the next day, there are already badges and songs.
N-X-211
CAPTAIN CHARLES "PLUCKY" LINDBERGH
CAPT. LINDBERGH
Dedicated To
CAPT. CHAS. A. LINDBERGH
AMERICA'S FLYING HERO
AS A TRIBUTE TO HIS SUCCESSFUL
TRANS-ATLANTIC NON-STOP FLIGHT
NEW YORK TO PARIS
MAY 20-21, 1927
No one is more jubilant than Jamie.
His magazine is the Aero, after all!

But after a while, all the hero worship for Lindy makes Jamie gloomy.

"I used to be that young," he says.

By which he means before the war, the divorce. When anything seemed possible, even flying across the Atlantic in a biplane.

And I have to admit that in the harsh light of mid-day, his face looks creased and bloated. Nightly Montparnasse drinking bouts are taking their toll.

"Please. Don't talk like that," I say. "Look at what you've done. Founded the Aero. Published writers no one else dared to."

"Just my point. Look at the Aero. Every quarter it sinks deeper in red ink. I'll be all out of money pretty soon."

Sketched from life at Fashion Park

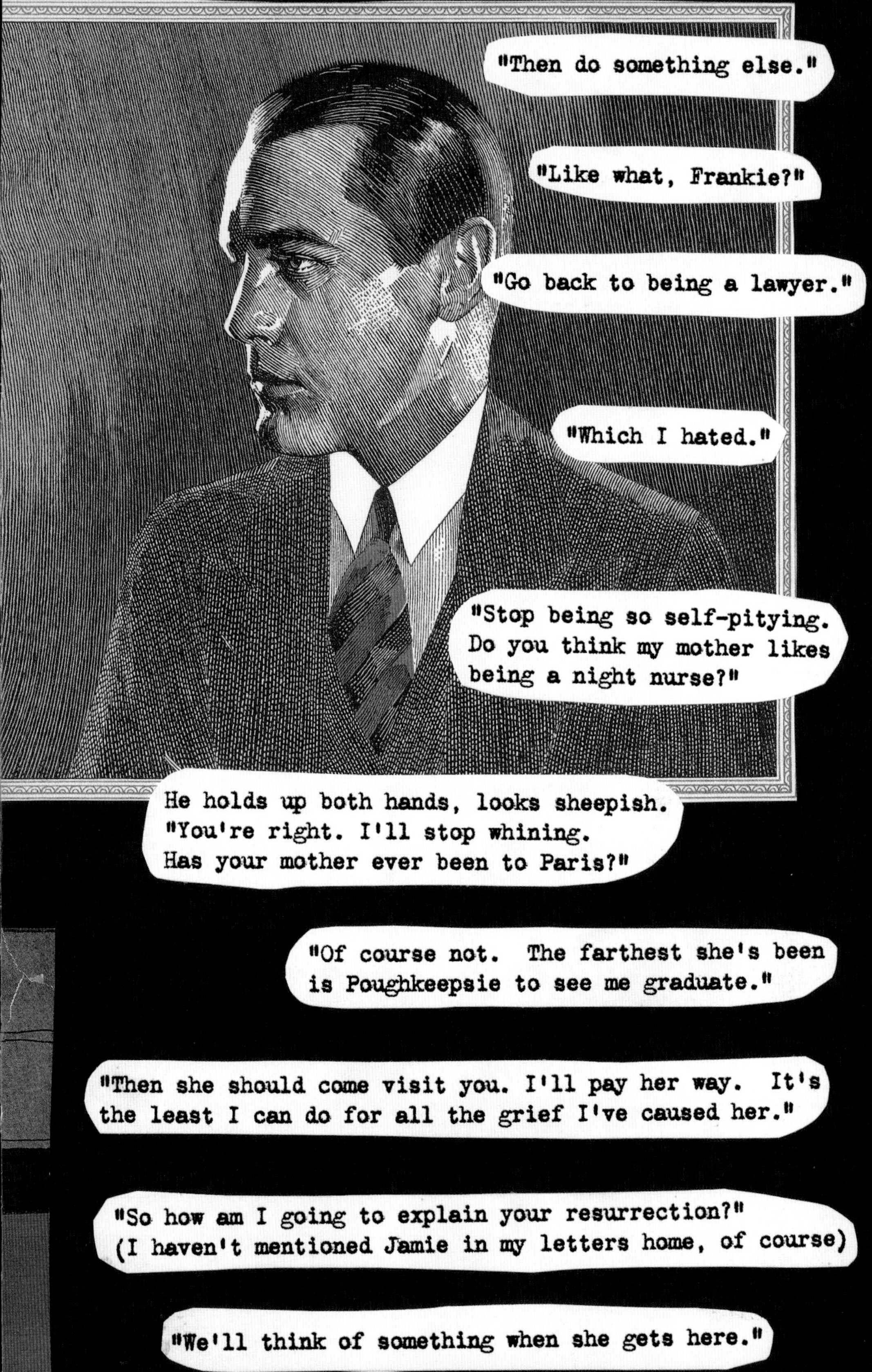

"Then do something else."

"Like what, Frankie?"

"Go back to being a lawyer."

"Which I hated."

"Stop being so self-pitying. Do you think my mother likes being a night nurse?"

He holds up both hands, looks sheepish. "You're right. I'll stop whining. Has your mother ever been to Paris?"

"Of course not. The farthest she's been is Poughkeepsie to see me graduate."

"Then she should come visit you. I'll pay her way. It's the least I can do for all the grief I've caused her."

"So how am I going to explain your resurrection?" (I haven't mentioned Jamie in my letters home, of course)

"We'll think of something when she gets here."

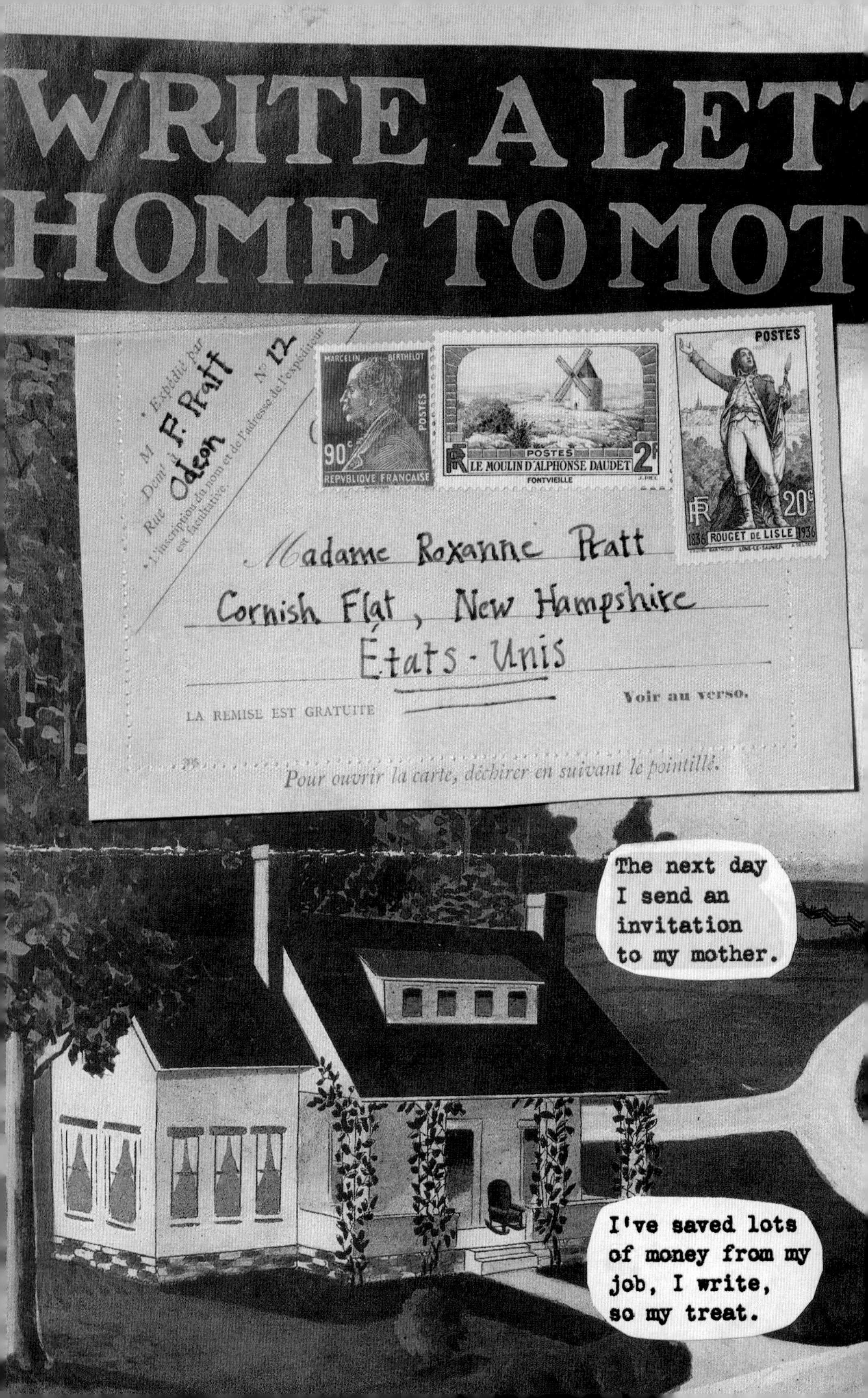
WRITE A LET
HOME TO MOT
M · Expédié par F. Pratt
Dem' à Rue Odeon N° 12
L'inscription du nom et de l'adresse de l'expéditeur est facultative.
MARCELIN BERTHELOT
90c POSTES
REPVBLIQVE FRANCAISE
POSTES
LE MOULIN D'ALPHONSE DAUDET 2F
FONTVIEILLE
POSTES
20c
1836 ROUGET DE LISLE 1936
Madame Roxanne Pratt
Cornish Flat, New Hampshire
États-Unis
LA REMISE EST GRATUITE
Voir au verso.
Pour ouvrir la carte, déchirer en suivant le pointillé.
The next day I send an invitation to my mother.
I've saved lots of money from my job, I write, so my treat.

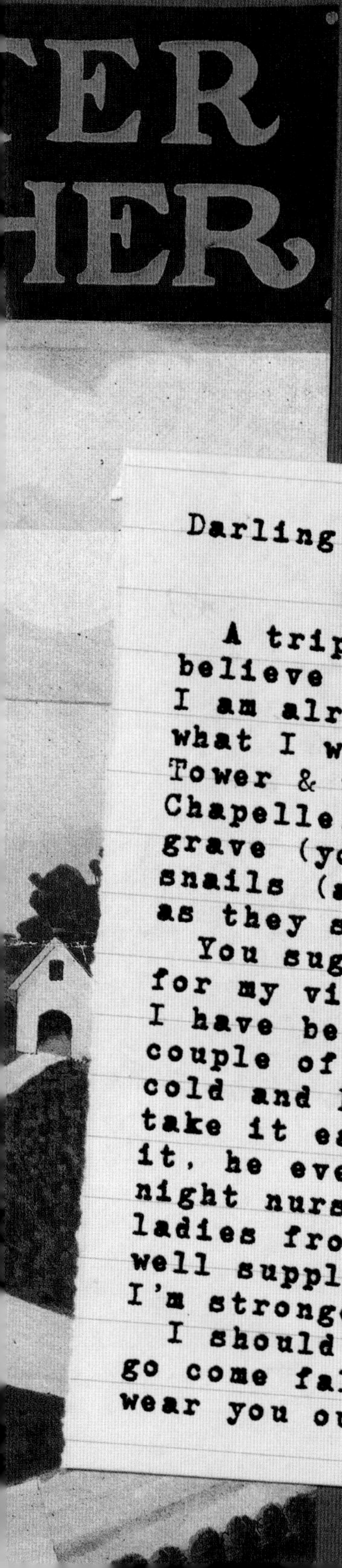
ER
HER.

Will she ever accept my relationship
with Jamie? I wonder.
Probably not.

Would she be happier if he made an
honest woman of me?
Probably not.

(Would I be happier?
Probably not...)

Darling Frankie,

Her Answer

A trip to Paree??? I can hardly believe it! Thank you, dear girl. I am already a making list of what I want to do. See the Eiffel Tower & the windows of Saint Chapelle. Visit Louis Pasteur's grave (your father's hero). Eat snails (are they as revolting as they sound?)

You suggested June as a good time for my visit, but could I postpone? I have been laid low for the last couple of months with a nasty chest cold and Dr. Hardy has ordered me to take it easy. During the worst of it, he even wanted to get me a night nurse. Imagine that! The ladies from St. Luke have kept me well supplied with beef tea, and I'm stronger every day.

I should be ready and raring to go come fall. Be prepared-- I will wear you out.

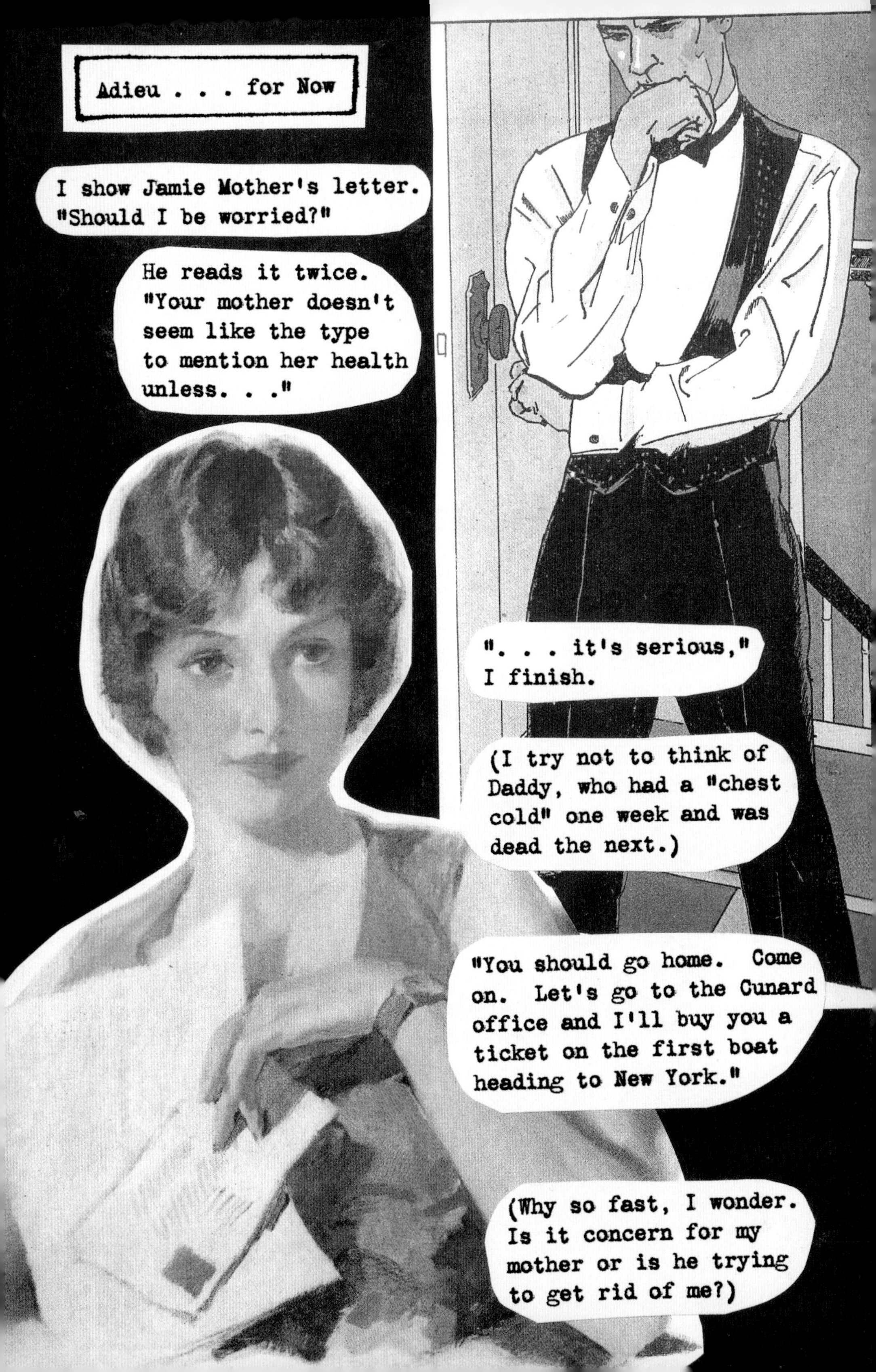
Adieu . . . for Now
I show Jamie Mother's letter. "Should I be worried?"
He reads it twice. "Your mother doesn't seem like the type to mention her health unless. . ."
". . . it's serious," I finish.
(I try not to think of Daddy, who had a "chest cold" one week and was dead the next.)
"You should go home. Come on. Let's go to the Cunard office and I'll buy you a ticket on the first boat heading to New York."
(Why so fast, I wonder. Is it concern for my mother or is he trying to get rid of me?)

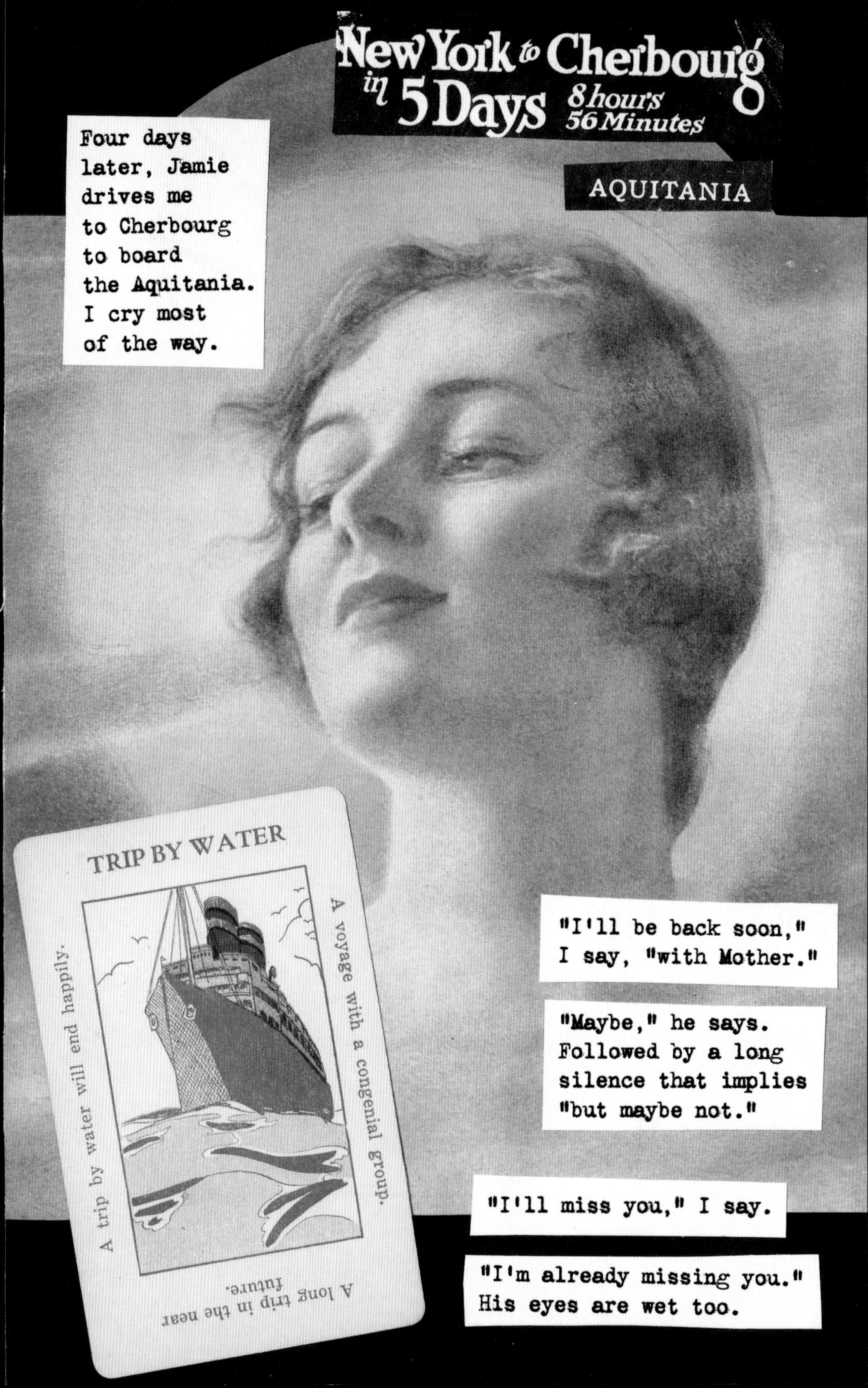
New York to Cherbourg in 5 Days 8 hours 56 Minutes
AQUITANIA
Four days later, Jamie drives me to Cherbourg to board the Aquitania. I cry most of the way.
TRIP BY WATER
A trip by water will end happily.
A voyage with a congenial group.
A long trip in the near future.
"I'll be back soon," I say, "with Mother."
"Maybe," he says. Followed by a long silence that implies "but maybe not."
"I'll miss you," I say.
"I'm already missing you." His eyes are wet too.

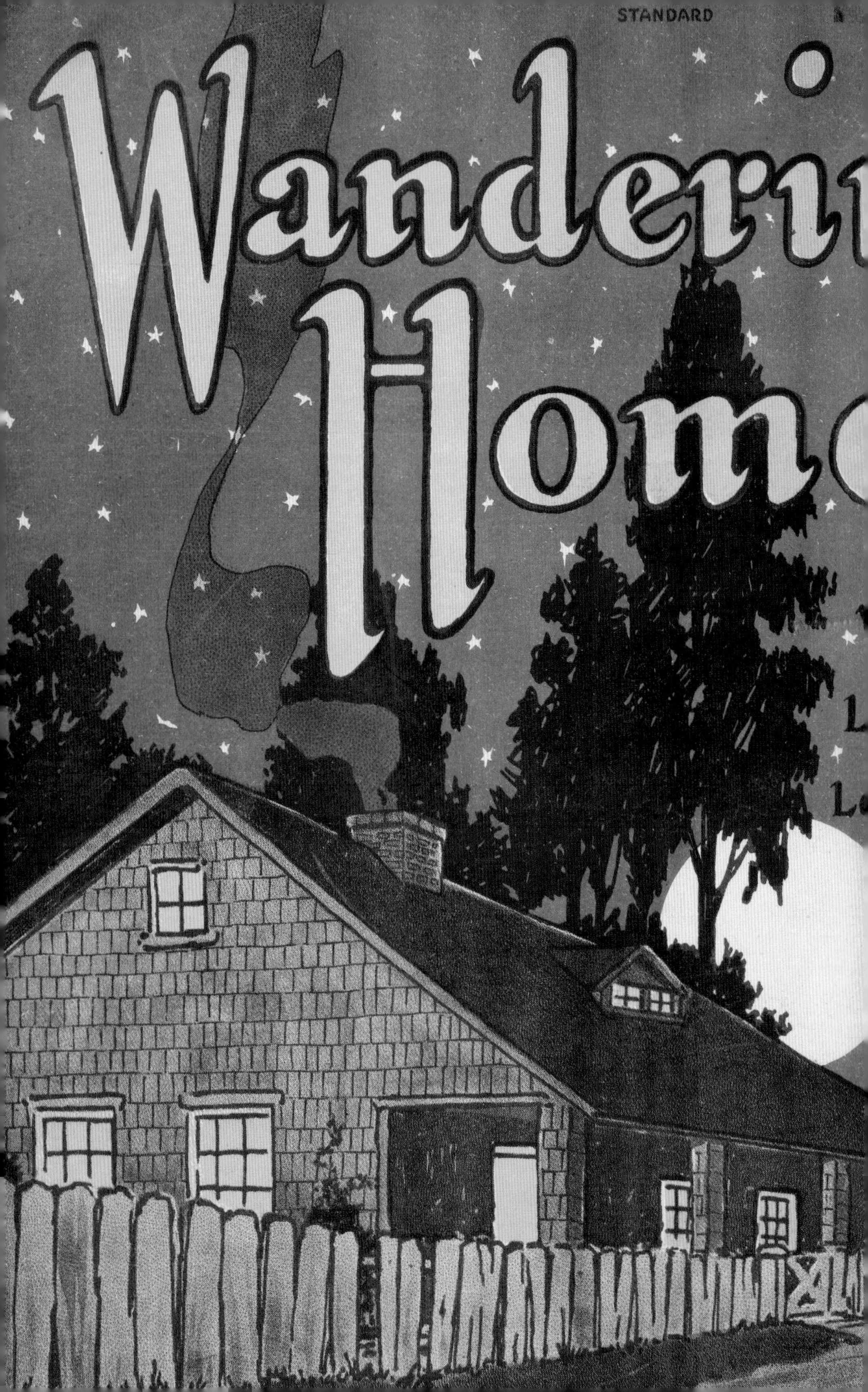
STANDARD

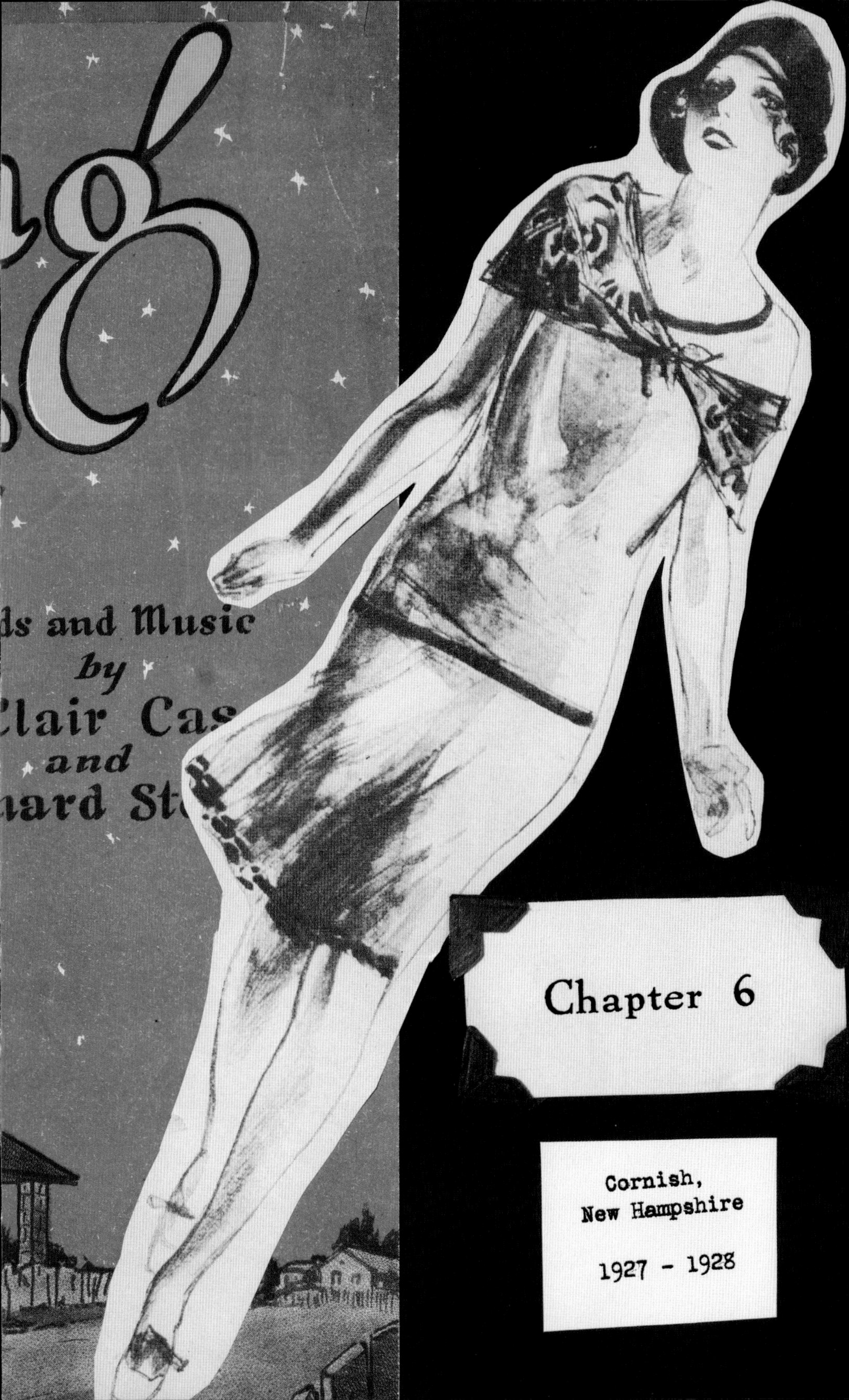
ds and Music
by
lair Cas
and
ard St

Chapter 6

Cornish,
New Hampshire

1927 - 1928

The Return of the Prodigal Daughter

With Wally and Teddy off at college, the house seems eerily quiet. The only light is a flickering lamp in the kitchen.

WESTERN UNION

JOSEPH L. EGAN
PRESIDENT

1204

SYMBOLS
DL = Day Letter
NL = Night Letter
LC = Deferred Cable
NLT = Cable Night Letter
Ship Radiogram

CLASS OF SERVICE
This is a full-rate Telegram or Cablegram unless its deferred character is indicated by a suitable symbol above or preceding the address.

The filing time shown in the date line on telegrams and day letters is STANDARD TIME at point of origin. Time of re... at point of destination

C34 CABLE = AQUITANIA

LC ROXANNE PRATT

CORNISH (NH) 1927 JUNE 29

DOCK NY 7 AM WILL BE HOME FOR SUPPER

HUGSANDKISSES FRANKIE

THE COMPANY WILL APPRECIATE SUGGESTIONS FROM ITS PATR... ...RVICE

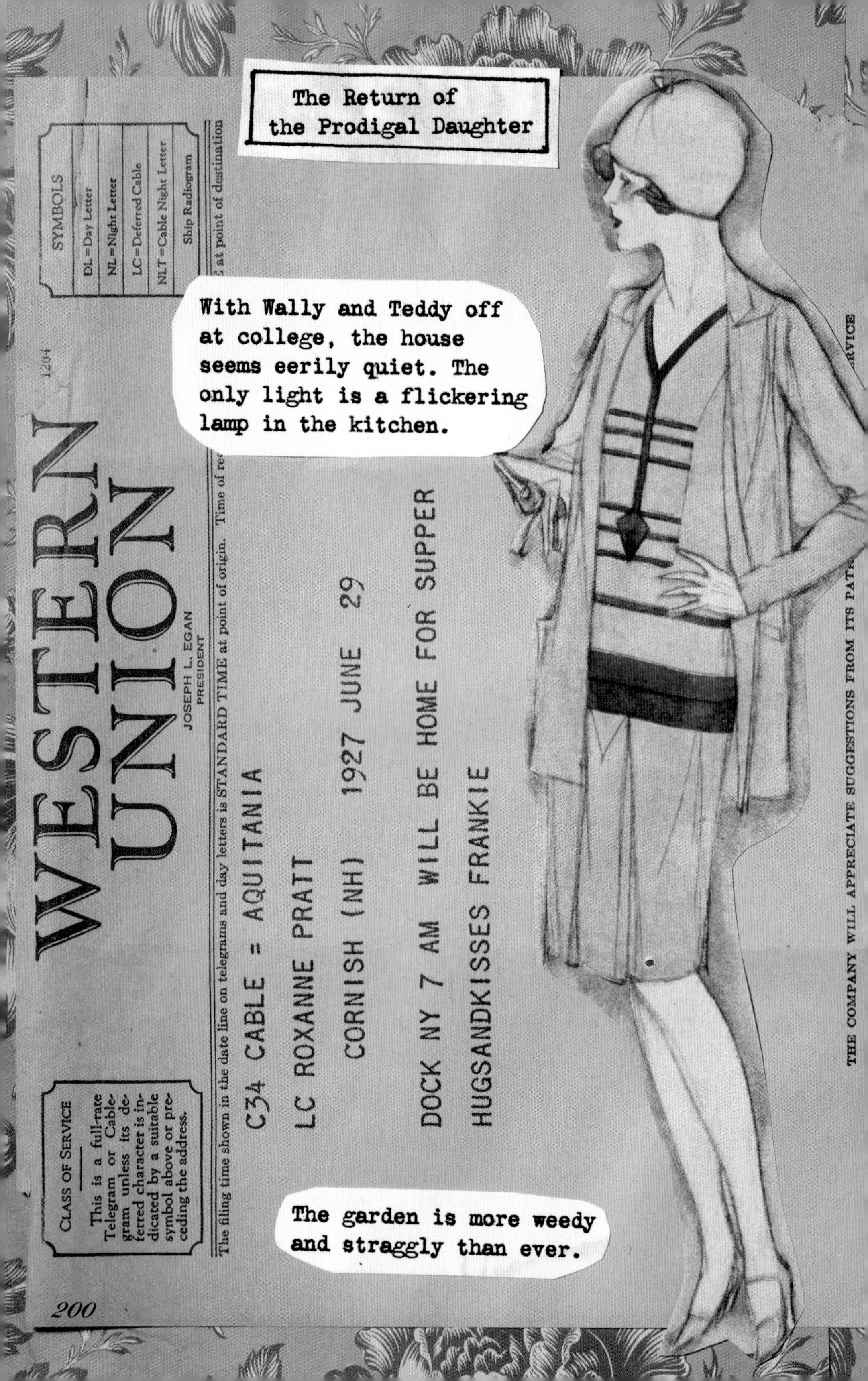

The garden is more weedy and straggly than ever.

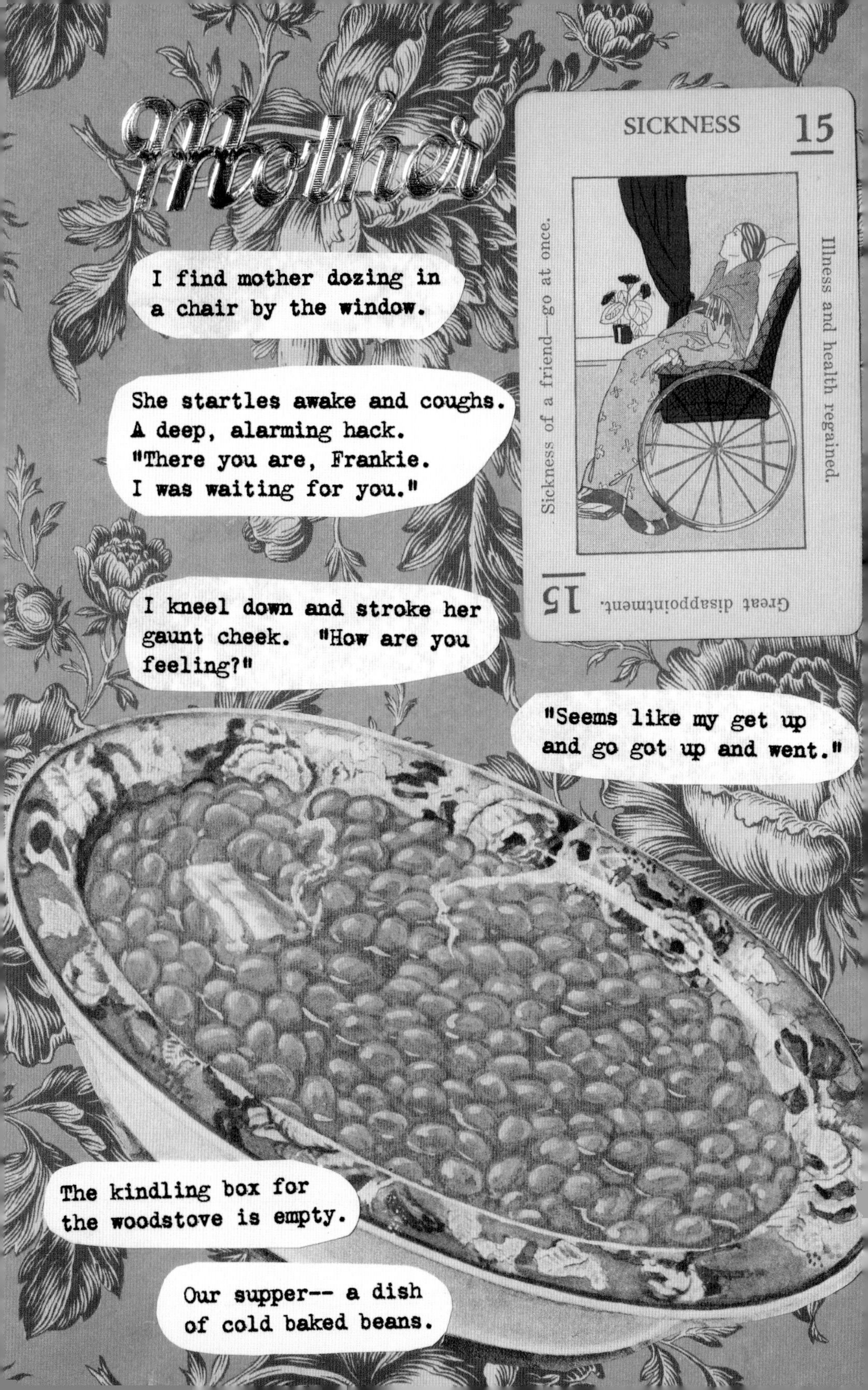
Mother
SICKNESS 15
Sickness of a friend—go at once.
Illness and health regained.
Great disappointment.
15
I find mother dozing in a chair by the window.
She startles awake and coughs. A deep, alarming hack. "There you are, Frankie. I was waiting for you."
I kneel down and stroke her gaunt cheek. "How are you feeling?"
"Seems like my get up and go got up and went."
The kindling box for the woodstove is empty.
Our supper-- a dish of cold baked beans.

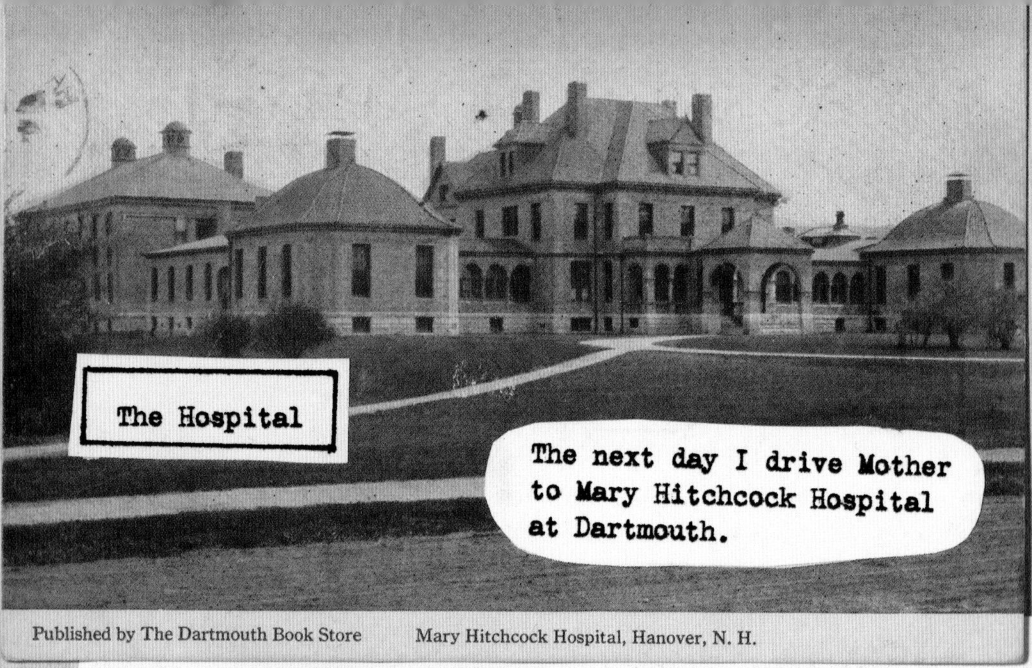
The Hospital
The next day I drive Mother to Mary Hitchcock Hospital at Dartmouth.
Published by The Dartmouth Book Store
Mary Hitchcock Hospital, Hanover, N. H.

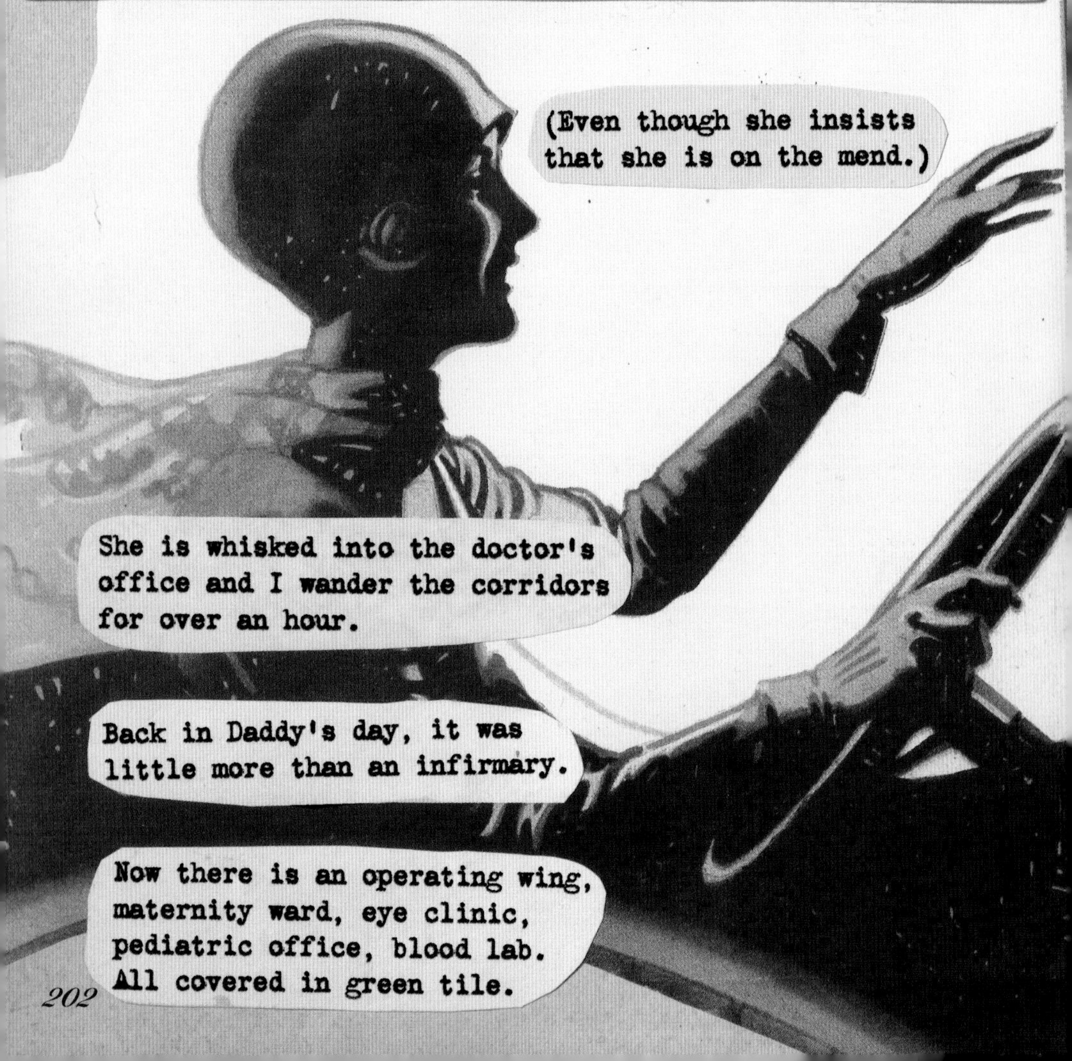
(Even though she insists that she is on the mend.)
She is whisked into the doctor's office and I wander the corridors for over an hour.
Back in Daddy's day, it was little more than an infirmary.
Now there is an operating wing, maternity ward, eye clinic, pediatric office, blood lab. All covered in green tile.

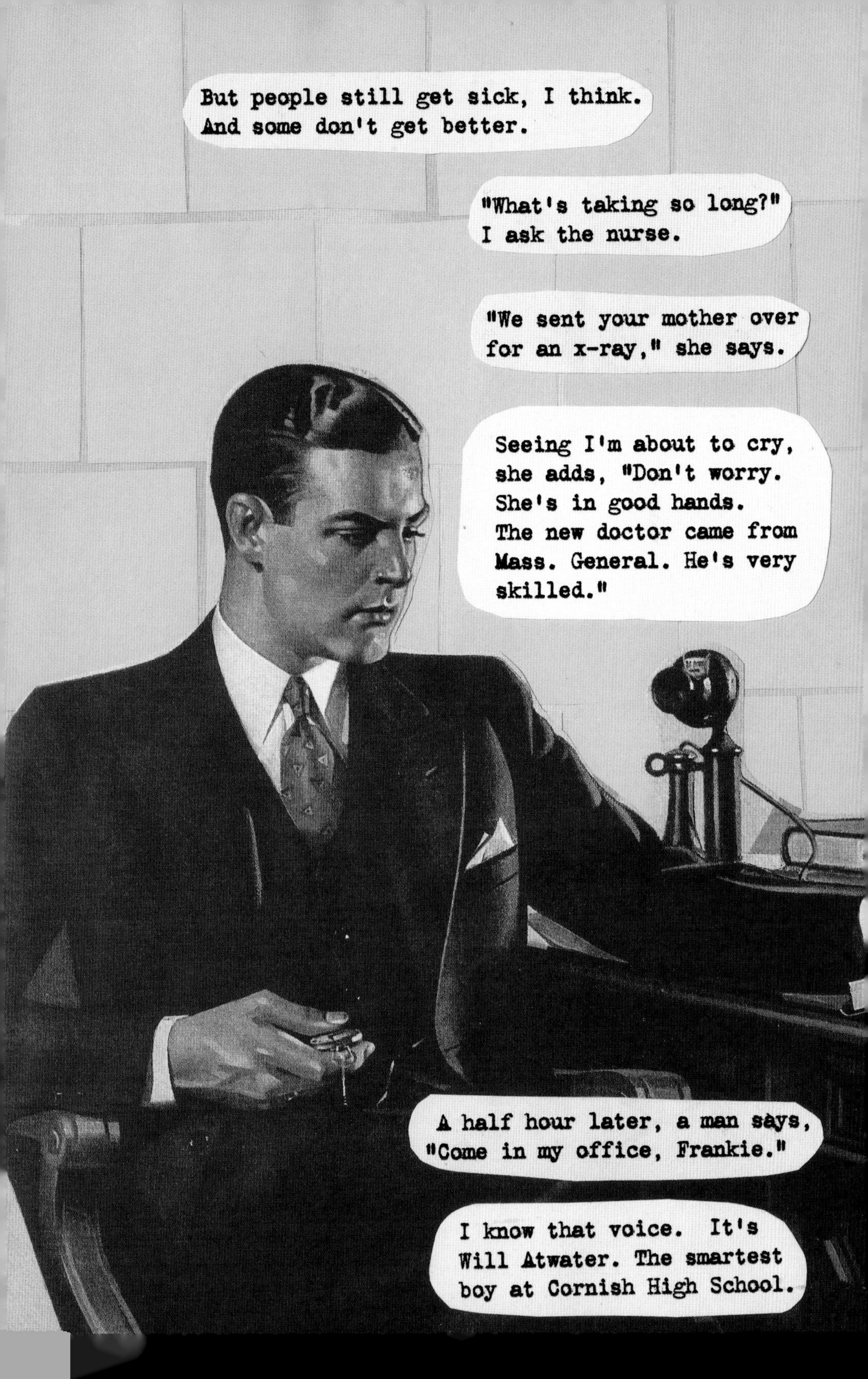
But people still get sick, I think. And some don't get better.
"What's taking so long?" I ask the nurse.
"We sent your mother over for an x-ray," she says.
Seeing I'm about to cry, she adds, "Don't worry. She's in good hands. The new doctor came from Mass. General. He's very skilled."
A half hour later, a man says, "Come in my office, Frankie."
I know that voice. It's Will Atwater. The smartest boy at Cornish High School.

The Diagnosis

He ushers me in and closes the door. "I wanted to talk to you privately. Your mother is still getting dressed."

The room is dark except for a light box on the wall, illuminating a lung x-ray.

"We found a spot here." He points to a blurry shadow on the right side.

"A spot?" Such an innocuous word.

"Tuberculosis."

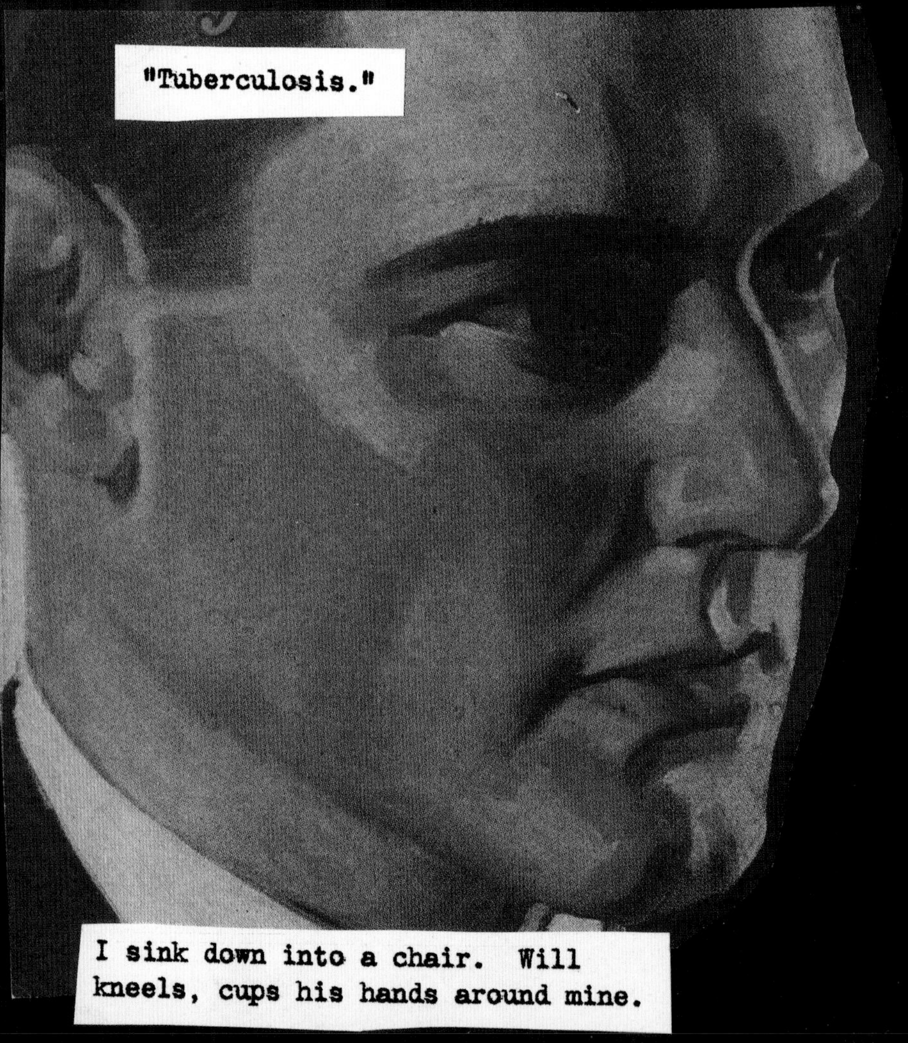

I sink down into a chair. Will kneels, cups his hands around mine.

"It's still small. I'm sure she can make a full recovery," he says.

I look up at his handsome, solemn face. His diplomas hanging on the wall-- Harvard magna cum laude, Harvard Medical School, Pasteur Institute.

(The last time I saw him was when I ducked his kiss after our disastrous date. I hope he doesn't remember)

"How? Tell me what to do," I say.

Dr. Atwater's Instructions

1. TB brought on by damp, unhealthy living conditions and exhaustion. The goal is to create a "Home Sanitarium."

2. Patient must have complete bed rest for weeks or maybe months.

3. Diet should be rich in calories. 3 meals plus 2 large snacks per day. Large quantities of dairy and fresh vegetables.

4. Remove all sources of mold and smoke from house. Replace wood-stoves and kerosene lamps with central heating and electricity.

5. Rigorous sanitation of bathroom, linens and utensils to prevent further contagion to patient with weakened resistance.

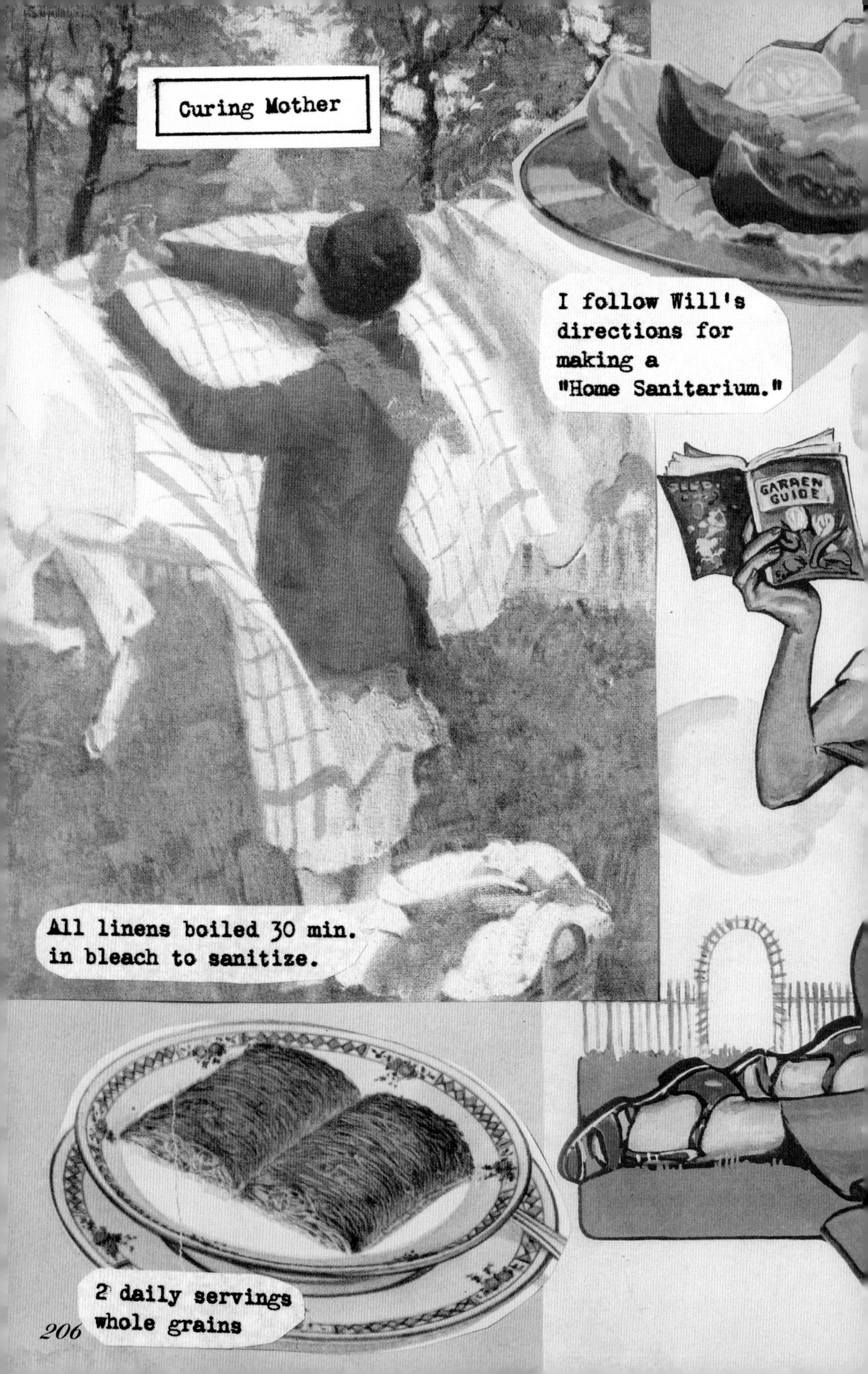
Curing Mother
I follow Will's directions for making a "Home Sanitarium."
All linens boiled 30 min. in bleach to sanitize.
2 daily servings whole grains

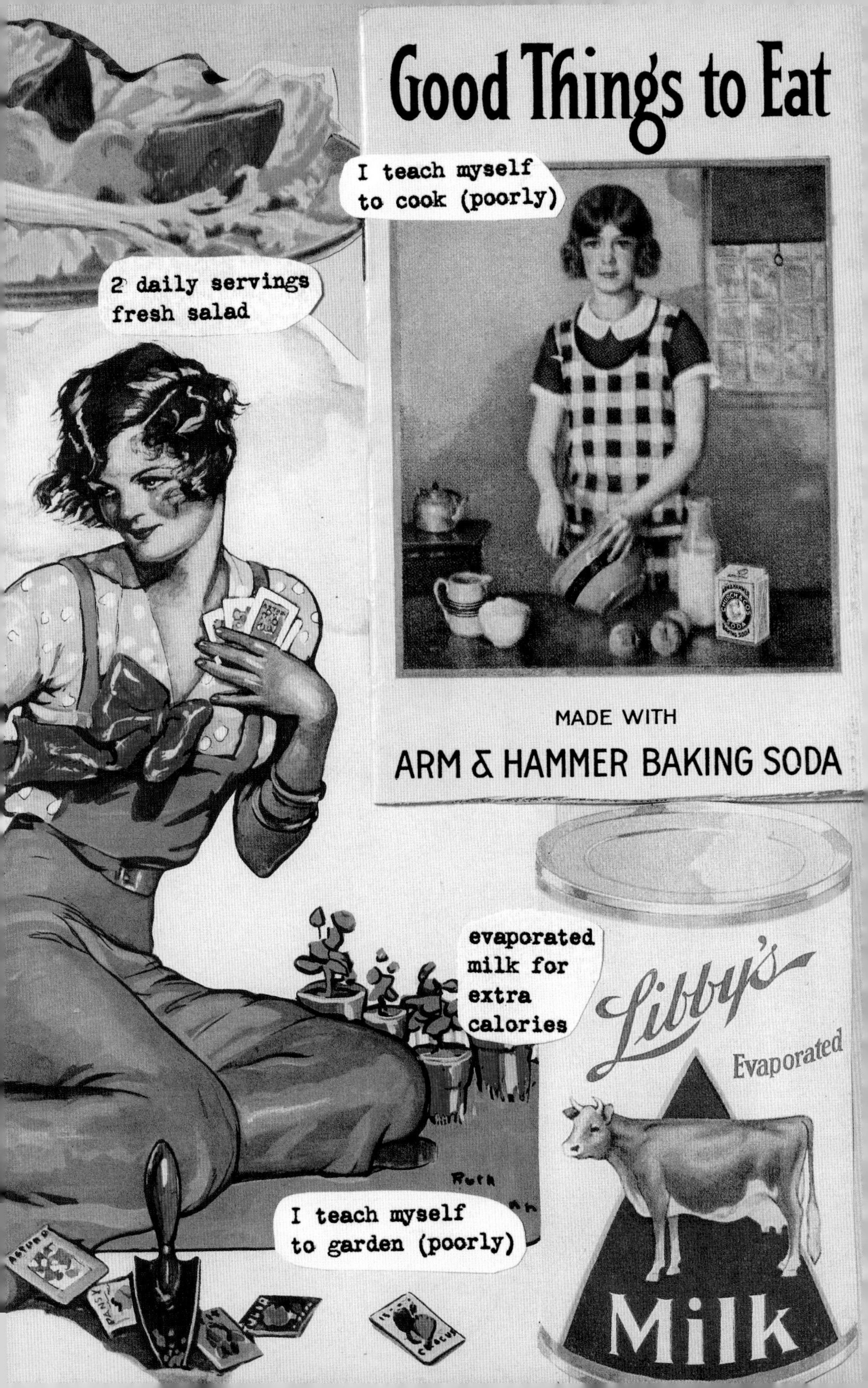
Good Things to Eat
I teach myself to cook (poorly)
2 daily servings fresh salad
MADE WITH
ARM & HAMMER BAKING SODA
evaporated milk for extra calories
Libby's
Evaporated
Milk
I teach myself to garden (poorly)

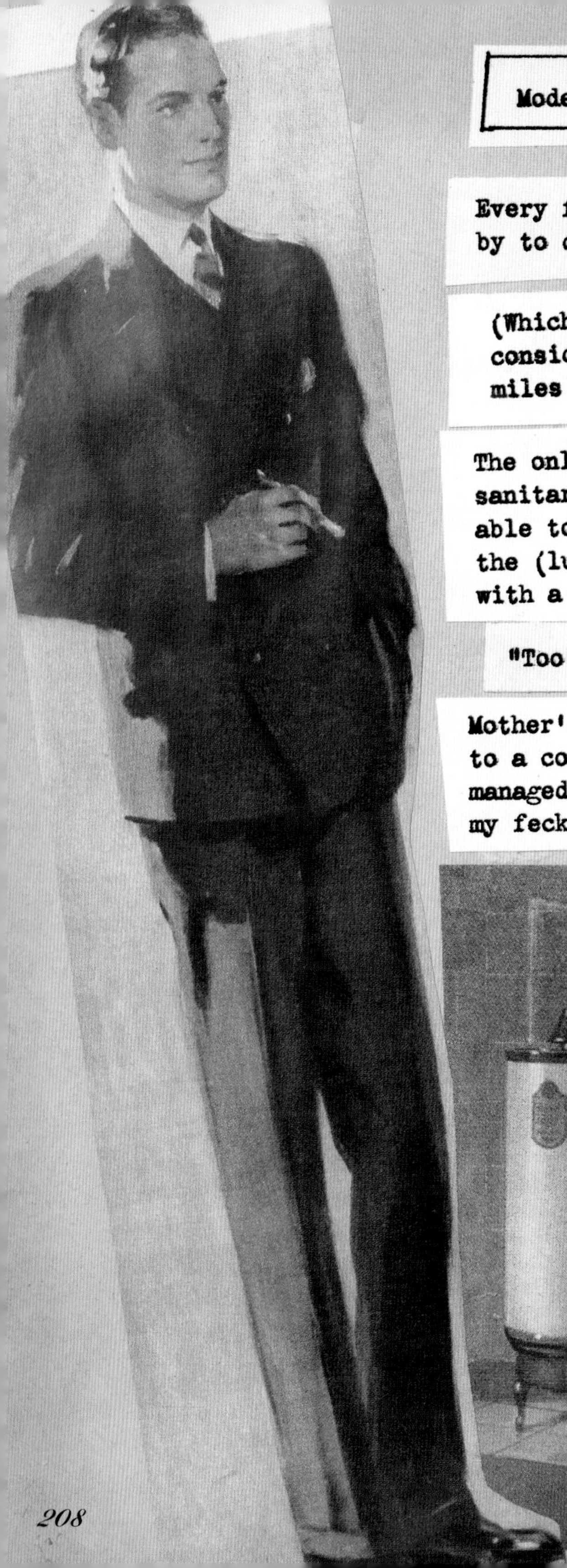

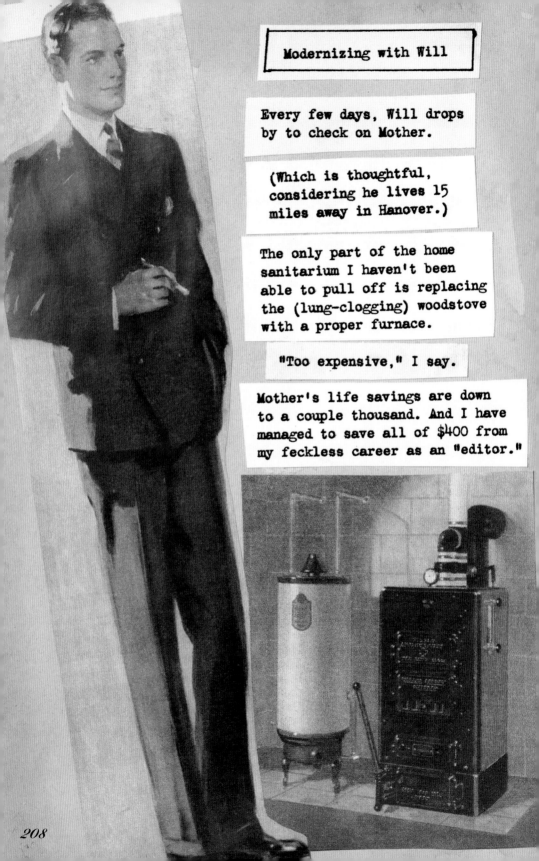

Modernizing with Will

Every few days, Will drops by to check on Mother.

(Which is thoughtful, considering he lives 15 miles away in Hanover.)

The only part of the home sanitarium I haven't been able to pull off is replacing the (lung-clogging) woodstove with a proper furnace.

"Too expensive," I say.

Mother's life savings are down to a couple thousand. And I have managed to save all of $400 from my feckless career as an "editor."

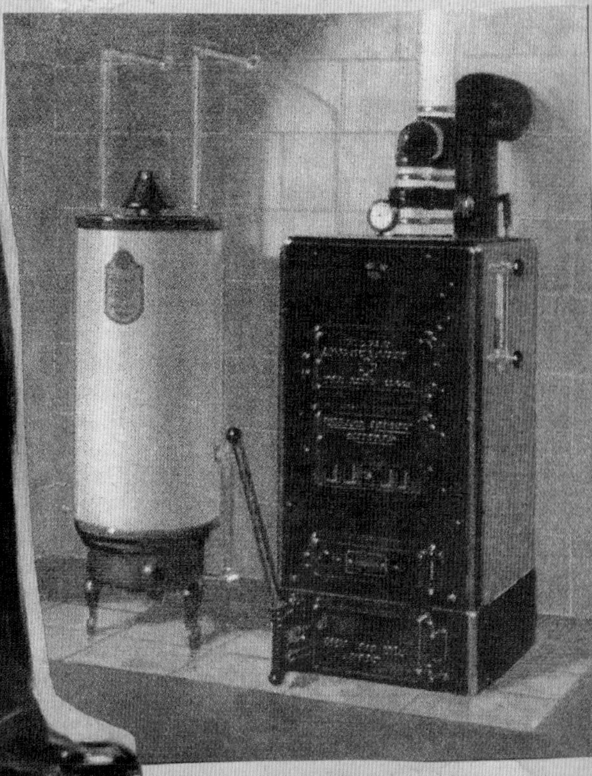

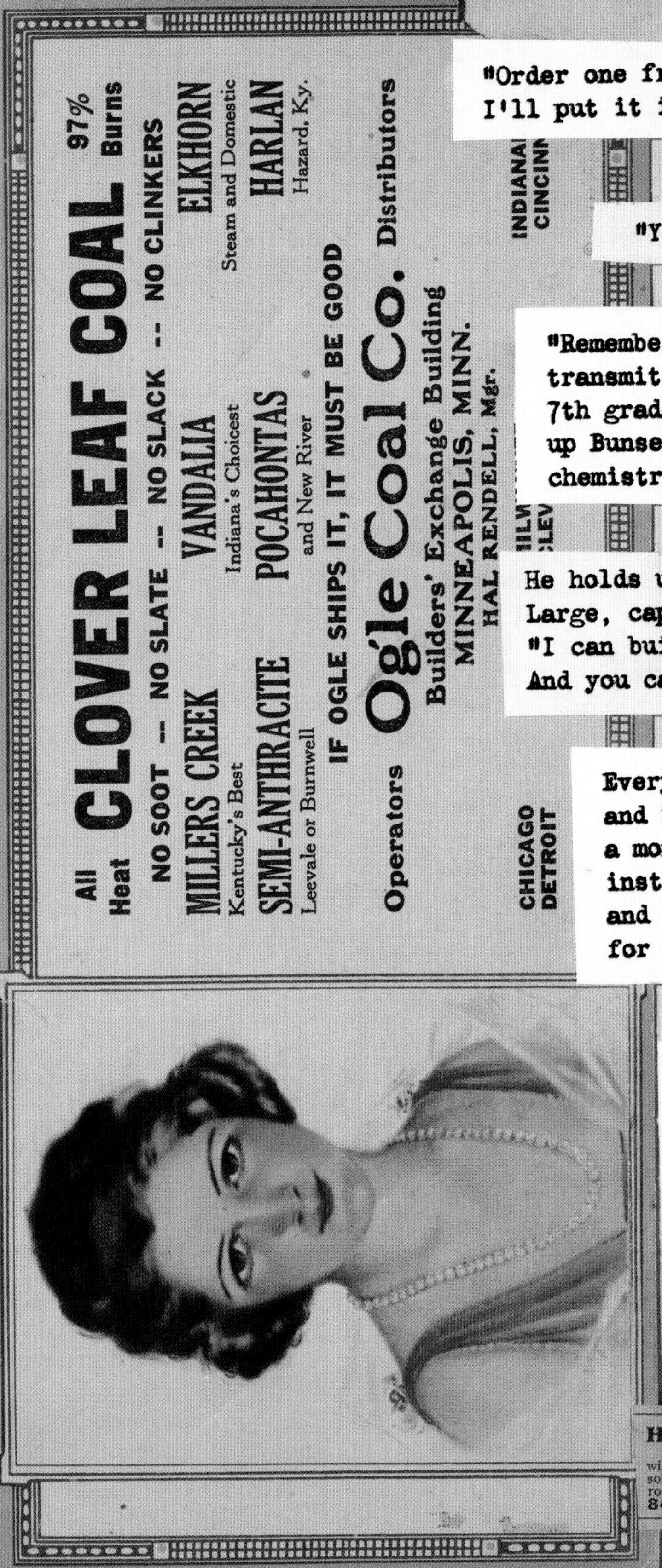
All Heat
CLOVER LEAF COAL
97% Burns
NO SOOT -- NO SLATE -- NO SLACK -- NO CLINKERS
MILLERS CREEK
Kentucky's Best
VANDALIA
Indiana's Choicest
ELKHORN
Steam and Domestic
SEMI-ANTHRACITE
Leevale or Burnwell
POCAHONTAS
and New River
HARLAN
Hazard, Ky.
IF OGLE SHIPS IT, IT MUST BE GOOD
Operators
Ogle Coal Co.
Distributors
Builders' Exchange Building
MINNEAPOLIS, MINN.
HAL RENDELL, Mgr.
CHICAGO
DETROIT

"Order one from Sears and I'll put it in," says Will.

"You?" I say.

"Remember the radio transmitter I built in 7th grade? And rigging up Bunsen burners in the chemistry lab?"

He holds up his hands. Large, capable hands. "I can build anything. And you can be my helper."

Every Saturday and Sunday for a month, Will installs ducts and floor registers for a coal furnace.

And I, Vassar class of 1924, winner of the Addison Prize, learn how to clamp pipes and solder.

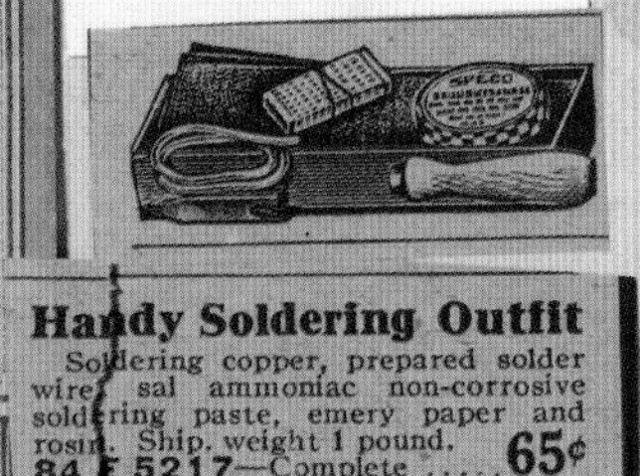
Handy Soldering Outfit
Soldering copper, prepared solder wire, sal ammoniac non-corrosive soldering paste, emery paper and rosin. Ship. weight 1 pound.
84 E 5217—Complete ..... 65¢

> I write Jamie long letters about the wonderful doctor who is curing mother. I'll be back in Paris by the spring, I write.

Dear, dear Frankie,

Please excuse th[e] ... can see that my expert[ise] ...

Thank you for all your lovely letters. I have read them over and over and I apologize for not answering them p[romptly] ...

> All I get back for 2 months are a few breezy postcards.

> And then this letter. . .

So, my news. I have [pulled the] plug on the Aero and have even found a sucker to take it off my hands. Nancy Cunard, the shipping heiress, who has decided a literary magazine would be an amusing pastime.

And now to the hard part of this letter— you coming back to Paris.

If you are coming back to be with me then no. Please don't.

You are the best thing that has ever happened to me. I am still amazed that such a dazzling, wise girl could love me.

But what can I offer you in return? More evenings with the other "wastrel" expats. Lugubrious strolls through Paris cemeteries.

You deserve a much fuller life. A young husband (just writing this makes me jealous). Children. A real home. All the everyday pleasures that I seem incapable of providing. (Just ask my ex wife.)

I suspect you may agree with me; may be a little relieved that you have my blessing to move on.

Now I am going to mail this letter before I change my mind...

Love Always J.

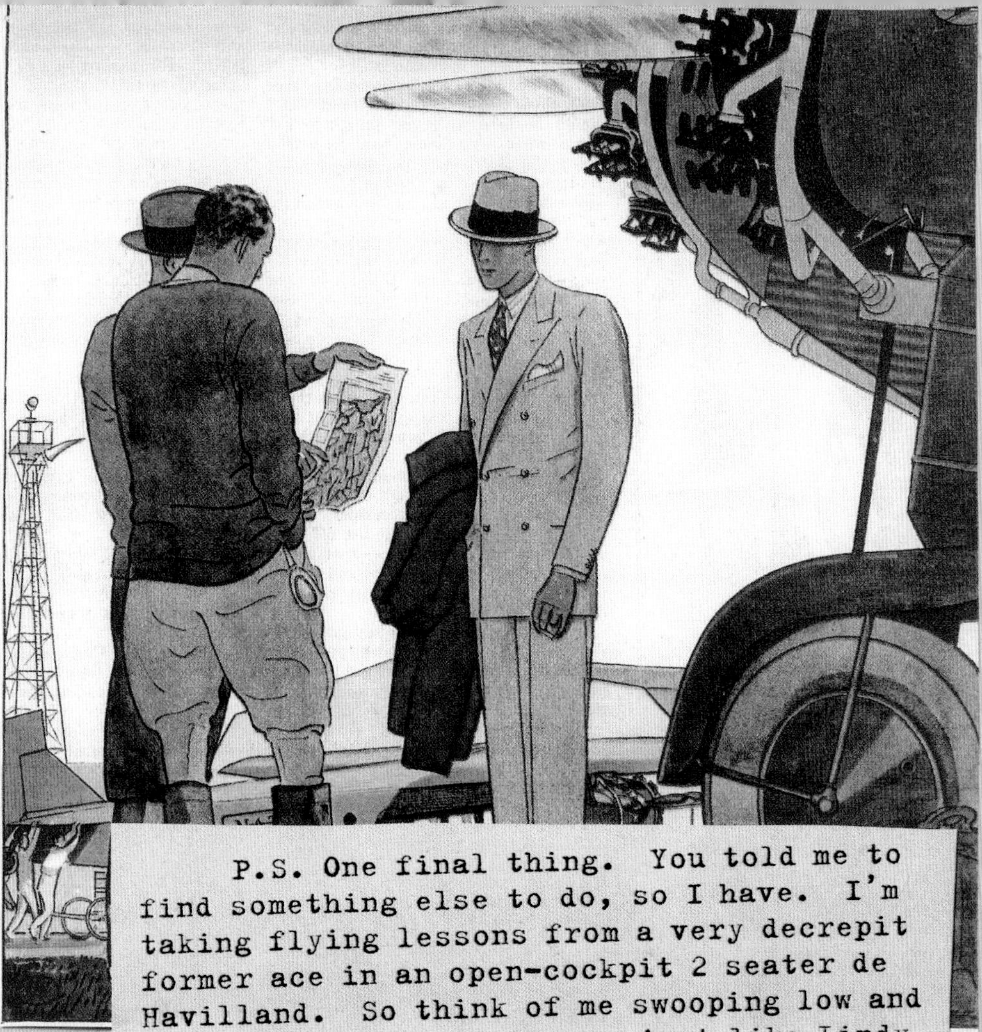

P.S. One final thing. You told me to find something else to do, so I have. I'm taking flying lessons from a very decrepit former ace in an open-cockpit 2 seater de Havilland. So think of me swooping low and circling the Eiffel Tower, just like Lindy.

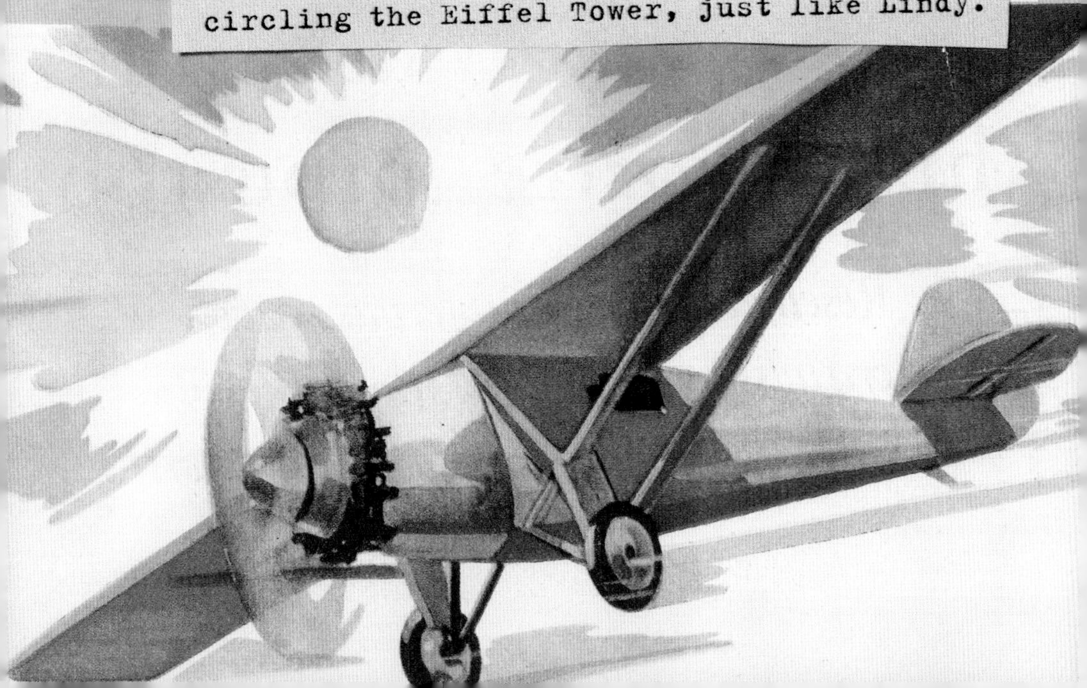

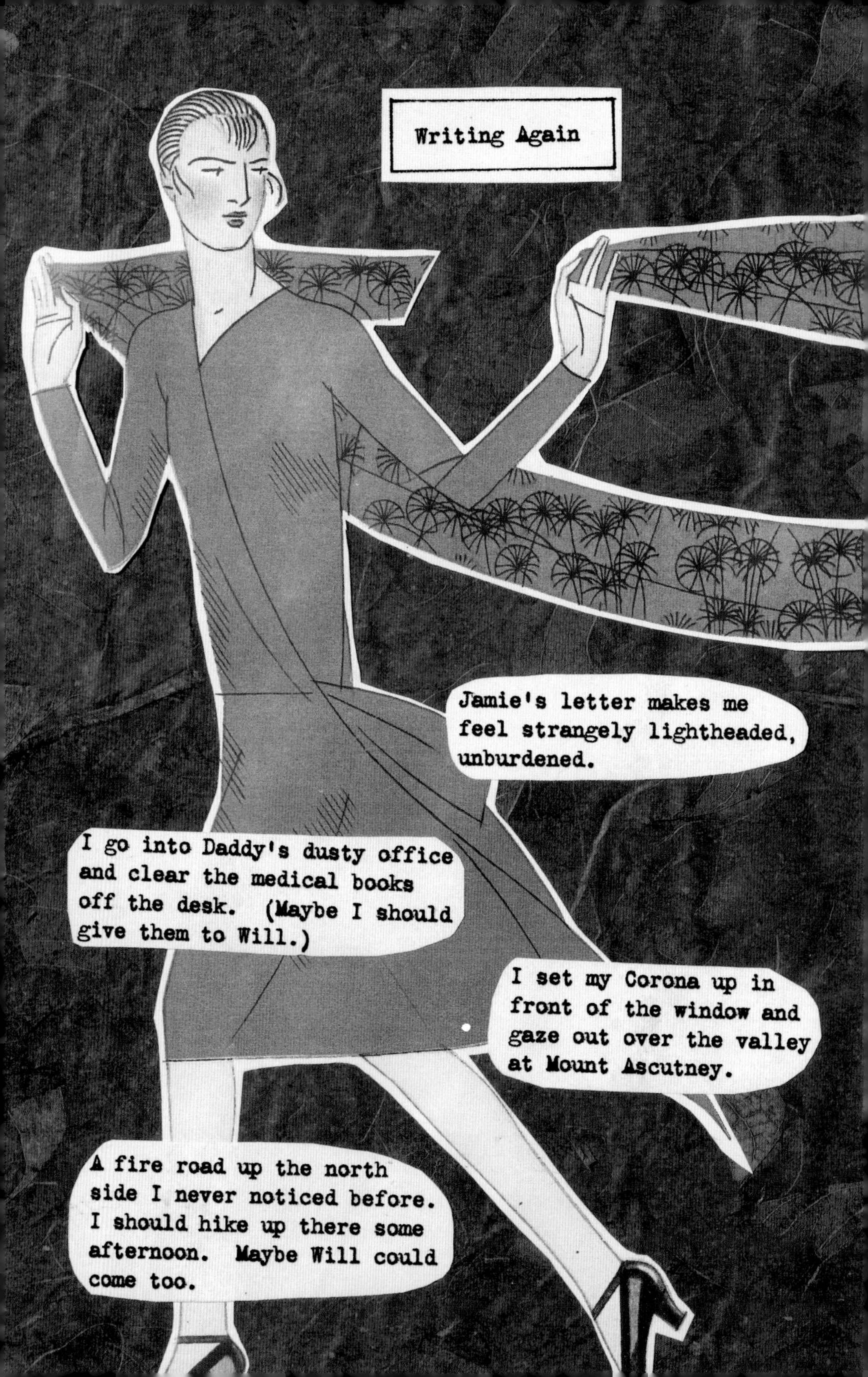
Writing Again
Jamie's letter makes me feel strangely lightheaded, unburdened.
I go into Daddy's dusty office and clear the medical books off the desk. (Maybe I should give them to Will.)
I set my Corona up in front of the window and gaze out over the valley at Mount Ascutney.
A fire road up the north side I never noticed before. I should hike up there some afternoon. Maybe Will could come too.

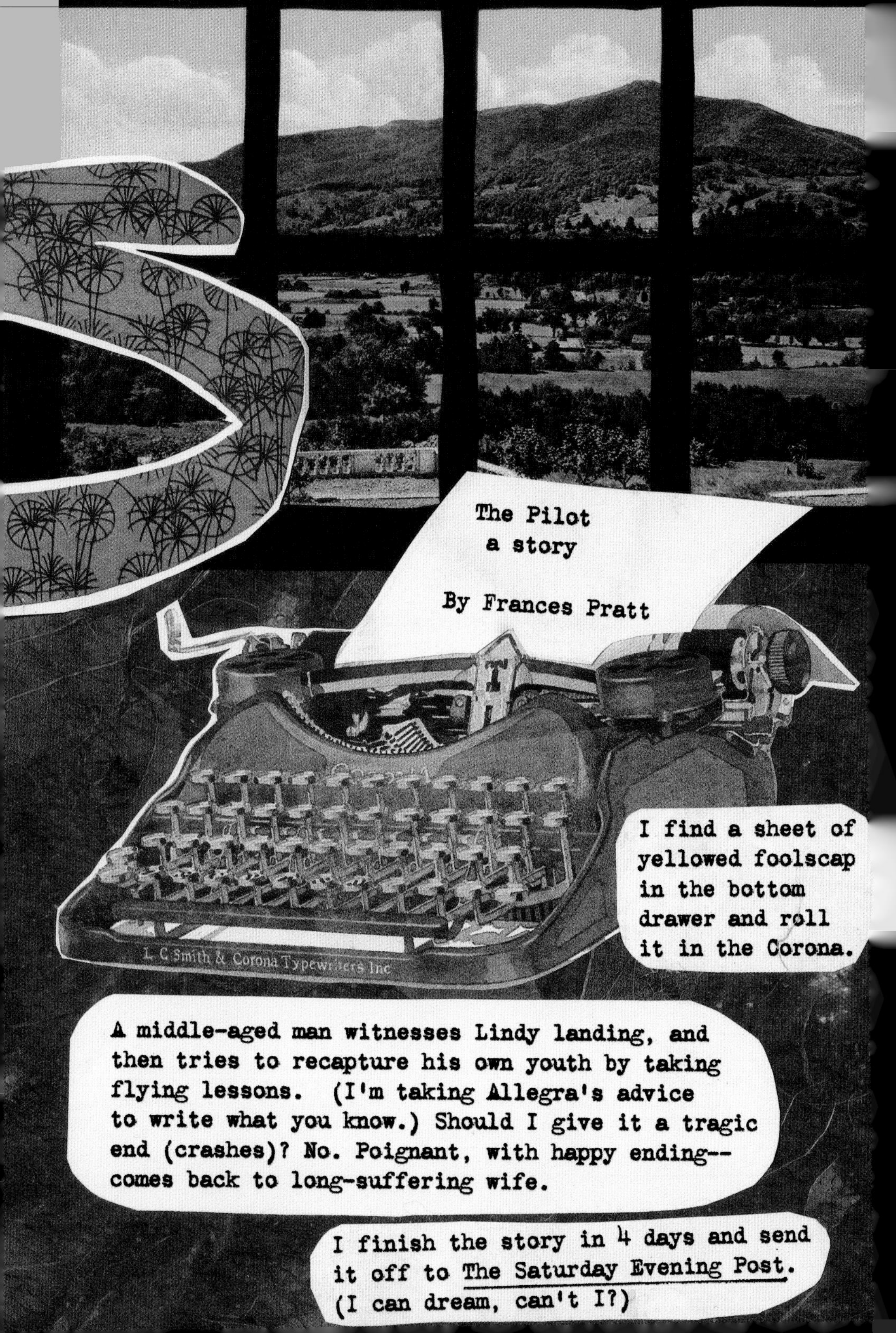
The Pilot
a story
By Frances Pratt
L. C. Smith & Corona Typewriters Inc
I find a sheet of yellowed foolscap in the bottom drawer and roll it in the Corona.
A middle-aged man witnesses Lindy landing, and then tries to recapture his own youth by taking flying lessons. (I'm taking Allegra's advice to write what you know.) Should I give it a tragic end (crashes)? No. Poignant, with happy ending--comes back to long-suffering wife.
I finish the story in 4 days and send it off to The Saturday Evening Post. (I can dream, can't I?)

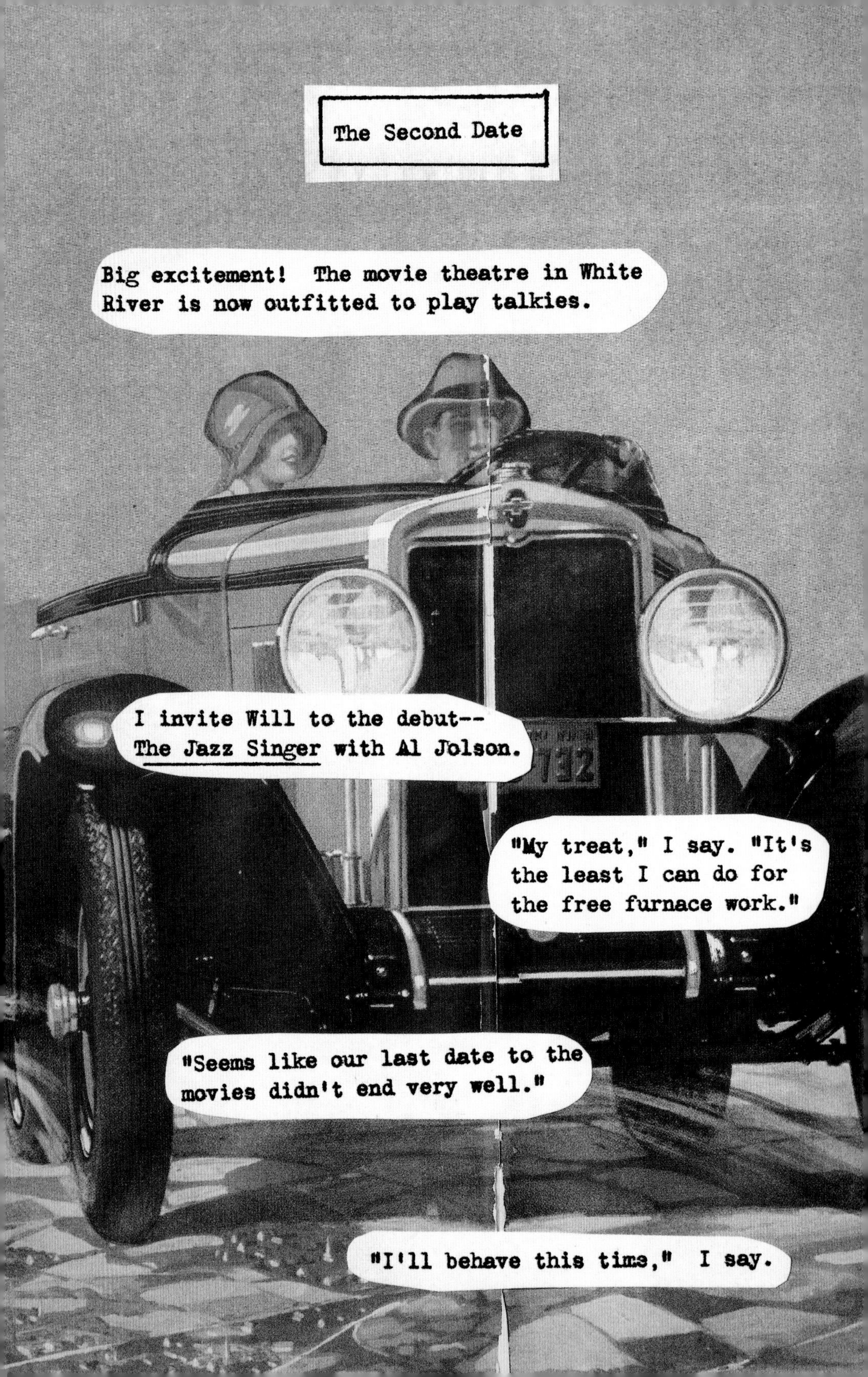
The Second Date
Big excitement! The movie theatre in White River is now outfitted to play talkies.
I invite Will to the debut--The Jazz Singer with Al Jolson.
"My treat," I say. "It's the least I can do for the free furnace work."
"Seems like our last date to the movies didn't end very well."
"I'll behave this time," I say.

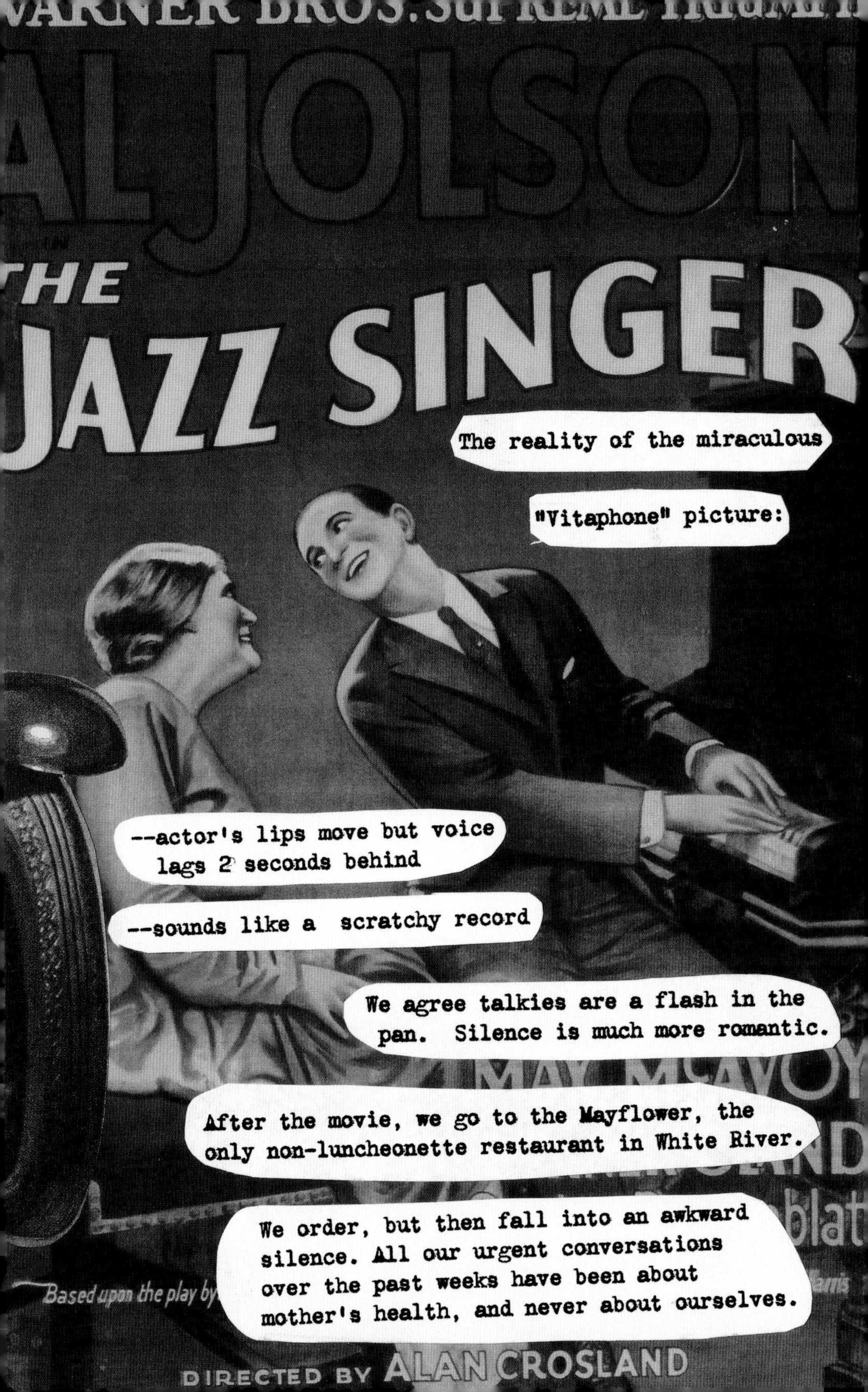
AL JOLSON
THE
JAZZ SINGER
Based upon the play by
DIRECTED BY ALAN CROSLAND

The reality of the miraculous

"Vitaphone" picture:

--actor's lips move but voice lags 2 seconds behind

--sounds like a scratchy record

We agree talkies are a flash in the pan. Silence is much more romantic.

After the movie, we go to the Mayflower, the only non-luncheonette restaurant in White River.

We order, but then fall into an awkward silence. All our urgent conversations over the past weeks have been about mother's health, and never about ourselves.

Talkie

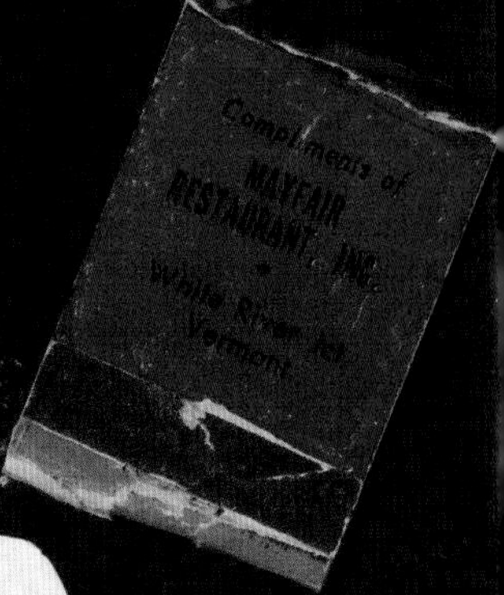
Compliments of
MAYFAIR
RESTAURANT, INC.
White River Jct.
Vermont.

And then we settle back and start to chat, like the old days back in the lunchroom at Cornish High School.

I tell him about my slow start at Vassar and the glamorous Wolfs. About my not-so-glamorous jobs at True Story and the Aero.

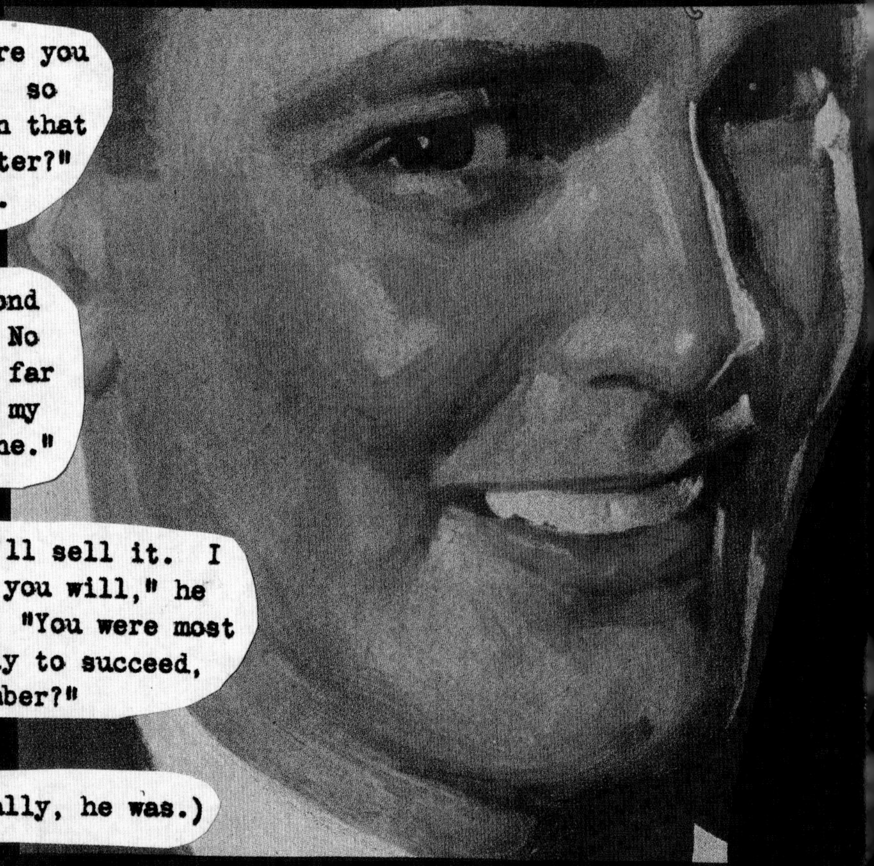

"What are you writing so madly on that typewriter?" he asks.

"My second story. No luck so far selling my first one."

"You'll sell it. I know you will," he says. "You were most likely to succeed, remember?"

(Actually, he was.)

I ask him why he became a doctor.

"Because of your father." Daddy paid a house call when Will was 8 and sick with the measles. He showed Will all the instruments in his bag and let him listen to his own heart with the stethoscope.

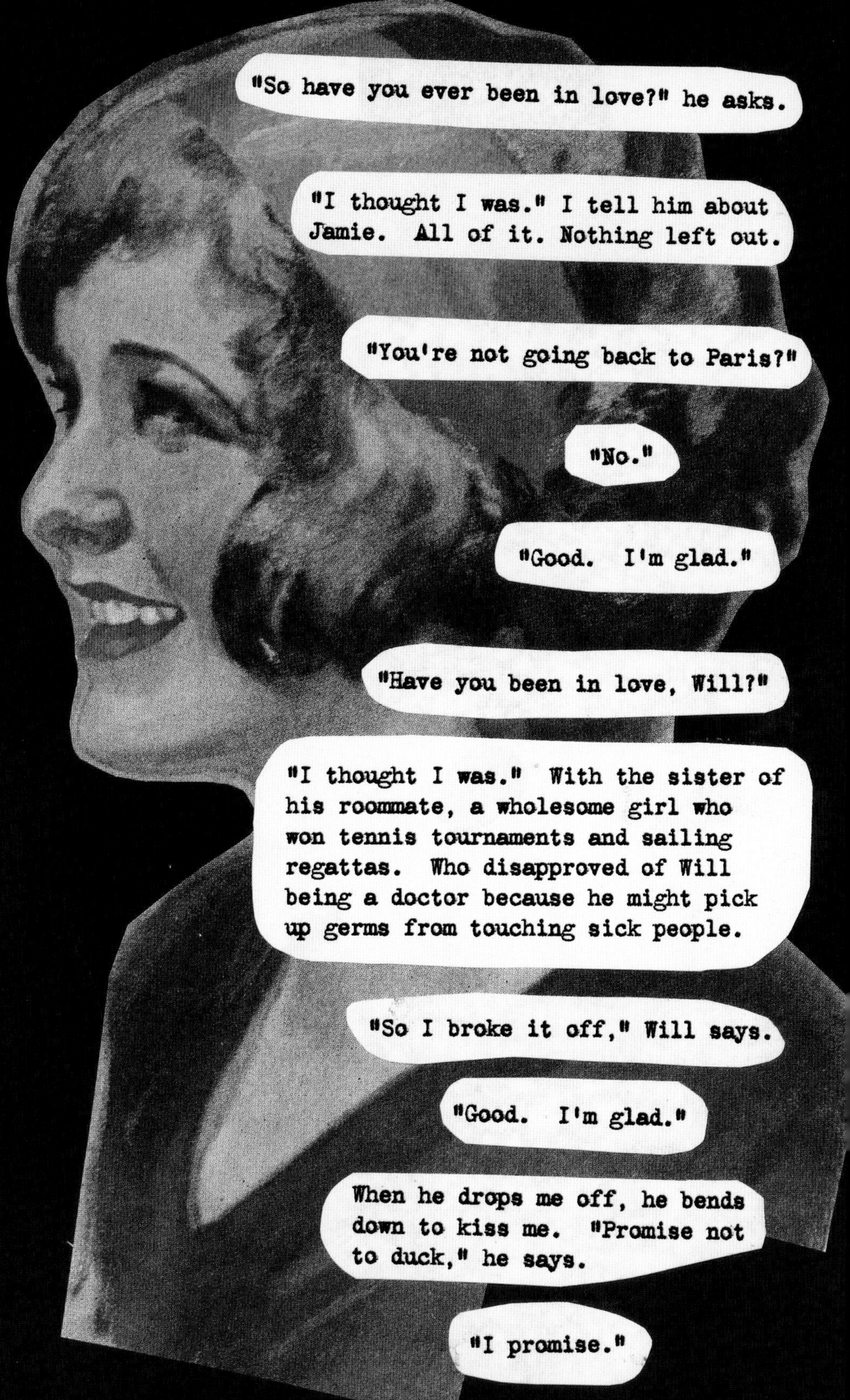

"So have you ever been in love?" he asks.

"I thought I was." I tell him about Jamie. All of it. Nothing left out.

"You're not going back to Paris?"

"No."

"Good. I'm glad."

"Have you been in love, Will?"

"I thought I was." With the sister of his roommate, a wholesome girl who won tennis tournaments and sailing regattas. Who disapproved of Will being a doctor because he might pick up germs from touching sick people.

"So I broke it off," Will says.

"Good. I'm glad."

When he drops me off, he bends down to kiss me. "Promise not to duck," he says.

"I promise."

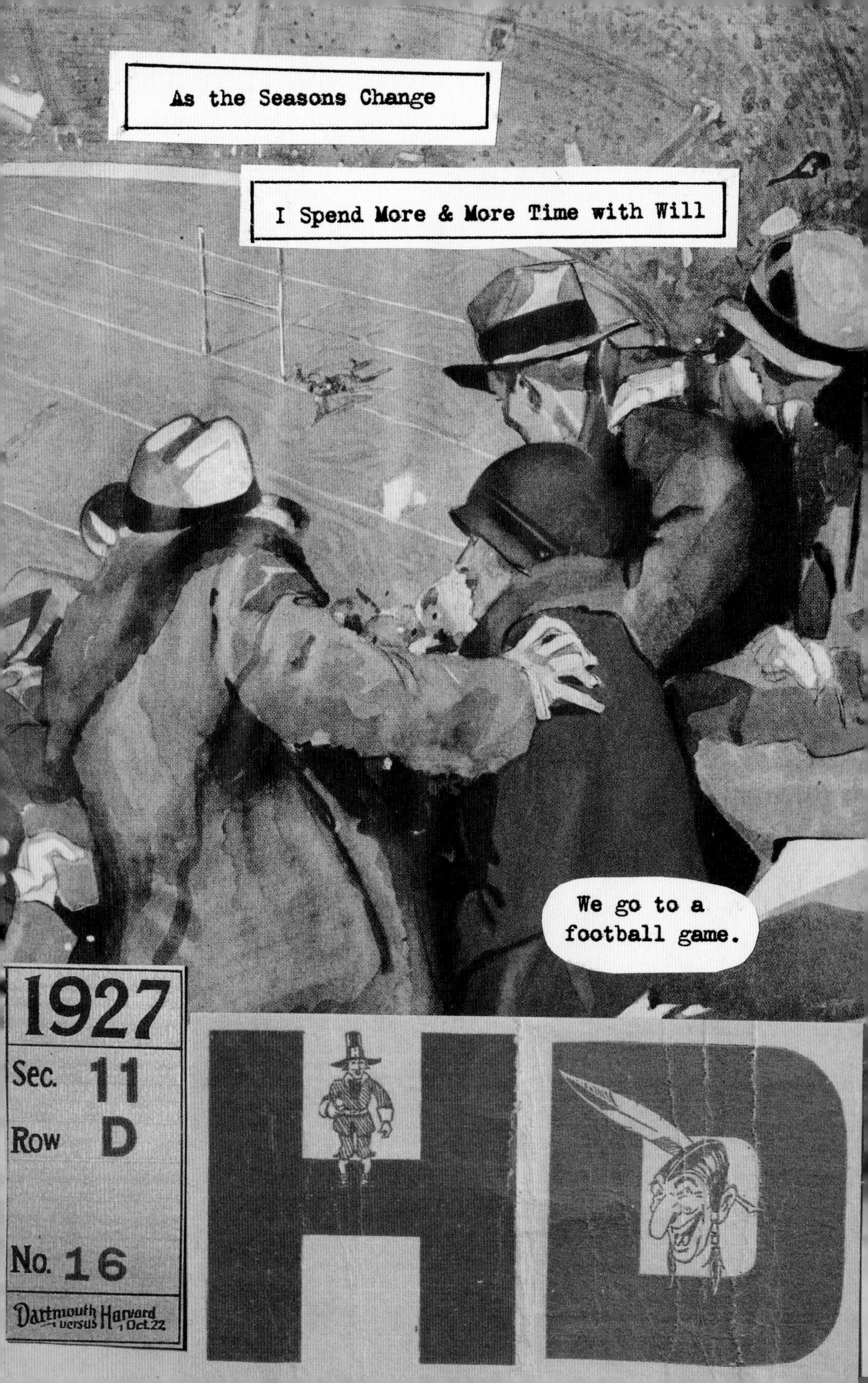
As the Seasons Change
I Spend More & More Time with Will
We go to a football game.
1927
Sec. 11
Row D
No. 16
Dartmouth versus Harvard Oct. 22
HD

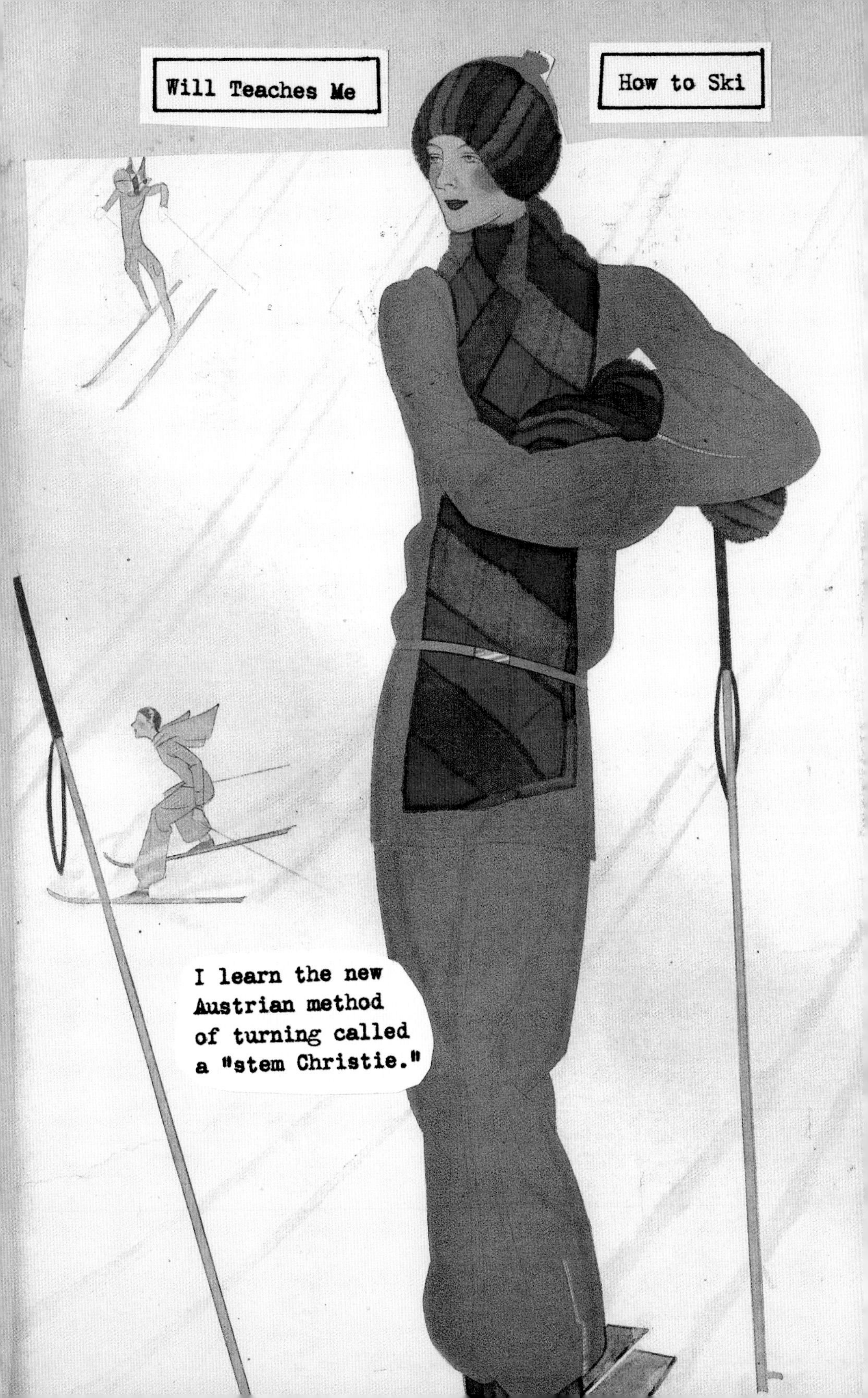
Will Teaches Me
How to Ski
I learn the new Austrian method of turning called a "stem Christie."

THE SATURDAY EVENING POST

Founded A°D¹ 1728 *by* Benj. Franklin

November 13, 192[

Success at Last

Frances Pratt
Cornish Flat,
New Hampshire

Dear Miss Pratt,

We are returning "The Pilot."
Unfort[unately] this story does
not m[eet] [our edi]torial needs
at th[e present ti]me.

Saturday Evening
Post rejects
"The Pilot"

Liberty
A Weekly for Everybody
**247 Park Avenue
NEW YORK, N. Y.**

And so does
Liberty,
Cosmopolitan,
& McLure's

Maybe I should drink Coke when I write

Collier's

THE NATIONAL WEEKLY

William L. Chenery, *Editor*

Frances Pratt
Cornish Flat,
New Hampshire

January 19, 1928

But Collier's says yes!

Dear Miss Pratt,

We are pleased to accept your short story "The Pilot" for publication. Your description of the Paris streets after Captain Lindbergh's landing was extremely vivid, as if you had actually been there.

The story will appear in the May 24, 1928 issue. Enclosed is a c[illegible] $400.

We would be very interes[illegible] any additional stories.

Sincerely Yours,

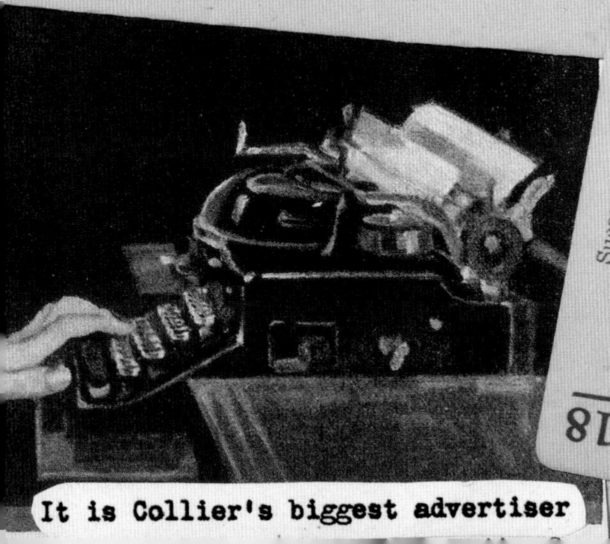
It is Collier's biggest advertiser

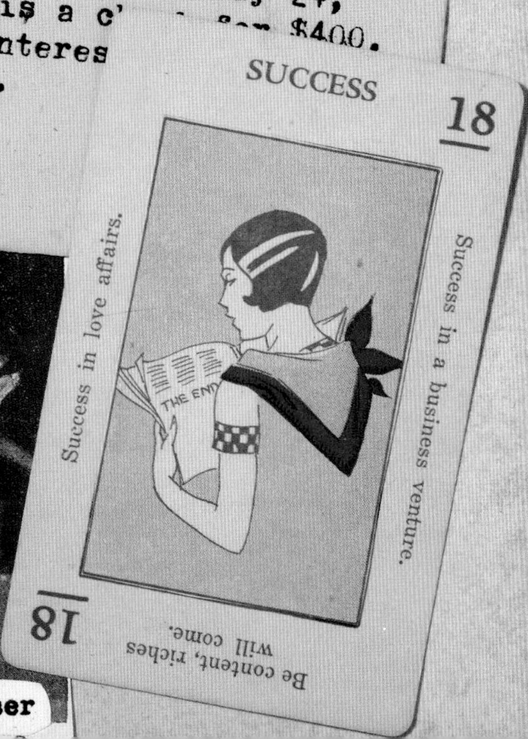
SUCCESS
18
Success in love affairs.
THE END
Success in a business venture.
18
Be content, riches will come.

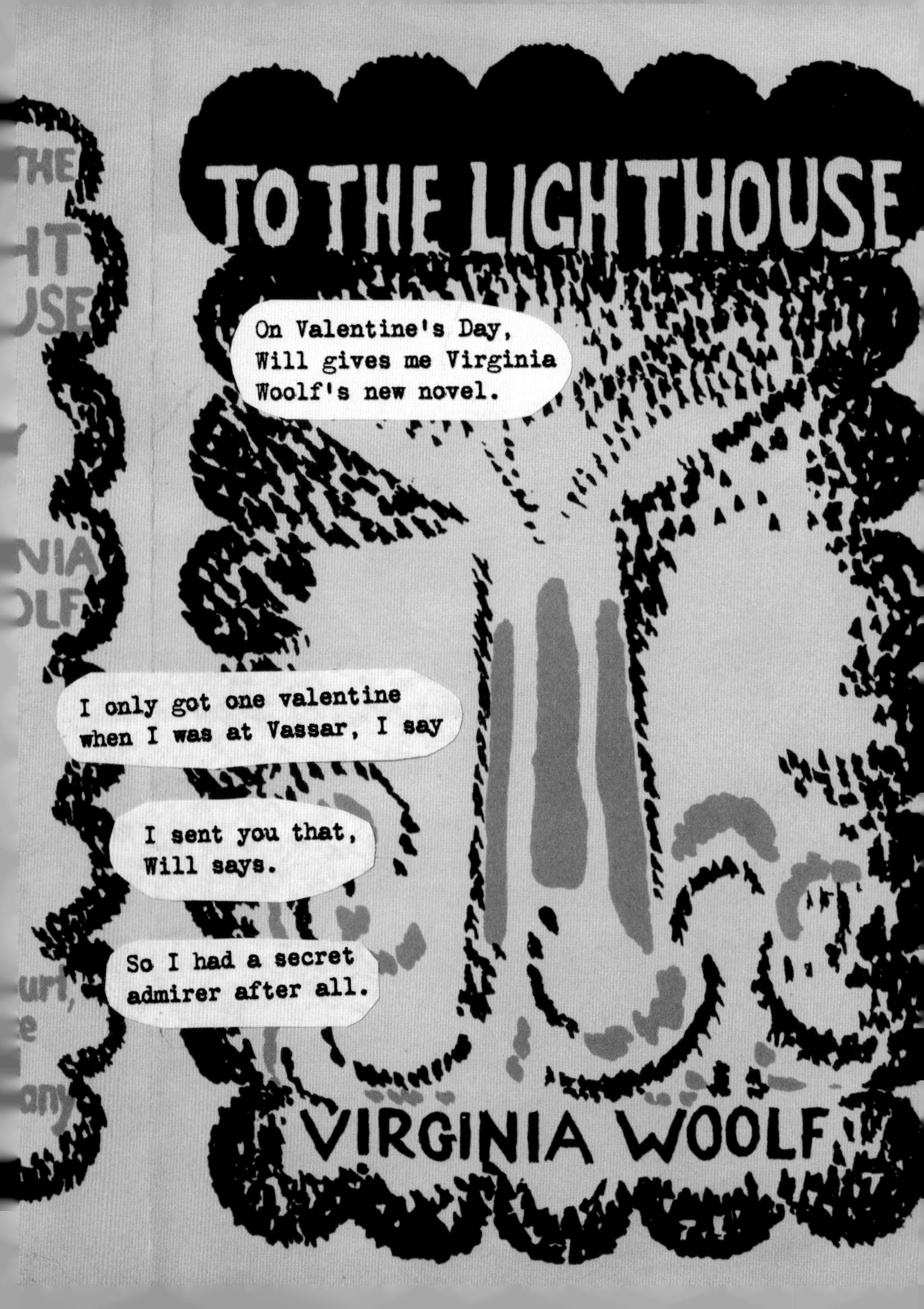
TO THE LIGHTHOUSE
On Valentine's Day, Will gives me Virginia Woolf's new novel.
I only got one valentine when I was at Vassar, I say
I sent you that, Will says.
So I had a secret admirer after all.
VIRGINIA WOOLF

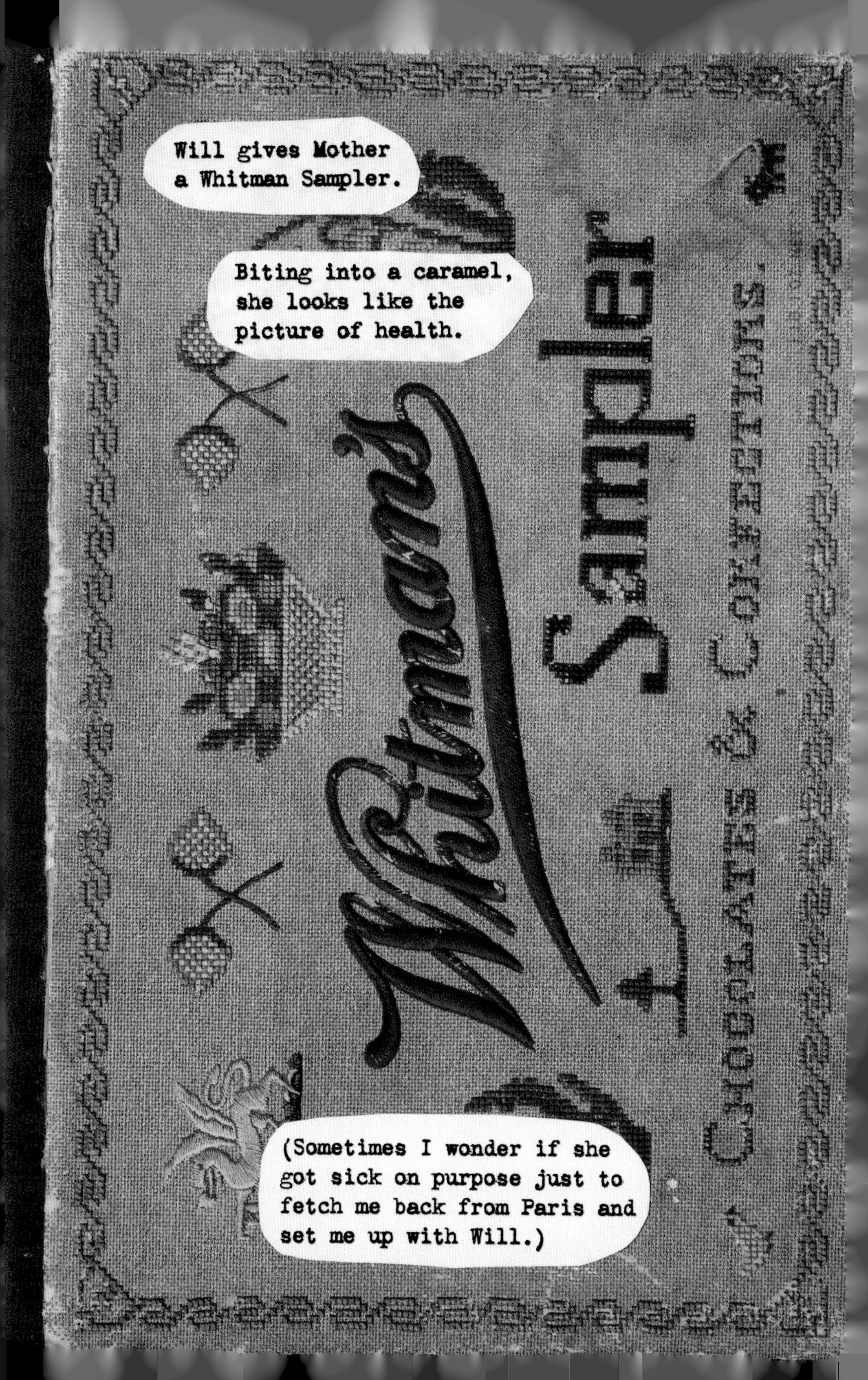
Will gives Mother a Whitman Sampler.
Biting into a caramel, she looks like the picture of health.
Whitman's Sampler
CHOCOLATES & CONFECTIONS
(Sometimes I wonder if she got sick on purpose just to fetch me back from Paris and set me up with Will.)

Eclipse of the Sun

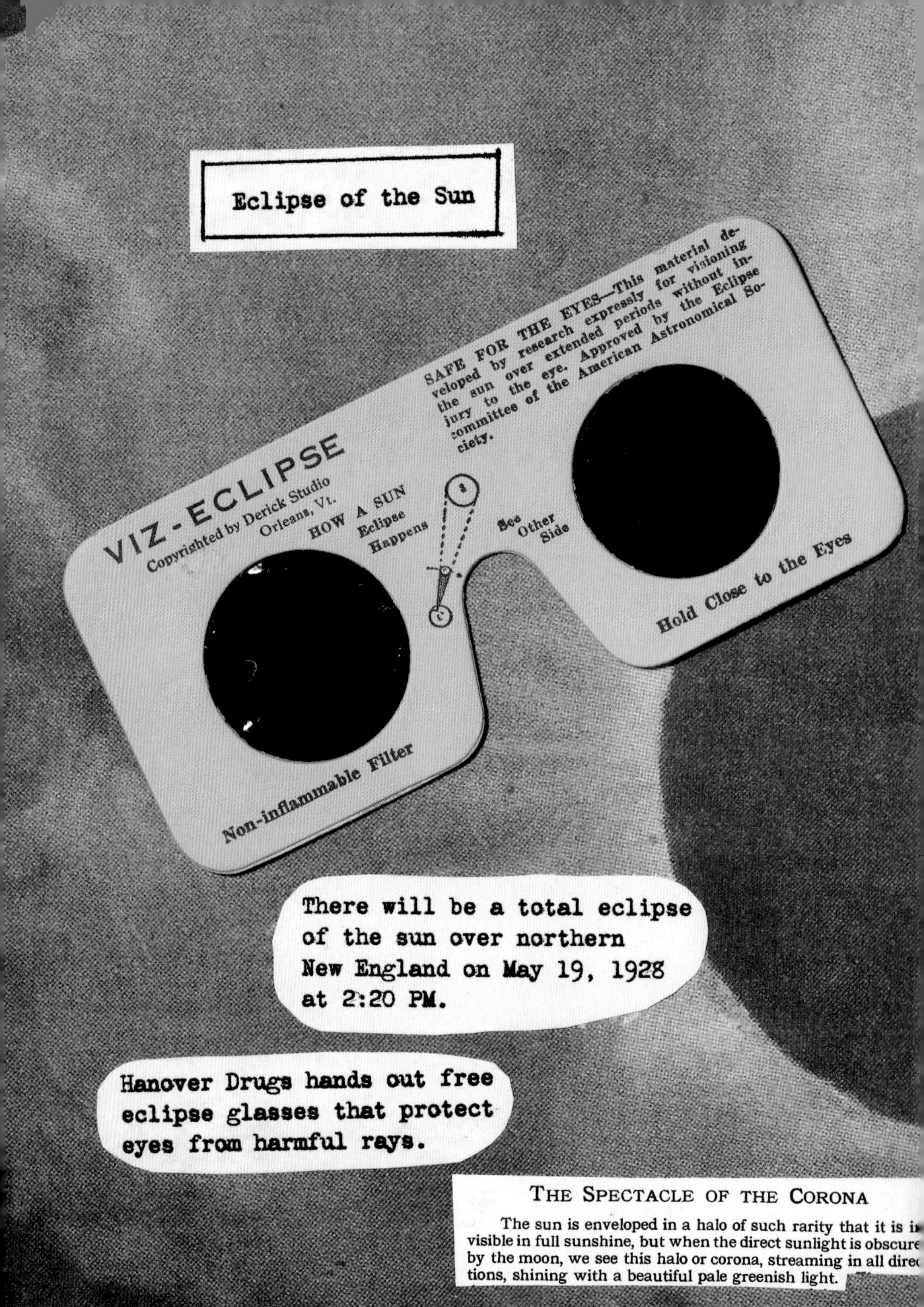
SAFE FOR THE EYES—This material developed by research expressly for visioning the sun over extended periods without injury to the eye. Approved by the Eclipse committee of the American Astronomical Society.
VIZ-ECLIPSE
Copyrighted by Derick Studio
Orleans, Vt.
HOW A SUN Eclipse Happens
See Other Side
Hold Close to the Eyes
Non-inflammable Filter

There will be a total eclipse of the sun over northern New England on May 19, 1928 at 2:20 PM.

Hanover Drugs hands out free eclipse glasses that protect eyes from harmful rays.

THE SPECTACLE OF THE CORONA

The sun is enveloped in a halo of such rarity that it is i visible in full sunshine, but when the direct sunlight is obscure by the moon, we see this halo or corona, streaming in all direc tions, shining with a beautiful pale greenish light.

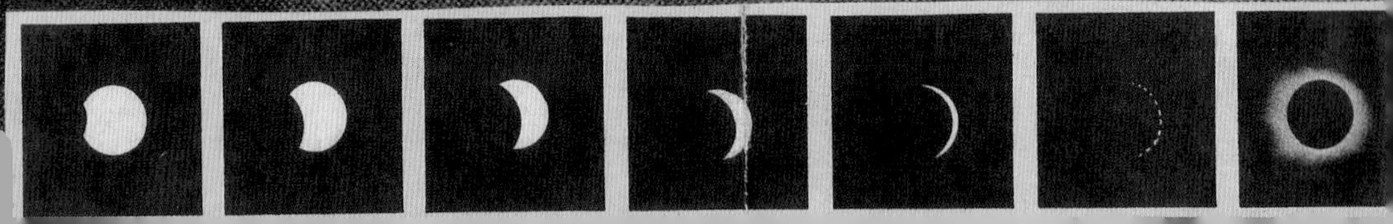

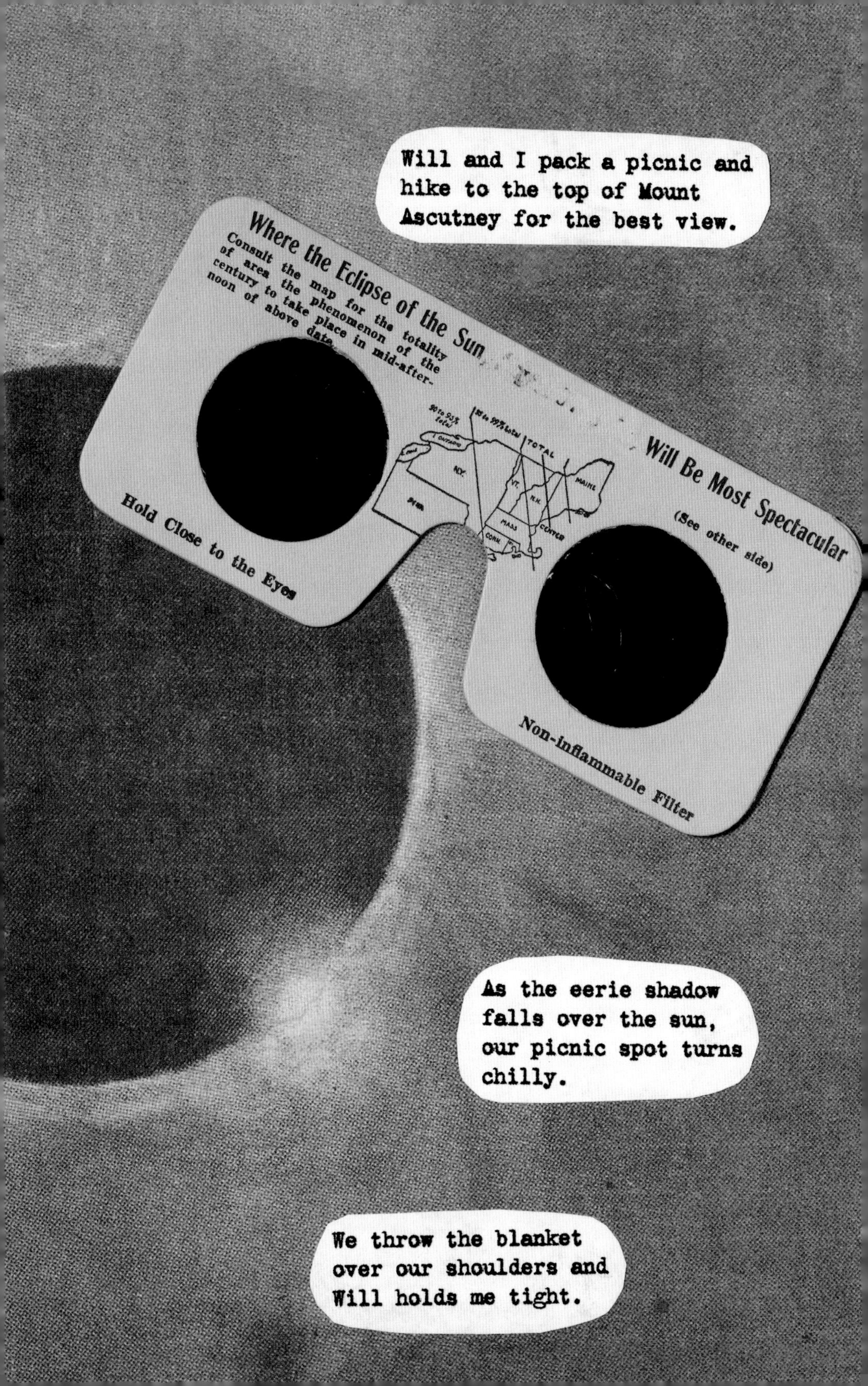
Will and I pack a picnic and hike to the top of Mount Ascutney for the best view.
Where the Eclipse of the Sun
Will Be Most Spectacular
(See other side)
Consult the map for the totality of area the phenomenon of the century to take place in mid-after-noon of above date.
Hold Close to the Eyes
Non-inflammable Filter
As the eerie shadow falls over the sun, our picnic spot turns chilly.
We throw the blanket over our shoulders and Will holds me tight.

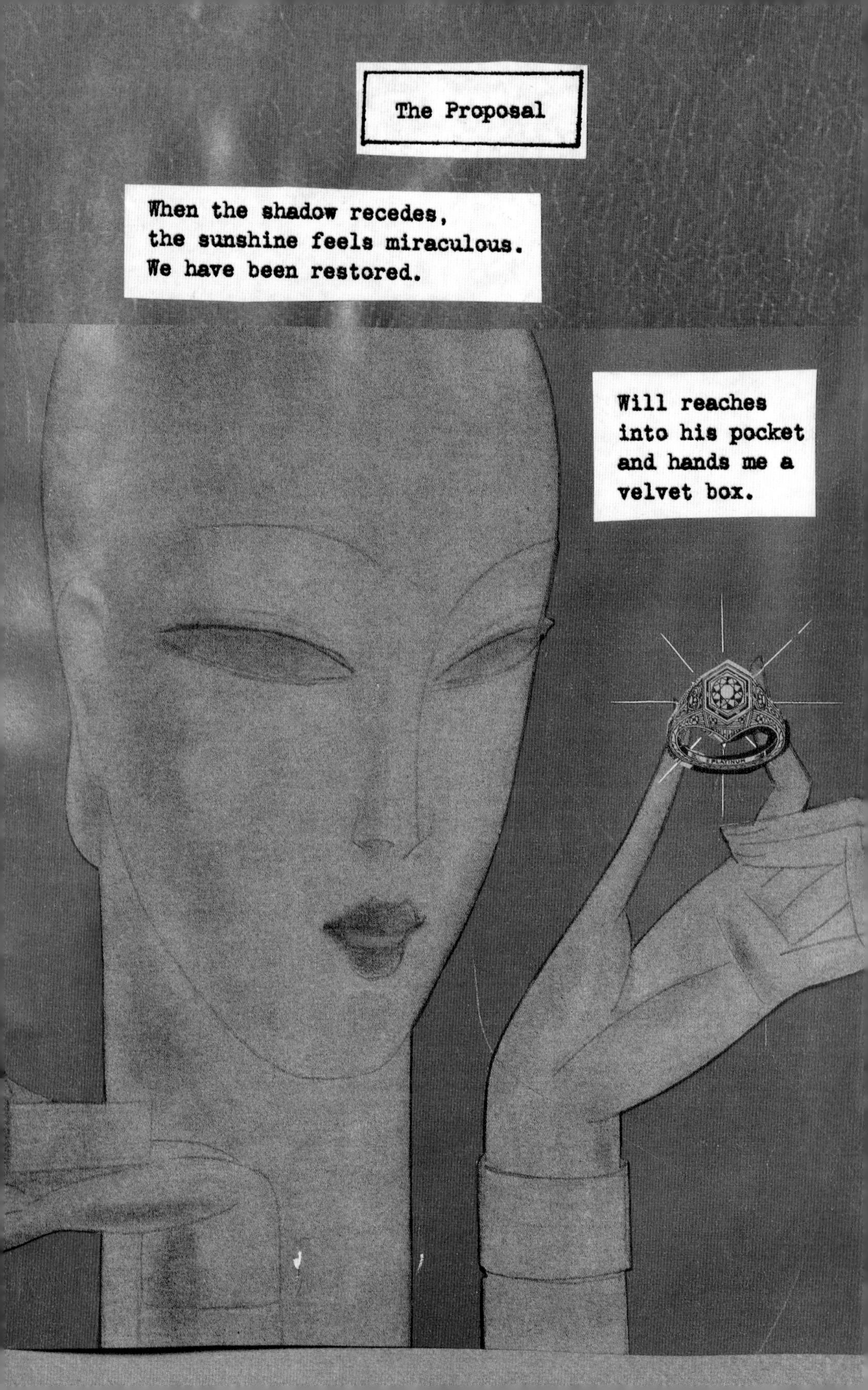
The Proposal
When the shadow recedes,
the sunshine feels miraculous.
We have been restored.
Will reaches
into his pocket
and hands me a
velvet box.

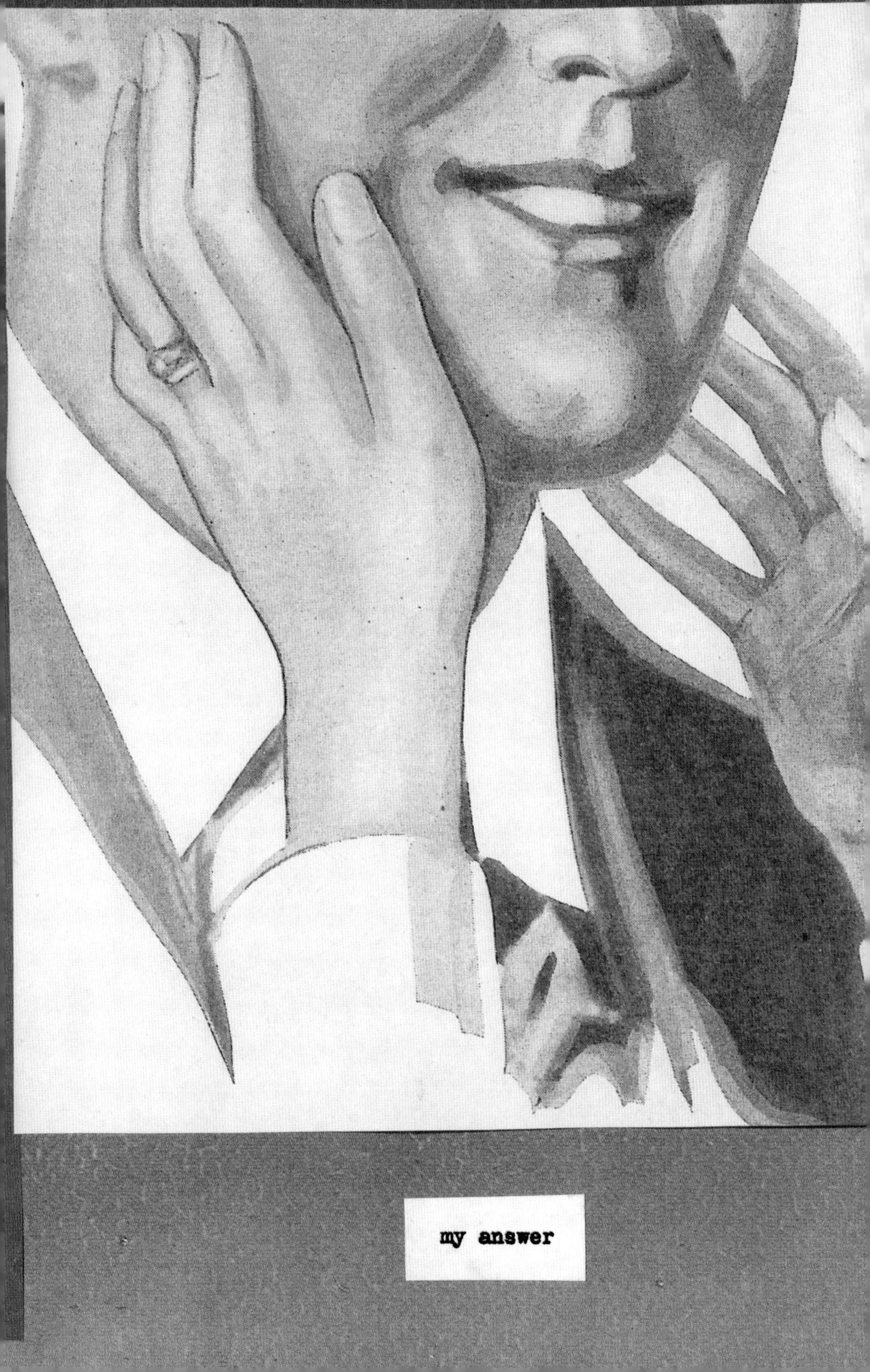

my answer

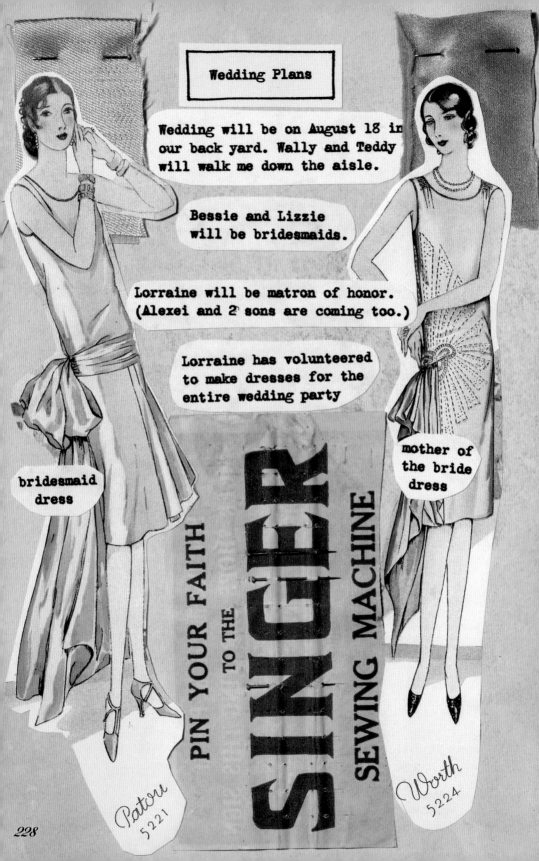

Wedding Plans

Wedding will be on August 18 in our back yard. Wally and Teddy will walk me down the aisle.

Bessie and Lizzie will be bridesmaids.

Lorraine will be matron of honor. (Alexei and 2 sons are coming too.)

Lorraine has volunteered to make dresses for the entire wedding party

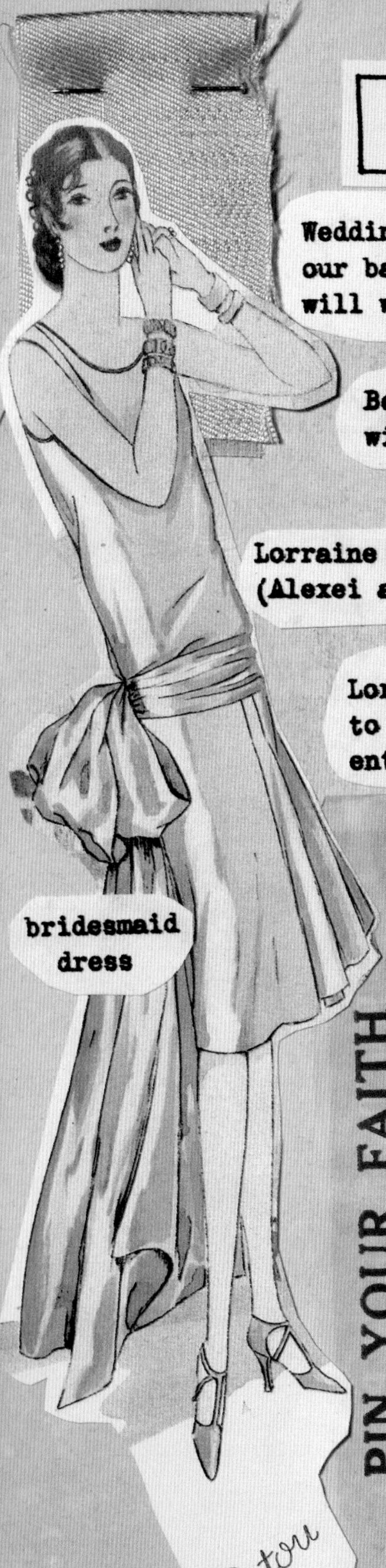

bridesmaid dress
Patou
5221

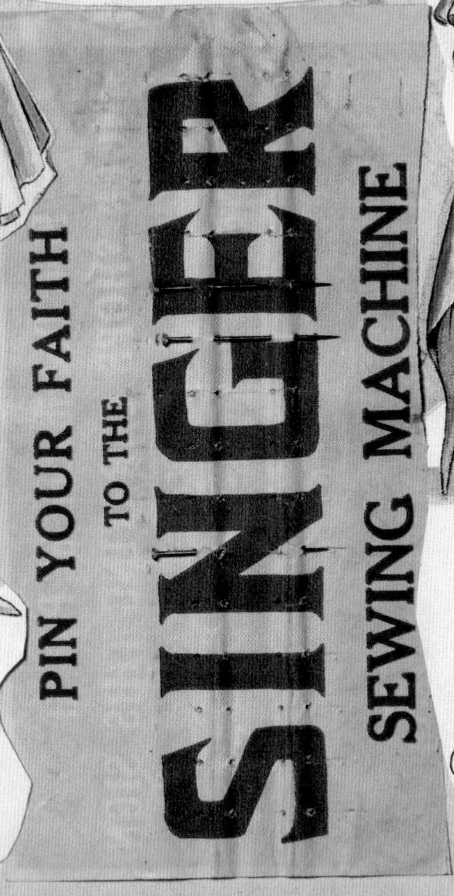

PIN YOUR FAITH
TO THE
SINGER
SEWING MACHINE

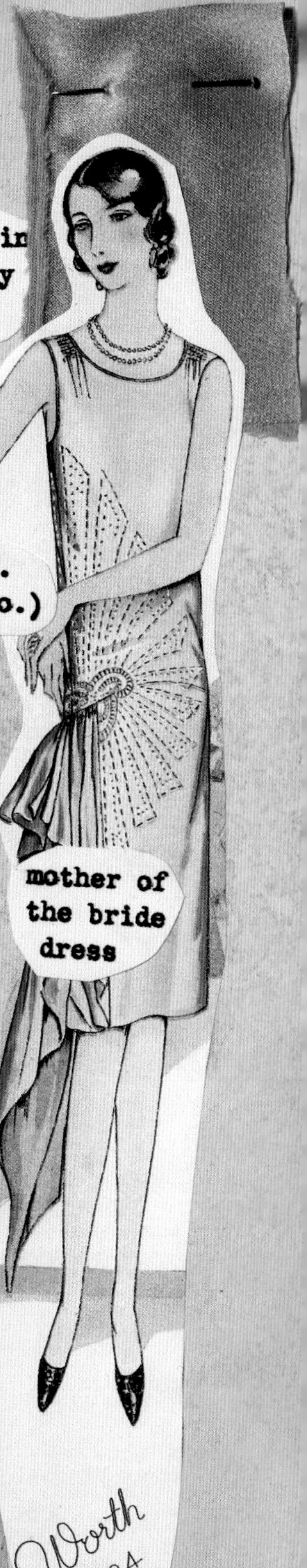

mother of the bride dress
Worth
5224

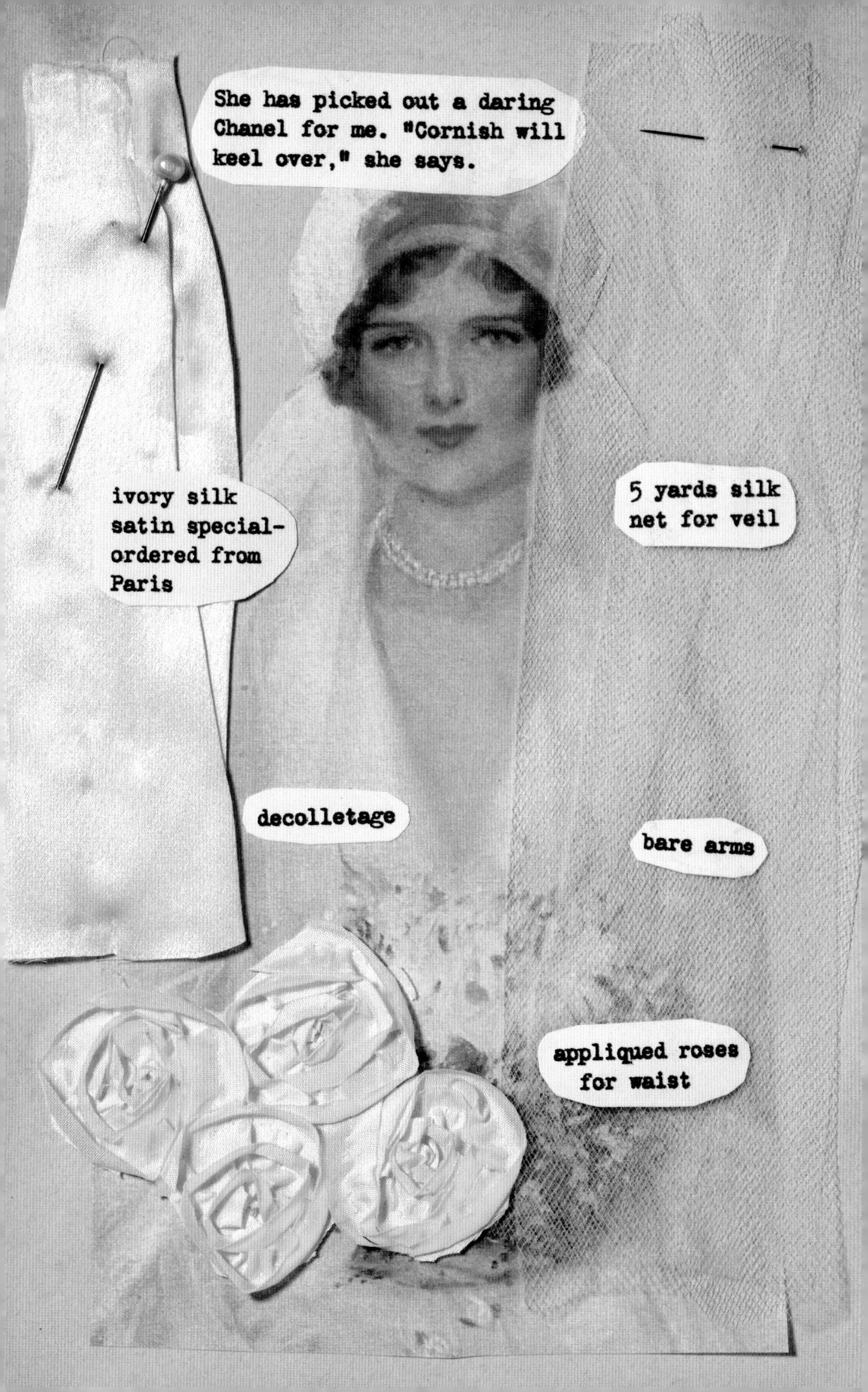
She has picked out a daring Chanel for me. "Cornish will keel over," she says.
ivory silk satin special-ordered from Paris
5 yards silk net for veil
decolletage
bare arms
appliqued roses for waist

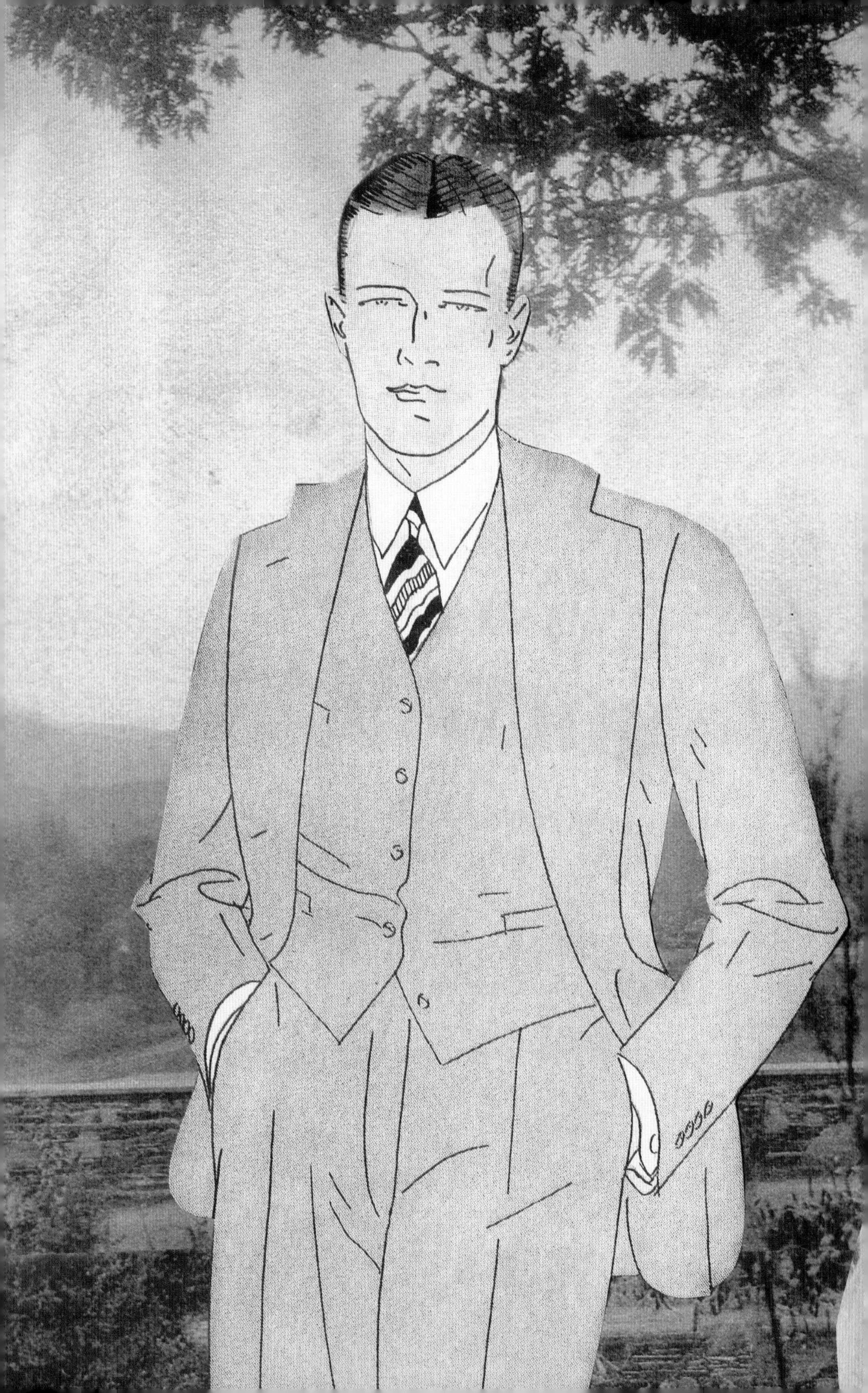

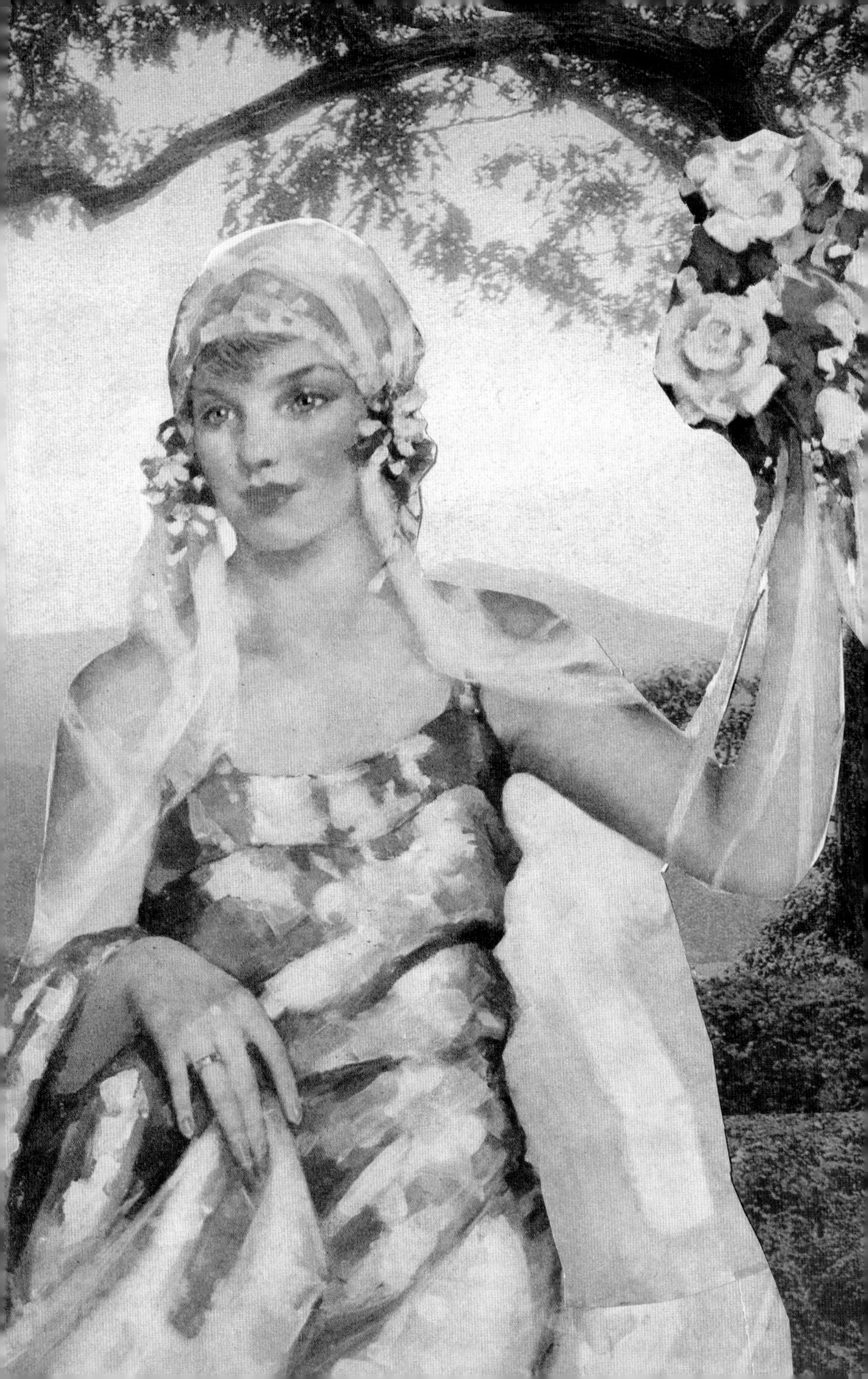

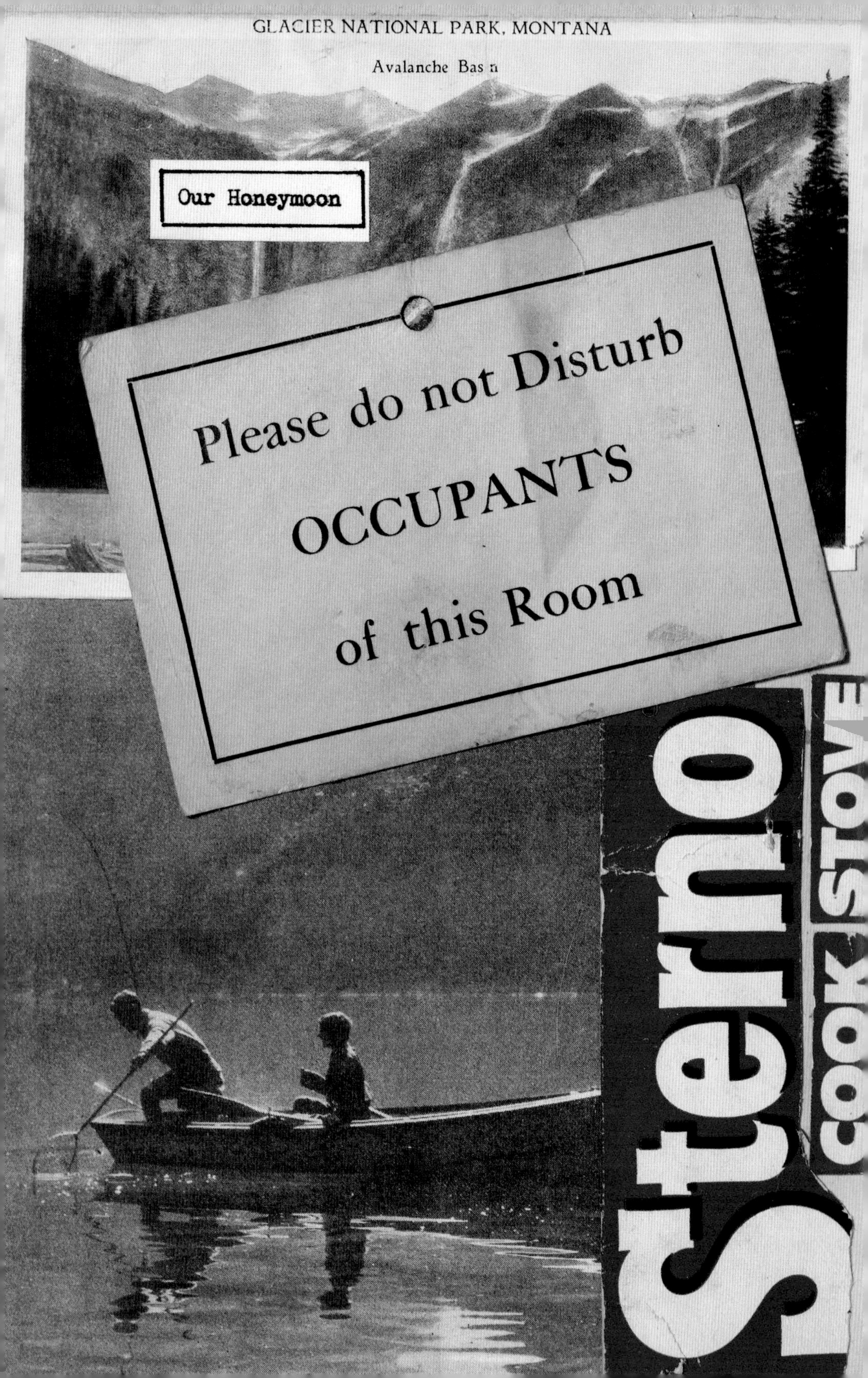
GLACIER NATIONAL PARK, MONTANA
Avalanche Basin
Our Honeymoon
Please do not Disturb
OCCUPANTS
of this Room
Sterno
COOK STOVE

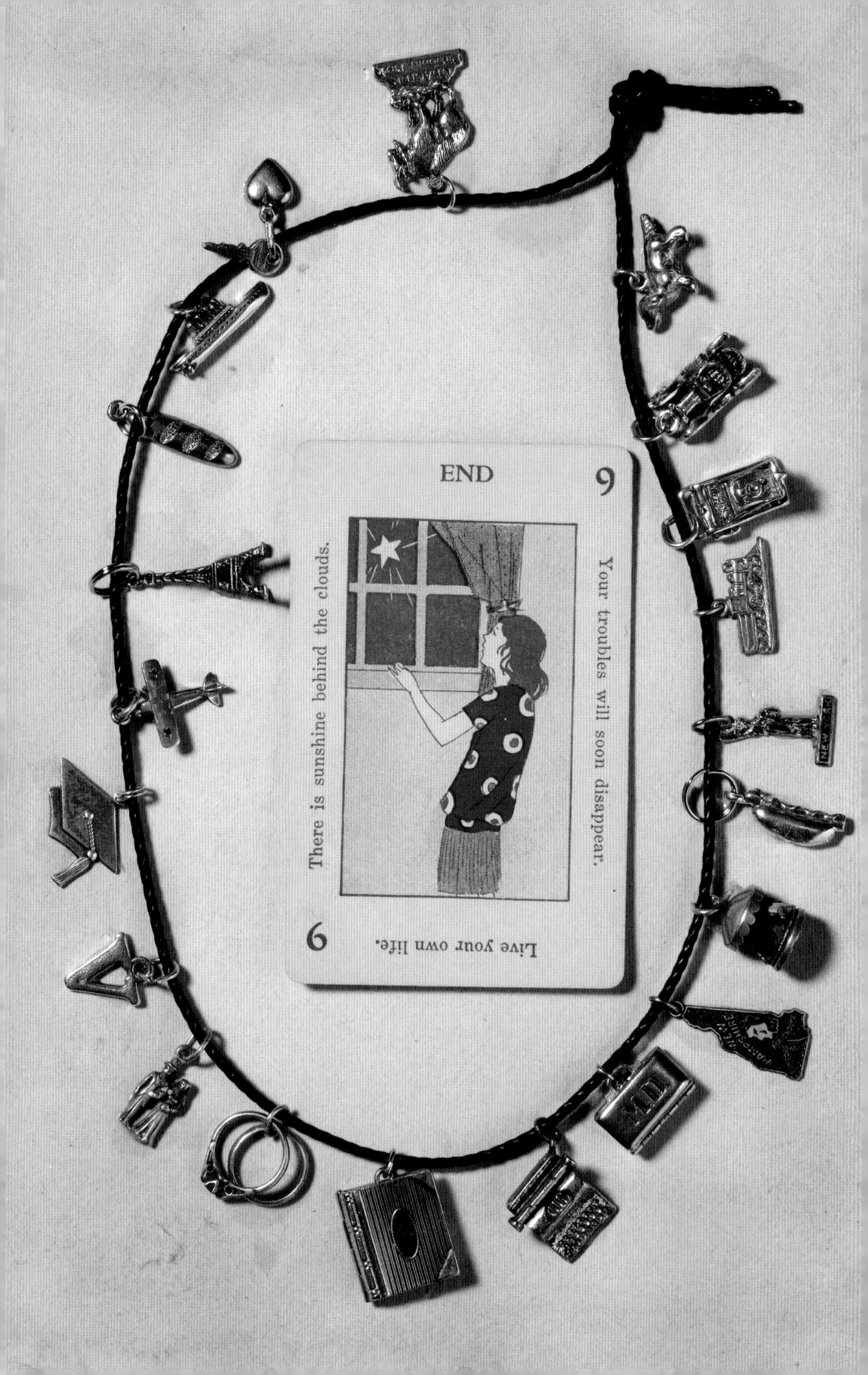
END
9
There is sunshine behind the clouds.
Your troubles will soon disappear.
Live your own life.
9

⊰ ACKNOWLEDGMENTS ⊱

Sylvia & Sylvia
Paris, 1924

My deepest thanks to:

My mother, Sylvia Peter Preston (1918–2011), for inspiring me with her own scrapbooks and memorabilia from her godmother, Sylvia Beach.

My first readers—Rosamond Casey, Chris Tilghman, Donna Lucey, Henry Wiencek, and Mameve Medwed.

Luke Tilghman, Margo Beck, and Trisha Orr for essential help.

My wise and tireless agent, Henry Dunow.

My fantastic editor, Lee Boudreaux, and the crack team at Ecco/ HarperCollins: Abigail Holstein, Mary Austin Speaker, Alison Forner, Daniel Halpern, Rachel Bressler, Ben Tomek, Michael McKenzie, Kim Lewis, Andrea Molitor, Eric Levy, Mark Ferguson, Andrea Rosen, Doug Jones, Carla Clifford, Kate Pereira, Jeanette Zwart, and Catherine Barbosa-Ross.

Richard Sheaff for choice items from his ephemera collection.

Deborah Paddock for her father Erwin's 1927 Dartmouth scrapbook.

Dean Rogers at the Vassar College Archives.

The Ragdale Foundation and the Virginia Center for the Creative Arts for residencies.

My sons—Matthew, Luke, and Will Tilghman—for always cheering on their mom.

And to more than 300 eBay sellers—A+++ rating.

ALSO BY CAROLINE PRESTON

Jackie by Josie

Lucy Crocker 2.0

Gatsby's Girl

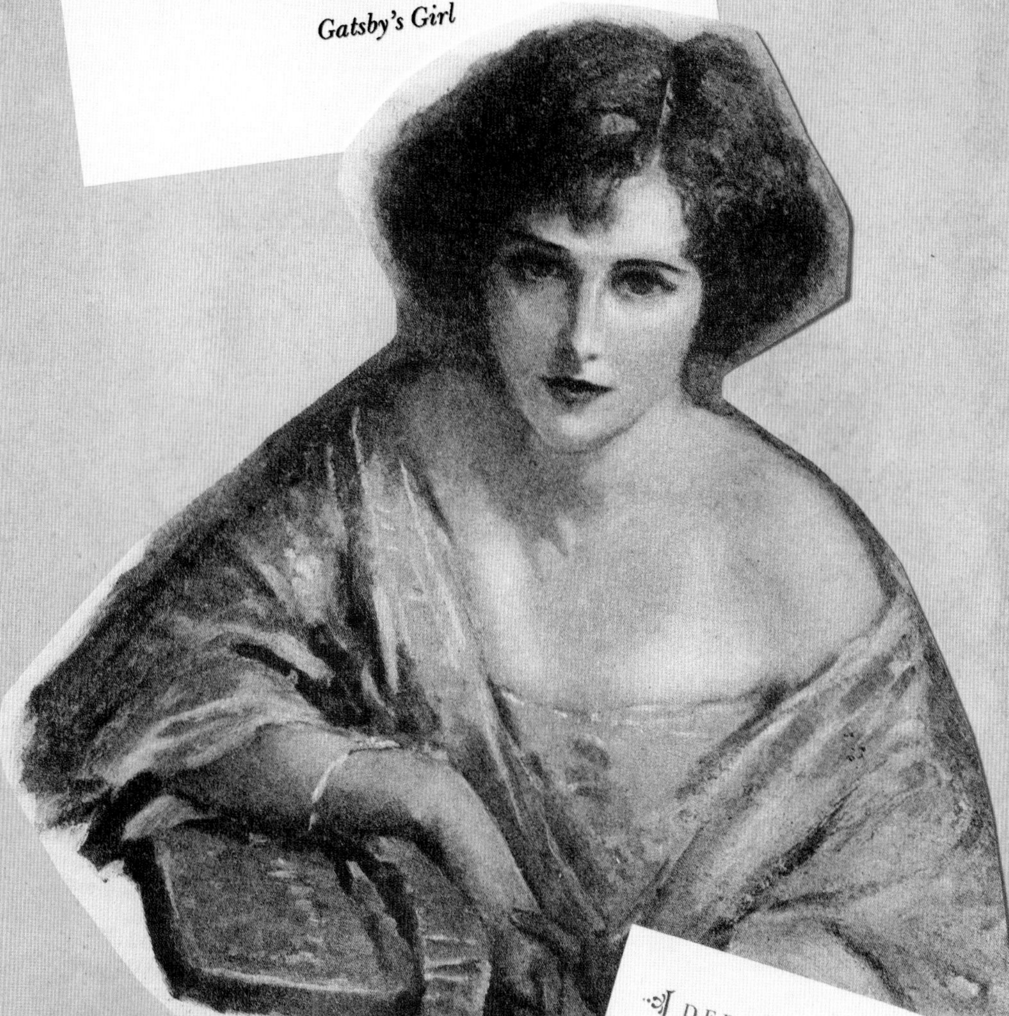

DEDICATED TO

my sisters

Margo & Marion

HarperCollins books may be purchased for educational, business, or sales promotional use. For information please write: Special Markets Department, HarperCollins Publishers, 10 East 53rd Street, New York, NY 10022.

FIRST EDITION

Designed by Caroline Preston

Background image for endpapers taken from Baroque, *published by the Pepin Press, www.pepinpress.com*

Photography by Ray Buonanno

Library of Congress Cataloging-in-Publication Data has been applied for.

ISBN 978-0-06-196690-3

11 12 13 14 15 / SCP   10 9 8 7 6 5 4 3 2 1